The Sun of God

Zoë Tavares Bennett

To my parents, for always supporting my dreams
and forever answering the question: What is love?

To my fellow Centristi, and your enthusiasm for
a forbidden love story.

And lastly, to Rome, my first true love.

Annos undeviginti natus exercitum privato consilio et privata impensa comparavi, per quem rem publicam a dominatione factionis oppressam in libertatem vindicavi.

At the age of nineteen, by my own initiative and expense, I raised an army to restore freedom to the Republic, which had been oppressed by the tyranny of a faction.

Emperor Augustus, *Res Gestae*

She clothed her children in strange raiment and gave them masks, and at her bidding the antique world rose from its marble tomb. A new Caesar stalked through the streets of risen Rome, and with purple sail and flute-led oars another Cleopatra passed up the river to Antioch. Old myth and legend and dream took shape and substance. History was entirely rewritten, and there was hardly one of the dramatists who did not recognize that the object of Art was not simple truth but complex beauty.

Oscar Wilde, *The Decay of Lying*

Italy, 1st Century B.C.E.

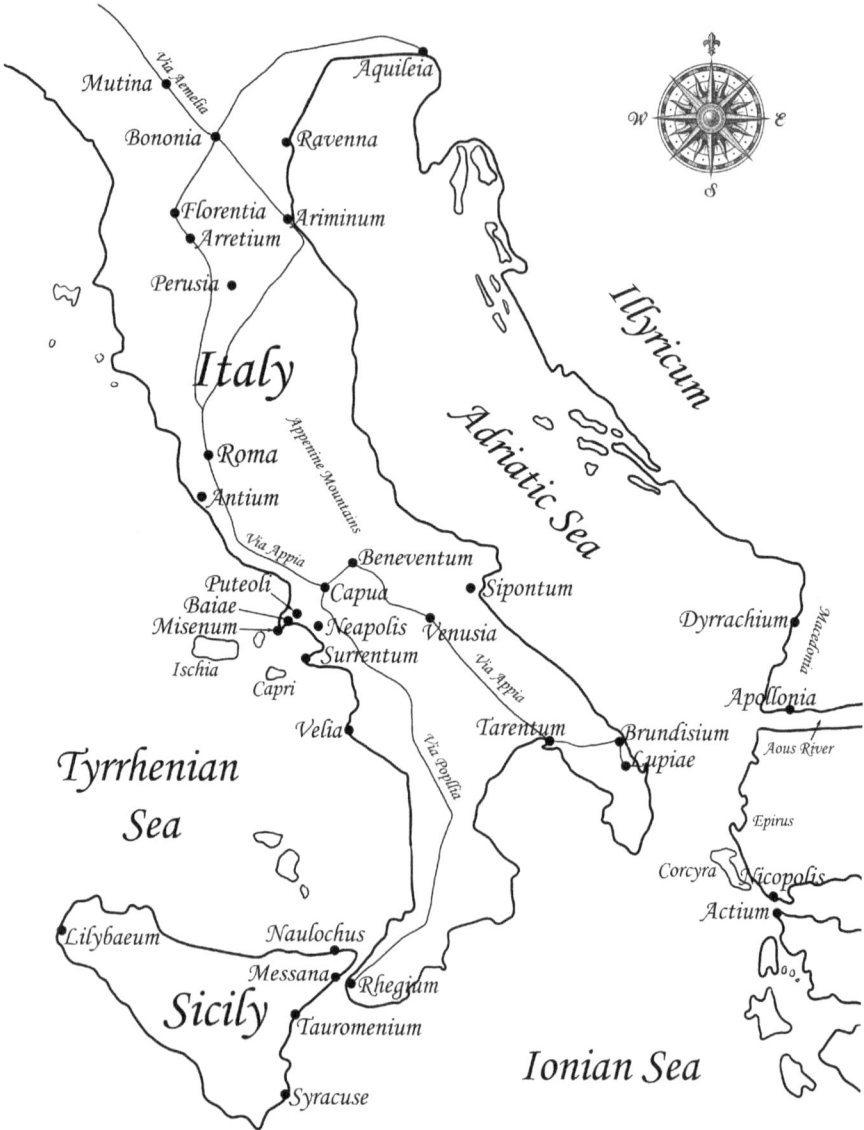

Mutina

Via Aemelia

Bononia

Aquileia

Ravenna

Florentia

Arretium

Ariminum

Perusia

Italy

Illyricum

Appenine Mountains

Adriatic Sea

Roma

Antium

Via Appia

Beneventum

Puteoli

Capua

Sipontum

Baiae

Misenum

Neapolis

Venusia

Surrentum

Ischia

Via Appia

Dyrrachium

Macedonia

Capri

Apollonia

Velia

Tarentum

Via Popilia

Brundisium

Lupiae

Aous River

Tyrrhenian

Sea

Epirus

Corcyra

Nicopolis

Actium

Lilybaeum

Naulochus

Messana

Rhegium

Sicily

Tauromenium

Ionian Sea

Syracuse

Rome, 44 B.C.E.

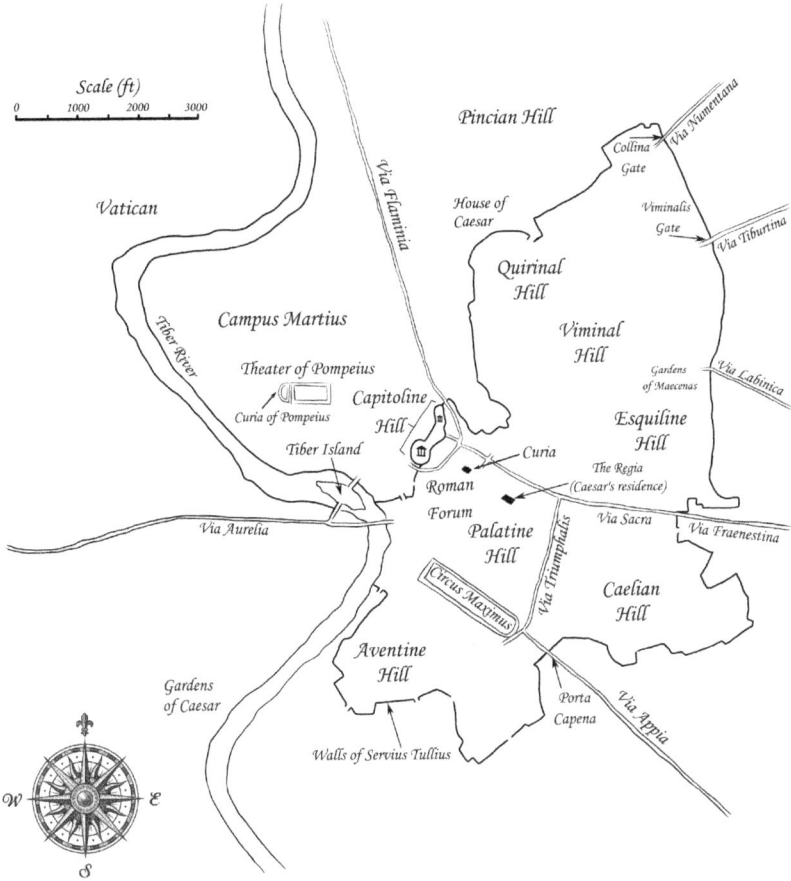

Scale (ft)

0   1000   2000   3000

Vatican

Pincian Hill

Via Flaminia

House of Caesar

Collina Gate

Via Numentana

Viminalis Gate

Via Tiburtina

Campus Martius

Tiber River

Quirinal Hill

Viminal Hill

Theater of Pompeius

Gardens of Maecenas

Via Labinica

Curia of Pompeius

Capitoline Hill

Esquiline Hill

Tiber Island

Curia

The Regia (Caesar's residence)

Roman Forum

Via Aurelia

Palatine Hill

Via Sacra

Via Fraenestina

Via Triumphalis

Circus Maximus

Caelian Hill

Gardens of Caesar

Aventine Hill

Porta Capena

Via Appia

Walls of Servius Tullius

W   E

S

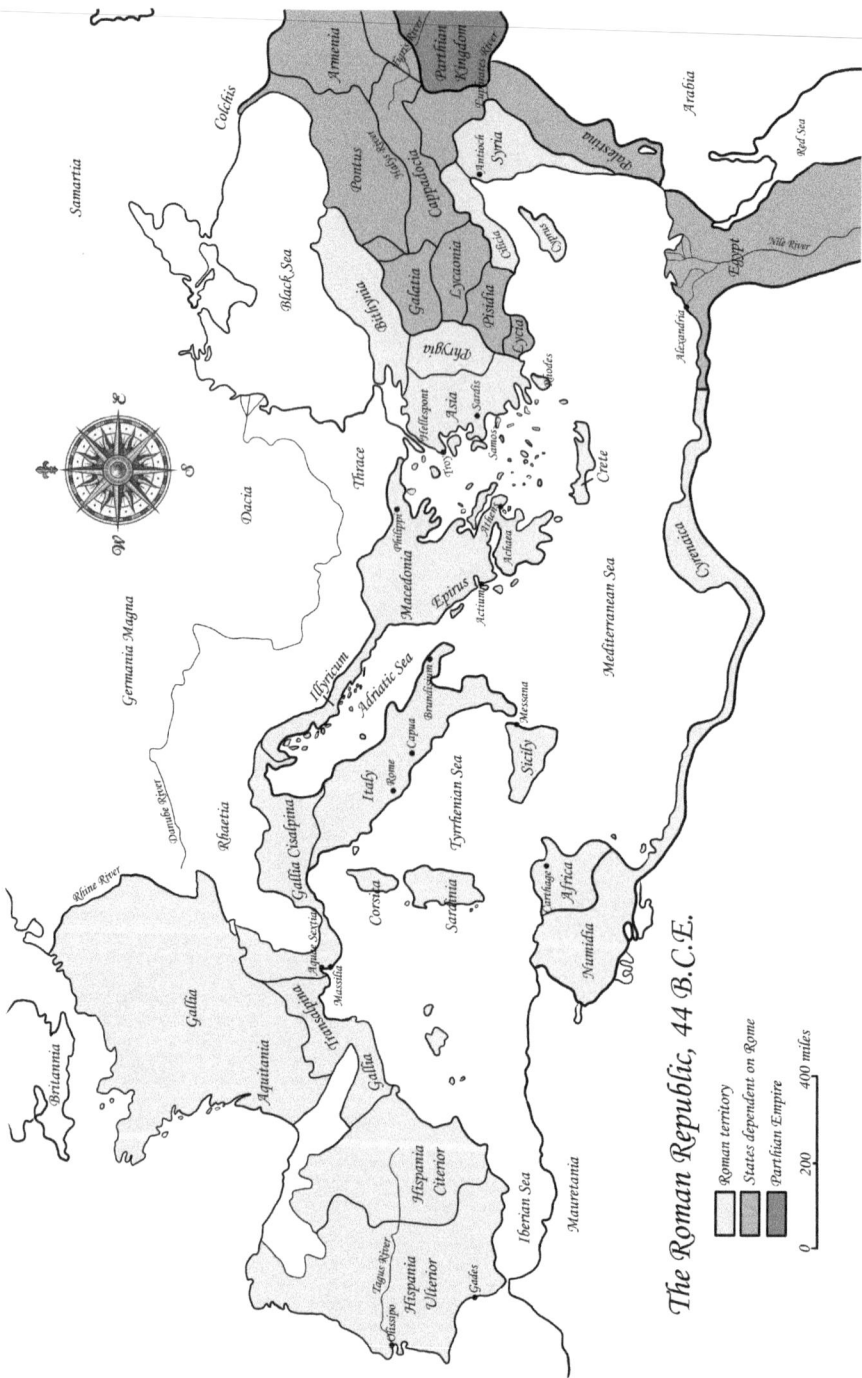

The Roman Republic, 44 B.C.E.

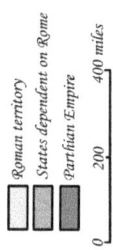

Roman territory
States dependent on Rome
Parthian Empire

0   200   400 miles

Britannia
Germania Magna
Rhine River
Gallia
Aquitania
Transalpina
Gallia
Massilia
Rhaetia
Dacia
Danube River
Gallia Cisalpina
Illyricum
Thrace
Macedonia
Philippi
Epirus
Actium
Achaea
Adriatic Sea
Italy
Rome
Capua
Brundisium
Tyrrhenian Sea
Corsica
Sardinia
Sicily
Messana
Hispania Citerior
Hispania Ulterior
Gades
Tagus River
Iberian Sea
Mauretania
Africa
Carthage
Numidia
Mediterranean Sea
Crete
Cyrenaica
Alexandria
Egypt
Nile River
Red Sea
Arabia
Palestine
Syria
Antioch
Cyprus
Cilicia
Phrygia
Rhodes
Lycia
Pisidia
Lycaonia
Galatia
Asia
Sardis
Samos
Troy
Hellespont
Bithynia
Black Sea
Pontus
Cappadocia
Armenia
Parthian Kingdom
Colchis
Samaria

CONTENTS

Volume I: Octavianus   1

Prologue   3

1. Marcus Vipsanius Agrippa   10

2. Gaius Octavius   20

3. Marcus Antonius   31

4. Marcus Vipsanius Agrippa   41

5. Gaius Octavius   48

6. Marcus Antonius   59

7. Marcus Vipsanius Agrippa   67

8. Gaius Cassius Longinus   79

9. Gaius Octavius   86

10. Marcus Antonius   95

11. Marcus Vipsanius Agrippa   104

12. Gaius Octavius   114

13. Marcus Tullius Cicero   125

14. Marcus Vipsanius Agrippa   132

15. Gaius Octavius   140

16. Marcus Antonius   150

17. Marcus Vipsanius Agrippa   156

18. Octavia Minor   164

19. Gaius Octavius   172

20. Marcus Vipsanius Agrippa   181

21. Marcus Antonius   189

22. Gaius Octavius   196

23. Marcus Vipsanius Agrippa   203

24. Marcus Junius Brutus   213

25. Gaius Octavius   220

26. Marcus Vipsanius Agrippa   228

27. Clodia Pulchra   237

28. Gaius Octavius   244

29. Marcus Vipsanius Agrippa   253

30. Scribonia   259

31. Marcus Antonius   266

32. Gaius Octavius   275

33. Octavia Minor   284

34. Marcus Vipsanius Agrippa   291

35. Gaius Octavius   297

Volume II: Augustus   305

36. Livia Drusilla   307

37. Marcus Vipsanius Agrippa   315

38. Gaius Octavius   324

39. Livia Drusilla   331

40. Marcus Vipsanius Agrippa   338

41. Sextus Pompeius Magnus Pius   345

42. Octavia Minor   351

43. Gaius Octavius   359

44. Marcus Antonius 367

45. Pomponia Caecilia Attica 373

46. Gaius Octavius 381

47. Marcus Vipsanius Agrippa 389

48. Octavia Minor 399

49. Gaius Octavius 405

50. Marcus Vipsanius Agrippa 413

51. Livia Drusilla 421

52. Gaius Octavius 427

53. Marcus Vipsanius Agrippa 436

54. Cleopatra VII Philopator 444

55. Gaius Octavius 455

56. Marcus Vipsanius Agrippa 460

57. Marcus Antonius 468

58. Gaius Octavius 473

59. Marcus Vipsanius Agrippa 479

60. Cleopatra VII Philopator 486

61. Gaius Octavius 493

62. Marcus Vipsanius Agrippa 500

63. Octavia Minor 509

64. Gaius Octavius 515

Epilogue 520

Acknowledgements 524

Historical Notes 526

About the Author 529

Appendices: 531

The Julio-Claudian Family Tree   533

Timeline of Historical Events   535

Real Names of History Mentioned   539

Latin & Greek Words   543

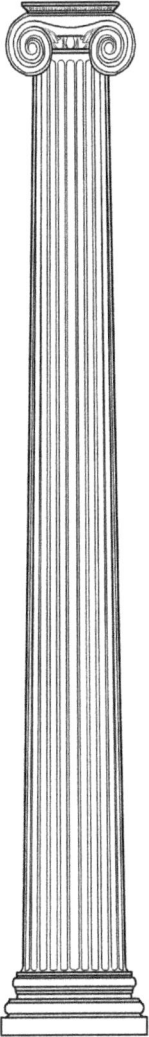

VOLUME I

Octavianus

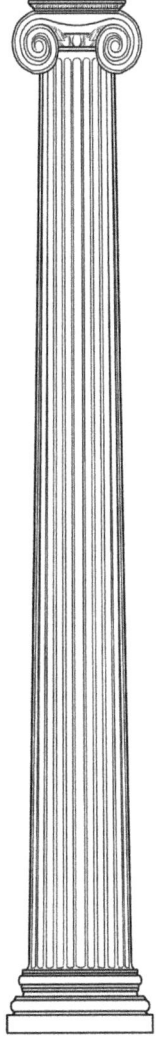

PROLOGUE
MARCUS ANTONIUS

MARCH 59 BC

MARCUS ANTONIUS HAD A lot of debt.

That was the first thing on his mind as he entered the luxurious villa of Gaius Octavius. The second was how much he hated funerals.

Antonius could already hear the faint voices of mourners in the house. Gaius Octavius had up until very recently been a popular politician and general, but he had died at his villa in Nola from a lingering battle wound.

His widow, Atia Balba, was holding a ceremony at their family home in Velitrae, just over a day's ride from Rome. The journey had been smooth but boring, and Antonius itched for a good bottle of wine and a game of dice.

A short hallway opened onto a shaded courtyard, a shallow impluvium at the center, its clear waters sparkling under the sunlight. The villa dripped in money wherever Antonius looked. Silver-veined marble coated each column and the walls were all painted with elaborate scenes from the Iliad. Antonius squinted at one, and sure enough, there was the Trojan Horse before the walls of Troy.

Gaius Octavius came from a wealthy equestrian family and it showed in every corner of his glamorous house. *New money always left a trace*, Antonius thought dryly, glancing at the statues of no-name ancestors standing proudly around the atrium.

"Marcus Antonius."

Antonius started at the voice and looked around for its source.

Atia Balba.

The widow of Gaius Octavius stood across the atrium in a white stola, her brown hair undone in mourning. She was so still, as still as the marble statues adorning the colonnade, that Antonius had not noticed her until she spoke.

Atia had always terrified him.

3

He crossed the atrium and kissed her in greeting. "My condolences."

"Thank you, Antonius."

She turned away with her usual cold indifference. While her husband had been born to an equestrian family, Atia was the daughter of Julia Minor and therefore descended from the Julian family, which legend told began with the noble Julus, son of the famed Trojan hero Aeneas. Antonius thought it all ridiculous.

Atia glanced at him sharply. "I am sure you are well?"

Antonius frowned. Everyone knew he had been struggling to stay afloat recently, amassing debts greater than any his stepfather had before him. Atia only asked him to be polite, however frosty the courtesy.

"Very well, thank you."

They walked in silence to the gardens behind the house, just as Antonius had suspected. There were already people lounging in couches set up across the grass, mourners milling about in quiet discussion. The men wore dark tunics with somber frowns, while the women were robed in white and wore their hair down like Atia. Some cheeks were still damp with tears, while others cried openly.

Antonius resisted the urge to scoff. Hardly any of these people knew Gaius Octavius. They were here for one reason only, and it had everything to do with Julia Minor's watchful eyes surveying the crowds from the far side of the gardens.

Julia Minor was the older sister of the *Imperator* Julius Caesar and mother to Atia Balba. But if they hoped to gain favor with Julius Caesar through his sister, they were greatly mistaken. Julia was just as ambitious as her brother, and no less ruthless.

Closer to the house stood—to Antonius' surprise and disdain—Lucius Marcius Philippus. Philippus was the rumored suitor of Atia Balba despite being a known critic of her uncle Julius Caesar.

Many guests flocked to him as a wealthy, well-connected politician, but many others kept their distance, catching the displeasure flitting in Julia Minor's eyes. There were many men like Philippus in the Roman Senate, who openly denounced their political enemies only to turn around and conspire with them behind closed doors.

Antonius did not know why Julia Minor tolerated such a man for her daughter—a woman Antonius had always considered very beautiful and proud, too beautiful for an old and arrogant man like Philippus. But that was not the question.

Philippus' old age and wealth provided a generous assurance for Atia and her children which Antonius could not have hoped to challenge even if he hadn't gambled all his money away. The real question was what Atia provided *him*.

"Well, if it is not young Marcus Antonius," Philippus called out to him, motioning Antonius over with his hand and a smirk.

Antonius reluctantly walked over to him as the crowd around him quietly dispersed. If there was someone at this funeral more disliked than Philippus, it would be Antonius himself, just shy of twenty-five and known more for his growing debt and scandalous love affairs than his familial connection to Julius Caesar.

But Antonius dared not offend the old man, though he felt Julia Minor's burning gaze from across the gardens as he kissed Philippus. "It is good to see you, sir."

"I heard you had some trouble with creditors in the city," Philippus said as a way of greeting, then dropped his voice, pretending to look around before he spoke. "I suppose the *Imperator* cannot vouch on your behalf?"

Philippus never missed an opportunity to remind Antonius of his mother's distant connection to Julius Caesar. Though she was indeed a third cousin to the current consul, unless Antonius married Atia instead of Philippus, Caesar would do nothing for his debt.

"Naturally he cannot." Antonius saw Philippus' smirking face and could not resist a little dig himself. "But rumor has told me that you are courting Atia Balba. Perhaps you might supplicate the *Imperator* for me?"

His smirk dropped. Philippus glanced across the gardens at Julia Minor, who held the same carefully polite expression that her daughter had so coldly offered as a welcome. "Very funny, Antonius. You know, when I was your age, I had already joined the army and was making a name for myself. If you don't quit your gambling and girls, you will amount to much worse than a mere debtor like your step-father."

Antonius tried not to betray his annoyance and snap back an insult. "And what is that?"

"Someone nobody remembers."

The words stung more than Antonius wished. He did not give Philippus the satisfaction of an answer. Instead, he watched Atia at the center of the gardens, a small child with the blonde hair and quick smile of her late father running about her legs. She was a girl of about seven or eight, who shrieked and laughed happily at something so loud in the quiet murmuring that Atia promptly slapped her across the face. At once the girl's eyes welled with tears and her bottom lip wobbled.

A few paces beside her stood a little boy no older than four years old, with closely cropped brown hair and steady brown eyes. He seemed scarcely moved by his sister's pain. In fact, he looked so different from his sister with olive dark skin beside her fair, rosy face that Antonius doubted for a moment whether they were even born of the same father.

Antonius watched the scene curiously. He had difficulty imagining Philippus holding any real fatherly affection for them, as he already had three grown children of his own by a first marriage.

"Those are the children?"

The boy turned and looked at them, as if sensing Antonius' eyes on him, angling his head to the side like a small, dark sparrow. Antonius did not break his gaze, but the boy only stared back, unmoving.

Philippus made a noise following his line of sight. "Unfortunately. The girl never shuts up and the boy never opens his mouth. But the girl will grow up beautiful like her mother. It's the boy I will have to worry about."

"Why?" Antonius asked, but he thought he already knew the answer. The boy had a strange air about him, too quiet and still for his age.

"He is stunted. Weak. The child falls sick every time the wind blows. If he does not die before manhood, his life will be very sorry indeed."

Antonius raised a brow. Those were bold statements to make of Julius Caesar's grand-nephew. But he supposed they were true. The boy did look sickly, his tan skin almost sallow.

"What was he named?"

Philippus glanced at him as if surprised Antonius would care. "Gaius Octavius. The only thing he inherited from his father."

Antonius nearly grimaced. He could sympathize with the poor child on this. His own father, Marcus Antonius Creticus, had fallen to disgrace trying to hunt pirates and in a fit of delusion became a pirate himself—not a very good one of course, because in the end he was caught.

Though his father had long since passed away, it was a legacy that never died, and as the eldest son and namesake, Antonius has borne the brunt of it.

"There is trouble in the air, I have no doubt," Philippus murmured thoughtfully. He was looking right at Julia Minor, who had taken hold of little Octavius' hand and was stroking his hair with uncharacteristic gentleness. The boy did not return the affection, but Antonius thought he saw a glimmer of satisfaction in those dark eyes. "I would advise you to escape the storm while you still can."

Now Philippus had his attention. There had been rumors of a growing discontent among the senators with Julius Caesar. Caesar's own co-consul, Marcus Calpurnius Bibulus, had always opposed him every chance he had and hated him still, despite holding the same office. It seemed any day the tension between the two men would boil over into something far more dangerous than a mere Senate speech. Could Philippus know more than he let on?

"What kind of trouble?"

Philippus cut him a sharp glance of disapproval. "The bad kind."

"I see." Antonius was suddenly thankful Julia Minor was occupied with the child. In a family such as the *gens* Julia, there was no room for treachery.

6

"You know, the *Imperator* cannot help you with your debt, but I can," Philippus said, eyeing him meaningfully. "If you leave the country, it would be easier for me to manage your affairs."

"And what would you like in return?" Antonius asked with a touch of mockery, though his thoughts quickened at the possibility of escaping his creditors. He had buried himself in a hole too deep to get out of himself, and time was running out.

"Consider it a favor." Philippus smiled, but it held too much cunning to be considered kind. "I only ask that you remember my generosity in the future."

Antonius hesitated, considering. "And where do you suggest I go?"

"Greece. Study in Athens. You can always join the military later. But when the time comes and you must pick a side, make sure it's the right one."

Antonius wondered which side Philippus would consider the right one. On the one hand, he opposed the *Imperator* at every turn. But on the other hand, Philippus appreciated power, and Julius Caesar certainly had a lot of it.

"Perhaps if I study philosophy I will learn how to distinguish between right and wrong," Antonius said, hardly hiding his sarcasm.

He did not trust Philippus, and besides, Atia Balba was now making her way towards them with the little boy shuffling in front, her daughter trailing behind tearfully.

"You do not use your wit enough, Antonius," Philippus said dryly, watching Atia approach, her stola falling elegantly around her legs.

"Only with the women, Philippus," Antonius muttered, before Atia stood before them.

Atia cast her eyes down in an affectation of innocence, but not before Antonius glimpsed a hard look of disapproval. Though Julia Minor could not hear them, she had been watching them and had sent her daughter over to end their conversation.

"What gossip have you two been cooking up?" Atia asked lightly, but there was a warning in her words.

"We were wondering where your uncle was to be found," Philippus answered without delay, looking at Atia with a smile, as if this were already their wedding day and not her husband's funeral. "He is very much missed today."

"He had business in Rome, but has already sent his condolences," Atia said. She looked down at her son, then Antonius, her face a picture of matronly duty save for the eyes, which bore into him like Athena herself. She was only two years older than Antonius, but it felt like she had lived a lifetime more. "Have you met my children, Antonius?"

"I'm afraid I haven't had the pleasure," Antonius said.

Though they were related, he usually saw Gaius Octavius and his family only every few years when someone either married or died. Even then, they had always been a very reserved family.

Antonius looked at the young Octavius, who stared at him in quiet curiosity. Atia pushed him toward Antonius with her knee and the boy limply moved forward. He dipped his head and kissed the boy's cheek. "Marcus Antonius."

The boy stepped away, wiping at his face.

His mother jostled him again. "Tell the young man your name."

He remained stubbornly silent. Antonius raised a brow, but Octavius only shook his head defiantly. Philippus shifted impatiently beside him, and Atia sighed.

"His name is Gaius Octavius Thurinus," she said. Her voice did not waver, instead sharpening around the name, like stone against metal. "He prefers his own company to that of others."

"That is one way to put it," Philippus muttered under his breath.

Atia ignored him, pushing her daughter forward, who brightened up with a smile when Antonius kissed her soft cheek.

"Octavia," she said in a gentle, lilting voice. "It is nice to meet you, Marcus Antonius."

He held back a smile at the way she said his name. "And you, Octavia."

Now that the child business was done, Atia shooed them back to their grandmother and returned her attention to Philippus.

She drew up her shoulders, as if the presence of her children had been weighing on her, and from one moment to the next she looked as Antonius remembered her from when he was still a boy and she had been newly wed to Gaius Octavius. A beautiful and proud young woman, the kind of woman Antonius was always trying to find, but instead only finding the bottom of a wine glass and a brothel.

"Well then, what news?" Atia asked.

"Nothing troubling, to be sure. Only Antonius here was telling me how he'd like to study in Athens," Philippus said, nodding towards Antonius.

Atia turned to him in feigned approval. "That is wonderful, Antonius. I will be sure to mention something to my uncle. He has many friends in Athens."

Antonius realized with a sudden anger that they had planned this all along. Perhaps it had even been Atia's idea. Or, more likely, Caesar had given the suggestion along with his condolences, if he had any, to brush aside a troublesome family member and secure his bribed support at the same time.

He was again reminded of the power extending beyond the tips of Julius Caesar's fingers, like stealthy tree roots wriggling their way into every home through the soil.

If someone were to ask him now, Antonius would bet on Caesar and his sway with the mobs to win, whether it was the right side or not. Politics, after all, was just like gambling, except in this game, one bet with their life. But the storm had not yet landed, and it was always better to wait until the wind began to blow.

"That would be very kind of you," Antonius said with a curt nod.

Philippus patted him firmly on the shoulder. "I do not doubt that Greece will do you good, son, and soon you will return a learned military man and we will hardly recognize you."

But the curl of his lips suggested otherwise. In their eyes, Antonius was nothing more than a gambling drunk, and perhaps it was best to let them think it. *For now.*

"Just do not marry a foreign woman while you are there," Atia added, "and we will welcome you back home with open arms."

He could not help a small smile at that—which Atia eyed curiously—because since the moment Philippus had suggested it, Antonius had been picturing a beautiful Grecian woman in his head, her hand already straying to her belt.

Antonius always did have a thing for accents.

I

Marcus Vipsanius Agrippa

JANUARY 44 BC

"I bet fifty *aurei* that I roll a Senio."

Octavius pushed forward a mound of gold coins, raising a challenging brow around the table. The soldiers crowding the tavern shouted their approval as the stakes were raised at last.

Agrippa shared disbelieving glances with Maecenas and Rufus. Fifty gold coins was over double the pot when all night long they had only raised the bets by increments.

Octavius looked all too satisfied at their hesitation. "Well?"

They all reluctantly matched the bet and threw in their coins. Octavius shook the dice in his hand, closing his eyes with a small smile. The tavern quieted before his throw as all the men watched Octavius take a deep breath and release the dice across the table. They skittered and settled loudly in the silence.

Agrippa reached over and flipped the first die face up. "Three." The next. "One." The next. "Four."

He hesitated on the last. It had to be a six to make a Senio. He glanced at Octavius, but he only smirked. Agrippa picked up the die and showed the room.

"Six."

The tavern broke out into rowdy cheers, the soldiers lifting their glasses high. Everyone looked at Octavius in open admiration as he kissed the dice in reverence and began dragging the pile of coins toward himself.

Agrippa shook his head in disbelief.

Octavius leaned over to him with a smile. "It appears Fortuna was on my side tonight."

"It was luck indeed, Octavius," said Maecenas loudly, who sat opposite Agrippa, "and you had best hope it does not run short." He hated gambling nights because he usually lost, but he loved spending money, of which he had a lot. "I raise your bet to one hundred *aurei*. But this time, the first person who rolls a Venus takes home the pot."

There were murmurs among the other men gathered around them. A Venus was the best throw in a game of dice when all four numbers were different. It was also notoriously rare to roll.

Agrippa shook his head. One hundred gold coins were nearly a fourth of his savings, and he would not risk it on an impossible bet. Besides, he had already lost much tonight. "I must concede."

Rufus, who sat opposite Octavius, leaned back with a frown. "Me too."

"And you?" Maecenas asked, turning to Octavius.

Octavius looked at Maecenas for a long moment, contemplating. He glanced around the room, a gleam in his eyes. Everyone was watching, waiting for his response. Octavius was at his best when there was a crowd.

He smiled and pushed forward a large pile of coins. "Two hundred and it's a deal."

Maecenas merely raised a brow, then nodded, adding his own coin to the pile which now towered in gleaming gold, comically large upon the stained wooden table beneath.

The soldiers in the tavern shifted on their feet, staring at the pile hungrily. Many of them had never glimpsed so much money in their entire lives. The shabby tavern packed with army men and smoky-eyed girls suddenly looked especially barbaric and dirty, though Octavius and Maecenas continued as if they had grown up betting on dice rolls in dingy taverns all their lives. Agrippa supposed it was not so far from the truth.

Octavius handed the dice to Maecenas, who eyed them warily. He gave them a quick shake, then released them onto the table without another word. Octavius leaned over the table to flip the dice one by one.

"One, six, three...and one," Octavius said, giving Maecenas an apologetic smile, which Maecenas returned with a scowl. "My turn."

He scooped up the dice and rubbed them between his hands, blowing gently. Maecenas sighed irritably at the theatrics but did not look away as Octavius rolled the dice, a reluctant smile tugging at his mouth. He had always found Octavius equally infuriating and charming.

"Don't say I didn't warn you," Octavius murmured, right before he rolled the dice. They flew and scattered across the table. One dropped off the ledge and landed by Rufus' feet.

Rufus reached across the table and flipped the first die. He showed the room. "Four." He flipped the next. "Six." There was a murmur among the men. Rufus flipped the next die. "Three."

11

"It is not possible," Maecenas whispered, staring at Octavius in disbelief.

Rufus picked up the die on the floor. Octavius had his eyes closed, but he was smiling triumphantly. He already knew. Somehow, he knew.

"One."

There was a stunned silence, before the soldiers exploded into violent shouts and cheers, crowding about Octavius to congratulate him. Maecenas alone looked miserable, staring dumbly at the four dice.

Octavius grinned, slapping Maecenas on the back, who half-heartedly shoved him away. "I told you Fortuna was on my side tonight." He raised his arms. "Another round on me, boys!"

The men could not contain their excitement at this, and wine sloshed across the tavern floor as another round of drinks was served. They began shouting his name and dragging him towards the bar, shoving a pretty Gades girl his way.

Agrippa stood up to join the festivities, but not before he glimpsed the white knucklebone of a fifth die disappearing in Rufus' hand as he slipped it into his pocket.

Don't say I didn't warn you.

He turned towards Octavius but he was already swallowed up by the crowd.

⁕⁕⁕

"You cheated," Agrippa said, halfway through the next morning.

Octavius glanced up in surprise from his couch. No, not surprise, Agrippa thought, but amusement. Had he known Agrippa would find out? Octavius paused his work, setting down his stylus and tablet.

They had been writing letters all morning to family and friends back in Italy before they worked on their assignments for tomorrow. Strategy lessons by their Greek tutor, Athenodorus, would begin early, followed by their first parade drill of the day and sword training.

"Yes," Octavius said simply.

Agrippa stared. "Why?"

Octavius looked at him curiously, half-smiling already. "To win, of course."

"It is not winning," Agrippa argued, though he felt the conversation was futile. He never had the wit and charm of Octavius, who could turn his enemies into friends with one bawdy joke and convince a crowd that he was right with a mere smile. "It is cheating. There is a difference."

"In war, there is no such thing as cheating," Octavius said with a smirk.

It was something Athenodorus had taught them. But he had also taught them that there was such a thing as dishonor in war and that it was to be avoided even at the cost of death.

"It was just a game, Octavius, not a war. And games have rules."

"Was it just a game?"

Agrippa shifted uneasily in his seat. Moments like these reminded him that they came from very different places.

Octavius, born into the Julian family, grand-nephew to the *Imperator* Julius Caesar, knew wealth and power that stretched beyond Rome, beyond the sea to lands of foreign tongues and strange peoples. Agrippa, descended from the humble beginnings of an immigrant family, born to a farmer and his wife, knew only what it meant to be a soldier turning the cogs of a machine much greater than himself.

"Nothing is *just* a game, Agrippa." But he spoke lightly, catching Agrippa's frown and shaking his head ruefully. "Life is the greatest game of all, and the rules are written by the winners. One day all of those soldiers may be under my command. If I cannot win a simple game of dice now, why should they believe I will win a war?"

Agrippa fell silent. He had no argument against this. There were already rumors that the *Imperator* favored his grand-nephew and had adopted him in his will. Caesar had promised him the position of Master of Horses, a very high honor indeed, which was currently held by Lepidus, a man more than twice Octavius' age.

Yet as they spoke the Egyptian queen Cleopatra resided in Rome as Caesar's mistress in hopes of forging an alliance between East and West. There was even talk of a rebellion among the senators against Caesar, who kept the Senate close but powerless, like a dog on a leash.

"You understand, then?" Octavius demanded.

He seemed keen to have Agrippa's approval. The thought pleased Agrippa, but at the same time, a doubt lingered in his mind.

For a moment neither of them spoke, and Octavius sighed, returning to his tablet.

"Rufus," Agrippa said suddenly. Octavius looked up, this time in surprise. "You did not explain Rufus."

"What of him?"

"Why did you have *him* swap the die?" Agrippa asked. He did not know why this bothered him most of all, except that he and Rufus had never been as close as the rest of them. Agrippa was a better soldier and student despite Rufus' more dignified background, which made Rufus endlessly jealous, and it took much of Agrippa's patience to ignore his harsh jokes meant only to humiliate him. "Why not ask me?"

Octavius raised a brow. "Would you have done it?"

"You are my closest friend, Octavius. I would have done it if you asked it of me."

Then Octavius smiled. "I know. That is why I did not need to."

"I see." Agrippa nearly smiled, before he realized what it was that had been truly nagging at him since the moment he saw Rufus slip the fifth die into his pocket. "But I was the one who flipped over the dice when you rolled a Senio. How did you manage that?"

"Ah."

Octavius reached into his pocket and pulled out four dice with a flourish. He tossed the dice on the table between them. They rolled to a gentle stop.

Three, one, three...six. A perfect Senio.

It was impossible, and yet the truth gleamed as white as those knucklebones. Octavius grinned, and Agrippa's breath caught. "That, my dear Agrippa, was pure luck."

"I don't believe it," he whispered, but as he looked at Octavius and his unwavering brown eyes, Agrippa thought he would believe anything.

"Then call it fate."

⤜⟩⟩⟩ ⟨⟨⟨⤛

Later that night they dined in the modest summer house of a client family of Caesar, who had invited Octavius and his friends to spend the weekend there despite his absence.

Although the house was not very spacious and poorly lit, it was a luxurious retreat from their daily military training, which more often than not consisted of marching endlessly through grassy fields and mud, erecting and disassembling camps, and swimming great distances in the sea for physical conditioning.

"I still cannot believe you won last night," Maecenas said, shaking his head and taking another sip of his wine.

Octavius grinned, but this time, Agrippa had trouble joining in. He refused to look at Rufus reclining right beside him, though Agrippa thought he glimpsed a tinge of a flush on his cheeks out of the corner of his eye.

"What can I say?" Octavius stretched his arms out. "I'm a lucky man."

"Are you sure it was luck?" Maecenas asked, arching a brow.

Agrippa's heart pounded. He glanced at Octavius, but he hardly seemed to be bothered, smiling into his cup as he drank. This time Agrippa stole a glance at Rufus. He was looking down at the floor and remained silent.

"You're right," Octavius said, and Agrippa looked at him sharply. "It was not luck. It was destiny."

Maecenas rolled his eyes and Agrippa relaxed. "Oh, spare me Aeneas."

It was an age-old joke they had with Octavius, whose family insisted they were de-

14

scended from Aeneas, the famous Trojan hero and founder of the Roman race. While Octavius always took the jest with ease, Agrippa sensed it bothered him more than he let on.

"What? Do you not believe in fate?" Octavius asked teasingly. He smiled still, but his eyes grew serious, looking at Maecenas with a familiar intensity.

For Octavius believed in things like fate and glory, and though he did not often voice them, he harbored plans of following in his great-uncle's footsteps. But while Julius Caesar was a seasoned and well-loved war general who had conquered not only armies but empires, Octavius was not yet nineteen and still in army training.

"Naturally I do," Maecenas drawled, though he suddenly looked very uncomfortable on his couch, glancing at Octavius cautiously. "With men such as Aeneas, at least. Achilles. Agamemnon. Odysseus. Menelaus. You know, the great heroes."

"You forgot Hector," Rufus interjected with a mocking smile.

"Everyone forgets Hector," Maecenas shot back.

"The great heroes," Octavius echoed, setting down his cup. "You know, there will come a time when the world will need another hero. Like Alexander the Great."

"You mean a conqueror," Agrippa said quietly. "Alexander the Great was not a hero."

"Oh, Agrippa, ever the moralist," Maecenas said with a dismissive hand.

He always picked Octavius' side, even if he did not exactly agree with Octavius himself. They came from the same social circles back in Rome after all, and Octavius had always been more charming than Agrippa.

But there was a hunger in Maecenas' eyes as he glanced at Octavius that made Agrippa stiffen. He thought their friendship strange, since Octavius surely knew of Maecenas' habits. It was not exactly a secret that Maecenas enjoyed the company of some of the younger boys now and then.

Yet when Agrippa had mentioned something about it off-hand some years ago, Octavius had only smiled at him.

"Maecenas is harmless," Octavius had said lightly. "He is a good friend."

"Because he has money?" Agrippa had asked, a touch angrily. He knew it was part—if not the only—reason Octavius was friends with someone like that, and it infuriated him to no end.

Octavius had given him a hard look. "Do not criticize his wealth when your problem lies with something very different." He paused. "He is a good friend to have."

Agrippa did not mention anything again after that.

But Agrippa was not surprised that Maecenas found Octavius attractive. It was not exactly his looks, which were dark and oddly delicate, almost feminine. His physique was slim and angular due to the illnesses which had riddled his childhood, and which he still suffered from occasionally. In fact, if one looked at him carefully as he walked, there was the slightest limp in his step, as if one leg had grown longer than the other, or he was born with some deformity.

But there was an air to him, a confidence in his eyes, a secret in his teasing smile like he knew something that no one else did, but that if you got close enough he might just tell it. It was one of the reasons Agrippa had always found himself gravitating towards Octavius, hoping to learn that secret, or perhaps simply wishing to be more like him.

Agrippa still did not know exactly what Octavius had seen in *him*, in his modest upbringing, his unartful conversation, his unexceptional intelligence. But he must have found something worth holding onto, even if it was only a boy who was desperate for a friend.

They had studied together at the same school in Rome since they were nine, under the tutelage of Apollodorus of Pergamon, a notable Greek teacher. His father had sent Agrippa to school there in the hopes that he would rise above his station.

The boys at school were all sons of rich politicians and lawyers, like Maecenas and Rufus, and they hardly spoke to him at first. It would take many months and the unlikely attention of Octavius to rope him into their summers vacationing in luxury villas on the bay of Naples and dinner parties at their father's stately homes on the Palatine.

Only later as they grew older did Agrippa feel more at ease among them, joining in their gambling and drinking sprees across Rome and exploring the back rooms of brothels. It helped that he had grown tall and strong, and excelled in all kinds of sports, so that he earned the respect of more than just his few close friends.

But that all came to an end at seventeen when Julius Caesar confronted the forces of Pompeius—his established rival by that time—in Hispania.

Octavius had wanted to fight alongside Caesar, but he fell ill before he could leave, and remained bedridden for weeks.

It was not the first time Agrippa had seen Octavius sick, but this time had been different. Agrippa would never forget the conversation they had on one particularly bad night.

Octavius had been lying in bed, his face deathly pale and gleaming with sweat, his dark eyes sunken and ringed gray. Agrippa had been so sure, then, that he would die, so he had spent all his days ceaselessly by his side, while even Maecenas and Rufus had left to attend to other business.

"You are afraid," Octavius had said, weakly, coughing at the effort. Agrippa thought he saw blood. "You are afraid I will die."

"Yes." His voice had been less than a whisper. To his horror, Agrippa had felt his eyes sting, and tears had welled in his eyes.

"Me too." Octavius' breath had rattled in his chest, and he would not look at Agrippa, staring at the ceiling. "Will you stay?"

Agrippa had stayed by his bedside through the entire night, and every time Octavius had closed his eyes, his breath so weak it appeared he was not breathing at all, Agrippa's heart would stop. But by dawn, Octavius had still been alive, and day by day he had recovered and regained his strength until he could walk again.

Soon after that, Octavius had begun talking about joining Caesar in Hispania, though his mother Atia flatly refused. Agrippa himself had not been sure that Octavius was well enough for the journey, but Octavius was adamant not to waste any more of his life at home, so together with Maecenas, Rufus, and a few others they journeyed north.

It seemed like the wrath of the gods when a violent storm hit them off the coast of Hispania, dragging their ship in the wrong direction and landing them on the shores of enemy territory.

Yet somehow they had survived, sleeping during the day and marching at night, until they arrived at Caesar's camp, where most of the fighting had already concluded.

Caesar had been so impressed by their survival that at the end of the year, he had them all accompany Octavius to the Academy in Apollonia for military training, where they would eventually join his Macedonian troops preparing for war in the East.

Months passed, and Octavius never spoke of that terrible night again. Agrippa was not even sure Octavius remembered it.

But Agrippa did, and he could still feel Octavius' limp, feverish hand in his, and for some time afterward his dreams were plagued with visions of Octavius' chest growing still, and Agrippa failing to shake his dead body awake.

Their early days in Apollonia, however, were not so easy, despite Octavius' wealth and favor with Caesar. The soldiers had already been circulating rumors about Octavius, especially as the grand-nephew of Caesar, who now had the Republic completely at his mercy. His youth and delicate constitution were an easy mark for slander.

"I heard he's a favorite of Caesar's," one would say in admiration.

"Aye, you know what that means. I heard he sold himself to Hirtius for a pretty sum." The soldiers found that particular joke awfully funny.

Even then, another would defend him. "Well, *I* heard that he fought against the eldest son of Pompeius in Spain earlier this year, and Caesar named him his heir because of it."

This quieted most of them, since the name of Julius Caesar carried a certain awe, and already people speculated about his successor. But when Octavius spent time among the men, all of the rumors came to an abrupt stop.

One of the first weeks there, Octavius had joined a night of games at the tavern. He gambled so much money away with such good nature that the boys all warmed up to him at once. By the end of the week, he was surrounded by a slew of young soldiers, leaning over the game board as Octavius played against the veteran soldiers.

There was one night that Agrippa will never forget. Octavius had been playing an older man who was at the time unbeatable in the game of mercenaries. Octavius had found himself in a tight spot, with most of his pieces confiscated, and his opponent closing in on the rest.

Suddenly Octavius had leaned back, looking around the room. His eyes had settled on Agrippa, sitting in his own corner, watching the night's events around him quietly so as not to draw attention to himself.

"Agrippa," Octavius had said. "Come here."

"The gladiator!" someone called out.

There was a ripple of laughter among the men. They jokingly called him a gladiator because of his strength and size, which was all the more amusing because of his rather soft-spoken nature.

Agrippa had walked over and sat down beside Octavius nonetheless, feeling very self-conscious, though he tried not to show it.

"Tell me, Agrippa," Octavius said, motioning to the game board. It was hard to tell if he was being sincere or not. "What do you think I should do next?"

Maecenas, who had attached himself to Octavius' side for as long as Agrippa could remember, frowned. "I already told you, Octavius. You should move that piece and block his attack."

But Octavius only looked at Agrippa. "Well?"

It was not unusual to ask for advice from friends during a game, but Agrippa was his social inferior, known more for his tavern brawls and boxing matches than anything else.

Luckily, his father had loved the game of mercenaries, having served in the army himself, and together at home they would play for hours, adding makeshift boards to enlarge the grid and make the games even longer and more complex. Agrippa had understood the strategy of Octavius' opponent since the beginning, and Octavius was falling right into his trap.

"The attack is only a distraction," Agrippa said finally. "He will use it to corner your offense and you will have lost before you have even begun to defend. It would be best to stage an attack yourself."

Octavius raised a brow but did not speak. The room hushed as Octavius made his next move, and by the end of the hour, he had defeated the reigning champion. Since that day, Octavius had insisted that Agrippa remain at his side during game nights, and as each night passed the bets staked on his victory rose to ever greater heights, much to the jealousy of Maecenas.

Even now, Maecenas disliked how close Agrippa was with Octavius, and in arguments such as these, he often argued merely to make Agrippa look bad.

"So what if he was a conqueror?" Maecenas asked flippantly, glancing at Agrippa with poorly veiled annoyance. "Alexander the Great was the best general to ever live and he was only twenty years old."

Octavius held up a hand to quiet Maecenas and looked at Agrippa thoughtfully. "Let him speak, Maecenas."

Maecenas was stunned into silence. Agrippa felt his heart move to his throat at the sudden attention. Even Rufus turned to him now.

"Alexander the Great only knew how to fight, not to rule. It was his downfall," Agrippa said quietly. "A true hero must know how to do both."

"Nonsense," Maecenas said, though he sounded unsure, shooting Octavius a quick glance. "Achilles never ruled and he was the greatest hero of all."

But Octavius was still looking at him steadily, as if Agrippa had understood something that only Octavius had known all along. "That, my Agrippa, is why we are friends."

2

GAIUS OCTAVIUS

FEBRUARY 44 BC

"WHEN YOUR ENEMY IS on the offensive, *that* is when he is at his most vulnerable," Athenodorus, one of their Greek tutors, said as he strolled in front of them. "And the same goes for yourselves."

The boys following after him carefully etched the words onto their tablets. In the center of the town was a shaded courtyard where Athenodorus liked to lecture. He believed in the ancient teachers, Socrates and Plato, and followed the Greek style of teaching, taking long strolls in the garden and lecturing them to boredom.

"Say, what about when he's bent over?" Maecenas asked, though he spoke in Latin and not Greek, so their tutor would not be as quick to understand.

The other boys held their laughs, and could hardly contain them when Maecenas made a crude gesture with his hands and hips. Many of these boys had gone to the same school in Rome as them, or else they knew each other through friends of family.

Octavius had specially invited some teachers from Rome to accompany him to Apollonia in order to continue their education in military strategy and rhetoric, since many of them would go on to become politicians after their time in the army.

Athenodorus glanced back with one raised, bushy brow. Agrippa, walking quietly beside Octavius, stiffened slightly. He hated it when they got themselves into trouble, although Octavius always reassured him that nothing bad would happen to him.

"A man's at his most vulnerable," Octavius announced, this time in Greek, feigning the deeper, gravelly voice of their elderly rhetoric teacher Apollodorus, "when he has his—"

"That's quite enough, boys," Athenodorus interrupted, turning around in annoyance at the choked laughter from the group. "Now since you all found that very entertaining, I shall increase your exercises for tomorrow and require the rest of Polybius' *Histories*."

There were groans from some of the boys who had barely begun reading the *Histories* in the first place.

"And," Athenodorus continued, "I will also require a spoken analysis of the strategies employed by the Romans against the Carthaginians throughout the Second Punic War by tomorrow afternoon."

Agrippa sighed beside him.

Octavius stepped forward in the following quiet. "My apologies, sir, but I am afraid that is not possible."

Athenodorus turned on him in annoyance, but already the corner of his mouth was twitching. Octavius was his favorite, after all, and everyone knew it. "And pray tell, Octavius, why is that?"

"Well, sir, it is only that tomorrow is the Lupercalia. We cannot possibly work on a festival day."

There was an agitated silence. While it was true that tomorrow the Lupercalia would be celebrated, the most important rituals occurred in Rome, and the festivities here would involve more revelry than worship. But Athenodorus was a Greek and did not need to know that.

"Please, sir," Octavius continued. "If it is necessary to punish someone, then punish me. I may give an analysis of the Second Punic War tomorrow if you wish."

He had already read the *Histories* a few times. Besides, he had a knack for public speaking, and he was at his best when he spoke off the cuff.

"What about your friend Maecenas here?" Athenodorus asked, gesturing to a blushing Maecenas, though his eyes were already softening. "Ought I not punish him as well?"

"Maecenas? Oh, but he's harmless isn't he," Octavius said, ruffling Maecenas' hair roughly with a grin.

Beside him, Agrippa tensed, though everyone else laughed. No one ever took Maecenas too seriously.

"Oh, very well," Athenodorus said at last, but not without a twinkle in his eyes. "The rest of you have until the day after next to prepare your analysis. But you, Octavius, since you so kindly offered yourself up for punishment, shall give it tomorrow morning before the ceremony."

"Yes, sir," Octavius said with a slight bow, ignoring Agrippa's eyes on him.

Athenodorus turned back around at that and began walking once more through the courtyard, shaded gently with fruit trees and decorated with statues of Greek and Roman deities. "As I was saying, your enemy is most vulnerable during his attack..."

Octavius and Maecenas shared a glance and had to look away before they began laughing again.

The steam of the *caldarium* clung to his skin. Octavius breathed in deeply, and his lungs burned slightly from the effort. Ever since he was young, he had to fight off countless illnesses, and his lungs never quite recovered from them.

But he loved the baths, the quiet calm of the waters, the oil coating his skin. His best ideas came to him in the baths, if only for writing bad tragedies and inappropriate verses. He was working on one now in his head but he did not know quite how to finish it off.

> *Claudia, Claudia, pulchrior est mea Claudia sole*
> *Quod ludamus ego et tu paulum, Claudia bella,*
> *Immo! Claudia, Claudia solum destituebat,*
> *Cum nihil ei plus nummi solvendae mihi dixi...*

> *Claudia, Claudia, more lovely is my Claudia than the sun,*
> *Why don't you and me, beautiful Claudia, have a little fun,*
> *Oh no! Claudia, Claudia she left me all alone,*
> *When I told her I had no more money to pay...*

Octavius was never meant to be a poet anyway. He lowered himself until the water reached his chin. There was a long silence, so long Octavius would have thought he was alone. But he was not alone.

Across the small pool sat Agrippa, his eyes closed, the steam from the water curling his dark hair against his forehead. Maecenas and Rufus had long left, wishing to exercise in the palestra, leaving the two of them in a painful silence.

"I am sorry about earlier," Octavius said at last. He knew Agrippa would never complain openly about his tendencies to joke around, even though the words were written plain enough on his face.

Agrippa's eyes opened a sliver. "It's alright."

"It's not. You hate it when we get in trouble." He paused. "But you know you don't have to worry about that anymore."

"I suppose." He sounded sullen, like Maecenas when he didn't get his way.

"Agrippa, I promise."

This time Agrippa looked at him, but strangely, as if embarrassed. "I don't need any favors, Octavius."

At those words, Octavius was suddenly reminded of a conversation he had with Maecenas about a year ago, when the wars between Caesar and Pompeius still raged in Africa.

They had received news that Agrippa's older brother had been taken prisoner by Caesar's army, having fought on the side of Pompeius. Agrippa had been devastated, but hid it well, even attending the lecture that day. He hated missing class for anything.

Octavius knew what he had to do, even if it cost him. His great-uncle had a soft spot for him, and if he did not say anything on Agrippa's behalf, he knew no one would.

"You know you are not obligated to hand out any favors," Maecenas had said quietly, glancing at Agrippa across the palestra, who had been wrestling another student. They had tousled on the ground for a few moments, locked in each other's flexed arms, before Agrippa had suddenly flipped the boy onto his back and won the match. "Though I suppose he is good in a fight..."

But Octavius had caught Maecenas' stare lingering on Agrippa's heaving chest—which had filled out with muscle over the summer—for a moment too long, and he pushed down a wave of irritation. Maecenas was always a bit ridiculous. "I am sure that is reassuring for *you*, Maecenas. But this has nothing to do with obligation."

Maecenas had glared at him. "If not obligation, then what?"

"You know there's much more to him than meets the eye," Octavius had said, giving Maecenas a hard look when he had smirked. "Did you know he sketched a map of the entire Republic by the time we were fifteen?"

"What would you need that for?" Maecenas had asked, perplexed, but he did take a second glance at Agrippa in newfound approval.

"And he is loyal," Octavius had continued sternly, ignoring Maecenas' frown. "That is worth more than all the money in the world."

After that, Maecenas had ceased questioning Agrippa's presence among them, even though he continued to make snide remarks that Agrippa understood all too well. It was a point of tension in their group, which Octavius was never sure how to resolve without picking a side.

Octavius looked at Agrippa across the bath, who avoided his gaze and ran a hand down his arm, which was turning red from the hot water. "I have been thinking a lot about what you said."

Agrippa frowned in confusion. "What?"

"About Alexander the Great." Octavius smiled, but it faded quickly. He had trouble joking about things that truly mattered to him. Agrippa stared at him as if he had spoken in another language. "And how he only knew how to fight, not rule. That it was his downfall."

"Oh." Agrippa scratched at his neck. "I didn't mean anything by it."

Octavius shook his head, and a few water droplets rolled down his face. He wished he could put it into words, the burning in his chest as if his heart were set aflame, whenever he thought of his future.

Ever since he was young, the world had tried to get rid of him, the gods, even his step-father, casting him aside, ill and unwanted. He remembered long nights lying in bed, unable to get up nor call for a doctor, and he would lie helpless for hours, wasting away on the brink of death.

But slowly, slowly, he would crawl back to the light, to life, each time more determined than before to make something of himself, his weak body, his legacy, his name. He did not fear death anymore, but a life unworthy of remembrance.

While a part of him longed for a glorious end, like that of Achilles, or an army to lead to countless victories, like Alexander the Great, there had always been a yearning in his soul for *more*. More than mere glory, more than victory.

Octavius longed, somehow, to forge a legacy that no one, from the far borders of Germania to the deserts of Ethiopia, would forget. He wished his name to be known beyond the outskirts of India, where they say Alexander once reached.

He did not know if it was because of his many illnesses, his weakness, that he strove for a far greater life than the one promised, or if it was because of some fate assigned to him. It did not matter. Long ago the desire had settled in his bones and each year the feeling grew stronger, that he would fight and never stop fighting to reach heights more lofty than even those of Caesar.

"Rome needs someone to rule her," Octavius said quietly, his voice echoing along with the *drip drip drip* of beaded water falling from the ceiling onto the slick marble floor. "Too long have generals fought over her. Too long have pirates ruled her waters. Too long have stingy Senators allowed Rome to fall into rot and ruin. The people believe Caesar will be the one to cleanse the streets, to return Rome to her former glory."

"And do you believe it?" Agrippa asked carefully.

"Perhaps."

Agrippa was silent. He had only ever heard Octavius speak his great-uncle's praises. Maecenas and Rufus, like most army men, were staunch supporters of the new regime and the defeat of Pompeius and his supporters. But his great-uncle would not be around forever.

Already there were rumors of backlash in the Senate, and it was not always certain how far deceit ran. Some days it seemed like time was running out, and they were only a step away from revolution and chaos.

Octavius leaned forward, and Agrippa tensed, watching him. "We only have one chance in our lives to do something great. If we miss it, then no one will remember us. Our lives will mean nothing."

Inexplicably, a smile tugged at Agrippa's mouth. "That is not what Athenodorus taught us."

Octavius sat back with a sigh. Agrippa had a habit of reminding Octavius of his immaturity, that all his dreams were simply youthful fancies. "Well, you know I don't listen during his lessons. You are the only one who does."

"Someone has to make sure we pass our exams," Agrippa said jokingly.

Octavius could not help a reluctant smile. "Don't tell Maecenas that."

Agrippa laughed, and it was an odd sound in such a quiet place, as if they were the only two people in a wide, empty field.

He could feel his fingertips beginning to prune. He leaned back and rested his head on the ledge, sweat rolling down his neck, and looked up at the ceiling, where paintings of men and women in close embraces encircled the room. Across from him, Agrippa tilted his head back too.

For a long time, they were silent. All that could be heard was the gentle lapping of the water against the sides of the pool. In Rome, the baths sprawled entire blocks, and they were always crowded. But here, the facilities only served the local townspeople and the army. The pool was small enough that if Octavius moved his leg, it would brush up against Agrippa's.

After another long minute, Octavius stood up, carefully stepping out of the bath.

He felt Agrippa's eyes lingering on him. "Octavius."

"Yes?"

"You know Alexander the Great died at thirty-two."

Octavius turned towards him and grinned, if only to hide the slight disappointment he felt. "I know."

But Agrippa was serious. "They say he was murdered. Poisoned. Some say it was done by one of his own men." He lowered his voice. "That's what happens to those who call themselves king."

"Ah, but that's the thing, *mi Agrippa*," Octavius said with a smirk. "I wouldn't be a king at all."

"No?"

"I'd be a god."

He had meant it as a joke, but the words fell heavily on the marble floor. Agrippa closed his eyes with a sigh, stretching his legs out until they nearly reached the other end of the pool. He floated in silence as if there was nothing more to say.

Octavius moved to the *frigidarium* in the next room, struggling to catch his breath, though he had hardly moved at all in the past hour. As he plunged into the cold water, he felt the burning in his heart cool until he could almost breathe normally again.

⠀⠀⠀⠀⠀⠀»»» «««

The sun lit the polished stone of the street, crowded with naked men holding out leather thongs, and women dressed in their best, screeching as a man got close and whipped her outstretched hand with his strip of shaggy leather.

Octavius glanced at Agrippa. He stood next to Octavius, his muscles gleaming in the noonday sun, a slash of blood from the sacrifice smeared on his forehead. He was slightly out of breath from running, his chest rising and falling rapidly, and he played with his leather thong, stroking the fur as if it were still on a live animal.

Maecenas suddenly ran up to them with a grin, his blonde hair damp with sweat so that it looked brown, the curls between his legs only a slight shade darker. He slapped his leather strap across Octavius' naked stomach so hard and fast it stung.

"Fili canis!" Octavius tried to get him back with his own whip but Maecenas twisted away, dodging the blow with a laugh. "You're only supposed to hit the women, Maecenas!"

"Oh, I know!" Maecenas laughed and ran off, his buttocks small and pale compared to his tan, wiry legs. While Maecenas was not very well-built, his quick instincts and determination made up for it, and he could be difficult to pin down in a fight if he would take any of it seriously.

"We'd better go on," Octavius said, motioning to the group of naked boys already far ahead of them.

He had paused in the shade to catch his breath from the initial sprint they had run from the altar through town. Agrippa had stayed with him, though it only made him more embarrassed. No one dared mention his weakness to his face, but he knew they talked about it when he was not around.

"On three," Agrippa suggested. "One, two—"

Octavius shot off, not looking back to see if Agrippa was following. He smiled to himself, knowing he would be passed, and soon enough, Agrippa flew past him, whipping the outstretched hands of women who pretended to trip and fall in his way, shrieking in delight and fear at the slap.

It was freeing to run like this, the wind pressing unfamiliarly close against his naked body as he and the other boys in town frolicked together through the streets, whipping the women to their hearts' content, whipping each other until fights broke out and they cast aside their whips and swung at each other with fists.

There was nothing like a group of boys running naked in the streets, Octavius thought, their strong legs tense as they ran, their arms swinging, their waists still slender and flexible in youth.

It felt as though they would be forever young, forever causing mischief, grabbing at women, who held their hands out but turned their bodies away, just out of reach, like nymphs. The boys were the centaurs in the woods, they were gods, hunting and howling in the wild parts of the world. A part of Octavius wished it would never end.

After they returned to the altar to finish the remaining rituals, they all meandered to a meadow just outside the town, flasks of wine in hand, as the sun set gently on the horizon.

Below the fields lapped the Aous River, spilling out into the Adriatic Sea. A few boys wandered down to the shore, wading out into the water despite its chill winter currents. It was the only barrier between them and the shores of Italy, and yet they might as well have been on opposite ends of the earth. Caesar and the political turmoil of Rome were like a distant dream.

Maecenas plopped down onto the ground, lying on his side as if they were about to dine. "That was fun."

"That was exhausting," Agrippa muttered from the ground beside him, taking a swig of his flask, his throat working.

Octavius always thought Agrippa's neck too slender, somehow, too delicate, for his large limbs, the curves of thick muscle, so that he still had a strange, boyish look about him despite his visible strength.

Maecenas was staring at him. He had the sudden awareness—as if they hadn't been all along—of their nakedness. Octavius resisted the urge to cover himself, instead lying flat on his back, his arms and legs spread out, completely exposed to the sky. His bare skin prickled in the breeze off the water, and he nearly shivered.

"What do you think they are doing in Rome?" Octavius asked, watching a cloud crawl its way across the purpling blue sky. It was painful in its slow, imperceptible movement, and Octavius had to look away, turning his head.

Agrippa now had his arms stretched behind his head, the hair underneath his armpits dark and curled, but cropped close to the skin, as if he had singed them off once.

Octavius occasionally removed the hair from his legs, though he barely had any to begin with, and they were blonde and thin. Agrippa, on the other hand, had thick brown hair everywhere, on his legs, his arms, his chest. Instinctively, Octavius felt his own chest with the palm of his hand, felt the bare smoothness of the skin, as it had been since he was a boy.

"Probably the same as it always is. Naked drunk boys slapping rich old women who couldn't get pregnant anymore if they tried," Maecenas said, yawning. He looked around. "Say, where is Rufus?"

"I thought I saw him over there." Agrippa nodded to a crowd of standing men taking long gulps of their flasks, stumbling against each other in drunken laughter.

"I bet the wine is better back home," Octavius continued, watching Agrippa shake the last drops of cheap wine from his flask into his open mouth. "And the women."

Agrippa's eyes flickered to him.

"Hey! Rufus!" Maecenas called out across the field, and soon Rufus appeared, his shaggy, red-brown hair matted with crusted animal blood from the sacrifice. "Come here!"

Rufus smiled, but it was mocking, and he ambled his way over to them. He sat down close beside Maecenas, his cheeks flushed red from the wine, and allowed Maecenas to stroke his hair.

"Those men were talking about you, Octavius," Rufus said quietly.

"Oh really?"

"Actually, they were talking about Caesar." Rufus glanced at Octavius to gauge his reaction. When Octavius only raised a brow, he continued. "They were saying he was the new king of Rome."

Agrippa glanced at him sternly, and Octavius ignored him. *That's what happens to those who call themselves king.* "Then they are mistaken. Rome has no king."

"Not yet," Rufus said with a mischievous smile that made Octavius' stomach drop.

It was not a new rumor, but no one had yet spoken of it to his face, fearing to voice the implications, which have been unprecedented for centuries and would warrant a prosecution against his great-uncle if anyone dared to speak out against him.

"You are drunk, Rufus," said Maecenas, giving him a warning glance.

Rufus leaned back against Maecenas' chest, closing his eyes with an indulging smile. "Aye, we are all just drunk."

Maecenas was silent. When Rufus got in one of his moods, there was not much they could do.

Octavius stared up at the sky, now night black, shining with stars. He felt Agrippa shift beside him, a flickering glow on bare skin from their lanterns, a glimmer in the darkness that closed in on them so that the meadow stretched out around them like dark rippling waves at sea.

They lay there in silence for some time, until Rufus' gentle snores could be heard, and even Maecenas half-slept curled up on his side, his eyelids drooping closed. Others were slowly leaving, while some stretched out on the grass and stared up at the constellations in murmuring conversation, the drunken revelry dwindling as the moon rose in the east.

"It does not mean anything," Agrippa said quietly, hardly more than a whisper, not wanting Maecenas to overhear and wake up. "It is only a rumor."

"Rumors often hide a seed of truth." Octavius turned onto his side, facing Agrippa, who looked at him under half-lidded eyes. "My great-uncle...he has always known what he wanted."

"That is not a bad thing."

"It is when the rest of the world knows it too," Octavius said.

His mother had been sending letters from Rome. She wrote anxiously of the various Senators opposing Caesar, and the rising hatred against him as he rose in power unparalleled since the kings of old. Not only that, the Egyptian queen Cleopatra still resided in Rome and it was becoming quite the scandal with circulating rumors of an illegitimate child.

Octavius remembered Caesar very well from the times he had seen him, which were fewer than some might think. Julius Caesar traveled much, campaigning in far-off places in the East, summering near Egypt, and then governing in Gaul.

While Octavius had lived with his grandmother, Julia Minor—when he was still very young and ill and his new step-father, Philippus, did not want to deal with him—he often saw Caesar as he passed through Rome and visited his sister.

Caesar was proud, but quiet, with a subtle sense of humor that often pleased the ladies of his company. Octavius had fond memories of his visits when he would share stories of his times abroad, the men he had killed, the places he had seen, the important people he had dined with, kings and queens and emperors.

He was well-liked, by his men and by the people of Rome, who would flock to the docks and the streets whenever he returned in order to greet him. While Caesar stayed in Rome he would throw the most magnificent parties, filled with wealthy senators and their beautiful, young wives, accompanied by the best poets and finest musicians the Republic had to offer.

If Octavius was lucky enough to remain unnoticed for the rest of the night, he would be able to hear the symposium gathering close to dawn, Caesar and his closest friends shut up in the dining room. He would only be able to hear their drunken voices and boisterous laughter from out in the hall before one of the servants found him and shooed him off to bed.

Yet underneath all of Caesar's charm and pomp, there ran deep a passion, a desire to be ever more powerful, ever more in control of Rome. He would talk at length about it to Julia, and to his guests, and even to Octavius when he had joined him in Hispania this last year. He obsessed over the vision of Rome he had, the new Rome, rising out of the ashes of civil war.

There were those who fought him relentlessly in the Senate, like Pompeius and Cicero, but they all quaked in his presence as if they were speaking with a god. Octavius remembered the way they looked at him, half-mesmerized, half-afraid, as though Caesar were either going to destroy or save Rome, and there was nothing they could do but wait and see.

He felt a hand on his arm in the dark. Their lantern had gone out a long time ago, descending them in darkness all around.

Octavius could hardly see Agrippa, but he felt him, his fingertips pressing into his forearm. They were rarely affectionate with each other, not like Maecenas at least, but the touch was like stepping on firm ground after weeks at sea.

"Whatever happens," Agrippa said quietly, "you have me."

Just then, Maecenas stirred, and Agrippa's hand left him. Octavius turned onto his back again, his skin warm against the chill air of the night, the wine still working in his veins.

Above him shined Orion the Hunter, his bow eternally taut in the sky, like the god Apollo. They slept there until Dawn rose in the sky and sought in vain for Her starlit lover before they returned to town.

3

MARCUS ANTONIUS

FEBRUARY 44 BC

ANTONIUS DECIDED HE HATED Julius Caesar.

The party was already in full swing, so there was not much he could do about it. Besides, he was drunk, and there were too many important people around him to risk anything.

Julius Caesar sat at the head of the left couch, looking smug. Beside him—as if she were his wife, by Jove—lay Queen Cleopatra, and beside her reclined Balbus, Caesar's finance manager and close friend.

A very uncomfortable Cicero, the senior of their party, took the place of honor on the middle couch, Antonius and Hirtius beside him, while Pansa, Brutus, and Cassius had been placed on the right couch. The rest of the guests, various Senators and lawyers and other prominent people such as Gaius Trebonius and Decimus Brutus, wandered about the house, mingling with the other guests or finding their own couches in other rooms.

It was a party fit for a comedy, Antonius thought, as he watched Cicero fail to hide yet another frown at something Caesar said, and Balbus intervened in his thick Gades accent to appease both of them.

Balbus did have a gift for reconciling rivals, having once reconciled Caesar with his rival Pompeius the Great. That is, of course, until Caesar had Pompeius killed, so that Balbus now had to play mediator between Caesar and the entire Republican party of the Senate.

Antonius did not know what was more shocking, however, the fact that Caesar had invited Brutus and Cassius to the dinner or that Brutus and Cassius had deigned to accept. For there were rumors of their anger at Caesar because of his—and Antonius supposed, his *own*—actions at the Lupercalia.

While Antonius had indeed offered a gold crown to Caesar during the festivities, Caesar had publicly refused and dedicated the crown to Jupiter, more to appease the crowds than any religious duty.

No one really cared that Antonius had been the one to offer the gold crown to Caesar in the first place. Antonius, after all, held no real power next to that of Caesar, and that was their true grievance in the end.

For most of the dinner, however, Brutus and Cassius had remained in quiet discussion with Pansa and Hirtius, both of whom Caesar had designated for consul next year. It would have been an acceptable dinner party if not for one thing.

The queen.

Cleopatra reclined beside Caesar as naturally as if she *were* his wife, which only infuriated Antonius more. She was dressed in robes of white linen, a purple embroidered shawl—perhaps to mock the Roman senators—and layers of thick blue-beaded necklaces.

Antonius struggled not to stare at her dark eyes lined with kohl, her face framed by heavy gold earrings. She was the image of Egyptian royalty, and Antonius was hopelessly in love with her.

But she was completely forbidden, being the mistress of Julius Caesar, who was now the eternal ruler of Rome and the man that has kept Antonius close and docile like a slave for as long as he could remember.

Antonius hated him.

"Now, oughtn't we have food with our wine? Bring out the *gustatio,* Dionysios!" Caesar motioned to his slave, who hurried to the kitchens to pass on the orders.

A few moments later several platters of oysters and fresh lobsters were placed on the table before them. They all got to eating, if only to save themselves from an awkward silence.

After a few bites, Balbus complimented the freshness, with Cicero not far behind in complementing the cooking, though he looked wary as a platter of crabs and clams was set beside the rest. Nothing boded well when a Senator showed off at his banquet, and Caesar was no exception.

"So, Queen Cleopatra, how has Rome been treating your Ladyship?" Cicero asked after a bite of lobster.

Cleopatra flashed a red-lipped smile that had Cicero flushing darkly. "Very well, thank you, Father." She spoke Latin precisely and with a slight accent that had Antonius reaching for more wine. "I especially enjoyed the Lupercalia."

It was a provocative statement to make for several reasons, and the men all tensed. Her gaze slid imperceptibly to Antonius, and he felt his pulse quicken.

For Antonius had boldly worn nothing more than a loin cloth to the ceremony. Though the younger boys still went naked in the streets as was tradition, it had become frowned upon for the older Senators to participate in the nude. Antonius, of course, had done it more to scandalize the likes of Cicero than any true religious feeling. And sure enough, Cicero was quick to denounce him for it, though with much exaggeration as always.

But Antonius was long accustomed to his rivalry with Cicero. He remembered a particularly scathing charge many years ago of improper sexual relations with his friend Scribonius Curio. When someone had asked him about it, Antonius had said that if it had happened at all, he did not remember it—but that Cicero certainly did. Needless to say, Cicero had not appreciated getting wind of *that* joke.

"Ah, yes, the Lupercalia is a very ancient festival in Rome," Cicero said, nodding his head and reaching for another oyster. Caesar did have an excellent cook, and he had spent quite some money to fund this particular banquet.

"But may I ask why the women must be whipped as if they were schoolboys who misbehaved?" There was a glimmer in Cleopatra's eyes and Antonius wondered if it was meant for him.

Caesar laughed beside her, a rumbling like the start of an earthquake. "It is quite a show, isn't it?"

Antonius felt the wine hot under his skin before he spoke. "It is believed, my Lady, that when the *Luperci* whip the women, they become more...fertile."

"Ah, I see." Cleopatra looked at Antonius, her eyes dark and unreadable. "My people believe that if a woman lifts her robes and presents her sex before the Apis Bull, she will be blessed with fertility."

Cicero coughed. "How fascinating!"

After the main course of roasted wild boar and vegetables was served, Antonius excused himself and wandered the house. The party was being held at Caesar's villa on Quirinal Hill just outside the city walls, where Cleopatra lived as his guest, since no foreign heads of state were allowed to enter Rome. Somewhere inside the house was Caesarion, the illegitimate child of Cleopatra and Caesar, though he was too young to be of much consequence.

The villa itself was grand and stately, fit for a Roman senator, even a king. Surrounding the house were large gardens and parks sloping along the hill, its trees and bushes still bare of flowers at this time of year. Many guests were enjoying the mild evening temperature and were milling about the pathways that snaked through the gardens, bending around gently flowing fountains and tall, brilliant statues. Antonius found himself in a small corner bordered by rose bushes where a statue of Eros and Psyche stood.

"Why did you leave before dessert?"

Antonius whirled around. He had not heard anyone approach, but there was Cleopatra, beautiful and proud as ever. She lifted her chin slightly, as if in challenge, though her mouth held a small smile.

"I prefer a different kind of sweet."

If Cleopatra understood his meaning, she did not show it, taking a few steps closer until he could have reached out and taken her hand. "But who does not love honey cake?"

Antonius had difficulty moving away, even though he knew they were too close for comfort. At any moment another guest could walk past and see them, ruining their brief moment of respite.

Perhaps it was the wine, but Antonius found himself taking a step closer anyway. "We have met once before, long ago. Do you remember?"

A shadow passed over Cleopatra's face. "What?"

"Do you really not remember?" Antonius asked teasingly, taking another step towards her despite himself. "You were still very young. I was only a cavalry officer at the time."

"I'm afraid I do not," Cleopatra said, her voice faltering when Antonius stood only a breath before her. "I have met many cavalry officers in my lifetime."

"Ah, but none like this one," Antonius said quietly. He grazed the lightest fingertip against her hand, looking into her brown eyes which flickered with the warm light of a nearby lantern. "He was the most handsome cavalry officer to ever live."

"I cannot say I had the pleasure."

Antonius glanced at her red lips, the color of the sun before it set, aflame above the Seven Hills. He nearly leaned in to kiss them before he realized what he was doing and stepped away. "I believe this has become too dangerous, my Lady."

Cleopatra raised a brow. "You say that every time, Marcus."

No one else called him by that name, but Cleopatra had insisted from the beginning of their affair that she liked it better. She stepped away, her face flushed, before walking towards the statue at the center of the bushes.

"But this time is different," Antonius said, hating himself for saying it, though he knew he must. "Caesar is not one to be deceived. I fear for your safety."

"For *my* safety?" Cleopatra smiled, but the red of her lips looked as dark as blood now. She glanced up at the marble gods and slowly traced the strong arm of Eros as he gripped Psyche in his embrace. "You should look after yourself first, my love."

"But you are a woman."

Cleopatra laughed. "Precisely."

Antonius felt his chest tighten. He loved her laugh. It was the most careless thing about her, where everything else was controlled and carefully planned. "You do not know Caesar like I do."

"No, I would think not," Cleopatra said, disdain in her voice. "He fucks me after all."

"Gods above." Antonius *hated* him. "You do not need to speak so…"

"Honestly?"

"It does not become a lady," he said, though he sounded rather petulant. "A woman should not speak of such things."

"But I am not a woman." She touched the hand of Eros as if she had the power to bring the statue to life. Her voice turned cold and superior. "I am a queen. I can do whatever I wish."

"Caesar may as well be a king," Antonius spat. "And he will not suffer the rule of another, be it man or woman."

"If I know anything," Cleopatra shot back, "it is how to deal with kings."

Antonius was silent. He had never known a woman who made him feel as a mortal to a goddess, who looked at him with a smile that hinted at all the hidden knowledge he would never know, before casting him aside as if he were nothing. She had been a queen for almost as long as Antonius had known her, and in comparison, even his high station as co-consul with Caesar meant very little.

"There are other plans at work, which I have only heard whispers," Antonius added hesitantly. "I dare not say them aloud."

Cleopatra glared coldly at him. "Then, by all means, do not."

Antonius lowered his voice. "You may not be safe here if what I know comes to pass."

A sliver of doubt appeared in her eyes before she shook her head. "If these plans are as secret as you say, you had best keep them from *me*." Then she walked past Antonius.

Without thinking, Antonius' hand shot out and grabbed her wrist, yanking her back into his arms, her hands landing tightly on his shoulders to stop herself from colliding with him. He wished to kiss her, but their lips remained apart, their chests rising rapidly between them.

"As long as you are Caesar's," Antonius whispered, "you can never be mine."

Cleopatra laughed, but her eyes were tinged with sadness. "As long as *you* are Caesar's, you can neither be mine."

Then she moved out of his reach and disappeared behind the rose bushes, her laugh echoing in his mind like a warning, even though it was far too late for that.

Antonius stood there for a long time before he made his way back to the house.

⤜⟫⟫ ⟪⟪⤛

Antonius drank his wine slowly on the couch as he watched Caesar say goodbye to the last guest at the front door. Some would be staying in the many guest rooms of the house like Antonius, while the rest would return to their houses in the city.

Dawn crept through the windows so that the courtyard glowed a faint pink. Caesar sighed as the doors were shut at last, then came to sit on the couch beside Antonius.

"What a nuisance these parties have become!" Caesar passed a hand over his face. He looked exhausted and much older.

In Antonius' mind, Caesar always remained the young, ambitious general he had known since he was young. But now Caesar was fifty-five, his cheekbones stark in his face and his hair thin and gray. Antonius, not yet forty, was grateful he still had all of his thick dark curls.

"We used to party past dawn and attend our morning meetings still drunk," Antonius joked. "What happened to that?"

"I was still young, then." Caesar motioned for Antonius' glass, and he handed it over wordlessly. "Much has changed."

"Did Cicero give you a hard time?"

Caesar shrugged, his eyes seeing far away. "He did mention the gold crown. But otherwise, he was quite agreeable."

"That's a surprise."

"Ah, Cicero loves to hate." He paused. "It was Brutus that I found most strange." He took another sip of the wine before handing it back to Antonius, but he no longer had the desire to drink it. "He spoke to me and touched my arm with all the air of friendship. He even asked after his mother. You know how sensitive he is about all that."

Antonius nodded slowly. It was well-known that Caesar had a very long, passionate love affair with Brutus' mother, Servilia. "Did he mention the crown?"

"Not at all." Caesar sighed. "That was what I found most strange."

"Perhaps he has had a change of heart," Antonius suggested hopefully. "Maybe Servilia has managed to convince him of things after all."

"I do not think so." Caesar stood up with a yawn, stretching out his arms. "But he is not the only one who has been deceiving me."

Antonius felt his stomach drop. "No?"

Caesar looked at him, his eyes cold in their amusement. "Did you think I would not notice?"

"Notice what?"

"The way you look at her," Caesar said, and there was a vicious triumph in his eyes as he stared at Antonius' shocked face. "Everyone can see it. You always did have a penchant for foreign queens, didn't you, Antonius?"

Antonius could not breathe, and the words struggled to come out. "I—I do not understand, Caesar."

Caesar took a step towards him and bent down so that they were face to face, his voice low and dangerous. "Go on, then. Fuck her. But every time you are inside of her, just remember that I was there first, that she came to *me* first. You are nothing more than a distraction."

Antonius kept very still, his heart hammering in his chest, and he tried to bottle up the hatred rising in his throat.

Then Caesar stood tall, looking down at Antonius with a curl of his lip as if he were truly nothing. Or worse than nothing—simply not worth his time.

"Goodnight, Antonius."

Caesar turned and walked away, following the hall down to his bedroom in the back of the house, where surely Cleopatra waited for him still. The very thought was like poison in his mind, turning his limbs heavy and his stomach sick.

Antonius laid on his back and took another long swig of his wine, watching the sun rise above the hills like a fiery stain in the sky.

⤛⤜

MARCH 44 BC

Antonius turned as he stretched in bed, the light of dawn piercing through his eyelids. His eyes flew open, and he nearly groaned aloud.

He was going to be late.

Someone stirred beside him. Antonius glanced at his wife as she slept, her pale flaxen hair, already silver at the roots, loose from her braids, and her stocky limbs covered in a thin, long-sleeve tunic.

Fulvia was not very beautiful, but Antonius had always felt an affection for his wife, albeit his third. She was a capable woman who never panicked in a crisis, practical in all her decisions, and economical with her money, which she had much of thanks to familial inheritances.

Antonius had needed her financial support after his second divorce, and Fulvia had been very supportive of his political ambitions. It was the perfect marriage despite their lack of passion, though she had borne him two sons. In fact, last night was the first time in many months that they had spent the night together, as they were used to sleeping in their separate rooms.

He reached out and lightly tapped her nose.

Her eyes opened in reproach. "I was sleeping, Antonius."

"I am going to work," Antonius said. "I am late as it is."

37

"Am I stopping you?" Fulvia asked, raising a brow.

Antonius grinned and grabbed at her waist, and she shrieked like a girl at her wedding. "No, but you could."

"Put me down, Antonius, do I look young enough to be handled like this?"

Fulvia struggled out of his embrace, and she had a bitter look on her face. Rumor had gotten around of his affair with Cleopatra, though Fulvia never brought it up with him. As the good Roman wife she was, Fulvia never mentioned any of his affairs to his face, though she would cease speaking with him for a time before he gently coaxed her back to his arms with gifts and poems.

She readjusted her dress, then paused. "Say, is it not the Ides of March today?"

"Yes, the consuls take up office today," Antonius said through a yawn.

"No! It is the start of the new year!" Fulvia was suddenly wide awake, scrambling out of bed. She began untangling her hair and called out for her handmaiden. "We are hosting a New Year's party tonight! How could I have forgotten..."

"Not anymore, remember? Thanks to Caesar, the new year starts in January now."

Fulvia caught the sarcasm in his voice and looked at him sharply. "Cease your complaining and get to work. You are a consul for Jove's sake."

"Calm down, woman." Antonius swung his legs off the bed and stood up. "See? I am already out of bed."

"Why are you telling me? I am not your mother—ow!" Fulvia massaged her head which her handmaiden was already brushing and yanking into tight braids. "But you must be home by sundown for the party. Don't forget!"

Antonius held back a laugh and called his manservant to shave and dress him. Soon he was on his way to the *curia* in his small carriage, the tall, crowded buildings of Rome passing by in the window as his horses trotted down the bumpy road.

Memories of growing up in the city rose in his mind like ghosts, roaming the streets at night with his brother and their friends, stumbling drunk into brothels, gambling until the sun rose.

It had all been a blur, the years before he fled to Greece, all of his youth spent chasing foolish desires, wasting his nights on the filthy backstreets of Rome, a Rome he hardly saw anymore in his lofty house up in the hills, untouched by the grime of the seething city below.

Suddenly they came to an abrupt stop, and he heard his driver drop down from his seat. Antonius looked out the window. The *curia* of Pompeius, where the meeting was being held, was still a block ahead, but Antonius could already see senators pouring out of the doors in panicked streams.

Antonius opened the door, and after a moment of staring at the scene, he began making his way down the street. His driver called after him worriedly, but Antonius ignored him.

He soon reached the crowds of senators, a sea of white and purple. An elderly man—of the Velina tribe, he thought— with white tufts of hair crowning his head, grabbed Antonius roughly by the sleeve of his toga.

"Caesar," he wheezed, as though he were out of breath.

"It is Antonius, old man," he snapped angrily.

"Caesar is dead!" Tears shone in the old man's eyes. "Stabbed to death. By the young Brutus. Stabbed to death by his friends!"

"Brutus..." Antonius hardly felt the hand clutching his arm in an iron grip. "Caesar..."

"Are you listening to me, boy? Dead! Right in front of the statue of Pompeius no less."

Antonius shook the man off his arm and wove his way to the doors where senators pushed each other in their scramble to exit the crime scene, as if the murderers were on the loose and anyone could be the next victim. He was almost inside when he was yanked backward, and he turned angrily to see Trebonius standing behind him with a pale but stern face.

"It would be better if you didn't," Trebonius said coldly, grabbing Antonius and leading him out of the crowd. "Nothing good would come of it."

"But Caesar—"

"—is dead." Trebonius placed a strong hand on his shoulder. "Listen to me, Antonius. It is too late. The deed is done. There is no going back now."

"What about the body?"

Antonius imagined Caesar, the man who had always dictated his life, his career, whom he had drunk with and laughed with and fought with side by side, his chest bloodied and cut up by countless wounds, lying dead on the Senate floor.

Then he saw Caesar's face close to his, that cold amusement in his eyes. *Go on, then. Fuck her.*

He looked to see Trebonius staring at him incredulously. Antonius seized Trebonius' arm, if only to steady himself, surprised to find tears clouding his eyes when he felt nothing at all.

His voice was demanding. "Will there be a funeral?"

"I cannot promise your safety, consul," Trebonius said slowly, as if Antonius were deranged. "You had your chance to pick the right side. If I were you, I would leave the city. Immediately."

Another surge of senators flooded out of the *curia*, pressing close to them. Antonius thought he glimpsed the silver flash of a dagger. He did not hesitate, releasing Trebonius, who scurried away from him fearfully.

After shoving his way out of the crowds, Antonius made it back to his carriage, out of breath with sweat beading on his forehead. He climbed in hurriedly and rapped on the roof to alert his driver.

"Drive, Tertius! Drive like the very hounds of Hell were after us..."

4

Marcus Vipsanius Agrippa

APRIL 44 BC

J ulius Caesar was dead.

No, *murdered.*

Agrippa stared at the waves glittering like metal armor under the sun. He should feel angered. Maybe fearful. The Republic had crumbled overnight, leaving a wasteland of power in the wake of its destruction. Instead, he only felt a vague sense of relief.

They were safe on this side of the sea.

Agrippa glanced at Octavius, who sat beside him on the sand.

They had been sword training since dawn when their commander, accompanied by one of Octavius' household messengers, pulled Octavius aside and handed him a letter from his mother.

Agrippa had overheard their low, urgent voices while pretending to readjust his training pads. He had been worried that Octavius would need time alone to grieve the loss of his great-uncle. Instead, after training was done, Octavius merely beckoned Agrippa and together they took a walk down to the water, discussing their training and dinner plans as they usually did.

When they had wandered to a secluded stretch of the shore and sat down by the water's edge, Octavius turned and told him the news, as plainly and indifferently as if he were pointing out the weather.

"Julius Caesar is dead."

Agrippa remained silent.

Annoyance flashed across Octavius' face, the first sign of emotion he had seen from him since the message arrived. "Well?"

41

"I don't know." Agrippa crossed his arms as if the breeze off the water made him shiver. "He made too many enemies, didn't he?"

Octavius shrugged, but there was something in the set of his shoulders, the slightly lowered eyelids, which betrayed a restlessness that did not break his calm surface, like a peaceful lake concealing the flitting shadows of sea monsters below.

Most people would have thought Octavius did not care, but Agrippa knew him better. This external peace sheltered a war within him, a war nineteen years in the making, since Octavius had opened his eyes in this life and knew he would have to fight for every breathing second to keep it.

"I might be named his son and heir in his will," Octavius said, looking out at the horizon. "If I were to claim my inheritance..."

Agrippa felt a thrill at the words despite the dread that dropped like a stone in his stomach. *The son of Julius Caesar.* While the implications were endless, one thing was as clear as the sun in the sky: Octavius would inherit an empire.

But it was impossible. While Octavius was safe on this side of the sea, the moment he set sail he would be surrounded on all sides. Agrippa knew Caesar's army would be waiting for someone to take command, and that Octavius would want to be the one to do it.

The son of Julius Caesar, however, would be no more welcomed by the Senate than Caesar himself, and it would be foolish to think that the current consul, Marcus Antonius, would hand over command any time soon. If Octavius were indeed named his son and heir, any claim to it would be considered a threat.

"Let them all kill each other fighting over power," Agrippa said, keeping his voice firm. "You owe them nothing."

Octavius cut him a glance. "It is not about debt, but duty."

"Since when do you care about duty?"

"Everyone has their duty in life," Octavius said, watching a bird arc in the sky, pause as if suspended midair, and then dive pin-straight into the water. "It would be cowardly to flee from it."

Agrippa raised a brow. "That sounds more like fate to me."

Octavius shook his head. "Fate is different. Not everyone is born with one."

"Were you?"

"Yes."

Agrippa did not answer. He had always found Octavius' beliefs very strange, given he descended from such a traditionally religious family.

For Octavius believed in his fate over everything, even the gods, with a possessiveness bordering on obsession. He held onto his fate like a soldier to his sword in the midst of battle, as though without it he would not survive.

"I must return to Rome," Octavius said quietly, cutting into the silence broken only by the tide lapping against the shore. "This is what I have been waiting for all my life. I know it."

"It is impossible."

"I must return to Rome."

Agrippa spoke through gritted teeth. "You will die."

Octavius paused, then looked at Agrippa, studying him. Agrippa held his breath. He knew that look. It was a look he gave before they sparred, as if Octavius could read every weakness of mind and body Agrippa had.

Although Octavius was not very strong physically, he had a cunning and daring while fighting which always left Agrippa slightly shaken, even when he won the round.

"Come with me," Octavius said, finally, the words hitting Agrippa a second later.

"What?"

"You heard me." Octavius raised a challenging brow. "I know no better tactician. If anyone can find me a way safely to Rome, it is you."

While it was true Agrippa had a knack for strategy, marching on Rome as the heir to a dictator recently assassinated was nothing more than a death wish, not to mention Agrippa had hardly any experience in war besides Athenodorus' rigorous exams and a few brief months of army training.

"Everything we have learned would call it suicide," Agrippa said.

Octavius leaned forward suddenly, taking Agrippa's hand in his. The touch was as shocking as a midwinter swim in the Adriatic. Far off memories crept in the back of his mind. *You are afraid I will die.*

"Forget what we have learned, Agrippa. Athenodorus has never fought in a real war. He has taught us to obey, that is all. We must learn to rule ourselves."

"The Republic has burned to the ground," Agrippa said angrily. "You wish to rule a desert alone."

Octavius' grip tightened. "Think, Agrippa. Think like a god, not a soldier."

"You are not a god, Octavius."

"Not yet."

He leaned back and released Agrippa's hand, his mouth tense and almost bitter. Agrippa watched him close his eyes briefly, then open them, the sun reflecting harshly in the dark pupils. He looked almost like a god, then, cold and distant as the stars, but young in the eternal flush of his cheeks.

It was useless to argue, of course. Agrippa knew this, the futility of fighting against Octavius. Since the day they met, Agrippa knew he would follow Octavius wherever he went, even if he led him straight to Hades himself.

Think like a god, not a soldier.

No, Octavius was not a god, but that did not matter if the people believed otherwise.

Agrippa looked out across the river, its rippling blue current. A bird shot up into the sky, fish scales glinting in its beak, soaring until it was eclipsed by the sun.

A thought began to form in his mind, like the beginnings of a dream—no, a vision—sent in his sleep by the gods above. Agrippa turned.

Octavius was already looking at him, as if all this time he had known Agrippa would say yes, that he would find a way, even an impossible one.

"I trust you with my life," Octavius said in a low voice.

Agrippa's heart clenched painfully in his chest. He nodded. "I have a plan."

⊷⊷⊷ ⊶⊶⊶

"Absolutely not." Maecenas shook his head in disbelief. "You cannot sail to Rome without an army. I thought, Agrippa, that you were supposed to be the best strategist of our year?"

Agrippa felt himself flush at this particular comment. He looked to Octavius as though he would defend him, but he merely drank from his glass of wine and waited.

They were having dinner at the house of Athenodorus, who had invited them to escape the chaos of the town, which had nearly erupted into riots when the news of Caesar's murder broke out.

The soldiers especially were outraged and expected—if not outright demanded—that Octavius lead them in revenge across the sea to Italy. But there were murmurs of Antonius seizing the treasury back in Rome and Lepidus swooping in with his army to stabilize the mobs rioting in the streets. Not to mention the Marius scandal, a young man who falsely claimed kinship with Caesar and who was now drawing a formidable number of supporters to his cause.

"If we land in Italy with an entire army of Caesar's men then we risk open warfare with either the Senate or Antonius," Agrippa said coldly. They had finally told Maecenas and Rufus their plan to sail to Rome without more than an armed guard and so far they were not taking it well. "But if Octavius accepts his inheritance, he may have time to garner support among the troops as Caesar's son and heir."

"*May* have time?" Rufus asked, raising a brow. "This plan of yours seems to hinge on more than one uncertainty."

"There is always risk in uncertain times," Octavius said, fixing Rufus with a challenging look. "If the risk is too great for you to take, however, I would understand."

"Nonsense!" Maecenas exclaimed indignantly. Rufus, on the other hand, remained silent. "My only concern is that we leave ourselves vulnerable to attack on the mainland, with or without an army." He looked pointedly at Agrippa as he spoke those last words. "How are we to convince troops loyal to Antonius and Lepidus that they ought to join our side if we have no army of our own?"

"There are troops stationed in Brundisium," Agrippa explained. "First we sail to Lupiae, then travel on land. At Brundisium we can survey the people's sentiments after the assassination and hopefully receive an oath of support from the local troops. They will welcome the son of Julius Caesar."

"Let us say all of this goes exactly as planned," Rufus drawled, rolling the stem of his chalice between his fingers. "What happens when you show up in Rome claiming to be the son of Julius Caesar?"

Octavius stood up, walking over to the pitcher of wine and pouring himself another glass. "As long as I am not trying to raise an army illegally, I am merely a private citizen claiming my inheritance. I'm only in my nineteenth year after all."

Agrippa sighed softly, glancing out the windows. The night sky was tinged with blue as the dawn rose in the east. Time was slipping away from them with every moment they waited, every moment they spent arguing about risks and uncertainties.

Already a month had passed since the assassination, during which many generals had advised Octavius to lead the Macedonian army overseas, though Octavius seemed to share Agrippa's hesitation.

For Agrippa knew all too well the forces they faced ahead of them, as if he could see the gameboard before him, the armies of Antonius and Lepidus spanning far and wide, and themselves merely a few pawns. He knew, somehow, that the key to their success would lie in the very fact that it seemed impossible that they *should* succeed.

"We are running out of time," Agrippa interrupted. "The longer we stay here, the more time and support we surrender to Marcus Antonius or that Marius pretender or anyone else who fancies an empire."

"You don't mean to leave now, do you?" Maecenas asked, his eyes wide, as though it were only occurring to him now that these plans were not simply another strategy exam they had to pass. He glanced nervously at each of them. "There is no turning back once we sail to Italy."

"We plan to set sail in two days," Octavius said quietly. "Speak of this to no one."

⟫⟩⟩ ⟨⟨⟨

Agrippa paced the deck of the ship. *Think like a god, not a soldier.*

But they were still mortal. The wooden planks beneath his feet strained and groaned as the ocean playfully rocked their ship side to side. Would they even take a step on Roman soil before they were snatched up by one of their many, many enemies?

Octavius sighed impatiently from his perch looking over the side of the ship, keeping his eyes trained on the horizon. Sailing usually disagreed with his constitution.

"You act as if we were facing monsters," Octavius said without looking at Agrippa. "They are only men."

Agrippa joined him, looking down at the waves cresting against the hull of the ship. He had always enjoyed sailing, the salty wind stinging his cheeks, the horizon unfolding before him as the heavens did above. But today the wind only made him shiver.

"How are you so sure?" Agrippa asked, though he did not know what he meant by the question. *How are you so sure they are not monsters? How are you so sure of yourself?*

How are you so sure of me?

"Because I am with you," Octavius said with a grin, as if that answered every question. *I trust you with my life.*

Agrippa glanced at Octavius from the corner of his eye. His face was pale, with twin flushes on his cheekbones. It reminded him of the day they first embarked on their ship to Apollonia.

Octavius had been thinner then, still recovering from his near-death illness a few months prior, and at his mother's demand had been wrapped tightly in a thick cloak and broad hat despite the sun beating down upon them. Agrippa had been caught staring, though Octavius had not been embarrassed about it.

Instead, he had flashed one of his smiles. "My mother thinks I will fall ill."

"Will you?" Agrippa had asked, unsure how to reply. He never had the right words, not like Octavius.

As if remembering that night when he almost died, Octavius' smile had faded, and he looked vaguely at the sea. "No, I will not."

It was true enough that day, though he looked sickly when they anchored in Apollonia. It was as if from that terrible night on, there had formed a quiet understanding between them, and it was Agrippa whom Octavius called for when he fell ill in December.

Agrippa had always thought that was how his life would be forever, training with the army, eventually being sent off to war, with Octavius always by his side, his closest friend, and Agrippa would always be there to make sure Octavius lived through the night. Now everything had changed, and they were sailing to the most hostile country in the world with nothing more than their own wit and luck to arm them.

"Our plan has too many unknowns, too many risks," Agrippa argued, knowing he was voicing the same doubts of Maecenas and Rufus but unable to help himself, a cold fear gripping his limbs at the thought of anything going wrong. "Maybe if we had more time in Apollonia—"

"There was no time," Octavius interrupted calmly. "You said that yourself."

Agrippa lowered his voice. "We are not even sure Julius Caesar named you his son."

Octavius' eyes flashed. "He did."

Agrippa let out a long breath. He looked at Octavius, the familiar features he had known for so long, and tried to see the face of Julius Caesar he had only glimpsed now and then. But all he could see were the boyish lashes, olive skin, and brown locks which had become as familiar to him as if they were his own.

"That is a risk," Agrippa said at last. "We have no way to prove it until we read the will ourselves."

Octavius was silent, his eyes growing distant as he watched the horizon sway side to side, the ship swinging with the wind and the waves. Then he spoke, and his voice was quiet and serious.

"After my father died, my mother married Philippus, who did not care for me. So he sent me to live with my grandmother, Julia Minor. She would tell me stories of her brother from when they were younger. Caesar was brave and intelligent, even as a boy. He had been fated for something great since the beginning. That is what she told me.

"But one night she told me something that I never forgot. She said, 'There is a very old story, a story of a woman who weaves. It is the job of the Weaver to weave the tapestry of eternity which adorns the palace of the gods. But not every blade of grass nor every ordinary man does the Weaver weave into this tapestry, with only enough room for those who will impress the gods forever. That is why the great men of history feel as though their hearts are pulled in one direction over another. The Weaver had her hands tight on the threads of their souls. That is how you know, my child, whether you are destined for greatness.'"

Octavius fell silent once more. His hands gripped the wooden ledge so tightly the knuckles grew white.

Agrippa placed his hands on the ledge, before hesitantly covering one of Octavius' hands with his own. It was ice cold and chafed from the excessive time he spent in the baths, though he always swore bathing helped with his health. Distantly, he thought of Maecenas and Rufus, who were on a different ship sailing close by.

"Do you know where my thread leads?" Agrippa asked quietly.

Octavius only looked at him from under those half-lidded, curious eyes.

"You," Agrippa said. "The Weaver pulls my thread to you."

The shadow of a smile flitted across Octavius' lips. "Then together we will conquer the world."

5

GAIUS OCTAVIUS

APRIL 44 BC

Octavius was exhausted when their carriage rolled to a stop in the dead of night.

Several hours ago their ships had anchored discreetly in the Port of Lupiae as the sun had begun to set. There, a few informants loyal to Caesar had related a report of Roman sympathies, accompanied by another anxious letter from his mother, who warned him of the danger they were in and urged him to travel directly to their family home in Velitrae.

He ignored her, instead traveling swiftly from Lupiae to the nearby city of Brundisium under cover of darkness, hoping to prevent news of their arrival on the mainland from reaching Rome. If they wished to enter the city safely, they would need surprise on their side—and the support of the troops in Brundisium.

But that required an inspiring leader, and as of now, Octavius presented more convincingly as a vagabond rather than the potential son and heir to Julius Caesar.

He limped out of the carriage, and his skin felt paper thin against the bones of his face. The nearly two days traveling on both sea and land had weathered his health more than he had anticipated. Unfortunately, Agrippa noticed his weariness too.

"We can wait until the morning," Agrippa suggested. "A few hours of rest and you will feel more alive."

Octavius shot him an irritated glance. He always became less agreeable when he was ill. "I am very much alive. And we do not have time to rest. By morning we must be on our way to Rome. That is the plan."

"That is the plan," Agrippa repeated with a sigh, and did not bring it up again.

So they made their way quietly and only with a few guardsmen to the soldier's quarters where Caesar's former finance manager, Lucius Cornelius Balbus, awaited them. Maecenas and Rufus had gone ahead and prepared the venue for Octavius' speech to the troops, which he would give soon while it was still night and the men were drinking.

They walked inside the tent where Balbus awaited them. He was the same short, well-built man with tan skin, sleek black curls, and a charming smile that Octavius remembered.

A foreigner hailing from Hispania, Balbus became a wealthy politician and business-man after serving in the armies of Pompeius, who gave him Roman citizenship, and after Pompeius' death, he grew to be the closest confidant and chief operator of all Caesar's affairs.

Octavius had encountered him at several of Caesar's dinner parties and knew he would be most helpful in acquiring Caesar's will, so he had arranged to meet with him before they traveled to Rome.

"Octavius!" Balbus chuckled, kissing Octavius affectionately as an uncle might. "The last time I saw you I could barely pull at the scraps of your beard." He paused, lightly brushing the stubble along Octavius' jaw, which he was allowing to grow in the usual style of grieving. Balbus' eyes grew heavy. "You are no longer the little boy I knew."

Octavius nodded and placed a hand on Balbus' arm. "That boy was murdered along with my father."

Balbus' thick brows quirked at the reference to Julius Caesar as his father, but he only nodded. He always had the tact of a diplomat, and would not offend a fly if he could help it. "I imagine so, I imagine so." Then his eyes wandered to Agrippa. "And who is this?"

"A comrade from school," Octavius said carelessly. He saw Agrippa turn slightly red at the words as he greeted Balbus with a kiss. "Marcus Agrippa."

"Ah, I see," Balbus said, his gaze sliding back to Octavius, though he sensed his mind still lingered over Agrippa's presence in such an intimate setting. "What is your plan?"

"We ride to Rome by morning," Octavius said.

"No, no, no," Balbus whispered urgently, looking around nervously as if someone might be eavesdropping outside, though his guards were lining the perimeter of the tent and had strict orders not to let anyone inside. "It is not safe. Rome is not safe. Antonius has stirred the people into violence and the senators had to barricade themselves on the Capitoline. He has even eliminated the Marius pretender. You cannot go to Rome."

"I wish to claim my inheritance, Balbus. It is my right," Octavius said, a hint of moral reprimand in his tone. He knew if he were to bring Balbus to his side, he would need to play on his feelings of loyalty to Caesar. "I shall not let my father's death be in vain."

Balbus frowned, and looked at him carefully, his eyes scanning his face as if he could decipher the hidden meaning in his words. "I see a lot of him in you." He paused. "If you wish to go to Rome, I will not stop you. But I cannot promise your safety, only my support."

"Your support alone is worth more than you know," Octavius said, catching the flicker of approval in Balbus' eyes. "But I must speak with the soldiers. I would like to have their support as well before I ride to Rome. After all, they were Caesar's men before Antonius took control."

Balbus looked startled, but he consented when it became apparent that Octavius would not budge on this particular point. He led them swiftly down the road to the forum. He glanced hesitantly at Octavius every other step, as though he wished to advise him but was at a loss for where to begin without offending him.

When they were only a block away, Balbus stopped them, grasping Octavius' arm. They could already hear the crowds of troops drinking in the forum.

"The soldiers are not an easy group to pacify," Balbus said, his eyes darting to the direction of the forum after a loud roar went up amongst the throngs. "They loved your...your father, but—"

Octavius placed a hand on Balbus' broad shoulder. "I loved him too. We will mourn his loss. Together."

Balbus nodded hurriedly, giving up his attempts at dissuading him. The three of them entered the forum where a wooden stage had been built at one end, flanked by Octavius' personal guards. Balbus remained at the side of the platform, not wishing to be seen fully by the mob of soldiers already flocking towards the stage. He was not a public speaker, after all. Not like Octavius.

Agrippa tensed beside him as they looked out on the crowd.

Octavius turned to Agrippa with a smile, then glanced up at the sky. "A storm is coming."

"Be careful," Agrippa warned.

Without another word, Octavius ascended the stage, his arms wide open in welcome, and his eyes cast to the heavens above. At his appearance the crowd surged around the stage, shouting drunkenly.

Not only did they recognize him, but they were calling to him, and only after a few moments did Octavius comprehend what they were saying. His agents had done their job well after all.

Fili! Fili! Fili Iulii...

Son! Son! Son of Julius...

"Father!" Octavius cried out.

The clouds above were dark and rumbling, and the light from the surrounding torches cast the passionate faces of the soldiers in an eerie glow as they continued to chant furiously. *Fili Iulii!*

"Father, hear my voice!" Octavius shouted, and the soldiers shouted back, raising their flasks of wine in the air. "Do you wish me to avenge your murder?"

The din of the mob rose to a feverish pitch, many beating against the side of the stage so that the flimsy wood trembled. Octavius never looked away from the sky, which rumbled again, and he knew it was close, so close. He lifted his arms higher.

"Father, speak! If this is what you wish, give me a sign!"

Crack! A flash of lightning lit up the sky, followed by the crash and rumble of thunder. The soldiers cheered blindly as the heavens opened their wide skirts and rain poured down on them in icy sheets.

Octavius remained standing with his arms spread wide while the storm broiled above them, his eyes closed and his chest rising and falling rapidly. He did not need to respond to his father anymore. The crowds could be heard as clearly as the next clap of thunder.

Divi fili! Divi fili! Divi fili...

Octavius allowed himself a small smile as he glanced at Agrippa, who stared at him from beside the stage, his face unreadable in the near dark.

Son of god! Son of god! Son of god...

⋙⋙ ⋘⋘

"Octavius?"

He looked up and blinked.

Agrippa watched him across the table worriedly. He was always worried. Perhaps this time he had good reason to be.

Octavius felt on the verge of collapse, his head pounding, his bones aching against the chill of the night. It had been a risk to stand out in the rain, even if the effect had been perfect. More than perfect.

Divi fili! Divi fili! Divi fili...

He could still hear their cries, each shout tugging at his heart, as if the Weaver had his thread of fate pulled taut tonight. It would be ironic if the rain would now be the death of him.

"What?"

Agrippa stared at him for a moment longer, then said, "You look tired."

"Oh, do I?"

"You should rest."

Agrippa never took the bait of an argument, always preferring to calm the situation rather than escalate it, so very different from Maecenas and his provocative, snide comments. Ever since their boyhood, Agrippa had never lowered himself to another's insult, as if he were afraid to confirm the suspicions of his social rank.

"I can rest as we travel," Octavius said. "First we must finish our business here."

Agrippa relented, pushing aside his cup of wine. They were weathering the storm in Balbus' tent, who had left them to attend to his own business before they departed for Rome together. It was thanks to the reaction of the soldiers more so than his devotion to Caesar that confirmed Balbus' decision to help him claim his inheritance.

The flap to the tent opened, and in walked Maecenas, drenched and shivering, with Rufus and Balbus in tow, also soaked from the storm. They all drew up stools around the table, and Maecenas slapped Octavius' back.

"Well done, Octavius," Maecenas said. "Could not have done it better myself."

Rufus only smiled, but it was tempered. He had disagreed with their plan from the start and was still wary of any success.

"Now we must speak of logistics," Balbus said, passing around a small platter of bread and fruit brought in by his attendants, as well as another pitcher of wine. "For instance, money."

Octavius tried to think, but his mind felt muddled. The last time he fell ill was late December, a week of chilly days and feverish nights, Agrippa appearing hazily in the pockets of his memory, placing a cool cloth on his forehead.

Agrippa was the only person he could suffer to see him like that, ever since the illness which had prevented him from fighting in Hispania. Before then, his illnesses had always been moments of weakness which left him ashamed. But Agrippa treated them as one might a storm, the only priority to find shelter and wait for it to pass.

"We have no money," Octavius said at last.

Balbus nodded slowly, stroking his chin. "But the son of Julius Caesar does."

They lapsed into silence. That was the problem. While Caesar's soldiers might believe Octavius was now his son, the Senate surely would not until he completed the legal process of adoption, which would be difficult if not impossible with Marcus Antonius in charge. And everything was wholly dependent on Julius Caesar's will explicitly naming him as his heir, which was less than certain at the moment.

That left only one option.

"Balbus, tell me," Octavius said. "Brundisium is responsible for conveying money to Macedonia, is it not? And tribute from the East?"

Balbus glanced at Agrippa as if to gauge the seriousness of the question. When Agrippa merely shrugged, Balbus nodded reluctantly. "Yes, yes of course. Brundisium is one of the principal trading posts on the eastern coast. You know this."

"Are there any shipments currently being held here?" Octavius pressed.

Now Balbus caught on to the purpose of his questioning. Balbus' usual cordial expression gave way to a stern frown. "Seizing public money without the approval of the Roman treasury would be a crime deserving of death. And the Senate only needs one good reason to kill you."

Octavius did not respond. Balbus was right, though he disliked admitting it. As the potential son and heir to Julius Caesar, the seizure of public money would be a rash decision, one Octavius had trouble excusing without incurring the wrath of the Senate and simultaneously handing Antonius the Republic in a single blow.

"What if we didn't *take* the money?" Agrippa asked suddenly. Everyone turned to him in surprise.

"And what would you suggest we do instead?" Maecenas asked, raising a skeptical brow.

"Nothing." Agrippa looked at Octavius, almost smirking. "The soldiers will give it to us."

Balbus looked outraged, his face growing red. "That's—that's preposterous!"

Octavius ignored the doubtful looks from Maecenas and Rufus. For there was something in Agrippa's eyes that made him pause. "Explain."

Agrippa leaned forward, speaking quietly. "We ask the soldiers for support and in return we promise to settle them in the colonies once we have the power and money to do so. The solution will be obvious. Then if *they* are the ones to hand over the money, *we* will be entirely blameless in the transaction. And as the son and heir to Julius Caesar, you have the rights to a certain amount of the money anyways."

Balbus was staring at Agrippa in surprise, perhaps even a grudging respect. Rufus, on the other hand, could not hide a glance full of envy, and he remained stubbornly silent.

"By Hercules..." Maecenas shook his head, but he was grinning. "Now that is one hell of a plan."

Octavius tapped his fingers against the wooden table, a smile forming on his face despite the exhaustion he felt. "Balbus, please take a message to the general. Tell him the son of Julius Caesar sends his regards."

⤞⟫⟫ ⟪⟪⟩⤝

The carriage jolted along the muddied road, waking Octavius from the dreamless fog that Sleep had pulled him under. He could barely breathe from the pain between his temples as he lifted his head upright.

On the seat opposite him, Agrippa slept, curled up against the wall of the carriage. Octavius studied his friend's face, which he so rarely could do while he was awake.

Agrippa still looked troubled, his dark brows furrowed, as if he never stopped worrying about Octavius, even in sleep. The dark brown hair was still as curly as ever, the fringe carelessly falling over his forehead. He never did care much about his appearance.

He had a strong jaw, which was softer at rest, and an elegant, aquiline nose. His strong limbs had difficulty arranging themselves comfortably in the small carriage seat. Agrippa had always been well-built, since they were young, so that at nineteen years old he was teasingly called a gladiator amongst the soldiers at Apollonia.

But Octavius' favorite feature of Agrippa could not be seen while he slept. His eyes. They were sea-green, the color of the Tiber River on a hot August day.

Agrippa shifted in his seat, his eyes opening. He saw Octavius looking at him and sat up straight. "Do you need something?"

"A drink, please," Octavius said hoarsely, resenting the tremor in his voice.

At least none of the others would be a witness to this weakness, as they were traveling in other carriages. Even Maecenas had not been jealous of Agrippa riding with him, as he hated being near the sick.

Agrippa rummaged in the sack at their feet and pulled out a small flask of wine. Octavius took a sip, closing his eyes as the dull burn traveled down his throat. He felt a cool hand on his forehead.

"You are too hot," Agrippa murmured, his voice barely heard over the grating of the metal wheels against the stone road beneath them.

Octavius almost laughed. "And yet I feel too cold."

"You know one day you will have a wife to nurse you to health instead of me."

He said it jokingly, but his gaze did not quite reach Octavius'. He thought distantly that Agrippa sounded bitter.

"I will always ask for you," Octavius said with a small smile.

Agrippa paused, before he leaned back against the side of the carriage, half-closing his eyes.

Octavius knew, of course, how Agrippa felt about him. It was not well disguised. He could read it plainly in his eyes, lingering on him when he thought Octavius was not paying attention, glancing at the corner of his mouth, the curve of his collarbone, the dip of his hip bones before they bathed. And when it was handed to him like that, like a gift with no expectation of one in return, Octavius could not help himself.

For everyone always assumed he knew nothing, that he was too young, or too weak, to understand. But Octavius had not been raised by just anyone. Julia Minor had taught him much in the time he had lived with her.

She had shown him the art of listening, the skill of thinking quietly, never allowing a thought to betray him on his face. But most importantly, she had shown him how to ensure people underestimated him, only to slip past them when they were not looking anymore, their most precious secret dangling from his fingers like the key to their coffers.

"Agrippa," Octavius whispered.

Agrippa stirred, blinking open his eyes. "Hmm?"

"I need to ask you something."

"Anything," Agrippa said with a yawn.

They had hardly slept much in Brundisium, eager to get to Rome before it was too late. But the closer they got to Rome, the more uncertain Octavius felt, and all those careful plans and passionate dreams he held secret for so long seemed now as flimsy and insubstantial as sand in the wind.

"When we arrive in Rome, I will claim my inheritance immediately," Octavius said.

"Yes?"

They had already agreed to this plan, but there was something else Octavius needed to confirm. Something more important than all the money and soldiers and inheritance combined.

Agrippa looked at him as if he thought his fever was making him more than just ill.

"It is very likely that I will be surrounded by enemies on all sides, and that even my friends will desert me out of fear. So I must ask that you fight for me when that time comes, and that you remain loyal to me, and only me." He paused. "You are the only one I can trust."

"I will," Agrippa said cautiously.

"Swear it."

Agrippa looked hurt but nodded anyway. He was a soldier, after all. "I swear by Jupiter—"

"No," Octavius said. "On me."

A shadow flickered across Agrippa's eyes. Octavius knew asking for this was taking it too far, but he also knew that Agrippa would agree to it, and perhaps that was the only reason he wanted him to say it, so he could hear the words aloud.

Agrippa lowered his eyes. "I swear by you, Gaius Octavius..."

"That I will be loyal to you," Octavius said.

"That I will be loyal to you," Agrippa echoed.

"And only you."

At his words a sudden gust of wind blew through the window and put out the small darting flame of the carriage lamp, throwing them both into darkness. It was not an uncommon occurrence, but just then it felt like an omen, though good or bad Octavius did not know. He could just make out the unmoving shape of Agrippa across from him.

Agrippa hesitated before speaking again. "And only you."

"In word, in deed, and in thought."

"In word, in deed, and in thought..."

"Regarding your friends as my friends, and your enemies as my enemies."

"Regarding your friends as my friends, and your enemies as my enemies," he repeated slowly.

"And who you regard as enemies I will by land and sea, with weapons and sword, pursue and punish."

A ghost of a smile appeared on Agrippa's face. "And who you regard as enemies I will by land and sea, with weapons and sword, pursue and punish."

"All my life."

To Octavius' surprise, Agrippa reached out and took his hand, holding it loosely. Octavius' hand looked delicate in comparison to the firm, capable fingers encompassing it, which arranged themselves with the strength and deftness of a skilled soldier.

Then Agrippa lowered his mouth and kissed the back of Octavius' hand, right on his signet ring, a ruby red stone engraved with a sphinx. It was a sign of submission, or perhaps of something more.

"All my life."

⟫⟫ ⟪⟪

"There are rumors," Balbus said as he took a seat beside Maecenas. "From Rome."

They occupied a private corner of a popular tavern near the soldiers' encampments at Beneventum, a city nearly one hundred and thirty miles from Rome. It was their fourth day on the road, but it might as well have been a month.

Octavius hated traveling by ship, but at least he had room to walk on the deck and stretch his legs. Even Agrippa looked exhausted, though perhaps that was on account of trying to lessen Octavius' high fever for the first three days of their trip. Octavius was just beginning to notice some strength returning to his aching muscles, which had weakened from the travel and sickness.

"What rumors?" Octavius asked, holding back a long sigh. It seemed every day there were new rumors, each one worse than the last.

"Marcus Antonius has compromised with Brutus and Cassius." It was telling that Balbus gave him the news so quickly instead of delaying it with pleasantries or casual banter. And indeed, the news was grim.

"He is a traitor, then," Maecenas said angrily.

Balbus shook his head. "Not in the eyes of the Senate."

"But he is in the eyes of the people," Agrippa pointed out, the severity of the news seeming to pull him out of his exhaustion. "We ought to conduct a campaign and recruit veterans who served Caesar. Then we march on Rome. It is the only way to oust Antonius from power."

"No," Octavius said immediately.

Agrippa raised a silent brow.

"Though I rarely agree with Agrippa," Maecenas said, "I must say he is right."

Rufus nodded in agreement. "You cannot possibly challenge the Senate *and* Antonius together."

Octavius looked at Balbus, who frowned, troubled. "I find it impossible to guarantee your safety in Rome without an army," Balbus said cautiously. "Besides, there is more news."

"More?" Octavius echoed.

Balbus nodded gravely. "Your father's will was read at his funeral. By Marcus Antonius." He looked at Octavius intently. "You were named his son and heir."

Octavius stared, uncomprehending. His heart pounded. A part of him was thrilled, but Balbus remained solemn, and the excitement quickly settled into unease. "What else?"

Balbus hesitated. "Antonius claims you have refused the heirship."

"Why?" Agrippa demanded.

Maecenas slammed his fist on the table. "It is an outrage!"

"Do the people accept this?" Octavius asked, struggling to keep calm.

"Yes," Balbus said, almost whispering. "His speech at your father's funeral sparked rioting. But that is not all. He has also claimed to be the head of your father's cause. Lepidus has returned with Caesar's soldiers to protect him. He has even received ownership of Caesar's property from his widow. Ultimately, the people needed an outlet for their fear and Antonius has given them one."

Agrippa leaned forward worriedly, but Octavius refused to meet his eyes. "This is exactly why you must campaign for soldiers, Octavius. If we defeat them in battle, the people will consider you a hero. With the people on your side, no one will stand in your way."

"No," Octavius said, more adamantly. He just needed to think. He knew the missing piece of the puzzle was there if he just looked hard enough. "I would only be a conqueror. You said so yourself."

Maecenas threw his hands up exasperatedly. "I do not understand you, Octavius. Are you the son of Julius Caesar or not? The soldiers will follow Antonius if you do not step up and oppose him."

"Do *you* believe I am his son?" Octavius asked sharply, looking around at each of them. He leaned towards Balbus, who eyed him warily, perhaps even fearfully. *Good.* Fear often worked better than flattery. "If I were the begotten son of Julius Caesar, would you advise me to march on Rome with an army at my back? Like the exiled son of a tyrant king returning to burn the city with my vengeance?"

"No," Balbus answered reluctantly. "Antonius would certainly use it against you."

"I suppose the Senate would be all too willing to support Antonius at that point," Maecenas muttered, and he looked disheartened at the narrowing list of options in the face of a mounting opposition.

Agrippa turned to Octavius with a sigh. "Fine, I agree with you. But then what do you suggest? Do you wish to conduct an assassination yourself?"

Octavius only smiled at him. "No. I wish to ally myself with Marcus Antonius."

For a moment, no one spoke, and Octavius took pleasure when Balbus' face paled. Maecenas' mouth had fallen open, Rufus' brows furrowed, and even Agrippa's eyes widened, before lowering pensively.

"He will kill you!" Balbus protested at last. A few soldiers glanced their way. Balbus lowered his voice. "As your father's most *trusted* advisor, I cannot stand for this."

Octavius leaned forward. "As my father's most *trusted* advisor, you should know Marcus Antonius fervently supported Caesar before he was assassinated. Why? Because the people loved my father, and the people would burn the city to the ground if only someone let them. Now the same Marcus Antonius has found his way to a half-hearted alliance with Caesar's very assassins. Why? Because that way he ensures the support of the Senate along with the people, an unbeatable combination. *Marcus Antonius has no loyalties.* He only respects the odds, and as of now, the odds are not in my favor."

Balbus appeared to be struggling between denial and admiration. He shook his head. "By the gods, Octavius, you are something else."

"So you wish to convince Antonius that he has chosen the losing side," Agrippa said slowly.

Octavius sat back, spreading his arms wide. "He has stolen my inheritance. He is consul and controls the Senate and the treasury. Lepidus has dropped an army at his doorstep. And the people support him as the successor of Julius Caesar. He has everything he could possibly have to raise his own odds." Octavius paused. "But no matter what he *has*, one thing will always be true: Marcus Antonius is not the son of Julius Caesar. *I am.*"

6

MARCUS ANTONIUS

APRIL 44 BC

"Praetor Antonius?"

Antonius ignored the voice, turning around in his bed.

"Praetor Antonius, sir?"

He buried his face in his pillow, determined to stay in bed. The warmth from the night still enveloped him, like a sweet perfume that bordered on poison.

"Darling." A hand gently caressed his arm.

Antonius groaned but stirred at this new voice. "What?"

"Business calls, my love."

He raised his head, looking at the woman lying close beside him. Her honey-colored shoulders were bare above the bed sheets, her thick, dark curls spilling around her face like violet grapes from the vine.

Not everyone thought her beautiful, but Antonius had long ago fallen in love with her sharply curved nose, the barely smirking lips, and the way she said his name in Greek. He had fallen in love with her the moment he had met her, but she had chosen Julius Caesar as her lover instead.

Antonius had to wait many long, patient years, but now he has finally found the woman he has been searching for since he learned the difference between love and respect. A beautiful and proud woman, at whose feet he wanted to lay the whole world.

He reached out and tugged at one of her curls, watching it bounce back once released. "But I still have business with Queen Cleopatra."

Cleopatra arched a dark brow. "If you do not wish to manage Rome, I will gladly do it for you."

Antonius almost responded when he heard a cough across the room. He looked and saw one of his manservants still at the door, his eyes trained on the ground. Antonius had spent the night in one of his other houses outside the city walls, where he had snuck Cleopatra in once Caesar's villa had been compromised after his death.

"Well?" Antonius asked irritably. "Speak."

"Please, Praetor. I would not dare interrupt, only that Gaius Octavius and his companion Marcus Agrippa are downstairs in the atrium," the boy said. "They request your presence immediately. They say it is urgent business, and apologize for any inconvenience."

Cleopatra looked at Antonius fiercely. "Gaius Octavius? Does he mean the boy named in Caesar's will?"

Her question stung. Antonius knew, of course, that Cleopatra remained in Rome after Julius Caesar's death to secure the inheritance posthumously for their illegitimate son, Caesarion. Now that the will had been read and Caesarion unnamed, Cleopatra has settled on the last option which could provide her with another avenue to power—himself.

While he knew Cleopatra calculated love as much as her political ventures, Antonius harbored a quiet hope that she loved him as much as he loved her.

"Unfortunately," Antonius said with a scowl. He had met the young Octavius a few times in Rome and once in Hispania, but could not think of why the boy had the nerve to show up at his doorstep now. "He surely could not have come to claim Caesar's inheritance. That would be foolish."

"But don't *you* possess his inheritance now?" Cleopatra asked, sitting up as the conversation took a weightier turn, the bed sheets pooling around her hips.

A noise of protest came from the corner of the room, and Antonius waved him away in annoyance.

"Tell Octavius and his companion that I have just awoken and need a few minutes to organize my affairs for the day," Antonius said, without looking away from Cleopatra's dark eyes.

The manservant left quickly, the door shutting behind him with a soft click.

Antonius grinned at her. "The nuisance can wait."

"If he is such a nuisance, why not get rid of him?" Cleopatra looked at him pointedly.

He knew she wanted him to bestow Caesar's inheritance upon her son now that Antonius possessed part of it. Antonius would have done it on account of *her,* but to give up the inheritance for the illegitimate son of Julius Caesar? By the gods, no. Besides, the people would revolt if he touched a hair on that boy's head.

"I do not need another martyr."

"I see," Cleopatra said, studying him carefully.

Her look unsettled him, so Antonius slid a hand around her waist, pulling her close and kissing her shoulder, then kissing her again below the jaw, trailing up her neck until he reached her mouth.

"Enough of that," he murmured against her lips. "He can wait a few minutes more."

But when he kissed her again, she pushed him away with a hand against his bare chest. "You ought to bathe before meeting with your *guests*."

"Why do you keep yourself so far away, when you are already in my bed?" Antonius asked to lighten the mood, but the words fell accusingly, and he blushed.

"Men know so much and yet understand so little," Cleopatra said mockingly, that ghost of a smile lingering at the corner of her mouth. He thought he would die if he did not kiss it, so he did. She pushed him away again. "You must go."

Antonius sighed. She was right. Octavius could not be kept waiting for much longer. "I will return to you the moment they leave."

Cleopatra laughed, so suddenly he flinched. She looked at his surprised face and smiled. "Did you think you would meet them alone?"

He only stared at her, too shocked to respond.

She shook her head, laughing to herself. "So little, so little."

⤞⤝

"You must be joking," Antonius said flatly. He stared at Octavius, who only looked back at him in polite expectation.

Octavius and Agrippa had joined them in the triclinium where Antonius and Cleopatra were already reclining, eating the fresh fruit of the season from expensive bronze platters he had custom-made in Greece. At first, it appeared the visit was merely conventional, and Antonius had relaxed.

"My condolences for the loss of your great-uncle," Antonius had said as the two boys had taken their places on the other couch. "He was my closest friend and mentor, and I miss him dearly."

"I have no doubt," Octavius had said, his eyes flicking over to Cleopatra, who had narrowed her eyes at the boy but remained silent.

Antonius had felt his face grow hot. It occurred to him then that it had been a bad idea to allow Cleopatra's presence at the meeting, though he knew deep down he didn't have a choice in the matter. When it came to women, Antonius never had much constraint.

"And who is this?" Antonius had motioned to Agrippa, wishing to bite back.

The strapping youth had not said a word, clearly leaving Octavius to do the talking. Antonius had thought the pair strange, what with Octavius' prestigious family background and his companion's more than insignificant one. He thought he had seen Agrippa tense under his attention.

"My schoolfellow, Marcus Agrippa," Octavius had said lightly, and Antonius had to

61

hold back a laugh. *Schoolfellow?* With that physique and silent countenance he was more akin to a bodyguard than a scholar.

"Please, let us discuss what you have come here to discuss," Antonius had said, growing impatient. He had more business to attend to later and there was a beautiful woman lying on the couch next to him.

Then Octavius had smiled. "I require the rest of my father's inheritance."

Cleopatra had looked at Antonius in surprise. Fury had struck him like a lightning bolt. Who was this boy to try and humiliate him, in front of the Queen of Egypt no less?

"You must be joking."

"He is not," Cleopatra said with an amused smile, and to his horror she sounded impressed.

"Firstly, Julius Caesar is not your father," Antonius spat. *Why must everyone want Julius Caesar as their father?* "Until you acquire the proper adoption papers, that inheritance is mine to safeguard as Caesar's lieutenant."

Octavius did not appear insulted, and Antonius hid his surprise at how composed the boy remained. "I was under the impression that he named me in his will as son and heir, not you. I was also under the impression that you read this will at his funeral. Or was I misinformed?"

"You were not here to receive the inheritance," Antonius said, though even to his own ears the argument sounded weak. "Calpurnia entrusted it to me."

"You mean his widow?" Octavius asked with a raised brow. "And not the *praetor urbanus?*"

Antonius remained silent. The *praetor urbanus* rank was currently held by none other than Marcus Brutus, the principal man responsible for the assassination of Julius Caesar. He and Brutus were already on very unstable ground without undergoing a formal claim of Julius Caesar's inheritance.

"I am the rightful heir to Julius Caesar's inheritance," Octavius said calmly. "Besides, it is in your best interest."

"Oh, really?" Antonius mocked. "How so?"

Octavius leaned forward as if he were about to reveal a secret, and the movement was so alike to Caesar that Antonius nearly shivered. "Brutus and Cassius will only lead you to destruction, even if they provide a temporary solution. You will have no enemy for the people to hate except yourself."

"Are you not my enemy?" Antonius asked. "Because I am having difficulty deciding whether I should exile you or kill you."

Octavius laughed. "You are not going to kill the son of Julius Caesar."

Antonius glanced at Cleopatra, who looked on impassively, though he was sure she hung onto every word. The boy had turned out more meddling than Antonius had anticipated. But one thing was certain. Antonius would not give up Caesar's inheritance only for this wily snake to stab him in the back once he no longer carried a weapon.

"You would be surprised by what I am willing to do," Antonius said coldly.

"Then you will have no one to point to when the people grow restless," Octavius countered, his eyes flashing dark as though he knew something Antonius did not. "Rome needs me. *You* need me."

"I need no one."

"If you shall not give me the money," Octavius said slowly, "the least you could do is dedicate a temple to my divine father with a part of the funds."

This time Antonius could not prevent the laugh that burst from his chest. "Make Julius Caesar a god! Did you hear the boy, my Lady? A god!"

Cleopatra only looked at Octavius curiously. "My people would not find this very strange."

"Your people worship men while they are still alive," Octavius said dismissively.

"And women," Cleopatra amended, to which Octavius glanced at her with disdain.

"Regardless," Antonius interrupted, "that is impossible. The Senate would never stand for it."

"And tell me, Antonius, how the Senate *would* stand?" Octavius motioned around them with his hands. "With what army?"

Antonius called a nearby slave to clear the plates of food. He did not want to waste another second on someone who was only trying to make him look the fool. "I'm afraid we must conclude our meeting. I have another appointment soon."

Octavius did not look disappointed or angry. Instead, he nodded as if he had expected the dismissal. Perhaps he had.

Antonius did not care in the slightest. There was no chance Antonius would let this child take control of an already precarious seat of power. He felt better once they had left the room.

He walked over to Cleopatra and lay beside her with a sigh, kissing her hair which was tied in a tight bun and covered by a fine golden net. She never wore her hair down in public, and sometimes even wore a perfumed wig. But Antonius preferred her natural hair, and already his mind drifted to the night ahead when he would reach out and unpin her hair, watching it unravel in those loose curls down her back.

"A foolish boy, is he not? And what a ridiculous pair they made! Why does the boy lug that hulk of a man around? For protection?"

Cleopatra laughed, kissing him softly. "Oh, men. So little. So, so little."

He did not quite understand, but she was kissing him again in earnest, and he forgot what he was going to say. Then she pulled away, her eyes cast down, but not before Antonius glimpsed the glittery sheen of tears. He gently touched her chin, turning her face towards him until he could see the tears welling in her eyes.

"Why do you cry, my love?"

She did not answer, but the tear that slid down her face spoke the words she could not.

Even though Antonius knew it was inevitable, that Rome was no longer safe for the former mistress of Julius Caesar and their illegitimate child, Antonius had hoped against reason that she would remain for him.

"You are leaving," Antonius said dumbly. He understood, but his heart did not, and he struggled to take another breath. He had the sudden urge to follow after Octavius and murder him. "Where will you go?"

"Home."

"You have a home here," Antonius whispered. "With me."

Cleopatra smiled sadly, touching his cheeks with her fingertips. "Not anymore."

⤞⤟ ⤜⤝

"We ought to have him killed!" Antonius shouted, pounding his fist on the table, ignoring the drops of wine flying from his cup as it rattled from the tremors.

Across from him, Lepidus sighed, scratching at his graying stubble.

Once Cleopatra had left Rome a few days after his meeting with Octavius, Antonius had returned to his house and shut himself inside, drinking every night in his office despite Fulvia's insistence that he pull himself together. He had not attended to any business until he had gotten wind of Octavius' latest shenanigans and had sent an urgent message to Lepidus, who showed up at his house an hour later.

"You ought to have killed him when he dined with you," Lepidus said idly.

He had sat and endured much of Antonius' ranting in silence. Lepidus was not a very amicable man, but he was a respected politician, a brilliant negotiator, and in command of an army, which were all useful to Antonius at the moment. However, he had never loved Antonius as much as he had loved Caesar, to whom he had been a devoted follower for his entire career.

Antonius glared at the old man. "Do not mock me, Lepidus. The boy has been selling off Caesar's property to people on the streets like sweets for children!"

"Did you not take his rightful inheritance from Caesar's widow?" Lepidus asked, shrugging. "He needs the money because you did not give him yours, which some would call illegal."

"Calpurnia knew I was the rightful heir," Antonius snapped, and Lepidus raised a

64

brow. "She was grieving, and I was the only one who would defend Caesar after the assassination. Now this—this *pretender* has turned me into the villain of his ridiculous fancies!"

"If you had stood firm with Brutus and Cassius, perhaps the Senate could have handled him," Lepidus said pointedly. "Or if you had taken my advice in the first place and killed the assassins when you had the chance instead of entreating with them out of fear, perhaps we would not be in this mess to begin with."

Antonius shook his head, wanting to scream his rage. The boy had them trapped between allying with Caesar's assassins and thus betraying the people, or alienating the Senate and thus endangering the power he had so carefully cultivated. And it was all Antonius' fault. It did not help that the love of his life was now on the other side of the Mediterranean.

"Unfortunately, the boy was right. The *Conspiratores* are liabilities rather than assets. If they had not fled from Rome I would have killed them to appease the riots."

"But that is all said and done, leaving us in the same position as before. What would you like to do *now*, Antonius?"

Antonius no longer cared about the consequences, the thought of Octavius ruining everything he had rightfully earned boiling the blood right under his skin. "Get rid of him! Assassinate him and make it look like another crime of the *Conspiratores*!"

Lepidus looked up at the ceiling in exasperation. "That is impossible. Stop behaving like a woman and think like a man."

Men know so much and yet understand so little.

Antonius groaned, dropping his head in his hands. But her voice remained in his mind even after he closed his eyes and tried not to imagine that smile always hidden in the corner of her mouth.

He had thought he had it all figured out, inheriting Caesar's power and mistress in one fell swoop without a drop of blood on his hands. But the arrival of one boy suddenly threatened the tenuous threads he had woven to keep his enemies at bay, who surely regretted sparing his life in the ensuing chaos as he did theirs.

"The boy wants me dead, Lepidus. You would be a fool to deny it."

"And? The Senate also wants you dead. If you murdered Octavius, your own men would murder you for them. The Senate would not stop it. And even if they deigned to try, they would have no army to protect you!"

Antonius took a long drink of his wine. He set the near-empty cup down with a thud. Lepidus eyed it with distaste. He knew Lepidus called him a drunk behind his back, but for the first time, he did not care. "Since you are so wise, what do you suggest instead?"

"Nothing," Lepidus said. "You must not send this boy away. He has a god on his side, even if that god is a dead man."

"Julius Caesar will not command me from the Underworld," Antonius retorted.

He recalled the ghost of Caesar he had seen in Octavius, as if his old master were haunting him in the shape of a boy, and it was all the more humiliating because Antonius was, indeed, terrified.

"*Use* the boy, Antonius. He is still young. Do you not remember what it was like at his age? The entire world seemed to glitter at your feet like a gem at the bottom of a lake. All you had to have was the courage to reach down and pluck it."

Antonius recalled his younger years prowling the streets of Rome at night, gambling every last cent he had for a roll of the dice. He had no prospects at the time except a far-off education in Greece to keep him out of the way and a mediocre rank in the army afterward.

But he had waited patiently, waited as the winds blew in one direction, then turned abruptly in the other. He had respected the odds, never gambling unless the odds were firmly his. Now Antonius finally stood at the top of the world, and all he could see below was ruin.

He ruled an empire, yet he ruled alone. Her laugh echoed in his mind, a constant reminder of all the things he did not know, and never would.

So little, so little.

Antonius clenched his fists. He has allowed Octavius to send his woman away as if she were a concubine and not a queen. Antonius wanted to burn the entire world to the ground in revenge, only to build it back up again for her. Yet still it would not be enough. It would never be enough.

But it was a start.

"I will not kill Octavius," Antonius said darkly, staring at the swirling tendrils of wine at the bottom of his cup. "But I promise you he will wish I had."

Let the dice roll.

7

Marcus Vipsanius Agrippa

APRIL 44 BC

"**I** told you Antonius would never cooperate," Balbus said after a bite of his fish. He turned to Cicero, who reclined beside him. "The fish is excellent, Cicero."

Although Agrippa had heard many things about the famous orator, none had prepared him for his squatness, his labored breathing as he gave a tour of the house—newly furnished, with an extension added to the library, and a renovated bath complex—and especially his preoccupation with everything other than politics.

Agrippa could not tell if his reluctance to discuss the current political situation was on account of his skepticism of Octavius, his disappointment with the rise of Antonius, or his own old age, but it seemed he now found more comfort in the production value of his rustic villas or the pleasant breeze in his seaside houses than anything else.

"Thank you," Cicero said with a bright smile. "Caught fresh this morning."

Agrippa wished to knock the plates from both their hands. They were dining at Cicero's villa in Cumae in the hopes of ensuring his support of Octavius' cause, since Antonius had proved uncooperative.

They had left for Naples on the pretext of the dangers Antonius posed for them in Rome, but covertly they had begun recruiting soldiers in the region and formalizing a plan. Maecenas and Rufus had been left behind to look after their affairs while they were away.

Now Agrippa and Octavius were staying with Philippus, Octavius' stepfather, at his villa in Puteoli. And when they heard that Cicero was currently residing in Cumae—only the next town over—Octavius had wasted no time in sending the old senator a flattering letter and a request for dinner.

Yet not a single conversation had gone by without a remark about the food, either by

Balbus or Cicero, the former to praise it and the latter to praise the cook.

Octavius appeared unbothered, however, carefully cutting his fish and taking measured bites. He nodded and smiled politely, taking the diversions in stride, and complementing Cicero's estate and banquet just enough to have him beaming.

Agrippa knew that Octavius had been raised—even bred—for this purpose, to mingle politics with dinner, confident that in the long run the small nudges in one direction over another would eventually culminate into votes and legislation. But Agrippa had always been better in a fight when decisions were made in that split second between life and death.

He wondered how Octavius did it, the mask he slipped on so easily, how he knew exactly what to say to the right person at the right time. It was something that had always drawn Agrippa to Octavius, and yet at the same time unsettled him, and sometimes he doubted Octavius' sincerity, even with Agrippa himself.

"But as I was saying," Balbus said. "It was a mistake to try and cooperate with Antonius. He only understands violence."

"Quite right, quite right," Cicero agreed. "He is incapable of being rational."

Octavius was silent for a few moments before speaking. "No, but he will soon concede. I shall acquire my rightful inheritance whether he wishes it or not."

Balbus looked at him, too startled to reply. He had already been wary of dining with Cicero, as Balbus had been friends with him for many years and knew him to be staunch in his Republican beliefs.

Although Cicero had not been one of the assassins of Caesar, everyone knew he had supported them, and there were even rumors that he had advocated for the deaths of Antonius and Lepidus as well. The former, after all, would not be so surprising, considering their long history of rivalry and Cicero's outspoken hatred of Antonius in the Senate.

Cicero watched in wonder as Octavius took another calm bite. "How are you so sure he shall concede?" he asked suspiciously. "Antonius has just blocked every attempt of your legal adoption in court."

When Octavius looked up, he smiled good-naturedly. "For now. But when I have the people on my side, he will see the odds are no longer in his favor."

Cicero glanced at Agrippa as if to find the truth, but Agrippa did not speak. This meeting required a subtler skillset of the tongue than he possessed. They desperately needed Cicero on their side in the Senate, so Octavius had to appear in complete opposition to Marcus Antonius and yet appropriately vengeful towards the assassins. If he even suggested an alliance with Antonius, Cicero would be halfway to Rome to declare them a public enemy of the state.

"And how will you have the people?" Cicero asked, feigning curiosity. "Antonius has the plebs of Rome in his pocket thanks to Julius Caesar, not to mention the army and the treasury at his command."

"His public opinion is precarious," Octavius replied kindly, as if he were discussing the beautiful view of the bay from the windows. "After he executed the Marius pretender, the people are starting to question his loyalty to my divine father's legacy." Octavius paused. "They only need a little *push* in the right direction, and Antonius will be forced to flee."

Cicero raised a brow. "Oh is that why I'm here?"

"Rather, that is why *we* are here," Octavius said, so sincerely even Agrippa half-believed his gentle hand on Cicero's arm. "I cannot face Antonius without you."

"Well," Cicero said, trying not to look too pleased. "I dare say I don't mind. Marcus Antonius has always been a scoundrel." Then he glanced at the hand on his arm with a sudden doubt. "And what of Brutus and Cassius? Shall you support them when the time comes?"

It was a thinly veiled test, for they knew Cicero's greatest worry was the safety of his dear *Liberatores,* who had now freed the Republic from one tyrant only to find him replaced by his second-in-command, who was no less dangerous.

For now, Brutus and Cassius had stayed far away from Rome, fearing a delayed retribution from Antonius, and even Cicero continually put off his return to the city after rumors arose of a murderous plot against him.

Balbus had advised Octavius to tread on the side of caution with Cicero, as there would always be time later to deal with Caesar's assassins when Antonius no longer loomed over his shoulder.

"I shall support their return to Rome," Octavius said carefully. "While I cannot pretend to forgive them for their crimes against my father, peace must be restored to the Republic. But I believe now action must be taken against Antonius. Every day he grows stronger, and more Senators bend to his will."

"I have spoken with the designated consuls, Hirtius and Pansa," Cicero said hesitantly. "It is difficult to ascertain, at the moment, whether they shall cow to Antonius or fight for the freedom of the Republic. I hope they will choose the latter, but then again, it is impossible to say for certain."

"If I may speak freely, I do not trust Hirtius and Pansa," Octavius said. "Their positions of power make them all the more afraid to lose them." He paused. "I, on the other hand, have very little to lose except my honor. I would be ashamed to surrender the Republic to such a brute as Antonius."

It was the right thing to say. Cicero looked upon Octavius with unhidden approval. He leaned towards Octavius conspiratorially. "If I, too, may speak freely, I have more faith in you than in Hirtius and Pansa."

"I am very flattered, Cicero," Octavius said. "You have more faith in me than my own stepfather."

"Oh really?" Cicero popped a grape into his mouth, leaning back as if he were finally at ease enough to do so. "What a shame!"

"But when people see the true nature of Antonius, they will turn against him," Octavius said. "They will see that Julius Caesar is a god, and know I am his son."

"My influence only reaches so far," Cicero said hastily.

"Do not worry, my dear Cicero," Octavius said with a smile, and Agrippa thought he saw the mask slip into the barest of smirks. "I will take care of that part myself."

After dining, Cicero led them on a pleasant stroll through the grounds of his villa, which sat atop a large hill overlooking the ocean.

Octavius and Cicero spoke at first of philosophy, debating for a long time the tenets of Stoicism, and as they passed farther into the less cultivated parts of the estate Cicero took to pointing out the various trees and wildlife they saw. Octavius handled the conversation with good nature and impressive wit, and soon Balbus and Agrippa fell a ways behind to let them speak out of earshot.

Up ahead Cicero placed an affectionate hand on Octavius' shoulder as he passionately debated something. Balbus was looking at Octavius with a glimmering pride in his eyes. Agrippa wondered if Octavius reminded him of Julius Caesar and if that was a good thing or not.

"I dare say that boy will be written into *his* will too," Balbus said with a deep chuckle.

"We cannot count on Cicero's support," Agrippa said, and Balbus' smile faltered. "Politicians like to talk, but when it comes time for something to be done, they do nothing."

Balbus gave Agrippa a weary, sidelong glance. "You are still young, Agrippa. I have been around men like Cicero for a very long time. They know that true change, the change that lasts for centuries, only happens slowly. A war can incite rapid change, but even then, you might be surprised by how slow war feels in a standstill, and how little true change it ultimately brings about."

"Nevertheless," Agrippa said, "Octavius will need an army if he wishes to defeat Antonius."

"The soldiers support Octavius. That is not the issue." Balbus hesitated. "The issue is that they are also devoted to Antonius, and do not wish to fight against him."

"Money," Agrippa said with a shrug. Balbus raised a brow. "We give them more money than Antonius. Honor always has a price."

"That is a clever idea," Balbus said dryly, "if we had access to the inheritance money."

Agrippa was silent. It seemed of the infinite problems they had encountered in Italy, they all boiled down to the same thing. Money.

He did not have much experience with money, as his father's modest income hardly left anything over for an allowance. But his father had always made sure Agrippa lacked for nothing, especially when his mother passed away giving birth to his sister.

Now it seemed that nothing mattered more than money. Even the fanaticism of a soldier only went so far as the promised coin.

"I already sold all of his birth father's property, not to mention Caesar's property," Balbus added, almost apologetically, for he could tell Agrippa was frustrated. "But I could not sell them wholesale without triggering all the lawsuits Caesar had incurred over the years."

Agrippa sighed. "Octavius has already asked some of his relatives for loans. His cousin Pedius seems to be willing to help at least."

Balbus patted his shoulder lightly. He had warmed up to Agrippa's presence despite his initial skepticism. When he had discovered Agrippa's affinity for making maps, he had been fascinated and pestered him with all kinds of questions.

His ability to get Agrippa talking about himself—a thing he avoided if he could—reminded Agrippa that Balbus was no fool, and his keen understanding of other people and their desires had certainly saved his life many times in the past years of civil wars.

"Do not worry, son," Balbus said at last. "The money will come. I have seen it happen many times before, and it can happen again. Caesar himself was in debt nearly all his life before he rose to power."

They had followed the edge of the property to the cliffside, where a rugged pathway cut into the rock and snaked its way down to a beautiful, secluded beach. It was surely the grand finale that Cicero had waited all day to reveal to his guests, and even Agrippa understood why. He could see Cicero and Octavius on the sand, attempting to skip rocks on the calm water, as if they were already father and son.

"Do you think it will come to a war?" Agrippa asked idly, watching as Octavius skipped his rock four times before it disappeared underneath the waves, and Cicero congratulated him with a hand on his back.

"Oh yes," Balbus said.

Agrippa glanced at him in surprise.

Balbus had a grim smile on his face. "And if Octavius does not win it, he will be in grave danger." He looked at Agrippa sadly. "We all will."

After a long moment, they descended the path down to the beach. By that time Cicero and Octavius had given up skipping rocks and instead, Octavius was trying desperately to convince the old man to go in for a swim.

Agrippa thought that he would surely refuse, but after Octavius pleaded again, that the water was warm—"By the god of truth, it is like a hot bath!"—Cicero mumbled an answer and swiftly removed his tunic, casting it proudly on the sand.

"Well, come on then, Balbus," Cicero said impatiently, and Balbus laughed and threw off his clothes too.

Together they walked hesitantly into the shallow water, a most comical sight Agrippa had never thought he would see in his lifetime. Octavius watched them in barely concealed amusement from the water's edge.

"Like a bath, my beard!" Balbus grumbled.

Octavius laughed, because it was too late, and he slipped out of his tunic too. The fading light of the evening sun lit up his hair so that it appeared golden, his slim frame dark and lithe like a shadow. Agrippa stood still, thinking that if he moved, the moment would pass, and all would fall to war and ruin.

Then Octavius glanced back at Agrippa with a smile that seemed to hold a secret. "Coming?"

Agrippa nodded, carefully removing his tunic and following after Octavius, gasping when the ice-cold water hit his bare thighs. "You bastard!"

"Well, if I said it was cold would you have gone in?" Octavius asked, flashing a smile before he dove under an incoming wave, coming up for air and shaking out his wet hair which fell in dark brown clumps over his eyes.

Agrippa did not answer that he would have followed Octavius across the widest seas, across the coldest oceans, if he asked him to.

Cicero and Balbus waited for them further out, so they waded through the deeper water to meet them. Octavius swam out and out until Agrippa could only see his head bobbing on the water. Then Balbus swam after him, and there was a chase that ended shortly when Balbus conceded, out of breath and red-faced, though by then everyone was laughing.

Agrippa wondered if this was the calm before the storm, before Cicero had to pick a side and Antonius declared war and Octavius found himself caught in the middle of it.

But as Agrippa watched the sunset, embracing them in an inviting glow, their voices and laughter as natural as the wind and birds above, Agrippa wondered why there need be any war at all.

⟫⟫⟫ ⟪⟪⟪

They drove back to Puteoli early the next morning, having slept a few hours in Cicero's guest rooms. Agrippa watched the land unfold gently outside the window, the slopes of green farmland and fields rising and falling to the coastline, which gleamed blue under the sun.

Their route swung around Lake Avernus, a large crater filled with water as smooth as glass, and turned south and east along the bay until they approached close to the shore, docked with small boats and pleasure cruises. In spring, the coastal cities of the Bay of Naples were warmer than Rome, so that the wealthier citizens flocked to their shores.

Soon they rolled to a stop in front of Philippus' sprawling villa. The house itself was very large, climbing to three stories built on terraced hills facing the harbor. But the most impressive feature of the estate was its grounds, spanning several miles of wild fields and woodlands, where Philippus often took guests hunting.

Octavius looked out the small carriage window silently, staring at the path winding up to the front door. Although it had been a successful dinner with Cicero, dealing with Octavius' mother and stepfather had proven to be another kind of challenge.

"You do not owe them an explanation," Agrippa said quietly. "You are nearly in your twentieth year."

Octavius did not look at Agrippa, frowning. "If I owe anyone an explanation, it would be my parents."

Agrippa fell silent. He hated Octavius in this mood, unresponsive and far away, as if he were not in this carriage with him, but somewhere else, somewhere more real. But for Agrippa, nothing was more real than Octavius. It made him want to grab him by the chin and force Octavius to look at him.

"They are expecting us," Octavius muttered, before tapping the door for a servant to open it. Agrippa followed behind him sullenly.

They entered a very spacious atrium, and only the small fountain at its center could be heard in the hush that cloaked the house. Since the assassination, Atia had taken many precautions and had not invited any guests so long as Octavius was staying there. Light filtered from the opening above so that the marble columns nearly blinded him.

Octavius turned as if to say something to him when Atia rushed into the room, dressed in a very plain tunic with her hair wrapped in a linen cloth. She hurried to embrace Octavius in her arms. Atia held him tightly, her eyes squeezed shut, before she let him go with a kiss on his cheek.

"Mama, I was here yesterday," Octavius said with a boyish smile that Agrippa had rarely seen since they landed in Italy, kissing his mother on the forehead. "Did you miss me already?"

Atia looked at Octavius' face as if she would never see him again, her eyes sad. "I always miss you."

"I promise I will visit more often now that I have business in Rome," Octavius said, but Atia seemed to be speaking of something else entirely.

"Business in Rome?" a voice called out. Philippus entered the atrium, shaking his head. Agrippa saw Octavius tense slightly. "I had hoped you would forget this foolish idea you have taken up without a thought for either your mother or me."

Atia looked at him warningly. "Philippus, please."

"He is putting us all in danger, my dear!" Philippus said, kissing Octavius coldly, who stood as still as a statue while receiving it. He greeted Agrippa formally before leading them all into the dining room for some refreshments.

Agrippa had met Philippus many times growing up, and he had always been intimidated by him. After all, he had once gone toe to toe with Crassus and Pompeius for the consulate elections and would have won if not for the armies of Caesar who had voted against him. Yet his influence was great enough that Caesar appointed him consul even after he was named dictator.

In the wars between Caesar and Pompeius, however, Philippus had skillfully remained neutral, in part because of Atia and her familial connections, and had otherwise withdrawn from politics since the assassination.

"I do not wish to put anyone in danger except myself," Octavius said defensively as he reclined beside Agrippa, who felt he was intruding on a familial argument. But for whatever reason, Octavius had wanted him to hear it, otherwise he would not have been there.

Philippus shook his head. "You are still young, Octavius. There is much you do not know."

"I am willing to learn," Octavius said calmly, but Agrippa saw a muscle in his jaw clench.

"This will be harder than you think." Philippus barely looked up at Octavius as he cut himself a slice of bread. "Julius Caesar knew the game well and he still got himself killed."

"*Philippus,*" Atia whispered harshly.

"It is only the truth, Atia." Philippus glanced at Octavius sternly. "You must not take the name of that family. It will only bring trouble."

Octavius ran a hand through his hair, struggling to remain calm. "It is the only way," he said. "The soldiers will not support me if I am not his son."

"Don't you understand, boy?" Philippus snapped. "If Antonius does not squash your sorry excuse of an army, then afterward the Senate will chew you up and discard you like a dog with his bone. And the people! Do not speak to me of the Roman *people,* Octavius. They will adore and praise you as long as they fancy, but just as easily they will turn their backs on you and despise you."

Octavius seemed to bite back a retort. He turned to his mother, deferring to her as the final verdict. Even Philippus waited for her response.

Atia's face was as still and pale as if carved from stone, and her lips barely moved as she spoke. "They will kill you."

"He is not a child," Agrippa said angrily, the words slipping out before he could stop them. Atia looked at him in surprise, Philippus in annoyance. He ignored the heat rising to his cheeks when he felt Octavius' eyes on him. "He is a man now," he continued, keeping his voice steady, before addressing Atia alone. "Are you not the daughter of Julia Minor? He has the blood of the *Julii Caesares* in his veins. He has as much right to that name as you."

Octavius looked away from Agrippa and to his mother, lowering his voice. "I must do this. Father would have wanted me to."

Philippus sneered. "Which one?"

Atia cut him a scathing glance, but her eyes softened when she looked upon her son, and her voice was thick with emotion. "You are strong-willed, like my mother." Her gaze flickered to Agrippa. "And I am too old to stop you from playing with fire. You know the risks."

Octavius nodded solemnly. "I do."

"Then I wish you all the good fortune," Atia said, the sheen of tears in her eyes glinting like the sun on the edge of a sword. "*Caesar.*"

⇛⇚

Agrippa's arms burned, and beads of sweat rolled down his temples. The afternoon sun baked the palestra in the sweet smell of warm grass. He squinted at the sun, reckoning he had been exercising for almost an hour.

Octavius was nowhere to be found. He had acted as if he needed time alone from him, which hurt more than Agrippa would admit aloud.

After dining with Philippus and Atia, they had planned to go to the baths together. But while they were leaving the villa, Octavius had said he wanted to take a walk on the beach before bathing.

"Alone," Octavius had added with an apologetic smile, though he did not quite meet his eyes.

Agrippa did not understand.

After setting down his weights, Agrippa made his way to the *tepidarium*, which contained a large swimming pool encircled by a shaded colonnade. He took a few laps in the warm water, free to use the entire length of the pool since Philippus had the bath complex closed off for their use as an added protection.

While they were fairly certain Octavius would not be murdered in the baths so far from Rome, stranger things had happened in the last year alone. Even the slaves had been dismissed save those who kept the furnaces lit, so that it felt as though Agrippa were entirely alone, floating in a wide sea. Above the pool, the ceiling opened to the sky, and he wondered idly if anyone would even come looking for him if he slept under the stars all night.

When he grew accustomed to the warm waters of the *tepidarium*, Agrippa followed the hall to the *caldarium*, his damp footsteps echoing on the tile floors. He slipped into sandals before entering the hot room, taking a deep breath of the thick, humid air that rolled out of the entryway like fog. He paused when he saw a movement across the room.

Octavius.

He was sitting in the bath, submerged below the steaming water halfway up to his chest, his head thrown back so that his throat glistened under the lamplight. Unlike the *tepidarium*, this room did not have any windows except for small slits in the wall, which hardly let through any light, and left them in a quiet gloom.

Agrippa took a step backward, not wanting to bother him.

"Stay." Octavius' eyes opened a sliver. He gestured to the water.

Agrippa nodded, but could not speak, walking towards the bath. He slipped off his sandals before stepping into the tub, hissing at the scalding water.

Octavius did not look away as Agrippa slowly slid inside the other end of the pool, his eyes closing of their own accord as his limbs relaxed into the heat.

"Things are about to change, Agrippa," Octavius murmured. Agrippa opened his eyes. "I can feel it. Right here."

Octavius was touching his heart. But he had a faraway expression that left Agrippa lonely, as if there were oceans between them instead of a small stretch of bathwater.

"Things have already changed," Agrippa said before he thought better of it, hating how bitter he sounded.

Octavius opened his eyes fully, staring at Agrippa in surprise. "How so?"

Agrippa swallowed, looking away. "I do not know."

"Tell me," Octavius said softly.

He looked so vulnerable, then, his brown hair curling darkly against his forehead, a single droplet sliding down the delicate bridge of his nose, the water lapping gently against his chest, naked and lean.

"I cannot—I cannot touch you," Agrippa said, then flushed hotly. "As if you were far away."

Octavius smiled. "But I am right here."

"You do not *look* at me anymore."

"I am looking at you now," Octavius said. And he was, those dark brown eyes looking right through him. Agrippa nearly shivered.

"You are no longer Octavius. You are the son of *Divus Iulius.*"

He cocked his head. "With you, I am always Octavius."

Agrippa did not answer. Octavius stood up and reached over the side of the bath, picking up the oil flask left for them to use. The water of the pool reached his hips, and it took every drop of self-control Agrippa had not to stare.

Octavius glanced at Agrippa, then held out the flask. "Would you?"

He nodded, wading over to Octavius, who turned around so that his back faced him. Agrippa then poured some oil onto his palm, spreading it on Octavius' exposed skin.

Octavius' muscles tensed under his hands as they glided over his back. He passed down the ridges of his spine, the slender muscles between the sharp blades of his shoulders, the wet curls at the nape of his neck.

They were so silent that Agrippa could hear his own heart beating, could feel the rush of his pulse in his ears. He realized distantly that he was trying to pinpoint when, exactly, he had begun feeling like this.

While Agrippa had always found the curves of a woman, the feminine body, the soft thighs, more beautiful, more arousing, some time along the road from Rome to Apollonia, from boyhood until now, Agrippa had begun feeling a certain kind of attraction for Octavius. It was different from that burning look in Maecenas' eyes whenever he chanced upon the naked body of a man. For Agrippa it occurred at the strangest of moments, Octavius half-smiling at a joke, or the curve of his throat at dusk, or the way he said his name, like it held a promise.

But had he really not known? Had Agrippa not known from the beginning, when Octavius chose him all those years ago? Perhaps it was inevitable that Agrippa would come to feel this way about him. Perhaps it was even, to a certain extent, his fate.

Agrippa still remembered sitting alone with Octavius in his room, when they could not have been older than ten years of age. Already they had been close friends, and Agrippa had followed Octavius everywhere.

"You know if I were Achilles," Octavius had said importantly, "you would be Patroclus."

Agrippa had only known then that Achilles was the greatest hero of that age, and he had felt it only natural that Octavius would want to be like him. He himself had no issue playing the lesser part of his comrade, if only to please him. But Octavius had leaned in close with a wicked grin.

"That means you have to kiss me," he had said, glancing down at Agrippa's mouth.

After a moment of hesitation, Agrippa had shoved him away, crying out against it much to the absolute delight of Octavius, who rolled onto the floor in laughter as though it had all been some grand joke.

Soon they moved on like nothing had happened, and Octavius forgot about it entirely. But Agrippa never forgot.

Octavius turned around in the bath, facing Agrippa. He waited, as if he expected Agrippa to continue, though he did not meet his eyes, his gaze falling somewhere behind Agrippa's shoulder. Hesitantly Agrippa placed a hand against Octavius' chest, on the breastbone. Octavius' chest rose and fell quickly beneath his palm, but he otherwise remained still.

With a tightness in his throat, Agrippa skimmed a hand haltingly across Octavius' chest, daring to skirt the smooth skin of his stomach, his abdomen quivering under Agrippa's touch.

Octavius' eyelids fluttered shut as if against his will.

They were one dizzying breath apart. What would happen if Agrippa closed the space between them? What would happen if Agrippa were to lean down and kiss him?

You would be Patroclus. But it was always followed by endless laughter, cold and harsh.

"Octavius," Agrippa started, as though he were about to say something, his voice hardly a whisper.

Octavius looked up in question, but nothing in his eyes gave him away, and he did not speak. The silence was stifling in the heat. Agrippa felt his throat close up, his head light.

He stepped away before it was too late, turning his heated face from Octavius' dark eyes. "Done."

"Thank you," was the careless reply.

Agrippa heard him step out of the bath silently. He refused to look at him, to know for certain, lest it pain him even more.

Instead, he sank back into the water as the sound of Octavius' footsteps receded into silence, hoping the heat would swallow him up into oblivion.

8

GAIUS CASSIUS LONGINUS

JUNE 44 BC

C ASSIUS HAD ALWAYS LOVED philosophy.

Since he was young, he had fallen in love with it, the careful logic to explain the world, to give guidance to men in what was right and what was wrong. Cassius had even traveled to Rhodes in his youth and became fluent in Greek.

Philosophy made sense. Philosophy gave meaning to the world. Philosophy ensured that each man had certain basic rights. In a time when civil wars threatened the very foundations of their Republic, when dictators marched on Rome and proscribed thousands of citizens to their death, when tyrants pretended to be divine kings, Cassius looked to philosophy as a lit candle in the dark.

But he learned early on that not everyone cared for philosophy, much less lived by it.

Some men would see to their own power over others, would seek to cause evil upon their fellow men, and would even kill those who spoke against them.

Indeed, Cassius learned that most men were weak, their souls corrupted, and when it came to those men, not even philosophy could save them. Only violence defeated the violent, and only murder defeated tyranny.

These were the tenets he lived by, and he had seen it happen firsthand, beginning with Pompeius and now with Caesar. If it must happen again with Antonius, so be it. If it were up to Cassius, he would have been dead already.

Cassius could hear people arguing down the hall in the dining room, and he set his tablet and stylus down with a sigh. They were hosting a meeting of the *Liberatores* in his villa at Antium, a half-day's ride from Rome.

He had been shut up in his office to answer some correspondence which he had put off since fleeing Rome. Too many people wished to know his whereabouts, and too many people wanted him dead.

After he finished his last response, Cassius decided it was time to join the meeting. The gods knew there were very few in that room with enough brains and courage to do the right thing. He strained his ears as terse words floated from the closed doors.

"...you should accept the grain commission in Asia!" Cicero was arguing, as always. Cassius had heard his voice the most clearly from his office.

He entered the dining room, and immediately all fell silent, turning towards him. Reclining on the couches were Cicero, Favonius, Brutus, his mother Servilia, his wife Porcia, and Cassius' wife Tertia. The rest sitting around the room were either participants in the assassination or known supporters of it, but regardless, everyone was gathered here for one reason, and that was to know what happened next.

"Ah, Cassius, you have finally joined us!" Cicero said, though he eyed Cassius warily. "Please, sit down, we have been waiting for you."

Cassius surveyed the room from the doorway, noting those who were present, as well as those who were absent. Many faces were filled with fear, others carefully concealed their true feelings, waiting perhaps for the conclusion of the meeting before making any judgments. Very few showed any bravery, and none spoke loudly save for Cicero.

"I was just telling our dear Brutus that he ought to accept the grain commission in Asia. And you, Cassius, should take up your post in Sicily. There is nothing left for us to do but to see to your safety," Cicero said. He turned again towards Brutus. "You are the last defense of the Republic."

Brutus frowned, and it aged his face. Cassius had known Brutus for a long time, but never before had he seen him so devitalized. It was as if all the passion and strong will he had before the murder had been drained from him along with the blood from Caesar's body.

He shook his head, and at last, took his spot beside his wife. Tertia was ten years younger than he was, but she too, like her brother Brutus, looked much older, as though new lines had been drawn on her face in the last few months. In meetings such as these, she preferred to stay silent and listen, while her mother and brother did the talking.

"What say you, Cassius?" Cicero asked hesitantly.

"I will not go to Sicily," Cassius said coldly. "Should I accept an insult as if it were a kindness?"

Ever since Antonius assigned Brutus and Cassius the commission of grain, which was an insulting office for various reasons, Cicero had been trying to convince him by letter not to do anything rashly, and to accept the degrading position of legate until it was safer to make their next move.

Cicero sighed. "What then will you do?"

Cassius shrugged. "Go to Greece."

"And you Brutus?" Cicero asked, as if he cared more for his answer than Cassius', which was probably true.

Most people favored Brutus, as he was the more approachable of the two of them. Cassius was told once that he had a burning look about him, as if at any moment he might burst into flames and declare war.

Brutus hesitated in replying and glanced at his mother, Servilia.

While the death of Caesar had been quite devastating for her, as it was widely known she had kept up an amorous affair with Caesar, her attention was now completely fixated on her son, whose wellbeing she obsessed over nearly as much as Cicero did. Brutus himself had lost that surety that initially made him the face of their cause, and his lack of confidence worried Cassius in the long run.

"To Rome, if you think it right," Brutus said cautiously, addressing Cicero, whose eyes widened at his words.

"No, no, I don't think it right at all." Cicero shook his head. "You won't be safe there."

"But if it was safe, that is what you would want me to do, is it not?" Brutus asked.

Cassius knew Brutus desperately wished he could be in Rome however much he feared the city at the same time, and leaving had cost him much of his pride. Perhaps he hoped to make a martyr of himself, though Cassius doubted Servilia—or his wife Porcia for that matter—would allow it.

"Of course," Cicero said impatiently. "If it was safe I would not want you to leave for Asia now or after your praetorship. But as it is, I don't advise you to put yourself at risk in Rome. If what they say is true about Antonius stirring the Macedonian legions that Caesar left behind, then you had best leave Italy altogether. He already has his sights on poor Decimus in Gaul."

Cassius scoffed. "Poor Decimus? He commands Cisalpine Gaul and remains much safer than we. He is to blame for the position we are in. If it were not for Decimus, perhaps we would never have compromised with that brute Antonius."

There were murmurs in the room, and many added on other complaints. Decimus, they knew, was one of the first to come up with the plan of assassination along with Cassius. But at the end of the day, Decimus had been one of Caesar's men and was so loved by him that he was even named in his will like a son. It was not the first time someone suggested that Decimus had been too soft on his former comrades-in-arms.

Yet Cassius trusted Decimus, more than he trusted Brutus, while many turned rather to Brutus as a descendent of the kingslayers all those years ago. The more weeks that passed since their carefully planned execution, however, only proved that Caesar's corruption reached far deeper than they had thought.

Cassius now obsessed over the past, wondering where they had gone wrong, what they could have done differently, and Decimus' absence made him an easy target.

For, of course, he dared not speak of *Brutus*, who had begged them all to spare Antonius and Lepidus in the murder, and which had cost them dearly. Not with Servilia in the room, at least, who may as well be their best hope in removing the insulting grain commissions from the senatorial decree thanks to her influence with a few prominent senators.

"What is done hardly matters now," Cicero said, though his long sigh said otherwise. "Besides, the mistakes of the past do not only lie on the head of Decimus. You both ought to have called a meeting of the Senate after the whole affair. Perhaps if you had simply stirred up the people with more vigor, more passion, then the entire Republic could have been yours."

"Really!" Servilia mocked. "We have not heard *that* one before."

Cicero fell silent at that, his face sullen. He would not argue with Servilia, especially not when she was right. They had already debated to death the mistakes they had made, and Cicero was not putting forth any new ones.

"If you think it right," Brutus said at last in the silence, "I will go to Asia."

"But what of the games you are to give?" This question came from Favonius, who reclined beside Cicero. "Would it not be a sign of *weakness* to surrender the games to Antonius?"

Favonius was notorious for his espousal of the Cynic philosophy, though most people called him an imitator of Cato the Younger behind his back. If Cassius could have helped it, Favonius would not have been involved in the assassination at all.

Servilia huffed. "Nonsense!"

"The games would still be given in my name," Brutus said curtly. "I would merely be...absent."

"So then you agree to go?" Cicero asked.

"Yes." Brutus nodded firmly and looked at Cassius expectantly. He had made up his mind, apparently, and now wished Cassius to follow in his footsteps. The room waited for his reply, and Cassius knew the courage of many in this room hung upon a thread of hope.

"I will think about it," Cassius said finally.

"Then there it is." Servilia held her head aloft, as if daring anyone to go against her son's plan. She was a formidable woman, but with a sensitive streak, like her son. Cassius had always admired her ability to work her influence in the Senate. "Yes, that is best. And I promise to make sure the grain commission is removed."

"Then if I am to go, I had best leave directly," Brutus said, his eyes lit with a new determination, but to Cassius it only heralded recklessness. A desperate man was often the most bold, though it did not always make him right.

"So soon?" Cicero asked, also troubled.

"You were the one who wished us to leave," Cassius said, raising a brow.

He knew that Cicero would rather they lay low in Italy, though fearing at the same time that if they remained, they would attempt to confront Antonius in Rome.

But there was no more time to waste idling away in their countryside villas like Cicero. Either they surrendered to Antonius and returned to Rome, come what may, or they gathered a force large enough to defeat the Caesarian faction once and for all.

"Leave, yes, but not without a plan," Cicero said reproachfully.

"Do not worry, old man." Cassius grinned. "Leave that to me."

~∞⟫⟫ ⟪⟪∞~

"You know you do not have to listen to Cicero."

Tertia stood in the doorway of his bedroom, her dark hair brushed into a long braid. She wore a white linen dress down to her ankles, and her pale face was free from any makeup.

Cassius always thought Tertia beautiful, from the day they met, and much more attractive than Brutus, though they shared an uncanny similarity with their dark, almost black hair and pale skin. Her brother, however, had a hungry look in his eyes, a desire to prove himself and his lineage, that Tertia never had.

"Are you already going to bed?" Cassius asked. "I should not stay up for much longer."

"Did you hear me?" Tertia shook her head. "If you go to Greece, you will start a war."

"Sometimes war is necessary."

"It is dangerous," Tertia said, her voice low. "If Antonius defeats Decimus, there is no telling what will happen." She paused. "You may never be able to return to Italy."

Cassius stood up and walked over to her, kissing the top of her hair. "Not without an army I won't. But do not fret, *mea Tertulla*, I do not leave in vain. The Republic can still be saved."

A shadow darkened Tertia's eyes. "My mother says you and Brutus are the last hope we have."

"That may be," Cassius said sadly.

While he regretted having to leave his wife for such a long time, he knew it was the only way to ensure the safety of both their lives in Rome.

Besides, Tertia was a very independent woman, like her mother Servilia, and she would

83

survive without him just fine. Cassius had always allowed her to do as she wished, to see whomever she liked, which sometimes caused rumors to float back to him. She had never confessed to any kind of infidelity, however, and Cassius had never sought to know for certain. Some things, he found, were better left to rest.

"I worry for Brutus," Tertia said. "He puts so much of himself in these things. I doubt he will be left with much when all this is over."

"Brutus is sensitive, that is all." Cassius still remembered the look Brutus had on his face after the murder, as if he alone had struck the dagger into Caesar's body those twenty-three times. Even weeks after the Ides of March, Cassius would catch Brutus glancing at his hands, like he was checking for stains of blood. "He and Caesar were rather close after all, almost like father and son."

Tertia had a troubled look. "Yes, I suppose."

One of the rumors that had reached his ears was that Servilia had arranged an affair between Tertia and Caesar while Cassius had been away, perhaps in the hopes of gaining his favor. The thought had struck him as ridiculous at the time given Servilia's passion for Caesar, but every so often Cassius wondered.

As if to prove the rumor wrong, Cassius took hold of Tertia's arm, pulling her closer. He leaned down and kissed her cheek. "It has been a long time since we slept together."

"Oh, I don't know, Cassius…"

Cassius felt a fire kindle inside at her resistance. It was the same feeling he got when Caesar had been named dictator for life, as if his heart were white hot iron in his breast. "Come, Tertia, I may not be here for much longer."

Still, Tertia pulled away. "Really, Cassius, I cannot."

"Why not? Shall we only have one child?" Cassius was only joking, but he went still when Tertia's eyes filled with tears.

Her hands fell to her stomach, and she flattened her dress against her belly, which curved against her hands, undeniably pregnant.

Cassius could hardly think. "Since when?"

Tertia avoided his gaze. "I knew in April for certain."

"Why did you not tell me?" Cassius placed a hand on her belly, the skin warm through the thin linen.

She shook her head, and tears fell down her cheeks. "I did not want to worry you."

"Oh, *mea Tertulla*." He kissed one of her tears as it slid down her cheek. "A life for a life. It is a good omen."

After Tertia went to bed, Cassius returned to his office, where he found Brutus pouring over a map, carefully tracing the drawn lines and making a mark here and there with his pen. He looked up when Cassius entered.

"Took you long enough," he muttered, though he had a small smile on his face. He was looking more optimistic since their meeting, if only because now he had something to do.

"Tertia is pregnant," Cassius said as a reply.

Brutus raised a brow. "She just told you now?"

"You knew?"

He laughed. "I'm her brother."

"And I'm her husband. I had a hand in it, after all."

"More than that, I'd reckon."

"Careful, Brutus. That is my wife you speak of."

They settled in their chairs, sensing that the times for joking were over. Brutus handed over his map, pointing out the cities of the East in which he thought they had the best chance of campaigning for soldiers. Cassius made a few marks of his own. It was not a plan, but it was a start.

Cassius smiled. "Let's kill another king."

9

GAIUS OCTAVIUS

JULY 44 BC

*W*AR.

Octavius could taste it on the hot, summer breeze crawling through the windows of the house. The people in the city were restless in anticipation, as if there were a storm brewing on the horizon, which he supposed was not far from the truth.

In the east Marcus Antonius gathered the Macedonian troops that Julius Caesar had stationed before his death, while Octavius heavily recruited from Campania in the west, paying each soldier who would join his cause five hundred *denarii*. Lepidus held an army in Spain, Brutus and Cassius struggled to establish legions of their own, and senators were fleeing Rome with their tails tucked between their legs, not wishing to get caught in the crossfire of civil war.

He was walking a thin line himself, balancing on pure luck alone. Octavius was a step away from death at all times, where the only way to reach the other side safely was to look straight ahead.

Sea-green eyes caught the corner of his gaze.

Octavius felt his concentration stutter.

Nothing had been the same since Puteoli, the steaming waters of the baths and Agrippa's smooth, firm palm clinging to his memory. Octavius had supposed he went too far, and he wondered if their friendship would ever recover from it. But who was he trying to deceive? Agrippa would never desert him. That was precisely why he had tested him in the first place, to see how far he could go and how long Agrippa would allow it.

They did not talk about it afterward. After all, what was there to discuss?

"Caesar?" Balbus asked worriedly from the opposite couch. "Are you with us?"

It took a moment for Octavius to realize the address was for him, as he had only recently taken up the name of his great-uncle. He looked at Balbus, ignoring the watchful eyes beside him.

They had been debating the next steps in their plan while they dined at one of his family homes near the forum. Octavius was tired from a long day of courting senators and prominent elite families in Rome, hoping to gain their support and money for his cause. For they had returned to Rome to put on the games in honor of Caesar and Victory, and it had cost him quite a bit of money, though he hoped the result would be worth it.

"Yes, Balbus. What is it?"

"I said your tutor, Athenodorus, has landed in Italy," Balbus said slowly. "He plans to join you here in Rome shortly."

"Good. He will be useful to me."

Octavius had sent a message to Athenodorus, requesting that he join him in Rome. Athenodorus had many valuable connections with certain senatorial families, and Octavius hoped he would speak with them on his behalf.

"We should run through the numbers once more before I return home," Balbus said, sharing a concerned glance with Agrippa. A quiet companionship had grown between the two of them in the past few months, and Octavius wondered if it was on account of their similarly humble backgrounds.

Agrippa hardly mentioned his hometown, or his family, though Octavius knew that his father managed a modest farm somewhere in the countryside, while his mother had died when he was young. The only other thing Agrippa had said about his life before Rome was that he learned how to hunt in the untamed fields beyond his house, and that when he had killed his first bird, he had cried.

"Go on," Octavius said with a sigh.

"We have successfully recruited over three thousand men, nearly all of them loyal veterans of your father's cause. And the plebs have reacted well to Caesar's donations. But due to the games, our funds have significantly depleted."

"In other words," Agrippa said, "we need more money."

Octavius shook his head. They have had this conversation many times, and they always reached the same conclusion. "We need more support. People do not believe I can defeat Antonius, that is the problem. The people who have something to lose, at least, and those are the people who have the money to give."

Bablus smiled apologetically. "You are young, Caesar. Antonius has years and years of experience."

"I am not a child," Octavius said in reproach.

"To a sixty-year-old senator, you might as well be," Agrippa said, his voice chilly.

Octavius had not really looked at him this entire meeting. He did now and regretted it. Agrippa was staring at him intensely, his eyes cast in shade to a gray-green.

He nearly scowled. "Then I will not try to convince them otherwise. But when the time comes, they will wish I had."

Octavius thought of Cicero, how easily he ate up his flattery, the gleam in his eyes when Octavius spoke of defeating Antonius. They so desperately desired someone foolish enough to go to war against him, in the hopes that Antonius would be taken care of and the Senate may once again secure ultimate authority over Rome.

He knew Cicero wished to use him to this end and then discard him. For his part, Octavius would not dissuade him from this plan, and in fact, he would encourage it whenever possible. For the more they underestimated his power, the less time they would have to prepare when Octavius fully unleashed it.

"Regardless of whether the Senate is deceiving you, or you are deceiving the Senate," Balbus drawled in his thick accent, "you still have to defeat Antonius, and he has shown that a mere name will not be enough to oust him. A name, I might add, which he has continuously prevented you from adopting legally through the Curiate."

"The people will turn against him with Cicero's help. And my money," Octavius argued, though he knew at the end of the day that Balbus was right. "Already his soldiers are defecting. As for my adoption, his refusal only makes my cause the more righteous."

"That is not enough," Balbus said urgently. "The Senate hates Antonius but they still fear him, especially after he granted himself governorship over the Gallic provinces and threatened to oust Decimus. He has even scared Brutus and Cassius from Italy with a mere charge of grain supplies."

Agrippa snorted. "They will never accept that insult."

"Perhaps, perhaps not," Balbus continued, waving his hand dismissively. "It does not matter. Antonius will easily defeat them in battle if he gets to Decimus in Gaul first. Your best hope at that point would be enough destruction on both sides to give you a fighting chance. If the *Conspiratores* defeat Antonius, then you must turn on your dear Cicero or give up your plans. But if not, and Antonius proves totally victorious, then the Senate will truly cower, and no one will dare go against him, not even for the son of a god."

Silence. Octavius knew his greatest power lied in his new name, the fear it instilled in Cicero when he spoke of his divine father, how the people, the soldiers, all cried out to him as some kind of savior—no, a *restorer*—who would bring back the Republic for the people instead of the rich, and burn the dirty streets and rundown temples and build a city of marble, like a phoenix rising from its own ashes. But none of that mattered if Antonius took control and used that very name against him.

"What if we came to the aid of the *Conspiratores*?" Agrippa asked suddenly.

Balbus and Octavius exchanged an uneasy glance. He knew Agrippa had a keen grasp of military strategy, but Octavius could not see a world in which he aided the very men who killed Julius Caesar.

"You mean to suggest I openly support the assassins of my father?" Octavius asked doubtfully. "My soldiers would not stand for it."

"They would stand for the right price." Agrippa leaned forward intently. "Think. If you support the *Conspiratores* in defeating Antonius, just as Cicero wants you to do, then the Senate will gladly give you money and more troops. *Legally.* Your soldiers would be under your command."

"But even if you and the *Conspiratores* defeat Antonius, the Senate will kill you the moment they regain power!" Balbus argued. He lowered his voice. "You would be walking into a trap, Caesar."

Octavius saw it, then, like a rush running through his head, the future unraveling before him. He locked eyes with Agrippa, who smiled with him when he knew Octavius had understood.

"Perhaps, perhaps not," he said, echoing Balbus' own words with a grin. "Let the Senate think so. Let them underestimate my name, my men. But when the time comes, the people of Rome will answer to me, and with my army, they will be powerless to stop it."

Agrippa nodded, smirking. "Brutus and Cassius will not stand a chance."

"And if the Senate suspects this?" Balbus asked, though it was clear he was beginning to agree with their plan. "Will they so freely hand over their armies to another Caesar? Will they not fear that you will betray them too?"

"Do you not remember, Balbus?" Octavius asked mockingly. "Because to them, I am only a child."

⟫⟫⟫ ⟪⟪⟪

Agrippa held a blade in front of Octavius' throat, the edge gleaming in the weak light of the morning. A slave held a large mirror in front of him so that Octavius could watch Agrippa shave his face. Agrippa's reflection in the mirror raised a brow questioningly, and Octavius closed his eyes.

"I am sure," Octavius whispered, careful not to swallow. "I must appear as youthful as possible."

He felt the blade slide up his oiled neck, clearing the stubble he had grown since Apollonia. Usually, he had a barber come to the house and shave him, or else had one of his slaves do it, but nowadays enemies were easier to come by than friends, and he would not take his chances.

Octavius found it strange that Agrippa was one of the only people alive whom he could trust with his life, yet they could barely look each other in the eyes.

"Stay still," Agrippa murmured from above him. Octavius could feel his fingertips pressed against his chin, steadying him.

Octavius focused on the blade instead as it shaved close to his lips in delicate, short strokes, followed by the light splashing of water from a bowl beside them. Next, the blade curved up his chin, stopping right below his jaw. A finger ghosted along his jawline where he had grown out his stubble these past few months. Octavius opened his eyes.

Agrippa was looking at him, his fingertip still tracing the edge of his face. "A shadow of mourning."

"Or a shadow of revenge," Octavius countered, looking back until Agrippa turned away, then in silence shaved the rest of his face, leaving it more round and youthful.

When he was done, he picked up a wet cloth and gently cleaned Octavius' face. Then with palms damp with perfumed oil, Agrippa lightly patted his skin. Octavius breathed in the scent of roses, watching Agrippa's hands around his face in the mirror.

They locked eyes again, and Agrippa blushed. "The parade will begin soon." He collected the shaving supplies and avoided Octavius' gaze. "I believe Rufus and Athenodorus will already be at the stadium. Maecenas cannot make it. Says he is traveling to Arretium. Oh, and the *venationes* will be the first games, as you wished."

"Good," Octavius said, standing up. He took one last look at himself in the mirror before gathering his things. "Will you walk beside me?"

Agrippa looked at him in surprise. "During the parade?"

"Yes."

"I am hardly a priest," Agrippa said cautiously.

Octavius could not help but smile. "And I am hardly a consul. But we paid for every cent of these games. It is only right that we hold a place of honor."

Agrippa frowned, but before he could answer, one of his guardsmen approached, signaling that they must be on their way to the stadium. They rang to have their best togas wrapped around them before following the armed guard onto the street.

When they stepped out into the blazing summer sun, Octavius shared a glance with Agrippa. It had to be the hottest day of the year. The humid heat cloaked his skin like a second layer, reminding him of another festival years ago, and his mother warning him to cover his head. That day ended in dizziness, feverish cramping, and weeks recovering in bed. He could not afford another such moment of weakness today.

Agrippa seemed to be thinking the same thing. "Perhaps we can postpone the games for the evening when it is cooler."

"I am perfectly capable of sitting in the heat," Octavius said with a confidence he did not feel.

"The stadium does not have an awning."

Octavius only smiled, waving at the crowds of people watching him go by and calling out his name. "I will be fine."

He was saved from another argument by their arrival at the Capitolium, where sacrifices would be made before the parade began. The temple of Jupiter Optimus Maximus loomed over them at the top of the hill.

Already crowds of people had swarmed around the temple, the lictors in their traditional garb, as well as the athletes and musicians performing during the games. Even soldiers and citizens had flocked nearby to witness the entire procession, trying to push past the guards that lined the vicinity.

Balbus was waiting for them at the base of the temple, and when he saw them, he approached hurriedly.

"Caesar," Balbus said in a low voice, keeping stride with them. "I have bad news."

"Naturally," Octavius said.

Balbus gave him a hard look. "Antonius has blocked your request for displaying the throne and wreath of Caesar in the stadium."

Octavius shrugged. "Good."

"How so?" Balbus asked, exasperated, and also struggling to keep up with the fast pace as the parade goers moved to get in their positions.

"It makes it easier to name him the villain."

"A war of words," Balbus said, shaking his head, almost fondly. "You are truly your father's son."

Octavius did not react, but he noticed Agrippa glance at him curiously. He wondered what he saw in that glance. The ghost of Julius Caesar? A memory of a boy always falling ill? Or just someone he desired? Octavius did not know which he despised more.

Suddenly the crowd of trumpeters ahead of them began the commencement song, and the parade started to trudge a path of music and cheers down to the Circus Maximus. Octavius counted each inhale and exhale as he walked along the procession, the sun beating down on his neck. He felt a bead of sweat slide down his back, and he knew his cheeks must be flushed red.

Much to his annoyance, Agrippa kept a steady eye on him throughout, but he did not say anything, for which Octavius was grateful.

Soon they approached the stadium, which was already teeming with crowds of citizens donned in their nicest togas and tunics. The entrance never ceased allowing people into the stadium, the wooden bleachers straining under the weight of the crowds.

Octavius could hear someone calling out his name in a familiar voice. He turned around and ignored how the movement made his head feel faint.

In a nearby throng of people stood Athenodorus and Rufus, the former furrowing his bushy brows as he surveyed the rowdy citizens, looking hunched and frail beside the energetic, youthful figure of Rufus worming his way through the crowds of people to greet Octavius and Agrippa.

"Friends!" Rufus exclaimed, kissing Octavius and then Agrippa, who tried not to laugh at the unruly red-brown curls and wide eyes that sometimes made Rufus look like a startled puppy. "It feels as though I have not seen you in years."

"It has only been a few weeks, Rufus," Agrippa said lightly, though Octavius saw right through it.

Although the three of them were close friends, Agrippa had never quite gotten along with Rufus, and though they both pretended it was merely friendly competition, Octavius knew it was very serious to both of them.

Rufus ignored Agrippa's comment, turning to Octavius with a smile. "I am glad you are back. Rome needs you."

"Thank you, Rufus," Octavius said. "It is good to see you."

Then Athenodorus hobbled towards them. He grasped Octavius and Agrippa's hands and spoke to them in Greek. "It is a blessing to see both of you again. I have sorely missed being your teacher."

"I am sure you now have more competent students to teach," Octavius replied warmly, also in Greek.

Ever since they had left so abruptly, Octavius found himself missing the long lectures while strolling in the gardens, the tricky questions in which his tutor had found pleasure testing them, and Agrippa's silent presence beside him. Athenodorus was a symbol of a different time, however, and one which had forcibly come to an end.

"None shall ever be as bright as you," Athenodorus replied, squeezing both their hands in his wrinkled ones before letting them fall.

Octavius thought he saw Rufus' jaw clench at the words. He had always been a few steps behind in their tutoring, much better with the sword and shield than words. But even then, Agrippa had always managed to find the edge in their spars and win.

At that moment trumpets blared again, and Balbus appeared, calling his attention. Beside him was Gaius Matius, who partnered with Octavius to fund the games, as well as Gaius Oppius, a wealthy friend of Julius Caesar.

"The games are about to begin, Caesar. You ought to take your seat."

His guardsmen escorted them all up into their seats, where they had the best view of the ring below. As Octavius walked along the pathway to his row, the stands erupted in applause, chanting his new name. He greeted them all with a smile, although he feared his step would falter at any moment.

They sat down side by side, Octavius between Rufus and Agrippa, while Balbus, Matius, and Oppius took the row behind them. They were surrounded by a sea of people, their voices raised and their shoulders jostling each other as they made their way into the bleachers.

The sun was now high above them in the sky, shining with more intensity, baking the stadium in its heat. The dirt of the track shimmered, and dust rose in clouds above the ground. They could hear an animal growling somewhere, and the banging of a metal cage.

A fading dizziness made Octavius grab Agrippa's arm. He would not faint. "Do not let me fall."

"What?"

Octavius stood, using all his strength to keep himself upright. He felt Agrippa's hand hover nervously at his lower back. The people closest began chanting his name, so that soon the entire arena seemed to be looking at him, and Octavius had to raise his hands up to quiet them.

A wave of hushed whispers ran through the stadium until the entire arena was quiet, listening to what Octavius was about to say.

"People of Rome!" he cried out. "Today we honor my father's death with games. He was murdered by the same men who claim to free us. What do we say to that?"

The crowd yelled their disapproval, the soldiers making crass gestures that only served to stir the people into greater hysterics.

"And to the man who calls himself a friend of *Divus Iulius,* who has not only yielded to my father's assassins but even denies me the right to honor him properly. What do we say to *him*?"

Immediately the stadium shouted the name of Antonius, calling him a traitor and stamping their feet on the bleachers so that the arena shook as if with an earthquake.

He glanced at Rufus and Agrippa, who both nodded. Everything was set in place, everything was planned to the last word, the last pause.

"In honoring my father, I must do what he would have wanted to do if he were still alive!" The crowds began murmuring at this, wondering what he was going to do next. "My father would have wanted to reward each of you in coin for your loyalty and support!"

Before anyone could react, someone began shrieking in delight, pointing up at the sky. More people looked up, gasping and crying out in surprise. This had not been a part of the plan. At last, Octavius looked up too, his heart beating loudly.

He could not believe his eyes. It was a comet, burning a fiery white streak across the blue sky, its tail scorching a path in its wake. Octavius did not need to say much. Already the chanting had begun. He saw Balbus laughing in delight out of the corner of his eye.

Divi fili! Divi fili! Divi fili!

Octavius pointed at the comet. "Divus Iulius!"

The people echoed his words, raising their hands to the sky as if they could touch the comet's fading tail.

At that moment, it began to rain. Except that it was not rain at all, but money, small coins showering from above, landing all around them, catapulted by Octavius' men from around the stadium's bleachers. The people cried out once more, scrambling to grab as many coins as they could under their seats, holding out their hands to catch them as they fell.

Dive Juli! Dive Juli! Dive Juli!

Octavius raised his hands to the sky. "Let the games begin!"

Then he promptly sat back down, his face flushed, and his breathing shallow. He wordlessly accepted the flask of wine that Agrippa handed to him and took a long gulp.

Agrippa shook his head fondly. "You keep forgetting you are not a god."

Octavius grinned. "Why be a god when your father already is one?"

IO

Marcus Antonius

AUGUST 44 BC

Antonius crumpled the letter in his hand, angrily slamming it on the desk among the rest of his morning correspondence. He was swimming in bad news, even though he was currently consul and in command of Julius Caesar's remaining legions.

There were Brutus and Cassius amassing their own armies, Lepidus weaseling his way into the powerful position of Pontifex Maximus, Plancus and Pollio securing their provinces up north, and the Senate colluding behind his back, with Cicero being the most obnoxious and vile of all. Not to mention Octavius, who was stirring up the soldiers in Campania with claims of Julius Caesar's divinity.

The city was bad for him. He had returned to Rome, quite unwillingly, to settle his quarrel with Octavius once and for all. Now he was already regretting that decision.

It was as if no time had passed since Antonius was twenty years old, wasting nights in gambling dens, then suffering the daylight and the inevitable itch to throw the dice and drown his worries in a single number. But he was no longer that boy, and he had the entire Republic at his feet.

He smoothed out the letter after a deep breath, reading it through once more. It was from Lepidus, who was now in Hispania with part of Julius Caesar's army, keeping the Senate's anxiety of an alliance with him at bay.

Antonius had previously written asking for advice about Octavius, who would simply not go away. His own soldiers were switching allegiances, just for a quick stash of coin. It was despicable. It was embarrassing. And then the boy had the audacity to request a display of Julius Caesar's throne and crown in the theater like he was some kind of god? How could he have allowed it with the Senate breathing down his back?

As if matters could not have gotten any worse, a comet appeared in the sky during the games like a forsaken sign from the gods themselves. A comet! Now all anyone ever talked about was the spirit of Julius Caesar ascending to the heavens. And Antonius would lose all his soldiers if he fought against *that*.

So there remained the issue of reconciling with the boy while retaining authority over his soldiers. Antonius could hardly think of him without a rush of hot anger choking his throat. He wanted to have him executed, but that would only ensure his own death. Perhaps he could conceive of a clever assassination, but he recalled the aftermath of the Ides and shuddered.

Every way he turned, Antonius was blocked by the unfortunate truth that his soldiers liked the boy more than him. The last defense he had was denying his legal adoption by Caesar in the *curia*, where at least he still held some influence.

Lepidus advised him to set up a public meeting with Octavius where his soldiers could witness a reconciliation of sorts. Then behind closed doors, Antonius could continue to scheme against him in peace and without suspicion of disrespecting Caesar's son. But what if his public apology only humiliated him in front of his men? The thought made him sick.

However, it was the only civil option which gave him time before the violence began and his hand would be forced. Even now Decimus Brutus was situating his legions in Cisalpine Gaul, which would be legally transferred to Antonius on the first of January. But Antonius would be a fool to believe Decimus would give up one of the last defenses of the *Liberatores* without a fight.

The other letters piled haphazardly on his desk were mostly terse correspondence with various senators, complaints from the provinces, and general news from his legions. It was the kind of chore that Julius Caesar had usually managed, but now the responsibility had fallen to him, since his new co-consul, Dolabella, remained far away in the East secretly gathering forces.

He sighed, running a hand over his face. In the back of his mind, he knew these letters meant nothing, the endless grabs for power and the insults tossed his way in the name of politics.

Ever since *she* had looked at him, laughed, and with an idle gesture of her hand revealed the secrets of the universe, Antonius had known with a sharp certainty that nothing else mattered.

Nothing, nothing, nothing. But nothing would not bring her any closer, so he banished the thought from his mind and called one of his slaves to fetch his general. A few minutes later he stepped into the room with a hesitancy that irked Antonius.

"At your service, praetor."

"Varro, tell your men to bring Octavius to me at the temple of Jupiter," Antonius ordered. He swallowed down his boiling resentment. "I believe it is time we made some amends."

Varro brightened, and Antonius held back a grimace. "Wonderful news, praetor! We will bring him to you immediately. The men will be delighted to hear it, sir."

"Yes, yes," Antonius said, unable to hide his impatience. "You are dismissed."

Once the general was gone, Antonius made his way to the forum, flanked by his bodyguards, whose numbers he had increased as of late. He felt an animosity lurking in the people, in this miserable wreck of a city, with its filthy streets, the noise of the mobs clamoring out of gambling dens and brothels, marketplaces and baths, their protests in the forum and at the steps of temples.

He was once connected to those people, to the back alleys of the city, the grinding days at work, plowing through the mud and madness of Rome. Now he was responsible for it, and all he could think about was a woman. *Perhaps not much has changed after all.*

Antonius ascended the steps of the temple of Jupiter Optimus Maximus, stopping before the altar and looking out at the forum in the valley below.

A sea of soldiers had followed him, hearing the news of the reconciliation, gossip running through the ranks like wildfire. They stood restless, murmuring and looking up at him from around the base of the steps.

"Praetor?"

"Not now, Varro," Antonius snapped. He did not need any distractions, the fate of his authority resting on this meeting.

"*Praetor.*"

Antonius turned to his general angrily. "What?"

The frightened man looked past his soldiers to the entrance of the forum, where a crowd had gathered, too distant to make out clearly. "It is him."

"Who?" Antonius did not understand.

The crowd was approaching, and he realized they were shouting—no, *rejoicing*—their fists thrown high. They were soldiers, Antonius saw with a sinking dread, Octavius' soldiers, and many, many of his own. And in the middle of the mob was a small figure walking solemnly, a muscular shadow trailing close behind.

He whirled upon his general. *"What have you done?"*

"Nothing, sir, I only did—"

"Never mind what you did," Antonius interrupted scathingly. "It is too late."

Octavius was quickly nearing the temple, his head lowered piously as if he were leading the procession before a sacrifice, though he smiled and conversed with the soldiers around him. His trusted companion, Agrippa, seemed to stand at guard an arm's length away, carefully watching the closest soldiers who joked and jostled with Octavius as though he were one of them.

Antonius watched impassively from behind the altar as his own soldiers parted like water around Octavius, staring at him in barely hidden awe. *Filius Divi Iulii,* they murmured. *Filius Divi Iulii.*

The Son of Divine Julius.

When Octavius reached the base of the steps, he looked up at Antonius. "Hail, Marcus Antonius! My soldiers have brought me to you in the hopes of reconciliation. I could hardly refuse them what they so clearly desire from me."

"But is it what you desire, *Octavius?*" Antonius sneered, catching the slightest flinch in Octavius' face at the name. He was no longer Octavius to his soldiers, but to Antonius, he would always be the little boy had he met twenty years ago.

Octavius slowly ascended the steps, holding out a hand to stop his armed guard from following him up, until he was standing a few feet from Antonius. The soldiers below waited in anxious silence, straining to hear every word.

"I desire only what we all desire," Octavius said, sweeping an arm across the ranks of soldiers.

"And what is that?"

"Peace."

There was a murmur from the soldiers. They were all veterans of Julius Caesar and desired a unified front fighting against the *Conspiratores.* But Antonius knew it was futile. There could be no unity while both of them were still alive.

"To have peace you must have war," Antonius said at last. "What do you know about war, boy?"

"I may be young," Octavius replied, though he seemed to address the soldiers now, "but I am sincere. I only fight for the people, and for Rome, as my divine father did. What do you fight for, *consul?*"

An uneasy whisper could be heard faintly in the wind. Antonius tried to hide his surprise at the boy's ability to make him appear just as guilty as Caesar's assassins. But Octavius was a liar. Every man only wanted power for himself, and if anyone claimed otherwise, they were wrong. Yet the soldiers seemed to look at Octavius as a kind of savior. Antonius had to switch tactics before a riot broke loose.

"I thought you wished to reconcile, not throw stones," Antonius said, trying to sound lighthearted. "You ought to show more respect for your elders."

Octavius hardly looked at him, facing the crowds with an air of righteousness, and Antonius swore he could have dueled him right then and there. "I have trouble respecting those who disrespect my divine father."

"If by father you mean my dearest friend, Julius Caesar, then I have disrespected him as much as you have."

There was silence. It seemed they would remain at an impasse, the soldiers exchanging worried glances. But Octavius only turned to him with a smile, though Antonius could see the contempt in his dark brown eyes. He cocked his head, and he was suddenly reminded of that day long ago at Gaius Octavius' funeral. He remembered how strange he had thought Octavius, a small, silent child, no more than Atia's son. He wondered when that had changed, and if he was responsible for it too.

"Then let us reconcile," Octavius said. He motioned to the temple and lowered his voice. "In private."

Antonius nodded, unable to hide his surprise now, but returning the smile mockingly. "In private."

He motioned to his guards, who produced two wooden chairs and placed them at the top of the stairs, where they could still be seen by their men but not heard. Octavius took his seat beside Antonius silently.

They could hear the crowd of soldiers discussing urgently amongst themselves, but they appeared more at ease with their masters sitting down for a civil discussion. For now, a disaster had been averted, but the next time Antonius would not get so lucky.

"I am not a fool," Antonius said, unable to hold back any longer.

Octavius raised a brow. "I do not consider you one."

"Your soldiers led you in a triumph," Antonius said angrily. "You wish to embarrass me."

"You were the one who called me to you," Octavius replied, smiling and waving at his men to reassure them that all was going well. He spoke without looking at Antonius. "My soldiers were only protecting me."

Antonius was done with theatrics. He leaned towards Octavius. "Do not play games with me," he spat. "If you wish for war, you will get war. Some soldiers may be enticed by money alone but the rest will not be so easily deceived. And when your men see the forces they must fight against, they will flee."

"I do not wish to fight with you," Octavius said earnestly, looking at him intently, and for a moment Antonius almost believed him, before he caught the flash of hatred in those eyes. They shone the truth while his mouth lied. "I only wish to honor my father's legacy."

"He is not your father," Antonius hissed. He hated him, with every part of himself. He hated the boy to Hades and back.

The earnesty dropped, and Octavius smiled coldly. "Not yet."

"You insolent—"

But he was standing up, motioning for his guards. The soldiers strained their necks to ascertain the conclusion to the day's dramatic events. Octavius paused as he descended the steps, looking back with that infuriating smile.

"I am glad we could reach an agreement, Antonius. Do send my regards to my father's Macedonian troops. I hear they will be arriving in Italy soon."

Before Antonius could respond, Octavius was walking away, disappearing into the crowd which led him back through the forum. Antonius stared at the spot where Octavius had been standing, wondering how everything had turned upside down in only a few months.

Distantly, the soldiers could be heard cheering as his men followed after him on the streets, singing out a jaunty tune that Antonius could not make out. His general, Varro, made a move to follow, but Antonius held up a hand. It was no use. The winds were already blowing, and they pointed in only one direction.

Antonius made a sign and his guards began to escort him from the temple. He lowered his voice. "We must prepare for travel."

Varro looked at him, shocked. "But sir, the men will desert you if you leave them now."

"They are coming with me," Antonius replied with a smirk. "Octavius has picked a side, and so will I. War is upon us."

"Where shall we go?"

"Brundisium." Antonius could not stop the grin on his face. "You heard the boy! The Macedonian legions will be arriving by October. I must be there to welcome them."

The city had always been bad for him anyway.

⟫⟫ ⟪⟪

She was dead.

That was the first thing on his mind as he crossed the threshold of Philippus' grand villa, perched on the slope of a hill overlooking the bay of Naples.

The second thing was that it felt like only yesterday he had attended Gaius Octavius' funeral at twenty years old, and saw Atia, serene and elegant, standing in the atrium. Now he was nearly forty and it felt like no time had passed at all.

He walked into the atrium. Atia was not there. She would never be there again. His head felt light, his chest hollow. Antonius passed the atrium without another glance. He entered the second inner courtyard, where the evening light hardly reached, and it seemed as though the house was deserted. Not even the lamps were lit.

"What is he doing here?" a voice asked angrily, coming from down a dark hallway.

Antonius turned and saw Atia approaching—but no, it was a girl—who had reminded him of Atia only in the stern expression directed at him, before he looked closer and noticed all the things that were wrong. The bright blue eyes, the dull blonde hair, and the pale skin reddened at the cheeks. No, this was not Atia.

This was her daughter.

"Octavia," Antonius said instinctively.

The girl stuttered to a stop. She was not really a girl anymore, though, Antonius reminded himself, noting the metal ring on her left hand. He now recalled hearing of her marriage to a certain Marcellus, though at the time she had still been very young.

Antonius raised a brow. "We met many years ago. Do you remember me?"

Surprise quickly morphed back into anger, which did not suit her delicate features. "You should not be here."

A calm voice replied from the other side of the courtyard, followed by a familiar slim figure and dark brown eyes. "Why, sister? I invited him."

"You *invited* him?" Octavia looked at her brother with bitter contempt as he made his way over to them. "You should know not to allow your own enemies into the house. Even I know better than that."

"You have always been smarter than me, so it is no surprise," Octavius replied with a smile, dipping his head to kiss her cheek briefly, which Octavia allowed with reluctant satisfaction. "But it was what Mother would have wanted."

"My condolences," Antonius said quietly. "Your mother was a very pious woman."

Octavia turned on him sharply, her eyes flashing with indignation. "*Piety.* Men throw that word around as if they had any idea what it means."

Men know so much and yet understand so little.

"Pray tell, what does it mean?" Antonius asked, conscious of Octavius watching the conversation unfold.

"It means death, Praetor Antonius," she whispered, a tear escaping down her cheek. "It means death."

Then she walked past him quickly and disappeared into the house once more. Octavius approached slowly, an apologetic frown on his face.

"She has been like this since our mother passed away," he said, looking down the hall where Octavia had gone, though he seemed anything but wistful, perhaps simply resigned.

Antonius could hear other female voices now, many crying aloud, some even singing, the notes faint and trembling from deep within the house.

"It is normal," Antonius replied.

He did not wish to speak with Octavius, and he regretted having carried on a topic that pushed his sister away, who interested him more. In a way, she had been right. Antonius should not be here. He should be preparing for his relocation to Brundisium, which was only a month away, and there was still much to do. But when he received a single terse letter from Octavius two days ago, he found himself driving in his carriage down to

Puteoli.

"She has grown up a lot since the last time I saw her," he said, glancing at Octavius. "So have you."

"I remember you," Octavius said, turning towards him.

Antonius could not contain his disbelief. "You do?"

He nodded absently. "Yes, I do. You were sitting beside my stepfather. You were both laughing at me."

"Laughing?" Antonius did not remember finding anything very funny that day. "No, I was not laughing at you. If anything, I pitied you."

"Pitied me?"

"Yes. Your father had died when you were young, like mine. It is something that you can never escape, no matter how hard you try."

Octavius looked at him strangely, and Antonius felt his skin prickle. "And why would I try to escape it?"

"Brother."

Antonius turned at the voice, grateful not to be obliged to answer. Octavia had returned, her eyes red, but she looked calmer and more composed than before.

She glanced at Antonius briefly and impersonally, then slid her gaze back to Octavius. "The reception is about to start. Most of the family are already gathered. They wait for you."

Octavius nodded and followed after her silently to a further part of the villa, with Antonius trailing behind them. They soon arrived at a small room where Atia herself, dead and pale and covered with a gauzy shroud, lay on a low wooden table at the center in preparation for the procession and burial.

Relatives and members of the household stood around it, packed tightly together. Octavius and his sister made for the head of the group, where Philippus, Agrippa, and Atia's sisters were already standing, while Antonius lingered at the edges of the room. But no one spared him a glance, as if when it came to death, all the family became unified as one, no matter the hatred and bitterness between them.

"We gather here today in remembrance of Atia Balba Secunda," Octavia said, her voice low but echoing in the somber space. "She was a beloved daughter, wife, and mother, and it is our duty to keep her alive through our devotion to her memory."

Then everyone was silent, and even the air seemed to hang suspended above them. Antonius saw Octavius take one of Octavia's hands in his, giving her a reassuring nod. Octavia kept her eyes tightly closed, and Antonius held his breath.

Then she began to sing.

Her voice trembled, breaking, before lifting over her tears, growing stronger as Atia's sisters joined in the familiar mourning song. Soon the other women of the household began singing too, forming a chorus of grief threaded from a common pain that Antonius did not understand, that remained locked up in Atia's brown eyes which he would never see again.

Antonius watched Octavia as she sang, one hand gripping her robes tightly, the other in her brother's hand, the knuckles white, her face deathly pale, and for a moment, a brief moment, he thought he might understand.

Piety means death.

Octavia opened her eyes, and she seemed to look right at him, the blue clear and sharp as a deadly winter sky, and he knew she had dared him to understand, dared him to take part in the cutting pain of piety, and he had failed. He always failed to understand, in the end.

Then he recalled another face, all wine-dark curls and olive skin, like a hot summer evening—so different to this one cut out of ice. The thought of her left him breathless in an instant, as if the floor had suddenly disappeared from under him. But if he was given the chance, would he have what it takes to love her?

And if it was demanded of him, would he die for her?

The answer terrified him.

II

MARCUS VIPSANIUS
AGRIPPA

SEPTEMBER 44 BC

I T FELT LIKE THE worst time to have a party, but Octavius had insisted.

Maecenas had recently bought a magnificent house on the top of the Esquiline hill, already equipped with large gardens, gently climbing terraces, and libraries, though Maecenas planned to make many more additions. He already had a hot swimming pool especially constructed in the gardens.

The guests were invited from all the wealthiest families in Rome, and Agrippa felt very much out of place among the familiar greetings and distant familial connections. He reclined beside Balbus, as if he might feel less alienated next to a foreigner, but it turned out that Balbus had the most friends of all and was constantly being pulled into different conversations.

"That is absurd!" Balbus exclaimed. He was speaking with Maecenas, Octavius, and a wealthy couple whom Maecenas had invited from his social circles in Arretium.

"It is more than absurd," Maecenas said. "It is an offense!"

They were discussing the most recent rumor that Octavius had attempted to assassinate Marcus Antonius. It *was* absurd, but the guests never tired of asking Octavius about it, hoping for a reaction worthy of more gossip on the morrow.

But Octavius only laughed. "It is just a rumor, my friends."

Yet as he spoke his eyes lowered to the ground, and he frowned, lapsing back into silence. Octavius had often slipped into spells of quiet like this since his mother's funeral.

"Surely started by Antonius himself," the wife, Cornelia, said, nodding her head.

She was dressed in an atrocious yellow *palla*, weighed by several necklaces of amber and emerald stones. A gold necklace that must have cost a fortune clasped her throat, and there were even golden threads woven into her hair.

Cornelia was much younger than her very elderly husband, but she was not young herself, and her hair already bore white streaks. She gently touched Maecenas' arm as she spoke—a most open flirtation if Agrippa had ever seen one—and Agrippa nearly laughed at Maecenas' astonished face, though he knew Maecenas loved to be admired.

"No doubt!" Balbus agreed.

"Let him investigate me," Octavius said with a smile, holding out his hands as if to show they were empty. "He will find nothing."

"Oh, I do not understand you, Caesar," Maecenas said, a touch dramatically. He liked to draw as much attention to himself as he could at dinner parties. "The consul himself has accused you of attempted assassination. Enough of these politics and take him straight to war! That will teach him to respect your name."

"Oh dear!" The old woman laughed nervously. Though she was clearly interested in Maecenas, her husband was apparently unbothered, standing aloof beside her in his gold embroidered tunic. "A war!"

A few guests in the room glanced their way before returning to their own discussions. It was not as if they did not know that war was coming. Many of them had come today to show their support for Octavius, while others were more curious than anything. A war may stop many things, but it never stopped a party.

"There will be war regardless, I am afraid," Octavius said with a sigh. "Antonius is preparing to leave for Brundisium as we speak."

The woman clutched at Maecenas. "You don't say!"

Agrippa moved from his seat before he acted improperly. He wove his way through the guests until he reached the back doors and walked out into the gardens.

The night was clear and brilliant, the stars spread across the sky like a blanket sewn of bright jewels. A full moon shone on the lip of the horizon, shedding a hazy glow on the flower bushes and tall, looming pine trees. Once again, Rome reminded him of her breathtaking beauty.

Then he heard a crack behind him.

Agrippa turned, half-expecting to face a sword, but it was only Octavius. He must have followed him once he left.

Even though nothing had happened, nothing had changed, Agrippa still felt as though nothing was the same as before. *Before what?* Agrippa asked himself, and he did not know the answer.

Octavius smiled at him as if nothing were any different, though Agrippa sensed he avoided being alone with him as of late. Was it his mother's death? Was it the newfound pressure as the son of Julius Caesar? Or was it something else?

And why was he here now?

"I only needed some air," Agrippa said quietly, though he did not know why he felt the need to explain himself.

Octavius nodded, standing beside him and staring up at the sky. "I do not blame you. I am not sure how Maecenas does it."

"He was born to entertain," Agrippa said, half-smiling, but it faded as he remembered the conversation he had abruptly left. "I have been thinking...Perhaps we ought to trap Antonius in Rome before he flees to Brundisium where an entire army awaits his command."

He shook his head. "I need the Senate on my side first."

"Your army is already in Campania, all you need to do is lead them."

"If I raise an army without the Senate's approval, they will declare me a public enemy. It is too big of a risk without knowing the reward. We must wait for a sign before taking such an action."

"The comet was not enough?" Agrippa muttered and immediately regretted it.

But instead of being angry, Octavius laughed, shaking his head as if fond of Agrippa's wit. "Antonius will depart for Brundisium soon. That is when we call on my soldiers. Self-defense will suffice as an excuse, though the Senate must still give me *imperium*."

"We are not even certain he will leave," Agrippa argued. "To welcome the Macedonian legions at a time like this would mean an open act of war against Rome. He has already threatened to remain consul in the new year. The Senate would not stand for it and he knows that."

Octavius smiled, mocking. "The Senate does not have a choice. They have no army."

"And you suppose the Senate will turn to you for help?" Agrippa asked, raising a brow. "You have much faith in the Senate."

The smile dropped into a scowl. "I have no faith in the Senate. Cicero is my only hope at the moment, and he refuses to return to Rome and do anything about it. Believe it or not, I have actually thought up a more direct influence to steer the Senate into my path." He paused. "The tribune of the plebs."

"The tribune? You must be joking."

Recently one of the tribunes had died, and Agrippa recalled hearing the news that the position was open. But Octavius was too young to be elected, unless he had already secured an illegal means. It seemed impossible, but Octavius had already achieved more impossible things in the span of three months.

"I will not elect myself tribune if that is what you are thinking. Rather, I will propose *another* for the position. And if the people claim they want me instead despite my age, well, that is not my doing, is it?"

"Why not simply elect yourself?" Agrippa asked dryly. "You have the money."

Octavius grimaced, perhaps recalling their conversation about cheating all those months ago. "It is not only about winning. Caesar knew how to win, but not how to write the rules. And that got him killed."

"The Senate will surely block you," Agrippa said, his mind running through the possibilities—and traps—that this new plan posed. "To be tribune would give you the power to bring the *Conspiratores* before the popular assembly for a trial. Only Antonius has enough power to get you into that office now, and he's the last person who would want to."

"I suppose this will be the first test of my reconciliation with Antonius, then," Octavius said lightly, though his eyes told a different story. "Either he will pass the test and give me the office of tribune, or he will fail."

"And if he fails?" Agrippa asked. He had more faith in the assassins of Julius Caesar than Antonius.

"Then he fails Divine Julius, and his soldiers will defect." But Octavius looked grim as he spoke the words. They both knew Antonius would not support Octavius in any way when his soldiers were already transferring allegiances to Octavius without a second thought. "Then it will be war."

"Then it will be war," Agrippa repeated.

And if Octavius does not win it, he will be in grave danger. We all will.

Agrippa only hoped they would be ready when it came.

⤜⟫⟫⟫ ⟪⟪⟪⤛

OCTOBER 44 BC

Agrippa kept his balance centered as he and Octavius circled each other slowly in the open grass of Maecenas' gardens.

They had been invited to stay there despite Maecenas' departure to Arretium, where he was checking on the renovation of a family villa that had been passed down to him from a childless aunt recently deceased.

The early autumn sun warmed their skin. They had decided to train outside while the weather still allowed it. He watched Octavius' measured steps, the careful concentration on his face, the lean muscles of his chest flickering as he prowled.

"We can do this all day," Agrippa said, smirking.

Octavius moved.

Agrippa barely dodged a sharp stab of Octavius' wooden dagger, twisting out of his reach and landing a blow to Octavius' exposed side—more to force him off balance than inflict any damage—before retreating once more.

"You are slower than you were at Apollonia," Octavius taunted.

"We have not had much time to train in Italy."

"Speak for yourself."

Octavius sprang forward as he spoke, jabbing Agrippa's thigh before he could avoid it, eliciting a hiss of pain. At the sound, Octavius' eyes flickered up to his and Agrippa used the distraction to aim his own dagger at his chest while he was still within reach, but Octavius side-stepped with quick footwork and knocked the dagger clean out of Agrippa's hand.

A bare smile appeared on Octavius' face.

Agrippa stepped back without a second thought and delivered a kick to the stomach which left Octavius gasping in surprise as he retreated. Octavius seemed to be tired as they returned to circling each other, though he eyed Agrippa intently.

"Perhaps we should rest," Agrippa suggested, feeling somewhat guilty. He knew Octavius had struggled to reach full strength after his last illness in April.

"If I cannot handle a sparring match, how will I survive in war?"

Agrippa shrugged. "Perhaps there will be no war."

"If Cicero remains skittish, that is very possible," Octavius said wryly.

While Cicero was biding his time, Octavius was running out of it. The Senate was like a boulder at the top of a hill, indifferent and immobile to the problems of those below, but it only required a strong push in one direction to build momentum, before flattening everything in its path. Cicero could be the strong push to bring the Senate and Antonius to the brink of war. Yet nothing was ever certain in politics.

"Even if Cicero complies, the Senate may still seek another answer," Agrippa reminded him.

"Not if Antonius makes his move, which I know he will."

"Until then?"

As if in reply, Octavius tossed his wooden dagger to the ground.

"You wish to wrestle?" Agrippa asked, surprised. Octavius always preferred to have a weapon in his hand.

"We are already dressed like the Greeks," Octavius said, gesturing to his naked chest and the cloth tied around his hips.

He stepped closer and assumed the fighting stance of the *pankration,* his legs lean and gleaming in the sun. Agrippa followed suit, his heart beating faster.

Usually, he gained the upper hand in this kind of combat with ease, thanks to his stronger build, but today he was not so sure. Something had changed between them, ever since they had left Apollonia. He wondered if Octavius was using it against him now.

"ξυνὸς Ἐνυάλιος, καί τε κτανέοντα κατέκτα," Octavius said, a glint of mischief in his eyes. *The War-like god is even-handed, and he kills the man who kills.*

"Quoting the Iliad will not help you win," Agrippa replied calmly, but his muscles were taut, hating the lull before the fight, hating the tug of a smirk at the corner of Octavius' mouth.

Agrippa swung.

His fist was blocked, but he expected this, and he thrust his knee up. Octavius evaded the attack and struck his ribs, but fell back when Agrippa kicked out at his legs, trying to get him off balance.

While Agrippa's fighting style was more direct and offensive, Octavius liked to counterpunch, using Agrippa's momentum to his advantage and exposing his weaknesses.

"Is that all you have?" Octavius asked, clearly goading, though his mouth frowned, irritated. He knew Agrippa was holding back, and resented him for it.

In response, Agrippa advanced with a new burst of energy, kicking at Octavius' legs and then striking at his face, fending off Octavius' blocks until he was close enough to lock his arms around Octavius' chest, trapping his right arm.

It was a dangerous move, giving Octavius the same chance to lock his left arm, keeping them in place until one of them gained an edge. Agrippa felt Octavius' rough breath in his ear, his strength waning ever so slightly, his center of balance shifting just enough—Agrippa moved.

He aligned their hips, leaning in with his left leg before he arched his back, lifting Octavius up and throwing him down on the ground. Agrippa followed him down, splitting Octavius' legs with his right and lacing Octavius' left with his own.

Now Octavius was pinned beneath Agrippa, a bead of sweat rolling down his chest. Octavius was breathing harshly, his face flushed but his eyes narrowed. The wind was knocked out of him, though Octavius would never admit it.

"I suppose the War-like god does have his favorites after all," Agrippa said quietly, feeling more apologetic than satisfied.

Suddenly there were arms wrapped around his chest, squeezing hard as he was thrust up and shoved to the side with surprising, wiry strength.

Agrippa gasped as he rolled onto his back, and then Octavius was on top of him before he could retaliate, straddling his hips, a hand gripping his throat making it difficult to breathe.

Blood rushed to his face as time seemed to slow, and he was intensely aware of the dull thuds of his heartbeat at the base of his neck, the grass tickling his cheeks. He looked at

Octavius, his half-closed eyes, the arm stretching to his throat nearly trembling with the effort, the fingers at his throat tightening as Agrippa swallowed.

Then Agrippa struck at Octavius' chest with his palm, sweeping Octavius' arm to the side so that he lost his grip and caught himself with two hands on either side of Agrippa's face. Agrippa hovered his hands over Octavius' hips in warning. They were no longer fighting, but they were not at a truce, not even close.

Octavius did not move, his body still waiting in case Agrippa tried to move again. It was as if he wanted Agrippa to know that he had the upper hand now, that the game they were playing was not really a game at all, that this had been, all along, about power.

Agrippa wanted to shove him away. He wanted to fight him. He wanted to hook an arm behind Octavius' neck and kiss him.

Octavius looked down at him with a challenging brow. "I suppose you were right."

Agrippa imagined pressing his fingers into Octavius' waist, either to throw him away or bring him closer he did not know. The curve of his neck was invitingly bare. If Agrippa kissed him there, would Octavius stop him?

"τέτλαθι δή, κραδίη," Agrippa whispered, almost unconsciously. *Be still, heart.*

Surprise kindled in Octavius' eyes, a flicker of light in that deep brown, like the sky at dawn. He studied Agrippa's face, half-sitting up, momentarily forgetting their fight. For he knew the end of that line as well as Agrippa did.

καὶ κύντερον ἄλλο ποτ᾽ ἔτλης.

You suffered worse things than this.

Suddenly there were footsteps, and Octavius stood up calmly, as if they had not just wrestled each other to the ground, as if Agrippa had not nearly betrayed himself.

Agrippa sat up.

One of Octavius' messengers was waiting across the garden, standing at attention, out of breath but eager.

"What news?" Octavius asked, his shoulders tensing as if he knew what was going to be said before the boy said it.

"Marcus Antonius has left for Brundisium, sir."

Agrippa looked at Octavius, but he was staring at the ground, lost in thought. There was no celebration, not even an acknowledgment, though the sign they had been waiting for had finally appeared. For the first time, Agrippa wished it had stayed away a little longer.

Ever since their departure from Apollonia, they had skirted danger with Antonius, but they had never faced a true challenge. It had all been merely talk, a stage set up for the real action to play out later, always later. This changed everything.

"Then it will be war," Agrippa said softly. Octavius seemed not to hear, but Agrippa saw his hands tighten into fists at his sides.

Be still, heart: you suffered worse than this.

⭆⭅

Agrippa stepped into the room hesitantly. The steam was already hot and thick in the hallway, but inside here it clung to his skin like morning dew.

After news of Antonius' departure to Brundisium, Octavius had disappeared inside the house, and Agrippa thought it a good idea to give him some space. Besides, Agrippa still felt shaken after his sparring loss from earlier, so he had attended to some affairs he had neglected as of late, if only to distract himself.

But after a few hours of Octavius' absence, he had begun to wonder. He asked someone in the house where he had gone, and they pointed him to the baths. Agrippa nearly did not seek him out, but Octavius had been in the baths for several hours and it worried him. They still had not discussed Antonius and what they would do now.

"Octavius?"

"I am here."

Octavius was lounging in a marble bath full to the brim with steaming hot water. To Agrippa's surprise, he had a wax tablet in one hand and a stylus in the other, looking more alive and animated than he had for weeks.

"What are you doing?" Agrippa asked before he could help it.

"Thinking, mostly," Octavius said. He frowned. "Writing, less so."

"Poetry?"

"No, tragedy. I find the peace of the baths helps me focus." He beckoned Agrippa over. "Please, sit. Sometimes you act like a stranger."

Agrippa had been standing awkwardly by the door. He walked inside and sat at the edge of the glistening, marble pool.

These were Maecenas' private baths, and properly luxurious. Bronze lion-heads decorated each water spout of the bath, the walls were painted with nymphs and sirens, while large octopuses and fish covered the tile floors. Agrippa thought it all rather distasteful.

"Sometimes I feel like a stranger. I never knew you wrote tragedy in the baths," Agrippa said. It was half a lie. He had found one of Octavius' tragedies in his room back in Apollonia once, scratched haphazardly on used papyri. It was about Agamemnon, and it had not been very good.

"Well, I rarely finish them. And if I do, I always destroy them," Octavius said, his mouth lifting into a smile. "We all have our vices, I suppose."

Agrippa's stomach turned. "Yes, I suppose."

111

Octavius nodded slowly, his gaze settling somewhere beside Agrippa, who took the time to study him. His face was damp, cheeks flushed from the heat, eyelashes beaded with water, but he did not look ill, just thoughtful, perhaps a little weary.

"My mother is dead," he said suddenly, the words stated merely as fact.

Agrippa was startled into awareness, the words echoing in his own heart like an ominous drum beat.

Octavius repeated the phrase as if trying to convince himself of their truth. "My mother is dead."

He was silent. Octavius looked at him sharply, then, his eyes fever-bright.

"I always thought death was my father," Octavius said slowly. "And for so long it was him, a face I did not know, a voice I had never heard, waiting, just waiting." He closed his eyes, a hand fluttering to the place right above his heart. "But my mother is right here, now, like a weight on my chest, suffocating me, clinging to me in every memory I have of her."

"The dead never truly die if they are preserved in memory," Agrippa murmured.

It was what his father had taught him when his mother had died, and for many years he had believed it religiously. But as time passed, the memories had faded to half-imagined smiles and embraces, and he could only love the mother he once had. Though the grief never truly left, he had long ago learned to live with her loss.

Octavius opened his eyes, watching Agrippa from beneath lidded eyes. He looked so vulnerable then, as if Agrippa could break him with a single touch. "Will you preserve my memory, if I die?"

Agrippa's heart jumped into his throat. He tried to imagine it, his life without Octavius leading the way to some higher purpose. A long life in the army perhaps, with a wife and children he rarely saw, until one day a sword or a stray spear struck him in the right spot and killed him. Long forgotten would be those dreams of legacies and heroes, and the memory of Octavius would fade to nothing.

A cold fear laced his limbs at such a life, but he forced himself to say it anyway. "Yes. I will."

"Promise," Octavius said, hardly a whisper, and Agrippa realized he sounded afraid. "Promise I will live on in you."

"I promise," Agrippa said, the words heavy in his mouth.

So many promises, so many lies. He did not know how it had happened, how his fate had tangled itself with the boy looking at him like this now, as if his life were a precious jewel and he trusted no one else with it besides him. Now they were on the brink of war with the most powerful men in the country, and any chance of surviving was like an arrow shot in the dark.

Inexplicably, Octavius smiled, though it was grim. "Good. *For the War-like god is even-handed—*"

"*—and he kills the man who kills,*" Agrippa finished quietly.

War had come.

12

GAIUS OCTAVIUS

NOVEMBER 44 BC

T HEY WERE WALKING ALONG the edge of a knife.

Antonius was gathering the Macedonian troops in Brundisium, and it seemed like war would descend upon them any day. Everything Octavius strived after hung in the balance as they decided what to do next. The right step could mean an empire, while the wrong step could mean death.

Agrippa was standing over the table in the center of the tent, looking worriedly at the large scroll he had pulled across it. It was his masterpiece, an intricately measured and drawn map of the world, stretching from the far north where the Rhine met icy, open sea to the southern borders of Egypt, and spanning the many miles between the Pillars of Hercules in the west and the kingdoms of Parthia and India in the far east. He had started it in Apollonia out of a love of cartography, but now it served a very different purpose.

"We are nearly ten thousand strong after securing Calatia and Casilinum," Agrippa said, his finger hovering over a region on the map.

Octavius got up from where he was reclining on a couch, walking around the table and standing beside Agrippa. He was pointing at Campania, the land penned between the Apennine mountains and the Tyrrhenian Sea. He spotted the town of Capua, their base of operation thanks to Balbus' estate, nestled in the valley, with the towns of Calatia and Casilinum as two tiny dots nearby.

"What about the region of Samnium?" Octavius asked, looking at the vast lands to the east of Campania, where they had been campaigning for the last week.

Just yesterday they had passed through Cales and stayed the night at Teanum, where crowds of Caesar's veterans and countrymen had gathered to greet him and promise their support.

"Our scouts report a growing following," Agrippa said. He hesitated. "Any news from

Cicero?"

Octavius could not help but sigh. "Nothing useful. He refuses to meet me at Capua. Says it is impossible to keep secret. Perhaps he is right, but it would not be on account of *me*. Does he think a few half-hearted speeches in the Senate will scare Antonius? He is a coward. They all are, of course. *Politicians*. And senators are the worst of them."

"It is not too late to turn your back on the Senate," Agrippa suggested, though he knew well that Octavius would never agree to it. Winning over the Senate was the only way to get what he wanted. It was the biggest mistake Caesar had made, and Octavius would rather die than make the same mistake again.

Octavius gestured to the map with a sweep of his hand. "When you look at this map, what do you see? Perhaps you see territories, regions, tribes, legions. Cities and towns, and the roads in between. You see the rivers and mountains and where to cross them. Maybe you even see kings and consuls. But do you know what I see?"

Agrippa shook his head.

"An empire, Agrippa. Armies only build empires, they do not lead them. You need politicians for that. Cicero may be cowardly, but he knows how to talk and make friends as well as enemies. And we need more friends to outweigh the enemies we have made."

Agrippa remained silent, thinking. Then he asked, "If Cicero does not cooperate, how do you plan on convincing the Senate to give you *imperium*?"

"There is still a chance he will show himself worthy of the Republic he claims to support," Octavius said, recalling his last letter urging Cicero to save the ideals he had always fought for, to fight against the threat of Antonius, though it had been impossible to hide his obvious desperation for support.

He could only hope that his words, however false they rang, would still strike a chord with Cicero's pride, for that was where men usually found either the courage or stupidity to act. Octavius did not want to consider what would happen if he failed.

"But for now, we must trust that Antonius will do the work for us. Have we any report on our campaigning amongst the Macedonian troops?"

Agrippa fiddled with the wooden pawns placed over Brundisium, which signified the Macedonian legions there. They had sent ambassadors to campaign among the troops in secret ever since they had heard news of the legions' arrival on the coast. Besides offering money and gifts to soldiers who would switch allegiances, they had been feeling out support for his cause and Divine Julius.

"If our efforts have the effect we desire, we will know soon enough," Agrippa said at last. "Antonius' temper is short, as we know, and he will be less than delighted when his soldiers begin defecting."

"But if he marches to Rome, do we cut him off before he can arrive?" Octavius murmured, looking at the land between him and Antonius, and felt that it was not far enough. "Or do we take a stand in Rome?"

Agrippa's eyes followed the path from Brundisium to Rome while he thought over Octavius' words, following the Via Appia as it curved its way from the Adriatic coast, cut across the mountains, and passed through Capua on its way up to Rome.

It was the same route they had taken when they had first arrived in Italy, and they both knew how quickly the road could be traveled in an emergency. Agrippa looked at the map carefully, as if the snaking lines of roads and rivers, the gently shaded peaks and valleys, could reveal the future.

"What say Cicero?" Agrippa asked finally.

"He advised returning to Rome," Octavius replied. "He thinks my popularity with the mobs will sway the Senate before Antonius arrives."

"Hmm."

"Do you disagree?"

"I do not think it wise to cut him off without *imperium* from the Senate to lead your army in the first place," Agrippa said slowly, tapping the map thoughtfully. "But to take a stand in Rome without the Senate's backing could be equally as dangerous."

Octavius nodded. "We would be relying on the soldiers and the people of Rome to stand with us against Antonius and his army. We would be inviting civil war. Nay, we would be starting it." He remembered what Antonius had said to him on the Capitoline. *When your men see the forces they must fight against, they will flee.*

"It is a risk," Agrippa said, his gaze sweeping over the map.

Octavius waited, watching him work through the various options, weighing each one against the other. He still remembered the first time he had noticed Agrippa's uncanny ability to assess the odds, his keen grasp of strategy, even if at the time it had only been pieces on a gameboard. But at the moment, the small wooden pawns scattered across the map hardly looked any different.

At last, Agrippa tapped Rome. "But perhaps we need not risk everything at once."

"What do you suggest?"

Agrippa drew a line to a city north of Rome on the slopes of the Etruscan region. Octavius leaned closer, noticing Agrippa go still when their arms brushed. "Arretium. We could station the majority of our soldiers there as insurance, and move with only a few thousand. If we encounter any trouble in Rome, we retreat and play for time."

"I believe we know someone in Arretium who might be useful," Octavius said, glancing at Agrippa questioningly. He found it hard to believe that Agrippa would willingly suggest it.

As if Agrippa read his thoughts, he winced. "Yes. I know."

Octavius raised a brow. "Do you doubt Maecenas' loyalty? He has always been a friend to me."

"I wonder why," Agrippa said dryly.

"I know he has not always been entirely kind towards you."

Agrippa hesitated. "It is not that."

"Then what is it?" Octavius pressed.

This only made Agrippa more uncomfortable, avoiding Octavius' searching gaze. "He is ridiculous."

Octavius knew it would be better to drop the subject, but whether it was the impending war or the way Agrippa tensed every time Maecenas touched him, Octavius felt the urge to rile him up, if only to see his reaction.

"Pray, tell," Octavius asked, "what do you find ridiculous about him?"

"He believes himself descended from an Etruscan king, for one."

At this, Octavius smiled. "Does not every man believe that he was descended from a king?"

Agrippa gave him a hard look. "Not me."

"Of course not." He paused. "What else?"

"He is too...excessive," Agrippa said hesitantly.

"Other men would consider him luxurious," Octavius said, raising a brow. "Is it a crime to enjoy comforts?"

A mocking smirk tugged at Agrippa's mouth. "I do not mean with his wealth."

Octavius knew he was playing a dangerous game, but he could not help it, as if he wanted to hear Agrippa say it for once. "If not his wealth, then—"

Agrippa grabbed his wrist in a tight, unforgiving grip, his face dark and still in its anger. "You find it funny, do you?"

"What?"

He tried to move away but Agrippa held him steadfast. His eyes flickered to Agrippa's hand in surprise. It was as if they were wrestling again, except this time it was Agrippa who held the hand against his throat, so that Octavius struggled to speak.

"Not everything is a *game,* Octavius," Agrippa said accusingly, and despite himself, Octavius felt his face flame in embarrassment. No one ever dared use his words against him, and he had grown used to casting them out carelessly. "Do not give hope where there is none."

Anger shot through him at the suggestion. He yanked his wrist and brought Agrippa closer. "You think Maecenas ridiculous? You do not know the first thing about him. You never bothered. Do you think his parties are merely for fun? Do you think he spends all of his time with some young poet for nothing? Do you think he does not know what you think of him, or what anyone in any given room is thinking? Well, he figured you out from the beginning, and let me tell you, it was about as nice as what you think of him." Agrippa flinched. "So if I were you, I would be careful who you crucify when you cannot even name their crimes."

Agrippa stepped back, releasing his wrist quickly as if it had scalded him, and Octavius could finally breathe. He knew he had been too harsh, but he would not allow Agrippa to make such scathing suggestions of his character that were entirely unfounded.

Maecenas, like Octavius, had been born into a family of politicians, and they had long ago understood the value of alliances. But Agrippa had gotten one thing very wrong. Maecenas expected *nothing* from him. Their alliance was built entirely on the fact that Maecenas could benefit from Octavius as much as he could benefit from Maecenas. And until that changed, they would remain—if the word could be so used—friends.

He watched Agrippa turn away coldly. "We ought to make for Rome," Agrippa said, barely loud enough for Octavius to hear, refusing to meet his eyes. "Antonius could be halfway there by now."

Then he was gone.

⟫⟫ ⟪⟪

"πάντων μὲν κόρος ἐστὶ καὶ ὕπνου καὶ φιλότητος
μολπῆς τε γλυκερῆς καὶ ἀμύμονος ὀρχηθμοῖο,
τῶν πέρ τις καὶ μᾶλλον ἐέλδεται ἐξ ἔρον εἶναι
ἢ πολέμου: Τρῶες δὲ μάχης ἀκόρητοι ἔασιν."

*There is enough of all things, of sleep and love-making,
of sweet song and blameless dance,
yet some would rather rid their lust of these
than of war; the Trojans cannot have enough of battle.*

Octavius looked up at the familiar lilting voice echoing from the atrium before Athenodorus appeared in the doorway of his office, and for a moment, Octavius was in Apollonia again, his tutor's gentle but demanding voice finding him just when he needed advice the most.

Except he was in Rome now, preparing to give a rallying speech in the forum, and his schoolboy days were long over. He set down his stylus and writing tablet.

"Homer, *Iliad*," Octavius said, then frowned. "Are you suggesting we are like the Trojans?"

His tutor laughed, stepping inside the room, his bright eyes winking. "You always assume I harbor a prejudice against Romans simply because I am Greek."

"Well?" Octavius challenged.

"Perhaps," Athenodorus replied with a smile.

He loved to give ambiguous replies and force his students to the conclusion. Octavius understood what his tutor was implying with that quote, and the thought sat uneasily in his mind.

"You think I am too hasty in preparing for war?"

Athenodorus walked slowly about the room, his hands loosely laced behind his back. "I am only observing. Rome has been at war for a long time."

To have peace you must have war. What do you know about war, boy?

Octavius hated that Antonius had been right. Although he had not been so naive as to expect Antonius to surrender easily, Octavius had not thought war would become this complicated before it had even begun.

"There can be no peace while Antonius and my father's assassins live. The sooner they are brought to justice, the sooner there will be peace."

Athenodorus was silent, wandering over to the couch placed before Octavius' desk, and sitting with a deep sigh. Then he said, "We have a famous saying in Greek: σπεῦδε βραδέως."

"Make haste slowly," Octavius translated.

"Precisely," Athenodorus said, as if this were an exercise and Octavius had answered correctly. "When a lion stalks his prey, he may spend hours crouched in the tall grass, waiting and watching silently until the perfect moment to strike with all the speed and precision of a lightning bolt. The lion is quick in his stillness. That is the key to his success."

"Then what of Antonius and my father's assassins?"

Athenodorus held out a hand in response, and sitting in the wrinkled palm was a small red rosebud, not yet bloomed. "Vengeance is a delicate thing. It requires a gentle hand to nurture."

As he spoke he carefully pinched the bottom of the bud between his fingers and teased the tips of the petals. Then he gently blew on it until the rose petals began opening, as if yearning for air. Athenodorus smiled fondly at his trick.

Octavius looked at the rose and raised a brow. "You speak only in metaphor, my dear Athenodorus, and this war will not be metaphorical."

His tutor shook a finger at him. "On the contrary, my son, war is always a metaphor.

119

It is death that is not."

"Antonius marches on Rome in less than a day's time," Octavius said sharply. He held up his writing tablet, his careful script carved into the wax. "I must call on my soldiers to fight, or retreat. If I fight, the Senate may still choose to ally with Antonius out of fear and name me an enemy of the state. Yet by fighting I will be avenging my father. If I retreat, Antonius may convince the Senate to name me *hostis* regardless, but my enemies slip past my fingers."

"Ah, have I taught you nothing?" Athenodorus chided gently. "A true retreat is merely an attack in disguise. Sometimes the advance of your enemy can be used to your own advantage."

"You are most vulnerable while attacking," Octavius murmured, half-smiling. "I remember."

"Good," Athenodorus said. "Then I have taught you something."

"There is still more," Octavius said, without thinking. "There is still more you could teach me." He looked at Athenodorus meaningfully. "In Rome."

Athenodorus eyed him curiously. "My strengths lie in philosophy and rhetoric, not strategy. That is best left to your friend, Agrippa. He is gifted and loyal, a rare combination and one worth keeping close." He paused. "But I suppose you already know this."

Octavius hesitated, thinking back on that argument in Teanum, and the harsh words they had thrown at each other. Agrippa had been avoiding him ever since, and Octavius himself was not keen to apologize for a wrong he had not committed. It seemed Athenodorus sensed the tension between them, even if it was only indicated by Agrippa's absence.

"Yes, I know."

"Do not doubt your own heart, Octavius."

His eyes were not exactly sad, but heavy, as though weighed down by the knowledge of the world, of time sinking below the horizon, of bittersweet Past and the glimmer of Future. Besides Agrippa, he was the only other person Octavius would allow to address him by the name of a boy who had stayed behind in Apollonia.

Octavius nodded, silent.

Athenodorus stood up with a grimace, his back hunching against the pain of age, but his eyes were clear and sharp as a hawk. He bowed his head. "I shall remain in Rome as long as you wish, but I can only advise you as a friend, not a teacher." He walked towards the door, then paused at the threshold. "You know, it was not the Romans who reminded me of the Trojans. And I was thinking of a very different kind of war."

The War-like god is even-handed, and he kills the man who kills.
Be still, heart: you suffered worse than this.

Octavius did not return to his speech for a long time.

⟫⟫ ⟪⟪

"My friends! Oh, my good friends!"

Octavius slipped on a smile as he and Agrippa walked from their carriage to the front door of the vast estate that sprawled among the gentle hills and valleys of Arretium, lush gardens and expansive vineyards hugging the outskirts of the villa.

A wiry, energetic figure appeared at the door, robed in richly colored fabrics that seemed to glitter under the sun like gold.

"Maecenas," Octavius said warmly. "I hope our stay is not too burdensome."

He laughed, coming closer and kissing Octavius. Agrippa stood beside him like a silent mountain, tall and cold.

"Burdensome? Nonsense!" Maecenas brushed a careless hand against Octavius' cheek. "There is nothing burdensome about that face."

"Maecenas," Agrippa said, quiet but firm. "We are truly indebted to you."

Maecenas turned to him as if he had not noticed him before, laughing again and kissing him. "Agrippa, always so honorable! I've missed that frown. Oh, how I long for those simple days in Apollonia. Say, have you heard anything from dear Athenodorus? Oh, and Rufus? It seems as if ages have passed since I last saw them."

Octavius suppressed a chuckle. Maecenas always pretended to know less than he did. He was an expert in extracting the truth from those who most wished to hide it. Agrippa once called it manipulation, but Octavius had always preferred to think of it as *negotiation.*

"Athenodorus is in Rome," Octavius said, finally. "He is taking his leisure at Balbus' estate."

"And Rufus?"

"I have asked him to manage a few affairs of mine in Ravenna."

"That is where you have just come from, is it not?" Maecenas asked offhandedly. "You said in your letter that you could not visit me even though you passed straight through Arretium."

"I was occupied with an urgent matter."

Maecenas nodded as if he had hardly heard him, but Octavius saw his eyes cloud in thought before he turned back towards the house and led them inside.

Ever since Octavius had known him, Maecenas was clever enough to disguise his own intelligence with a frivolous attitude towards most life, while harboring an intricate understanding of those around him. It was what Agrippa failed to see in his dislike.

121

Octavius and Agrippa walked side by side as they followed Maecenas across the atrium and around the courtyard, which encircled a large water garden at its center.

The interior of the villa was just as extravagant and grand as the grounds outside, with colored marble facing every inch of the walls, mosaics of gods and heroes tangled in battle stretching across the floors, and gold, silver, and bronze accents everywhere they looked.

They stopped once they reached the triclinium, the couches covered in plush purple cloth. A seven-tiered fountain against the wall trickled water down into a pool at the center of the floor.

Maecenas' face hardly concealed his pride. "It took five months for them to renovate this place, and another two for the furnishings and accents to be shipped and put in their proper place."

"It is marvelous," Octavius said. Agrippa merely inclined his head. Perhaps it was best he did not try to respond.

Maecenas waved a hand and a minute later a large silver platter was placed on the table, laden with cheeses and bread, honey and fruits, and a large pitcher of wine painted as if it had been made in the East.

As they reclined on the couches, Octavius was reminded of Maecenas' charm despite being known for a rather unharmonious face, his lanky limbs seeming to contain a mysterious energy as he lounged among the cushions.

He plucked a grape from a nearby cluster. "So tell me, why have you fled so soon from Rome?"

Octavius swallowed a slice of bread and cheese with the wine, ignoring Maecenas' impatient eyes fixed on him. "Marcus Antonius has proved too volatile to remain in the city. I trust you have received wind of this."

"Yes, I suppose. I had hoped you would tell me the truth. You know how Rumor likes to twist Her words."

"What has She told you?" Octavius asked, hiding a smile.

Maecenas frowned at Octavius' deflection. He preferred to let others do the gossiping for him, though Octavius knew him too well for this to work on him. In fact, Octavius did not know another person as well connected and informed as Maecenas, and he intended to make use of that.

"People said war would come any day now, but then it did not. Some said Antonius wished to name you *hostis,* then he did not. Others said he claimed you had an unnatural relationship with your divine father, though only *you* can answer to that. Yet still others said you occupied the forum with armed men. See, it is hard to know what to believe."

Agrippa's face darkened. "Antonius always resorts to slander when he lacks evidence."

"Naturally," Maecenas said with a mocking smile. "Although he seemed to think he had enough evidence to name you *hostis.*"

"He fears my popularity with the people," Octavius said before Agrippa could say something reckless again. Although they were friends, asking for favors was always a delicate matter, and Maecenas liked to feel as though he had something to offer.

"But I heard the people were not so pleased with the possibility of a civil war," Maecenas countered.

It was true. Antonius' approach with his army had nearly sent Octavius' troops into riots, and they refused to fight against their fellow soldiers. In fear that Antonius would use the chaos against him and arrest him in Rome, Octavius had taken Agrippa's advice and retreated to Arretium, where they hoped to ask Maecenas for supplies and food for their troops.

While Maecenas had been eager to aid Octavius with his affairs upon arriving in Rome, publicly aiding Octavius' private army now with no legal sanction from the Senate was a risk he was not entirely sure Maecenas would be willing to take.

"No, I suppose they were not," Octavius said hesitantly. "They had hoped Antonius and I would ally and exact vengeance upon my father's assassins. But Antonius had other plans. We can only hope now that the small pebbles we pushed might cause a landslide."

"You speak in riddles, just like Athenodorus. Perhaps you two have spent too much time together."

"Perhaps," Octavius said with a smile.

"Oh, you are infuriating as always!" Maecenas exclaimed. He called over a nearby slave. "Bring Demetrius here." He turned to Octavius with a smirk. "Perhaps some poetry will loosen your tongue better than wine."

A moment later, a boy only a few years younger than Octavius walked inside. He was unabashedly beautiful, with dark black curls, glowing skin, and light eyes. Octavius thought he saw Agrippa flush when Maecenas patted the couch beside him, smiling when Demetrius reclined close to him.

"Sing, my dear," Maecenas said softly in Greek, a hand trailing to Demetrius' arm. Octavius ignored the sharp look from Agrippa.

Demetrius blushed and nodded silently before beginning to sing. "μῆνιν ἄειδε θεὰ Πηληϊάδεω Ἀχιλῆος οὐλομένην, ἣ μυρί' Ἀχαιοῖς ἄλγε' ἔθηκε..."

Sing, goddess, the cursed wrath of Peleus' son Achilles, which placed thousandfold pains on the Achaeans...

The boy's voice was gentle and rhythmic as he sang the familiar verses, his eyes closed and his forehead creased as if he could see the fast ships of the Achaeans moored by the shore, Agamemnon and Achilles looming as large as gods. Maecenas watched the boy with an enchanted look.

"Is it not strange and terrible how one man can change the course of history?" Maecenas asked. He turned to Octavius with a keen glance. "I see it in you. I have seen it since the first day I met you. But I still do not understand. How did you escape Antonius? The Senate? *How are you still alive?*"

"As Athenodorus likes to say, when your enemy is on the offensive, that is when he is at his most vulnerable," Octavius said. "We hope to buy some time in our retreat. And that is why we have come here."

Maecenas grinned wickedly. "Ah, so this was all to say you need my help! Why did you not say so in the first place?"

Just then a messenger burst into the room, panting and clutching a bundle of letters. "Master, I have news from Rome!" He fell silent when he noticed the guests, his eyes widening.

Maecenas sat up impatiently. "Well, speak, boy!"

The messenger nodded quickly. "It is *Praetor* Antonius. He has fled the city and marches against Decimus up north. They say two of his legions have deserted him for...for Caesar, sir. Cicero wants to declare Antonius *hostis*. War has come."

Maecenas looked at Octavius in awe as the missing pieces of the puzzle fell into place. "The gods are watching you, my friend."

Everyone in the room was looking at him. His heart marched a steady beat up to his fingertips, and for a moment, Octavius thought that if he touched anything, it would turn to gold. At last, the odds were turning in his favor.

"Let the gods watch us," he said. "After all, there is nothing they enjoy more than war."

Agrippa raised his cup of wine with the shadow of a smile. "To war."

Maecenas looked carefully between Agrippa and Octavius, contemplating, before he raised his glass high. "To friendship."

Octavius could not hold back a smirk, joining his glass in the air. "To the Republic."

13

MARCUS TULLIUS CICERO

DECEMBER 44 BC

CICERO HAD ONLY EVER loved two people in his life, and one of them was dead. The other would have a lot to say about the guest he was entertaining this evening.

Indeed, there was something about the young man reclining on the opposite couch, his dark brown eyes determined and thoughtful, that Cicero could not quite name.

He sipped his wine and watched Octavianus carefully eat his food. Cicero refused to call him Caesar—which the boy, unfortunately, insisted upon using despite lacking legal documentation—instead preferring to call him the less political name *Octavianus*, perhaps also to remind the boy that Cicero did not forget his former name. Could this mere boy be the answer to all the questions Cicero has had about the Republic?

Despite himself, hope swelled in his chest. He could just see it, the greatness for which he had always aspired, the city of Rome restored to its former glory and freedom, where intellectualism and wealth ran through the streets and cleansed them of their violent, hateful mobs.

Perhaps he could be, but Cicero knew how easily men's hearts were corrupted. Octavianus was young, and he needed guidance.

The time had come for the first true test. Cicero wished Octavianus to march against Marcus Antonius, who was already closing in on Decimus Brutus in Gaul. This required imperium to be given to Octavianus, a power which had been abused even by grown men, let alone a boy who was scarcely in his twentieth year.

"The fact of the matter is, my dear Octavianus, that Decimus needs our help," Cicero said, piling his plate with more roasted meat, along with another glass of wine. After all, the gods only knew how long these small comforts would last.

From the corner of his eye, he watched the boy nod, his face clear and concerned.

125

"I hear that Antonius has a strong cavalry," Octavianus said gravely. "It will be difficult for Decimus to resist him if it comes to a fight. Is Decimus prepared for a siege?"

"By Jove, let us hope it does not come to that!"

"One should always be prepared for every possibility."

Cicero chuckled. Though Octavianus was quite mature for his age, Cicero saw his youth glimmering in moments such as these. "If that were possible, I hardly doubt we would be in this conundrum to begin with, would we?"

Octavianus merely smiled. "Or no one was prepared for this possibility."

This surprised Cicero, but then again, the young were always more unyielding than the old when it came to war. "Perhaps you are right. But that does not help us. We must aid Brutus now or forever hold our tongues. For Antonius does not like those who talk back."

"Where are Brutus and Cassius? Did not the Senate grant them imperium?" Octavianus asked.

"They are caught up with their own barbaric gladiator, Dolabella, who now fully supports Antonius," Cicero said impatiently. He had hoped as consul, Dolabella could be convinced to side with the Senate and restore order to the Republic, but he seemed only to prove that once a man of Caesar, always a man of Caesar. "Besides, if I called them back now, by the time they arrived, the battle would have been already won or lost. No, we must call for aid elsewhere."

"And Hirtius and Pansa? Are they not to be consuls come the new year?"

Cicero sighed, and lowered his voice, though they were the only ones in the room. "If I may be frank, they do not have the dispensable men at hand like you do."

Octavianus had the grace to blush. "You know, Cicero, you are like a father to me, if I may say so. If you need me to aid Decimus, you need only ask."

"I only hesitate in asking because of what feelings you may harbor towards him."

"I cannot disguise my anger towards those who murdered my father," Octavianus said carefully, then his eyes flashed darkly. "But I promise you that it is Antonius whom I truly loathe, for he was one of my father's closest friends, and thus his betrayal is worse than any simple wrongdoing."

"Wisely put my dear boy, wisely put. Therefore I will not try to dissuade your feelings, but remind you of what is right and what is wrong, as a father might to his son." Cicero hesitated, deciding on the best way to phrase his instruction. "If Antonius should be defeated, the Republic that Julius Caesar built will still stand. But if Antonius should prove victorious, gods forbid, then any trace of that Republic will diminish to no more than dust and ash."

Octavianus nodded solemnly. "I know what my father would have wanted me to do.

He only ever wished to serve the Republic and its people."

"Of course, of course," Cicero said quickly. He did not wish to turn the conversation into a funeral *laudatio* for Julius Caesar. "And there is no better way to honor his legacy than by fighting for the Republic."

"I would be honored to fight for the Republic," Octavianus said, then paused. "Though I am not sure the Senate would be so willing to give me such an honor."

"Nonsense!" Cicero smiled. "You forget who you are speaking with, my boy. I am no everyday buffoon. The Senate will hear what I have to say, and they will soon be persuaded if they had not already been before."

"I am very grateful, *pater*, if I may call you that."

"Naturally, my son!"

"But I must request a few provisions, as I am sure you understand," Octavianus said, so off-handedly that Cicero nearly nodded absentmindedly, as if he had noted the quality of the wine instead of the quality of *imperium*.

"Oh?"

"Please, do not mistake my intentions. I fully intend to fight for the Republic. I only wish to ensure that the Senate will also fight for my return, so to speak."

"Do you doubt my influence in the Senate?" Cicero asked, unable to hide the sharpness in his tone.

"I only doubt that others will be as reasonable and honorable as you."

Cicero nodded, though he still felt uneasy. "I suppose that is true enough. What provisions would you propose?"

"Firstly, that I be appointed proconsul with the fullest powers of that office."

"Proconsul?" Cicero exclaimed in disbelief, unsure whether he ought to laugh or admonish the boy. "Either you must think I am a god, or that you are, to be proposing such an impossible thing!"

Octavianus did not appear perturbed. "I understand what I ask will be difficult to acquire—"

"Difficult? Difficult? My boy!" Cicero threw up his hands. "You must be at least forty-two years old to be consul, let alone proconsul!"

"If my youth is a concern, then I suppose I must be too young to lead an army against Antonius," Octavianus said quietly, and Cicero's heart dropped as the sharp features of his face honed into an echo of another man who knew the power of desperation and had ultimately been killed because of it.

Although it was no secret that the Senate needed to raise an army and fast, Cicero had thought they would have the upper hand in this alliance. Perhaps they still could.

"No, of course not," Cicero whispered, then cleared his throat. "Alexander the Great was the greatest general to ever live and he was only twenty years old."

Octavianus frowned as if he disliked the comparison. "I do not pretend to be like Alexander the Great. But historically in times of war, even private citizens were appointed as proconsuls to aid the efforts of the consuls. Cornelius Scipio Africanus was the first such man to receive this rank and he was never defeated in battle." He paused. "And he also refused to accept any perpetual office afterward."

His argument was convincing, but Cicero knew there was no world in which the Senate would allow this boy to reach the same rank as Hirtius and Pansa so soon after they had just rid themselves of another Caesar. But Cicero also knew their only chance of defeating Antonius lay in relinquishing some power to this boy, however painful it was to do so.

"I will not pretend that I can appoint you proconsul, but may I propose another solution?"

"Of course."

"We can appoint you propraetor with all the power that office entails. It will be difficult to persuade the Senate to admit your youth, but I believe I can manage it. Would that satisfy you?"

Octavianus nodded thoughtfully. "I also request that I be made a senator."

"Anything else?" Cicero asked dryly.

"A few more things," Octavianus replied in all seriousness. "I request permission to speak my opinion on the praetorian benches. I would also request that for any magistrate I seek, my candidature be legally accepted as if I had been quaestor the preceding year. I also request, on behalf of my army, that all of them and their children be exempt from further service, that lands be enquired for them, and that whatever sum of money I have promised them be given as soon as possible."

Cicero was silent. It was now impossible to hope that Octavianus would allow the Senate to string him along like the puppet they had planned him to be. Perhaps that was Cicero's fault, though he would deny it if anyone ever accused him so.

Besides, it hardly mattered now. The Senate needed an army, and the only one at hand was sitting in this very boy's lap, waiting for his command. Cicero saw no other solution, and he doubted anyone else would think of anything half as useful before it was too late. Ultimately, the decision had fallen upon his head, and it would be he who reaped the most of its fruit, be they bitter or sweet.

Octavianus got up from his couch and circled around to sit beside Cicero, taking Cicero's hands in his own. "I know what you are thinking. You fear that I will grow too big for my own shoes, that I will crave more honor and recognition after I have had but the barest taste. And you would be right to warn me of those things, pater, as my elder and one who has cared for me as if I were his son.

"So I will not tell you to stop caring, for indeed it is the greatest honor that could be bestowed upon me, and instead I will listen and heed your most welcome advice. I wish to fight for the Republic as you have fought your entire life, to fight for the Republic and the Republic alone. If that means fighting alongside men who have wronged my family, then I will put aside my anger for what is right, and what is far nobler than any kind of revenge. Please, allow me to fight for the Republic. Let me save her."

Cicero swallowed, his head light. He squeezed the gentle hands in his, smiling but feeling as though he might faint if he stood up. For he had realized what it was about this boy that he could not quite name, and it was staring right back at him in those dark eyes.

Let me save her.

It was his dream. His vision. And here was a young, willing boy, his own love for the Republic—his Republic, really, the true beloved of Cicero's life—reflected in his eyes.

For he would have been nameless without the Republic, a man no one knew or cared for, all of his talents and ideas wasting away in some small town, waiting for time to bury him in a cold eternity. But the Republic had given him a path to greatness, perhaps even immortality. So how could he deny this boy when those eyes offered up that woman to him like Victory herself?

"Yes, my boy, let us save her." Cicero nodded, more confidently as relief flooded his chest. "Let us save her before it is too late."

After all, if there was anything he had learned about Caesars, it was how easily they died.

⁂

JANUARY 43 BC

"There is news from the Senate, sir."

"Tell me." Cicero looked away from the window, where the forum spread out below, bustling and crowded as usual. He felt that familiar contempt rise up before he pushed it away. These people were not aware of their own ignorance, their own bliss.

"Gaius Vibius Pansa sends his greetings to Marcus Tullius Cicero. Antonius has sent a response to our embassy. He agrees to relinquish Cisalpine Gaul to Decimus in exchange for the Transalpine province and that all his acts be ratified. Please meet with me at your earliest convenience to discuss this. Vale."

Cicero sighed. His slave lingered to see if Cicero would write back. "You may go,

Hector. I will not be making any replies yet."

He turned back to the window as the sound of footsteps receded and the house fell back into silence save for the distant clamor of the crowds below, the familiar murmur of the city. The sun was already dipping below the hills, dotted with trees as black as night, their trunks twisting elegantly to the sky and their ever-green branches yearning for the lost warmth of the sun. It was still the most beautiful view he had ever laid eyes upon.

Cicero sighed again. This news changed nothing, despite what most of the Senate thought. Antonius still lay siege to Decimus, as Octavianus had predicted, trapping Decimus' army inside Mutina with his cavalry like dogs herding sheep. War had been postponed, not avoided, and Antonius remained in control of a formidable army.

He watched all those tiny dots scurrying around the forum. He pictured the senators as small as ants crawling frantically about the *curia*. They had no sense of loyalty or pride. They quivered in the safety of their name, their rank, fearing a man like Marcus Antonius after they had just killed another like him.

But Cicero did not fear Antonius—he only loathed him. He loathed his arrogance, his brutish nature, and his desire to dominate his fellow men. In comparison to Cicero and the ideals he sought after, Antonius was nothing more than a barbarian.

Octavianus promised more. Though he was the son and heir of Julius Caesar, there was a sensitive streak in him, a sensibility to the arts, an appreciation of the ideals Cicero had written about in countless letters, countless books. Cicero wondered if in another world, they could all have lived peacefully, if Octavianus would have called him *pater* and Cicero would not have felt a twinge of guilt.

Suddenly he heard a young girl's shrill shriek caught on the wind, followed by a faint laugh, and without warning, Cicero was swept into the past, his daughter's little footsteps dawdling throughout the house, her voice high and piercing as she called for him to *look, papa, come look!*

Then the wind howled as it beat against the house, and Cicero blinked, looking away, alone once more. His daughter had long ceased running through these halls, though she continued to haunt them in his memories, the pain of her death a hollow echo in his heart.

Yes, he wondered much about other worlds, but if they existed, they had not changed this one.

"Apologies, sir, but another message has arrived from consuls Pansa and Hirtius. They request your presence in the *curia* immediately. There is to be a meeting concerning Marcus Antonius."

"Of course there is," Cicero muttered under his breath. "Do not bother with a reply. I will be there soon enough."

He stood up despite the reluctance of his body to move from his comfortable position.

Though his mind retained its ever-constant stream of thoughts, his body had already begun slowing down.

Somehow he would have to find a way to convince the Senate that Antonius still posed a big enough threat to their hard-earned Republic, that there would be no peace while he still lived. Octavianus was already marching towards Mutina to confront him, but the Senate cared not for the boy and would abandon him at the last moment if it ensured that Antonius would spare their lives.

Cicero knew all too well that Pansa wished to restore harmony, even if it meant cowing to Antonius and his Caesarian party. Hirtius, on the other hand, was already bending towards Cicero's mind. They merely needed a push, a nudge in the right direction, and Cicero was the best man for the job.

The stage was set, his pen at the ready as if it were a sword. For the battlefield never held the same appeal as a courthouse, and Cicero was never as good a soldier as a statesman.

And if this were to be his last war, then Cicero would die with a pen in his hand, fighting for the Republic he had loved since she had cast her eyes upon him and rescued him from oblivion.

14

Marcus Vipsanius Agrippa

JANUARY 43 BC

T HEY HAD BEEN MARCHING swiftly for three days on the Via Flaminia with minimal rest.

Agrippa watched Octavius as he sat by the small fire where they had boiled some meat. They had pitched camp near Spoletium for the night, still a long way away from Ariminium, their final destination. Most of the camp had gone to sleep already. It felt like they were the only two people alive on Earth, the only witnesses to her velvet darkness.

Octavius picked at his food as if he had no appetite, despite the day's rigorous climb up and through the Apennines.

"You ought to eat," Agrippa said, despite himself. "We have a long day tomorrow."

They had not spoken much more than necessary since their argument last November. Although it was months ago now, there was an undeniable rift between them that had not been there before. Agrippa wondered if it was his fault.

Octavius avoided his eyes. "You ought to sleep. It is late."

"I could say the same to you."

He did not respond, merely staring at the small flickering flames of the fire as it died. Agrippa could see the flames reflected in his dark eyes, red in a sea of black like a lonely star in the night sky. His face looked hollow, sunken, as though he had hardly eaten for several days.

"You are sick," Agrippa said.

Octavius' eyes flicked over to his, then firmly away. It was not confirmation, but it was enough.

Agrippa walked over to Octavius and knelt beside him, pressing a hand to his forehead. It was burning. "How long have you had a fever?"

Octavius shrugged. "I hardly noticed."

"Answer me, Octavius. This is serious."

"After the first night on the road. It is a chill from the cold, that is all."

Agrippa pushed down a wave of annoyance. "You should have told me." *I could have helped.* But he bit back the words.

"There is nothing to be done," Octavius said, and his mouth twisted into a bitter smile. "Besides, we are going to war. There is no place for a sickly soldier on the battlefield, much less a sickly general."

"Self-pity does not suit you," Agrippa retorted, unable to check his anger before he spoke.

Octavius' mouth tightened. "Self-pity and self-awareness are not the same thing."

Agrippa shook his head. "You wish to see yourself as one man alone against the world. But you are not alone, Octavius, and the world is not against you. There are many who love you, whether you wish them to or not."

"We are all alone in this world," Octavius said with an ironic smile. "Love is simply an illusion. It is the utmost selfishness disguised as self-sacrifice."

The words sent Agrippa reeling. But hadn't he always sensed this in Octavius, this isolation in him—not to keep to himself, but to keep others out? It left him wondering if Octavius had kept Agrippa out too, if all those secretive smiles, all that talk of conquering the world together, the many oaths and promises they swore, meant anything to him at all.

"How noble of you," Agrippa said mockingly, his initial hurt now stinging more like an insult. "I suppose you are above such illusions."

Octavius looked at him, then, and brought a hand up to Agrippa's face, touching his cheek lightly. Agrippa stilled, his heart jumping to his throat at the contact. "Then what is love, if not illusion? Is it self-sacrifice? Trust? Loyalty? Or is it merely another word for lust?" His voice was taunting, but Agrippa thought he sounded almost pained. "What is love, my dear Agrippa?"

"If I knew," Agrippa said coldly, his face hot where Octavius' fingertips touched, "why would it matter to you?"

Octavius' hand dropped, and he turned away, frowning. A bristling wind whistled down the mountain, hugging the valley as it descended. Octavius shivered, pulling his cloak around his shoulders. Agrippa gave him a sidelong glance before pity won over his anger and he sighed.

"Here." Agrippa grabbed a nearby flask of wine and handed it to Octavius, who took it reluctantly and drank, wiping at his mouth with his sleeve. "If you lie down I can try to lessen the fever."

Octavius hesitated, then nodded silently. He followed Agrippa back inside the small tent where their mats were rolled out side by side. Without looking at him, Octavius lowered himself onto the mat quietly, resigned.

Agrippa left him and gathered some snow outside, wrapping it in the stiff cloth of a spare military cloak. He ducked inside the tent and paused. Octavius was already asleep, his brows furrowed, as if he were arguing with Agrippa in his dreams.

He knelt beside Octavius, gently brushing loose strands of hair from his forehead. Octavius did not stir. Agrippa lightly placed the makeshift compress on his feverish skin, ignoring the pull of sleep on his own eyelids, listening to Octavius' labored breathing.

What is love, my dear Agrippa?

If I knew, why would it matter to you?

But he did know. Agrippa knew, as he knew the rolling hills of Italy's countryside, as he knew all of the rivers and roads that snaked his homeland, what the answer was to that question. Perhaps he had known the answer to that question for a long time.

"If love is selfishness," Agrippa whispered, "then I am the most selfish of all."

He remained by Octavius' side until the fever quelled, and sometime in the night, Agrippa fell asleep at his side, their hands lying a breath apart until they were awoken by the rosy fingers of Dawn.

⟫⟫ ⟪⟪

"Today we march," cried out Carfulenus, "in honor of Aulus Hirtius and Gaius Julius Caesar!"

Agrippa watched Octavius look out over the crowd of soldiers, absorbing their cheers and shouts with a charming smile. He looked better these past few days, his fever having lowered, but Agrippa still felt his exhaustion like being buried beneath a deep layer of snow. They could only hope to reach Ariminium without any incidents.

Hirtius stood beside Octavius, grinning and waving as the soldiers marched into formation behind them. He had joined them yesterday with the legions granted to him by the Senate. Pansa would most likely join them at Forum Gallorum in a month's time, but until then, Hirtius and Octavius were charged with breaking Antonius' siege at Mutina and freeing Decimus.

Now they marched to Ariminium, the nearest town on the road. Maecenas and Rufus were somewhere behind him in the procession, in charge of their own cohorts appointed by Octavius himself, as Agrippa had been.

It was an important day, perhaps the most important day to have passed since they had landed in Italy, because today marked the granting of *imperium* by the Senate and the assuming of the *fasces*. Today Octavius did not merely have an army.

He commanded one.

"Your father would be proud to see you today," Hirtius said, laying a hand on Octavius' shoulder, who stiffened at the touch. "He always wanted to see you succeed one day. Of course, he thought he would be around to see it."

The processions had begun, as was custom. Lictors led the march with the long wooden rods of the *fasces* over their left shoulders, twelve for Hirtius and six for Octavius.

Hirtius and Octavius themselves were escorted by the soldiers. Agrippa walked a few paces behind them, far enough to give them distinction but close enough to overhear their conversation.

"My father still watches from above," Octavius said carelessly. It seemed he did not deem Hirtius worth the theatrics.

"Do you remember that campaign in Hispania? I believe you were only seventeen years old," Hirtius continued with a sly smile as if Octavius had not said anything.

Agrippa recalled that Hirtius had once been close friends with Julius Caesar and even Marcus Antonius, and that only recently had he been persuaded by Cicero, also a close friend, to join the Republican cause.

He had seen Hirtius a few times in Hispania, but they had never spoken much. Octavius had enjoyed his company, however, and had often joined Hirtius and Caesar on their nightly trips to inns and brothels. He was quite charming, being both handsome and intelligent, but Agrippa found him more arrogant than anything else.

"I do remember," Octavius said, though he did not share his smile.

"Do you?" Hirtius persisted. He lowered his voice so that Agrippa strained his ears to hear. "Perhaps some memories were washed away with wine."

Octavius hardly glanced at Hirtius. "I am not seventeen anymore, Hirtius."

Hirtius paused, eyeing Octavius carefully, and nodded. "I see."

They marched in silence after that, leaving Agrippa to wonder at what that all meant. Octavius did not look behind him, and Hirtius maintained a careful distance.

It took them several hours to march into Ariminium proper. Their camp had already been established by the cohorts they had sent ahead of them. When they arrived, Octavius went straight into his commander's tent without speaking another word to anyone.

Agrippa followed after him.

"Octavius."

He was standing across the table where they had yet to unravel a map of the region. "I am not Octavius anymore. You might as well stop calling me that."

"If you are not Octavius, then who are you?" Agrippa asked, surprised to find himself sounding angry.

While Octavius' official name was now Gaius Julius Caesar Octavianus, in private Agrippa had been silently allowed to call him by his former name. The thought of Octavius forcing him to call him Caesar felt like a punishment.

"I am who I always was," Octavius said, his voice oddly calm. "You are just seeing me for the first time."

"I do not believe that."

"No?"

"Hirtius said something to you. That is why you are like this."

"Hirtius is a traitor, for all I care. Worse than a traitor, for he did not even have the guts to betray Caesar in the first place. Now he thinks he can treat me like I am still a child."

"I thought you liked Hirtius," Agrippa said. "It certainly seemed so in Hispania."

"I was seventeen," Octavius said dismissively. "And Hirtius was a close friend of Caesar. They liked to go to brothels and drink. I went with them a few times. He was worldly, I was young." Octavius looked away, troubled. "He always favored me."

Agrippa imagined Hirtius, his easygoing smile, his clever eyes, and then Octavius, only seventeen. He remembered the jokes the men would make in Apollonia, the slander of Antonius, and he wondered if that favor ever slipped into something else. The thought made him jealous, though he knew he should not be. Octavius did not owe him anything.

"It does not matter anymore," Octavius said with a sigh. He sounded exhausted, though Agrippa doubted it was only from the fever. "Antonius may still yet make corpses of us all."

Before Agrippa could respond, Carfulenus entered the tent, and Octavius turned to him and smiled easily.

"My good Carfulenus, what news?"

⤜⤛⤜⤛

MARCH 43 BC

Octavius paced the tent. Agrippa sat by the wall, half-hidden in shadow. Hirtius and Carfulenus stood by the table, studying the map which was now littered with wooden pawns signifying each army. In the dim light, the map seemed more akin to a gameboard. But war was not a game. It was more like a dance, and even then, war was only ever war.

The pleasant gardens and classrooms of Apollonia, the wooden swords and shields, had kept the ugliness of war at bay, the grime of blood and dirt, where the thread of one's life was so thin, so delicate, that the hands of Fate need only tug to unravel it all.

"We ought to attack Antonius as soon as possible," Carfulenus said, looking at Octavius, who stopped pacing. "It has been almost a month. Antonius has already begun drawing our soldiers from their camps. War is upon us. If we wait for Pansa, Antonius will gain the upper hand."

"Antonius is only baiting," Agrippa said. Carfulenus looked at him in surprise. Agrippa rarely spoke, and then only when he knew he was right. "We would be fools to bite."

Hirtius nodded. "I agree with Agrippa. We cannot allow Antonius to engage us in battle before we have a full force behind us."

"Pansa marches the Via Cassius, does he not?" Octavius asked, his eyes searching the map.

"As we speak," Hirtius said, flashing a smile that Octavius did not reciprocate.

"And he commands four legions of fresh recruits?"

"What are you suggesting?" Hirtius asked.

Octavius picked up the wooden pawn signifying Pansa's legions, sliding it up the Via Cassius and stopping near Mutina. "Antonius knows that we await Pansa and that we will not attack him until he arrives. But if Pansa arrives, he would be outnumbered. That is why we wait, after all. There is only one logical move left for Antonius."

"And what is that?" Carfulenus asked.

"Attack Pansa," Agrippa said grimly. "He will be most vulnerable after traveling in the harsh weather. Not to mention that his troops are merely recruits."

Octavius moved Antonius' marker down the road, in between Pansa's forces and theirs. "Pansa would be helpless."

"That is an interesting theory," Hirtius said, crossing the tent and returning the markers to their original places on the map. "But I will not risk leaving Antonius unchecked while we aid Pansa in a fight which may or may not occur."

"Yet you risk Pansa and his recruits," Agrippa insisted. "They are an open target."

"What would you have me do?" Hirtius asked, slightly mocking. He was the more experienced general, but sometimes experience led to complacency and carelessness.

"Send a smaller contingent of troops under cover of darkness," Agrippa said. "It must be done secretly and silently. Antonius will sense a trap a mile away. Whether Antonius attacks here or there, we buy ourselves enough time to come to each other's aid."

Hirtius sighed reluctantly. "I suppose it is the safest course of action. But safe does not always mean right!"

"Naturally," Agrippa said, slightly mocking in turn.

Hirtius looked at him irritatedly but did not respond, instead turning to Carfulenus. "You will march the *Legio Martia* and join with Pansa, while two cohorts will march with me," he said. "Caesar, you will remain here."

Octavius' nostrils flared angrily. "But—"

"I will not risk leaving Antonius unchecked," Hirtius interrupted sharply. "You remain here. As I am consul, I ask that you respect my decision."

Agrippa watched the indignation and shame flicker across Octavius' face like flames fighting against the wind, before they sputtered and died into careful obedience, his eyelids lowered to hide his true emotions.

"Yes, *Praetor.*"

Hirtius nodded curtly, then beckoned Carfulenus. "Let us prepare. Pansa will be arriving in a few days, and we must be ready to move."

They left the tent swiftly, leaving Octavius and Agrippa in a loud silence, the wind whipping through the open flap before an attendant sealed up the tent.

"It is not fair," Octavius whispered. "*I* ought to aid Pansa."

"Why are you so intent on hurrying your fate?" Agrippa asked. "You know nothing of battle."

"And you do?"

Agrippa stood up from his seat. "You are being irrational."

"You do not understand."

"I never do, do I?"

Octavius looked at him coldly. "This is not about you. This is about my name."

I am not Octavius anymore.

"No," Agrippa said, his blood hot in his cheeks. "It is more than that."

Silence. It was louder than words these days. Octavius bit his lip, perhaps regretting having said anything, but it was too late.

"Maybe you are Octavius. Maybe you are Caesar. But do you know what I think?" Agrippa paused. Octavius looked at him sharply. "I think you do not know who you are. Perhaps you never did. That is why you crave some name that is not even yours. That is why you dragged us across the sea for an heirship that may get us all killed."

Octavius' voice was low. "You swore an oath."

"And I shall keep it," Agrippa said softly. "But you seem to forget that there are greater things than a mere name. Greater than glory. Fame. Even empires." He shook his head. "You once said the world needed a hero. But no hero fights alone, even if they think they do."

If I were Achilles, you would be Patroclus.

Octavius did not speak. He looked caught in time, one hand touching the table beside him, the other halfway up, as if he considered reaching out to Agrippa but suddenly forgot how. Then his mouth twisted bitterly, and he turned around.

Agrippa's face burned in that familiar embarrassment. He should not have said so much. He made for the exit, refusing to give Octavius any more leverage than he already had.

Before he walked outside, Agrippa hesitated, his heart slowing his feet despite the warning in his head. He thought he heard Octavius look up across the room. The words came easily, as they always did, but Agrippa bit them back.

He did not need to speak them. The silence already did.

15

GAIUS OCTAVIUS

MARCH 43 BC

"**Q**UICK! HURRY!"

He could hear the voices, see the blurred shapes caught by lamplight. The camp outside their tent pitched in the darkness of the night like a small boat at sea. Octavius listened carefully to the muffled sounds.

Someone burst into the tent and Octavius nearly flinched, his hand moving to the hilt of his dagger.

But it was only Agrippa. His face was desperate. "It is the consul, Pansa. He was badly injured."

Octavius felt his stomach drop. It had felt like hours of waiting for any news, and now it was coming all at once. "And Hirtius?"

Agrippa grimaced. "He was too late. He surprised Antonius on the road and chased off much of his army, but Pansa had already been forced to flee by then. There were many casualties."

"They never listen to me," Octavius said, more to himself but Agrippa still heard.

"Perhaps it was a good thing," Agrippa countered. Octavius looked at him in surprise, but Agrippa stood firm, his eyes challenging. "If Pansa does not recover, the consulship is open."

"Do not speak of Death when He already lingers," Octavius whispered, though his mind raced with the possibility, as if he had drunk a strong glass of wine. "It is bad luck."

"You and your luck, Octavius," Agrippa said, shaking his head. "Death does as He likes, whether Fortuna smiles upon you or not. It is best to remember that."

"Where is Pansa?" Octavius asked, changing the subject. Agrippa had not forgotten Octavius' wish to aid Pansa on the battlefield, and Octavius did not plan on resuscitating a dead argument, especially since he was now bound to lose it. "I want to speak with him."

"He is in Hirtius' tent. They are arranging his affairs in the case of his death," Agrippa said, then hesitated. "Be gentle, Octavius. These may be his last days."

"I am not a child," Octavius shot back. "Lead me to him."

Agrippa eyed him warily, then walked out of the tent. Octavius followed, ignoring the chill that crept up his neck, which he doubted came from the cold.

There were soldiers everywhere, some huddled in gloomy groups, others tending to the wounded who had been laid out on the ground, peppering the patches of snow and dead grass with armor caked in mud and blood.

So many had died, so many would die soon. There was a silence in the air as loud as a tomb. Octavius knew it well.

They reached Hirtius' tent stationed in the center of his camp. Octavius steeled himself, but the thick, musty smell of sickness and medicines filled his nostrils and made him dizzy.

Agrippa took a seat in the corner of the tent and nodded towards a room in the back, separated by a thin curtain, betraying the outline of two standing figures whom Octavius assumed were Hirtius and Pansa's doctor, Glyco.

A few moments later Hirtius walked out of the small room, stopping short when he saw Octavius, then looking away. They had not spoken since the battle, but they both knew it had been a failure.

Antonius still had Mutina in his grasp, and their casualties were not insignificant. If it hadn't been for Octavius' foresight and Agrippa's suggestion, Pansa's legions of recruits would have been crushed seven miles down the road with no time to send for aid.

"He is stabilized," Hirtius said at last. "You had best let him rest."

A feeble voice reached their ears. "No, Hirtius. Let the boy come here."

Octavius raised a brow, then lowered his voice to a whisper. "What have you told the Senate?"

Hirtius straightened himself with the last bit of pride he had left. "The truth. We have won a great victory tonight. Though many lives were lost, we still have strength enough to defeat Antonius once and for all." Hirtius paused, glancing behind him where Glyco tended to Pansa. "Pansa was wounded in battle, but is recovering."

Octavius felt Agrippa's eyes lingering on him from the corner of the tent. "I am sure the Senate will celebrate our triumph."

Hirtius looked at him for a moment longer, then nodded. He left the tent without another word. Octavius waited until he was gone before he entered the small room where Pansa was laid out, pale and still, his abdomen stitched up and wrapped with gauze. Glyco hovered at his side.

Octavius had spoken much with Pansa in the weeks approaching the new year. Pansa had wanted to unite the Caesarian factions, but Octavius had refused to ally with Antonius, at least not while he remained the Senate's pet. It had come at a steep price, though one which Octavius had not yet paid.

Pansa observed him silently. He was quite different from Hirtius, Octavius had discovered. Where Hirtius was bold and charming, Pansa was quiet and friendly. They both had supported Julius Caesar and Marcus Antonius, but Hirtius had quickly sided with Cicero after Caesar's assassination, while Pansa had maintained his support for the Caesarian party, wishing for peace. It was a noble dream, but a dream Octavius knew would never come to pass without war first.

"You fought bravely," Octavius said. "I wish I had been fighting alongside you."

Pansa smiled weakly. "Thank you, my boy, but you had your own battle here, with Antonius' brother."

"Lucius was merely a distraction. Otherwise, we would have come to your aid."

"An enemy spear struck me," Pansa said, his cheeks flushed with fever. "I am dying. I know it."

Octavius looked at Glyco, but the doctor did not meet his eyes. "Hirtius said you were recovering."

Pansa nodded. "He will believe what he wants to believe. And I may yet live long enough to see the end of this war, but not the end of them all. For there are still more wars to come."

"With Antonius?"

"No," Pansa said after a labored breath. "With you."

"When Antonius is defeated, the Republic will be restored," Octavius said defensively, his heart beating loudly. He had not expected Pansa to accuse him of treason. "There will be peace."

"*If* Antonius is defeated, there are still others," Pansa said, coughing into a piece of linen. Octavius thought he saw flecks of blood before it was hidden again.

"Others?"

Pansa glanced at Glyco, who seemed to understand the command because he administered two drops of brown liquid with a sharp smell into Pansa's mouth. He swallowed and winced. "Yes. Some who still support the Caesarians. Others who wish to see all of them dead, including you."

"Me?" Octavius betrayed nothing, his voice measured. "I have only ever aided the Senate."

Pansa smiled wryly. "You are sharp, Caesar. I see it in your eyes. Sharper than Julius Caesar had been. You know the Senate only intends to use you to defeat Antonius and then discard you. They fear your power with the people, and they always will."

Octavius was silent. He could not deny it, but he would not admit how much he knew, not until he was sure of Pansa's aim.

"The lots have been cast," Pansa said fervently. "Some have already fallen into place. Brutus and Cassius are far away. They will not return until the victor is decided. Antonius is surrounded by enemies, but he also has many friends. If he is defeated, it will be up to *you* to gather those who supported your father and bring peace to the Republic." His eyes were pleading. "It is what Caesar would have done."

"And Caesar is dead," Octavius said flatly. "I wonder where *his* friends were when he was pierced by daggers twenty-three times."

Pansa only looked at him, his eyes growing heavy and solemn with understanding. If Pansa did not know before, he knew now. Octavius did not intend to keep many friends.

"You see, my dear Pansa, friendship only means so much. It is loyalty that stays the hand which would stab a friend in the back."

"What do you know of loyalty?" Pansa asked sadly.

"Enough to know it is rare, if it exists at all," Octavius said. "Loyalty is more than friendship. It is bound by an oath which the gods hold."

Another cough hacked up Pansa's throat, the hand gripping his linen pale and trembling. He eyed Octavius warily. "What do you plan to do when the Senate turns its back on you? Who will you turn to when you refuse the friendship of those who would support you?"

Octavius did not reply. The answer was obvious.

Pansa sighed, reading his thoughts. "An army is a dangerous weapon, Caesar. Are you so sure you know how to wield it?"

"A weapon is just like any tool," Octavius said, glancing at the bottle of medicine that Glyco still held in his hands. He had recognized the scent of the plant, ἀριστολοχία, from the moment he had entered the tent. Not a few times had a doctor prescribed it for him, with the warning that a few drops would cure him, while one too many would kill him. "It can be used for healing and harm, depending on whose hands it is in."

"And what will you use it for, Caesar?" Pansa asked mockingly. "Will you use it for healing or for harm?"

"That depends," Octavius said with the barest of smirks. "Will the Senate take their own medicine or not?"

⟫⟫⟫ ⟪⟪⟪

APRIL 43 BC

As recruits, they were first taught how to march.

There was a science behind it, even an art, learning to move as one body, one mind, weighed down with heavy equipment but steps light and timely, the central beat to the song of war.

Octavius recalled once marching twenty-four miles in six hours under a hot sun, the fatigue that made a home in his very bones, and the mild, persistent cough that plagued him for weeks afterward.

Then they were taught silence.

It was silly in practice until the *Optiones* hit them with their long sticks, bruising beneath the armor. Then silence was learned. It was meant to scare the enemy as a display of efficiency and make any commands easily heard in the quiet, but Octavius considered it merely a premonition of death.

Today the silence hung heavy in the fog of the morning. Octavius could hear the rattling of armor, the tides of heavy breathing from men and horses, and the occasional shouts of a general calling order to his line as their legions readied themselves for battle.

His head was hot in his helmet despite the bite of a cold spring dawn stinging his face. Antonius' muddied campground stretched before their ranks, his soldiers scrambling to retreat and form lines, their faces frantic. Beside him, Agrippa watched the scene carefully.

"War does not seem so glorious now, does it?" Agrippa asked softly, smiling wryly, perhaps to lighten the mood. "Rather wish you were in your bed, do you not?"

"I would rather die on the battlefield than in my bed," Octavius murmured, though his pulse stuttered at the thought.

Agrippa's smile fell, then, and his voice was dark. "Only men who cannot find honor in life wish to find honor in their death."

Octavius did not agree. He thought there was great honor in dying on the battlefield. When he had been young and bedridden he had often dreamed of dying in war, strong and fearless, cut down by Apollo's arrow like Achilles. But at the time he had nothing, no prospects, no army. His father had been dead, his mother overshadowed by a lesser man, and he, merely a boy whose name no one knew.

Now things have changed. He was no longer nameless. In fact, his name was the only sure thing he had these days. Agrippa was right. He had honor still to gain in life, and his mind leaped ahead with visions of a land unified under one empire, one name which they would chant in the streets as if to a god. No such honor awaited him in death.

Yet a part of him still yearned for it, the deathblow of which ballads were sung. He thought of his father, his true namesake, Gaius Octavius, who had died valiantly from a fatal wound in war.

As a child, Octavius had been ashamed of how different they had been, how he had failed his father as a son, always on the verge of dying from another illness. He wondered if that shame would ever truly go away.

"Caesar!" Hirtius called from down the line, before he strode up to them, his face lined with worry. "We ought to advance while Antonius' troops are scattered."

"Send the cavalry ahead," Agrippa said, looking out at Antonius' camp as if he could see the battle there before it had even begun. "Antonius will try to stave us off with his own *equites*. They are strong, perhaps stronger than ours, but time is on our side. Then we break a passage through the camp and funnel supplies to Decimus. Hopefully, he is waiting for us on the other side."

Hirtius looked at Agrippa in surprise, then a reluctant respect. He nodded firmly, turning to the soldiers and shouting, *"Parati equites!"*

Octavius watched the cavalry form lines before the camp, the horses stomping and snorting at the weight of the heavily armed soldiers sat astride them.

Before Hirtius could give the next command, they heard shouting from the camp, then hooves beating against the dirt. Antonius' cavalry emerged onto the field before their campground, spears at the ready.

Hirtius moved back towards his legions. *"Ciringite frontem!"*

The infantry held their ground, silent and still with the utmost discipline. Their cavalry grew restless, however, the horses sensing the growing hostility in front of them. Hirtius looked to Agrippa, who held out a hand. *Wait.*

Antonius' cavalry inched forward. Agrippa's hand fell, and Hirtius cried out, *"Cursu mina!"*

Their cavalry charged, hurtling towards the enemy at full speed while the rest of the legions remained in their places, unblinking, and silent. Always, always silent. Octavius felt the urge to move forward, to fight, but he held back, keeping very still, knowing any slight movement from him would rattle his troops and break their formation.

Clashes of weaponry and the cries of falling soldiers were as clear and cutting as the swords they wielded. Soon they heard the command from within the campgrounds and Antonius' cavalry fell back, retreating as their own cavalry pursued them.

"Cuneum formate!"

The soldiers uniformly moved into lines resembling the tip of a sword, with broad shields in front, and daggers ready to slice through the enemy.

Octavius gripped his shield and dagger tightly, his heart pounding loudly in the silence before the storm. Agrippa whispered something under his breath. Perhaps a prayer.

"Percute!"

They moved as quick and silent as sharks. Distantly they heard the shouts of soldiers deeper within the camps as the cavalry sent them running. Other groans were heard closer, softer and duller, followed by a thump as bodies hit the ground around them.

Octavius and Hirtius' men entered into the main camp and met the rest of Antonius' forces, his infantry struggling to hold their lines and fend off the attack. Octavius glanced at Agrippa, who nodded.

"*Contendite vestra sponte!*" Octavius shouted. The command only meant one thing. Chaos.

Octavius surged forward with his men, immediately coming face to face with one of Antonius' soldiers who had broken through their ranks. There was no time to call for help. He lifted his shield just as a dagger swung, the blow rattling Octavius' teeth.

Another blow hit his shield, clanging in the silence. Octavius was only aware of his breath, shallow and quick. He could not feel his body. Another blow. He could not hear anything except the distant cries of the slowly dying.

The soldier struck again, but this time Octavius moved in time, some nameless will within controlling his limbs so that from one blink to the next he dodged the blow and struck out behind his shield with his own dagger. His blade missed but the attack forced his enemy to retreat, while Octavius followed with another cutting swipe, nicking his armor. He heard a humming now, like the persistent thrumming of a bird's wings, just beside his ears.

Octavius feinted right, then attacked, thrusting his dagger into the soldier's abdomen, the blade sinking into the body as if it were meant to be there all along. He yanked it out, and just like that, the man's mouth fell open, and he was dead. Octavius did not wait around to see him fall.

"*Ad latus stringe!*" Octavius shouted, his voice a mere echo in a cave, his vision sharp except for the edges which were tinged with darkness.

His soldiers reformed the line and continued advancing through the camp.

Octavius looked around for Agrippa but only saw a sea of helmets glinting in the sunlight. A slight panic gripped him before another soldier was upon him, and his thoughts narrowed to the swing of his blade, the weight of his shield.

Another dead.

Octavius forged onwards.

Another dead.

A voice called out in the punctuated silence. He knew this voice, but at first, he could not remember the name to which it belonged. A night of wine and women flashed through his mind, an easy smile. Hirtius.

"*Equaliter ambula! Invenite Antonium!*"

For a moment, Octavius watched uncomprehendingly as Hirtius led his *Legio III* away from their ranks. They quickly disappeared deep into the camp, cutting down the enemy's reinforcements that rushed to join their comrades in battle. Hirtius' words returned to him. Octavius realized they were searching for the commander's tent.

Hirtius planned to kill Antonius.

A trumpet sounded from far away before Octavius could decide to follow or stay. Many soldiers lifted their heads briefly before they pursued the enemy again with more vigor. Because that was not Antonius' trumpet.

It was Decimus Brutus. He was joining the fight.

Octavius called out again. *"Cum ordine seque!"*

His soldiers surrounded him as they forced a passage through the camp. The fighting grew thick as they advanced through Antonius' ranks, attempting to clear a path to the river, across from which stood the city walls where they would send supplies to break the siege.

Bodies piled up like sacks of grain, no more heeded than the slick mud they stomped through or the tents that burned as Octavius' men stormed the camp. They reached the central part of the campground and Octavius saw Hirtius' legion struggling to hold their ground. He tried to search the faces but they were mere unfamiliar blurs. Where was Hirtius?

Then he saw him. On the ground, his head lolling, mouth bloody. Dead. No. They were in Spain. Octavius was drunk. Hirtius smiled at him. *Have you ever kissed a man before?*

"Dirige frontem!" Octavius shouted.

His soldiers reformed the front lines and charged at Antonius' forces. Octavius slashed his way to Hirtius' body. His knees hit the ground. The body was heavy. Octavius' arms strained to pick up the weight. He called to his men, and two soldiers quickly moved to grab the body and send it back down the ranks.

Antonius' troops were retreating. They moved away from the camps, begging for their lives or a quick death as Hirtius and Octavius' legions swept through the field, killing anyone in their path and burning the tents. Octavius' hands were slick with blood as he gripped his dagger.

They had won. Barely. Smoke curled in the air. Blood and death sat heavy on the wind. Octavius looked around. Too many bodies. Too many blank faces. His teeth chattered, but he was not cold.

The remaining soldiers conducted a survey of the abandoned campground in case some of Antonius' soldiers had lingered.

Octavius did not remember how he returned to his own camp. His soldiers led him away. Hirtius was dead. The siege was broken. Blood and death. Death and blood. His mind reeled, and he swallowed bile as it climbed up his throat. The inside of his tent swayed as his eyes struggled to see straight.

Then it struck him like a blow to the chest.

Agrippa is dead.

No. He pushed the thought away. Agrippa had not yet returned.

But his breath left him, as though the air had suddenly disappeared. He had lost Agrippa in the chaos of battle, and his own fear of death had driven his body on when his mind had failed him.

Octavius refused to believe that Agrippa could still be on that field, one more body cast among many, and Octavius had not known it.

Agrippa is dead.

"Octavius."

No. It was a ghost come to haunt him for the rest of his days, just like his father, just like his mother, just like Hirtius.

Octavius opened his eyes.

Agrippa stood across the tent, his helmet held under one arm, those dark curls matted with either mud or blood, Octavius could not tell. He looked so painfully beautiful, then, like a Greek warrior returning from the very depths of Hell, like the hero Patroclus after fighting Hector.

He did not speak a word. His legs moved forward and then Agrippa was right there, standing in front of him. He placed a hand against his armored chest, as if to make sure he was real, that he was alive, that his chest rose and fell beneath his palm.

"Look at me," Agrippa whispered.

He shook his head, not trusting himself to look up, to move his face. Not when they were this close. Not when Octavius already felt reality slipping through his grasp like a bad dream.

Then Agrippa grabbed his chin and kissed him.

Silence. He was back on the battlefield, feeling his pulse right in his head. Agrippa's mouth was unexpectedly soft against his own. Octavius heard Agrippa's helmet drop to the ground with a dull thud, and the sound alone made him light-headed.

He pulled away, his breath labored, his thoughts muddled. Agrippa stood still against him, his entire body stiff, as if now he were truly dead.

You know, it was not the Romans who reminded me of Trojans. And I was thinking of a very different kind of war.

But Octavius no longer wished to fight.

He took Agrippa's face in his hands and pulled him close until he could taste blood.

He was dead. They were both dead. This kiss was nothing more than a dream. Even their mouths were speaking tongues unknown to the living.

Then arms circled his waist, tight and warm. Octavius tilted his head until their teeth scraped, dizzy with a rising want. He wanted to make Agrippa say his name. He wanted Agrippa to swear on his own life, to swear on everything and anything. He wanted heat and hands until he forgot that death was more than just a dream in the dead of night.

He was dizzy. So dizzy.

Octavius stepped backward, his vision blurred. He heard his name as if down a long tunnel. He tried to call out but his voice was gone. His body loosened like a knot unraveling.

Strong arms caught him, voices called out, shadows moved.

Then, darkness.

16

MARCUS ANTONIUS

APRIL 43 BC

B EFORE MARCUS ANTONIUS WAS a politician, he had been a soldier. In fact, he had been a very good soldier, and there was nothing he did better than retreat.

They had hardly escaped from the battle at Mutina before Antonius commanded his troops to cross the valley and hike into the Alps. Retreating to Transalpine Gaul without a single army supporting him other than his own was a gamble, but for the first time, Antonius liked his odds better than anyone else's.

They were camped along a slope deep in the mountains where it always snowed. Antonius pulled his cloak tighter over his shoulders, bracing himself against the icy wind that still managed to sweep through his hastily erected commander's tent.

Outside a horse whinnied and a man's shout quickly followed. There was a murmur that came either from the mountains or the soldiers, Antonius could not tell. His men knew the precarious situation they were in well enough, with Decimus Brutus only a two-day's military march behind them. But these mountains had a mind of their own.

Suddenly there were muffled shouts outside the tent. Antonius did not move from his seat, but his right hand tightened on the hilt of his *gladius.*

"*Praetor* Antonius!"

One of his generals hurried into the tent and stood at attention.

"Speak," Antonius said impatiently. He sensed the urgency and feared bad news.

"One of our men who we thought dead has returned," he said hurriedly. Then he added emphatically, "Unharmed."

"Unharmed?" Antonius could not hide his perplexity. "How?"

"The young Caesar himself allowed him to return to us." There was a tone of reverence in his voice that Antonius disliked, but his kindled curiosity distracted him for the moment.

"Bring him to me," Antonius said dismissively. "I wish to hear this miraculous tale myself."

The general complied and quickly fetched the soldier, who Antonius was surprised to see was hardly older than seventeen. His eyes flickered nervously to Antonius, then down to the ground.

"I am told you were set free by Caesar?" Antonius asked.

The boy nodded quickly.

"Why do you tremble before me when you have so nearly escaped Death himself?" he asked angrily. "Do your duty and explain how this happened, then return to your post."

"Yes sir," the soldier replied automatically. He avoided Antonius' gaze but did not cower. "During the battle, I was knocked down by a blow to the head which I thought would surely kill me. I lay wounded on the field, at times awake, at other times unable to open my eyes. Hours or minutes passed, I know not. I am lucky not to have been trampled in the fray. Then I heard voices in the quiet. The battle was done and I knew I would either be imprisoned or killed.

"One voice suggested piercing a dagger through my heart, but another voice silenced him. *Get him up and well enough to walk. He is to return to his commander.* The other voice tried to protest but then agreed, and soon I was lifted from the ground. When I opened my eyes, I thought it was a god before me, but as I looked closer I saw it was Caesar himself. He said: *The Fates have smiled upon you this day. Send my regards to Praetor Antonius.* Then I was sent on my way. They released others as well, but I got here as fast as I could to tell you. That is the full truth of it, sir."

An uneasy silence fell at the words, and Antonius quickly dismissed the soldier, having heard enough. Was that impertinent boy goading him by returning his fallen soldiers unharmed and bearing messages of friendship? Or was the young Caesar quicker to understand the game of war than he had thought?

He stood up from his chair with a grunt and walked to his desk, where he kept his most private correspondence locked in the drawer with a key he kept on his person at all times. He picked up the letters, unraveling the most recent one.

It was from his old friend Lepidus, who was currently occupying Transalpine Gaul, the province nestled at the confluence of the Rhine and Durance rivers. He wrote in his typical sparse fashion, vague enough to be of no consequence if intercepted by enemy troops and sent to the Senate, but Antonius knew his friend well enough to read between the lines. Ultimately, Lepidus wished to know the odds before he rolled the dice, and Antonius was only too happy to provide them.

He began pacing the room as he unraveled the next letter, scanning the words he had already read several times over.

This letter was from Plancus, the current proconsul of Gallia Comata further north, who Antonius knew was in a long communication with Cicero in Rome. The Senate believed him more secure than Lepidus in his loyalties. But Antonius had information that he was sure Rome—along with her senators sitting comfortably in their estates far from the bloody battles and snowy mountain peaks—did not know.

While Plancus repeatedly assured Cicero that he would be promptly joining Lepidus to counter Antonius, his own scouts reported that Plancus and his legions remained quiet and unmoving in Cularo, his military camp in Gallia Comata, with no intention of taking a stance. While Antonius knew that Plancus was only loyal to himself, he would be swift to join Antonius if the winds were favorable.

The last letter of immediate consequence was from proconsul Asinius Pollio, whose legions were immobile in Hispania Inferior, too far away to commit to any side, and too sensible to join when the scales were still swaying.

Antonius put the letters back in the drawer and locked it. What did the Senate expect from three men who had been loyal to Julius Caesar and his cause? They had more to lose by backing the Senate than aiding Antonius against Decimus' weakened army. The Senate would only try to lessen their power, while Antonius would give them more of it.

Yet there was one piece of the puzzle that did not fit.

Octavius.

The boy definitely recognized his power over the soldiers. As far as Antonius could tell, he was still camped near Mutina, refusing to aid Decimus and the Senate. However, Octavius was also reluctant to join Antonius and the Caesarian cause despite messages of friendship, leaving himself unnecessarily stranded.

Antonius did not understand. What was his aim? Why not take a stance and fight, either for or against the Senate? How did he expect to come out of this civil war unscathed if he lingered for too long on his own?

He could hear the voice of his lover as if she were in the room with him now, listening to his thoughts. *So little, so little...*

"Then what would you do?" Antonius asked sharply, then blushed when he heard his words spoken aloud to nobody. Now was not the time to gain a reputation of insanity amongst his troops.

He recalled the letter he had sent to Octavius and Hirtius before the battle at Mutina, when he had realized his army would not be able to withstand such a force, urging them to see reason and join his cause before it was too late. They had answered with war, pitting former comrades against each other in battle, aiding Decimus and his ilk in the Senate.

But now that Decimus marched forth to finish the job, Octavius dithered the time away, walking a dangerous line between Antonius and the Senate.

"*Praetor* Antonius, sir."

It was one of his messengers, Publius Decius, who was responsible for the correspondence between his legions and those of Octavius. Antonius motioned for him to enter the tent without delay.

"What news?"

"It is the consuls Hirtius and Pansa, sir," Decius said. "They are both dead."

⤞≫ ≪⤝

MAY 43 BC

"He wants the consulship, that much is clear," Lepidus said in his dull drawl. He reclined beside Antonius as they took their meal. "Now that Pansa and Hirtius are dead, there is nothing in his way. The Senate has no army."

"Yes," Antonius said impatiently, "but why?"

It had taken a month of persuading, along with the close proximity and mingling of their troops, to convince Lepidus to aid him against Decimus' impending arrival.

Soon Ventidius Bassus and his legions approached after their long march from Rome to join him. Miraculously—or not so miraculously—they had not been hindered by Octavius or any other legion along the way.

Their numbers were steadily growing, and it was only a matter of time before Plancus and Pollio marched to his side, forming a blockade in the west from which Decimus could not possibly hope to escape.

Still, Octavius waited. Antonius' scouts reported that Pansa's troops—whose command Octavius would not relinquish—refused to fight for Decimus, that they did not wish to go to war against their own comrades, and that the Senate would not pay them anyway. But Antonius knew these sentiments always had a source, and Octavius was certainly responsible.

Lepidus mulled his question over as he sipped his wine. "I suppose he means to play a bigger part in this war than a mere ally to either us or the Senate."

"But the consulship is nearly over. He would be powerless by the end of the year," Antonius argued.

"It is a strange strategy, I confess, as it seems to be fruitless with both the Senate and the Caesarian cause. I do not pretend to understand his aim, but surely it cannot matter too much either way. He is powerless to stand against us when Plancus and Pollio join our ranks."

Antonius still felt uneasy despite the compelling argument of his friend. His instincts

153

told him that Octavius would not be so easily swept aside.

Over the past year, he had developed a grudging respect for the boy. He was so much like Julius Caesar. Infuriatingly ambitious. Efficient and calculating. Charming and well-spoken when need be. But he was more dangerous, at least to Antonius' eyes, for Octavius had the good fortune to be able to learn from Caesar's mistakes.

"He is never powerless as long as his soldiers consider him the son of a god," Antonius said reluctantly. "He is a threat that must be eliminated either by joining me or the Senate if he cannot be outright killed."

Lepidus shook his head with a condescending smile. "You think too much like a soldier, not like a politician. He can be an asset, not a threat, if only you make him so. His influence over the soldiers is great, but he is only a boy after all. If he goes for the consulship, let him. There is no power in the Senate anymore. And if he wishes to ally with us, I do not see a reason why we should fear it. Together, Brutus and Cassius would fall at our feet."

"Your words are pleasant to hear, my friend, but they seem too sweet for my liking," Antonius said with a bitter smile. "Do you not remember the alliance formed between Caesar, Pompeius, and Crassus? Do you not remember which name rose up from the ashes of that civil strife? And who bears that same name?"

"A name is not enough to rule an empire," Lepidus said loftily.

"A name is all Octavius had to begin with," Antonius countered. "And he has made it quite far without much more."

Lepidus sighed in irritation. "Ever since that woman took hold of your heart, you have softened. Where is your courage? Where is your daring? One year ago you saw the Republic crumble and you took action, picking up the good work that Caesar started but failed to complete. Where has that man gone?"

Antonius could not help seeing her face then, the dark eyes flashing, lined with kohl, and that smile, hinting at a knowledge only found at the tips of fingers brushing skin in the dark.

He shook his head, pushing thoughts of her from his mind. Lepidus was right, however much he would deny it aloud. She had played him as a bard played his lyre, and now Antonius could not forget her, even to save his own life.

"I am still the same man," Antonius snapped. "And I will not bow down to another Caesar."

"There he is," Lepidus said with a small, dangerous smile.

"Let us send a message to Plancus. He will soon see there is no future in the Republic," Antonius said, smirking as he saw the various pieces falling into place, his own larger and more powerful than all the rest. He picked up his glass of wine and raised it. "To the good work, my friend."

Lepidus raised his glass with a smirk of his own. "To the good work."

17

MARCUS VIPSANIUS AGRIPPA

JUNE 43 BC

"I T HAS BEEN TWO months since the battle at Mutina," Rufus said to Octavius, catching the attention of the others dining beside them who had until now been engaged in their own conversations. "Much has changed. Pansa and Hirtius are dead. Antonius gathers more power in the north. Lepidus has joined his cause, and I am sure Pollio and Plancus are not far behind. When will we take a stand?"

All eyes turned to Octavius, who merely looked at Rufus steadily and smiled. *"Patientia,* my dear Rufus."

They were gathered in the commander's tent, everyone of importance. Agrippa reclined beside Octavius, who had not looked at him a single instance the entire dinner.

Beside him reclined Balbus, then Oppius, another former close friend and advisor of Julius Caesar, and Matius, who had helped Octavius put on the games last July. On Octavius' left was Maecenas, looking positively indulged, and beside him was Rufus, who looked quite the opposite after Octavius' dismissive tone.

"I have patience, but I also have honor," Rufus said, still blushing at the slight. "We continue to flatter the Senate when we ought to be aiding Antonius against Decimus' approach. The Senate has already insulted you with a mere ovation as their thanks, while Decimus has received a triumph. I understand you wish to tread carefully, but now is not the time to remain idle when we risk becoming an enemy to both sides."

"Your sentiments are noble, but your logic is flawed," Agrippa interjected curtly. Rufus narrowed his eyes. "The best course of action now is to wait until the fates of Antonius and Decimus are decided."

"Naturally, I agree," Maecenas drawled, with the intention of either playing mediator or inciting an argument, Agrippa could not tell. "But is it so bad to consider other options?"

Balbus cleared his throat. "Besides, there is the question of payment."

Octavius raised a brow at the rising doubts in their party. Agrippa could sense his slight embarrassment that his own closest supporters did not trust in his plans, but it did not show on his face, and he merely waited for further explanation.

"If the Senate does not pay the troops—which they will not—then it is only a matter of time before your legions begin to desert you," Balbus said cautiously. "Especially with Antonius as a growing threat. If our scouts have calculated correctly, by the end of the year Antonius could amass more than twenty legions under his command."

"The soldiers may love you," Oppius added, half in jest, "but love always has a price."

"Quite right," Maecenas quipped, smirking at Octavius—much to Agrippa's annoyance—but Octavius only half-smiled in response.

"Please, Caesar," Matius interjected in his quiet, thoughtful voice, "do not think for a moment that we doubt your cause. We are only advising you the best we can."

They all watched in a restless quiet as Octavius thought over these suggestions. Agrippa wished that Octavius would look at him, if only for reassurance, but since the aftermath of the battle at Mutina they had scarcely spoken to each other.

He could still see the moment with clarity, the widened eyes of Octavius across the tent, as if he had seen a ghost, red drops of blood bright against his pale face, before the space between them had disappeared and Agrippa forgot the battle entirely.

Then Octavius had fainted, either from exhaustion or heightened nerves, and Agrippa should have known it was a bad omen.

Thereafter Octavius had succumbed to illness, which would not have been unusual if Agrippa had been there to nurse him back to good health. But Octavius had refused to admit Agrippa into his quarters, and even after a few weeks of rest restored some of his health, his eyes never quite reached Agrippa's again.

If coming to Italy had changed everything between them, then their kiss had altered the very air they breathed. Agrippa felt the resistance in Octavius' limbs as if he were touching them.

He knew now it was not a question of desire—that kiss erased all such doubts. But this was different. Much different. Because now it was a question of power, and power was not love.

"My friends," Octavius said at last, "you ask important questions, and questions I have asked myself often since I heard that Pansa and Hirtius were dead. So let me ask you this, Rufus, you who display such valor in wishing to join Antonius. What do you think will happen if I ally with Antonius? Do you think he will be so generous as to share his power with me?"

Rufus colored when everyone who had supported his criticism looked at him now. "No," he muttered, his eyes lowering, but not before Agrippa caught a flicker of resentment in the dull blue. "He would not."

Octavius smiled, but it was merciless. "And what do you think would happen if we join forces and defeat Brutus and Cassius in the East? Would he make sure I retain command over his soldiers? Would he consider me an equal and allow me to remain alive and powerful in Rome?"

"No. He would cast you aside," Rufus said reluctantly, "just as we know the Senate wishes to do with you."

"Precisely, Rufus," Octavius said, and he looked around at each of them, daring anyone to challenge him. The room was deathly silent, and Agrippa had to wonder if the silence came from respect or fear. "I cannot ally with Antonius when he has the power to cast me aside after I have offered my help. I must have a better bargain when the time comes to join forces. It is the only way."

"But are we really in a position to bargain?" Balbus asked carefully. "Soon the Senate will understand your true motives if they do not already, and they will name you *hostis*. Cicero will turn on you without a second thought. Antonius will not bother saving you. If we do not take action soon, we will be trapped between Antonius in the West and Brutus in the East, with no hope of escape."

Octavius raised a brow, a smile already playing at his mouth. "The answer is clear, is it not?"

No one answered, realizing that Octavius had already foreseen these obstacles and made a plan, however daring and risky. But he was waiting for an answer, relishing in the blank, uneasy faces around him. Agrippa could hardly stand it.

"The consulship," Agrippa said, his voice loud in the silence. Octavius looked at him in surprise, as if he had truly forgotten Agrippa was there, but the heated flash in his eyes before he looked away told Agrippa otherwise. "It is the only way. Rome is practically defenseless. We must secure her before Antonius has the chance to march against her."

"But the consulship will end in December. What could you possibly do—" Balbus began to ask, confused, before the answer to his unspoken question dawned on his face, and he looked at Octavius in wonder, smiling slowly and shaking his head in defeat. "You are truly Julius Caesar's son."

"As I am sure you have guessed," Octavius said, "I was not able to be legally adopted by Julius Caesar while Antonius still held influence in the *curia*. I was also unable to bring my father's murderers to trial as a private citizen. But if I were consul, there would be no one to stop me." He paused to let his words settle in. "The Senate would be completely at my mercy, and Antonius would be forced to ally with me if he wishes to avoid an outright war. Then, we defeat Brutus and Cassius once and for all."

Octavius spoke unsmiling, but his eyes glittered. Maecenas was the only one who did not look away from his fierce glance, staring at Octavius in unabashed admiration.

"The Senate would never let you run for the consulship," Rufus countered, seemingly envious that Agrippa had understood the secret plans of Octavius before he had. "Do you plan to march against the city with your army just as Antonius had threatened?"

"We will send an embassy to Rome," Octavius said carelessly. "My soldiers, I believe, would be very willing to demand the consulship for their commander along with the money which was promised to them."

"And if the Senate refuses?" Oppius asked warily, sharing meaningful glances with Balbus and Matius. After all, it was not only the lives of soldiers at stake anymore.

Octavius scarcely smiled, but Maecenas beside him grinned. "Then we march."

⟶⟫⟫ ⟪⟪⟵

"You think you are clever," Agrippa said.

The others had all left the tent once the meal was done and they had finished preparations for the sending of an embassy to Rome.

While Maecenas and Balbus had been thoroughly convinced of his plan, Rufus, Oppius, and Matius required more convincing before they saw the merit of the consulship. It did not matter. Octavius had his heart set on obtaining the consulship, and there was no changing his mind now.

But Agrippa had stayed behind, wishing to speak with Octavius, who allowed his manservant to clean his face and hands as if Agrippa were not there. Finally, the manservant retired to his quarters, leaving them truly alone for the first time in weeks, save the armed guard standing at attention outside the tent.

"Clever is not the word I would use," Octavius muttered. "You sound critical. Do you disagree with the plan?"

He did not look at Agrippa but proceeded to walk to his desk and study the map that had been spread across it as if there were nothing the matter, as if nothing had happened between them.

"You know I could not disagree with a plan I had a hand in making," Agrippa said with an edge of mockery.

Octavius looked up at him sharply. "You?"

"Yes, or did you forget?" Agrippa walked closer to him. "When Pansa was ambushed, I had suggested the opportunity his death would provide. You chastised me for it if I remember correctly, but I suppose one can always change their mind."

159

"I would never wish death on another to further my own cause," Octavius said, but without the passion he had when Death had been much nearer.

"Of course not," Agrippa said, taking another careful step forward, catching Octavius' eyes flicker at the movement. "Is that what you will tell yourself when you sentence Julius Caesar's murderers to death?"

Octavius gave him a long, stern look, but remained silent. Ever since they were boys, Octavius had never given anything of himself away. Once upon a time, Agrippa had thought it a strength, something to be envied. But now Agrippa knew better.

"Will you be so merciful then?" Agrippa continued. He was on the other side of the desk now, facing Octavius, who did not look away, his dark eyes startlingly familiar after so long chasing even a glance.

"Pansa was not a murderer," Octavius said quietly. "There is a difference."

Agrippa leaned forward, knowing Octavius would rather die than back away and admit any sign of weakness. "And what if the difference is not so clear? How will you decide a person's fate?"

"I decide no fate," Octavius countered. "That is the work of the gods."

"Do you believe yourself innocent?"

Octavius frowned. "There is no such thing as innocence in war."

"But there is such a thing as mercy."

"Why do you say such things to me?" Octavius asked indignantly, a reluctant hurt bright in his eyes.

Suddenly he appeared to Agrippa as he remembered him from their younger years, when Octavius had been nothing more than a rich, charming schoolboy who had fanciful dreams of playing the hero like any other boy their age. But now things were different. Those fanciful dreams were not so far out of reach, and every decision they made would determine the fate of others besides themselves.

"You never questioned my motives before. Why now do you consider me a monster?"

Agrippa was silent.

"You are angry with me," Octavius said, his eyes searching Agrippa's face, who stood perfectly still. "You believe me unthinking, unfeeling. But you mistake me. This is bigger than us. Bigger, even, than war. This is about power, Agrippa, and those bold enough to seize it."

Agrippa stared at him, the words escaping him as they always did.

Octavius looked satisfied, as if they had been sparring and he had won, though the weapons this time were words. He began moving away when Agrippa shot his hand out and grabbed Octavius' wrist, keeping it caught above the desk between them.

"Octavius."

Octavius looked at the hand encircling his wrist carefully, then up at Agrippa, his expression unreadable save for the red flush creeping up his neck.

"Yes?"

Their last kiss rose up in Agrippa's memory like the tide of the ocean, strong and clear. Agrippa ignored the sudden racing of his pulse.

"I do not consider you a monster," Agrippa said slowly. He felt the slender muscles in Octavius' wrist tense against him, resisting him, and he swallowed. *This is about power, Agrippa.* "I am only afraid that you may become one."

The silence between them was stifling. Octavius had a surprised look on his face, his mouth slightly parted, as if he had not expected the words from Agrippa, as if Agrippa had somehow betrayed him, when it had always been the other way around.

He immediately regretted it, regretted trying to reach out only to grasp air, left with that cold and cruel laughter that always followed in his dreams. Suddenly a sliver of doubt appeared in Octavius' eyes. *If I were Achilles, you would be Patroclus.*

"Octavius—"

But before he could speak, Octavius moved away abruptly, forcing his hand free. He returned to examining the map just as Rufus entered the tent.

Agrippa pretended to study the map as well, ignoring the flush rising on his face.

"Caesar."

Octavius raised a brow, for all the world perfectly composed. "Yes, Rufus?"

Rufus cast Agrippa a furtive glance. "One of the commanders wishes to speak with you. The soldiers are restless. They demand more money."

"And money is what they will receive," Octavius said, his voice terse. Agrippa could not tell if it was because of him or Rufus' unwelcome news. "But only if they remain loyal to me."

"Loyalty has a price," Rufus replied, raising a brow.

"It seems everything has a price these days," Agrippa muttered.

Octavius ignored his comment, looking at Rufus with a cold smile. "And it is a price I am willing to pay. Are you?"

Rufus' face turned red, flustered. "Yes, of course, Caesar."

"Good," Octavius said calmly. "Then tell the soldiers to be patient." He looked at Agrippa, smirking, and his eyes alone left Agrippa breathless. "If there is anything I have learned, it is that vengeance is a delicate thing, and requires a gentle hand to nurture."

"Yes, Caesar." Rufus looked between Agrippa and Octavius with a bemused frown, before he left the tent.

Agrippa looked at Octavius carefully, feeling a boldness enter his heart before he could stop it. "Do you suppose a kiss has a price?"

Octavius stared back, his eyes steeled. Was it a warning, or a challenge? "Perhaps. But are you so sure you can pay it?"

⟫⟫⟫ ⟪⟪⟪

JULY 43 BC

Octavius stood before a desk, but the room was entirely different from the military tents they had been accustomed to these past few months. The painted walls, gilded furniture, and the familiar high hills of Rome rolling like ocean waves outside the window all indicated that they were in Julius Caesar's estate on the Palatine Hill, rifling through the papers he had left behind.

"My great-uncle truly kept his affairs in order," Octavius said quietly, unraveling another letter and quickly reading through the contents. "Though I suppose not orderly enough."

"It is difficult to foresee what one does not wish to see," Agrippa said.

Octavius looked at him, his eyes flashing darkly, sensing a double meaning in his words. "It was a weakness of his. I will not be so easily deceived."

Agrippa did not answer, and a moment later the door swung open with a slam. He drew his *gladius* quickly before he saw who stood in the doorway. A woman, fair-haired and pale-skinned, the light from the windows shining on her blonde hair, with a determination in her eyes that immediately struck Agrippa as familiar.

Octavia.

She entered the room, eyeing Agrippa in annoyance. "Put away your sword, Agrippa, though I cannot promise I will not try to strangle my brother!"

Octavius had not even flinched, as if he had expected his sister all along. He grinned wide. "My dear sister, welcome home."

"Home?" Octavia laughed scornfully. "This is a tomb if it is anything at all. What were you thinking, marching on Rome while your sister was still here? I could have been killed!"

"I knew you would be smart enough to hide before anyone could find you."

"That is beside the point, brother!"

But Agrippa thought he saw a grudging fondness creep into Octavia's eyes as she stared down her brother. Octavius raised a brow, a playful smile on his lips which only served to distract Agrippa from what they were saying.

"...you are safe now. From whom did you find protection?" Octavius asked.

Octavia smiled triumphantly. "The Vestal Virgins."

162

"Oh, you *are* smart," Octavius said, nodding. "I will be sure to repay their kindness."

"But what are you going to do now?" Octavia asked, looking out the window where the tall columns of the temple to Jupiter could be seen towering over the city. "The Republic has fallen."

"That depends on how you look at it," Octavius replied, his voice turning diplomatic. "I will be consul soon. I will have the power to right wrongs and return order to Rome and her provinces. The Republic has not fallen. It is only being reborn, and birth requires pain before there is life. But these are things best left to men, my sister, who cherish their country as a woman her child."

"Oh really?" There was a glint in her eyes that Agrippa did not like, reminding him too much of Octavius right before he said the exact thing that would anger him beyond all evil. "Then I suppose you must have the most important political alliance already established?"

"And what is that?"

Octavia smiled, and as if he knew before she said it, Agrippa's heart dropped.

"Marriage, of course."

18

OCTAVIA MINOR

AUGUST 43 BC

THE DAY HER MOTHER died, Octavia became a woman.

She felt it in the looks cast her way by their household, the searching glances that once fell on her mother, and which now settled on her. She felt it when her brother was fighting at Mutina, the brewing war far away from Rome, when Octavia stood as the sole representative of her parents and their legacy. But most of all, she felt it in her marriage.

"My love."

Octavia turned her head. Marcellus, her husband, stood in the doorway, scarcely hiding his affectionate smile as he watched her weave by the window, bathed in a gentle sunlight. She blushed and turned back to her weaving.

They had not always been so coy with one another. When they had first married, she had just turned twelve, with Marcellus in his thirty-fourth year. The marriage had secured political and familial ties more than anything else.

In those early years, Marcellus had been more like a guardian than a husband, teaching her to manage the affairs of the house, discussing the philosophy and literature he took up in his spare time, and gossiping about the tumultuous politics of the Senate.

She became his closest confidant, his dearest friend, and he became the man she loved for his gentle and patient nature, but more than that, for the respect he paid to her opinions and beliefs on all subjects. Never in their nearly ten years of marriage had she felt belittled, never had he looked at her with anything more than respect and care. For nearly ten years, they had been more like the best of friends than man and wife.

But over the last year, something had changed.

Octavia noticed it in the way her heart beat faster when he walked into the room. She caught herself staring at the dark locks curling over his forehead, the familiar blue eyes that softened when he looked at her. While he spoke with her, an easy smile playing at his lips, his brow lightly creased, she would lose track of her words and stutter a reply.

And she could tell he had begun noticing her as well; a lingering gaze on the curve of her cheek, a pleased flush when she laughed at one of his bad jokes and could not help but smile.

She was twenty-three years old. They had skirted the issue long enough, Octavia thought, and she would not always be young enough to have children. But they hesitated like blushing newlyweds, as if they had not already known each other for a decade.

Perhaps that was the problem, though. They had been friends for so long that they did not know how to be lovers.

"Yes?"

Marcellus walked over to her. "I ran into Cicero at the forum today."

"That is hardly a surprise."

He laughed. "I suppose. He does not cease a day."

"What did he have to say? For he *always* has something to say, and I am sure it was about my brother."

"Oh you do love to make fun of the poor man," Marcellus said jokingly, though his eyes were sad. "But be gentle, my love. He is a long friend of mine, and his days may be few."

"What are you suggesting?" Octavia asked sharply.

Marcellus raised a brow at her tone. "I hardly think I must explain to you the…unfortunate circumstances he has found himself in. You know well enough the new political establishment will no longer tolerate his voice in the Senate."

"Then it *is* about my brother." Octavia had long stopped weaving. She turned around, facing him, ignoring the pang of her heart when Marcellus frowned. "Do you believe him to be such a monster that he would silence a man simply for holding power in the Senate?"

"Power is like a drug, my Octavia. Men will do unthinkable things to keep it."

Octavia pursed her lips. She always thought men gave too many excuses for their actions. "My brother has only ever called Cicero a friend. It was Cicero who wished to use him and kill him if he could. If Cicero would only keep quiet for once then maybe he would not find himself surrounded by enemies."

"Do you wish to live in a world where one cannot speak their mind freely?" Marcellus asked.

"Oh, Marcellus, we women already live in that world," Octavia said with an arch smile. "Advise your friend to be more subtle in his attacks. Perhaps he will find others more tolerant of his voice if he used it less."

Marcellus laughed. "Cicero is anything but subtle, my dear, and I am afraid he is long past the age when men are still capable of changing their ways. But your point is well taken.

And as long as your brother does not attempt to end our marriage as Caesar did, then I will not complain too much. You are the only thing that truly matters to me anyway."

He leaned in and kissed Octavia's cheek, lingering for half a moment too long. She blushed and turned away. "Speaking of marriage, I have been meaning to speak with you about something."

Marcellus stepped back, eyebrows raised. "Not *our* marriage, I hope?"

Octavia shook her head. "Of course not. I mean the marriage of my brother."

"Your brother?" Marcellus looked amused. "Does he approve of you meddling in his affairs?"

"It is my duty as his older sister to meddle in his affairs. And besides, men are completely hopeless when it comes to marriage."

"Oh, are they now?" Marcellus lightly brushed her hair with his fingertips, as if he wished to touch her but was afraid she would scold him for it. "I suppose you do not need my help then."

"I never said *that*," Octavia muttered childishly.

He could not hide the satisfaction at her answer, but he took her hand gently and kissed her knuckles. "I only tease, my love. Tell me who you have in mind for your brother."

"The daughter of former consul Publius Servilius Isauricus. He was a supporter of Caesar's cause and although he opposed Marcus Antonius, his loyalties lie firmly with my family." But Octavia hesitated, remembering how her brother had reacted after she had mentioned his inevitable duty to marry.

"Marriage," her brother had said, "can be as politically disadvantageous as it can be advantageous, Octavia." His tone had been playfully dismissive but Octavia had noticed an edge in his voice. "There are more important political alliances to establish at the moment."

Octavia had raised a brow, glancing at Agrippa in surprise, but her brother's friend had merely looked at her, quiet and serious. "It is your duty to marry. If Mother were here—"

"Mother is dead," Octavius had interrupted, and she had nearly flinched. "I will marry when I wish to, or not at all. How can I be united with a woman I do not know, let alone love?"

"Love?" A rush of anger that she had not expected nearly choked the word. "Love? What do you know of love? What do you know of marriage? You must join yourself to another for the sake of our family, for the children who will bear your name. You will marry because it is right, then we may speak of *love*."

"I know more about love than you know," Octavius had retorted with a smirk, clearly meaning something very different than what *she* had meant by the word.

Then her brother's gaze had flickered ever so quickly to Agrippa, before returning to her, his smile quickly fading. A thought flowered in her stomach uneasily, but she pushed it aside.

"We will continue this conversation another time," Octavia had said gravely. "Until then, I advise you to think hard of that love, and whether it is worth sacrificing your reputation." She had left them in a deadly silence, her head light at what she had suspected.

Octavia was drawn from her thoughts when Marcellus kissed her hand again, encouraging her to continue.

"It is a good match," Octavia said finally. "Her mother is sister-in-law to former consul Marcus Lepidus, another man loyal to the Caesarian party. But she is young, and I am not entirely convinced my brother will agree to marry her."

Marcellus frowned. "I am sure he is merely scared. A man's first marriage is as terrifying as his first battle. If anyone can convince him to see reason, it is you."

"I hope so," Octavia said, troubled. She wondered whether she ought to tell him her suspicions. Perhaps he would think she imagined what she saw. Or worse, he would believe her.

He saw her pause and squeezed her hand. "What is on your mind? Speak. You know you may always confide in me."

"It is nothing." Octavia knew she could not betray her brother, not in this. She would find a way to make things right before anyone was the wiser. "I love you, that is all."

He smiled, his brow cleared of worry at her words, pulling her close and kissing her. "And I love you."

⋙ ⋘

She found him in the gardens of Julius Caesar's estate, staring out across the hills of Rome, rolling back like green waves, embracing the heart of their people.

Octavius did not look at her as she approached, his hand brushing a flower nearby which had already begun drooping in the late summer sun. These were their grandmother's gardens, but they did not stir the same sympathy in her as they did in him. Julia Minor had always loved Octavius more than her.

"I used to spend hours in this garden with *Avia,*" he said as a way of greeting once she stood beside him. "I used to pray that Caesar would come visit, but he was always traveling. He rarely stayed for long even if he did return, and when he left again, I hated this garden, and I hated that I had to remain with *Avia*. It was only when she died that I realized how much I would miss this garden, and her."

"I never spent much time here," Octavia said. "And then I married, and I had a garden of my own. Though I cannot pretend to have spent a single day in it."

"You never did like gardening."

Octavia laughed, the sensation startling after several tense months of war and looming death. Her brother gave her a wry smile. "No, I never did. I was much better at weaving. You were the one who could force a seed to grow even in the wrong season. That is why *Avia* loved you best."

"Nonsense," Octavius said, shaking his head. *"Avia* always praised you. She would tell me to be more like you. You did everything asked of you. I was troublesome to our parents. That is why they sent me here."

"Did you know that you hardly cried? Mother worried herself sick over it. But when you did cry, she worried even more. You were the baby of the family. It was Phillipus who thought it would do you good to spend time with *Avia*. You were never truly troublesome."

"Ah, the woes and whimsies of childhood. I cannot say I particularly miss it." Octavius had a faraway gaze that was tinged with bitterness. "But you did not pay me a visit to reminisce. What is it you wish to speak about?"

Octavia remained silent.

Her brother sighed. "Just say it."

"Do you love him?" she asked, surprised at her boldness.

Octavius flinched at the words and his eyes hardened, but it was enough confirmation for her. "Who?"

"You know of whom I speak. I saw the look on his face. I saw you notice it too. I shall ask you again. Do you love him?"

His mouth opened as if about to deny her accusation, then closed. After a long pause, he shook his head. "No."

"No?" Octavia turned towards him and he looked back at her fiercely. She saw her mother in those eyes, reflecting an unbending will in their dark depths. "Does *he* love *you*?"

He did not speak at first, but his eyes betrayed a struggle within as he decided how to respond. "It is harmless. It is nothing."

"I do not care," Octavia said curtly. "I do not care if you love him or not. More is the pity if you do not. It is the people who will care. It is your enemies who will care. I only wish to protect you."

"I do not need you to protect me," Octavius retorted.

"Then prove it," she said. "I have found a nice girl from a prominent family who supports your cause. Her name is Servilia. She will strengthen your ties with former consuls Isauricus and Lepidus. Maybe in time, you could even come to love her. You would be a fool to reject her."

Octavius did not answer, but he was listening.

"Maybe it is not marriage that you fear," Octavia said, studying his stern frown, the familiar defensiveness that has walled her brother's heart for as long as she could remember, wishing that she could break it, if only a little. "Maybe it is loving him which you fear, and that even marriage would not stop it."

The words seemed to glance off him like arrows against glinting shields. He smiled at her. "I already told you, sister. It is nothing."

"I believe you," she said, smiling sadly. "Do you?"

⟫⟫⟫ ⟪⟪⟪

Steam rose up from the water, cloaking Octavia in a warm mist. Her Greek handmaiden, Prima, rinsed her skin, smoothing a sweet fragrant oil across her shoulders and down her arms.

Octavia closed her eyes, feeling the gentle hands wash her neck and travel down her back. "Prima?"

"Yes, my lady?"

"Have you ever been intimate with a man before?" Octavia asked before she lost her nerve.

Her handmaiden laughed, before schooling her features into a suppressed smile when Octavia opened her eyes and half-heartedly glared at her. "Sorry, my lady. I do not mean offense. I only laugh because I am surprised."

"Why are you surprised?" Octavia was not offended, merely embarrassed. "I am married."

"Well, my lady, it has been many years since you were married." Prima shrugged and began rinsing her hair. Octavia closed her eyes again, relaxing into the sensation. "Sometimes it is not meant to be."

"I love my husband," Octavia protested.

"Ah, but you see, my lady, there are different kinds of love." She paused as if unsure how to explain it, then added, "There is the deep love of husband and wife, but there is also the flame between man and woman, the flame that makes life."

"I see," Octavia said, her face burning. She was quite humiliated that she did not already know these things, but also intrigued to know more. "And this flame, how does one go about making it?"

"Not one, but two, my lady." Prima stopped washing her hair and touched a light hand under her chin.

Octavia opened her eyes, staring into the kind dark eyes of her handmaiden, her tan

169

skin already wrinkling around her eyes. She had been Octavia's maidservant since she married, only five years older, and in many ways, they had grown as close as sisters. But in this moment Octavia was reminded of the life Prima had before her, however brief.

"It starts with a kiss, no? The sweet mouth, then the soft neck, and down below the stomach. The rest is up to the man."

"So you have, then, before?"

Prima smiled gently, then kissed Octavia's cheek. "Yes, my lady, I have, and it is like touching Olympos in the sky above."

"Really?"

"Oh yes, when the flame is there."

"How do you know if the flame is there?" Octavia asked, unable to hide the eagerness in her voice.

Now Prima laughed unapologetically. "That, my lady, you will know."

Octavia flushed, thinking of how her stomach burned every time Marcellus' kiss lingered on her skin. Immediately her heart began to pound, and she suddenly felt like a little girl again, awaiting the night of her wedding.

"I am afraid."

Prima stroked her head, nodding. "That is normal, my lady. But I have found a trick that works every time. Shall I tell it to you?"

Octavia hesitated, then nodded.

⟫⟫ ⟪⟪

"Marcellus."

Her husband turned in surprise.

She stood at the frame of the door, watching Marcellus prepare for bed. They had always slept in different rooms, and she rarely approached his bedroom if ever, and especially not in the night. She wore a thin nightgown that Marcellus eyed with slight surprise, before reluctantly moving his gaze to her face.

"Yes, my love?"

Octavia took a few hesitant steps forward. Marcellus remained still, watching her approach silently. She swallowed her nerves, daring to glance up into his eyes, and paused at the heat flashing in them.

Before she could change her mind, she reached out and took his hand in hers, pulling him closer to her. Then on her tiptoes she pressed a kiss on his lips, hardly more than a brush.

Marcellus closed his eyes as if the kiss had pained him. "Octavia."

A doubt crossed her mind when he did not move, and she felt ashamed to have kissed him. But then he lowered his face and kissed her, a knuckle lifting her chin towards him, his mouth warm against hers. A flaming heat seared inside of her, and she could not stop her arms from circling his neck and bringing him closer.

When they pulled away, for a moment neither of them spoke, their breaths loud in the darkness.

"Please, Marcellus," Octavia said at last, breathless, her whole body humming, a deeper want rushing to the surface of her skin like a wildfire burning up a grassy field. "Bring life into this world with me."

Marcellus' eyes widened. One of his hands skirted her waist, brushing against her stomach. "Are you sure, my love?"

She nodded, feeling the flickering flame where he touched her. "Yes."

Suddenly Marcellus scooped her up in his arms as if it truly were her wedding night, and he led them to a small bedroom deep in the house which she knew was kept shut except for special nights between a married man and woman. They should have consummated their marriage there, but she had been too young, and as far as she knew the room had been left unused for years.

They entered the bedroom. Even after Marcellus lit the few lamps on the walls, darkness still lingered in the corners. But they were bright enough to cast a glow on the typical paintings along the wall of men and women tangled in sweet embraces, and the single bed inviting in its vast emptiness.

Octavia blushed.

Marcellus lowered her onto the bed, hovering above her. She lied back carefully, staring up at him, his soft blue eyes, now serious and enraptured as they gazed upon her, wandering from her face down the white folds of her nightgown.

She recalled the words of Prima, and before she doubted herself, Octavia took Marcellus' hand and placed it on her stomach, pressing his palm down. He did not speak, waiting for her, as if he could sense her purpose. She guided his hand further down until his fingers slipped underneath the hem of fabric and brushed the soft skin of her inner thighs.

"Oh, Octavia," Marcellus breathed. Then he kissed her.

It was late in the night when Octavia finally fell asleep, their bodies pressed close as though still in embrace, and Octavia dreamed of the flame of love between them, growing in her hips as strong branches yearned for the sky.

19

GAIUS OCTAVIUS

AUGUST 43 BC

THE CROWDS RUSTLED AS Octavius stepped onto the *rostra* and stood before the Roman forum. Clouds gathered above in dark gray turmoil, threatening a storm. In a single glance, he saw senators, veteran soldiers, and other prominent citizens crowded around, waiting for him to speak. Some looked on warily, others hopeful.

Everyone seemed to hold their breath, watching him carefully. He was twenty years old now, but the creased, critical faces in the crowd made him feel fifteen again, when he donned the *toga virilis* for the first time.

Agrippa, along with Lucius Cornificius, a man of plebian birth but passionate in his beliefs, were seated on the benches to the right of the *rostra*, ready to testify, as well as other prosecutors, while a few defendants occupied the benches to the left. Stern jurors sat on either side of them, their faces cautious and withdrawn.

Octavius avoided the lingering gaze of Agrippa, whom he had studiously kept at a distance these past few weeks.

"Conscript Fathers," Octavius began, his voice cutting through the murky silence.

A few senators exchanged glances. There were many who were eerily absent. Cicero had disappeared, most likely to one of his many beloved villas, though Octavius would not be surprised if he had fled to Greece. Brutus and Cassius were fortifying their positions in the East, while Antonius and Lepidus were building dangerous alliances in Gaul.

Octavius ignored the unease settling in his stomach at the uncertainties that had sprung up so easily in the past month, finding that ever-present heartbeat that drummed deep within his chest. *That is how you know, my child, whether you are destined for greatness.*

"Conscript Fathers," he repeated more firmly, "and citizens of Rome. We are gathered here today for the trial of those responsible for the murder of Julius Caesar."

The special trial had been set up after his co-consul and relative Pedius passed a law condemning the murderers to banishment. Octavius felt the disapproval of the senators who had supported the *Conspiratores,* as Octavius and his men liked to call them. Only the veteran soldiers and poorer citizens gathered were eager for justice.

"Let the first prosecutor step forward and make his case to the judges."

The first prosecutor, Cornificius, stood up solemnly. His eyes flickered over the crowd, flashing with purpose. Despite his negligible lineage, Cornificius was a brilliant public speaker, and the combination of obscurity and passion was precisely why Octavius had chosen him for this role.

"It is no secret, O judges," he began, "what took place in the Curia of Pompeius on the Ides of March just last year. In fact, these murderers boasted of their crime to the public, claiming that the Roman people were now free." He paused significantly. "We know what the Roman people thought of that hollow freedom."

The crowd murmured, remembering the burning of the Senate House and Julius Caesar's bloody wax statue paraded about this very forum not two years ago.

"But instead of justice for their crime," Cornificius continued, "the people saw those murderers—still stained with the fresh blood of twenty-three stab wounds—pardoned. Now they have fled to the East, illegally amassing armies with the intention of bringing civil war and needless death to Rome and her children. Our fathers and sons, our brothers, killed—for freedom! A bloody freedom indeed!"

Another rumbling spread throughout the crowd. Despite the slight inflection of emotion in his voice, Cornificius' expression remained calm and serious in its passion as he now looked around at the spectators and, finally, settled on the judges present.

"As prosecutor, I accuse Marcus Junius Brutus of knowingly plotting against and assassinating the former consul of Rome, Gaius Julius Caesar."

At his name, a groan rose up from the crowds, though it was impossible to tell if in lamentation for the murdered or the accused. But it did not matter; the judges would not vote for the *Conspiratores* in the face of his army.

Nonetheless, Octavius felt a rising indignation in his chest at the hypocrisy of the senators, their speeches of freedom and democracy from the tops of their lofty estates, now hiding in their sprawling villas adorned with gold and bronze.

He suppressed it, however, without a flicker of emotion on his face, remembering what he had been taught as a child, when his stepfather had sent him away to his grandmother as a lost cause.

For everyone thought him too young, too inexperienced to walk in the wake of the man Julius Caesar, let alone the god, and too sheltered for a world where cruelties abounded as numerous as birds in the sky. They waited for him to falter, to take a wrong step.

But they did not know that he had been taught by Julia Minor herself, who had perfected the art of stillness, the silence of a marble statue.

Julia Minor had never been a particularly warm woman, but Octavius knew she had cared for him in the best way she could. Her faded voice echoed in his mind, recalling those endless days trimming leaves and picking flowers in her gardens.

Never reveal your true feelings, my dear child.

Words can only incriminate, not vindicate.

If you keep quiet, your enemies will do the work for you.

A herald then mounted the *rostra*, as was custom, to summon the accused to trial. Brutus' name rang clear as a bell three times. Then, silence.

The crowds looked around as if the man would appear, before settling hesitantly on Octavius. For everyone knew Brutus was far from Rome, somewhere in the East, though dead or alive no one could say for certain, as communication during the current turmoil had become sparse. The silence drifted into a subtle murmuring as they awaited the votes of the judges.

Suddenly one of the judges rose, his face contorted in pain. Tears wetted his cheeks as though his face were a mask of the theater, a near-comical picture of grief.

Octavius recognized him as Publius Silicius Corona, a known supporter and friend of Brutus, though he had not been implicated in his crime. *Yet,* was the grim afterthought that pierced Octavius' heart like a dagger.

Agrippa glanced at Octavius as if he had heard it. He ignored him once again, but Agrippa's warnings crept into his mind anyway. *Is that what you will tell yourself when you sentence Julius Caesar's murderers to death?*

Will you be so merciful then?

Silicius looked out at the crowds silently, before turning his gaze upon Octavius, the hatred in his eyes unmistakable. "Brutus was a brave man who risked his life to free the Roman people of a dictator who wished to be *king*. I vote for the acquittal of the accused party."

A hush descended over the crowd. Silicius sat down slowly, his burning gaze never leaving Octavius, who merely nodded and signaled for the next judge to vote. Agrippa visibly relaxed when Octavius did not retaliate, and even Silicius himself could not hide a resentful surprise. But despite the display of resistance, the rest of the judges voted one by one for Brutus' banishment and the forfeiting of his property, as the law had stated.

Octavius remained impassive as the final vote was cast, then addressed the crowd. "The court has found Marcus Junius Brutus guilty of knowingly plotting against and murdering the former consul of Rome, Gaius Julius Caesar, and is condemned to banishment."

The next prosecutor to stand before the judges was Agrippa. He gave no passionate speech, but spoke succinctly and to the point, his sea-green eyes roaming the senators and crowds as if he dared any to speak out against him.

"I stand before you, O judges, knowing you will exact justice as the gods above command, else that divine justice be exacted upon yourselves."

The threat was clear, and spoken from one in the very inner circle of Octavius rather than a little-known upstart caused the words to carry menacingly in the air. The judges shifted uneasily in their seats.

"While Brutus may be considered the face of their murderous plot, it was his co-conspirator, Gaius Cassius Longinus, who had equal if not more responsibility in the conception of the plot to murder a current consul. His undeniable calculation and execution of the assassination of Gaius Julius Caesar leaves him no less guilty than Brutus. Therefore as prosecutor, I accuse Gaius Cassius Longinus of knowingly plotting against and murdering the former consul of Rome, Gaius Julius Caesar."

Again, the judges voted him guilty one by one. Again, Octavius remained impassive as the vote was tallied. And so the trial passed without incident.

Several others knowledgeable of, involved, or associated with the plot to assassinate his great-uncle were tried and found guilty, including the Sicilian pirate Sextus Pompeius, son of Pompeius the Great.

The weak daylight waned to a dark gloom as the proceedings reached an end. Droplets of rain began to fall, slowly and sparsely at first, before they poured from the sky when the clouds above thundered. The trial was broken up as the crowds flocked to find shelter under nearby porticoes, prosecutors and judges alike hurrying down from the *rostra*.

Octavius immediately felt Agrippa by his side, leading him skillfully through the crowds to where Maecenas, Rufus, Balbus, Oppius, and Matius were already clumped together inside the Basilica Aemilia, their clothes and faces damp. They kissed each other in turn, relief visible on their faces now that the trial had concluded successfully and without any real resistance.

"That was a marvelous display of self-restraint and patience, Caesar," Balbus said at once, his rich accent thicker with emotion. "The daring of that Silicius Corona! Had Julius Caesar still lived he would not be so quick to speak!"

The comment irked Octavius immediately, and he wished to retort back that Silicius would not have spoken if he knew Octavius' true plans. But he was prevented from responding when his name was called.

He saw former consul Publius Servilius Isauricus making his way across the basilica towards them.

"Servilius Isauricus," Octavius said, smiling as Isauricus joined them. "You came to the trial?"

"I'm afraid I had some business to attend to," Isauricus said apologetically. "But I heard it was a success."

Isauricus had recently supported the Senate against Antonius, so it did not surprise Octavius that Isauricus wished to remain neutral before taking so bold a step as supporting his cause. Still, everyone knew he had been a close friend to Julius Caesar long before then.

Octavius raised a brow. "The judges voted for what they deemed right, if that is what you mean by success."

Isauricus nodded slowly, then smiled. He had night black hair, a clean-shaven face, and bright blue eyes, the kind of contrast at once eerie and beautiful. Octavius wondered briefly if his daughter would look the same.

"Would you care to take a stroll, Caesar?"

His entourage drifted away to give them some privacy. Agrippa was the last to walk away, giving him one last glance before following behind Rufus.

Isauricus allowed Octavius to set the pace as they strolled under the portico, sheltered from the pelting rain that drenched the courtyard and made the marble floor gleam.

"I hear you have just now entered into your twentieth year," Isauricus said with a raised brow. "Caesar was over twice your age when he was first consul."

"Indeed, it is an honor," Octavius said, keeping the indignation out of his voice. "You served as consul with him, did you not?"

"Yes, I did, once. Caesar was a brilliant man. He knew how to touch the hearts of many. The people loved him dearly." Isauricus glanced at him meaningfully. "But love brings just as much hate."

"It is impossible for one to be loved by everyone. Besides," Octavius added quietly, "sometimes an enemy is better to have than a friend."

"Well, I hope my friendship will still be welcomed," Isauricus answered wryly, then paused. "And that of my daughter Servilia."

They were coming to the other side of the portico just as the rain began to let up and the sky allowed sunlight to pierce through from above.

Octavius flashed his most charming smile. "Naturally, Isauricus. Your friendship is more like family after all."

⫸⫷

SEPTEMBER 43 BC

Laughter floated into the triclinium from throughout the house. Voices, men and women, filled each room, each couch.

Wealth oozed from the guests effortlessly at every turn as they flitted among each other. Here a golden bracelet entwining a delicate wrist like a snake. There a collarbone decorated with colored beads shipped from the East. Hair braided with gold leaves. Well-weaved togas clasped in bright red jewels.

It reminded Octavius of the banquets and parties Julius Caesar would host here on the Palatine after his long travels, all of his friends and their wives hiding laughs in their wine, eating delicacies only found across the ocean, their gold and jewels glittering in the fading light of evening.

He had been young then, and had not understood the importance of such gatherings, running about with the other children who understood even less. Now he understood all too well.

Octavius sensed Agrippa's discomfort from across the room. His glance kept finding its way back to Octavius even while he was speaking with some important wealthy citizens who had secretly supported Julius Caesar during the past few months of civil war.

"To think we almost lived in a time where murderers were not punished for their crimes!" someone said, feigning worry.

"These are dark times, dark times indeed," someone replied.

"And what do you think of Antonius?"

"Well, what about him? He is far away."

"And Lepidus! What a man to turn traitor..."

"They will see reason soon enough," another interjected. "Antonius has always been a friend of Caesar. He will be the friend of his son as well. Lepidus too."

"Then there's Brutus and Cassius."

"They are banished! What more can be done besides war?"

"Ah, war is inevitable these days, is it not?"

"Seems so, my friend. But Rome has survived war before."

"I am dreadfully tired of wars."

"So is everyone, my dear. But if it is for the sake of peace..."

"That is what they all say, my love. Men love war more than peace, that is the problem."

"Men? We all know it is women who start the wars. Just look at Helen!"

"Helen? What are we, Greeks?"

There was a lull in the conversation. A few heads turned his way, eyes blinking and uncertain. Most of them had hardly seen Octavius, let alone heard him speak.

"Caesar, what do you think?" one man asked him. "Do women start wars or men?"

Octavius raised a brow and smiled. He had only been half-listening to the conversation as it fluttered here and there among the current politics, his mind elsewhere. "The answer is quite obvious, is it not?" he said, then smirked. "Men start wars out of love for their mistresses, while women start wars out of spite when they find out."

The guests laughed, taking a drink of their sweet wine and moving on quickly. No topic held long in conversation, else the mood became too heavy and life had to be taken seriously.

"So Isauricus, are the rumors true?"

Isauricus reclined near Octavius, between Oppius and Maecenas, the latter quietly observing the room with a pleased smirk as if he had personally paid for the entertainment.

Servilia was somewhere in the house with her mother and other women who had migrated to the gardens, perhaps to escape the unceasing talk of politics. As Octavius braced himself for more gossip, he did not blame them.

Isauricus smiled knowingly. "I suppose it depends on what rumors you are referring to."

A tittering laugh. "Oh, be serious, Isauricus. You know I meant your daughter's engagement to the young Caesar himself."

"Ah, that rumor," Isauricus said, his icy blue eyes glittering in amusement. "I will let the young Caesar answer that."

"I will not address rumors," Octavius said. "But if you must hear it for yourselves, I am happily engaged."

"Ah! Here is a man mature beyond his years, Isauricus."

Octavius smiled politely as the conversation turned to the cost of grain, which had recently risen along with tensions in the East. Soon he felt those eyes returning, seeking him out, and Octavius in his boredom at last allowed himself to look.

He regretted it. Agrippa was already taking his leave, and his eyes merely glanced at Octavius, a silent beckon that nearly made him tremble. It was a strange feeling, like a deep, burning curiosity that hooked itself in his chest, drawing him towards that familiar shadow disappearing down the hallway.

Octavius remembered what his sister had said, the words which he had tried to bury, but which kept circling in his mind whenever he allowed it to wander. *Maybe it is loving him which you fear, and that even marriage will not stop it.*

But she was wrong. This was not love, not even close. He may love his mother, may love his wife, may love a woman he knew only for her body. But this was nothing like that.

Agrippa was a constant, a face he knew like a dream he had over and over, the only person who had seen him at his weakest and had not even flinched.

Even though he knew it was a mistake to follow after him, Octavius got up and excused himself on the pretense of making his rounds as host, hoping they could not hear the beating of his heart which roared in his ears. Only Maecenas watched him for a moment longer as he left the room.

He found Agrippa lurking around the corner of the courtyard near the private quarters of the house, where no guests had yet wandered.

"Agrippa." They locked eyes, and Agrippa's flashed dangerously. "What—"

He could not finish, his breath knocked from his chest when he was shoved into the nearest room. Julius Caesar's old office. Octavius barely registered the large wooden desk and the traditional wall paintings before Agrippa pressed him up against the wall.

"Every day, Octavius."

Octavius stared at him. His chest was rising and falling too fast. Agrippa hovered in front of him, hands braced against the wall on either side of Octavius' head, his eyes shut tight as though he could not stand to look at him.

"What?" Octavius sounded breathless.

He could hardly comprehend anything. He felt Agrippa's lips brush his, then pull away, the brief sensation like a dull ache in his chest.

"Every day I want you," Agrippa whispered against his mouth. "Every day I must stop myself from kissing you. I cannot do it anymore."

Do you suppose a kiss has a price?

"Agrippa."

"Do not say my name," he said quietly. "I cannot bear it."

But it was the only thing he could say. The only word that could make it past his tightening throat, like a warning, a question. "Agrippa—"

Agrippa kissed him, as if it were the only way to shut him up.

For a moment Octavius forgot how to resist, the mouth on his sweet from fruit and wine. Then his body moved automatically, his hands grasping the thick strands of Agrippa's hair, tugging at the curls, bringing him closer, his mouth closer, hips closer, until the world narrowed to the space between them.

Octavius felt reckless. Dangerous. Anyone might find them, anyone might stumble upon this room. Yet with Agrippa's hands traveling up his arms, down his sides, tracing a dangerous path, Octavius could not find it in himself to care.

Their kiss was more heated than the first they had shared after the battle. He felt Agrippa's hands rifling with his tunic, fingertips brushing cold sparks against his warm skin. If he never pulled away, how far would they go?

Footsteps.

He pushed Agrippa away without a thought, who was too unaware to protest. Octavius rapidly adjusted his tunic as he ran to the door, which in their rush had been left open a sliver.

There was no one there. Octavius looked across the courtyard and thought he caught sight of the swish of a stola disappearing around the corner. Impossible. Even in the heat of the moment, Octavius would have known if someone had been watching, wouldn't he?

It is the people who will care. It is your enemies who will care.

Octavius shivered. "I thought I heard..."

He felt rattled, as if a broad sword had slammed into his helmet and left the world quaking in its wake. He glanced at Agrippa, who was watching him carefully, quietly, but he did not move to make him stay. They both knew what had happened could not happen again.

"I must return to the guests," Octavius said, his voice steady, though he could not meet Agrippa's eyes. "Do not follow me right away."

Agrippa nodded, looking away, still flushed. "Yes, Caesar."

Octavius stared at him in surprise and opened his mouth to speak before he thought better of it. After a beat of silence, he left.

20
MARCUS VIPSANIUS AGRIPPA

SEPTEMBER 43 BC

T HERE WAS NO FEELING like leaving Rome.

Although he had not grown up in the city, Agrippa had long ago felt the allure of its power, like standing at the breathing, beating heart of the world. The past enveloped the city walls in a timeless spell, while the towering columns of temples stood as beacons of the future.

In fact, he believed as an outsider the city spoke to him the more, beckoning him to explore her winding roads, intoxicated by the grime, the noise, and the crowds, dizzying in their simultaneous grandeur and depravity.

To leave such a place, to watch the lofty temples and extravagant villas, the stacked apartments and narrow streets, the people crowding the forums and gathering in basilicas, to see all of it swallowed up by the high, ringed stone wall, sinking like a ship amidst rolling hills, caused the breath to leave his chest, as if the city's very air had been necessary for life.

Yet the moment he lost sight of that precarious place, the urban tether cut and the rambling Italic countryside seamlessly unfolding as the carriage trudged onward, oblivious to one's heartache, the world itself suddenly felt pure, untouched, even peaceful in its eternal equilibrium, a darting animal in the grass, a bird singing in the distance, an overgrown thicket of brambling trees appearing effortlessly on the slope of a hill.

Agrippa was reminded that the world was wide and welcoming, and that nothing truly mattered but the sun on one's face.

Except everything mattered nowadays.

"Agrippa."

Octavius sat across from him in the carriage. He looked at Agrippa with the intensity of the setting sun, half-hidden under lidded eyes.

Agrippa looked back warily, his chest knotting up and making it difficult to breathe. "Yes?"

"We are staying the night in Arretium." Then Octavius looked away, and the feeling faded. "The camp is five miles away, but I thought we could stay with Maecenas."

Agrippa nodded, trying to appear unbothered. Why did Octavius look at him like that? Ever since they had almost gotten caught at that banquet, Octavius had been strange, somewhere between flighty and heated, but never settling.

They both knew it was unavoidable. When they were with other people they could hardly look each other in the eyes without flushing or losing track of the conversation. Yet Agrippa sensed Octavius' reluctance to give in entirely, as if he were afraid of what would happen when he did.

"Will Maecenas come with us to Bononia?" Agrippa asked, less because he was curious and more to prevent Octavius from returning to that stubborn silence.

"No. Maecenas is entertaining some guests. He wished me to meet them tonight."

Octavius continued to look out the carriage window, watching the wild hills grow higher and higher as they climbed the incline into town. His brows were furrowed, and he sounded distracted, as if he were thinking hard about something else.

"Oh?"

"Poets, supposedly." Octavius glanced at Agrippa, then quickly returned to staring out the small window. "Maecenas hopes I will invest."

"Poets?" Agrippa watched Octavius' eyes flit back and forth as the first farms and houses appeared along the road, the brown irises reflected with blue and green. His brevity annoyed Agrippa more when they had so much to talk about, and he could not refrain from bickering. "What good are poets in political negotiations? This is a time of war and weapons, not words."

"The weapons of poets *are* words, my dear Agrippa," Octavius said coolly, not taking the bait. "Poets can be very helpful if they are paid well. In time you will see that a spear cannot pierce hearts like a well-turned phrase, and hence why Maecenas is such a valuable friend."

"That may be true," Agrippa said, sounding sullen. "But poetry will not help you with Antonius and Lepidus if it comes to a fight."

"Neither will weapons if it comes to negotiation."

"You are impossible, Octavius."

Octavius raised a challenging brow. "So it is Octavius, then? Not Caesar?"

Agrippa's face grew hot, and he could not look away from that dark gaze. "Do not act as if I am in the wrong."

"Oh, so I am, then?"

"You can hardly look at me," Agrippa said angrily. "When I have been nothing but honest with you."

"Honest?" Octavius repeated, disbelieving. "There is nothing honest about this."

Agrippa felt the words as sharp as a dagger. Perhaps Octavius was right about poets after all. The thought made him laugh, and the sound was jarring in the small carriage. Octavius looked at him in reproach.

"War is coming," Octavius said quietly, as if that explained everything. "We cannot afford a mistake."

Agrippa was silent. Octavius' expression was shuttered, impenetrable like a wall of ice. It terrified Agrippa as nothing had before.

He had been so wrong, so terribly wrong, to hope that Octavius would surrender after a mere kiss. The carriage jolted violently as they left behind the dirt roads of the country and rode on the muddy stone streets of the city.

"We are almost there."

Agrippa nodded. His chest tightened when Octavius returned gazing outside the window. They remained in silence for the rest of the ride.

⭑⭑⭑

"Welcome, Caesar!" Maecenas could not hold back a smile as he greeted them. "I am so glad you found the time to dine with us tonight. I know you are a very busy man now."

Ever since Octavius had become consul it had been fashionable to host him, and Maecenas loved that he had gained a reputation as one of Octavius' oldest friends.

Octavius returned the smile easily, as if nothing had happened in the carriage ride. Agrippa supposed nothing had. "I always have time for you, my friend."

Agrippa followed silently as Maecenas led them into the house. He heard a cough behind him and realized he had forgotten that Rufus would join them instead of retiring in the camps.

Rufus lingered between him and Balbus, looking slightly dejected, while Oppius and Matius were dismounting their carriage nearby.

"Tell me, Caesar," Maecenas began. "What has happened since I last left you all in Rome? How is my dear Octavia and Marcellus?"

"All is well," Octavius said with clear amusement at Maecenas' questioning. "Pedius is managing my affairs while I am traveling."

"Oh dear, I hope the Senate does not trouble him too much!" But Maecenas did not sound like he really cared for the fate of Pedius. He gave Octavius a side glance full of that

183

sharp curiosity that truly kindled his heart. "I suppose you must be thinking of war if you are traveling with your troops."

"Nonsense," Octavius said with a grin. "I am sure all the fighting will long be over by the time my troops and I find either Decimus or Antonius. Besides, Decimus' recruits have already abandoned him. Our scouts have notified us that they plan to join me as we march north."

"Well, that is convenient," Maecenas muttered. "Decimus will not last long on his own so far north. It is only a matter of time before Antonius finds him, or worse. And the only thing worse than a Roman enemy is a barbarian one."

There was an uncertain pause as they walked down the hall, Octavius and Agrippa sharing a glance, their footsteps loud in the silence. Soon they reached the triclinium where his guests were reclining.

Besides a few familiar faces who had dined with Maecenas before, Agrippa noticed a large figure confidently draped on the couch, glancing at them with interest and an indulgent smile. Beside him, barely noticeable, was a boy who flicked his eyes to Octavius and then Agrippa before quickly looking away.

Maecenas smiled widely as they entered the room. "My lovely guests, though he needs no introduction, I am happy to welcome the current consul and my most beloved friend, Gaius Julius Caesar, to our party."

All the guests bowed their heads respectfully, concealing their wide eyes. Agrippa wondered if he would ever become accustomed to such a grand reception.

"And these are our most trusty friends," Maecenas added. "Lucius Cornelius Balbus, Gaius Oppius, Gaius Matius, Quintus Salvius Salvidienus Rufus, and Marcus Vipsanius Agrippa."

"Thank you for the introduction," Octavius said warmly, but otherwise unaffected by such an entrance. "Now, please, Maecenas, introduce your guests."

Maecenas pointed to the taller man whom Agrippa had first noticed. His hair upon closer observation was such a reddish auburn it gave a glow to his face like a flame. "This is Lucius Varius Rufus, the next great poet of Rome."

"You flatter me, Maecenas," Varius said carelessly, a knowing smile on his face. "But I assure you I merely cannot succeed at anything else."

"He is humble too," Maecenas added, and the room laughed. "But he has read some of his verses to me and they are simply delightful." He laid a hand on Octavius' arm, and Agrippa swore Maecenas did it just to infuriate him, though there was no reason for him to know that it did. "For the many years I have known Caesar, I have never met a man so keen on the arts. It quite becomes a great leader, does it not?"

"I am sure Varius will accomplish great things in the years to come," Octavius said, inclining his head politely. Then his gaze passed on to the thin, lanky boy beside Varius, who seemed to shrink under the attention. "And who is this?"

Maecenas smiled as if he knew all along the boy would catch Octavius' interest. "This is Publius Vergilius Maro, whom Varius says will be the best poet in Rome."

"In the *world*," Varius said, his smile teasing but in such a serious tone that Octavius raised a brow. "I said Vergilius will be the best poet in the world."

Vergilius, who had not spoken a word yet, shook his head, embarrassed. "Homer is the best poet in the world. I am only his disciple."

At the low voice, Agrippa suddenly realized he was not a boy at all, but at least a few years older than Agrippa himself. His features were soft but strong, with full lips and a firm brow, high cheekbones balanced by a square jaw, a straight nose, and a dimple in the chin. The strangest feature was his hair, cut short and rough, somewhere between blonde and light brown, like a field of wheat after it rains.

Octavius looked at Vergilius in surprise. "You are from the north, are you not, Vergilius?"

"Yes." There was a tinge of pride in his voice, though it was said quietly. "Cisalpine Gaul. Near Mantua."

"Do you like Rome?" Octavius asked, though it was clear Vergilius did not wish to converse any longer, glancing at Varius as if he wished him to continue the conversation for him.

"Yes, I do."

"You prefer the country," said Octavius, watching him in amusement. "I can tell."

"Who does not?" Maecenas interrupted, leading them to their seats. Vergilius looked relieved at the deflection, but wary as Octavius and Agrippa reclined opposite him. "Nature is the purest setting for life."

"I did not realize civilization made humans unnatural," Agrippa murmured, though not truly meaning to voice his thoughts aloud. Varius glanced at him curiously.

"Are we not unnatural?" Varius asked. "We alter the land to fit our needs. No other being does such a thing."

"What is the difference between an anthill and a house built of wood?" Agrippa countered.

He ignored Octavius' glance his way. He rarely spoke during dinner parties, but for some reason, he felt the need to speak now, if only for the sake of arguing with someone when Octavius would not.

Varius smiled. "We are the difference. Humans are too interesting to be mere creatures."

"And yet," Agrippa said, smirking, "what more do we want than food, drink, and pleasure?"

Varius laughed but did not answer, his gaze lingering on Agrippa in approval. He felt rather than saw Octavius' heated gaze on him, and he ignored the rush of satisfaction that followed.

"Knowledge of the gods," Vergilius suddenly said. "Ants do not pray. They do not need to."

"Why not?" Octavius asked. There was a murmuring laugh among the guests. "Perhaps ants have their own gods."

"Only the gods would know," Vergilius replied.

"Or the ants," Octavius countered with a smile as the rest of their company laughed.

Vergilius nodded in reluctant agreement, and the conversation turned to the latest harvest, which Maecenas argued was the most plentiful his villa had ever had.

It was not long before most of the party retired besides Maecenas, Octavius, Rufus, and the two poets, leaving a more intimate group in the lamplight. Agrippa remained quiet and disinterested until talk circled the current situation of Decimus Brutus and Marcus Antonius.

"The Senate must know Decimus does not stand a chance," Maecenas said, looking at Octavius in concern. "They can hardly expect him to defeat the forces of Antonius *and* Lepidus with hardly an army at his back."

"It does not matter what they expect. The Senate had a chance to do right by the memory of my divine father and they chose to pardon his murderers," Octavius said. "They could not expect Antonius to remain on their side for long. Now it is only a question of whether Antonius will return to Rome as an ally or an enemy, and whether we should join or fight him."

"There are also the *Conspiratores* to think about," Rufus added. "Even if our troops did wish to fight Antonius—which they do not—and they miraculously defeated him, could they sustain their strength enough to then face the armies amassing in the East?"

"Antonius is now allied with Lepidus, Pollio, and most likely Plancus as well. A win against such an army could not be guaranteed," Agrippa said gravely. "Besides, if we wish to defeat the *Conspiratores,* we will need more troops. There is only one course of action which would truly secure the downfall of Brutus and Cassius."

"An alliance with Antonius," Maecenas said with a sigh.

"But it is dangerous," Rufus pointed out. "How can we guarantee Antonius will not betray you after you pardon him?"

"Oh he will betray me," Octavius said calmly. "In fact, I am counting on it." He looked at Vergilius. "What say you, Vergilius?"

Vergilius' cheeks stained with a blush at the attention, but he did not back down from the critical eyes of Octavius, who waited patiently for his answer. "Antonius would be a valuable ally at the present moment, but he is not to be trusted. His actions allowed the *Conspiratores* to be pardoned. His only aim is power, nothing more."

"And you believe mine is not?" Octavius asked, testing.

Agrippa held his breath as Vergilius paused. Maecenas glanced between them nervously. At that moment there was a flash of steel in Vergilius' eyes that had until then remained hidden. *The weapons of poets* are *words, my dear Agrippa.*

"I believe your aim is peace," Vergilius said finally. "But as with our founder Aeneas, power is the road you must take to find it."

Octavius smiled.

⤜⤛

The carriage rattled as it traversed the rough dirt paths winding from Arretium up toward the mountains in the north. Octavius was staring out the window, just as he had on the journey here, so that the night spent with Maecenas and his poets felt like a dream.

"Antonius will try to gain the upper hand in any alliance," Agrippa murmured. "If he does not try to kill you first."

"Let him have the upper hand." Octavius did not look at him. "An alliance would be temporary."

"Still, he is dangerous."

A small smile. "You sound like Rufus."

"Octavius," Agrippa said, his voice low. "Look at me."

Octavius looked at him, his smile fading and his eyes dark and piercing.

Suddenly they were too close to each other and too far away at the same time. Agrippa wanted to touch him. He wanted to leave the carriage. It was almost too much, then not enough.

"You are not only bargaining yourself," Agrippa whispered. "You are bargaining *lives.*"

"What are you suggesting?" Octavius asked angrily.

"I'm merely reminding you that this is more than politics." Agrippa leaned forward, watching Octavius lower his eyes, as though the mere sight of him was disagreeable. "This is the future of the Roman people."

Before Octavius could respond, the carriage jolted to a stop.

Agrippa sat up straight, his hand finding the hilt of his dagger that he kept hidden at his hip. There was a knock on the door of the carriage.

"Caesar, sir," said a young but authoritative voice. It was one of their men. "A scout has returned with a message from Marcus Antonius."

"Open the door," Octavius said, meeting Agrippa's eyes briefly before facing the soldier, who turned toward the scout standing at attention beside him. "What news?"

"Decimus Brutus has been killed, sir. Marcus Antonius requests a meeting."

21

MARCUS ANTONIUS

OCTOBER 43 BC

A CRISP WIND RUSTLED through the hills as they approached the Rhenus River snaking around the city of Bononia.

Antonius caught sight of a small island enveloped by rushing streams, crossed by a bridge on both banks. He lifted a hand as he eased to a stop on his horse, hearing his cavalry clatter to a halt behind him. Lepidus did the same from the other side of the river.

Ahead of Antonius a third cavalry unit approached slowly over the horizon, one horse slightly ahead of the rest, creeping closer until he could make out their faces. The figure leading them faced the sun, and for a moment the sharp silhouette lit up like the carved gold bust of Julius Caesar.

Then a shadow covered his face and Antonius was reminded of a very different person, standing in a shaded atrium all those years ago, cloaked in an indifference that hid within an even harder spirit. He remembered being terrified of it.

"Salve, Marcus Antonius," Octavius called out once he was a few feet away, reigning his horse to a stop, his cavalry doing the same.

Antonius could just glimpse Octavius' infantry marching in the distance, matching the infantry that he and Lepidus had brought with them as agreed upon prior to the meeting. Octavius' second in command, Marcus Agrippa, rode next to him, though he remained silent as always.

"Who shall secure the island?"

"Lepidus," Antonius said, turning his horse aside and trotting to the edge of the river where the bridge began.

Octavius did the same, sidling up beside him. Perhaps the boy thought pleasantries would still get him far, but the time for niceties had long since passed.

Lepidus dismounted his horse and crossed the other bridge alone, dressed in his priestly garb for the occasion. He scouted the island, searching around trees and bushes for any

189

sign of mischief before waving his cloak.

"All clear!" Lepidus called out.

Antonius motioned for one of his attendants, who brought forth three chairs. Then together he and Octavius dismounted their horses and crossed the bridge, meeting Lepidus in the center, on full display for their legions but conveniently out of earshot.

"*Salve*, Praetor Caesar," Lepidus said politely, though his eyes briefly met Antonius' with a glimmer of playfulness. "*Salve*, Propraetor Antonius. Shall we sit?"

They sat, with Octavius in the center as consul, Lepidus and Antonius beside him. Antonius disliked the apparent importance this displayed to his troops, but everyone knew Octavius did not have the upper hand today.

For a moment, no one spoke, each of them looking at the other two men, as if attempting to read each other's thoughts. Lepidus gestured for Octavius to begin—not as a sign of deference, Antonius knew, but as a challenge.

Octavius nodded, and gazing at the crowds of troops watching them intently, began to speak. "We gather today as three men, devoted to the cause of my divine father Julius Caesar, not as enemies. For the real enemies lie in the East, those who murdered my father, and we are the only ones who can defeat them. Thus I propose an alliance of three men, charged with the restoration of the Republic and eradicating anyone who opposes it."

"And so it begins," Lepidus said softly, eyeing Antonius curiously, waiting for his response.

"An alliance of three men, you say?" Antonius smiled, staring at Octavius, who sat perfectly calm, as though he forged alliances every day. "I suppose you think we will be like Pompeius, Caesar, and Crassus. But with a different ending, I would hope?"

"Yes, this would be different," Octavius said, the ghost of a smile appearing on his lips. "Our alliance would be law. We would legally and equally hold dominion over the entire empire, with Italy remaining neutral territory of course."

"And how do you propose we divvy up the empire amongst three men?" Antonius asked with a sneer. "Draw lots?"

"Not unless you wish to, *Propraetor,*" Octavius said, infuriatingly polite. He did not show it but Antonius sensed the taunt in his voice.

"I will not gamble the empire away, *boy,*" Antonius snapped. "I will govern Cisalpine and Transalpine Gaul or I will end this alliance before it begins."

Lepidus eyed Antonius warily. "As I am currently proconsul of Transalpine Gaul as well as Hispania, it only makes sense for me to retain command of those provinces. Perhaps you may be persuaded to govern Gallia Comata instead?"

Antonius knew he would have to give up some power to his allies, and it was still not in his best interest to anger Lepidus while he still held command of formidable forces.

Besides, it was better that Lepidus controlled Transalpine Gaul than the boy.

"I accept the offer. Then that leaves Africa, Sicily, and Sardinia for you, *Caesar*."

It was not a question. Antonius and Lepidus looked at Octavius as he realized he would be left with the only provinces which still needed to be conquered, and with no say in the matter.

But the boy merely inclined his head, his eyes steady and undaunted. "Then that covers it."

"There is still the matter of legality," Antonius said. "The Senate will see us as nothing more than dictators."

"Not dictators," Octavius said, then paused, thinking. "We will be *Tresviri*. It is the truth after all."

"The three men?" Antonius grinned. "You have a way with words which could get you in trouble, boy."

Octavius looked annoyed at his patronizing tone but did not reply. Lepidus cleared his throat. "I do like the sound of that. *Tresviri rei publicae constituendae.* The three men who will establish the Republic."

"With consul power," Octavius added quietly. "We must limit our terms as well, perhaps to five years. We would hold equal power to the consuls with the ability to pass laws. Of course, we must also attend to our troops. I have already marked out the cities most productive for farming."

Antonius waved a hand, disliking the natural authority in the boy's voice and wishing to think more on the subject before agreeing blindly to whatever he proposed.

"We can discuss the details later. But first, we must cement this alliance properly before moving forward. Therefore, *Propraetor* Lepidus, I offer my daughter, Antonia, as a wife for your son, Marcus Aemilius Lepidus Minor."

Lepidus nodded. They had discussed this part of the alliance between the two of them beforehand. "I accept your offer."

Antonius turned to Octavius, and he was surprised to see reluctance as their eyes met. "And *Praetor* Caesar, I offer my step-daughter, Clodia, as your wife. She is young, but then again, so are you. It would be a good match. You must not worry about Isauricus—he will be rewarded for his sacrifice."

Octavius paused as he thought over the implications of this engagement, his jaw tightening before he nodded. "I accept your offer."

"Good. And there was another thing," Antonius said, feigning to ponder something over, then raised a finger in the air. "Ah, yes. The consulship."

Octavius raised a brow.

"You will step down for the rest of the year." Antonius gauged his reaction, but

Octavius merely looked at him. "I propose Ventidius as *consul suffectus.*"

"Agreed. And *I* propose we appoint consuls for the next five years," Octavius said, smiling when Antonius could not hide his surprise. "It would promote good faith, and ensure a peaceful transfer of power."

"Agreed," Antonius said, beginning to feel that uneasiness that had become familiar around Octavius creep into his stomach again.

It was more than his uncanny similarity to Julius Caesar; the ambition, the charm, the edge of cruelty necessary to rule. What Antonius feared lurked far deeper than the traces of a dead man, but rather flitted in those dark eyes like a shadow in the night, a natural secretiveness which was more dangerous, more powerful, than any outward display.

Antonius had only ever seen this in two people—a mother and a queen—and they were the most terrifying people he had ever met.

"We must not forget my divine father and his supporters," Octavius added. "The Senate and magistrates must swear an oath to maintain all the acts of Julius Caesar as dictator. He ought to be deified according to custom, with a temple to Divus Iulius built in the forum."

"These are no small demands," Antonius said sarcastically, though he felt his dread grow heavier in his chest. "But I suppose they are necessary."

"Necessary and right."

"We shall see," Antonius muttered, unable to admit that the boy might, after all, be right.

"Let us conclude this meeting and retire for the afternoon," Lepidus said wearily, standing up. The troops watching across the river shifted at the first sign of movement. "We may reconvene later to discuss the finer details of our alliance. Then we may also announce the good news to the soldiers. But first, let us dine."

⇻≫≫ ≪≪↢

"The young Caesar is much more amiable than you have made him out to be," Lepidus said, taking a careful sip of his wine.

They were sitting in Antonius' tent, drafting letters to their constituents and agents in Rome and abroad. After two full days of negotiations and dinners, they had reached an agreement on all facets of their new alliance and the legal technicalities. While Octavius certainly had a knack for politics, Antonius had made sure he strengthened his own position by appointing consuls whom he knew would ultimately support himself over Octavius if it ever came to that.

Then Octavius had announced to their soldiers the terms of the new alliance, including the cities chosen for the promised settlement of veteran soldiers—eighteen in total—and the soldiers had turned their minds to celebration.

Now the night brought on more dangerous conversation, along with that paranoia peculiar to politicians which Antonius had come to know all too well.

"That is merely an act, my dear Lepidus," Antonius said impatiently. "He chooses his battles well."

"I fear you give him far too much credit," Lepidus drawled. "He is only a boy."

"And I fear you give him too little. We are entering into an alliance with him after all."

Lepidus frowned. "He is no longer consul. He will govern provinces against which he will have to win wars, not mere battles. His popularity will wane, his name will fall into oblivion, and the people will turn to the true restorers of the Republic."

"He is no longer consul because of *us*," Antonius countered. "We have given him much more power than he deserves."

"What other choice did we have?" Lepidus asked with a yawn. "It is not worth worrying over when we will have much greater worries in the near future. Brutus and Cassius have not been idle all these months abroad, I assure you that."

"Yes, I suppose," Antonius agreed grudgingly.

Suddenly there was a shuffle outside their tent, and his guards entered and announced the presence of Gaius Julius Caesar. He and Lepidus shared a glance before the boy was admitted into the tent.

"Propraetor Antonius. Propraetor Lepidus," Octavius said, bowing his head, though Antonius thought he saw the edge of a smirk on his mouth before it disappeared. "Good evening."

"I am glad you could join us, Caesar," Lepidus said in his offhand manner.

"Of course," Octavius said lightly. "There is still much to discuss." He took his place on the third couch they had left empty.

"Then let us begin," Antonius said. "Naturally, the Senate will sanction our alliance and approve all our acts. Then we will declare war on Brutus and Cassius."

"I will remain in Rome as consul with Plancus for the following year," Lepidus added, reiterating what they had already decided upon. "I will retain command over only three legions, while the rest will be transferred to both of your commands for the duration of the war."

"Correct." Antonius paused. They all knew the dangers of leaving Rome so vulnerable after the recent turmoil. "But now we must decide on a course of action pertaining to certain enemies in Rome who could prove a threat to the restoration of the Republic while we are at war."

Octavius raised a brow. "And by that, you are referring to Cicero?"

"Not only Cicero," Antonius said with a wry smile. "One thing you will learn, Caesar, is that power always makes more enemies than friends. And we cannot afford to keep around any more enemies."

"I see," Octavius said, nodding slowly. "You wish to proscribe them, as Sulla did."

"It is the only way."

"How many?" Octavius asked.

"As many as those who supported Brutus and Cassius, as well as any wealthy private citizens who might harbor resentment towards the Caesarian cause," Lepidus replied grimly. "We must take no chances."

"You will have a say in the composition of the list, of course," Antonius said. "And we will not be merciful, even to our own families. This is a matter of their death, or ours."

"Then let us begin," Octavius said, echoing Antonius' earlier phrase. "But I do have a suggestion, if I may."

Antonius raised a brow, and Lepidus nodded. "Of course."

"There are certain persons who must be eliminated for the safety of our cause, are there not? Such as Cicero, for one."

"Yes." Antonius was already weary of the boy's incessant suggesting.

"And there are others who must be eliminated for their wealth more so than the immediate danger they pose alive," Octavius continued.

"What are you suggesting?" Antonius asked impatiently.

"I am suggesting that a preliminary list be sent to my colleague, Pedius, before the people are notified. Then the city gates can be closed, and we may ensure that those *proscripti* will be eliminated without risk of their escape. If the list is short, the people will be less likely to revolt or flee, believing that no more will be proscribed. Once our alliance is affirmed by the Senate, then we may publish a longer list, and allow those *proscripti* to choose whether they flee or not, and give the citizens the power to dispense justice. After all, it is important that we remain the saviors of the Republic, not her executioners."

Lepidus stared at the boy in surprise. He glanced at Antonius as if *he* had been the one concealing this plan all along. "You speak sense. But how can you guarantee that the people will turn against each other so easily?"

"Money," Antonius said, unable to hide his annoyance at the boy's uncanny ability to wriggle his plans into theirs, just as Julius Caesar had his whole life. "I suppose we can offer provincial offices and city magistracies as rewards to those who prove their loyalty. After all, nothing ensures murder more than a bounty on another man's head."

Octavius nodded. "The results will certainly not be orderly, but that can hardly be expected. The most important thing is eliminating our most dangerous enemies and raising enough funds to declare war against Brutus and Cassius."

"Then we are in agreement?" Lepidus asked. "These times are not for the faint of heart."

"Yes," Octavius said, his expression unreadable beyond the outward calm he wished others to see. "We are."

Antonius smiled, procuring a piece of parchment and a metal pen, the tip stained with ink, the black shining red like blood in the lamplight. "Then let us begin."

⁂

Several hours passed before the list was completed in full. Then Lepidus and Octavius retired to their camps for a night of rest before beginning their long march back to Rome.

Antonius lingered by his desk where the only evidence of the list remained in a bottle of ink and scrapped parchment. The preliminary list had already been sent ahead to Pedius as Octavius had suggested. Antonius envisioned the ensuing chaos, and then the silence of death as the sword swung.

He should rest, but his thoughts kept him awake. A few months ago he had thought a more stable position of power would solve all of his problems, but now he felt less secure than before. There was no one he could trust, not even his closest friends, not even his family.

Lepidus and Octavius knew as well as he that their alliance was temporary, and not only due to the limited term. The day would come when one of them would rise more powerful than the others, and Antonius intended it to be him.

There was only one person he could trust, and she was far, far away. Still, her location in the East and her fresh supply of soldiers and resources could be valuable in the upcoming war. Antonius knew she would come to his aid if he asked. If all else failed, he had her.

He unrolled more papyrus and dipped his pen in the ink.

My dearest Cleopatra...

22

GAIUS OCTAVIUS

OCTOBER 43 BC

OCTAVIUS ENTERED HIS TENT where Agrippa, Balbus, and Rufus were waiting for him. It was well into the night but no one seemed tired in the slightest, all of them standing up quickly at his entrance.

"Well?" Agrippa asked when no one else spoke.

He sighed, unable to hide his exhaustion. "It is done. We make for Rome at dawn."

Only Agrippa did not look relieved, his brow raised. Balbus stepped forward and embraced Octavius, his tenderness hardly a comfort to the heaviness within, but Octavius returned the embrace nonetheless.

"You did well, son," Balbus said.

"Thank you, Balbus. But I assure you there is still a long way to go."

Rufus embraced him next. "I shall ready the troops."

"Thank you, Rufus."

Octavius remained standing until Balbus and Rufus left the tent.

Agrippa stood across from him, who had been watching him in silence as the others had congratulated him. They did not move for several long moments, the quiet filling the space between them. Octavius wondered when it had become so difficult to say even the most simple words, and whether he was responsible for it.

"Speak, Agrippa."

"It is done?"

"Yes," Octavius said wearily.

"Then there will be death." Agrippa looked grim, and Octavius nodded, his head heavy. "How many?"

"Seventeen." A twinge of guilt. "Cicero included."

"As I expected," Agrippa said, not meeting Octavius' eyes. "Has the list been sent already?"

"Yes. Soldiers, too," Octavius said, and paused. "It will be over when we arrive."

Agrippa nodded, taking a deep breath. "Then we best ride quickly. Pedius will need support when the chaos begins." He looked at Octavius, started as if he were to approach him, then stopped short, looking away. *This is the future of the Roman people.*

Octavius envisioned Rome as he saw her, tall and proud, and the future he had in mind for her which even Agrippa did not know entirely, the reformed government and army, the paved roads snaking far and wide to places yet unseen, temples and forums and basilicas shining in marble and gold from his many conquests, newly built and towering towards the sky. Then he saw the streets running with blood, bodies piled on burning pyres in the forum, and the Tiber flowing red.

Agrippa watched him carefully as if he could read his thoughts. "Octavius?"

He nodded, Agrippa's voice pulling him from dangerous thoughts. "There is something else."

Agrippa paled. "Yes?"

"I will be breaking off my engagement with Servilia," Octavius said, the words spoken without emotion. "Antonius has offered me his daughter, Clodia, in marriage."

"And you accepted?" Agrippa asked after a long moment.

"Yes."

There was another silence. It was nothing. It meant nothing. And yet, Octavius could not look at the hurt that flashed ever so briefly on Agrippa's face. Why did every choice feel like a betrayal, no matter which he chose? How could they be so close and so far away at the same time?

"We must rest," Octavius said finally.

Agrippa nodded. He walked towards the exit, passing Octavius without looking at him.

For a moment, Octavius thought he would leave, just like that. But then his hand was around Octavius' neck, and their lips brushed with such suddenness that Octavius reeled back, caught only by Agrippa's arm around his waist. They were breathing hard, too hard for nothing. *Nothing, nothing, nothing.*

Agrippa's eyes searched his, the sea-green as startling as the first day they had met. Octavius could scarcely hold himself up, as though only a touch from him and his body forgot its own strength. This was dangerous. A wave of want rippled through him so intensely that Octavius closed his eyes.

The arm left his waist.

Octavius staggered and his eyes opened. The flap of the tent rustled in the wind.

He was alone.

⤜⤛⤚ ⤝⤞⤟

NOVEMBER 43 BC

Their carriage rolled swiftly down the Via Flaminia as Rome came into view on the other side of the hills ahead.

Agrippa was asleep across from him, resting his head on the side of the carriage which rattled with every small bump and dip of the muddy stone road beneath them.

Octavius watched as Agrippa roused himself and yawned. It was a simple, innocent gesture that reminded him of their days in Apollonia, sleeping on the beach after a long day of training and waking up when the tide tickled their feet.

"We are almost there," Octavius said quietly.

Agrippa nodded, avoiding his gaze. The latest report was that Rome had descended into a frenzy when the people woke up to the death of four senators in the streets, the city gates locking the rest of them in. Pedius had the list published the following day according to the instructions of the *Tresviri,* promising in a public statement that only those on the list would fall. Since then, they had heard nothing else from the city, as if life had simply stopped. For some, Octavius supposed, it had.

"Antonius is already in the city," Octavius said. A messenger had reached them on one of their brief stops while Agrippa remained in the carriage to sleep. "Lepidus will arrive tomorrow or the next. We will begin the process of legalizing our alliance as soon as possible."

"I hope you know what you are doing, Octavius," Agrippa muttered, his voice still laden with sleep. "There is a fine line between revenge and murder."

"I do," Octavius said. "And this is not revenge. It is justice."

Agrippa nodded again, but his eyes told a different story.

"It is the only way," Octavius said, turning away.

There was no point justifying it anymore. This was murder, names written in cold blood. It was no battle. It was not fair. But it was war, and war was many things.

Soon they stopped just outside the city gates. From here they would march, as vehicles were prohibited within the city at this hour. Octavius had scarcely exited the carriage when one of his messengers approached, running frantically up the road to their party.

Octavius stepped forward, his heart beating loud. Had it already happened so soon?

"What news?" Agrippa asked when Octavius did not speak, cutting him a questioning glance.

The messenger slowed to a panting stop. He had to have sprinted several miles at the very least. "It is Praetor Pedius, sir. He died late in the night. The doctor said it was from a sudden illness."

The chaos had begun.

⤜⤜⤜ ⤛⤛⤛

He sat in Julius Caesar's old desk, staring out the window at the city below. Never had he heard Rome so quiet, so still, as if it had been abandoned overnight. No, as if she were a graveyard.

A gentle breeze, too gentle for the circumstances, rolled into the room, carrying the sickly sweet scent of decaying leaves and rotting, overripe fruit from the gardens. He thought he heard a scream far off in the distance, but it could have just been the wind in the trees.

The door opened. Agrippa walked in.

Octavius turned and tried to hide his alarm. "What are you doing here?"

"You have been avoiding me," Agrippa said, with a calmness that Octavius feared more than his anger, for it meant disappointment.

"I have been busy." Octavius looked away from the fierce green of his eyes which lit up with indignation at his words. "We have been arranging Pedius' funeral. And a *consul suffectus.*"

"When were you planning to tell me?" Agrippa asked, and Octavius nearly winced when his voice wavered.

"Tell you what?" Octavius asked. Why was he always in the wrong these days?

"A second list," Agrippa said flatly. "That there was a second list of names."

Octavius stood up and walked towards the window, if only so he did not have to look at Agrippa. "We swore an oath of secrecy. I could not risk it. Besides, I knew you would find out eventually."

"You could have told me." Agrippa joined him by the window, looking out at the empty streets. He sounded more resigned than anything else, as if he had expected nothing less but had hoped for more anyway. "You could have trusted me."

"You are the only person I trust," Octavius said bitterly. He knew it was useless to lie any longer. Agrippa could always see right through him.

"Then why?" Agrippa turned towards him and placed a hand on his arm. The firm touch alone was dizzying. Octavius swallowed as his stomach turned, desire bordering on nausea. "Why did you not tell me?"

"I could not say it." His voice was a mere whisper. "I could not..."

"Do you regret it?"

"No," Octavius said harshly, his unbending will saving him from further embarrassment. It was the truth, after all. He did not regret it. He moved his arm abruptly and

199

Agrippa's hand dropped to his side. "It is necessary."

"Just tell me this. Are there more?"

Octavius did not answer at first. A faint scream rose up from somewhere in the hidden alleys not visible from their vantage point. *These times are not for the faint of heart.* He shivered. "Yes. There is another list."

"I see."

"Most will not die," Octavius said, though he did not know who he was trying to convince anymore. "The gates have been opened to allow for their escape."

Agrippa was silent.

"You think it wrong."

"Yes."

I do not consider you a monster. I am only afraid that you may become one.

Octavius shrugged. "There are times when one wrong is necessary for a more necessary right."

"This is more than wrong. This is slaughter."

"Oh really? What about soldiers in war?" Octavius shook his head, refusing to be named the villain when it would have been his name on the list if they had not beaten the Senate into submission. "We send men to their death every war. This is no different."

"It is different and you know it."

"What would you have me do?" Octavius demanded, for he had the sudden realization that this argument had nothing to do with war, at least not this kind. Somehow with Agrippa, every argument felt like a war. "Allow the likes of Cicero to live and wait for them to name me *hostis*? It would not only be my name on his list. No, yours would be too, my innocent Agrippa. And Octavia's. And anyone else whom I love. Cicero would kill them all with a *smile*."

Agrippa stared at him with a strange look, caught halfway between defiance and fear.

"Oh yes, he would," Octavius continued. "No one is innocent in war. You simply do not want to face it."

He thought of Cicero's joke, a witty claim that he would raise Octavius up and immortalize him in a single stroke, though Octavius knew Cicero had never meant for him to hear it. And then he thought of the endless illnesses dragging him to the very gates of Hell, the feverish days, the nightmares, the numbness creeping under his skin, waiting helplessly for the end. *No.* No, Octavius would not suffer an ignoble death at the hands of the Senate when he had fought so hard all these years to keep himself alive.

"And the others?" Agrippa asked. "Are they not innocent in this?"

"The others?" Octavius laughed, but it rang hollow. "The people who celebrated Caesar's death? The people who wish to see my head nailed in the forum? Who sat in their estates far away from where his blood stained the ground? *Those* people?"

"Yes. *They* did not murder Julius Caesar."

"I do not need to convince you why this is necessary," Octavius said with a tight smile, taking a step forward, hating how he noticed the unwilling flicker of Agrippa's eyes towards his mouth before they locked with his. "For you already know why. And if you really thought I was wrong, your name would be on that list too."

Agrippa's eyes widened slightly before his face shuttered, and he shook his head. "Only the gods know which way the scales will tip. But these murders will not go unpaid for."

"I will pay for them with my own blood if I must," Octavius said angrily. "I will pay for them my entire life. But if we do not defeat Brutus and Cassius then we may forget what is right and wrong. Death will answer for it."

⟶≫ ≪⟵

DECEMBER 43 BC

The days dragged on in grays and blues as winter brought more death and decay. He walked through his grandmother's gardens, the withered leaves and blackened flowers and fruits so different from the blooming pinks and yellows, the lush greens of spring.

Octavius had not spoken to Agrippa much in the last month, both of them busy with various affairs around the city, and he only saw him at the solemn dinner parties he hosted for his friends. It would be foolish to pretend that there were no doubts, that Balbus did not glance at him in worry, that even Maecenas rarely spoke in conversation, often caught lost in thought. But no one dared counter the new policy of the *Tresviri,* especially when their own party benefited from it.

Especially when the possibility of an alternative series of events, where their own names were publicly displayed on a long list, was much less desirable.

"Brother."

Octavius whirled around, his heartbeat in his throat. He saw Octavia standing like a ghost, her pale skin glowing faintly in the moonlight, the round curve of her stomach, which had grown so quickly these past few months, visible even beneath the thick fabric of her stola. "Sister. I did not hear you."

"Cicero is dead," Octavia said in answer. She walked towards him in her elegant stride despite the heavy weight of her pregnancy. "But I suppose you already heard."

"Yes."

Octavia had surprised him in the events following the formation of the *Tresviri.* He had

201

expected her to be furious, to demand his reasons, to criticize him as Agrippa and others had. Her husband, after all, had been close friends with many who had been proscribed. Instead, she had simply embraced him tightly.

"You are my brother," she had said. "I will live and die by your side."

Perhaps her pregnancy had given her a new understanding of life—and death. Regardless, it had been a relief that there was one person in this world who would not question the decisions he made, especially those that were the hardest to make.

"It is unfortunate," Octavia said now, standing beside him and gazing at the dead leaves and flowers of the garden. "He was a brilliant man, despite everything."

"Yes, he was."

There was nothing else to say. Good men died every day. Octavius could not regret it. He refused to regret it, not when there was still so much to lose. Not when he had already lost many whom he loved.

"I have also heard you are betrothed to Clodia, Antonius' daughter. It seems everyone heard before me." Octavia gave him a teasing smile. "Why did you not tell me?"

Octavius could not help a smile at his sister's familiar taunts. "I feared you would not approve my breaking off the engagement to Servilia, which you yourself had a hand in making."

"You have nothing to fear," Octavia said warmly. "My concern lies with your happiness, and yours alone. I am sure Clodia will make a suitable wife, though she is quite young."

"We will marry in the new year. It will mark a new beginning."

Octavia looked at him worriedly. "Is it?"

"Is it what?"

"Is it a new beginning?" Octavia asked. He heard the subtle challenge in her voice. *Maybe it is loving him which you fear, and that even marriage will not stop it.*

Octavius touched a gentle hand to her stomach, feeling the movement within almost immediately. The midwives had all agreed the child would be a boy. *Marcellus.*

Children had always wearied him, but there was a surety in Octavia's eyes and flushed cheeks that made him curious for the child, and he wondered what the child would be like, if he would have Octavia's poise and passion, Marcellus' thoughtfulness and patience, and whether he would love Octavius even with all the blood on his hands.

Octavia kissed his cheek as if she knew the answers to all his questions and more.

"Yes," Octavius said at last. "It will be a new beginning for all."

23

MARCUS VIPSANIUS AGRIPPA

JANUARY 42 BC

T HE ROOM WAS SO loud with conversation and laughter that Agrippa was nearly dizzy. He drank more wine though he knew it would not help him suffer the tedious events of the day.

The wedding party had settled in Antonius' largest triclinium for the banquet, which still raged on despite the approaching dawn.

Antonius reclined beside Fuvlia, his wife. Octavius reclined in the place of honor, more for Antonius to show off the new alliance than to follow custom, though they scarcely acknowledged each other. Clodia, Octavius' new wife, reclined between Octavius and Agrippa, dressed in priestly white and veiled in yellow, silent and still as a young deer caught by a hunter in the woods.

"Felix! Bring more wine, for Jove's sake!" Antonius called out to a nearby slave. The guests laughed, though Agrippa noticed Octavius and Clodia did not.

"Oh, but you mustn't drink any more wine, husband," Fulvia said, resting a hand on his shoulder.

In Rome and even beyond, Fulvia was the epitome of wealth and womanhood. Her neck was laden with large jewels, her wrists shined with gold, but it was her air—the very way she sat and spoke and smiled—that exuded a life of luxury and power.

She looked for all the world secure and content, but Agrippa caught her subtle, sharp glances at Octavius. Beside her vast, inherited wealth, Octavius, with his unforgiving ambition and vulgar popularity, appeared nothing less than an interloper.

"Soon you will not be able to walk the newlyweds to their home," Fulvia added lightly, though her eyes narrowed.

"Nonsense, Fulvia," Antonius said, but his cheeks were flushed and he set down his glass of wine. Octavius watched him with a bland curiosity which, Agrippa knew, meant he had noticed something of importance. "A little cake should do the trick. Felix! Bring out the *mustaceus!*"

The weary attendant had just returned with pitchers of wine but quickly retreated to bring out the traditional wedding cake. Agrippa never quite found the fruity wine-cake to his taste, but the rest of those banqueting were pleased at this new addition to the already overflowing treats and delicacies before them.

"Shall we toast to the newlyweds?" Antonius asked. He lifted his glass, not waiting for a reply and ignoring the pursed lips of his wife. "I believe we shall. Let us toast to the union of my daughter Clodia and her husband, the *Tresvir* and son of *Divus Iulius,* Gaius Julius Caesar Octavianus *divi filius!*"

Octavius merely inclined his head, thanking the guests as they cheered with suitable good humor at Antonius' exuberance. He gave Clodia a smile, which she returned shyly, and Agrippa felt his face grow hot for no good reason.

The festivities continued with no less enthusiasm for several hours until it was time to escort the bride and groom home, when the husband would carry his wife across the threshold and to the bed where they would consummate their marriage. Agrippa's stomach turned at the thought, but he knew it was inevitable. Marriage was a duty, after all, and this marriage was nothing more than an alliance.

It meant nothing, but Agrippa knew it still meant more to him than he wished. Octavius, as if he were thinking the same—though more likely feeling Agrippa's eyes on him—looked at Agrippa and raised a brow. Agrippa shook his head, turning towards another guest and joining their conversation.

They had reached a sort of truce after their argument during the proscriptions. Octavius had been right as much as he had been wrong. Besides, the argument had less to do with the proscriptions and more to do with trust. So Agrippa had held his peace.

Since then much had changed. The Senate had sworn an oath to maintain the acts of Julius Caesar and confirmed his presence in the heavens. Octavius was now officially *divi filius,* the son of god, which he used to the fullest advantage as his title. Even a temple to *Divus Iulius* had been decreed and would be built in the forum where Caesar's funeral pyre had burned.

But not everything had gone so smoothly. Though all the *proscripti* had either been killed or escaped to Sextus Pompeius' protection in Sicily, the proscriptions had not yielded nearly enough money to fund the war against Brutus and Cassius. Instead, the new consuls Plancus and Lepidus were forced to resurrect antiquated taxes on men and women alike, which had been resisted, to say the least. They had resorted to confiscating temple treasuries, including personal savings entrusted to the Vestal Virgins, nearly leading to riots.

The most shocking change, though, had been the official recognition of Caesarion, Cleopatra's illegitimate son by Caesar, as king of Egypt, thanks to the aid she sent to Dolabella in opposition to the *Conspiratores*. Octavius had not exactly supported it, but he also knew that useful allies today could become useful enemies tomorrow, and Cleopatra should certainly not be brushed aside quite yet.

Overall, the new year had brought as many problems as it did successes, but the world, Agrippa discovered, continued on as it always did, and there was nothing—not even a war—that could stop a wedding.

Indeed, everyone here this evening was too alive and too wealthy to care for the unfortunate souls who found themselves on the wrong side of the war. So they readied to parade the married couple through the streets without a second thought to the murders that took place there only a few weeks ago.

At long last Octavius stood up, and the room quieted to excited murmurs and stifled laughter as he pretended to prowl the room like a lion waiting to pounce on its prey.

Clodia remained mute on the couch. Her expression was partially obscured by her veil, but Agrippa thought he saw fear. She could not be older than fifteen.

Octavius feigned grabbing at a few of the older women also donning yellow veils like the bride, and they shrieked with laughter when he got close to them, a scarcely hidden desire lurking in their eyes at the young and handsome bridegroom. He strolled past Agrippa as he reached Clodia, swiftly lifting her up into his arms as she faked a scream and reached for her mother. Octavius grinned as the room cheered.

The procession led Octavius and Clodia to his home on the forum, which he had recently moved into after abandoning Julia Minor's property on the Palatine. The house was strategically closer to the *Curia Julia* and the sacred fire of Vesta. Agrippa had tried to persuade him to remain in the Palatine home for its connection to the gens Julia, but Octavius had refused, claiming everyone needed a new beginning, including his family.

Although it was a significant walk from Antonius' home to the forum, Agrippa felt the miles passing quickly, as if he were running out of time. When they reached Octavius' home, Agrippa found himself near the front of the group, dreading what he knew he would see and yet unable to resist, like a moth drawn to a flame.

Octavius and Clodia gave their last waves to their family and friends. The guests called out their final blessings to the newlyweds. Then Octavius crossed the threshold and disappeared inside the house.

Agrippa stood staring at the closed doors, unable to cheer along with the rest of the guests. He closed his eyes briefly, wondering what Octavius would say to her, how he would touch her, each thought more nauseating than the last.

He remembered telling Octavius that one day he would have a wife to care for him. At the time it had been nothing more than words. He also remembered what Octavius had replied. *I will always ask for you.*

He remembered believing it.

"Agrippa."

He opened his eyes, startled. But it was only Marcus Antonius who stood before him, blocking his view of the house, a wide smile on his face. It unsettled him, and he did not return it.

"*Tresvir* Antonius," Agrippa said reluctantly. "Congratulations."

"Thank you," he said, still smiling, undeterred by Agrippa's hesitation. "I suppose I must congratulate you as well."

"Me?"

Antonius brought a large hand down on his shoulder. "Yes. I have always understood you are like a brother to Caesar, as I once was to his divine father."

"A brother," Agrippa echoed. "Yes."

"Then I have a gift for you, since that makes you family," Antonius said, grinning now. Agrippa wished to shrug his hand off, but he did not dare offend. "I have arranged your marriage to Attica, daughter of Titus Pomponius Atticus. Close friends with Cicero, as I am sure you know. It will restore good faith."

Agrippa was silent. He heard Antonius say something else, but his eyes flickered to the windows of Octavius' house, where he thought he saw a light shine before it was dark again. Was that a shadow or a trick of his mind?

"Well? What do you say?" Antonius asked, jostling his shoulder. "I hear she is even-tempered. Something to be prized, let me tell you. Caesar has already approved, so I do not see why not—"

"What?"

"Oh yes, Caesar approved the match. He said you would be sure to agree. A friend of Cicero would be a valuable connection in the upcoming wars. Well? What do you say, Agrippa? Do you fancy yourself a wife or not?"

The betrayal was somehow worse than anything he could see in those windows. Agrippa let out a breath, pushing down the pain until he felt absolutely nothing. "You say she is even-tempered?"

"Is that a yes?"

He paused. Now there was definitely a light on the second floor. Agrippa turned to Antonius and smiled. "Yes."

Nothing, nothing, nothing.

⟩⟩⟩⟩ ⟨⟨⟨⟨

FEBRUARY 42 BC

"I am here."

Agrippa turned at the voice, and for a moment the screaming faded into the distance. Octavius stood at the doorway, his head silhouetted by the setting sun so that he seemed crowned in a dull gold. When he stepped into the house, Agrippa saw that his face was pale.

"You are late," Agrippa said. It was the first thing that came to mind. Either Octavius did not hear it or he ignored him.

"Where is she?" he asked.

"Upstairs," Agrippa said automatically, unable to look away from the delicate features drawn sharp by worry. He had scarcely seen Octavius this past month. "The midwife is already here."

Octavius walked past him swiftly, as if he barely registered Agrippa more so than the slaves and attendants lingering within the house who winced at the continued screaming from above. Agrippa followed after him as he climbed the stairs by two.

They reached the door to the room from where Octavia's cries could be heard intermittently. Marcellus leaned against the wall, his forehead resting on the door. His eyes were closed in pain.

Octavius stood beside him and rested a light hand on his arm. "They will not let you in?" he asked.

"This is the realm of woman, my friend," Marcellus said with a wry smile, though he looked exhausted. "A man would only get in the way."

"How long has she been in labor?"

"Not more than three hours." Marcellus passed a hand over his face. Suddenly he looked up and pressed an ear to the door. "She has stopped screaming."

"I suppose that is a good thing?" Octavius asked uneasily.

Marcellus glanced at him gravely. "Not always."

Then, a cry, a different cry, floated through the air, a mere whimper at first, which a breath later turned into a piercing scream. The baby was born. Marcellus could not help but smile in relief, and he embraced Octavius before he could speak.

After another hour, having been ushered to wait in the courtyard, the women supporting Octavia through the birth exited the room and called for Marcellus to enter at last. Inside the room, the midwife held a small, squirming child, bundled in fresh linens.

"A boy, my lord," she said, before stooping to set the child on the ground before his father.

After a moment's pause, Marcellus leaned down and scooped up the child, a wonder in his eyes. He lifted baby Marcellus above his head before kissing the red, squinting face and holding him close to his chest. But it was Octavius who continued to stare at the baby even as Marcellus moved his attention elsewhere, handing the baby back to the midwife.

"And my wife?" Marcellus asked anxiously.

The midwife nodded, glancing fondly at Octavia, who was already washed up and half-asleep on the bed, a blanket draped over her. Marcellus knelt by her side, while Octavius and Agrippa lingered at the perimeter of the room.

"You are warm," Marcellus said nervously, touching a hand to her forehead.

"That is normal," Octavia whispered, taking his hand gently away from her head and resting it on her chest, right over her heart. "I am fine, my love."

"It was an easy birth, my lord," the midwife said, gently placing the baby in Octavia's arms. She cradled him against her chest, a vigor returning to her limbs as the baby whimpered, and she smiled and kissed its forehead.

"But it sounded as if you were dying!" Marcellus protested.

Octavia did not answer, absorbed completely by the baby, so Marcellus turned to the midwife, who laughed.

"Nonsense," the midwife said. "The baby only needed a little push."

"He was eager to come into this world," Octavia said, tracing the baby's pink cheeks and puckered mouth. "It is a good omen."

"We must write to our friends," Marcellus said. "They did not expect the baby until March."

"Yes, you came early, didn't you?" Octavia crooned, tickling the baby below the small chin. "March was too late for you."

"He should have waited," Octavius said. His sister looked up at him for the first time, dazed, as though she had not noticed him before. "February is unlucky."

"Octavius," Agrippa reprimanded.

"It is alright, Agrippa," Octavia said with a smile. "My brother has always been suspicious. He just wants a reason for why things might go wrong." She nodded at him. "Here, Octavius. Come hold him."

At first, Octavius did not move. Then he started forward, kneeling on her other side. She held out the baby and he took it carefully, his face serious and focused, betraying no emotion. Agrippa had the sudden understanding that Octavia knew how to deal with Octavius much better than he did.

"Well?" Octavia asked, teasing.

But Octavius did not smile. He continued looking at the baby. "He is a miracle."

"Oh, Octavius." And she began to cry.

It was another hour before they left the couple to tend to their newborn baby, Octavia overcome by emotion and fatigue until she dropped off into a deep sleep, Marcellus taking the baby and sitting in a chair next to her.

Agrippa had also held the baby, and his little hand had latched onto his finger, unwilling to let go. But it was Octavius who was silently enraptured by the child, watching its every move with a genuine intensity Agrippa had not seen in a while.

Finally, they walked back down the hall, leaving Octavia and the baby to sleep peacefully. Octavius looked lost in thought.

"That will be you soon enough," Agrippa said wryly.

Octavius looked at him, startled. Agrippa realized it was the first time the two of them had really been alone together since his marriage to Clodia. "Why do you say that?"

"You are married, are you not?"

"And?" But he looked amused.

"Octavius."

"Yes?"

"Be serious." Agrippa could not help the annoyance that crept into his voice.

"I am very serious," Octavius said, looking him straight in the eye, though Agrippa spied the humor that danced there. He took a step closer. "What do you think happened on my wedding night?"

"You tell me," Agrippa answered sullenly. "You were there."

Octavius grinned. "Tell me, Agrippa." He was suddenly very aware of the darkness of the hallway, the muffled voices behind closed doors, and Octavius nearing him with a glimmer in his eyes which was nothing short of dangerous. "Tell me what you think happened on my wedding night."

"It would be improper."

"Spare me your propriety."

"This is childish."

Another step. "Agrippa."

He sighed. "You and Clodia—"

"No." Octavius shook his head, suddenly serious, coming to a stop before him. "We did not."

Agrippa held his breath. He wanted to kiss him. Despite everything he still wanted to kiss him.

Octavius looked up at him carefully but did not move any closer. At that moment Agrippa knew he would always come back to Octavius, no matter the cost, no matter the distance.

"Octavius—"

The door down the hall opened and Agrippa turned, his heart leaping to his throat, but Octavius was already a step away, looking calm and indifferent as if nothing had happened. And nothing had happened. It was only the midwife, but the interruption was enough for Agrippa to regain some of his senses.

"Goodbye, Octavius," he said, once the midwife had gone downstairs. He began to walk away. "Give your wife my best wishes."

"Give them yourself," Octavius said. Agrippa paused but did not look back. He wondered if Octavius knew the risks of the game they were playing. "You hardly visit anymore."

Agrippa nodded silently, then left.

⤜⤛ ⤜⤛

JUNE 42 BC

Dishes rattled awkwardly in the silence. Agrippa watched as Octavius picked at his food and Clodia reclined with her eyes trained on the floor.

He regretted this visit more with every passing second. It was the first time Agrippa had dined at Octavius' new place without a large party of guests, and he quickly learned why he had been avoiding it.

"Do you like the house, Clodia?" Agrippa asked, failing to think of another more interesting topic of conversation.

Clodia looked up at him. "Yes, I like it."

"Really?" Octavius asked. "I rather think it is too noisy."

"That is what you get for buying a house by the forum instead of up the hill," Agrippa said jokingly. He saw Clodia smile, but it quickly disappeared when Octavius glanced her way. "Have your mother and father visited yet?"

Clodia shook her head. "No. They are very busy."

Octavius made a noise. "Not that busy, I assure you."

"Caesar," Agrippa admonished. Clodia looked on the verge of tears. "I am sure they will visit soon enough."

"Do not give her false hope, Agrippa," Octavius said with a shrug. "She should know the truth."

Agrippa was silent. It was the truth, but it was cruel for a young girl to hear, and Clodia bit her lip, a tear escaping down her cheek. Octavius saw it and his face hardened, as if the sight of it irritated him. He called on a slave standing in the corner of the room.

"Charis, please escort my wife to her chambers," he said. "She is unwell."

Clodia did not protest as she was led meekly out of the room and upstairs, leaving Agrippa alone with Octavius, who took a sip of his wine as though nothing unusual had happened.

They were silent for a few moments until Octavius raised a questioning brow. "What?"

"You are too harsh on her," Agrippa said. "She is only a girl."

"I was her age once. I do not see why she must cry whenever I speak with her."

Agrippa shook his head. "I do not understand you sometimes."

"What do you mean?"

"This girl is your wife," Agrippa said. "She deserves your respect at the very least, if not kindness and generosity. Why marry if you intended to treat her like this?"

"I married to establish an alliance," Octavius replied. "She would be a fool to believe otherwise."

"It does not matter. She is your wife now, regardless of circumstance. You owe her and yourself a more loving relationship."

"A loving relationship, you say?" Octavius smirked. "I suppose you are readying for married life yourself. Please, let me know how that works out for you."

"If I did not know better, I would say you sound jealous," Agrippa said, his voice calm but scathing. Octavius went very still, narrowing his eyes at him. "But it was *you* who approved my betrothal to Attica before I even had the chance to deny or accept it."

"It was a necessary alliance. I had no choice."

"You always have a choice, Octavius, and it is your choice to punish this girl for something that you have only yourself to blame!"

Octavius sat up, his eyes blazing, but a part of Agrippa could sense that he enjoyed it. "Oh, there you go again, making *me* the monster. You are not innocent in this, Agrippa. You started this as much as I."

Agrippa could not stand it. He got off the couch and made for the door. He paused on the threshold. Octavius remained across the room, his eyes lowered in silence. Agrippa's heart ached at the sight. When had their lives become so complicated?

"Clodia is a sweet girl with a nice smile," Agrippa said quietly. "What more could you ask for?"

"Love!" Octavius shouted angrily, as if the words had been torn from deep within. He got off the couch, shaking his head. "I want love. I want someone who understands me, who has more thoughts in her head than weaving and children. I want someone who can listen to me and converse with me and advise me when I am wrong. I want someone who wishes not for a family but something more! Something greater. *That* is what I want."

"It is not always about what *you* want, Octavius," Agrippa said. "Love is shared, not mastered."

Octavius stared at him, breathing hard. Then he walked towards Agrippa and kissed him, a hand sliding in his curls and gripping tightly. Agrippa pushed him away, though every part of him yearned to kiss him back.

"Not here, Octavius."

"Then in my study," Octavius whispered, his eyes bright and his cheeks flushed, like they had been sparring instead of kissing. "She cannot enter there."

Agrippa knew he should not. He knew it was dangerous, and that he should leave immediately, so Octavius might learn for once that he could not get everything he wanted.

Instead, he followed Octavius up the stairs with a pounding heart, his vision dark around the edges, so that Octavius was all he saw as the doors shut behind them and Agrippa pulled him close, kissing him without another thought, the days—no, the weeks—without this making him desperate, making his hands tremble as he brought them to Octavius' waist.

Octavius was just as feverish, his fingers shaking as they undid Agrippa's belt which held his *gladius,* the sword falling to the ground with a loud thud. They both paused at the noise, their chests rising and falling rapidly. It was too much, too fast, and they both knew it.

"This is a mistake," Agrippa said roughly. He stooped down and carefully picked up his belt, ignoring how his head went light. "We cannot do this."

"You know as well as I that we can," Octavius said, strangely calm. "And we will."

Agrippa looked at him in surprise, unable to think of what to say. Instead, he strapped his belt back around his waist before turning away. He was halfway out the door when Octavius spoke.

"Come visit again soon." Agrippa heard rather than saw his smirk. "Clodia liked you. I could tell."

Agrippa nodded, swallowing hard, before he left the house as quickly as he could.

24

MARCUS JUNIUS BRUTUS

JULY 42 BC

*F*REEDOM.

That word had turned over in his mind since the hilt of his dagger met the lean chest of Julius Caesar and killed him. Was the price of freedom always death?

He remembered the man more than the murder. His own mother had been in love with Caesar, their affair lasting fifteen years with little interrupting their passion. Sometimes he wondered if his mother had loved Caesar more than him, even more so in her grief.

Julius Caesar had been a benefactor, a friend, even family in his own perverted way. But he had also been a dictator, nearly king, and it was impossible to kill one without the other.

When he was younger, Brutus had seen good in everyone, believing the world could be righted by courage and honor. His *gens Junia* was said to have been founded by Lucius Junius Brutus, who overthrew the last Roman king and was one of the first consuls of the Republic, when the people of Rome swore never to have a king again.

When Brutus' father had been killed by Pompeius the Great, he had lost that belief in others, though the hope lingered that the world could still be righted by those with enough daring. And when Julius Caesar had risen, like a king without a crown, Brutus knew it would be up to him to follow in the legacy of his bloodline and save the Republic before it was too late.

Had it been too late? Had the tides of power shifted towards dictatorship decades—nay, centuries—before Julius Caesar had come along and seized it? Brutus would like to blame the man, but after his death, he realized the cracks in the system ran deeper than he had thought, and that it would take much more than the death of one man to right the wrongs of half a millennium.

Was the price of freedom always death?

It certainly seemed so as his legions traveled towards Sardis, slowed by the bloodstained riches and slaves they had plundered throughout Asia to pay for the upcoming war. Not *upcoming*, Brutus reminded himself, for already Murcus sailed to blockade Antonius at the port of Brundisium now that Cleopatra had slunk back to Egypt, the fleet she sent as aid shattered in a storm. Indeed, war had begun two years ago, when Caesar was murdered, and the *Liberatores* drew first blood.

But perhaps it really had begun long before then, when the Trojan hero Aeneas first brought bloodshed to Italian shores, battered by another, even older war.

So Freedom and Death have gone hand in hand, since the beginning of time. Brutus would have written a treatise on this if he did not have more pressing matters to attend to. Cassius had already reached Sardis and was ready to march to battle with his usual vigor.

Both of them had spent the beginning of the year mustering troops and collecting money as they traveled from city to city, but now they had to put their Eastern wealth to use, which was another matter entirely. Unarmed citizens were easier to quell than the well-trained cavalry and foot soldiers of Antonius and the young Caesar.

Brutus twinged with regret at the thought of those two generals. He had hoped Antonius would relinquish his power for the good cause after Brutus had spared his life in the assassination. Alas, power had gripped him as a hand to the throat and had not let go. Cicero had warned against sparing him, but at the time Brutus had brushed that aside as Cicero's personal hatred.

Now he was paying the price, and Cicero was dead.

The young Caesar, on the other hand, had been a surprise. He had no money, no party, no army—nothing except his name, and that too was not even his—and he had defied the will of the Senate and the strength of Antonius within the year.

Unlike Cicero, Brutus much preferred Antonius over this boy. While Antonius was hotheaded and domineering with a strong army at his back, his motives could be anticipated, his desires predicted, as any brute could be.

The boy was trickier, his manners too reserved, his plans too concealed, to allow for even the slightest misstep. He might be easier to eliminate, but if he was anything like his new namesake, even his death could prove meddling.

Soon Brutus and his men reached the outskirts of Sardis where Cassius was encamped. Brutus allowed himself to be escorted to the commander's tent. Cassius was waiting for him, having received a message of his arrival, and they reclined for dinner.

"My scouts have reported that the Thracian chief at Cardia is friendly to our cause," Cassius said with a smile, as it had been his idea to follow the coast and cross the

Hellespont to reach Thrace. "We must march there immediately if we wish to have the advantage."

Brutus nodded absently. He remembered urging that they march to Macedonia earlier in the year to cut off the advancement of Antonius' lieutenants, Norbanus and Decidus Saxa, but Cassius had advised that they dispatch Antonius' Rhodian and Lycian allies first to prevent an unwanted attack from the rear.

While now they certainly had the advantage of funds, Brutus could not help but sense that time was not on their side anymore. Maybe it never had been.

"You have doubts, Brutus," Cassius said, studying his face with those shifting, eager eyes in his hardened face. "You wish we had remained in Macedonia."

"It was a more secure location," Brutus replied reluctantly.

"But we did not have as many men as we do now, nor the means to pay them," Cassius countered, his brow raised. "If we had remained, who knows what would have happened when Norbanus and Saxa reached us. We have bought ourselves time and money."

"It is not only Norbanus and Saxa that I worry about. Antonius sits in Brundisium with legions of his own."

"And Brundisium is where he will stay," Cassius said confidently. "Murcus will not let him cross the Adriatic unharmed."

"Antonius is cunning in battle. I would not so easily discount him."

"Then we shall send Ahenobarbus' fleet as reinforcement. Now pray, what else ails you, my dear Brutus?"

Brutus sighed. "I regret abandoning Macedonia so quickly, but perhaps you are right."

"There has been more on your mind." Cassius eyed him knowingly. "I can tell."

Cassius had always been attuned to the thoughts of others. Keener than Brutus, who often wished to see in others what was only in himself.

"Nothing of importance," Brutus said uncomfortably. "Or rather, nothing of importance now."

Cassius frowned. "Please tell me you do not regret the death of Caesar."

"No." Brutus hesitated. "I regret only that it did not yield the smooth transition of power for which we had hoped."

"That cannot be helped now," Cassius said gravely. "We underestimated the violence of the people and Antonius' influence. Now we must fight for the world we wish to live in or perish. This is the last stand of the Republic, Brutus. Cicero is dead. Many others have died too. Antonius and Caesar have shown their cards. If we fail, then the Republic will too."

"I do not understand," Brutus said, shaking his head in disbelief. "How can the people love someone who would rule as a king and deny them their freedom?"

"The people do not see," Cassius replied, his voice cold. He had always been more cynical than Brutus. "They are blinded by their poverty and ignorance. They cannot appreciate freedom when their minds have none."

Brutus nodded, but he found his friend's words left him uneasy. He had heard the frenzy of the people, he had seen the looks in their eyes after Caesar was murdered, and Brutus had known they had missed something very important. It was not blindness, nor enslavement, which he saw in them. The people had been angry, and they had known exactly who would fan their flames.

Perhaps it was not a king they wanted, but a champion, and it was *that* difference Brutus had failed to see before it was too late.

"We had better rest before the long march ahead," Brutus said at last.

Cassius nodded, getting up and resting a hand on Brutus' shoulder, his eyes holding that lingering sadness Brutus had become used to seeing. Two years ago to the month, Cassius' wife had miscarried as they fled Italy, and the weight of that loss had remained with him.

"Do not linger in the past, my friend, or you will find yourself stuck there, and then there is no coming back."

Brutus placed a hand over his. "You are the last of the Romans, Cassius. I am honored to know you."

A shadow passed over Cassius' face, and he smiled tightly. "Goodnight, Brutus."

⤜⤜ ⤛⤛

AUGUST 42 BC

"I am told Norbanus and Saxa have seized our Sapaean and Corpilean passes," the Thracian chief, Rhascupolis, said in his thick accent, stroking his dark beard.

Brutus and Cassius stood beside him, looking at the map laid out across the table in Cassius' tent. Neither of them spoke his dialect, but Rhascupolis knew enough Latin to guide their march through Thrace.

But this was bad news.

Even Cassius paled. "So soon?"

"We ought to have stayed in Macedonia," Brutus said immediately, closing his eyes. Time had officially caught up with them.

"Calm down, Brutus, we still have time," Cassius rebuked. He turned to Rhascupolis. "We must force the enemy to retreat. Then we make for Philippi. The hills behind will make for an advantageous campsite. The marsh to the south and the mountains to the east ensure our enemy cannot attack us from behind."

"How do we force the enemy to retreat after they have secured such difficult passes?" Brutus asked.

"Our fleet can outflank them," Cassius said with a confidence Brutus did not feel. "We force them to retreat from the Corpilean pass at least."

"And the Sapaean pass?"

Rhascupolis pointed to the map. He began tracing a winding route along the side of the Sapaean mountain, avoiding both sea and river. "My people know a way around the mountain. We will move safely behind Norbanus."

"Then we advance towards Philippi," Cassius concluded. He grinned, his eyes alight with that familiar passion Brutus had always admired, like flint awaiting flame. "We may still take the advantage. Norbanus will most likely retreat down the valley to Amphipolis. When we attack, it will be like running downhill."

"We must not forget Antonius and the young Caesar," Brutus said. "They are the true enemy. If we are not careful, they will destroy us from the inside out before they even land in Illyricum. Remember, many of our soldiers fought under Julius Caesar."

Cassius' lip curled. "I will kill anyone who is loyal to that tyrant-king. I would rather fight and die alongside honorable men than find victory among criminals and cowards."

"Then you had best hope no one reveals their true loyalties," Brutus said bitterly. "You might well fight alone."

Cassius looked at him with a sad smile, his eyes softening, as if he saw something in Brutus that he himself could not. "Do not lose hope now, my Brutus. You most of all, who have come so far. You cannot lose hope in the good of this world."

"What good remains anymore, my dear Cassius?"

"Our friendship," Cassius answered firmly. "And any honor left among Romans."

Soon after the meeting concluded they readied their troops to march into Thrace, sending messengers to their fleet and taking the waterless track around the mountain that Rhascupolis had shown them.

It took them the rest of the month to reach Philippi, in part due to the circuitous route they chose, but it worked. Norbanus found himself threatened and quickly marched back to Amphipolis to fortify his camps. Saxa, too, was successfully forced into retreat by their fleet and joined Norbanus in Amphipolis.

Rhascupolis led them skillfully through the woods to the north of Philippi by early September, and from there they approached the outskirts of Philippi, a dry area elevated by hills. They chose two of them to set up camp and looked down on the valley stretched out below.

Just beyond the hills, the city of Philippi crowned the top of the valley. Beneath her feet lay a vast, breathtaking plain that extended all the way to the towns of Municus and Drabiscus and the river Strymon.

Brutus looked out upon the plain, the beauty of it, and he felt the gods watching him. Indeed, it was in this very field they said Persephone had been carried off while picking flowers. He thought it a shame this field would likely see blood spilled on her soft grass.

"We must attack swiftly, while we still have the upper hand," Cassius said, joining Brutus on the lip of an overhanging rock, sweeping his eyes methodically across the plain.

"Do you not think it wise to wait?" Brutus asked.

He looked at the marshes and ponds spilling out to their left as far as the eye could see, the steep, impassable gorges to their right, the aloof mountain peaks at their backs, and the wide, endless plain before them, cut through only by the Gangites River.

Their own plentiful supplies were safely stored at Neopolis, a mere eight miles from their camps. The enemy, on the other hand, was blocked on all sides by nature and Brutus and Cassius' legions, with their camps in Amphipolis, forty miles away from Philippi. Not to mention that their funds must be nearly depleted thanks to the civil wars these last two years. Now that they were on this side of the sea, their supplies were restricted to the limited resources of Macedonia, since Murcus had cut off aid from Italy.

"We could starve the enemy," Brutus concluded. "It would be impossible for them to retreat or last the winter."

Cassius shook his head. "Norbanus and Saxa should be dealt with while we have the chance."

Brutus sighed and retreated with Cassius to their camps, where fortifications were already being made. He felt the familiar lull before the battle, breaths held and faces shadowed but brimming with that Roman fierceness, like the silent, dark clouds gathering before a thunderstorm. Brutus turned to look once more at the untouched plain and paused.

A small figure was racing up the field. Brutus recognized him as he neared. He was a scout, sent to report back on the camps at Amphipolis.

"Cassius," Brutus said, stopping his friend.

Cassius turned, and together they watched the scout expertly scale the hills and reach their camp, where he was pointed in their direction. Cassius watched the messenger warily as he approached.

"What news?" Cassius asked. "Quickly."

"*Tresvir* Antonius reached Amphipolis, sir. With all of his legions still intact."

"But Murcus—" Brutus began.

"Damn that Murcus to Hell," Cassius interrupted scathingly. He shook his head.

"It does not matter now. And what of Caesar? If anyone may sail past Murcus and Ahenobarbus then I suppose he has too."

"Yes, but *Tresvir* Caesar remained in Epidamnus with his army," the messenger said. "It is rumored that he is ill, and may not survive to see battle."

"I will believe it when I see his corpse and those of his men," Cassius snarled. He took a deep breath and turned towards Brutus. "Our plans must change. They will expect an attack on Amphipolis."

"Then we wait for Antonius to attack," Brutus said, looking out across the plain as if he could see a far-off city surrounded by enemy legions. "He knows time is no longer on their side. Their troops will succumb to famine soon if they do not draw us out. We must wait until then."

Cassius sighed, following Brutus' gaze to the horizon, where the fate of the Roman Republic seemed to hang suspended above the field like the setting sun. "Then we wait."

25

GAIUS OCTAVIUS

SEPTEMBER 42 BC

"LOOK AT ME."

The body aches came first, then the fever. Octavius remembered the chill off the Adriatic, the spray of salt from the waves, the vertigo weighing him down as the ship rocked side to side, before a darkness tinged his vision and he had to close his eyes.

Agrippa had him lie down in the cabin near the stern, and he had been too feverish by then to feel ashamed. It was the last memory he had of the ship before they landed in Epidamnus.

Since then his days have slipped in and out of dreams. He did not know what was real or in his mind. Agrippa appeared most days, but not always as he was now, and never did they speak. Sometimes he was the boy Octavius met at school in Rome. In others he was older, sleeping, or dead. Octavius would run to him but he never made it, always his draped form would remain just out of reach.

"Look at me," Agrippa whispered, and his fingers touched Octavius' chin firmly before they were gone, like a ghostly wind. Octavius reeled at the memory—or was it real?

"Agrippa," he murmured, his lips painful to move.

No one answered. He thought he felt the warm water of the *caldarium,* a gentle palm against his chest, before a chill ran up his spine and Octavius forgot the baths, forgot the touch entirely.

"Look at me."

The voice was everywhere at once, and it sounded nothing like Agrippa this time. Octavius tried to find the source but he only saw darkness. Was that a flash of light—Agrippa opening the flap of the tent—or a piercing pain in his head?

"Look at me."

Water rose up around him, past his chest, up, up his throat, bubbling into his mouth, choking him, and he coughed until the voice told him to breathe. Fingers touched his chin, and like a fragmented memory, he felt Agrippa's hands on his waist, fingers pressing into his skin. *Every day I want you...*

"Agrippa."

"Look at me."

But no, this voice was old, and not mortal. This voice was old like the light of the stars, beheld only from far, far away. Octavius shivered. Something cold touched his forehead. He turned and saw that he stood in a green field, alone.

"Agrippa?"

The name echoed across the field. He looked around at the flowers growing among the soft grass bending to the breeze. It was familiar, but only as a place was known through stories about times when gods still walked the earth. A delicate laugh was carried on the wind, then a scream, as if someone had been caught by something terrible. Was that a girl, or a goddess?

A dark storm rumbled overhead, threatening rain. Lightning flashed, and Octavius flinched. Then the voice came from everywhere at once.

"Look at me."

Thunder crashed again and the rain followed. The drops were warm, hissing on his skin. Octavius saw his arm was splattered red. Blood. It was raining blood. He looked up, his heart pounding, any desire to cry for help dying in his throat.

The vast valley was running with rivers of blood, and the grass heaved in torrents of red mud until the earth seemed to groan with the weight, and the bloody field around him began to sink into the ground, crumbling into the yawning black deep below.

A small chuckle arose from its depths before a figure ascended from the very darkest caverns of the world, cloaked in shadow. A burning wind ran across the valley, flattening the grass.

Octavius tried to run away but his legs would not move and he saw to his horror that his feet were stuck in a thick marsh, slick with blood, sucking him down to death.

"Octavius."

He tried to move his legs, straining against the marsh, sweat running down his back, dripping from his brow, but it was blood, it was all blood. The clouds grew denser, hotter, closing in on him as the figure approached, and Octavius saw a gnarled hand larger than life holding a ring of thick, black keys.

"LOOK AT ME!"

He looked and Octavius gasped as his knees buckled and the earth beneath him shook and finally fell, a hand reaching towards him, his name whispered softly in his ears, as if Death knew the language of love.

Then light flashed and Octavius opened his eyes.

⟶⟫⟫ ⟪⟪⟵

"The battle will start soon, I believe."

Octavius nodded absently.

Agrippa stood across the tent, looking down at Octavius curiously. It had been several days since his fever broke. Antonius had already been sent ahead to Amphipolis with most of their troops. Octavius swallowed, his throat sore. The doctor had ordered him to remain in bed for the time being.

"You were speaking," Agrippa said, apparently at ease, leaning against the edge of a table, though his brows furrowed. "In your sleep."

"I don't remember," Octavius lied.

"Was it a dream?"

Or a nightmare. Octavius shook his head. He did not want to describe the dreams he had, the terrors of the night, nor the memories that mingled among them. "I was unconscious."

At that, Agrippa glanced at him and blushed.

When Octavius had awoken from his dream, it had been Agrippa who was there, kissing him softly. At the time, Octavius had only enough wits to ask for some wine, but now he was well enough to remember the strange incident.

"You were lucid, at times," Agrippa said, and he sounded defensive.

Octavius' heart constricted. "Was I?"

"Yes." Agrippa paused, looking at him carefully. "You spoke of your mother."

The blank in his mind made Octavius uneasy. He did not remember speaking of his mother, or in fact, speaking to Agrippa at all.

"What did I say?"

Agrippa frowned. "You kept saying she was here, and that you could hear her."

Octavius nodded slowly, his cheeks growing hot. "I see."

"There is no need to be ashamed," Agrippa said softly, and Octavius closed his eyes, unable to bear it, the pity, as if he were still that weak child capable of nothing but dying slowly. "There was a night when I feared Death was close."

"I was fine," Octavius bit out. He opened his eyes and glared at Agrippa, who raised a brow. "It was nothing."

Agrippa did not reply, instead lifting his *gladius* off the nearby table and hooking it on his belt. He made to leave, and Octavius realized he was annoyed.

"Wait," Octavius said. Agrippa stopped, looking at him warily. "We ought to prepare to join Antonius in Amphipolis. You say the battle will start any time soon, if it has not already begun."

"Battle?" Agrippa repeated in disbelief. "You will not be in any battle while you are still in this state."

"I must. The entire Republic will mock me if I do not, including my own men." Octavius' jaw clenched at the thought, of him lying helpless while Antonius fought his battles for him, the rumors that would spread and take root like weeds. "It is not a suggestion. Prepare to join Antonius in Amphipolis."

Agrippa stepped forward, his hands in fists and his eyes flashing angrily. "You do not know anything. *I* was here, Octavius. I cared for you day and night. I saw your eyes roll behind your eyelids. I heard your labored breathing. I felt the heat of your forehead as the fever took hold and did not leave you."

"I did not ask it of you," Octavius said, his voice chilly.

"Except that you did," Agrippa replied bitterly. "Every single night."

Octavius flinched.

"You almost died, Octavius," Agrippa said, his voice breaking. He took a deep breath and looked away. "You are not well enough to go to battle."

The words rocked Octavius like a wave at sea, as if the ground beneath him would cave and he would fall, fall for eternity in darkness. Octavius pressed his lips together and did not answer, and let Agrippa walk out of the tent.

After a few hours, a local doctor arrived and administered the medicine Agrippa usually gave him. His head was heavy, but from the illness or the conversation, he did not know.

You almost died, Octavius.

It did not matter. He was alive. Octavius knew the importance of appearing strong and ordered his troops to ready for the long march ahead to Amphipolis.

The road wound through the mountainous terrain as they descended into the valley that cradled the city, bordered by marshes and gorges. A carriage was arranged for him instead of his horse to save strength, and he did not allow anyone inside, not even Agrippa.

Look at me.

Octavius closed his eyes and slept.

⇛ ⇚

OCTOBER 42 BC

"Glad you could finally join us, Caesar," Antonius said, the sarcasm slipping out in the last word.

Octavius merely smiled and embraced him with his usual distant politeness. His taunts held no more weight than those of a common barbarian.

"Glad to see the fighting has not yet begun," Octavius said, and though his tone never wavered, Antonius caught the slight and narrowed his eyes.

"Yes, Brutus and Cassius wish to hold out and starve us." Antonius' face darkened. "It is a smart move. We would not last the winter. The battle must be fought soon and we must win quickly."

Agrippa stood beside him, eyeing the map rolled out on the table. They were taking counsel in Antonius' tent, and though Octavius might wish to, he could not afford to face this war without Agrippa. While Maecenas and Rufus were somewhere in the camp, as Octavius had made them commanders of their own cohorts, he did not need them here.

"They have positioned themselves on elevated ground, surrounded on all sides by difficult terrain," Agrippa said finally. "It will be difficult to draw them out."

Antonius cut Agrippa a scathing glance. "I am well aware."

"Then what do you suggest?" Octavius asked impatiently. They had no more time for petty remarks.

"The marsh," Antonius said in a low voice, and Octavius nearly flinched. *Look at me.* Antonius gestured to his map, sweeping a finger around the valley directly below Philippi where they were stationed now. "We barricade here by day and build a causeway through the marshes by night. We must be silent. They cannot discover it. Then we attack from the rear."

"And if they find us out?" Agrippa asked pointedly. "It is a risk."

"Then we force the issue and storm one of their camps," Antonius said grimly. "It is death by sword or death by starvation, but triumph can only be found on the battlefield."

"Agreed," Octavius said. "So when do we begin?"

Antonius grinned. "We already have."

So the days passed quietly, the camps tense with the premonition of battle. At night, the troops silently built a causeway through the marsh, then returned before daylight and continued barricading the camp, fortifying walls and digging ditches, raising towers and arraying troops for battle with their standards.

Octavius spent most of his time resting in his quarters, but occasionally he would muster up the energy to pass through camp and encourage his men for the battle ahead.

Agrippa was avoiding him, but then again, Octavius did not seek him out. Perhaps it was for the best, though a part of him felt stung by the distance. If one of them fell in battle, it would be easier to grieve in anger than in love. Or so he hoped.

When war came on the tenth day, the news was less than welcome. Antonius summoned them to a meeting in his tent.

"Cassius has discovered our causeway," Antonius said angrily, ignoring the knowing eyes of Agrippa. They had almost finished planning their attack from the rear when they received news of the destruction. "They have blocked it off. We must storm the camp or risk starvation."

"We cannot simply storm the camp," Agrippa protested. "We must strategize. Try to draw them out, at least."

"There is no more time for strategizing, boy," Antonius sneered. "Unless you can strategize how to grow crops in a marsh. Now get your troops together and prepare for battle."

Octavius laid a hand on Agrippa's arm to silence any more protests and allowed Antonius to leave the tent in his rage. He knew the power Antonius' anger could fuel and thought it best to focus on their own legions.

"It is too late," Octavius murmured. "Death does not wait for our plans."

"You will remain in the camp," Agrippa said, turning towards him, pleading. "You cannot fight."

Octavius shook his head. "If we lose, I will die anyway, and I would rather die on the battlefield. But if we win, I would rather have died than look weaker than I already do."

"If we lose, you may still yet escape." But Agrippa's eyes grew sad. They both knew it was not true.

Octavius felt his throat close up. "Escape to where, my dear Agrippa?"

Agrippa stared at him, his brow creasing in despair. "I do not know."

"There will be nowhere that is safe for me if Brutus and Cassius prove victorious. I must stand with my men," Octavius said firmly, though he felt a tremor run through him. *Look at me.* "But I will hand over my command to you. I am not well enough for that."

Agrippa's mouth parted. Octavius had never given him command before. "Octavius—"

"I am not asking," Octavius interrupted before Agrippa could say something he could not bear to hear, stepping closer and taking Agrippa's hand in his. Agrippa looked down at their joined hands in surprise. "You are the only one I trust to do this."

After a deep breath, Agrippa nodded.

Octavius stepped back, releasing his hand quickly, and they left to join the troops.

Antonius had already mustered his forces in battle lines facing Cassius' camp. When Antonius saw Agrippa assume the position of command, he sneered at them.

"Stay close," Agrippa whispered to him as the silence before the storm descended on the field. "If you lose me, hide. I will find you."

Octavius looked at him, his heart skipping a beat, and for the first time, it occurred to him that Agrippa could die too. Finally, he nodded, unable to speak, for the sounds of clashes could already be heard from Cassius' camp as Antonius and his troops stormed the walls with their ladders.

Suddenly there was a far-off shout of command, before cavalry and troops burst forth from Brutus' camp like bees from a hive, barreling down the hill as though the grass spurred them on. And they were heading directly towards them.

Agrippa's eyes widened, and he pushed Octavius slightly behind him with his arm.

"Ordinem servate!" Agrippa shouted, drawing his sword and lifting his shield. Their cavalry shifted uneasily before them, the horses bucking at the oncoming danger, their riders raising their spears higher.

The stamping of the horses and soldiers as they streamed downhill made the very earth tremble, and Octavius held his breath as their cavalry clashed, the momentum of Brutus' forces rushing through their ranks with terrifying speed.

Agrippa assumed a readied stance, so Octavius did the same, his heart beating clumsily in his chest.

"Parati!" Agrippa cried out, just as the first foot soldiers neared them, and battle broke loose.

Octavius was instantly protected by his own troops, but Brutus' men were too strong, steadily cutting their lines and making for their camp. The sharp noise of battle, metal on metal, the grunts of falling soldiers, swirled in Octavius' head as he turned about nervously, waiting for the first soldier to break through his guard.

Look at me.

An armed shoulder rammed through his guards and then soldiers were upon them, Octavius swinging his sword blindly, the force of its clashes with enemy armor rattling his bones. He managed to throw the soldier to the ground and spear his abdomen before he looked up and saw that his guards had scattered and Agrippa was nowhere to be found. They were overrun.

LOOK AT ME!

Octavius swiveled around, his sword up, and saw the muddied field red with blood and scattered with dead bodies. He blinked and the plain was running with rivers of blood. Then he was on the ground, a horse having rammed him from the side on its way to his camp. He could not hear anything, all sound muffled as if he were underwater.

Octavius.

A woman's voice. Familiar, even tender.

Octavius glanced up through the grass. The dark figure loomed across the field, and the clanging of its keys echoed across the field as the sound of battle faded. He staggered up and it was gone, the battle rushing back around him. Octavius saw his men fighting for their lives, too few and far between, and still no sign of Agrippa.

"*Equaliter ambula!*"

The order came from up the hill. *Advance uniformly.* Octavius' stomach dropped. He saw another swarm of troops descend the hill from Brutus' camp. *If you lose me, hide. I will find you.*

Octavius had no choice. He ran.

He ran until he reached the marsh, where no soldiers had yet strayed alive. Octavius began wading across, the mud thick and slimy, his breath frantic as his steps became slower and slower. When he had no strength left to lift his feet, Octavius crouched, hiding in the tall reeds. His head pounded, still weak from his illness. He thought he heard a low, dark laugh, or was it the earth groaning beneath the battlefield?

Time passed slowly. The sky darkened gradually as night came on and obscured the field across the marsh. Octavius fell into a fitful sleep, unable to keep his eyes open, the pounding in his head growing until Octavius thought he might die right then.

"Caesar!"

"Octavius!"

His neck ached as he lifted it, but he could not see in the dark. There were footsteps, and water splashing close by.

"He is here."

A strong hand came down on his shoulder, and Octavius was dragged to his feet. Agrippa. He looked relieved, but grim. Maecenas was standing next to him, looking at Octavius worriedly.

Octavius leaned against Agrippa, not caring that Maecenas watched their every move, his skin numb and his vision beginning to spin.

Agrippa put an arm around Octavius to keep him upright. "It is done. The battle is done."

"For now," Maecenas amended, earning a sharp glance from Agrippa.

"Cassius is dead. Brutus has retreated," Agrippa said firmly.

Octavius nodded. He did not care, his whole body turning hot, then cold. "You found me."

Maecenas watched them silently.

Agrippa's eyes flickered to him, then to Octavius, frowning. "Yes, I did. I will always find you."

Then they picked a path through the marshes as they walked slowly back to camp, Octavius supported up by Agrippa, and Maecenas trailing behind them.

The silence of the dead descended on the field for the rest of the night.

26

MARCUS VIPSANIUS AGRIPPA

NOVEMBER 42 BC

Agrippa was only slightly aware of the ship rocking beneath him, the gentle sunlight on his face, and the warm wood solid underneath his back. His daydreams turned into memories easily.

There was Marcus Antonius, standing near Octavius, the battle won, and Brutus dead.

"You have your revenge, Caesar," Antonius had said, gesturing around the battlefield with his hands, the field strewn with corpses and bloodied armor. "You may finally rest."

Octavius had shaken his head. "I may never rest."

The dreamlike memory slipped away when he heard footsteps pass him on the deck. He had stolen a few moments to sleep while Octavius rested in the cabin.

Octavius had fallen ill sometime during the journey home. Whether it was the same illness or a different one, Agrippa did not know, but he feared if one did not take his life, the other would.

After the first battle, Brutus had held out for twenty long and tireless days. Every morning, they had formed lines and teased the enemy with javelins and arrows and rocks, taunting those on watch in Brutus' camp. Every night they had prepared to do the same thing again the following day. When they heard that their fleets in the Adriatic had been destroyed, they only dared the enemy more, their men spurred on by fear of starvation.

When Brutus' men finally stood and fought, victory had been decisive, and Brutus had died on his own sword, the last of the *Conspiratores*. The survivors of his army had sued for peace. Many had been Julius Caesar's men after all.

Agrippa did not feel sorry. The war had taken many lives, but it had also spared others. He thought of Octavius, half-unconscious in the marsh, and the knowing look on Maecenas' face. *You found me.*

They had almost died, but the gods were watching now, and Octavius' fate demanded a different ending. Agrippa only hoped it was peace.

"Sir, *Tresvir* Caesar asks for you."

Agrippa opened his eyes, shielding himself from the bright sun above with the back of his hand. He dismissed the soldier, then walked to the cabin.

Inside, the cramped space was dark, musty, and nearly chilled. Octavius lay on a makeshift bed, his cheeks flushed with fever. Agrippa sat on the edge beside him and pressed his hand to Octavius' forehead.

"You are still hot," Agrippa said. "But we will land in Brundisium soon. I will fetch a doctor when we arrive. You know it would be wise to remain there until you are well."

Octavius barely opened his eyes, nodding slowly. They both knew his illness was dangerous. Too dangerous. "I need you to write a letter."

"To whom?"

"The Senate." Octavius began to laugh, but it quickly turned into a cough. "It appears there is a rumor that I am dead."

"Antonius' work, I am sure," Agrippa said grimly.

Octavius smiled wryly. "I have many enemies."

"And it seems you always will."

He knew Antonius and Octavius would not remain peaceful for very long. Antonius had remained in the East after the battle, surely keen on visiting his Egyptian mistress, leaving Octavius to settle the discharged veteran soldiers in Italy.

Not to mention Sextus Pompeius still controlled Sicily, and therefore the grain supply itself. There were rumors that Lepidus had begun a communication with the islander, perhaps realizing that staying behind in Rome during the battle had rendered him near powerless.

"There will be a day, Agrippa, when the rest of the world falls at our feet and peace returns to the Republic," Octavius said quietly, his eyes dark and steady. "But until then, we fight."

⟫⟫⟫ ⟪⟪⟪

JANUARY 41 BC

Clodia sat weaving by the window, a small smile on her face, her flaxen blonde hair delicately pulled back in braids and pinned up high. She was lovely, her slim fingers working the loom expertly, her cheeks rosy in the afternoon sun.

Agrippa took a step forward, and Clodia looked up, startled as a bird in the woods when a branch snapped.

"I apologize," Agrippa said, inclining his head in greeting. "I did not mean to interrupt."

Clodia smiled brightly. "Nonsense. I was not doing anything important."

"You were weaving." Agrippa raised a brow and Clodia blushed. "That is important."

"Not to my husband," Clodia joked, but her smile faded. "I suppose you are here to see him."

He could not help feeling guilty. "Yes."

Clodia sighed. "I know he is troubled. He is quicker to anger these days. But he does not tell me anything. He says I am too young and sheltered to understand the ways of the world."

"Are you?"

She glanced at him with a sharpness that surprised him, tilting her chin up proudly. "I know more than he thinks."

"I am sure that is true," Agrippa said with a smile, nearing her. He nodded towards her loom, where the colored threads of silk wove a pattern into fabric. "It is beautiful."

Clodia lowered her head. "Thank you."

"Do not take what your husband says to heart," Agrippa said quietly. "He does not really mean it."

She lifted her head with a sad smile. "I know he does not. But that is worse, you see, for then he speaks only to hurt me."

Agrippa had no answer. The gods knew she was right. A tear slid down her cheek, but she looked up at Agrippa with tender eyes, as if he were the sun rising on a moonless night.

"Agrippa."

He turned, unable to stop the blush on his face. Octavius stood across the room, barely glancing at Clodia before fixing Agrippa with a stern look.

Agrippa inclined his head. "Good afternoon, Caesar."

Octavius' face hardened. "We have much to discuss."

"Of course, Caesar," Agrippa said. He thought he saw a shadow of a smile on Clodia's face. "After you."

He followed Octavius, who walked stiffly up the stairs to his office. Once the door closed behind Agrippa, Octavius spoke. "You are doing that on purpose."

"Doing what?" Agrippa asked, amused.

"Seducing my wife."

"She is a child," Agrippa said carelessly, but a twinge of guilt followed when he remembered the look in her eyes. Octavius looked as if he did not care anymore, walking around his desk and sitting down.

"We have much to discuss," he said, all business, and Agrippa had to hide his slight disappointment at the sudden formality.

"What about?"

"The people are demonstrating in the forum," Octavius said, a slight edge of resentment in his voice. "They protest the settlement of the veterans. But I have no choice. I cannot make everyone happy."

"The people love you. They will forgive you."

Octavius raised a brow. "Love has a price. Always."

"So it seems."

"And I will be the one to pay it," Octavius continued, regretful. "Not that any of them will have the slightest thanks for it."

"Would you rather have fifty thousand angry farmers or fifty thousand angry, armed soldiers?"

Octavius sighed. "Yes, yes, of course."

"You have greater problems to worry about," Agrippa reminded him. "Sextus must be defeated."

When they had arrived in Rome after Octavius recovered from his illness in Brundisium, Lepidus had indeed been intriguing with Sextus Pompeius. Antonius had then made preparations for Hispania—which was now well under Sextus' power—to be transferred to Octavius' command, while Transalpine Gaul would be transferred to Antonius'. Octavius had in turn offered Lepidus the African provinces as a chance for him to prove his loyalty, but it was merely a way to remove him from Sextus' influence. Sextus had become too powerful a naval force to ignore alongside the fleets of Murcus and Ahenobarbus, which had defected to his side after the battle of Philippi.

"I cannot abandon Rome at this time." Octavius sighed. "I will send Rufus and some legions to deal with Hispania. It is the only way."

"Do not send Rufus," Agrippa said, unable to hide the hurt in his voice. "I am the better general."

"I need you here."

"But—"

"It is done," Octavius interrupted firmly. "I need you here when Antonius' coward of a brother turns against me." Praetor Lucius, together with Praetor Isauricus, who no longer had any reason to support Octavius, was already gathering those loyal to Antonius, and now he had armies under his command. "Fulvia has also been meddling. They say she visits the camps and speaks to soldiers about Antonius. Lucius wishes to settle the veterans himself, so he and Antonius might reap the rewards."

"Let him," Agrippa retorted. "He will see it is not as easy as he thinks."

"No." Octavius shook his head. "It is not easy, but if I allow Antonius to do what I have promised, then the soldiers will owe their loyalty to him. And that cannot be."

"It may come to a fight, then."

Octavius smirked. "Yes. That is why I need you here, not in Spain. I am trusting you with military command."

"Octavius," he warned.

"I know. But I cannot risk losing this battle for the sake of my pride."

Agrippa remained silent. The illness which had kept Octavius bedridden in Epidamnus before the battle and in Brundisium afterward had only made Antonius look the true victor against the *Conspiratores*.

Now the resentment of the evicted farmers and the anger of the veterans whose settlements were being delayed by Lucius' antics only served to sink Octavius' popularity more. To hand over military command was to expose the same weakness that had given Antonius an edge in the first place.

But Octavius had one thing over Antonius in all this.

"I am here," Octavius said confidently. "Antonius is fraternizing with a foreign queen in the East. He will regret leaving his dirty work to lesser men."

Agrippa sighed. "So be it."

Octavius passed a hand over his face. Agrippa noticed then the exhaustion etched into Octavius' face, the dark skin under his eyes, the sharp cheekbones, as though he had not been eating enough lately. Octavius locked eyes with his, his face unreadable. An uneasy silence settled between them, the tireless months stretching behind and before them.

Suddenly Agrippa remembered. "And Clodia?"

Octavius blinked as if pulled out of a daydream. "What?"

"You plan to wage war against her family."

He shrugged. "She must be sent back to her mother."

"Octavius," Agrippa said reproachfully, though he knew deep down he was right.

"What would you have me do? She will hate me more than she already does if she stays. Besides, she is still a virgin."

Agrippa shook his head. "She will be devastated."

"She will be relieved," Octavius said, sounding angry now, and Agrippa was not entirely sure they were talking about Clodia anymore. "She never wanted to be my wife. This life is not for the faint of heart."

"You do not know what she wants," Agrippa countered, finding himself angry too, though it was only anger at himself. "You do not know anything about her. You never wished to learn."

Octavius' eyes flashed. "Well, since you seem to know my wife better than I, pray tell, what would you have me do with her?"

Agrippa turned on his heel, heading for the door. For he was angry at himself only because he knew he would be back. He would always be back for more, even if he knew he shouldn't. "Nothing, Octavius. For once in your life, do nothing."

He left, the surprise and hurt on Octavius' face the last thing he glimpsed before the door closed behind him.

⤚⟫⟫ ⟪⟪⟛

APRIL 41 BC

Agrippa paced his room. He had never felt so nervous, not even before a battle. The humid heat of the oncoming summer already weighing on the city did not help.

There was a knock at the door, and his footman entered the room. "Sir, your father has arrived."

Agrippa nodded with a deep breath. "I will be right down."

He had not seen his father in years. Despite his better sense, Agrippa was slightly embarrassed, as his father came from humble origins in the countryside. It was a fact that Agrippa concealed by avoiding his paternal name, Vipsanius, but the taint of his birth never left. Octavius took great risk ignoring his less-than-sterling family ties, and that was something Agrippa had never forgotten.

Agrippa went downstairs. Lucius Vipsanius stood in the atrium, looking around his newly bought house, only a few streets away from Octavius', with a barely hidden wonder.

Though it was a modest abode, Agrippa knew it might as well be a palace compared to the rambling country houses and farms his father knew best. He looked exactly as Agrippa remembered, so much like himself, except for the brown eyes—Agrippa had his mother's eyes.

When he saw his son walking towards him, Vipsanius grinned. "My son," he said, and opened up his arms.

Agrippa embraced him tightly, shutting his eyes against the sudden wave of emotion which threatened tears. *"Pater."*

Vipsanius stepped back and gazed at his son, taking in his expensive clothing and neatly arranged hair. "You have grown so much since I last laid eyes on you."

"I am a man now," Agrippa said, standing taller. "And soon I will be a husband."

233

His father's eyes glimmered with a mix of sorrow and pride. "Your mother would have been proud."

Agrippa nodded, and a tear that had almost dried escaped down his cheek, clinging to his jaw. He smiled and wiped it away. "She *is* proud. I am glad you came, *pater*."

Vipsanius took a deep breath and smiled with him. "Of course. A father cannot miss his own son's betrothal. I only hope you will not begrudge your father's common rank amongst such wealth and influence to which you now belong."

In an instant, the brief shame he had felt melted away, and looking at his father's warm face, Agrippa wondered how he could have felt it at all. "Never, *pater*. Never."

"I may not have riches," Vipsanius said, "but I do have something for you which I hope you will accept, be it small."

His father held out a small wooden box and carefully opened the lid. Inside sat a gold ring of two hands clasped at the center. It was his mother's ring, which Vipsanius' mother had given to her son when he had married, a token of their love for Agrippa's mother.

Agrippa shook his head, his throat tightening. "I cannot."

Vipsanius took the box and placed it in Agrippa's palm, covering Agrippa's hands with his own. "When I first gave this ring to your mother, I never thought I would see it on another hand. But any wife of my son is like a daughter, and I know I will love her as such."

The following day, Agrippa and his father made their way to the lavish house of Atticus which towered over the Quirinal Hill. Although Agrippa now mingled with the most powerful names of Rome, his father had been wrong in one thing.

Agrippa did not belong, and never would.

As they walked up the hill, Vipsanius began giving advice to his son. "A woman does not always want gifts, you know. Many times they only want you to *listen* as they complain that you do not give them enough gifts."

"Is that so?" Agrippa asked, his mouth quirking into a smile.

"No, not at all actually," Vipsanius replied, perfectly serious except for the amused glimmer in his eyes. "A woman always wants gifts. Your mother was only an exception."

"I see." Agrippa sighed as they reached the large entrance to the lofty estate, the walls painted in patterns of red and white. "And what would you give to a woman who could have all the gifts in the world?"

With sad, knowing eyes Vipsanius placed one hand on his son's arm, the other on his own chest, right over his heart. "Love, my son."

The doors opened. Atticus stepped out, dressed in an elaborately patterned tunic, his eyes wary despite his welcoming smile. Though he had been a close friend to Cicero the politician, Atticus himself was of the equestrian class, having inherited wealth and investing it in real estate. From then on he had confined himself to banking and publishing, thus escaping the proscriptions.

Agrippa could not help remembering the months of quiet and screams, the blood on his hands even if he would have it another way, and his heart sank. How could Rome move past the murder and death of these past few years, nay, past decades? It seemed impossible.

"Lucius Vipsanius," Atticus said as they neared. "And his son, Marcus Vipsanius Agrippa. Welcome, my dear friends. I hope the travel has not been too taxing."

"Not at all," Vipsanius said warmly, embracing Atticus formally. "Thank you for your hospitality."

Agrippa embraced Atticus. "It is an honor, sir."

Atticus looked at him for a moment, his watery gray eyes lingering on his face, before nodding. "Please, call me *pater*. We shall be family soon, after all. My daughter awaits us."

They were escorted to the courtyard in the back of the house. Agrippa could tell his father forced himself to keep his eyes forward and abstain from marveling at the high ceilings and meticulous mosaics stretching across the vast floors of the estate.

His stomach knotted more tightly with every step he took, and as they neared the courtyard where a figure stood veiled in the center, her head lowered, Agrippa forgot to breathe.

"Attica, my dear, please welcome Lucius Vipsanius, and his son, Marcus Vipsanius Agrippa."

The figure lifted her face, and the light that shone from the open sky above caught her veil, flashing on steady eyes and a full mouth. Agrippa could not help but mark the absence of her mother.

She turned to her father. "May we begin?"

At her voice, low and firm, Agrippa could breathe again. He shared a glance with his father, who raised a brow and smiled as if he approved.

Atticus nodded, chuckling at her insistence. "Yes, we may, *filia carissima*."

She turned and faced Agrippa, tilting her head as though to assess him as her father had. "Then let us begin."

"Very well." Atticus turned to Agrippa's father. "Do you, Lucius Vipsanius, promise the marriage of your son to my daughter?"

"Yes, I do," Vipsanius said with a smile. "And do you, Quintus Caecilius Pomponianus Atticus, promise the marriage of your daughter to my son?"

"I do," Atticus answered. "Do you, Marcus Vipsanius Agrippa, promise to take my daughter's hand in marriage?"

Agrippa locked eyes with Attica. "I do."

"Do you, Caecilia Pomponia Attica," Vipsanius said, "promise to marry my son?"

She paused, then, "I do."

"As the father of the *sponsa*," Atticus said, "I freely give to the *sponsus* the gifts of two slaves, a horse-drawn carriage, and a trunk full of the finest cloth from Egypt, as well as a dowry of five hundred thousand *sesterces* to be paid in two annual installments."

Agrippa bowed his head, more to conceal the initial shock those numbers still caused, then stepped closer and brought out the wooden box with his mother's ring. He could not hide his trembling hands as he opened the lid and took out the gold ring.

Attica lifted her left hand, and Agrippa gently slid the ring on the fourth finger. Their hands remained lightly joined.

"Along with my mother's ring," Agrippa said, noticing Attica's slight movement at his words, "I gift to you silks from Persia and India, a pearl necklace, and a bracelet of emerald and gold."

Atticus brought forth a piece of parchment, inked with the terms of their union. "If the *sponsus* and *sponsa* may sign the written oath."

Once Agrippa and Attica took turns carefully signing the parchment, they turned to her father.

Atticus, his eyes weighed with sadness, walked behind his daughter and lifted the veil back over Attica's head, revealing a youthful, pale face and warm brown hair, a shade lighter than Agrippa's. When their eyes met, Agrippa saw the same gray eyes as her father's, though there was a hardness to hers that he had not seen in the elderly man.

"Then the *sponsus* may kiss the *sponsa*."

Agrippa stood still, his chest tight, a pair of dark eyes flashing in his mind like a warning. Octavius had been too busy to attend the informal ceremony, but Agrippa knew the truth. *I need you here.*

Then he saw the gray eyes before him widen, and Agrippa leaned forward, closing his eyes, and gently kissed her lips.

Nothing, nothing, nothing.

27

CLODIA PULCHRA

DECEMBER 41 BC

WHEN CLODIA HAD TURNED twelve, her mother had sat her down and told her men would only ever want one thing from her. She had believed it. So it had come as a surprise when her husband had carried her over the threshold of their new home as she had always dreamed about and had put her to bed. Alone.

"Where are you going?" she had asked, her voice wavering. *Did he not want her?* She did not understand. But Caesar—for that was what he had asked her to call him—had only cut her a glance and smiled, though it was not warm, and she had shivered.

"I am going to bed. You should too."

"But—"

"A wife must listen to her husband, Clodia," Octavius interrupted firmly. "I would have thought your mother taught you that."

Clodia had not said anything after that rebuke, watching his figure retreat down the hall where a light flared to life, soon hidden by the closing doors of what Clodia later learned was his study. It was his favorite room in the house, and Clodia was expressly forbidden to enter it.

Caesar had a similar room now tucked away on the second floor of their new house on the Palatine Hill. The first night there, Clodia had thought perhaps Caesar would change his mind about her, but as evening drew on while Clodia wove silently by the window and Caesar read by firelight, he suddenly went upstairs, alone.

"Where are you going?" Clodia had dared to call after him, a tremor in her voice.

Caesar had paused on the stairs, almost smirking. "To Syracuse."

She learned later that this was the name of his office. *Syracuse.* Clodia thought a more apt name would be *Seclusus,* for he rarely left the room except for business.

He had acquired the modest house after the battle, selling the one by the forum. When she had asked who owned the house previously, he had only told her he was a disgrace to the Republic, and that she ought not ask so many questions. Regardless, she hated the new house, the quiet of the halls, where before she had grown accustomed to the clamor of the forum, the voices on the street so loud they seemed to be in the very room with her.

Now she spent her days in silence, waiting each night in her bed alone, waiting and yet still hoping that one night Caesar would come in and kiss her goodnight. The question flickered in her mind again. *Did he not want her?*

For it was not a crime to want her husband to love her, was it? And she knew enough to know that if they did not consummate their marriage, there would never be a child. And Clodia very much wanted a child, a little baby to amuse her all these long, lonely days and nights. She knew motherhood was difficult, but surely it could not be much worse than being a wife.

At least she had Agrippa.

He was her husband's closest friend and Clodia was in love with him. She wished she had married him instead, and wondered why her mother had let her marry such a heartless man when there was so kind and gentle a man in his friend. But it did not matter, for now Agrippa was to be married, leaving her alone once more.

Clodia hated Caesar, his hard eyes and even harder words, which always came out of such a soft, murmuring mouth. But she also loved him. He was *her* husband after all, and on one else's. *Or was that true?* A little voice in her head questioned his faithfulness. *Syracuse* or *Seclusus,* he loved that office more than her, if he loved her at all. But if he did not love her, whom did he love?

Ever since he had returned from the war, she noticed him shut up in his study well into the night, and would not emerge until morning. Clodia fell asleep with strange thoughts in her mind, imagining foreign women, barely dressed, excessively decorated and perfumed, being escorted into that office while she was sleeping, just as her stepfather had done when he thought she and her mother were asleep.

Could it be that Caesar was being unfaithful to her?

The moment she thought it, Clodia could not rid herself of the conviction. She watched his office door day and night, whenever Agrippa was not around, for then she liked to enjoy his company. Some days she almost mentioned it to Agrippa but thought better of it. He might not understand; men rarely did. But her husband's secrecy gnawed at her, until it was the only thing on her mind, and she was determined to know the truth.

"You seem distracted today," Agrippa said kindly.

He was reclining opposite her, picking at his plate of food. Caesar was out of the house, but he did not mind that she ate alone with Agrippa so long as they were chaperoned.

Clodia smiled. She had been thinking of going to sleep earlier, so as to prepare for her plan. Tonight she was going to discover the truth. "I am only tired. The crows woke me up at dawn today. They like to nest in the trees."

Agrippa smiled at her comment. He knew she disliked the Palatine Hill and had preferred the house by the forum. Clodia held her breath. She thought him so beautiful when he smiled, like the glimmer of sunlight on water.

"You say Caesar will return soon?" Clodia asked, changing the subject.

He stiffened at the name, and his smile fell. Clodia wondered if Agrippa loved and hated Caesar too. "Yes, he is with his sister, Octavia. She just gave birth to her second child."

A surge of jealousy rose in Clodia instantly. "Really! He didn't mention it to me. Is it a boy or a girl?"

"A girl," Agrippa said, watching her carefully. "Claudia Marcella."

"But didn't she just have baby Marcellus?" Clodia asked, sounding resentful even to her ears.

"March of last year. I was there." Agrippa's eyes clouded over, as they had tended to ever since his betrothal. "They are a miracle, children." Then he looked at her, smiling sadly. "You will have your day, Clodia, I promise. You will make a great mother."

Clodia blushed. "You think?"

"I know," Agrippa said warmly. Then he hesitated, glancing away. "But simply because one will make a great parent does not mean they are ready."

For the first time, Clodia felt hurt by something Agrippa had said. "How can you say such a thing?"

"I do not only mean you."

"But—"

The front door opened and shut. Clodia flushed. She felt a righteous anger seize her as her husband filled the doorway. He looked exhausted, as if the last few weeks had taken a toll on him. She knew he was having trouble at work. The servants gossiped as if he had done something wrong. The anger melted away into pity. Was Agrippa right? Was her husband simply not ready to be a father?

"Leave us, Clodia," her husband said quietly.

Clodia felt the anger return, swift and strong. She clenched her teeth and exited the room as her husband sat down beside Agrippa. Their broken conversation carried up the staircase where she lingered, straining to hear.

"...a message to Antonius..."

"...the meeting at Teanum..."

Why were they speaking about her stepfather?

"...now they are in Praeneste..."

"...have to tell her...not tonight..."

Her? Were they talking about Clodia? Or another woman?

"...tomorrow?"

"...she will stay the night I suppose..."

Clodia felt her face grow hot. *Stay the night?* So they must be talking about another woman. Although she had long expected it from her husband, to hear Agrippa so casually indulge it was unbearable. Clodia quickly climbed the last flight of steps and shut herself in her room. It was decided. She would wait until night, then find out once and for all the reason her husband did not love her.

It was much later when Clodia heard footsteps up the stairs. She had been half-asleep on her bed, struggling to remain awake. At the sound of voices, she leaped to her feet and rushed to the door, pressing her ear against the wood.

"...she is asleep, I assure you...come..."

Clodia nearly gasped, and her blood ran hot. She heard the door to his office open and shut. After several minutes, she carefully opened the door and stepped out into the dark hallway. Her heart pounded with each step closer she took to the office.

A few more. The door was just in reach. She heard the voices again.

"Octavius..."

Clodia hesitated at the low voice, somehow familiar, her neck burning. It was impossible. She thought for a moment about turning back and forgetting this ever happened. But no. She had to know.

The door opened under her palm, silent as a leaf on water.

Her husband stood behind his desk. Seated before him, his back turned towards her and his tunic pooled around his waist, was Agrippa. But that was not the worst of it. Agrippa's head tilted up, kissing her husband, his hand clutching the front of Caesar's robes and pulling him closer, as if any distance between them would pain him.

She made a noise. Agrippa turned, his eyes going wide when he saw her, his mouth falling slightly open in surprise. But her husband merely stepped away, looking unbothered.

Clodia was rooted to the spot, her breath having left her the moment she saw Agrippa. He was still beautiful, and without his clothes, the muscles in his back rippling, he was like a god. She had never seen anything like it save in the statues of Jove himself.

"She wants to know the ways of the world," her husband said, his voice as cold as night, colder than she had ever heard, so that even Agrippa flinched. Caesar looked at her and smiled tightly. "Now you see."

Clodia whirled and ran, shutting the door of her room so loudly the walls seemed to rattle with the force of it. She was breathing hard, stunned as if her mother had slapped her. For it was Agrippa who had betrayed her in the end, despite everything she knew.

Her mother had once told her that men always betrayed the ones they loved. Clodia had never believed her until now.

⤜⤛⤚ ⤚⤙⤘

FEBRUARY 40 BC

Fulvia reclined beside Clodia, huddled in large fur coats while she conversed with Lucius, her stepfather's brother.

Clodia had always thought her step-uncle a very small, pitiful man, always trying to imitate her stepfather, always trying to please her mother. While Lucius did look like his older brother, his build was weaker and leaner, and his face did not hold the arrogance and ease of her stepfather.

They were taking refuge in Perusia, a city Clodia had never been to before. War broke out here and there near the city walls, but mostly her days were filled with much the same activities as before, weaving by the window and bathing and dining, so that she thought war was far less exciting than men made it out to be.

Just as she considered retiring to her room to return to her weaving, a plate of roasted nuts appeared before her, as she had requested. Delighted, Clodia reached out, but her mother whacked her hand away, turning on her angrily.

"What did I tell you, Clodia?" her mother asked sharply. "There is a famine. We must ration, or we will die before the end of February. Terpia, take this away at once."

A slave came and took away the plate, but not before her mother snatched a nut and ate it herself, chewing furiously. Clodia's stomach grumbled loudly watching her. "But I am so hungry, mother."

"Well, maybe if you had pleased Caesar better we would not be in this situation," Fulvia said tersely.

Clodia felt a familiar shame well up, then anger, remembering how she had been betrayed.

She knew her mother secretly despised her for the failed marriage to Caesar and the siege they now suffered after their divorce, despite her lack of involvement on all points.

When she had been returned to her mother without a single goodbye from her husband or Agrippa, she had wanted to explain to her mother the strange, shameful event she had witnessed, but the words had failed her.

They were no use now, anyway.

"Now, now, my dear Fulvia," Lucius said from the other side of the room where he paced before the window. "It is not *her* fault Caesar was incompetent. Besides, war was inevitable."

Clodia could just make out from their vantage point the camps of soldiers surrounding the city walls like marching ants, clustered in orderly groups. She wondered idly if Agrippa was down there, then pushed the thought away.

"Oh, you wish to speak of incompetency?" Fulvia asked, arching a brow.

"Your words wound me, Fulvia," Lucius said, walking towards her. "The people hailed me *Imperator* as I walked through the city. They loved me. They would have followed me."

"The people will love anyone," her mother snapped. She could be merciless in her anger, Clodia knew well. "They would not be able to tell the difference between you and a donkey's ass if you shoved it in their faces."

Lucius turned away angrily and spoke under his breath. "I do not understand how they did it."

"How a mere boy managed to rout the armies of not one, not two, but *four* grown men?" Fulvia asked, feigning ignorance.

"Not just the boy, Fulvia," Lucius replied, though his cheeks flushed red. "You women do not understand the ways of the world. Marcus Agrippa was in charge of the army. He trapped me from behind while I was trying to cut off Salvidienus Rufus' approach from the north. I had no choice but to turn aside."

Clodia lay very still, listening now with her full attention. The name brought back the memory, as vivid as if it were before her eyes once more. *Now you see.*

"What? That no-name soldier?" Fulvia scoffed. "*You* failed to outwit a farmer turned general. If my husband were here—"

"But he is not here, is he?" Lucius interrupted quietly. Her mother glared at him. "No, he is not. He is off fucking an Egyptian queen—"

Fulvia gasped. "How *dare* you!"

"It is true—"

"And in front of my daughter! Clodia, cover your ears!"

She did not cover her ears, watching her mother stand up indignantly and face her step-uncle, her jaw twitching with repressed fury.

But Lucius held his ground. "Oh yes," he continued. "He will wait until his brother and his wife finish the dirty work for him, is that not so? You know my brother as well as I. He always uses those who love him until he does not need them anymore."

"Slander," Fulvia whispered. "Lies. You want the glory for yourself."

"I love you, Fulvia," Lucius said softly. "You and I both know Antonius does not."

Clodia felt her cheeks burn, despite herself. "Mother? Is that true?"

"Shut up, Clodia." Fulvia stepped closer to Lucius, her face trembling with rage. "Antonius loves me. It is *you* he never cared about, and that is why you will always—"

Lucius took Fulvia's face roughly in both hands and kissed her on the mouth, pressing hard. At once Fulvia wrenched away from his grasp and slapped him clear across the face, the clap echoing in the quiet room.

Lucius cradled the left side of his face, his eyes shut in pain. "I love you, Fulvia," he mumbled. "I have always loved you."

Her mother's chest rose and fell rapidly. She blinked furiously and then turned around, barely keeping herself upright, as if she were drunk, stumbling away.

Clodia did not move, worried that if she made the slightest sound they would send her away to her room. *Now you see.* She shivered as if his voice were spoken in the room now.

"Pollio, Ventidius, and Plancus march to us as we speak," Lucius said quietly, gingerly prodding his reddened cheek. "They will break the siege, defeat Caesar, and Antonius will return the victor. Then we may forget this ever happened."

Fulvia breathed in deeply, then turned around, her face stern and composed, a woman who had seen the world and knew it to be despicable. "Then you have more faith in men than me."

Clodia sighed at this, before she left the room silently, and returned to her weaving. And as she looked out the window and watched her former husband's army attack the city with their sling bullets and flaming arrows, saw the dead bodies of starved slaves and poor citizens heaped on the side of the streets, Clodia vowed never to speak to a man again.

Now you see.

28

GAIUS OCTAVIUS

FEBRUARY 40 BC

"I F I KNOW YOU at all," Balbus said wryly from across the tent, "you are planning something quite dangerous."

Octavius looked up from his desk, where Agrippa's map of the world, some recent letters, and his *gladius* were strewn, having grown disorderly throughout the long siege of Perusia. Now that Lucius and Fulvia had surrendered, Balbus knew Octavius would be looking elsewhere for his next move.

He raised a brow at his finance manager. "You are wrong, Balbus. It is *already* planned. I was merely reviewing."

After one last glance at the map, he picked up his *gladius* and hooked it to his belt, then called his manservant to pack the rest of his belongings and prepare to leave. Octavius walked over to Balbus with the first genuine smile he had had in a long time, feeling as light as a feather, as if at any moment he could dart off into the sky like a bird—no, like a *god*.

Balbus eyed him warily. "What have you planned?"

Before Octavius could answer him, Agrippa entered the tent swiftly, kissing Balbus in greeting before motioning in more soldiers who would pack up the tent. Octavius led Balbus outside as their men worked quickly and efficiently to disassemble the camp, load wagons and carriages with weapons and provisions, and begin the fast pace of a soldier's march.

Agrippa joined them a few moments later. "Caesar, we must stop on our way to find wool cloaks and blankets. Our men will not survive the north without warmer clothes."

Octavius nodded. "We shall stop at Arretium, then. Maecenas has already offered his aid. We cannot afford to delay."

Balbus looked between Agrippa and Octavius in confusion. "The north? But are you not going back to Rome?"

"Not yet, Balbus," Octavius said with a grim smile. "Calenus' legions in Cisalpine Gaul need our attention first."

Calenus and his troops had threatened to march on Octavius to break Lucius and Fulvia out of the siege. Although Calenus had not reached them in time, a threat was a threat, and this was a particularly dangerous one.

"You mean to replace him with one of your own generals," Balbus realized, then shook his head. "I would warn against it if I could, but I am sure you will not be swayed."

"I am merely doing right by my trusty colleague, *Tresvir* Antonius," Octavius said mockingly. "He would not approve of a governor who would march on a member of the *Tresvir*, now would he?"

"You are playing a dangerous game," Balbus warned. He had always advised caution when taking any political stance, but the time for caution had come to an end when Lucius drew first blood. "Antonius will see this as an open declaration of war."

"You wish to speak of war?" Octavius scoffed. "I have not been the one starting wars. He may thank his brother and wife for that."

Balbus winced, but it did not deter him from advising him in the best way he could. "Caesar, you must consider the ramifications of dealing such a blow. The governorship of Gaul is not to be trifled with, especially as the son of Julius Caesar."

Agrippa spoke for the first time, his voice calm but cutting. "The ramifications would be Calenus marching on us as we speak. War with Antonius is inevitable. It would be in our best interest that Antonius did not send the legions of Gaul marching on Rome when that time came."

Balbus glanced at Agrippa pointedly. "Just because you managed to trick that poor fool Lucius does not mean you will succeed in tricking his brother. Antonius is the better general and the viler man."

"And he will soon be the enemy," Octavius said in an attempt to end the argument. He had no need for fighting within his party. "Whether we wish it or not."

"If you make Antonius an enemy, he will make you one as well," Balbus said.

"Then we must be sure to win," Octavius said with a deep breath. "For the victors write history, do they not? Come, Agrippa, we must depart soon. I have a few things I must discuss with you. As for you, my dear *consul,* I have arranged your transportation back to Rome. I believe there are a few financial matters of mine to arrange. You know of what I speak."

Balbus bowed his head in concession, unable to hold back an exasperated smile, then left him alone with Agrippa, who narrowed his eyes.

"What financial matters?" Agrippa asked. "I am not aware of any new arrangements."

"That is because only my finance manager is aware of my financial matters, *general,*"

Octavius replied smoothly. "Besides, you will find out soon enough."

"I do not like it when you keep secrets from me," Agrippa said, a shadow crossing his face, as they both remembered the dark days of last winter. *You could have trusted me.* "You know I have only ever been loyal to you."

For a moment, Octavius recalled a memory he had tried to keep buried. A meeting with Antonius, sometime after the proscriptions. His wedding had been impending, and with every day Octavius had grown more and more uneasy. Antonius had proposed that Agrippa marry the daughter of Atticus, a friend of Cicero, in order to gain a powerful ally.

"Are you sure he will agree to marry?" Antonius had asked with a sly smile. "He does not seem to leave your side."

Octavius had flushed, despite all his self-restraint working to remain calm. Was it possible Antonius suspected something? No, he had decided. Antonius thought Agrippa nothing more than a henchman, a tool in his repertoire, which was the only way Antonius understood the world.

"Agrippa is loyal to me," Octavius had said slowly, the words in his mouth bitter. "He will say yes."

Then Antonius' smile had stretched into a grin.

"Octavius." A hand on his arm returned him from memories he would rather forget, and he focused on Agrippa, who watched him carefully. "What are you thinking about?"

"Marriage," Octavius said quietly. "He is arranging my marriage."

Agrippa nodded. "I see. You wish to ally with Sextus Pompeius."

"Yes. Before Antonius reaches him first. It is the only way." Octavius paused. "We both must marry."

"Who is it?" Agrippa asked, ignoring his last comment, though his mouth twisted slightly at the words.

"Her brother is Lucius Scribonius Libo, father-in-law to Sextus," Octavius said, then frowned. "But my personal affairs were not what I wished to discuss with you." He pulled Agrippa away from a nearby group of soldiers who were piling spears into the back of a wagon. Agrippa lowered his head to listen. "I need you to dispatch a small retinue to follow Lucius to Hispania."

Agrippa stepped back. "You do not mean to—"

"No." Octavius shook his head. Assassinating the brother of Antonius would not solve any of his problems. "But he must be watched. I do not trust him. Although he has surrendered, as long as he is alive, Lucius is still dangerous. I cannot afford another distraction."

"Anything else, Caesar?" Agrippa asked warily.

Octavius raised a brow. "Yes, in fact. I am planning to hand the governorship of Gaul to Rufus. I wished to tell you first."

"Rufus?" Agrippa's face hardened. *"No.* I forbid it. He is not to be trusted."

"I know," Octavius said with a tight smile. "That is precisely why I must do this. If he fails me, his position as governor of Gaul is too dangerous and powerful to remain unpunished. And the Senate will surely not prevent me from punishing one of my own. It is the safest manner of testing his loyalty."

"He may not prove loyal, but he is still your friend. It would be a risk to lose him," Agrippa said cautiously.

Though Agrippa disliked Rufus, nevertheless he had been their close friend for many years now. But Octavius had learned the risks of friendship long ago.

"Friendship is not loyalty," Octavius said coldly. "Never forget that."

"Then once you have eliminated Rufus, who will you appoint as governor of Gaul?" Agrippa asked, challenging.

They both knew the obvious answer, but Octavius was reluctant to speak it. He needed Agrippa in Rome for now.

"We shall see when the time comes," Octavius said finally. "He may still prove his loyalty."

"And what of Plancus? And Pollio and Ventidius? Their troops are already moving towards the Adriatic coast. They await Antonius."

Octavius waved a dismissive hand. He had more recent news than Agrippa. "Plancus has already fled to Greece with Fulvia and abandoned his army. As for Pollio and Ventidius, leave them be. We have no time for skirmishes when a war awaits. Calenus' legions are of the utmost importance now. Besides, if my reports are accurate, Pollio has left his station in Gaul and plans to join Ahenobarbus and his fleet."

"Even if all of this is true," Agrippa said with a sigh, "Calenus will not hand over Gaul without a fight."

Octavius paused as he watched a white flake of snow fall on Agrippa's shoulder. Then he realized it was not in fact snow, but ash. Octavius turned towards the city of Perusia, where flames had begun to rise up from the outskirts, devouring the houses and shops in its path, licking the sky with delicate, deadly tendrils. The soldiers had begun pillaging the city, and when they were done collecting the spoils, they would march north.

He bared a smile. "Really? I have a feeling there will be no fight at all."

⟫⟫⟩ ⟨⟨⟨⟪

MARCH 40 BC

There was a soft knock at the door. Octavius sat at his office desk, reviewing his records carefully. He did not answer, for he knew who it was when he heard his footsteps up the stairs.

It could only be him.

The door opened slightly, and Agrippa stepped inside. He looked at Octavius, hunched over his work in candlelight, and frowned. "How are you faring?"

"I am fine." Octavius set aside a letter from Rufus, who was now in charge of Gaul. He knew Agrippa was asking for another reason entirely. It was the anniversary of Julius Caesar's death, now four years past, but he felt nothing he had not felt then. Agrippa watched him warily as he stood up and walked around the desk. "Many more have died today."

It was true. Nearly three hundred senators and equestrians had been tried and executed for allying with Lucius. As war with Antonius approached, he could take no chances of treachery in Rome. But Agrippa did not come to speak about that.

"News has come from Egypt," Agrippa said without preamble. "The queen is pregnant."

The words hit him numbly. He leaned against the edge of the table, silent for a long moment. Then, "Antonius is the father." It was not a question.

Agrippa nodded. "If it is a boy, he will have an heir in Egypt."

"He wouldn't dare," Octavius said, his voice strangely calm at the bad news. "She is a foreigner."

"Love makes all of us fools," Agrippa murmured.

Octavius glanced at him, then away. "Fools allow love to cloud their judgment." He closed his eyes, the reality of what he had to do sinking into his stomach anxiously. Agrippa seemed to sense it too, but he remained silent, waiting for him to say it. "I must produce an heir."

"Yes." Agrippa's hand lifted up as if he wished to touch Octavius before he let it fall by his side, his face darkening. "There have been rumors."

His breath left him. "Rumors?"

"They are nothing new," Agrippa said quietly. "It is not your fault."

Octavius turned away, the pity in his eyes unbearable. "It is. I am weak. I cannot fight my own battles. I cannot last a winter without an illness. My first marriage was a disaster. It produced no heirs. It is no surprise they suspect. And then there was Hirtius..."

"Hirtius is dead," Agrippa said harshly, and Octavius glanced at him in surprise. "And...and you were young."

His heart thudded in his chest, and he did not know how the words left his mouth. "Have—have you ever?"

"Before you?" Agrippa hesitated, his gaze flitting away. "No."

Octavius could not stand it. He felt that familiar shame bubble up his throat, and his hands gripped the edge of the desk just to keep himself upright. Agrippa could never understand, even if he wanted to, and the thought left Octavius faint with nausea. Suddenly he could not bear to have Agrippa in the room.

He gritted his teeth. "Leave."

Octavius did not look, but he could sense that Agrippa had not moved, had not left the room at all, just watching him, always, always watching. The air of the room closed in, suffocating him.

"Leave," he repeated, his voice trembling. He looked up.

Agrippa stood there still, unmoving and silent as ever, watching him carefully like one might a wild animal.

Octavius walked over to him and lightly pushed his chest, as hard as iron against his hands. "Get out."

"Octavius," Agrippa said quietly.

"Leave, Agrippa." Octavius pushed him again, then again, until Agrippa stumbled back, trying to find his footing while Octavius now used all his strength to shove him towards the door.

But Agrippa had somehow known this was coming, for he grabbed his wrists so that both of them struggled to gain the upper hand.

"Stop," Agrippa grunted, forcing Octavius' arms by his sides. "Stop, Octavius. Stop fighting for once."

"No." He knew he was acting childish, angry that Agrippa had looked at him like that, with such pity. But his body had a mind of its own, wanting to fight, wanting to hit him, to *hurt* him, if only to punch that look off his face.

"Octavius."

"Get. *Out.*"

"Gods above," Agrippa swore under his breath, before he was kissing him.

Octavius went still under his touch, the brush of their lips. Agrippa pulled him close, too close. He ignored the pounding in his head, the beating of his heart, and tried to focus on this, Agrippa's hands tightening on his wrists, his unforgiving kiss.

Look at me.

He recognized the voice now. It was his mother, calling to him, waiting for him in the golden fields of Elysium. But if his mother was death, then Agrippa was life, all life, warm and alive against him, his skin hot, his mouth burning, everything alive, alive, alive, bringing him to the heart of life, right where the sun kissed the scorching earth.

"Look at me," Agrippa whispered against his mouth.

"Why?" he demanded, breathless, all the fight in him spent. "Why do you always want me to look?"

"Because when you look at me I know when you are lying."

Octavius was silent, his eyes fluttering shut as Agrippa traced a delicate fingertip on the edge of his mouth.

"Every lie you tell has a truth hidden inside," Agrippa murmured. "I only need to find it."

Then Agrippa kissed him again, a searching kiss, so that Octavius believed every truth he had never said aloud was spoken wordlessly between them.

Agrippa kissed him until the night passed into day and Octavius forgot why he would ever lie in the first place.

⤙⤚

When Dawn raised her rosy fingers in the east, Octavius rose from the couch.

The room murmured softly as the guests turned towards each other, watching Octavius, waiting for him to steal his newly wedded wife from her mother's side and return home holding her in his arms. He ignored the watchful eyes of Agrippa from across the room.

Scribonia reclined beside her mother, veiled and appropriately modest, watching him as well. They both knew what came next.

Octavius stepped forward. The room quieted.

Scribonia's mother, Sentia, watched him warily. This was not the first wedding she had witnessed, nor the first time her daughter had been stolen from her.

Octavius steeled himself as he lowered and gathered his wife in his arms, her body made heavier by the thick folds of her dress. Scribonia was stiff in his embrace, unyielding and alien, so unlike Clodia's soft, petite limbs.

"You are supposed to scream," Octavius muttered. "It is tradition."

Scribonia looked at him and frowned. "I know." She rolled her neck back and stretched out her arms, feigning terror. "Help! Mother! Help!"

It was a convincing act and the wedding guests trailing behind them laughed. Octavius' arms ached as he carried her through the streets and up the hill to his house on the Palatine. His house appeared and after they crossed the threshold and exchanged the customary vows, Octavius quickly set her down.

"Welcome home," he said quietly.

Scribonia looked around, nodding appraisingly at the sparsity of his decorations and the understated, elegant style of the walls. Clodia had thought it all too bare, but Scribonia came from a much more modest household. "Where is the bedroom, my dear?"

"What?"

She arched an eyebrow at him. "It is our wedding night." A pause. "I have done this before, you know."

"Yes," Octavius said uneasily. "I know."

Scribonia smiled, and it was a beautiful smile, bright and easy and mild. She was from a well-respected family with all the comforts and expectations of the wealthy, conservative circles of Rome, and she knew it too. She also knew Octavius had not consummated his last marriage. "I am not so naïve as to believe you have not been with a woman before."

Octavius had the self-composure to sneer. It was not difficult to find cheap pleasure in the darker, quieter streets of Rome, and he had never been one to refuse a drunken fumble after a night of games in the local tavern. But he had never seen the women in the light of day afterward.

"Then I will follow your lead, husband," Scribonia said archly.

He nodded, not thinking, not feeling, her presence as vague as wind at his back. Scribonia followed him to the back of the house where a small bedroom awaited, the door creaking loudly as they entered.

"Here," Octavius said.

Scribonia followed him into the room, looking at the bed and then back at him. "It is a small bed."

"Yes," Octavius said. She stood, waiting. He stepped forward, then hesitated. Octavius had the strange sense of betraying a lover, but pushed down the feeling.

At his hesitation, Scribonia walked closer to him slowly, her hands lightly clasped before her, her blue eyes serious and accusatory. His failure would not have consequences only for him. "We must consummate our marriage, my love. It is tradition, after all."

He winced at his own words so easily given back to him. *If it is a boy, he will have an heir in Egypt.* A flame of anger shot through him. "Take off your dress."

Scribonia raised a brow but did not protest, silently removing the bejeweled clasps on her shoulders, allowing the fabric of her dress to drop around her feet. She stood naked before him, her pale skin gleaming under the lamplight, her arms loose at her sides, framing wide, rounded hips, a curving stomach, and soft thighs.

Octavius quickly turned around before he looked any closer. He put out all the lamps until the room was as dark as night. There were no windows in this room. Scribonia was scarcely more than another shadow in the dark.

They met silently, and Octavius touched her side, fitting his palm against the supple bend of her waist. Where Clodia had been in every way a child, a girl, Scribonia was a woman, firm and solid under his touch.

"On the bed."

Scribonia lowered her head, her face featureless in the dark. She walked towards the bed, her figure pliant as she knelt on the sheets.

Octavius did not think, allowing his memory to move himself forward and kneel behind her so that her face was hidden. He fumbled with his own tunic with one hand while the other held her down by the hair. When she tried to move, Octavius held her steadfast, pressing her down with his hand. Something inside leaped to attention, and he felt a fire grow steadily inside him.

He breathed heavily as their bodies met in a steady rhythm. Octavius' grip tightened so much he heard her make a noise of protest, and that alone flared in him a piercing pleasure, as if the newfound power over this soft, curving body beneath him could move mountains in their wake. An heir. An empire. Was that not his fate? Was he not the son of a god?

His body pitched forward, his pleasure heightening all at once. Octavius shuddered against the damp skin beneath him, then carefully stood up, adjusting his tunic and wiping the sweat from his brow.

Scribonia sat up on the bed, eyeing him curiously. "You may stay here if you like."

"Goodnight, Scribonia."

Octavius left and wandered to his bedroom. He lay down on the bed, staring up at the patterns on the ceiling until he finally fell asleep.

29

Marcus Vipsanius Agrippa

APRIL 40 BC

"Y<small>OU LOOK VERY MUCH</small> like your father," Agrippa began carefully, glancing at the stoic face of Attica as she walked alongside him. "Especially—"

"My eyes," Attica interrupted softly. "I know."

Agrippa sighed quietly. They were on a chaperoned walk which he had requested of her father in order for them to be better acquainted before the wedding ceremony, but they had already walked one lap around the basilica and had yet to exchange more than a few words at a time.

Attica was as calm and collected as when they were betrothed. Though she was only in her eighteenth year, Agrippa found himself at a loss beside her quiet, cool demeanor.

"You did not know my mother," Attica said suddenly, and Agrippa raised a brow in surprise. She blushed, then, and glanced away from him. "But I look very much like her as well. She passed away six years ago."

"I am sorry for your loss." He hesitated. "I lost my mother as well. She died giving birth to my sister. In almost every way I look exactly like my father except for—"

"The eyes," Attica interrupted, this time with a small, sad smile. "I was wondering. She remains a part of you, then."

Agrippa hid a smile, pleased despite himself. Her attention felt like the faint warmth of sunlight on a cold winter morning. "I did not know you noticed."

"I notice many things," Attica said.

"Oh, do you?"

"I notice that you are ashamed of your father and do not use his name. I notice that you frown whenever you are thinking deeply about something. I notice how you fear mentioning your friend, Caesar, because my father's dear friend Cicero was slain by his

253

hand," Attica answered, her voice only wavering at the name of the famous orator. "Yes, I notice many things."

Agrippa was silent. He did not have an answer. But Attica merely looked at him, her eyes heavy with sorrow beyond her years.

"I know the cost of war, Agrippa, and the price of politics in Rome," she said gravely. "But I lost a friend, not a politician, and there is nothing in this world that will bring him back."

"I wish it were not so," Agrippa replied, his words hollow, useless. He had never felt so ashamed. "I am sorry your husband must always bear you such a reminder of grief."

"Grief, yes." Attica came to a stop and turned towards him slowly. "But also life. There is still good in this world. And I am blessed with much of it."

Agrippa felt his heart lighten, and his hand stirred at his side as if he wished to reach out and touch her. "You are too pure for these troubled times, *mea sponsa.*"

Attica smiled at his words. "You are too sweet, *mi sponse.* But a husband always believes his wife to be pure until they are married."

He laughed. "I suppose we shall see."

But she looked troubled. "We will marry, won't we?"

Agrippa did not answer right away. Though they had betrothed a year ago, the battle at Philippi and the siege at Perusia had kept him away. While he could marry her now, the looming war with Sextus and Antonius stayed his hand.

Of course, that was not the only reason.

"It is a dangerous time," Agrippa said. "If anything were to happen, it would be better to lose a betrothed than the husband of your child."

Attica lowered her head. "I understand. But I hear Caesar has married, has he not?"

"Yes." Agrippa's face burned. "He did. Scribonia's brother is father-in-law to Sextus Pompeius."

Her gray eyes flickered with a passing thought he could not read. "I see."

"I promise we will marry," Agrippa said, but even to his ears, the words rang false. "When the wars end, we will marry."

She smiled sadly. "But do wars ever truly end?"

⸙ ⸙

Agrippa hated dinners. They took too much time, everyone spoke too much while saying very little, and as Octavius rarely attended a dinner without his wife, Agrippa was always obligated to interact with Scribonia, whom he had disliked from the moment they had first met.

"My dear Agrippa, my husband tells me you have yet to set a wedding date," Scribonia said with a bright smile. Octavius lowered his eyes when Agrippa glanced at him sharply. "If I were you, Attica my love, I would be protesting!"

Attica only smiled gently at Agrippa, her eyes knowing. "Do not worry on my behalf, Scribonia. I assure you the choice to delay was mutual."

Agrippa felt his heart swell. He returned Attica's smile, ignoring Octavius' eyes on him.

"Well, when you decide on the wedding day, please let me know," Scribonia said, no longer smiling, though her eyes glittered. "I would love to help with decorations. A wedding is no trifle to execute properly."

"Of course," Attica said, lowering her head obediently.

Scribonia eyed her in slight disdain before she hid it with another easy smile. While Scribonia was more distinguished as the wife of Caesar, Attica was equally well-bred and knew how to dismiss the subtle attacks of wealthy, proud wives.

"Our wedding was splendid, was it not?" Scribonia said, placing a hand on Octavius' arm. He gave her a strange, subdued look before nodding.

"It was very tasteful, yes," Octavius said, his eyes briefly flickering over to Agrippa. "My wife has a good eye for decorations. Her dress in particular was beautiful."

Scribonia turned to Attica. "If you wish to have a similar dress made I can send a note over to my tailor. He has the finest fabrics in all of Rome."

"I was actually going to wear my mother's wedding dress," Attica said. "But I thank you for the kind offer."

"Naturally," Scribonia said with a careless hand, though her eyes told a different story. "But if you change your mind—"

"That is quite enough," Octavius interrupted mildly.

Scribonia looked slightly offended but laughed anyway. "I was only—"

"Silence, Scribonia." He gave his wife a cool look, who glared at him but did not speak. "It is getting late. Agrippa, we must speak business before you leave. Let us leave the women to their wedding talk."

Agrippa felt Attica's eyes on him, and he could not help the slight guilt he felt. "Caesar—"

"In private." Octavius stood up and walked out of the triclinium without waiting for him. Agrippa could do nothing else but follow. They took the stairs silently and went into his office.

"What did you wish to tell me?" Agrippa asked warily.

Octavius closed the door behind him. "It is as we feared. Antonius has allied with Sextus and Ahenobarbus. They are besieging Brundisium as we speak. I received the news just before dinner. We must prepare to travel in less than a month."

"Then it is war," Agrippa said, half-relieved. Perhaps Scribonia would be sent back to her mother too.

"No."

"What?" Agrippa watched Octavius across the room. "Antonius is marshaling all of his forces against you. How can you say there will be no war?"

"There will be no war because our men will not fight Antonius without just cause," Octavius said. "I will send Maecenas to arrange for an agreement."

Agrippa sighed. "Agreements will not ensure peace between you and Antonius."

"No, but they will buy us enough time before the next war. An alliance between Antonius and Sextus is too powerful to pit ourselves against at the moment. We must restore a semblance of peace."

He stared at Octavius, the exhaustion in his face, the tenseness of his shoulders, as if held the fate of the Republic on his shoulders. Perhaps he did. Agrippa thought he looked older, no longer the fresh-faced nineteen-year-old who dreamed of heroes and battle. No longer the boy Agrippa had known for so long, eager and charming and quick to smile.

This Octavius harbored a weariness in his eyes, a hardness around his mouth, that spoke of the horrors, the murders, that he had witnessed, that he himself had committed, since leaving Apollonia and landing on the shores of a war-ravaged land.

But Agrippa also saw that glint in his eyes, like sunlight glancing on the edge of a sword, that had always marked him out from the rest.

Fate is different. Not everyone is born with one.

Were you?

Yes.

Agrippa nodded slowly. "So we make peace with the pirate."

A dangerous smile hovered over Octavius' mouth. "For now."

⇝≫ ≪↢

MAY 40 BC

In the first week of May, Octavia's husband died quite suddenly in the night.

Their house was dark and eerily quiet, save for the wailing of a baby, the shout of a small child running somewhere inside, and the soft cries of women. Agrippa was escorted to the courtyard in the back of the house where many close family and friends had gathered before the funeral procession.

Octavius and Scribonia were already there, as well as Atticus, on whose arm Attica

256

leaned, her face cast darkly. This was not the first funeral she had witnessed recently, and it would certainly not be the last.

Octavia was nowhere to be found. Agrippa took his place beside Attica, and after a few moments, Atticus nodded at him and left them alone in the corner of the courtyard.

For the first time, he did not feel Octavius' eyes lingering on him in the crowd. He rarely saw Octavius these days, constantly occupied with the preparations to leave for Brundisium, taking long walks with Attica when he could spare them, and spending any quiet, lonely nights working on his maps.

"It is a shame, isn't it?" Attica asked, her voice heavy. "Two children without a father. The third will never even meet him."

"No one escapes Death," Agrippa murmured, another phrase he had learned, not from his father but from Athenodorus in Apollonia. He had been confronted with Death before he understood it, and he was not sure he understood it now. "I have been meaning to tell you. I must leave soon for Brundisium. There is to be a meeting with Antonius, or else war. But if I return, then we may marry."

Attica turned to him, her eyes pleading. "You know that is not the reason we delay."

"You see what Death can do, Attica," Agrippa said, looking at the drifting mourners, their hopeless faces, like a sea of ghosts. He thought he glimpsed a pair of familiar brown eyes before they were swallowed up by a passing group of guests. "I will not leave you widowed."

A tear fell down her cheek. "You wait for something that is impossible."

Agrippa stilled. "What do you mean?"

"I know, my love," Attica said quietly, nearly whispering. "I knew you loved him from the start."

Agrippa was silent. She stepped closer, taking his hands gently in hers. Agrippa could not look away from her sad, gray eyes. "But he will never love you like I would. He will never give up the world for you."

"You do not understand," Agrippa said finally, embarrassed that she had read his feelings so plainly, and wondered if others could too.

Attica squeezed his hands, and he swallowed painfully against tears he refused to shed. "He cannot be yours. He belongs to the gods." She kissed his knuckles quickly. "His fate is already written."

Before Agrippa could respond, the room went silent. He looked up and forgot his thoughts entirely.

Entering the courtyard was Octavia, a dark dress framing her pale skin so that she looked like Death itself. She walked slowly across the square, one hand firmly under her pregnant belly, the other loose at her side. Her hair gently fluttered in the breeze behind her, a few strands swept against her tear-stained face, eyes wide and unseeing.

For a moment, Agrippa wondered whether she would speak, but then she stumbled forward as if she had tripped, only to be held in the arms of her brother, who had been there waiting, hidden in the crowds.

Octavia's cries filled the house, until even Agrippa felt a tear slide down his cheek, and Attica's hand tightened in his.

30

Scribonia

MAY 40 BC

S CRIBONIA SWORE SHE WOULD never marry a man again.

She had been twelve when she first married. Her husband had been much older, having already been consul once before. He had been quite preoccupied with his mistresses, and for the most part, left her well alone. Scribonia hardly remembered him now, and she bore him no children as reminders of that time or him.

When her first husband died a few years later, she was promptly married again to Gnaeus Cornelius Lentulus Marcellinus, who had been twenty years older than her, also having served as consul. He was enamored with her, though he kept several girls and boys at hand.

Scribonia had thought him too large in the belly and careless with his business, but he lavished her with all kinds of gifts and was generally sweet in bed, so that she thought it a shame when she had been forced to divorce him to marry Caesar. But she had borne him a son, Cornelius Marcellinus, and a daughter, Cornelia, the latter alike to her in almost every way.

Cornelia had recently married, just shy of thirteen years old. It was young, but that was the best opportunity she could provide her daughter in a world where women could do little else. Her son had begun his schooling under the care of his father's family. Now Scribonia was married to Caesar, a change to her destined quiet life of motherhood that she had never expected.

She felt satisfied having married such an illustrious boy, but weary, as she was already in her thirtieth year, with Caesar seven years younger. While he seemed either not to notice her age or care in the slightest, Scribonia certainly noticed his. Caesar wanted to dominate her, as most boys his age wished to do, but he had only ever dominated men, and the gods knew women attacked and defended in much different ways.

Caesar was rarely home, but he did not neglect her like her first husband had. When night came, Scribonia left her weaving and went to their joint bedroom, where she liked to wait for him. It was a fun game they played.

And after all, he was quite beautiful, in a feminine sort of way, with a slender nose and high cheekbones, as well as lean, youthful limbs, so unlike his manly friend Agrippa. It was not dreadful to lie with him, except—

There was a noise down the hall. Someone entered the house, the door shutting softly behind them.

Caesar.

She was in the bedroom now, waiting.

Caesar lingered, giving last-minute orders to the household, pausing at his beloved office, named after some island or another. He liked to tarry, it seemed, as if he could not decide whether he wanted it or not. But every night, no matter how long he delayed, her husband always came to her.

The door to the bedroom opened a sliver, and Caesar slipped in. He was exhausted, but that was not unusual. Most nights he hardly slept more than seven hours as a strict rule, and he spent over double those hours working ceaselessly.

Scribonia shifted in bed, and Caesar looked at her briefly, then closed the door.

"How was your day, my dear?" Scribonia asked.

"Terrible." He unhooked his belt which held his *gladius*. He never left the house unarmed. Then he turned around, eyeing her. "Antonius and Sextus have come to terms."

"I was wondering whether you would tell me or if I must discover all the latest news from the porter," Scribonia teased with a smile, but Caesar did not return it. He rarely found her amusing, if at all.

"I was hoping our marriage would delay such an alliance," Caesar said, sighing. "But it seems not."

"Perhaps that is because we have borne no heir of consequence," Scribonia answered archly. She would not accept the blame for a problem she had not made.

"I have tried," Caesar said through gritted teeth.

"Not hard enough." Scribonia stood up and walked towards him. "You must keep trying if you wish my brother-in-law to be persuaded against Antonius."

"Maybe *you* should try harder," he said bitterly.

"Now *that* is not the task of the woman. Besides, *I* already have two children," Scribonia said, raising a brow. "I am not at fault here." She paused. "Perhaps it is because you do not love me."

"What?"

Scribonia nearly smirked. "Oh yes, I believe there is a difference. Children know the difference before they are even born, I assure you."

Caesar narrowed his eyes at her, though she saw fissures of doubt creep into his face. "That is impossible."

"My former husband loved me to death," Scribonia continued, nearly taunting now, and finding herself thrilled at the prospect of humbling him. "He never failed me in bed, and he was twenty years older than you are now. You, on the other hand, can hardly find pleasure if you see my face."

"And? What does it matter to you how I find pleasure?"

She shrugged. "I suppose it matters little unless you want an heir."

He was silent. Finally, she had beaten him at his own game.

Scribonia took another step closer. "Perhaps we may ask your friend Agrippa for assistance?"

Caesar looked at her sharply. "What?"

"You think I did not know?" Scribonia laughed carelessly, relishing in the flinch that passed across his face. "A wife always knows. But at the end of the day, my dear, only *I* can give you an heir."

"That is nothing," Caesar said coolly, realizing he would not be able to deceive her on this. "I am married."

"Oh, you do not need to explain anything to me. This is not the first I have heard of that sort of thing." Scribonia touched a gentle hand to his face, and he went very still at the contact. "Please, my love, you must trust me. I only want what is best for you. What is best for *us.*"

Caesar looked at her in silence, thinking, a battle in his eyes which Scribonia did not care to understand. Men always made the simplest things the most complicated, and the most complicated too simple. Finally, he nodded.

"Come," Scribonia said quietly, taking his hand. "And close your eyes."

She led him across the room to the bed, where she laid him down on the mattress. He looked at her warily but did not protest. Scribonia undressed quickly, then climbed over him before he could change his mind. It had been a long time since she had done this, but it had never failed her before.

For she was not just any woman. Scribonia was the daughter of Sentia, a noblewoman whose forefathers minted the coins of Rome, and Lucius Scribonius Libo, descended from the honorable Libones.

Scribonia was a woman of status and respect, who did her duty to her family without a single complaint. She always got what she wanted, and that was not about to change now.

So when Caesar's hips strained towards her in the dead of night, she knew he was finally conquered.

·»»≫ ≪««·

JUNE 40 BC

Agrippa hated her, Scribonia could tell.

Whenever she invited him and that poor girl, Attica, to dinner, he looked at her and understood more than she had initially assumed. Agrippa saw how Caesar looked at her, unloving and indifferent. But it was merely the game they liked to play now, for by nightfall he was beneath her, silent, straining, even pleading.

Somehow Agrippa understood that, or at least sensed it, and now despised her as someone else who had discovered the key to his lover's defenses which others were too daunted to try and break.

For the key was not to break, but bend, and she had certainly bent Caesar to her will.

But Scribonia had no interest in love, or even sex these days. She only wanted to conceive, as was her duty. Men held dominion over the Senate and over land and sea, but only women had the power to create life, and Scribonia intended to wield that power for her benefit.

"Attica, my dear, let us leave the men to their business," Scribonia said as the dinner came to a close. She did not wish to endure Agrippa's glare any longer. "I am sure they have much to speak about."

Attica followed her without protest after a shared glance with Agrippa.

Scribonia led her to the inner courtyard of the house where she usually kept her loom, and had another one brought out.

"There is no need," Attica said. "I prefer to read."

"Very well." Scribonia had a few scrolls of Homer brought out. "I assume you are learned in Greek?"

Attica bowed her head. "Thanks to my father's dear friend, Cicero, I had the pleasure to learn, though I know it is a useless skill."

Scribonia angled her head, studying the young girl before her. She reminded her of herself in many ways, long ago, before the glamor of marriage and children wore off to reveal the rest of her solitary life. A small part of her was undeniably jealous, jealous of her youth, her naivety, the enchantment of one's first marriage, no matter how miserable the man.

"A useless skill for women, no doubt, but I suppose your husband will not mind," Scribonia said lightly. "Not like mine would, at least."

Attica's brows raised slightly. "Yes, Caesar is quite conservative in his ways."

"All men are the same," Scribonia replied dismissively. "They only care about one thing."

"And what is that?"

"Power." She kept weaving, only glancing at Attica to see her reaction, but the girl merely frowned. "Never forget that, my dear Attica. Everything is about power. Who has it, but more importantly, who does not."

"I would prefer to live by love," Attica said coolly, picking up the undertones of her meaning.

"Men cannot love, not really. What they love is power, my dear, and it is best you learn that sooner rather than later."

When Attica refused to respond, Scribonia stopped her weaving and turned towards her. Though they did not get along, Attica was young, and could not understand. But she would. She would understand when it was too late, and for that Scribonia pitied her.

"I have been married three times, and bore two children," Scribonia said. "I have been loved and hated and everything in between. But what never changed was power. Men love power, and it is a woman's job to make him believe he has it. It is only when they believe they have the power that you are allowed to take it away. And *that* is when you know a marriage is successful."

"Agrippa loves me," Attica countered. "I know he does."

"And perhaps he does, my dear, but then why have you not married?" Scribonia asked. She did not wish to hurt the girl, but if she did not tell her the truth, who would?

"I have told you many times, Scribonia. The delay was mutual."

"Nonsense!" Scribonia shook her head ruefully. "It is about power. If not over you, then over another. You understand me, yes?"

Attica was silent. She had noticed. Of course, she had noticed.

"Men only care about power. It is the sad truth."

"Then we live in a sad world," Attica shot back, though her gray eyes grew darker in turmoil, betraying her carefully built confidence.

"That is why we have children," Scribonia said, smiling sadly. "Otherwise, what else would we live for?"

"My father," Attica said, her voice tight. "I would live for my father."

"I did as well," Scribonia murmured, returning to her weaving. A memory flashed through her mind, of her mother sitting at the loom, and her father gazing at her lovingly. "I did as well."

JULY 40 BC

Scribonia held the small child in her lap as he struggled to turn and reach for his mother. "Quite fond of his mother now, is he?"

Octavia looked up from where she sat, breastfeeding her daughter with motherly skill despite her very pregnant belly. "Oh, yes."

When Marcellus died, Octavia had been devastated and had not allowed anyone inside the house except her brother. Since then, she had completely preoccupied herself with her children, and only recently allowed Scribonia and a few other close friends and family to visit in her time of mourning. Though they had not become fast friends, they got along better than she and Attica, and had found common ground in motherhood.

"He will grow out of it," Scribonia said with a sigh, feeling an unexpected nostalgia as she remembered her own son, now almost ready to don the *toga virilis*. "Though you will always be like the sun to him."

"Until I am not," Octavia muttered, picking up her daughter and laying her over her shoulder, patting her back firmly. "But girls always love their fathers more."

"Not always." Scribonia could not help a smile. Cornelia had always loved her mother intensely, and when it had been time for her to marry, she had cried for several days before Scribonia could convince her that she would come and visit often. Only when her daughter had left did Scribonia allow herself to cry too. "But girls leave. Boys stay for longer."

"I suppose."

Marcellus began to cry, and Scribonia stood up, placing him on her hip. He had wispy blonde curls the color of white sunlight, and a round, angelic face like his mother.

She walked him over to Octavia. "See? Your mother is right here, darling. No need to cry. It makes her upset."

Marcellus sniffled, looking to Scribonia, and then to his mother, as if he had understood her words.

Octavia smiled half-heartedly. "You are a good mother. My brother is very lucky."

"It was not luck, though, was it?"

"No," Octavia said with a sigh. "It was not. He always seems to get his way, even if all the odds are against him."

"Not always," Scribonia said with a faint smirk.

Octavia raised a brow.

"I know your brother better than you might think." Scribonia lightly tucked a curling blonde strand behind Marcellus' tiny ear. She missed the days when her children were this small, so pliable, so needy, always, always needing her. The feeling swept through her so strongly she thought she could cry right then.

"As do I," Octavia said in a strange voice. "But he has always managed to surprise me."

Scribonia heard the warning in her words, but she was not daunted, not in the slightest. She had heard how his last marriage had ended. But Scribonia had given birth twice, and nothing Caesar could say or do would pain her half as much.

"Well, your brother will be the last man I marry. I can promise you that."

"Then I suppose you never loved the men you married," Octavia said, her eyes shining. She looked off into the distance as if the ghost of her husband were standing in the very room with them. "But I did. And I would have been married to him all the days of my life if I could."

"No, I have never loved a man. But I have loved my children, and that is enough."

Octavia circled a hand around her belly, smiling faintly. "I understand."

"Do you think it will be a boy or a girl?" Scribonia asked, glad to turn the attention away from herself. It was best not to linger on the past, or what might have been in the future. They were false dreams, sent through false gates from below.

"You know, we always hoped for another boy," Octavia said, a tear falling down her cheek, though she still smiled. "But I think Marcellus secretly wanted another girl."

"He lives on in your children, you know," Scirbonia said, laying a comforting hand on Octavia's shoulder. She had not noticed the tears welling in her own eyes until it was too late. "We all do."

Octavia looked at her, blue eyes bright and firm. She placed a hand on her heart. "I know."

31

MARCUS ANTONIUS

JULY 40 BC

T HE LIGHT OF THE moon shone through the curtains, lifted by a hot breeze. Laughter and shouting reached the windows of their palace despite the late hour. Alexandria was a city that never rested, never quieted. Always some gathering or festival or rebellion was taking place in the city, where people from all over the world, of all religions, came to the vast halls of her libraries and their endless scrolls of knowledge.

Something whimpered in the darkness of the room.

Antonius left the bed where Cleopatra lay sleeping, her hair curling darkly on the pillow, her face calm, peacefully dreaming. He walked over to the crib where he had heard the noise and picked up the small child. *Cleopatra Selene.* Her brother, Alexander Helios, slept soundly in the other crib. Cleopatra had given birth to twins not a week ago, and they were so small Antonius could cradle both in one arm.

He heard Cleopatra stir in bed, and she looked at him, smiling sleepily. "Come back to bed."

"I thought I heard her cry," he said.

"Then let her," Cleopatra murmured. "She will not learn to stop if you keep coddling her."

"You are cruel."

Cleopatra laughed. "She will sleep now. Come back to me, love."

Antonius could not resist when she told him like that, so he carefully placed Selene in her crib and climbed back into bed, wrapping his arms around Cleopatra's waist and kissing her.

"I love you," Antonius whispered. "Do you know that?"

She smiled against his mouth. "I do."

"You are very, very cruel."

"I know." She bit his bottom lip and smirked when he hissed in pain. "Lovers are always

266

cruel."

"Lovers can be sweet too."

Antonius kissed her cheek, then her neck, inhaling the perfume that clung to her skin, burnt cinnamon, and beneath that, the rose water she bathed in.

Cleopatra kissed him, opening her mouth to him gently, slowly, as if they had all the time in the world. He moved his mouth away, settling a kiss on her jaw, and she bared her neck for him, that smooth, supple olive Antonius dreamed about in his sleep.

"You know I would make you my wife if I could," Antonius said, kissing her hair.

"To me, you are no more married than your Romans would believe us to be married," Cleopatra said.

Antonius held her closer, not wanting to let go, even though he would have to. "You know it is different for me."

"You are scared," Cleopatra challenged. "You are scared of what the world will say about you."

He hesitated. It was not as if he did *not* want to marry her, but... "If I marry you, we will be enemies in the eyes of the Roman people. I do not wish to put you in danger."

"Forget the Roman people." She placed her hands on either side of his face, her dark brown eyes persuasive in their twisting shadows. "Your people are here. *I* am here."

Antonius placed a hand on her chest, above her heart, feeling the light pulse beneath, like drums in the night. "I—"

There was a soft knock at the door. Antonius groaned, and Cleopatra sighed. It seemed their time had run out. She turned over and lifted the sheets over her shoulders. Antonius went to the door and opened it. His lieutenant stood on the other side.

"What news?"

"It is from your friend, Cocceius Nerva, sir. He has sent letters requesting your presence in Brundisium. He has spoken with Caesar and urges that you come to terms."

"Is that so?" Antonius sneered. "Caesar wants peace now, does he?"

For the past few months, that boy had been nothing but trouble. He had besieged his brother and wife, stole the legions of Calenus after the poor man had the nerve to die before the battle, and then locked Brundisium's gates against Antonius' own men.

Antonius himself had not idled all his time away in Egypt, having gathered an army to repel an invasion of the Parthians into Syria. He had also been in communication with Sextus and Ahenobarbus, who controlled the waters. This should be the time for war, not peace, and yet Caesar offered him an olive branch as if it were his to give. The boy did not cease to surprise him with his audacity.

"Plancus and Fulvia have also sent letters, sir. They are in Greece, and await your command."

"Is that all?" Antonius asked.

The lieutenant nodded, and Antonius dismissed him. He returned to bed and gently touched Cleopatra's arm.

"It is time, my love," he whispered. "I must go."

She rolled over and clutched at his arm. It seemed as though she were about to say many things, but settled on the one she could speak in words. "Just do not get yourself killed."

Antonius kissed her forehead, then stood up, looking at her carefully until he realized he was trying to memorize every feature of her face, every soft curve of her body. "I will always find you, even after death. That is what your people believe of two lovers, is it not?"

"Marcus," she said, her voice wavering.

"I must go." Antonius set his jaw. "If I come back alive, I promise I will marry you."

"Then go." Cleopatra turned around. "I cannot bear to see you leave."

Antonius left.

⤜⤛

AUGUST 40 BC

"Antonius, are you even listening?"

He looked up at Fulvia, who glared at him from across the room, her daughter Clodia idly eating fruit beside her, seemingly oblivious to the conversation.

Lucius Munatius Plancus stood awkwardly on the other side of the room, observing them with his usual uncommitted patience. They had all gathered in one of Antonius' estates in Greece before deciding their next course of action.

"Of course, I am," Antonius snapped, though she was right. He had not heard a single word of his wife's useless debrief, his thoughts straying from Caesar to Cleopatra to the fleets of Ahenobarbus in a matter of seconds, making him tired and distracted.

"Then you heard my question," Fulvia said slowly. "You must invade Italy before Caesar musters up a force and storms your troops in Brundisium. Sextus has already attacked Thurii and Consentia. Why do you delay?"

Plancus stepped forward hesitantly. "Might I add—"

"No, you may not," Antonius interrupted sharply. "I will not take counsel from the very people who put me in this position in the first place. If it had not been for my brother's failure, or your cowardice, Plancus, or your interference, Fulvia, we may have defeated him months ago. As it is now, we must tread more carefully."

Fulvia stood up, her face livid. "We were defending your title while you wasted your time in Eastern debauchery, allowing your soldiers to die for you. The least you can do is thank us!"

Antonius strode over to her, and she lifted her head up and met his gaze. It had been the one thing he had liked about her when they first married, that she never backed down from a fight, that she would fight for him even if she was the only woman in a room full of men. But that was a long time ago. "You are foolish, all of you. Brundisium has locked her gates against me, forcing a siege. I will not invade Italy as if I were a foreigner!"

"Well, maybe you are!" Fulvia cried out.

Before he knew it, the back of his hand had struck her jaw, and she staggered back into the couch where Clodia looked up at him, her eyes wide. Antonius felt his face grow hot at her words, despite his defiance.

"You and Lucius are good for each other," Antonius spat in disgust, then walked over to Plancus, who was fiddling with a thread of his tunic. "I have heard from Cocceius that Caesar wishes to come to terms. If we make peace now, that will buy us time. War is inevitable, but my men will not fight a Caesar until he has proven his disloyalty or incompetence. Sextus is a mutual enemy of our families. It would perhaps harm my cause if our alliance continued, especially if we invaded Italy together. Then if Caesar wishes to wage war against Sextus, he may risk his own life doing so."

"Wise words, *Tresvir* Antonius," Plancus said with a mild smile as if he had not witnessed any of the familial dispute mere moments ago. He was an untrustworthy man, quite ugly in the face, ruled by fear more so than his own conscience, but he was a useful companion when his wants aligned with one's own. "Might I add that Sextus may in turn deal with Caesar? Perhaps, then, the Sicilian will be more reasonable than the boy?"

"Now that is a very good point, Plancus." He called for his lieutenant and a messenger. "Send a letter to Cocceius. Tell him I will meet with Caesar at Brundisium, and Pollio will be my envoy. Send also a letter to Sextus. Tell him the plans have changed, and to return to Sicily immediately."

"Yes, sir."

Antonius then retired to his bedroom, where his thoughts strayed yet again. He wondered whether the world would fall apart if he left and returned to Egypt. What would the people have to say about him? Was he a traitor, or a lover? Was he a general, or a fool?

No. He could not return. Not yet. First, he had to deal with Caesar, and when he had control of the empire, Cleopatra would rule at his side.

The door opened, and Fulvia stepped inside, her head held high.

Antonius sighed. "What do you want?"

"Is it a crime for a wife to seek her husband before bed?"

"You are not my wife."

Fulvia flinched. "I have been loyal to you."

"But I have not," Antonius replied. He did not wish to see Fuvlia's aged face looking back at him in reproach. Of the many sins he had committed in his lifetime, this had to be the least grievous. "I free you from the burden of my husbandry. You are welcome to marry anyone you like, even my fool of a brother."

Her lips quivered. "You are not the man I loved. Not anymore."

"You never loved me, Fulvia. Let us not pretend otherwise," Antonius said. "You and Clodia must go to Sicyon, where you will serve the rest of your exile until I can reverse it. Leave the wars up to the men."

"Just answer me this," Fulvia said, her eyes filling with trembling tears. "Do you love her?"

Antonius looked at her, his heart beating loud as he thought of that warm smile, her body wrapped around him in the dead of night. "Yes."

Her face turned deathly pale, as though he had fatally struck her with his sword. She clenched her hands in fists and spoke through gritted teeth. "You will rue the day you chose a foreign queen over your loyal wife. The gods will see to your punishment, and they will be as wrathful as Juno to Aeneas."

"Goodnight, Fulvia," Antonius said wearily, turning around.

For a moment, he wondered whether Fulvia had come to murder him, and he waited for the pain of a dagger in his back. But then he heard the door close behind him, and when he turned around, she was gone.

⤜⤜⟩ ⟨⤛⤛

SEPTEMBER 40 BC

He got a letter from Sicyon when he arrived in Brundisium. Fulvia was dead. They said she took ill after the travel from Athens, but Antonius suspected another cause.

In the end, she was just one more death on his hands of many. He thought briefly of Clodia, but decided perhaps she was better off now. Fulvia had never been particularly motherly, and it was time the girl remarried anyway.

"If you want some time to grieve, I am sure Caesar would understand," Cocceius said. He was acting as the intermediary between Antonius and Caesar, being a friend to both of them.

"No," Antonius said. "Let us get to business."

They rode to Brundisium from their military camp off the coast of the Adriatic. His company included Asinius Pollio, Plancus, and a few others. They met Caesar and his envoy, Maecenas, as well as a committee of officers appointed to negotiate peace between their respective parties. Maecenas and Pollio would stand on the council as their respective representatives, with Cocceius as the neutral body.

They met outside the *curia* of Brundisium, Caesar accompanied by his usual retinue. Agrippa and Maecenas on his flanks, Balbus, Oppius, and Matius behind him. Antonius noticed the absence of Rufus, who commanded the legions in Gauls, which used to be his own.

He nearly smirked, having been given a tip that Rufus planned to defect from Caesar and come to his side. It was not a surprise. In the face of Antonius and Sextus, powerful on both land and at sea, Caesar did not look so untouchable. But the time for war would have to wait.

"Χαῖρε, Caesar," Antonius said with a grin.

"*Salve*, Antonius," Caesar said, unsmiling. Perhaps he had given up on niceties. "I have heard your summer has been quite...productive."

A titter of laughter arose around them before Antonius' sweeping glare quelled them. "More than yours, surely. But not more than most men."

Caesar walked towards the doors of the *curia*, most likely to save himself from answering. Antonius followed suit, along with the rest of the attendees, and soon they stood before the makeshift council.

The courthouse they were using was small and modest in comparison to the *curia* back in Rome, but it would do for the treaty they needed to craft quickly and without too much fuss. After the formalities of introductions, the debate began, Caesar drawing the lot to speak first.

"I come to you in friendship," Caesar said, though his grave face said otherwise. "We are kin, your mother Julia close cousins to my divine father, and we are the defenders of the Roman people. Our men wish us to be friends, and for good reason. Will you allow this pirate, the son of Pompeius, to rule our waters, cut off our grain supplies, and give aid to our mutual enemies? Will you forsake your own kin for a traitor of the Republic?"

There was a murmur among the council as they listened. Caesar yielded the floor.

"You ask for friendship, and I freely give it," Antonius said. "But it was not I who replaced the governor of Gaul without consulting one of the *Tresviri*, nor did I transfer the standards of the remaining legions to mine. I have only been loyal to the Republic and our alliance."

"Your brother and wife waged war against us," Maecenas interjected calmly. "Caesar did what he had to do to protect the Roman people."

"Lucius and Fulvia acted without Antonius' command," Pollio countered in an equally even tone. "That is why Plancus, Ventidius, and I did not come to their aid when Perusia was besieged. Ultimately, Lucius and Fulvia did what they thought to be right as well, and protected the agreement which bound the *Tresviri,* which Caesar has been shown all too willing to ignore."

Cocceius stepped forward. "It is clear that communications have suffered dearly this past year. There were rights and wrongs committed on both sides. But now is the time to forgive the past and forge a new friendship for the future."

Caesar looked at him as if he were considering whether this new friendship would be worth it. But there was no doubt they would patch up this alliance, at least for the time being. Antonius had been curious as to what the bargaining chip would be, and as he looked into Caesar's unreadable gaze, he found himself wondering if it had been a mistake to cast Sextus to the wayside so soon.

"If grief is not too near, I offer you my sister, Octavia, as a symbol of my friendship. She has recently lost her husband while still with child, but she is an honorable woman, and will make a good wife."

For a moment, he remembered the funeral at Atia's home, the little girl saying his name and blushing. Then he remembered the woman, her bright eyes cutting as glass. *Piety. Men throw that word around as if they had any idea what it means.*

It was both a test and a trick, for Antonius did not wish to marry anyone else, not when he so desperately wished to be with Cleopatra. But if he did marry Octavia, she would give Caesar too close an eye and ear to his own private affairs, which could kindle rumors against him.

If I come back alive, I promise I will marry you.

When he had said the words, Antonius could not have predicted he would come back married to Caesar's sister. Pollio glanced at him, his eyes warning.

Antonius forced himself to grin. "I accept your offer of friendship, Caesar, and I very much look forward to the wedding night."

There were a few laughs, and Caesar smiled coldly. "In honor of our alliance, you must forbid Sextus Pompeius from attacking our shores."

"Then we must come to terms with him as well," Antonius said. "He will not surrender his fleet without a fight. If you wish to start a war with him, be my guest. Otherwise, peace must be restored. There cannot be strife in Italy while my legions campaign against the Parthians."

"Regardless, I must prepare for war." Caesar looked grim. "He has the power to blockade the coast of Italy and bring famine to our lands. I will not risk starvation for a failed peace with a *pirate.*"

"I propose a compromise," Cocceius interrupted. "Let each man raise an equal number of recruits in preparation for war with Sextus Pompeius and the Parthians, respectively. There can be no more misunderstandings henceforth."

"And what of the old alliance?" Maecenas asked pointedly. "Will Lepidus remain in Africa?"

Antonius shared a look with Caesar. On one thing, at least, they did agree.

"Lepidus will remain in Africa," Antonius said. Caesar nodded. "Now in the name of this renewed friendship, let us reestablish the agreements of our alliance."

Pollio stepped forward. "I propose a division of the provinces and islands into East and West. Antonius will govern the former, Caesar the latter. As a boundary line, we propose Scodra in Illyricum."

Caesar glanced between Agrippa and Maecenas, before nodding. "Agreed."

The rest of the day was spent drafting a more precise treaty of peace which would be the official record.

But before they retired for the night, Antonius drew Caesar aside. Their entourage trickled into the city to find a tavern where games would be played and bet on. He had once heard that Caesar never lost a game of dice, and Antonius desperately wished to call his bluff. But first, he had one last business matter to attend to, and he burned with curiosity to see Caesar's reaction.

"I must speak with you," Antonius said, then lowered his voice. "Privately."

Caesar was reluctant but followed him down the street a safe distance away from the others, their armed guards lingering nearby. A few of their friends glanced their way, questioning, but no one dared approach. "What is it, Antonius?"

"It has been reported to me by my procurator Marius that your friend and general, Salvidienus Rufus, intends to defect and join my ranks. As we have renewed our alliance, any enemy of yours is an enemy of mine," Antonius said, watching Caesar closely to gauge his reaction.

Instead of arguing in Rufus' defense—as Antonius half-expected him to—Caesar nodded pensively. "I thought he might."

Antonius could not resist. "What will you do?"

Caesar looked at him, his brow raised, as though surprised Antonius had asked him. "I shall charge him with high treason." He paused. "Then I will execute him."

Antonius was silent. He never had qualms about murdering those who would murder him, but to execute a friend by trial was quite different. There had to be another motive, not simply to punish betrayal. There was always another motive with this boy.

"But I will only execute him," Caesar repeated, "if I have proof of his treachery."

"I only have Marius' report," Antonius said in confusion. "There were no letters."

Caesar smiled, then leaned in close as if he were telling him a secret, and his voice was eerily familiar in its liquid cunning. "An informer must welcome treachery to hear of it."

Finally, Antonius understood. "You wish for me to execute Marius."

"Any enemy of mine is an enemy of yours," Caesar echoed mockingly.

For a long time, Antonius stood silently, looking at this boy pretending to be a man, and wondered if he would be the death of him. "So be it."

32

GAIUS OCTAVIUS

OCTOBER 40 BC

ONCE THE SCREAMS SUBSIDED and Octavia had time to freshen up, Octavius entered the room. His sister had been staying at his house ever since Marcellus' had been sold after his death.

Octavia was lying on the bed, her damp hair pulled from her head in loose braids, a small, pink child swaddled in soft linen cradled to her breast. The midwife hovered at the other side of the bed, keeping a careful eye on the newborn and the mother.

"Finally," Octavius said, smirking. "A boy?"

Octavia glared at him, but she could not fight the smile tugging at her mouth. "A girl, actually. Claudia Marcella Minor. I shall call her Claudia." She gazed upon her baby tearfully, sighing deeply, though her smile never left. "He lives through her the most. I can feel it."

Octavius tore his eyes away from the baby. He had other urgent business besides congratulating her birth. "The marriage has been approved by the Senate. Once you are well enough, you will travel with Antonius to Athens."

"Come here, brother," Octavia said as if he had not spoken, tickling the baby's nose, her eyes dreamy. "Say hello to your niece."

"Did you hear what I said?" Octavius asked, trying to hide his impatience. She *did* just have a baby, after all.

Octavia looked at him sharply. "Of course I did. What can I say? Ought I to thank you? You have married me off to a brute without consulting me because you knew I would say no. Now the Senate has approved the marriage. There is nothing I can say. This is my fate."

"I did not consult you because there was no time," Octavius said calmly, but it was a lie and they both knew it. He had known it would come to this, but if he had asked her, she would have said no, just like she said. And it was always better to ask for his sister's

275

forgiveness than permission.

"Do not lie to me," Octavia said. "I am on your side, after all."

"It was the only way to ensure Antonius held up his side of the agreement," Octavius said reluctantly. "Your presence will threaten him."

"*My* presence?" Octavia laughed. "I will be nothing more than a nuisance."

"Precisely. He wishes to be with Cleopatra. You must report to me if he leaves you to see her."

"Ah, so I am to be a spy now?" Octavia asked mildly, her attention returning to her child, who latched a hand onto her finger and shook with surprising strength.

"I thought you said you were on my side," Octavius said quietly. "I need you on my side."

Octavia frowned. "Of course I am on your side. It is only that no one is on *my* side."

"Here," Octavius said, holding his arms out as if in answer. Octavia raised a brow as she passed him the child. "You may rest now."

She glanced at the midwife with a wry smile. "You will keep an eye on him, won't you, Delphia?"

The midwife nodded with a knowing smile. Then Octavia laid her head back, closing her eyes. She fell asleep almost instantly, and Octavius walked as quietly as possible to the door, the baby beginning to squirm, noticing that she was no longer being held in her mother's arms.

"I will call if I need you," he whispered to the midwife, then stepped out of the room, the baby scrunching its eyes and swinging an arm wildly. He had enough practice holding her other children that he felt at ease, watching the baby's small mouth yawn.

"I never thought I would see the day."

Octavius looked up. Agrippa stood in the hallway, the light from the door shining around him, his face in shadow. Octavius' heart stuttered in his chest. "Why are you here?"

"Have you shut your doors to friends but welcome your enemies now, *Imperator Caesar divi fili?*" Agrippa asked, raising a brow as he walked closer.

It was meant as a joke, but Octavius could read the challenge in his words. It was always a challenge with Agrippa. Maybe that was why he kept coming back to him, never able to walk away from a bet.

"Oh, but we are not friends," Octavius said. "Not anymore."

Agrippa raised a brow as if considering. A thought passed across his eyes that Octavius could not catch before he nodded. "Where is Scribonia?"

"Visiting her daughter." He paused. "She will be gone for two weeks."

"I see." Agrippa's face was shuttered, unreadable, whereas before Octavius could always read him, like his thoughts were written in that familiar frown. When had they become more like strangers than friends? Agrippa came closer, his eyes lowered, looking at the baby. At his approach, she opened her eyes and peered at him. "She is beautiful."

"A boy would have been better," Octavius said distractedly. It had been months since they were this close to each other, and it felt like slipping back into the same dream.

Agrippa stepped away, and Octavius could breathe again. "I have come bearing news."

"Oh?"

From his furrowed brows, it did not seem good. "Sextus will not give up the Western coast. His blockade will send us into a famine. We must act soon, I am afraid."

Octavius raised a brow. "I will not surrender, if that is what you are asking."

Agrippa merely looked at him. "Menodorus has recaptured Sardinia. We cannot win this war today."

"Perhaps not, but tomorrow is a new day. We will build a fleet capable of destroying Sextus, and we will put an end to that pirate's reign."

"Then you will have to levy new taxes," Agrippa said, scratching at the stubble that shadowed his chin. "The people may well rebel against you."

"It is either war or death by starvation," Octavius countered coolly. "The people have no choice."

The argument returned to near silence, save the small noises from the baby. Agrippa stood pensive, looking lost in thought at the wall paintings gracing the hallway, the bright green wreaths and blushing cherubs, the golden candlesticks mimicking the warm glow of a lamp.

Octavius began strolling down the hall without speaking, and Agrippa followed. At last, when they reached the gently trickling fountain at the center of the courtyard, the small garden around it aglow in the sunlight, Agrippa spoke, his voice low and warning.

"Antonius advises peace." He paused. "The people will choose him as their champion if you do not come to some kind of agreement with Sextus."

A rush of anger rose in him before he could stop it. Octavius recalled Antonius' smug face at Brundisium, the arrogance in his voice when he told Octavius about Rufus' betrayal as if *he* knew anything about loyalty in the first place.

"Antonius advises peace because he knows an alliance with Sextus is the best chance he has in defeating me. He is only biding his time."

Agrippa sighed irritably, the first sign of his true emotions. "You have not been the same since you married Scribonia."

Octavius went hot at his words. "What is that supposed to mean?"

"Your judgment is clouded," Agrippa said. "You think only of yourself and not others. It is because you are so blinded by your hatred of Antonius, of your need for an heir, that you do not see how much power you lose in trying to gain more of it."

"I thought we wanted the same thing," Octavius said, his voice cold like the bite of a winter wind. "Perhaps I am not the only one who has changed."

Agrippa's eyes were sad. "I am still the same man who followed you from Apollonia."

"That is a privilege I cannot afford," Octavius said with a sneer he knew would hurt Agrippa more than anything else. "I cannot hope to defeat Antonius if I cower at his feet like you would. I suppose you wish to end up like our dear friend Rufus?"

"Is that a threat?" Agrippa asked sharply, though his eyes betrayed his hurt. "If you continue on this path, you will be dead before Antonius declares war." His voice was trembling. He took a deep breath and turned around, walking towards the front door. "I should never have come."

"That is what you want, is it not?" Octavius called after him, unable to stop himself. Agrippa went still at his words, his back tense. "You wish I were dead so you can marry Attica and not feel guilty when you do."

Agrippa turned around slowly, his face hardened. "My marriage to Attica has nothing to do with you."

Octavius laughed. He knew this would only push Agrippa away even more, but he did not care. He did not care about anything except that deep, lancing pain, the only thing he allowed himself to feel these days. "Your marriage to Attica has *everything* to do with me. You won't admit it because you are ashamed."

"Ashamed?" Agrippa repeated, disbelieving. "I am never ashamed to love. But you? You would rather die sad and alone than risk loving someone."

"Love is nothing but a weakness," Octavius said angrily, but before he could continue the baby began to cry, her wails growing louder and louder. He tried to calm her but she had her hands in fists, her head twisting furiously away from his grasp.

Agrippa walked back over to him and took the baby in his arms, lifting her up over his shoulder and patting her back soothingly. "Shh, shh, shh. Do not worry about him, my dear. He is just upset."

"I am not—"

"Shh, shh, shh." Agrippa raised a brow at him, his eyes dancing with amusement. "Babies can sense when their caretakers are angry."

Octavius took a deep breath in to calm himself, watching as Agrippa walked the colonnade slowly, rubbing the baby's back and bouncing her lightly until her cries quieted. Soon the baby was silent again, and Agrippa held her in his arms, smiling down at her.

"Love is the purest emotion in the world," Agrippa said softly. "A mother's love for her child is proof of this."

"Love is deadly," Octavius found himself saying, his voice a near whisper. Agrippa looked at him in surprise. "If it were pure, it would not feel like *poison*."

Agrippa came closer, avoiding his eyes, and held out Claudia, who yawned, once more pacified. Octavius took her in his arms, though he was exhausted, and her weight settled against his chest heavily. Agrippa's eyes were clouded in thought, and he turned to Octavius, a hand lifting ever so slightly at his side before he thought better of it and paused.

"Then it is not love," he said at last. "For love makes one feel lighter than air."

Octavius did not know how to respond. They were oceans apart, as though the waves of a storm had drawn them further away, and the harder they tried to reach each other, the more they found the distance between them had grown. The oaths sworn, the promises whispered, the kisses traded like secrets, it all felt so fragile now, ridiculous even, in the face of the wars ahead, the race to power, and Death that haunted their every step.

He ignored the way his heartbeat pounded at Agrippa's half-smile, his chest aching as he watched him shake his head and walk away, all the words he would never say bitter in his mouth.

"Love is a weakness," Octavius repeated under his breath, before he returned to Octavia, the baby fast asleep in his arms.

⋙⋙ ⋘⋘

JANUARY 39 BC

"We must be leaving soon," Scribonia said as her handmaiden adjusted the golden brooch in her hair. She gave him a stern look. "Otherwise we will be late to the party."

Octavius continued to read the latest letter he had received from Antonius, his lips curled in disgust. He was already dressed for the evening event, but then a messenger had come bearing more news of the blockade, and he had immediately taken up his business in the downstairs office. Scribonia had found him with her usual annoyance.

"We will leave within the hour," Octavius said, waving a hand at her dismissively. He wished to read through this letter carefully and draft a response.

Scribonia walked over to him, her head high and demanding. "I must request that we leave now."

Octavius raised a brow. "I am the man of this house. I will decide if we leave or not."

"And I am the woman of this house," Scribonia said lightly, undaunted. "If it were not for us women, there would be no parties at all!"

Octavius sighed. He knew she would not give up easily, and already his mind strayed from the letter to a night of rolling dice and drinking. He could use a break. "Fine."

She smiled triumphantly.

They were transported in a litter to Antonius' house, who was hosting an afterparty in celebration of his wedding to Octavia last week. Scribonia sat opposite him but did not bother to start a conversation.

While the beginning of their marriage had been marked by attempts at niceties and pretended interest, now there was no disguising the mutual dislike they shared for each other.

During the day, Scribonia occupied herself with a woman's adeptness at keeping busy, and Octavius remained out of the house on business for as long as possible or else shut himself up in his office, if only to prevent their paths from crossing.

He did not know what it was, except that every part of the woman was repulsive to him. Her eyes that bore into him as if she could read every little whisper of his heart, her soft hands a stark contrast to her harsh words, and the grip she had on his desires, the fear of never producing a suitable heir, a failed alliance, the revealing of his relations with Agrippa, all of it compounded into a single, unified hatred of her.

But then night came. He was lonely, tired, and afraid. Rome had been lowered to a state of famine, the streets broke out into riots daily, and Octavius could not escape the mess he had made so perfectly for himself. Scribonia waited for him, knowing he could not escape his own fears, his desperation for an heir.

"We are here," Scribonia murmured.

Octavius steeled himself as they went inside. Agrippa and Attica were already reclining near Antonius and Octavia, the latter looking serene but subdued, as if she were not really in the room at all, her eyes wandering with her thoughts.

Though she was still grieving Marcellus, they had ignored the usual waiting period before her next marriage in order to cement their alliances. Antonius, on the contrary, did not seem grieved for his late wife in the slightest, and he grinned and drank with the rest of the party.

"Ah, Caesar has finally deigned to show up," Antonius said, lifting his glass. "Please, take a seat and dine with us."

Octavius went around the room, giving his greetings before he took his place on the couch nearest to Octavia. Scribonia took her place beside him with ease, smiling at the other guests with her usual self-assurance.

"How are the newlyweds?" Octavius asked.

"Splendid," Antonius said, taking a long swig of his drink. He nudged Octavia. "Answer your brother. He asked you a question."

Octavia looked at Antonius with a delicate brow raised, and Octavius had to hide a smile. If Antonius thought demands would cow his sister, he did not know her very well at all.

She turned to Octavius, inclining her head. "I am well, thank you, brother."

It was later in the night when the rest of the guests trickled from the dining room out into the courtyard, some saying their goodbyes and leaving for home. Octavius and his wife were now alone with Antonius, Octavia, and Agrippa. Attica had long ago left, pleading exhaustion, and went back to her father's house, escorted by Agrippa's small retinue of guards.

The lamplights burned low and the hot flames cast the room in a flickering glow.

Antonius swirled the wine in his cup, before lowering his voice, and his eyes grew surprisingly serious despite his clear inebriation. "I have news which I did not mention in my letter to you, Caesar. Sextus is reported to have raided a few coastal towns just last night."

"That is not surprising," Octavius said, ignoring how all their eyes turned to him. He was the one responsible for the lack of peace, of course, not to mention the poll tax on slave-owners and a new legacy duty. "That is why we must defeat him."

"The famine grows worse every day," Antonius continued, though he looked unconcerned, stifling a yawn. "We will not last the summer at this rate, let alone the year. If we do not come to some sort of compromise, then he will grind us down until we cannot fight any longer."

Octavius looked to Agrippa, but he did not meet his eyes and remained silent. He was on his own. "You seem to forget he is our enemy."

"And our enemy he shall remain," Antonius said, then smirked. "But sometimes enemies must be kept closer than our friends."

"Naturally," Octavius said, not bothering to hide his sarcasm.

"Sextus will agree to peace at the right price. I am sure your brother Libo will speak to him on our behalf, will he not, Scribonia?" Antonius asked, happily ignoring Octavius' tone.

Scribonia smiled. "Of course he will. My brother is a very reasonable man. I may also offer to speak with Sextus' mother, Mucia, whom I know well."

"See?" Antonius said to Octavius. "Peace is not so hard after all."

"That is easy for you to say," Octavius said with a tight smile. "You may return to the East at any moment and leave me with a fleet of pirates who could starve us whenever they please."

"I am only advising you." Antonius shrugged. "If you think the people of Rome will stand for this, then I will not stop you. But they are already rioting. It is only a matter of time before you and I are both exiled from the country."

"Then I will speak with the people." Octavius glanced at Agrippa, who finally met his eyes, though they were filled with disapproval and doubt. Had he really changed so much? Did he not fight for the people now as he had then? "They will listen to me."

⤜⟫⟫⟫ ⟪⟪⟪⤛

He had not so much as stood on the platform before the crowds parted and surged together like waves tossing at sea.

His words were shouted uselessly as the mob screamed at him and each other in a confusion of bodies and noise. Octavius felt as if he had been thrown into battle, but of a very different kind.

"Come down!" Agrippa shouted as he and the rest of Octavius' bodyguards struggled to restrain the oncoming crowds in their zeal. "It is not safe!"

"I must speak to them!" Octavius shouted back. He muttered under his breath, "I must try."

Agrippa knocked someone to the ground who had nearly escaped past him. "They are not listening!"

Octavius tried to speak once more. "People of Rome! This is not the time for—"

Pain blossomed on his face, right above his brow. He touched his forehead and looked down at his hand. Blood. His body reeled at the sight, and he barely side-stepped the following stone that had been thrown at him from the mob.

They were stoning him to death.

Octavius hardly processed the thought before an onslaught of stones was showered on him. He was unable to move, his feet rooted to the ground in terror as he cowered and cringed under his arms. Was this how he was to die? By the very people he was fighting for?

Do not speak to me of the Roman people, Octavius. They will adore and praise you as long as they fancy, but just as easily they will turn their backs on you and despise you.

He heard chanting, but it was not until another stone hit his chest that he understood. *Morere! Morere! Morere!*

Die! Die! Die!

Suddenly he was dragged down to the floor. Agrippa had an arm around his waist, breathing hard. He tried to force Octavius away from the stage but he refused. He would not give up. Agrippa glared at him.

"Let it go!" Agrippa cried above the shouts.

"No!"

"I will not leave you to die!"

Agrippa held him tight, and Octavius could no longer resist, allowing himself to be

282

guided around the stage and safely out of the mob as his men created a passage for him through the pressing, ugly crowds.

They found their horse and carriage waiting for them, and they quickly entered and rode away a moment later. A few stragglers tried to follow them but their carriage quickly outran them. From afar they saw Antonius' soldiers descend on the mob swiftly, their swords and whips merciless.

When they reached a safe distance, Octavius forced the carriage to stop with a desperate rasp on the window. He stepped out, staggered away, and promptly vomited. His whole body was flushed hot as if he had a fever, and his stomach heaved.

Agrippa stood beside him, waiting. There were other soldiers accompanying them, but having been so close to death Octavius no longer cared if he seemed weak.

Look at me.

"No."

Agrippa placed a hand on his back, and Octavius shoved it off, standing upright.

"I am fine."

Agrippa took a step forward. "You are in shock."

"I am fine!" Octavius snarled. He wiped his mouth with his sleeve, breathing heavily. "I do not need your help."

"You almost got yourself killed," Agrippa said in disbelief. "If it had not been for me—"

"I might have made them listen!"

"They would have killed you!" His voice broke at the end. Agrippa stepped closer, his hands clenching and unclenching in fists at his sides, and he lowered his voice to a near whisper. "Stop fighting, Octavius. Please."

Octavius felt his will crumble. All he wanted to do was collapse back in the carriage and sleep, let Agrippa cool his forehead with a touch and a flask of wine, as he once did on their journey from Apollonia. Those days seemed so far away now.

Instead, he took a deep breath and nodded. "I will send a message to Libo. We must speak immediately."

Agrippa nodded, but he still looked weary, as though this was as painful to him as it was to Octavius, only for a different reason. But Agrippa knew when to back down, even more than Octavius himself did. "You may still win this war. Just not today."

Octavius closed his eyes, remembering the darkness of the carriage, Agrippa's kiss on his signet ring. Then he pushed the memory away.

At last, he nodded. "Not today."

33

OCTAVIA MINOR

JANUARY 39 BC

S HE HAD NEVER FELT pain like this before.

It ran deeper than her heart, through her very blood, and shadowed her soul. Octavia knew death. She had grieved for her mother, the guiding star in her life, the loss of it like losing the anchor to a ship. But this was different.

This felt like the end of the world.

"Your brother has agreed to peace," Antonius said. "After he was almost stoned to death, of course."

He was sitting near her in the courtyard, reading. Octavia worked at her loom. The house was large and beautiful, a testament to the great wealth and power her new husband had accumulated. She could hear the children playing in the gardens. In the most twisted way imaginable, it seemed, life went on after death.

"Do you blame him?" Octavia asked idly.

Antonius' mouth quirked into a smile, before he frowned, glancing away. "No, I suppose not."

Octavia had been surprised by Antonius. After their wedding night, when Antonius had carried her across the threshold, he had set her down and told her to sleep. But over the next few days, Antonius had used every excuse to spend time with her, throwing parties and reading his letters in the same room while she wove.

It seemed he was so in love with the Egyptian queen that he longed for some companionship, though they had yet to consummate the marriage. She could not tell if it was out of respect or insult.

"Once the treaty is signed, we will travel to Athens," Antonuis said, looking at her carefully to gauge her reaction.

Octavia continued to work at her loom. "Very well."

"Are you pleased?" Antonius asked suspiciously.

"Yes."

He glared at her. "Why do you speak so?"

"How so?"

"Before our marriage, when I last spoke to you, it seemed you hated me," Antonius said, his eyes flashing as if he remembered it well. Octavia herself hardly recalled what he was talking about, but she knew it had been at her mother's funeral, the blinding anger she had felt when he had entered the house. "Now you act as if you agree with everything I say."

"I do not understand," Octavia said, secretly enjoying the annoyance that flitted across her husband's face. "Do you not want me to agree with you?"

Antonius stood up angrily. "You are doing it on purpose. I know you hated me then, and I know you hate me still. You are a fool if you think I believe this...this act."

Octavia stood up as well, a familiar anger sparking in her which usually only broke through the fog of grief when she was with her brother. "What would you like me to do, dear husband? I have been nothing but cordial with you."

"You have been false." Antonius' lip curled, and he came close enough to touch her. "Speak your thoughts. I demand it of my *wife*."

The anger lit inside like a flame, and she tilted her head up, staring straight into his eyes. "Oh, it would not be proper to speak my thoughts."

Antonius smirked. "Try me."

"Then I think you are a coward," Octavia said angrily, all of her pain and frustration and sorrow honing into words, none of them cutting enough for the pain she felt in her heart, sharp as a knife. "I think you are afraid. Afraid of failure. Afraid of love. Afraid of losing it most of all. So you hide behind the façade of a man but really you are a scared little boy who understands nothing of this world and so you would rather destroy it to make yourself feel better. *That* is what I think."

Her husband's nostrils flared as he looked at her, but he did not speak. They were a breath apart, and it occurred to Octavia that he might kiss her.

She shivered, hating him, yet somehow wanting him to kiss her if only to know that he desired her, her womanly pride rising up against his manly arrogance. He was still infuriatingly handsome, almost rugged, like the first day she had met him as a child, more like a dream than a memory. But that only made her hate him more.

Finally, he stepped away, avoiding her eyes, suddenly unsure. Octavia felt both triumphant and miserable. She never had to fight Marcellus, never had to demand love and respect, and the thought made her weak at the knees.

Antonius left the room and went upstairs. Octavia sat down at her loom again, but her hands were trembling. She felt her eyes well up painfully, and she shut them tightly. How had her life changed so much so quickly?

She remembered sitting at her loom and feeling Marcellus' gaze on her when he returned home, like sunlight on a vast field in summer, warm and soft. He had loved her so much. Octavia would never be loved or love like that again.

Octavia remained at her loom until the sun set and the winter cold chilled the house.

⇶ ⬳

Octavia watched her son, Marcellus, not yet two years old, laughing on her brother's lap as he clutched his uncle's arms.

Octavius had a comically serious expression as he alternated bouncing his knees, beginning slowly and then quickening the pace. Since Antonius was traveling for some business matter or another, Octavius had invited himself over to see Marcellus without the risk of running into his rival.

"You must hold on tight to the reins, Marcellus," Octavius said with such gravity Octavia had to stifle a laugh. "If you lose control of your horse, you may very well fall off...and die!"

"Oh, brother," Octavia chided.

But Marcellus shrieked happily and clutched Octavius tighter as his legs bounced faster, until Marcellus toppled over and Octavius scooped him up, giggling, into a hug. "Again, papa, again!"

She and Octavius both went still. Neither of them had taught him the word, but there it was, unconsciously said. Octavia's heart beat loudly in her chest. Octavius stared at her, the most afraid she had ever seen him. Marcellus squirmed, sensing the uneasiness in the room.

"Ah, no more today, *mi aselle,*" Octavius said with another worried glance at Octavia, lowering Marcellus to the ground, who was still grabbing at his knees. He gave Marcellus a wry grin. "The horse is tired today."

Marcellus jumped on his tiptoes. "No! Again!"

"Come, my love, you may ride the horse tomorrow," Octavia said, her voice strained. She had not known hearing the word would hurt her so much. She took a deep breath as she picked up Marcellus and handed him to Prima for a nap.

"I am sorry," Octavius said carefully. "I did not know he would say it."

"No need to apologize, brother." Octavia smiled, and there was joy despite the pain. "You will be more like a father to him than anyone."

Octavius' eyes lowered. "I suppose."

"But why did you visit?" Octavia asked, raising a brow. "You never visit without a reason."

"Do you consider me so?"

"Yes," Octavia said teasingly. "I do."

"Then it is about Antonius," Octavius said, leaning forward, his eyes dark and intent. Octavia had not seen that look in a while, and her heart dropped. "What about him?"

"You will leave with him to Athens once the treaty is signed, correct?"

"Yes."

Octavius looked at her, pensive, then sighed and sat back. He had the ghost of a smile on his face. "You must try to get along."

"Me?" Octavia laughed. "It is not me you should be worried about. Surely you did not come all the way here to tell me that?"

"He does not respect his alliance with me. But if you had his child—"

"He would abandon me," Octavia interrupted, anger blooming instantly in her chest. She felt the truth in her words with a damning certainty. "He would not care in the slightest."

"I am not so sure," her brother murmured. He had a strange, knowing look on his face that she did not like one bit. "He might feel a certain obligation. Or else, he might feel threatened. I could claim the child as my heir one day."

"You assume too much of him," she said, shaking her head. "He is quite simple at heart. And as of now, his heart is set on one woman, and one woman only."

Octavius smirked. "Then let him die for her. Either way, a child is not a simple matter. They may claim more than just parentage when they are of age. Antonius would be a fool to ignore it."

"Nay, brother, you ask too much of me."

"Octavia," he said gently, pleading, something he rarely did. "There is no man in the world who has the power to touch Antonius' heart. Only a woman can do that. And you are the only woman I trust to do this for me."

She felt her heart sit heavily in her chest. What would Marcellus have to say about this? Her mother? The world was set against her, but that was not new. A woman had to fight to be heard, to be loved, to be respected. She had to fight every day of her life just to live it. But to submit to that brute of a man, that arrogant, violent general? It felt like a line she was not willing to cross.

Octavius knelt on the ground before her, taking both of her hands in his. She had never seen him beg before. Not once. He was her little brother, and if she did not help him, who would? "It is the only move against him that I could not make myself."

Octavia nodded. "Then I will try. But I cannot promise you he will do the same."

Her brother smiled. "But I promise it. He is only a man, after all."

⇒⇒⇒ ⇐⇐⇐

JULY 39 BC

The ship creaked heavily beneath her. Octavia nearly lost her balance and held Prima tightly with one hand, the other under her belly. She was now almost five months pregnant, and though it was her fourth child, she had not found pregnancy any easier.

"My lady, you must sit," Prima urged.

"If I sit I will vomit, I assure you." Octavia sighed. "I need to watch the waves."

Prima took her arm and steadied her. "Your husband would wish for you to sit."

"Where *is* my husband?" Octavia strained her neck, looking around the ship to see if she caught his face among the men scurrying across the deck, preparing to set sail. Perhaps he had not boarded yet, even though they would depart in less than an hour.

"He is there," Prima whispered.

Octavia turned and saw him. She was once again reminded of how different he was from her former husband.

Antonius walked as if he had all the power and time in the world, and his smirk and narrowed eyes surveyed his surroundings like a lion atop his kingdom of grass. Marcellus, on the other hand, had been humble, yet self-assured, and he had known the power of a well-placed compliment. But it was not the only difference, as she remembered that night in late January, the night everything had changed between them.

He had returned from work unusually early and had found her luncheoning with Scribonia, who had visited to ask for advice about Octavius and their failed attempts at conceiving. Antonius had practically sneered at them and demanded Octavia speak with him in his office. Scribonia had left quietly after that.

"You are a brute, do you know that?" Octavia had said as she entered his office. She had taken to speaking her mind with him, as it seemed to bring them closer, though not necessarily in a romantic way. It was something else, something she would rather not name. "Scribonia is a friend."

"She is also the wife of Caesar," Antonius had countered swiftly, leaning against his desk and folding his arms. "He might have sent her to spy on you."

"If my brother sent her to spy, it was not on account of me," Octavia had said archly.

"Fine," Antonius had said. "He might have sent her to spy on me. But it is the same difference. You are my wife now. My enemies are your enemies."

"If you mean my brother, he is no more an enemy of yours as he is of mine."

Antonius had spoken under his breath. "Foolish girl!"

"I am not a girl, Antonius!" Octavia had said, raising her voice. Then she walked over to him, daring to stand close, trapping him between her and his desk. He had nearly growled at her, like an animal caught in a cage. "And I am no fool. You fear my brother's power, so you wish to betray him before he betrays you. Perhaps you expect me to pick your side as my husband. Did you think I know nothing?"

Antonius had looked at her in uneasy surprise and tried to move away, but Octavia placed a hand on his arm, taking another step closer and looking into his eyes. She could see his resistance breaking, his eyes wandering down her face. Her heart had begun beating fast and would not slow.

"Oh yes," Octavia had whispered. "I see your soul. I see every thought and dream of that lost boy—"

He had kissed her, hard.

She would have stumbled back if not for his arms, which had wound themselves around her waist, pressing her flush against him. He did not kiss her like Marcellus had. Not at all. Antonius kissed her deeply, roughly, kindling not a spark but a wildfire in her, burning the grief and love alike. He took her right against that desk, with no ceremony and no loving words.

When they had finished, Octavia had not been able to speak, her legs trembling, and Antonius had left the office without another glance, the door slamming behind him.

She had felt a slight pity stir in her, but the feeling had quickly faded. He might have harbored some regret, but she knew he would be back for more. They always did. *He is only a man, after all.*

And sure enough, by nightfall, he had climbed into her bed, kissing her with that same unconscious abandon, his mouth everywhere, persistent, wordless, and they had been like two creatures wrapped tightly around each other, at times fighting more than making love.

Octavia shook her head and felt her pregnant belly. She had done her duty, and soon Antonius would cast her aside. But those nights haunted her, desire like a secret whisper in her heart.

"My love," Antonius said, kissing her cheek, while his knuckles skimmed her waist.

She glanced at him, and the heat in his eyes told her the touch had not been an accident. Prima averted her eyes and feigned caring for Claudia, who was sound asleep in her arms.

"You are late," Octavia said, turning away and looking out at the waves.

"I had some last-minute business to attend to."

"You could have sent a messenger," she admonished. "I have been waiting here."

"You ought to sit down," Antonius said, his eyes looking at her stomach briefly, frowning. "The wind off the ocean can cause illness. Besides, it is a long way to Athens."

Octavia did not protest this time, for her legs were aching, though she would loathe to admit it. Her pregnancy was the only thing Antonius refused to acknowledge. He seemed to be enraptured by everything about her, unable to stay away for more than a day, his hands and mouth searching her even after they had fallen asleep, waking her with no remorse. But when it came to her children or their baby, his eyes shuttered as if he were not really seeing them, and he stood aloof.

She knew that if the child proved to be a boy, Antonius would waver. Here she would be, a Roman wife and son, leverage against his rival and her brother, a chance to live respectably in the eyes of the Roman people. But if the child was a girl, Antonius would have no reason to stay. Octavia would have to fight for both their lives, as she had to fight for her own now.

"You can sit here." Antonius led her into the cabin of the ship, dismissing Prima and their bodyguards.

The door shut and they were standing in the dark.

She turned, ready to admonish him more. "Antonius—"

But he was kissing her, and despite the proximity to hundreds of people, all her thoughts fell away.

One day Antonius would leave her, yes, but that day was not today, so Octavia curled her arms around his neck and kissed him until a new dawn rose, as flaming and red as fire.

34

MARCUS VIPSANIUS AGRIPPA

AUGUST 39 BC

*P*ERHAPS *I* AM NOT *the only one who has changed.*

Agrippa tried to forget his words, but Octavius had a knack for saying just the thing that would stay with him most. Has he changed? Agrippa was taking a walk with Attica in the gardens of her father's estate, but he could hardly focus on their conversation with Octavius' cold laugh ringing in his ears.

You wish I were dead so you can marry Attica and not feel guilty when you do.

Attica looked at him worriedly. "You seem distracted. I thought the treaty with Sextus was all figured out?"

Agrippa nodded and tried to smile. "Yes, it was."

At first, it seemed a resolution would never be met. Sextus had demanded a place in the triumvirate and he had been unequivocally rejected. Therefore, the meeting had ended coldly, but Octavius and Antonius knew war was impossible, so they reconvened the meeting at Puteoli and came to an agreement.

In the end, Sextus would hold dominion over Sicily, Corsica, and Sardinia, and he would be consul in four years, while Antonius would concede Achaia and pay an indemnity of fifteen million *drachmae.* The famine ceased, grain supplies flowed into Italy once more, pirates were cleared from the seas, fugitive slaves were returned to their masters, and even the exiles not formally condemned to death for the murder of Julius Caesar were granted full amnesty and welcomed back in Rome. It seemed the world had found peace at last. But Agrippa knew it could not last.

"It is wonderful that Caesar was able to make peace with Sextus," Attica said conversationally.

"Yes, it is."

Attica eyed him. She knew him too well for him to lie. "You do not agree?"

Agrippa hesitated. "It is only that the peace shall not last."

"I see. But peace shall last a little while at least. *Tresvir* Antonius has already landed in Athens. He would not lose soldiers fighting the Parthians if he thought Caesar would need aid against Sextus." Attica looked at him doubtfully. "Would he?"

"It is hard to say," Agrippa said carefully.

He did not like discussing politics with Attica when their opinions and families differed so much, and when he knew certain things that she could not.

"The Roman people deserve peace," Attica said firmly. "We have suffered enough war."

"I agree."

Attica whirled on him. "But you do not! Caesar certainly does not."

"He does," Agrippa said defensively, though he recalled arguing the same against him. "But sometimes war is necessary."

"Why?" Attica asked with that tempered passion she rarely revealed so openly. "Why must there be war? It is because men like Caesar and Antonius want power. They wish to control the Senate and deceive the people with their promises of wealth and peace."

"But what has the Senate ever done for the people?" Agrippa asked, the words slipping out in a rising feeling of defense. Attica looked startled. He had never argued with her before. His next words he spoke softer. "The Senate also wants power and money. They have never truly helped the people, and the people know this. That is why they wish for someone who will change that."

Attica's eyes lowered, her passion subdued, though not extinguished. "The Senate is democratic. They are men voted by the people to represent their wishes."

"And so the Senate shall remain," Agrippa said gently. "But the people did not wish for Julius Caesar to die, and yet men in the Senate murdered him anyway."

Attica looked up at him with blazing eyes. "Let us not speak of murder."

Agrippa sighed, feeling deflated. He had not meant to begin an argument, but her probing and his weariness had caused him to let his guard down. A small tear slid down her face in frustration, and Agrippa held her cheek in his hands, sweeping his thumb across the soft skin. Attica leaned into his touch, closing her eyes.

"I'm sorry," he whispered.

"I love you," she said quietly. "You know that, don't you?"

Agrippa felt his throat close up painfully. He nodded, unable to say the words. "Yes."

Her eyes were wide and gray as the skies of a storm when she opened them. "I am not angry."

"Neither am I."

A smile tugged at her lips. "Good."

Then it occurred to Agrippa that he wished to kiss her. It was a fleeting thought, like a half-formed memory of a day long ago, but he thought it and now he looked at her and his gaze dropped to her lips, slightly parted, waiting.

He let his hand drop. Attica turned, seemingly unaware, and they continued walking.

He loved her, perhaps, but it was different than his love for Octavius. With him, his heart burned, and he felt intoxicated, irrational, as if drunk on wine. But with her, Agrippa had never felt so calm, so centered, his life making sense for the first time.

"Do you know how many children you would like?" Attica asked lightly, changing the subject.

They had become accustomed to asking each other such questions, now that Attica had accepted an indefinite delay to their marriage. It seemed as long as they spoke of it, she was reassured it would still happen. And so was he.

"At least five," Agrippa said, relieved.

"Five!" Attica laughed. "And I suppose you shall give birth to some of them?"

"Well, how many do you wish to have?" Agrippa asked, smiling as he took her arm in his. She smiled back and brought him closer as they walked so she could rest her head against his arm.

"Why, I always thought two or three at most," Attica said. "I am terrified of giving birth. I fear I may die from it."

"Don't say that," Agrippa said quietly.

Realization dawned on her face. "I am so sorry. It is only—many women die from it."

"I know."

"You will be a great father," Attica said fiercely, squeezing his arm. "You know that, right?"

"And you will be a great mother."

"Then our children will be very lucky because they will want for nothing." Attica smiled brightly, then her eyes lit up. "Come! Let me show you the new roses we planted late this spring. They have just bloomed."

Agrippa followed, and right when he thought everything was perfect, it all changed. A messenger found them by the roses, red as blood. Agrippa knew the moment he saw him arrive, and his hand gripped Attica's arm. Somehow, he just knew.

"Marcus Agrippa, sir. Caesar requests your presence. Immediately."

⟫⟫⟫ ⟪⟪⟪

"Why am I here?" Agrippa asked, closing the office door behind him. He ignored the

293

memories rushing upon him of all the times they had kissed in here.

Octavius was sitting at his desk, reading something. He set the scroll down and looked up at Agrippa, raising a brow. "May friends not call upon each other?"

"I thought we were not friends," Agrippa said dryly.

Octavius looked at him pensively for a long moment, as if he were also recalling that argument. *Love is deadly.* But either he had moved on or did not wish to revive the argument, because all he said was, "Scribonia is with child."

Agrippa paused, wondering what kind of child would come from those two, the ambition and charm of Octavius and the wit and calculation of Scribonia. He decided it would be nothing good. "The gods have blessed you."

Octavius smiled, but it did not reach his eyes. "If it is a boy. A girl is useless."

"Not always. They may be married off."

"I wish for an heir, not a bargaining chip," he shot back. "A girl is a burden."

"Then let us hope the gods have no reason to punish you," Agrippa said ironically. "Why have I come, Caesar?"

A sliver of hurt entered Octavius' dark eyes. "Oh is that how it is now?"

Agrippa stared at him. "What do you mean?"

Octavius stood up and walked around the desk leisurely.

He reminded Agrippa so suddenly of their days in Apollonia, Octavius striding into a tavern with a crowd of soldiers at his beck and call, his easy smile, that charm in his talk just before he shook the dice and rolled, that Agrippa forgot how to breathe.

Octavius lowered his eyelids. It seemed to take much pride to say the words, his voice low and almost pleading. "You know what I mean, Agrippa."

"I am not sure I do."

"Do not make me beg," Octavius said reproachfully.

Agrippa had half a mind to see him try. Instead, his traitorous hand caught Octavius' wrist, the underside as soft as the petal of a flower, and brought him closer. Then Agrippa lifted his other hand and skimmed his fingertips against the slant of Octavius' cheekbone. He remembered wanting so badly to touch him there every day when they were in school—no, since the day he had met him, when he had known there would be no one else he could love as much.

If I were Achilles, you would be Patroclus.

But in the end, their love was a tragedy, and the end of an even more tragic war.

"We cannot keep doing this," Agrippa said quietly, and he had not known he would say the words until it was already too late. Octavius' eyes snapped up to his, betrayal clear and bright in his eyes. *"I* cannot keep doing this. It—it hurts too much."

"You are a coward," Octavius said, almost in surprise, before he shook his arm from

Agrippa's grasp.

Agrippa grimaced. "Perhaps. But it is the truth."

Octavius was silent for a long time, a furious denial stark on his face, before his expression shuttered and he returned to his desk. He sat down and flashed him an easy smile, one of those charming smiles that told people he was unbothered, that made married women turn their heads, that Agrippa had always dreamed of kissing in his sleep.

But Agrippa had learned that even a kiss had its price, and he was no longer sure he was willing to pay it.

"That is not why I called you here," Octavius said coolly.

Agrippa's heart pounded. Of course, with Octavius, there was always something else. "No?"

"I have assigned you to the governorship of Transalpine Gaul." Octavius looked up, his eyes dark and cold, as remote as the depths of Hades, and Agrippa shivered, wondering when the darkness had crept in and never left, or if perhaps it had been there all along. "You must leave Rome immediately."

"Octavius—"

"Caesar," he said. "It is Caesar to you."

Agrippa felt a sharp pain in his chest, as though his words had truly turned to daggers at last, twisting deep in his heart. But there was nothing he could do. The world between them had spun them as far apart as he could imagine, and Agrippa could not stop it now even if he wanted to.

"Yes, *Caesar.*"

He thought he saw Octavius flinch imperceptibly. Then Agrippa left.

⟫⟫⟩ ⟨⟪⟪

SEPTEMBER 39 BC

"Drop anchor!"

The ship rocked slowly as they neared the port of Massilia. A fair breeze sprayed salty water overboard, and the sun shined bright above where birds circled the skies, eyeing the barrels of fish overflowing the harbor.

There were shouts of traders loading their ships full of olive oil and fish-smelling *garum,* shrieks of children running on the docks after their fathers and brothers, and women selling their wares on the side of the road to worn-out travelers and seafarers.

The Gallic coast, its sloping white rock dotted with young green trees, welcomed him as a new land, and a new life. Agrippa stepped off the ship and wandered the docks.

He would be escorted by a small retinue of soldiers to the military base camp to speak with his second-in-command. There would be letters to write, orders to give, and much traveling in the following months. Most likely there would be war, and Agrippa would risk his life yet again for the man who sent him here, no better than an exile.

Agrippa stopped and looked one last time at the ship preparing to return to Rome without him. He watched the horizon, blue melting on blue, all his love and loss left behind, and wondered if Octavius was also watching the horizon on the other side of the Tyrrhenian sea, longing for another world across oceans, or simply longing for things to be different.

But Octavius had been right. He was not the same boy who had followed Octavius from Apollonia into danger and death. Agrippa was a man now, and his thread of fate was bound to Octavius no more than to ocean waves swelling upon distant shores.

No, the Weaver had stayed her hand. His thread no longer pulled him to Octavius, or to anyone else.

For the first time in his life, Agrippa's fate was his own.

35

GAIUS OCTAVIUS

SEPTEMBER 39 BC

H E RECEIVED A LETTER from Athens in the morning. Octavia had given birth to a girl, Antonia. She had written that all was well for now, and Antonius had remained at home caring for her, though Octavius understood the implications of a daughter as much as she did.

It would not be long before Antonius left her for Cleopatra, and when the time came, Octavius had to be ready. But he was far from ready. The treaty with Sextus Pompeius was temporary, and already there were rumors of another blockade ever since Antonius refused to surrender Achaia to Sextus.

Even though Octavius and Antonius had made sure all their acts were ratified from their first day of power, Octavius still felt as helpless and alone as the day he set foot on Italian soil after Caesar's assassination.

There was a knock on his office door, and for a moment, Octavius' heart leaped at the thought of who it could be. But he knew it was impossible. Agrippa was on the other side of the sea, far away from here.

"Come in."

A servant opened the door. "The lady wishes to speak with you, sir."

He sighed. "Let her in."

Scribonia walked inside, her face flushed and bright, smiling with that prideful air he hated. Even though the folds of her dress were loose, he could still make out the slight curve of her stomach. She had her hands perched on top of her pregnant belly, and his servant closed the door once she was inside.

"Husband," she said. "We have received a last-minute invitation to the dinner of Tiberius Claudius Nero. They have recently returned from Sicily, you see."

"Ah." Octavius set down his papers. "And you wish to attend?"

"I suppose it matters little to *me*." Scribonia smiled, and it was all cunning. "But I thought you might wish to cultivate such a valuable friendship. They owe their return among Roman society to you, after all. Such generosity towards so prominent a family will pay well."

Octavius raised a brow. Despite his annoyance at the prospect of yet another dinner party, his wife did have a compelling argument. "And who did you say was his wife?"

"I did not say," Scribonia said, looking pleased, as if this had been the final card she had to play and she knew it would win. "Livia Drusilla, daughter of the senator Marcus Livius Drusus Claudianus. He died at the battle of Philippi."

"Oh yes," Octavius said slowly, vaguely remembering a report of the man. "He ended his life as Brutus did. A shame, really. But her husband fought as well, did he not?"

"Yes, I suppose he did."

Octavius knew Livia Drusilla came from two very prestigious families, as did her husband, Tiberius. In fact, the latter had been closely supported by Julius Caesar for some time. He had been appointed as consul in the second year after Caesar's death until he chose the wrong side, joining Lucius in Perusia, then Antonius in Achaia, and finally Sextus in Sicily. His reappearance in Rome and the late invite to Octavius was a humbling gesture of loyalty which Octavius would not brush aside lightly.

"Is it tonight?"

Scribonia watched him carefully as if she could read his thoughts. "Yes. They await our response."

"We shall be there," Octavius said. "Now leave me."

Scribonia left. Octavius worked in his office for several hours more until he rang for his manservant, and began to prepare for the party. He bathed, shaved, and dressed in his best toga before meeting Scribonia downstairs, who had her hair adorned in gold and ruby, dressed in a loose-fitting stola bordered with vines and flowers. The draping fabric hinted just enough at her pregnancy.

"You look beautiful," Octavius said with a smirk.

She only raised a brow, following Octavius to the litter, and they were carried to the house of Tiberius. It must have been recently bought, Octavius thought, since their previous houses had been abandoned and sold in the chaos of civil strife with Antonius' brother. It was more modest and humble than deserved a man and wife of such illustrious lineages, but Octavius and Scribonia were given a grand escort into the courtyard, where many guests were already gathered in lively conversation.

The room quieted when Octavius and Scribonia entered. Many turned and looked at him with carefully polite expressions, their gazes lingering on his wife, whose hands cradled her belly. He quickly spotted their hosts at the opposite end of the courtyard.

Together they walked over to them. Tiberius watched them warily as they approached.

He had harsh, aged features which were made more wrinkled by a seemingly permanent frown.

His wife reclined beside him, at least five months pregnant and forty years younger, her young face beautiful in contrast to her husband, her dark hair tied back effortlessly in a conservative style. She was radiant and serene, save for her eyes, which fastened on Octavius sharply. They reminded him of something, or someone, and he had to look away.

"Divi fili imperator Caesar," Tiberius said politely. "And his beautiful wife, Scribonia. Please sit, you are very welcome here."

As they reclined on the couches beside them in an awkward silence, Livia was the first one to speak.

"I was sad to learn, Caesar, that your friend Marcus Agrippa was not in Rome," Livia said kindly, her brown eyes warm but unreadable. Scribonia raised her brows. "I have heard you two are inseparable."

"He is a close friend from school," Octavius said automatically. "He has been appointed as governor of Transalpine Gaul."

"Ah, I had so hoped to meet him," Livia said, though her voice held a touch of something he could not place. She turned to Scribonia and smiled pleasantly. "I see you are also with child. The gods have blessed you."

"Thank you," Scribonia said, her voice cuttingly polite.

Livia raised a brow at her tone but did not lose her small, almost unconscious smile. She turned to Tiberius, resting a slender hand on his arm, looking all the more young and sweet next to his cautious old age. "This is our second child. You have two others from a previous marriage, do you not, Scribonia?"

Scribonia narrowed her eyes slightly. "Yes. A son and a daughter."

"Your daughter is already married, no?" Livia shook her head and sighed. "I cannot imagine my children so grown up."

"I would think not," Scribonia said with a shade of sarcasm.

Octavius cut her a sharp glance. Tiberius watched uncomfortably but said nothing. It was clear who had the power in his marriage, and it was not him. Though why that was so Octavius could not fathom, for Livia might be beautiful and pleasing, but she was also young and therefore naïve.

"I heard your father fought at Philippi," Octavius said to Livia, who turned towards him quickly at the words, and he thought he saw a flicker in her eyes that turned the warm brown colder. "I am sorry for your loss."

Livia was certainly smarter than she looked, Octavius realized, for she understood he was testing her and inclined her head gracefully. "Thank you, Caesar. He was an honorable man."

"I do not doubt it," Octavius said.

She had passed the test, but he could read her true feelings easily. Her father's death still hurt her deeply, and she blamed Octavius for it, that much was clear. But she was also a woman raised in a respectable Roman family, and she would never dare accuse him openly.

As the party grew more crowded, Octavius and Scribonia took their leave of Tiberius and Livia and made their rounds among the guests. Soon Scribonia found a group of women she knew and Octavius gladly took the chance to abandon her. Mere moments later, however, he was addressed by none other than Livia Drusilla.

He had been standing in a corner of the courtyard, admiring a statue of Apollo, or at least pretending to, so as to escape the greedy, often false pandering of the wealthy patricians and bankers present. But perhaps Livia was worse.

"This one is an original of Lysippos," Livia said when she approached, and he still could not decide if her smile was truly friendly or not, so beautiful and open it was. And her voice, gentle and kind, fell too softly on his ears for comfort. "Do you like it?"

"Yes," Octavius answered. "I have always favored Apollo over other deities."

"There is a beauty to him that seduces the viewer," Livia said quietly, glancing at him knowingly. "But beauty can be deceiving."

"His beauty is like the light of the sun," Octavius countered. "It serves only to illuminate the truth."

"Ah, but you cannot look directly at the sun, can you?" Livia asked teasingly, though her eyes had grown serious. Octavius found himself both fascinated and fearful of this woman. "You wish to be like him, do you not, Caesar?"

His heart beat faster. "I am not a god."

"Only the son of one?" Livia asked archly.

"What are you suggesting?"

"Nothing that you have not already thought about," Livia said with a slow smile. "Power is fickle. You wish for something more."

"And what is that?" Octavius asked carefully. Despite himself, he found the girl charming, and her words piqued his interest.

"Immortality," Livia whispered, her dark eyes so wide they could have held entire constellations.

Octavius stared at her. He did not know what to say. Livia's smile turned dangerous, but it was unlike any smile he had ever seen, for it was as pure and beautiful as a goddess, but hidden beneath were shadows of thought, dark and secretive.

"I can give you what you seek, Caesar," she murmured. "I can make you more than the son of a god."

"And why would I want to do that?" Octavius asked, his voice turning chilly. He no longer wished to have this conversation, for he sensed a trap and disliked the way he nearly shivered at her words. Many men have tried to sell him false dreams and empty promises, but never before had a woman dared to bargain with him.

"If not, I will reveal to the world your secret," Livia said, her smile disappearing. "I will tell your enemies the truth behind the sun. I will tell Marcus Antonius of your love for Agrippa."

Octavius could not believe the words he was hearing. At first, he struggled with a response, wondering how she knew, or whether she was only bluffing. But something in her dark eyes told him that she knew and that there was no escaping her.

In the end, only a single word clawed out of his throat. "How?"

"A few years ago I saw you slip away with him at one of your parties. I followed you and heard and saw many, many things." Her dark eyes flashed triumphantly when he flinched at her words, and at that moment Octavius realized that she had reminded him of his mother, Atia, and her mother before her, Julia Minor, a woman of honor, and a woman of secrets. He was suddenly very, very afraid. "And I have *never* forgotten."

Octavius moved forward and grabbed her arm tightly, and Livia gasped, looking at him in angry surprise. "Then that is why you have invited us tonight? You and your husband wish to plot against me?"

"My husband knows nothing of this," Livia said, lifting her chin proudly.

He stepped closer to her, looking deep into her eyes, his body numb, as if it no longer belonged to him. "Is it revenge for your father that you seek? Do you wish to ruin me as you were ruined? Is that what this is?"

Livia smiled but it was no longer sweet, and Octavius thought he tasted her bitterness. "Oh, this is so much more than revenge, *Caesar*. I thought of all people you would understand that."

"You have no proof," Octavius hissed, but even as he said it, he felt a sliver of doubt in his heart like a small cut left to fester. "No one will believe your lies."

"Oh is that so?"

"I ought to arrest you," Octavius said harshly. "Give me one good reason not to have you executed."

"On what grounds?"

"Adultery. Treachery." Octavius tightened his grip when she tried to yank her arm away. Her eyes glanced around the party, but no one had noticed them yet. "You may decide if you wish."

"You will regret it," Livia taunted. "If you arrest me, I have arranged for messengers to be sent. My death will be proof enough of your guilt."

Octavius noticed a few strange glances their way, and he quickly dropped her arm, turning again towards the statue of Apollo, ignoring Livia as she smiled once more and gazed at the statue reverently, almost knowingly, as if she had met the god in a past life. Octavius would not be surprised if she had.

He took a deep breath and forced himself to steady his voice. "I have never been threatened by a woman before. I must say, Livia Drusilla, I am impressed."

"Well?"

"I cannot marry you if that is what you want."

"Why not?" Livia asked demandingly. "A man may always divorce his wife."

"She is with child."

"So am I." Livia lowered her voice. "Your alliance with Sextus Pompeius will not last. I am your only hope in defeating Antonius."

He flashed her a cold smile. "Your promises are sweeter than your threats, but not as genuine."

But she was not deterred, and she spoke in earnest now. "Every day that Sextus blockades the West, Antonius grows more powerful in the East. He will have Egypt and Greece and more besides, and allied with Sextus, he will be unstoppable. But in the East, Antonius also remains most vulnerable. The Roman people wish for a mother as much as a father to rule, and they do not trust this Egyptian queen. Scribonia must be taken care of before you break ties with Sextus and you know this. *I* am your answer."

"Given that all of this is true," Octavius said dryly, "if Scribonia gives birth to a boy, I may have a chance to ally with Sextus instead. Antonius will be easily defeated in a naval battle. There would be no reason for me to marry you."

"And your secret?" Livia asked tauntingly.

"You may tell it to the world," Octavius whispered with a smirk, though his heart still clenched in fear. "I will execute Agrippa as the instigator of a plot you both designed to remove me from power. You will be pardoned in my mercy, or executed in my grief."

Livia's eyes clouded in doubt, and she hesitated. "You would so willingly execute him?"

Octavius felt cold and distant, untouchable, like the gods, like the light of stars far away. After all, Agrippa would not be the first traitor he has punished. "Yes."

"But if it is a girl?"

He bared an icy smile. "Then, *my love,* you have a deal."

OCTOBER 39 BC

There was a knock at his office door very late in the night. Octavius felt as if he were reliving many moments at once. His servant opened the door and announced his wife. It seemed not much had changed in his life, but it certainly felt as if everything had.

Scribonia entered the room. She looked at Octavius in disdain. Since her pregnancy, they had not touched each other at all, and the lack of attraction from both of them killed any last remnants of goodwill between them, if there had been any to begin with.

But this last month, Scribonia had become particularly aggressive, and Octavius did not know if it was on account of her pregnancy or their miserable marriage, but he was already sick of her.

"There are rumors that you are in love with that Livia Drusilla," Scribonia said without preamble, glancing at him to see his reaction. "Are they true?"

"Of course not," Octavius answered, perfectly cordial, but he knew she would hear the taunt in his voice. "If they were, I would tell you, wouldn't I?"

Scribonia sneered. "Arrogance does not become you, Caesar."

"Neither does jealousy become you, Scribonia," he countered. He has had enough of her pettiness and judgment. "You needn't worry. I am no more in love with her than I am with you."

"She has said something to you," Scribonia said resentfully. "I know it. She has said something to turn you against me."

Octavius nearly smiled. "You are mistaken."

"A woman is never mistaken when it comes to her husband," Scribonia snapped. "And I have had three of them. I know you better than you know yourself."

"Oh, I really doubt that is true, my dear," Octavius muttered, not without sarcasm.

"You think I do not know what will become of me if I give birth to a girl?" Scribonia asked with a laugh, her face twisted, the features he had once thought quite beautiful seeming as ugly as if they had been marred. "You believe there is someone better than me. Husbands always do. But then after their second, after their third, after their fourth wife, men always learn the sad truth that women knew all along. People are all the same, and you are better off alone."

You would rather die sad and alone than risk loving someone.

"Perhaps you are right," Octavius said coldly. "But I would rather be with anyone other than you."

Scribonia flinched, but then she smiled, and she looked even uglier than before, like a nymph caught in her true form before dawn. He wanted her out of this house for good.

"There are far worse, far more terrible things than a hateful marriage," she said. "But I will let you learn of those on your own."

Octavius shook his head with a sigh. "Your words have poisoned me for long enough. Your only duty to our marriage is that child. Nothing else."

Scribonia smiled sadly, but he saw no pity in her eyes as she turned towards the door. "I know my duty, Caesar. Do you know yours?"

She left before he could respond, but he realized that he did not have an answer anyway. Not anymore.

That is how you know, my child, whether you are destined for greatness.

When he had left Apollonia, Octavius had thought he knew his duty, to avenge the murder of Julius Caesar and restore the Roman Republic to its former glory. But now those murderers were dead, or else scattered powerless across the seas, and the Republic had survived as the legacy of a god bequeathed to his only son and heir. Octavius had the entire world at the tips of his fingers if he would only reach out and take it. So why did he hesitate?

You wish for something more.

Octavius looked out the window, the hills of Rome rising and falling like gods in slumber, the Temple of Jupiter a black silhouette against a rising dawn, bringing light to the houses and streets below, but casting shadows long and dark in their wake.

His heart pounded painfully, as if the Weaver had his thread of fate pulled so taut it might snap. For a brief moment, he wished Agrippa were here, and his heart ached. Then the feeling passed and he knew what he had to do. He had trusted his fate this far, and there was no reason to stop now, no matter the price he may have to pay.

Octavius took up a pen and parchment, the ink shining gold in the bright rays of the sun, like the spilled blood of the immortal gods above.

Dear Livia Drusilla...

His fate had just begun.

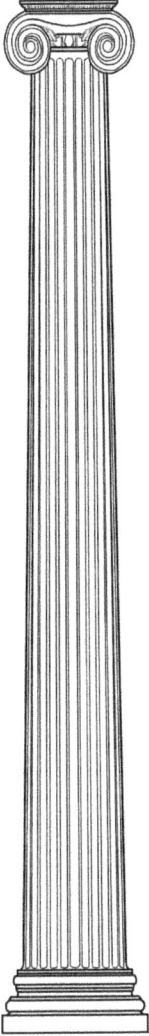
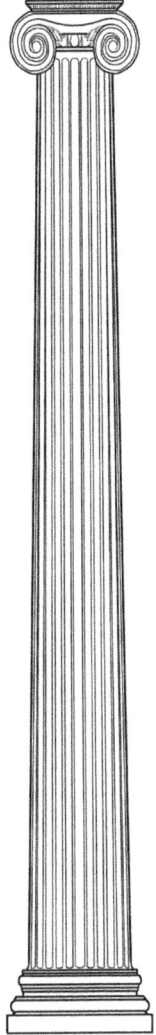

VOLUME II

Augustus

36

LIVIA DRUSILLA

NOVEMBER 39 BC

W HEN LIVIA WAS YOUNGER, her father had told her that she would accomplish great things one day. She was the daughter of a long line of senators, after all, and she was beautiful.

Livia used to believe him.

Then she got older, and she realized her father had simply wished she had been the boy all the midwives had predicted.

At sixteen she was quickly married off, a year later her father died, and then she gave birth to her son, Tiberius. Her family was on the run for a few turbulent years as Caesar and Antonius wavered between peace and open war.

Livia would have lived quite a comfortable, though monotonous life as the wife of Tiberius Claudius Nero, a wealthy politician nearly forty years older than her, if it had not been for a very unlikely incident five years ago.

The day remained as clear in her memory today as if she were living it. She had only just married when her husband had been invited to a dinner party of Caesar Octavianus, the son and heir of Julius Caesar, who had recently been betrothed to the daughter of Servilius Isauricus. It had been a purely formal matter of attendance, but that night Livia had seen something that would change the course of her life forever.

That night Livia saw her future.

Unlike what she had told Caesar, she had stumbled on the room thinking it was empty. She had left the party on the pretext of finding the latrines and had wandered into the back of the house looking for something quite different: Julius Caesar's study.

For Livia had always been a curious soul and never shied from danger, which her father had encouraged to the constant worrying of her mother. She had only wanted to read through the infamous man's letters, to glimpse into his mind, and be in the space he had spent so much time scheming both good and evil.

But the room had not been empty.

There, fighting against the strong arms of Marcus Agrippa, had been none other than Caesar, in his twentieth year at the time. At first, Livia had almost called for help, thinking he had been in danger, but something held her voice back. Because they were not fighting. No, they were not fighting at all.

They were *kissing*.

She had hardly been able to comprehend the pain on Agrippa's face as he fit his mouth against Caesar's, who, instead of protesting—as Livia half-expected him to do—had kissed back with a reckless abandon.

It had been too much. She had hardly kissed her husband, let alone watched others kiss. So Livia had fled back across the courtyard, hiding in a corridor for a few moments to catch her breath, before returning to the party and hoping the heat on her cheeks had faded. She had wondered if they had seen her, but both boys had been so wrapped up in each other they had not even heard her approach.

Soon Livia was forced to flee Rome anyway, and the incident was set aside in the face of exile and death. But she never forgot. And when her husband was allowed back in Rome, now controlled by the same ambitious and unforgiving Caesar she had seen helpless in the arms of his closest confidant, Livia knew this was her chance.

This was her chance to make her father proud.

Livia did worry for a time after their party when she had finally confronted Caesar that she would be quietly arrested and executed and all her plans would be foiled. She knew that at the end of October, Scribonia had given birth to a girl, Julia Caesaris filia. She also knew that on the very same day, Caesar had divorced her. It quickly became the scandal of the city.

She heard the news herself when Caesar had paid a visit to their house the next day and spoke with her husband privately. An hour later they had emerged, Caesar stoic but his eyes gleaming triumphantly. Her husband had not quite reached her gaze, but he never spoke ill towards her, so Livia knew Caesar had gently persuaded Tiberius to divorce her in exchange for generous compensation.

A few days later, Livia returned to her mother's house, where she planned to spend the remainder of her pregnancy. She had not seen Caesar, but she had heard much of his crumbling alliance with Sextus Pompeius after his divorce, as the Sicilian once more blockaded the Western shores.

But still, there had been no message sent to her that he planned to marry her, and she had become anxious that at the last minute, her plans would fall through. That is, until now.

Caesar had sent a discreet messenger at the beginning of November to arrange a private meeting. She was escorted by an armed guard in the dead of night to his house on the Palatine, since his wife, Scribonia, was away visiting her children. There would be no one to hear their conversation except them two alone, no one to stop Caesar from ending her life right then and there.

They sat in his office, Caesar behind his large desk, looking at her carefully.

A small part of Livia hated him, truly and deeply, as the murderer of her father. But that was locked and stored away in the most secretive corner of her heart. Because another part of her found Caesar quite interesting, if not even handsome, his young face so still and watchful, his dark eyes flickering with unreadable thoughts, the smirk always there at the edge of his mouth.

They were alike in many ways. Both their fathers were dead, both held secrets close to their chests, and both had desires far beyond the limits of their world. But in one thing they were different.

Livia was a woman, and therefore she could create life.

"You are quite far along," Caesar said, glancing at her belly. Indeed she was almost seven months pregnant, and the baby would most likely be born early in the new year. "I will not marry you while you are pregnant with another man's child. You must give birth before."

"It matters not. I will remain with the child until he can be nourished on his own. Then he shall be returned to his father."

He nodded in assent. These were only the customary legalities of divorce. "And you said you have another child?"

"Yes," Livia said. "Tiberius. He would remain with his father as well." Though her heart ached at the separation, her former husband was a good father, and besides, his old age would not keep her children away for long.

Caesar raised a brow. "He is a boy."

"Why have you brought me here?" Livia asked, masking her impatience with a smile. "Do you simply wish to know more about me?"

"If I recall correctly, *you* threatened *me*," Caesar said mockingly.

"Is that not what you men call a business deal?" Livia asked, equally mocking.

Caesar's eyes flashed. "You are smarter than you look."

"Because I am a woman?"

"Because you are beautiful," Caesar said, folding his hands on the desk in front of him as if this were truly a business deal. "It is hard to believe the gods blessed you with both graces."

Livia was pleased despite herself. "You had best believe it, Caesar."

"I still do not like it."

"You do not have to," Livia said with a smile. "You only have to hold up your end of the deal."

Caesar studied her, and her smile fell. He angled his head as if to get a better look, and she resisted the urge to squirm under his gaze. It seemed he saw something there that interested him, for he asked, "Did you even consider the risks of marrying me? It is a wonder you would give up a life of comfort and stability for a man you do not even know."

Livia paused, thinking how best to phrase it, without giving too much of herself away. "Tiberius is an honorable man," she said slowly. "But he is old and scared. He wishes only to remain safely out of the way and survive the civil wars. But I am like you. I want something more."

"And your children? Do you want *them* to remain safely out of the way?"

She was silent for a moment. Of all the questions he might have asked, Livia had not predicted this one. She thought of her eldest, Tiberius, a sensitive child who clung to her, who did not have her boldness and love of adventure. She thought of the child not yet born in her womb and wondered what kind of life she was bringing him into, the high risks that promised yet higher rewards.

"My son takes after his father," Livia said finally. "I see it in his eyes. He will amount to nothing great in that household."

"For that is what you want, is it not?" Caesar asked, smiling, but it was secretive, like her own. She understood, then, why Agrippa had wanted to kiss it, and why it had pained him, like wishing to kiss a god only to discover his own mortality in doing so. "You wish to be great. You wish your children to be great."

Livia met his gaze fiercely. "We are alike in that way."

Caesar looked away, thoughtful. "And you believe by marrying me you shall achieve that?"

"I do not believe it," Livia said. "I know it."

"How?"

His eyes burned with curiosity, despite his careful nonchalance. Livia had known he would want a reason that made him believe, a reason that defied reasoning. He wanted to know that the gods were watching them now.

"Ever since my father died, I have dreamt the same dream many times. I am walking in a garden at night, overgrown and lush, filled with birds and flowers. In the center of the garden stands a laurel tree, still young and growing, but majestic and powerful. As I approach, a light shines from within the tree, and the voice of a god speaks to me." She smiled, for she remembered how Caesar had looked at the statue in her courtyard, the look he gave her now. "The voice of Apollo."

Caesar stared at her, his eyes half-lidded, a divine fire kindled in them. "And what does he say?"

"*Look at me,*" Livia whispered. Caesar's eyes widened. "*I am your destiny.*"

⟶⟫⟫ ⟪⟪⟵

JANUARY 38 BC

"Are you ready?" Caesar murmured, standing above her.

She had given birth to her second son, Nero Claudius Drusus, nineteen days before the Kalends of February. Caesar had notified her of their wedding date that very day, and now only three days later, they were holding the customary wedding ceremony and feast at her former husband Tiberius' house, who had reluctantly agreed to send her off in the place of her late father.

Livia glanced at Alfidia, her mother, who smiled at her, eyes welling with delicate tears. Her mother had always been a sensitive woman, and ever since Livia's father had passed away, she cried often.

While her mother had approved their marriage, she had warned Livia not to love a man like him, for he would only hurt her.

"Do not worry, *mater,*" Livia had told her. "The only man I will ever love is dead."

Now Livia looked up at her new husband and smiled. "I am ready."

Caesar lifted her from the couch, carrying her towards his home on the Palatine while she feigned fright. Since she had just given birth, they had a litter bring them up the hill, then Caesar carried her across the threshold, his expression dark and silent.

Livia touched his cheek, and he tensed under her touch. "*Ubi tu Gaius, ego Gaia.*" *Wherever you are, Gaius, I, Gaia, am.*

She had said the vow before, but never had she felt the words stir in her like they did now with Caesar looking into her eyes. Then he leaned in and sealed the vow with a kiss. His mouth was soft and light against hers, then quickly pulled away.

Once they were in the empty atrium of the house, Caesar led her quietly to the back of the house into the shared bedroom, which was small and surprisingly cramped for a man of such great wealth. He moved deliberately, but Livia sensed a hesitancy to his step, a flitting of his eyes that betrayed his confidence.

"We may rest tonight if you like," Livia suggested.

Caesar gave her a sidelong glance. "No. Come here."

She stepped forward just as he reached out and unfastened her shoulder clasps, roughly dragging her dress down. Livia remained still as he removed the rest of her underclothes.

311

She still had a curve in her stomach from the recent birth, the skin wrinkled and stretched, but she was young, younger than his previous wife had been.

Yet Caesar hardly looked at her before he moved her back on the bed. With his hands on her shoulders, he turned her around and forced her down onto her knees. She tried to adjust herself, but Caesar laid a heavy hand on her back.

"Lie still," he said.

She remained unmoving as he knelt behind her. Her wedding night with Tiberius had been similar, and she closed her eyes tightly as she prepared for the unceremonious pain.

Then, nothing.

Livia opened her eyes. "My love?"

Silence.

"Caesar?"

"I—I can't." His voice sounded strangled.

She turned over. "What is wrong?"

He would not look her in the eyes. She dropped her gaze and understood.

"I can't," he repeated, almost brokenly, and for the first time, Livia felt pity for him. But this was not her first marriage, and this was not the first time she had dealt with this problem. It seemed for Octavius, it was.

"You needn't worry," Livia said gently. "We may try again tomorrow."

"No," Caesar whispered angrily. "We must do this."

Livia touched his arm, and he looked at her helplessly. "Not today," she said, quietly. "There is time."

"That is where you are wrong." He sounded defeated, and very young. "There is no time."

She placed a hand on his cheek, as she did to her son when he started to cry. "I have two sons. There will be another soon. I promise."

Caesar hesitated, pained but subdued, and to her surprise, he nodded. "Tomorrow."

She kissed him lightly on the cheek. "Tomorrow."

➤➤➤ ⫷⫷⫷

MARCH 38 BC

Tomorrow came and went, as did the next day, and the next, without another attempt at consummating their marriage, until January and February passed by swiftly, an early spring not far behind.

Livia had her hands full with both her own newborn baby and Scribonia's baby, Julia, and Caesar worked night and day to stop the blockade and end the famine which had returned to Rome with a vigor.

She heard the rattling of the keys at the front door, and she called over Phoebe, her handmaiden, who already had Julia in her arms, to take Drusus as well. Octavius disliked the noise of babies when they spoke, and they spoke often.

It seemed he liked her advice more than her body, though they did not always agree. Livia enjoyed these moments more than she would like to admit, for he made her feel useful—not despite being a woman—but because of it.

"It seems war with Sextus is inevitable," Caesar said as a way of greeting. He crossed the atrium and kissed her briefly, a rare, unconscious display of affection that Livia secretly enjoyed, if only as a sign of her success in winning him over.

"But you knew this, didn't you?" Livia asked, raising a brow.

Her husband sighed heavily as his manservant took off his cloak. "I suppose."

"Then what is the problem?"

"We cannot hope to win," Caesar answered reluctantly. "Sextus is too strong a naval power. We do not have enough men."

"Antonius will not send his men?"

Livia knew the alliance between Antonius and Caesar was precarious, but she had thought it would hold for long enough to defeat Sextus at the very least. Caesar seemed to have hoped for the same thing, but as each passing day brought less and less communication from the other *Tresvir,* that hope dwindled.

Caesar glanced at her, a thought hiding behind his eyes. "He may."

She read the thought more clearly when he looked away, hesitating. "You think it will not be enough even if he does."

"We have no fleet," Caesar said in explanation. "Our soldiers are useless against him."

"Then build a fleet of your own," Livia urged, placing a hand on his arm. "Build a fleet larger than his."

Caesar shook his head, covering her hand with his own. "We have no time. Besides, a fleet is expensive."

"Raise money, and make time," Livia said, her voice firm. She had seen men raise armies in the blink of an eye, and make money out of nothing. There was no reason Caesar could not do the same with a fleet. "Distract Sextus for as long as you can. Force his hand. There are those on his side who will be afraid, and desert him. Then when the time is right, you may strike again."

He looked at her with raised brows, then grinned. "You are too smart for your own good, do you know that?"

"Someone may have told me so," Livia said teasingly.

Then Caesar frowned as he thought over what she had suggested. "But who can I trust to build me a fleet of such large proportions? If I leave this task in the wrong hands, I may very well build the fleet that would destroy me."

"He must be someone loyal to you," Livia said quietly, squeezing his arm meaningfully. "And to you alone."

Caesar looked at her in surprise, then doubt. He turned away, and her hand dropped back to her side. He remained silent and pensive for some time. She thought she understood.

Finally, he sighed, glancing at her, his brown eyes hardening. "There is someone."

37

MARCUS VIPSANIUS AGRIPPA

AUGUST 38 BC

"CONGRATULATIONS, GENERAL." HIS LIEUTENANT, Manius, embraced him firmly. "You have done great work here, sir. You are the first general after *Divus Iulius* to cross the Rhine. *Imperator* Caesar shall certainly reward you for your victory."

"Thank you," Agrippa said, but he did not believe it. Octavius was unlikely to hand out rewards for the very task which had been meant more as punishment than anything else. "But we still have more work to do."

Although just last spring they had managed to quell a fierce rising of the *Aquitani,* a tribe that occupied the lands between the Atlantic Ocean and the Pyrenees, there were still other rebellions stirring among the Germanic tribes that needed his attention. Even if Octavius granted him a triumph for his victory in one battle, Agrippa could very well perish in another.

Despite his unofficial exile, Agrippa had enjoyed the Gallic landscapes and military escapades. His men loved and respected him, and together they fought well and enjoyed themselves afterward, gambling on dice and watching the performances of dancing women.

As they often did as night settled on his base camp along the Rhine river, Agrippa and his squadron had gathered in the local inn and drank, speaking of their various near-death escapes from dangerous rebels, as well as their recent conquests of the neighborhood women.

"There was one by the fish market in Massilia the other day," one of his men said with a touch of pride. He was really still a boy, just shy of his eighteenth year, and he felt the need to prove himself among the men. "Had to have been twice my size, that one."

"The fish or the woman, son?" Agrippa asked with a grin.

315

His men all laughed.

"Are you celebrating today, general?" another asked him.

Agrippa hesitated. "I don't know..."

"Oh, come on, Agrippa, it is not as if you are married to the girl!"

But it was not a girl on his mind at all. Agrippa glanced at the dancer walking towards them now, clothed in thin leopard skins and holding a small flute. Before he could protest she took a seat on his lap to the cheers and taunts of all his men, and began to play a jaunty tune, the flute pressed against her red-painted lips.

She looked as if she had come from somewhere in the East, with overlined kohl around her eyes and a strange perfume clinging to her skin, though he knew she most likely hailed from Hispania or Africa.

"Go on, then, my friend," Manius said, nudging his arm. "You deserve it."

He placed a hand on the girl's waist, which was soft and curved. She turned to him and smirked, but her eyes were dark and serious, reminding him all too much of someone else. It was not as if he did not enjoy himself from time to time. And why should he not? He did not owe Octavius anything.

Last he heard, Octavius had divorced Scribonia and married a certain Livia Drusilla. They even said he was in love with her. Agrippa only hesitated because it had been nearly a year since he had left Rome, and his thoughts strayed to him more than usual. That was all.

Agrippa moved his hand up her waist slowly. He could imagine it, then, slipping into a dark room in the back of the inn, sliding down the leopard skin and melting into the pleasure, the quick thrill of a nameless girl. It would hardly cost a fortune. Her perfume was like a spell, sweet and spicy at the same time, and Agrippa nearly stood up to leave with her when a messenger approached their table.

"There is a letter from Rome, sir," said the messenger. "Addressed to the general Marcus Agrippa."

He stood up, releasing the girl, who cast a disappointed look his way before settling on the lap of his lieutenant, who gladly held her in his arms. His heart beat fast as he imagined every scenario back in Rome that would warrant a letter. "Who is it from?"

"Caecilia Pomponia Attica, sir."

He sighed deeply as his men laughed, jostling each other with knowing grins. "It is the wife!"

"Ah, yes, the wife always knows!"

Agrippa quieted them with a hand, then followed the messenger to a private room, where he read the letter quickly. It was written in Attica's hand rather than dictated, which meant it would contain news she did not want the wrong people to hear.

Greetings to Marcus Vipsanius Agrippa, from Caecilia Pomponia Attica,

A shadow grows every day over the city. I find myself counting the days until you return, my love. Rome is not the same without our walks in my garden. Sextus continues his blockade mercilessly, and the people turn to a savior, though it seems there is none to be had. I am sure you have heard the news already, but I shall give you my account of it.

Only a week ago Caesar was defeated in a bloody battle at sea after attacking Sicily, though I hear a certain captain Menas has deserted Sextus for our side—if I may call it that. It was already a devastating loss before a storm destroyed the remaining ships the following day. Rumor circulates that he has asked Antonius for aid to no avail. I do not understand why he fights when we may have peace, but I suppose you would tell me it is necessary.

I await your return eagerly, but without worry, for I am sure you will return. However, in case you must hear it from me, please do return. I cannot endure the whims of our leaders without your reasoning voice to calm me. Vale.

He set the letter down, his mind reeling. The events of the year remained a vague jumble in his head, as Rome sent infrequent reports this far into Gaul and he had been so occupied with his own battles. But Agrippa had thought Octavius would at the very least inform him of his plans, especially if those plans included such a dangerous attack on Sicily.

While Menas' desertion was not necessarily a surprise, he doubted Octavius would consider that fact enough to stage an offensive move against Sextus' main naval base without a comparable fleet of his own. It simply did not make sense. And now he was asking Antonius for aid? The very man who had abandoned him in Rome to take the brunt of the people's unrest once famine returned?

It seemed the moment Agrippa had left, Rome had fallen apart. He needed to return, he *wanted* to return, despite his better sense warning him of the consequences. He imagined all the times they fought, then all the times they kissed, the feeling when Octavius finally surrendered—Agrippa stopped himself before his thoughts got out of hand.

He was only stationed in Gaul for the rest of the year, as he had been appointed consul for the following term. If Octavius did not change his mind about that, Agrippa would be back in Rome by December. And he knew he would quickly prefer to be back here, away from the boy who had only ever brought him heartbreak and pain.

Yes, soon he would be back in Italy, and Rome would embrace him in the heart of her valley again. But until then, Agrippa would enjoy the freedom and pleasures of the military camps, and the sheer, serene beauty of *Gallia Transalpina.*

He returned to the main room of the inn, where his men were still joking with each other about the flutist. When Manius spotted him, he quickly released the girl, and she waltzed over to Agrippa's arms as if she knew all along he would have her.

"Ready?" she asked, smirking, a slight accent as she spoke the word. He had been right—she was one of those infamous Gades women from Hispania.

Agrippa smiled, kissing her cheek. "Yes."

⭑⭑⭑

NOVEMBER 38 BC

Agrippa took a deep breath as his boat docked on the Tiber River. His stomach turned, looking at the crowded streets of peasants rushing to the markets and busy tradesmen unloading their boats, only for them to be rowed back out to the ocean and shipped around the empire.

He had received a brief letter from Octavius a month ago recalling him to Rome earlier than he had planned. There was no explanation, but his men considered it a reward for his victories in Gaul. Agrippa did not think so.

Octavius had an escort prepared for him, and Agrippa was taken up to his house on the Palatine. He had only been gone a year, but it might as well have been a decade. The gray skies broke out in a steady rain as the guards dropped him off in front of the house, where Octavius' porter opened the door for Agrippa and led him into the atrium.

Standing there in a modest tunic, his hair in dire need of a trim and a shadow of a beard on his chin, was Octavius. He looked at Agrippa, assessing him briefly before he stepped forward and smiled as though he was greeting an old friend. The familiarity of the movement made Agrippa's head light.

They embraced casually, their kiss nothing more than a light brush of their lips.

"You are back," Octavius said, sounding oddly relieved.

He led them to his office upstairs, though he did not take a seat, merely leaning on his desk, forcing Agrippa to stand awkwardly a meter away. How many times had he looked at Octavius in this exact position? How many times had he kissed him there?

"You called me here, Caesar," Agrippa said, keeping to formalities. He thought he saw a flicker of surprise in his eyes. "Why? I cannot imagine it is merely because of my consulship."

Octavius smiled apologetically. "I had no choice. It is Sextus."

Agrippa raised a brow. "I heard of your defeat. Antonius still refuses to send you legions?"

He cut him a sharp glance as if he had thought Agrippa would never find out. Then he nodded, scratching at his chin thoughtfully. "He sailed to Brundisium with troops but

318

returned to Athens when I was not there to receive him. Or so he says. I expected no less from *him*. But Maecenas has sailed after him. He will come around with some...convincing."

"And when Antonius arrives?"

"Then we will come to terms and extend our alliance before he returns to Athens." Octavius sighed, and he looked older, weathered, in a way that Agrippa had not seen before. Was it because of the wars with Sextus? Or something else entirely? "Antonius will never waste his time fighting Sextus. He will leave the dirty work to me."

"Then why am I here?" Agrippa asked, his patience worn thin already. He longed for his simple life back in Gaul, the tall mountains and flowering fields, the strict military schedule, and the nights drinking away his thoughts. "It seems you have everything figured out."

Octavius smirked. "I have a job for you."

Agrippa's heart dropped. "A job?"

"Yes." Octavius began walking towards him. "Fighting Sextus with an army is impossible. And peace would never last. The only way to defeat Sextus' fleet would be to build a fleet of our own. And *that* is why you are here."

"You wish for me to build you a fleet," Agrippa repeated slowly. He shook his head, exasperated. "That will take a year, at the very least."

"Two years is more likely." Octavius shrugged. "A fleet is the only way we shall defeat him."

"Then you will need to build a harbor," Agrippa murmured, his mind turning over the idea curiously despite himself.

He envisioned a large fleet, the largest fleet Rome had ever seen, more advanced and deadly than any before, setting sail and burning Sextus' fleet across the open sea. Octavius looked at him silently, waiting. *I know no better tactician.*

"Yes, you will need a better harbor than the land offers," Agrippa said at last. "A safe harbor. We will need crews to be trained. Before I left for Gaul I had been thinking of an improvement on the *harpax*. The hooks would be able to bring enemy ships closer so that we may board them."

Octavius nodded, intrigued. "And where might we build this harbor?"

Agrippa motioned for a servant to retrieve his trunk of belongings. He found his large map of Italy rolled up in a wooden box, and unfurled the scroll carefully, spreading it across the desk.

Octavius stood next to him, and the proximity was enough for Agrippa to tense up, though he forced himself to focus on the task at hand.

He circled the area east of Naples, near Baiae, then pointed to a lake a few miles inland.

"Lake Avernus." He drew a line to a smaller lake below, separated by a narrow strip of land, at the edge of the bay of Naples. "And the Lucrine Lake. If we join the two together then we create a safe enough harbor to build a fleet. We will probably have to dredge the lake, otherwise it will be too shallow to sail. But our problem will not be the lakes. It will be the manpower to row the ships."

"That can be taken care of," Octavius said quickly. "How soon can you begin the harbor?"

"Whenever you wish, Caesar," Agrippa answered, glancing at him.

To his surprise, Octavius blushed, and looked away, his eyes hesitant. "You still have not asked me of my wife."

Agrippa shrugged, then began rolling up his map again. "Is there anything to ask? You are in love with the girl. It is not my place to ask anything."

Octavius met his eyes. "But I am not."

"No?"

"I am not in love," Octavius whispered. "She threatened me. She said she knew. She said she knew about *us.*"

Agrippa paused, his heart beating painfully before he shoved the rolled-up map back into the box. "That is impossible."

"My party. After my betrothal to Servilia. She saw us." Octavius stepped closer to him. "She threatened to tell everyone if I did not marry her. And if I had her arrested or executed, there were messengers at the ready." His eyes clouded with the memory, and he turned away abruptly. Agrippa had the sense he was hiding something else about that conversation. "I told her if Scribonia gave birth to a girl, we would wed."

"Why are you telling me this?"

"I thought you would like to know," Octavius said coldly.

Agrippa pushed down a wave of anger. "You always have a choice. You were just too much of a coward to choose it."

Octavius stared at him in disbelief. "What ought I to have done?" he demanded. "Execute her?"

"At the very least call her bluff," Agrippa shot back. "Or offer her money, if that is what she wanted. Do you handle every threat to your honor by wedding them?"

"Only the ones I want to bed," Octavius retorted.

"You may marry whomever you wish." He spread his arms wide, and Octavius narrowed his eyes. "You may sleep with whomever you desire. I will not stop you. You never owed me anything and you know that."

"Then why do I feel like I do?" Octavius asked angrily. "You return as if you are so much better than me. But you are not. You are as guilty of this as I am."

"I have done what you asked of me," Agrippa said, exhausted, almost pleading. "I have quelled the rebellions of the *Aquitani*. I have risked my life for you and your cause. I have done my duty."

But it was the wrong thing to say.

Octavius' eyes blazed. "Your *duty*. Is it a triumph you want, then? To declare your *duties* to me fulfilled? You may have it. You may have a hundred triumphs if you wish!"

"I only wanted *you*!" Agrippa cried out, unable to hold his trembling rage back any longer. "Not a triumph. Nor riches. Nor fame. Not even greatness! That is what you have been incapable of understanding. I only ever wanted *you!*"

Octavius stood silent, staring.

Agrippa turned and left the room, taking the stairs quickly, and he was surprised when Octavius did not follow him.

As he was passing the atrium, he nearly ran into a woman he had never seen before. Except he had, nearly five years ago. She lifted her head elegantly, brown eyes glittering with recognition.

"If it is not the famous general Marcus Agrippa," Livia said, bowing her head. "It is a pleasure to finally meet you."

"Is it?" Agrippa asked, and Livia raised a brow at his lack of greeting, though she did not look offended. "Shall you threaten me before or after I kiss you?"

"He has told you, then," Livia said, though it held no surprise, only a slight resignation.

"Do you always bargain yourself to men for the right price?"

But Livia only smiled, and it was both gentle and dangerous. "I am a woman. I only have myself to bargain."

Agrippa looked at her, the subtle intelligence in her eyes, the graceful smile, so very different to the harsh independence of Scribonia or the childlike simplicity of Clodia. Here was a woman who had more than mere ambitions. She had dreams, and they did not only encompass her husband and children.

He recalled what Octavius had said all those years ago with a sinking dread. *I want someone who wishes not for a family but something more. Something greater.*

"Then I hope you are happy," Agrippa said quietly. "For he has bargained much less for you."

Livia only smirked. "Has he?"

Agrippa did not answer, but her question lingered with him all the way home, where he immediately went to bed, exhausted as he had never felt before.

As he began to fall asleep, his thoughts strayed to Attica, and her patience as she waited for them to marry, offering only herself, which was the most precious thing she had to give. Agrippa had just been too blind to see it.

But he will never love you like I would. He will never give up the world for you.
When he slept, he dreamt. And for the first time, it was not about him.

⟫⟫⟫ ⟪⟪⟪

DECEMBER 38 BC

On a cold night in December, Agrippa wedded Attica.

The ceremony was small and quiet, held at Atticus' estate with her family present, as well as Agrippa's. Octavius and Livia were present too, though Agrippa almost wished they were not. The former watched Agrippa carefully throughout the night, scarcely eating any of the food at dinner, and remaining silent unless spoken to.

Livia, on the other hand, seemed to enjoy herself immensely, becoming fast friends with Attica, the two of them laughing over a whispered comment as if they had known each other for years. Agrippa tried to smile.

As dawn rose above the horizon, and birds took flight with their shrill cries, Agrippa glanced at Octavius and their eyes met.

He has bargained much less for you.

Has he?

Agrippa thought he saw pain hidden in his brown eyes, but then Octavius looked away with his usual easy indifference, a charming smile on his face, and Agrippa sighed.

A weak dawn filtered through the room. The time had come for the bride and groom to depart the banquet. Agrippa stood up and walked over to Attica, before lifting her up in his arms. She smiled at him, her gray eyes knowing and tender. He returned the smile as the party followed behind them all the way to his home, and cheered them on as Agrippa carried Attica across the threshold.

She whispered the vow. *"Ubi tu Gaius, ego Gaia."*

Agrippa lifted her veil back over her head and kissed her smile. He held Attica's hand lightly as they walked to their shared bedroom downstairs. She blushed when Agrippa closed the door behind him.

"Are you afraid?" Agrippa asked softly.

"With you?" Attica smiled, then, and shook her head. "Never."

Agrippa walked over to the lamps and put them out one by one before he returned to Attica. She took off her veil and set it to the side.

He touched her chin with the tips of his fingers, then kissed her, and it was like watching the first flower blossom in spring. She kissed him hesitantly, then more sure, as he tilted his head and ran a gentle hand in the strands of her hair, the knot coming loose down her back.

Once he pulled away, Agrippa lifted her up and laid her carefully on the bed. He kissed her neck, soft and arched beneath his lips. She sighed into his touch, her breath trembling.

"Let me see all of you," he murmured.

He sat up and undid her dress, one clasp and then the other, his fingers deliberate, gentle. Attica helped him slip the dress off, laughing as they threw it to the floor together.

Then Agrippa unwrapped his toga, allowing the fabric to fall to the ground, and took off his tunic. Although he rarely had sex naked, he felt it was only right that she see all of him too, that they begin this marriage as a man and a woman, honest and bare. Attica's gaze traveled down slowly, a rosy flush blooming across her face.

He lowered himself over her, kissing her more fully, their mouths meeting in a sweet rhythm, like waves of different oceans mingling. Attica wrapped her legs around his waist tightly. She threw her head back and Agrippa found her hands with his, lacing them together on either side.

And as the sun climbed high in the sky, Agrippa fell into Attica's warm embrace, a soft glow within him kindling, a deeper kind of love settling in his heart, the kind of love that turned the moon around the earth, that healed scars of old, their limbs winding like trees deep in the forest.

Afterward, Agrippa kissed her cheek and brought her close. There was only one thought on his mind as they fell asleep to the same heartbeat, his body laden with an eternal slumber.

This is love.

38

GAIUS OCTAVIUS

DECEMBER 38 BC

O CTAVIUS HAD NOT SEEN Agrippa for two weeks, nor had he heard from him.
After he married Attica, they traveled to Naples and were staying in one of
Balbus' villas there to be closer to the lakes where Agrippa planned to build his fleet.
Octavius would not visit until some time in the spring when the project would be well
underway, so he would not see them again until January when Agrippa would assume the
consulship with him. For now, Octavius remained in Rome, where he had his hands full
with the blockade and famine, among his many other responsibilities.

In more dire news, Maecenas had recently sent a letter from Athens, which he was
reading now in his office upstairs. He reported that he and Octavia were trying to convince
Antonius to return to Italy and offer aid, but thus far they had been unsuccessful.

Octavius knew Antonius would only return if he promised to come to terms with
Sextus, but Octavius was not willing to surrender just yet. Antonius must come with aid.

He began drafting a reply when Livia called his name from the other side of the door.
He usually did not like others to enter his office unannounced while he worked, but Livia
was an exception, as he liked to hear what she thought about his problems. She always
seemed to have a solution.

"Come in," he said.

Livia entered. She was wearing her winter clothes, white bordered with gold and
purple, a restraint of decoration that only served to accentuate her elegance. Her cheeks
were rosy as though she had been walking outside in the gardens. Octavius was surprised
to find he had been looking forward to when she would finally bother him.

"I did not hear you come home," Livia said as an explanation. "Any news?"

"None that you do not already know about. Maecenas and my sister have yet to
convince Antonius to return. But we predicted this." Octavius paused. "Have you any

news from Attica?"

Livia raised a brow, coming around to his side of the desk and glancing at the letter from Maecenas. "She is well, last I heard. Agrippa is hard at work building your fleet. But does he not send a report himself?"

They both knew Agrippa was not communicating with Octavius more than he needed to, which was next to nothing. "His second-in-command sends the reports of my fleet." He felt his face heat up, and Livia waited, always knowing more than he would like. "I meant if there was any news of a baby."

Livia laughed. "They only just married! You can hardly expect them to know so soon. Besides, I believe Attica once mentioned to me her fear of pregnancy. She may prevent a child if she can."

"Can she do that?" Octavius asked, disbelieving. He had not known that was possible. It sounded like something only the gods were able to do.

"We women have our ways," Livia said, smirking.

Octavius reached out and grabbed her waist, pulling her onto his lap. She laughed as they nearly fell over, Octavius steadying Livia in his arms while she locked her hands behind his neck. Recently a kind of affection had sprung between them that Octavius had difficulty explaining. A red blush crept up her neck as she glanced at Octavius beneath long, straight lashes.

"Oh, *mi Octaviane*," she murmured.

It was her preferred name to call him, which had begun in jest and quickly became a form of endearment. Octavius felt so young when she called him that, as if he were back on the streets of Rome at sixteen, and had kissed a woman for the first time.

"Do you believe in love, *mea Livia?*"

He thought she might laugh again, but all she did was smile. "Yes, I do. Love is a beautiful and strange power. It comes in many forms, not only between man and woman, and can run deeper than time itself."

Octavius sensed the veiled reference, and he stiffened. "If you are referring to Agrippa," he said in a low voice, forcing himself to smirk, "love was not the question."

Livia smiled sadly. "It is not so bad a thing to love someone, you know."

He shook his head. "Love is a weakness."

It was the same thing he had told Agrippa all those months ago, but this time, Octavius was not sure if he believed it. He was not sure *what* he believed in anymore.

Livia lifted a hand and touched his face, brushing a strand of hair from his temple. "What do you know about love?" she asked.

Octavius closed his eyes at her touch, her fingertips that raked through his hair, traced a line down his jaw. She lightly skimmed a fingertip over the bridge of his nose, his brows, his mouth, as if she were sculpting him from clay.

"I know love is dangerous," he whispered. "I know it hurts more than anything to lose."

He felt her kiss the corner of his mouth, and he opened his eyes. It was the first time she had kissed him. Livia shook her head firmly. "That's the thing about love, *mi Octaviane*. It cannot be lost, only forgotten."

Octavius looked at her, his heart beating fast, and was surprised to feel a vague possessiveness, almost pride. Livia seemed the most beautiful woman in the world, then, more beautiful even than his mother. He leaned forward and kissed her, and she tasted of hope, the same hope Pandora trapped under the lid of her jar, the same hope he trapped in his own heart.

As she shifted closer in his lap, he felt his body stir with a forgotten feeling. Not desire, but pleasure, like the first bite of a ripe peach in midsummer. She pulled away, and placed a hand on his chest, above his heart.

"Love stays with us, even beyond death. Never forget that."

Octavius knew he never would.

⤞⤞⤝⤝

JANUARY 37 BC

Octavius watched Agrippa across the triclinium, reclining beside Attica, who glowed as if she were in love.

Agrippa looked at her differently, more satisfied, like they had a secret understanding between them that walled off the rest of the room from their true feelings. Octavius hated it.

"I love what you have done with the place," Maecenas said, looking around at the newly painted walls. He reclined beside Octavius and Livia, while Agrippa, Attica, and Athenodorus reclined opposite, Balbus, Oppius, and Matius reclining on the middle couch.

Octavius had invited his close friends to stay at the villa he had bought as a wedding gift for Livia, which he had renovated only recently. The estate was less than a day's ride outside the city and was in fact previously owned by Livia's family before the proscriptions.

It had initially been intended as both a threat and an apology, but now it was a retreat from the chaos of the city. Livia never spoke of the villa's history, merely thanking him for the generous gift, and in that way, they were both content.

"What say you, Agrippa?" Maecenas asked, for he had been silent all dinner. "Very tasteful decorations, are they not?

Agrippa nodded. "Very tasteful."

Maecenas raised a brow. "And if I had said they were tasteless? Would you repeat that too?"

"Only if I agreed," Agrippa said testily.

Livia laughed. "Stop teasing him, Maecenas. He has enough to mind as it is."

"Do you mean the consulship or his marriage?" Maecenas asked, smirking, much to the shock of the more elderly guests present.

"Maecenas!" Livia cried out in protest, but she was still laughing.

Balbus muttered something about the shameless nature of the current youth, and the other older guests heartily agreed.

Livia had loved Maecenas of all Octavius' friends the most, and the two had hit it off at once, though he supposed Livia had that effect with almost everyone. If he had any suspicion that either of them would be romantically interested in the other he would have prevented their friendship, but as it was, the only threat they posed together were the jokes they liked to tell to the mortification of their guests.

Maecenas raised a brow at Attica as if to prove a point, and she blushed. "Ah, so might we expect an announcement soon?"

"By Jove! Do stop, Maecenas, or the gods will punish your insolence," Livia said, though it appeared she liked that insolence very much. She turned to Octavius, who found himself glancing at Agrippa to see his reaction. "Tell your friend to stop torturing our guests at once."

"Please, Caesar, the gods know I have never been able to put that Maecenas in line," Athenodorus said in his thick Greek accent.

"You are better at flirting with married women than unmarried ones, Maecenas," Octavius drawled. "It is no surprise you remain a bachelor."

Maecenas laughed carelessly. "But the best women are forbidden. Even Jove knows that."

"Quite right!" quipped Oppius with a hearty laugh, earning glares from Agrippa and Athenodorus.

"Alright, settle down now," Livia said, looking at Maecenas meaningfully, and he nodded in assent, suppressing a smile. Octavius did not understand how, but Livia had managed to enchant and hold Maecenas under her sway, more even than Octavius. "There are serious matters we must discuss."

Their conversation then turned to the blockade, as it often did these days, with Attica and Athenodorus adamantly supporting peace, Livia and Octavius arguing for a calculated attack that would buy them more time, and Agrippa and Balbus toeing the line between the two. Maecenas acted mostly as mediator along with Oppius and Matius, though he was quick to check anyone's baseless claim.

Once the wine pitchers emptied, the women retired to their chambers, most likely to gossip about their husbands, while Athenodorus asked to be escorted to his bed. Oppius, Balbus, and Matius wished to take a walk in the morning light. Maecenas glanced at Octavius and Agrippa, hesitating when neither of them stood up with the rest, before claiming his need for further exercise, leaving them alone.

Agrippa glanced at him, a small smile dancing on his mouth. "Do you wish to join them? I will not hold it against you."

"You know I do not," Octavius said quietly. "Not with you here."

He looked at Agrippa steadily, his heart pounding painfully when Agrippa's brows raised in surprise. They remained silent for several tense moments. He had extended the most tentative olive branch, and Agrippa seemed to wait for it to be pulled away.

"What has changed?" Agrippa asked finally.

"Nothing," Octavius said, his voice rough. "Nothing has changed. I have always wanted you."

Agrippa narrowed his eyes, a bitterness in them that Octavius had never seen before. "You are a coward, then."

"Perhaps. But it is the truth."

Agrippa's brows raised at the same words he had spoken more than a year ago before Octavius had sent him away to Gaul, before they found themselves at this impasse, so that staring into the sea-green Tiber of his eyes was like waking up from a very long, very terrible dream.

Agrippa lowered his voice. "This is dangerous."

Octavius did not look away, his pulse racing. "I know."

"I am not the same man I once was," Agrippa warned. "We shall not be what we were."

"I know."

"I love you," he whispered, like a confession. "I cannot help it."

Octavius could not move, his body gone still under his heated gaze. "I know. I—"

There were footsteps. Livia entered the room. When she saw them, reclining on opposite-facing couches, rigid and flushed, she bowed her head and hid her face. "I apologize for the intrusion."

"No," Agrippa said quietly, his face shuttering. "Do not apologize. I wish to rest anyway." Octavius felt his breath leave him at the words. "May someone escort me to my bedroom?"

Livia glanced at Octavius, who did not dare move, then nodded. "Follow me."

Octavius watched Agrippa follow Livia down the hall. He remained alone for a long time after they were gone.

"I have a surprise for you," Octavius said, placing his hands over Livia's eyes before she could protest.

She had been weaving downstairs in the smaller courtyard, facing the doors that opened on a large field stretching from the back of the house for a few miles, bordered by a short stone wall.

"You know I detest surprises," Livia reminded him, though he felt her smile even without seeing it.

"Not this one."

He led her outside to a large shed with a set of locked doors that had previously held a storage room. Octavius secretly had a passage built underground while the house was being renovated. He walked her carefully down the stairs to a small hallway. The air was still damp from the recent construction, but the lamps flared bright against the tunnel walls.

When they entered the small room at the left end of the corridor, he released his hands. Livia looked and gasped.

They were standing in a garden, except that it was not a garden but a room, painted on all four walls with vibrant green flowers and foliage, laurel trees and bushes, birds flitting in the clear blue sky, perching on nearby branches. The ceiling appeared to be a cave, decorated with ornately painted squares, which opened onto the garden on all sides. Beyond the painted white fence were untamed forests and fields.

"Happy birthday," Octavius said.

"My dream," Livia whispered, turning towards Octavius, her eyes shining with tears. "You remembered."

"How could I forget?" he asked, and pulled her close, her brown eyes drawing him in. *"You are my destiny."*

Livia smiled, and it was like the sun. "Kiss me, my love."

He kissed her, and her mouth was sweet, tinged with a bitterness he almost enjoyed. She was nothing like Agrippa. Where he was passionate and demanding, Livia was gentle and firm. Octavius always felt unraveled with Agrippa, as if at any moment his life could suddenly end and he would not even notice.

But with Livia he was entirely himself, capable of anything, his future as near as her touch. He felt a deep pull towards her, a rising want from the inside, his hands skating her waist, brushing her neck.

"Livia—"

"I know."

Livia lowered herself to the ground, and Octavius followed, kissing the hollow of her neck, his hands tight on her waist. He kissed her as his hips joined with hers, her legs hooking around him, their bodies in tune to a rhythm far older than them, than even the earth, as ancient as the stars above.

He felt as though thunder rumbled above, the trees of the garden shaken by invisible gods. For was that not a flash of lightning above the garden? And was that not a cry of nymphs in the distant fields? The cave above shielded them from the light of day, but Octavius thought he saw the rays of the sun shine on the laurel tree at the garden's center as he held Livia close.

For he finally understood. Livia was more than his wife, more than a mother, more even than the daughter of a great man. She was a woman, and she was more than life.

I am your destiny.

She was immortality.

39

LIVIA DRUSILLA

MARCH 37 BC

L IVIA WATCHED AS ATTICA read silently on the couch, a strand of hair slipping
from her braids. She was only a year younger than Livia, but Attica always seemed
younger, more innocent, though no less intelligent.

Watching her eyes travel slowly over the parchment, Livia decided that over the last few
months being wed to Agrippa, Attica had changed. She had become more relaxed and
quiet, as if she had finally settled and did not wish to criticize the world any longer.

Attica was visiting her father in Rome for a few weeks and traveled without Agrippa,
who remained in Naples to oversee his project. Octavius was campaigning in the north
to recruit more men for the upcoming wars. This was one of those rare moments when
Livia and Attica had the house all to themselves, free to speak of whatever—and whomever—they wished.

"So, how are you finding Agrippa?" Livia asked idly, continuing to weave. She did not
particularly enjoy the activity, but the repetitive nature of weaving allowed for peace of
mind and ample time to ponder over one's life. "I always imagined he would be a good
husband."

Attica looked up from her parchment, surprised, as though she had not expected Livia
to ask her any questions. "I find him to be a very good husband," she said, then paused,
glancing at Livia. "I may ask the same of you."

Livia laughed. "He is better than I had expected."

Attica hesitated, and there was worry in her gray eyes. "You know, you are not the first
of his wives that I have met."

She raised a brow. "Yes, you knew Scribonia."

"Yes," Attica said quietly, "whose daughter you now house."

Livia frowned. It was customary for the father to remain with the children after a
divorce. Indeed, after a tearful parting, her son, Drusus, had returned to his father's house

331

with his brother, Tiberius. She now had Julia Caeseris filia under her care, but it was not the same as rearing a child of her own, and she longed for the day when Tiberius and Drusus were old enough to visit her more often.

"Do you think he loves you?" Attica asked when Livia did not answer.

"In his own way."

Attica nodded slowly, but it was clear that she did not believe it. "Sometimes I wonder if Agrippa loves me at all."

"Of course he does!" Livia exclaimed, shocked.

She had never heard Attica speak one bad word about her husband. Besides, she had seen the love Agrippa had for Attica shining in his eyes whenever he looked at her. Livia herself had often felt jealous of that look, the honesty in it, a simple kind of love. The gods knew that was not her fate.

"Sometimes I wonder if he will always love Caesar more," Attica said bitterly.

Livia felt her heart ache for Attica, for she had seen the pain etched into Agrippa's face as he pulled Caesar close all those years ago. She remembered thinking that their kiss was the most beautiful and tragic thing she had ever seen, though at the time she had been too young to understand.

"Agrippa loves you, Attica," Livia said firmly. "I am sure of it."

"And Caesar? Do you not wish for love? Real love?"

Livia shook her head, thinking of that night she struck a bargain with Caesar, his hand tight and unyielding around her arm. "I seek no such thing from my husband. We made a deal. That is marriage, after all."

Attica still looked troubled. "You must know that Caesar only wants one thing. And if you do not deliver, he will abandon you as he did Scribonia when she gave birth."

But Livia only smiled, touching her stomach. "Then it is a good thing I have it."

Attica's eyes widened. "Are you?"

"I believe so."

"Does he know?" Attica asked nervously.

"Not yet." Livia hesitated. "I must be sure."

Attica nodded, but her eyes were clouded. "I care for you. You are like a sister to me, Livia."

Livia sensed the other girl's doubts, and she could not help but feel some of her own. She considered herself capable of reading anyone's mind, but her husband's was particularly difficult to read entirely, though she certainly tried. Had she miscalculated his desires? His fears? She supposed she would simply have to wait and see.

"And you are like a sister to me too, *dulcissima* Attica," Livia said with a smile.

"I do not wish to see you hurt," Attica whispered, and her eyes welled with sudden tears.

Had she been waiting all along for Livia to be cast aside as Scribonia had been? Livia stood up swiftly and knelt beside her, hugging her shoulders.

Attica reached a shaky hand down and touched Livia's belly with her hand, her eyes dark with a terrible sadness. "If it is a girl...I could not bear to see you go."

"I will not allow it," Livia said, her throat tight against her own tears. "He would have to exile me first before I leave you."

"But don't you see?" Attica asked, her voice trembling. "He already did it once. Why might he not do so again?"

Livia brushed Attica's tears away, but she did not speak. It was the truth, after all, and there was no arguing against it.

They remained holding each other for a long time, until Phoebe entered with Julia, and Attica continued to read in silence.

⤙⤚

APRIL 37 BC

As spring descended on Rome and the flowers began to bud, she liked to stroll in the gardens of their Palatine house, though her husband spent more effort tending to them. He had a knack for growing things even when their season had not yet come. Livia watched him now as he gently touched a decaying leaf, snipping off the browning stem with a small dagger.

As she walked towards him, he looked up. His eyes saw her, but he did not smile.

Ever since Livia had interrupted them after the dinner party—her husband and Agrippa reclining alone in the triclinium—she felt that her husband was not the same. A part of her wondered if she had known all along that they were alone, and had purposely walked into the room at that moment to end their conversation.

It was impossible to know. Of course, she knew that her husband loved Agrippa. She knew it more than he himself did. But now the poor boy looked lost, as if he had thought the sky was above him only to find it below his feet. Livia almost pitied him.

"Come, my love, take a walk with me," Livia said, beckoning him with a hand.

He stood up, eyeing her curiously, before linking his arm with hers and walking down the rows of flower bushes. Most had not yet bloomed and would wait for the nearing heat and humidity of the summer to reveal their colors. But in the center of the garden grew a young laurel tree, its slender green trunk sprouting towards the sky, already budding with small leaves. Her husband had it planted after their conversation last year, one of the many surprising things she had discovered about Caesar.

"Do you like it?" he asked, looking at the tree, his cheeks slightly reddened from a cold wind rushing down from the north.

Livia smiled at him. "It is beautiful."

"The tree shall stand for generations to come," Caesar said, turning towards her. "The laurel will be a symbol of our family."

He brought her closer and kissed her, one hand cupping her cheek. Livia put a hand on his arm, and he stepped back, questioning. She had never stopped him from kissing her before.

For a moment, she wondered if she should keep quiet, hide the pregnancy until its very birth if she could. Caesar made a move to speak.

"There is something I must tell you," Livia said quickly before she lost her nerve.

He looked alarmed. "What is it?"

She took his hands and brought them to the curve of her stomach. He looked down, then up, uncertain. At last, she said, "I am with child."

He did not speak, only looked at her, then without another word, he knelt down and pressed an ear to her stomach. She dared not interrupt, dared not even laugh.

Caesar stood up after a few moments with a grin. "It is a boy. I know it."

"We shall see," Livia said, remembering with an uneasy feeling what Attica had said to her, and a cold murmur traveled up her spine, as though she had taken a step into a stream of icy water. *And if you do not deliver, he will abandon you as he did Scribonia when she gave birth.*

He shook his head in wonder. "We are going to have a *child*."

She could do nothing else but force a smile.

Once they walked the garden and returned to the house, Livia retired to her room for some much-needed rest. Phoebe was there, cradling Julia in her arms and cooing to her softly.

Her handmaiden was quite young, perhaps younger than Livia herself, too young to have already traveled from Greece, away from her family and native country, to a foreign land, fostering foreign children. They had taken to each other quite well when Livia moved in, and she had the sense that Phoebe would be in her life for a long time.

"Caesar is quite certain the child is a boy," Livia said softly.

Phoebe looked up, a laugh in her eyes. "Ah, yes, master wishes very much for a boy."

"Did you ever learn the ways known to your people?" Livia gestured to her belly. "I know it is early, but I hoped…"

There was a reservation in her eyes, but Phoebe nodded. "Yes, I learned. We all had to.

334

But some say it is wise not to cheat the gods of their surprise."

"I must know," Livia said, lifting her chin defiantly.

Phoebe set Julia down in her crib, then stooped before Livia, pressing the palm of her hand on the curve of her stomach, then her ear. She stayed there, listening, for what felt like a long time. Only the whimpering of Julia without the attention of her caregiver filled the silence.

At last, Phoebe stood up, but she did not smile, and her eyes did not quite reach Livia's gaze.

"Well?" Livia asked, and her heart clenched.

"Very quiet," Phoebe said hesitantly.

"He is calm. There is nothing wrong with that."

Phoebe nodded but did not answer, and she busied herself with Julia who squealed in delight as she was lifted back into Phoebe's arms. Livia felt slightly nauseous and wondered if it was merely the effects of her pregnancy, or if this was yet another warning.

"But is it a boy?"

That same reservation returned, but Phoebe finally nodded. "It is a boy."

Livia fell into a deep silence, thinking, the faint noises of the baby and Phoebe's murmuring breaking up the endless quiet.

⊱❯❯❯ ❮❮❮⊰

After the news of the baby, her husband had decided they ought to spend a few relaxing weeks in Livia's villa north of Rome. Caesar had gifted it to her for their wedding, but she merely considered it a debt paid to her by the murderer of her father. Her husband perhaps wished both to remind her of his power and ask for her forgiveness at the same time, and for that kind of cunning, Livia grudgingly respected him.

But during the first week, a violent storm had approached from the south. Wind rattled the window panes, and the house groaned loudly as the storm gathered all its strength and encircled their villa in its most powerful sheets of rain. Livia nearly flinched when a flash of lightning seemed to strike a hill in the distance, gathering the blankets on her bed over her shoulders. It was the middle of the night, and the storm showed no sign of letting up.

At last, she decided she would not sleep, and crept out in the hall, holding out her lamp, its flame flickering from the wind gusting through the windows. As she walked towards the courtyard, she saw that the door to her husband's room was wide open, his bed empty. It appeared she had not been the only one the thunderstorm had awoken from sleep.

Livia stopped a slave who was running with a large vase to the atrium, which had surely begun to flood.

"Where is my husband?" she asked.

The boy pointed to the other side of the house. "The room below."

The garden room. He had gone to the garden room. Livia hurried across the house, ignoring the protests of her servants urging her to return to her room, saying that it was not safe. She ran outside in the rain to the large shed and found the door, which used to open to storage rooms, and took the stairs down to the small tunnel.

Her husband was lying on the ground in the center of the room, curled up with his back facing her, unmoving and silent as if he were asleep. Livia approached slowly, for fear of startling him. But when she stepped into the room, his eyes opened instantly and he turned around.

"You should be asleep," he said quietly.

"So should you," Livia countered.

He sighed. "I could not. The thunder kept me awake."

Livia held back a smile. "Does thunder scare you?"

He scowled, but then a rumbling of thunder broke in the sky, shaking the house to its very bones, and Caesar flinched. Livia lowered herself to the ground next to him and took his hand.

"You needn't be afraid," Livia said. "I am here now."

"I am perfectly fine." But he tightened his grip on her hand at the next clap of thunder that made the earth tremble beneath them.

"You know, Phoebe has said that the child is a boy," Livia said softly.

He turned to her, startled. "She did?"

"Yes. I thought you would like to know."

But instead of the smile she expected to find, her husband frowned and turned away. Livia put her fingers under his chin and turned his face towards her again. "What is it? Are you not happy?"

He hesitated. "I am."

"Then what ails you?"

"The future," he said in a near whisper, as though there were others around and he did not wish them to hear. He glanced at Livia, and his eyes were dark, flashing with the glow of her lamp. "It is difficult to see at times, that is all."

"Is it the war with Sextus?" she asked. "You know you shall defeat him in time. Agrippa has not failed you before and he will not fail you now. You told me as much the other day."

"It is not that," he said, averting his eyes. "It is you."

Livia's heart stopped. "Me?"

He would have to exile me first before I leave you.

But don't you see? He already did it once. Why might he not do so again?

Caesar nodded reluctantly. "Yes. You see a future that is hidden from me. What if I spend my whole life searching for something that does not exist? What if I have already doomed my fate to oblivion? Will my life have been for nothing?"

Livia could breathe again. "Your fate is already written. As is mine. There is no use worrying about it now."

"And yet I worry," he whispered, placing a hand on the small curve of her stomach. "I worry for us."

"You must trust in the gods." Livia took his hand and kissed his palm. "They hold your fate in their hands."

A shadow passed across his face at her words. "And do *you* trust them? Do you trust the gods with your fate?"

Livia smiled, but it felt more like a smirk. "Of course not. That is why I married you."

A reluctant smile tugged at the corners of his mouth, and he looked at her with a tenderness she had never seen before. "I love you."

"Oh, I don't believe that," Livia teased.

But he remained serious, his hand at her waist pulling her closer. "I do."

Livia's smile faded, and she could not hide the doubt in her voice. "Do you?"

"Yes." He paused, a slight blush on his cheeks. "But I am not sure you do."

She looked at him silently, then traced a fingertip down the side of his face as she liked to do when they got this close, around his cheekbone, the sharp line of his jaw. He was still as beautiful to her as the first day she saw him, nearly six years ago now, when she had first married Tiberius and he was just a boy with a hidden dream, the son of a god.

"I shall love you," Livia said, finally, "if you love me."

He smiled, and then with his hands he gently lifted the skirts of her nightgown.

She reached out a hand and touched his arm to stop him. "You do not need to."

He only raised a brow and continued to lift up her nightgown. "The baby will know the difference."

"What?"

"That I love you. The baby will know the difference."

She meant to speak, but the words caught in her throat as he kissed her, and all she could think of was his gentle touch and the heat of her body. When she tried to turn over, he stilled her with a hand and continued to kiss her much slower and more deliberate than ever before.

As they fell asleep to the crashes of thunder above and below, Livia whispered in his ear softly. "I love you too."

40

MARCUS VIPSANIUS AGRIPPA

APRIL 37 BC

T HE LAKE GLITTERED BENEATH the sun like a silver shield of armor. Agrippa watched the small figures milling about the warehouses on one side of the shore, hard at work building the large, slender ships that would be necessary to destroy Sextus' fleet for good. He breathed in the salty air borne on the breeze coming off the bay.

If Rome was the center of the world, then Naples was the belly of the beast, where exotic foods and pleasures were consumed with such decadence and abandon, and the sea surged blue-green and warm against the sand, wide and intoxicating as a woman, that one forgot the troubles of politics and wars in the world abroad. There was only this moment and the best thrills that one could find at the best price.

"If I were an enemy, you would already be dead."

Agrippa whirled around, his heart beating fast at the familiar voice behind him.

Octavius stood at the other end of the dock, and as he walked closer, Agrippa felt the wood beneath him rock strenuously on the water.

Lake Avernus was not big enough to feel dangerous, but legend told that its waters were the entrance to the Underworld. Many traveled here to worship the lake, while others skirted death in their luxurious villas and bathhouses lining the curved shore.

"If you were an enemy, there are a thousand men here who would have killed you before you stepped foot on this dock," Agrippa said, raising a brow.

A shadow of a smile hovered over Octavius' mouth, but it could have been a trick of the light. "Ah, it is a good thing I am not an enemy then."

Agrippa watched as Octavius stopped three steps away, hesitating. "You have come to check my progress."

"Yes." Octavius paused, and Agrippa's heart skipped a beat as he saw a flicker of thought cross those dark eyes. Agrippa almost knew what it meant before he spoke. "And there is something else."

"What is it?"

He motioned back towards the military camp. "Not here."

Agrippa did not protest, following Octavius back to camp. They fell into step beside each other, the silence heavy in the midmorning heat. He wished to ask him a thousand questions, but Agrippa had never been very good with words, and soon they reached his tent. Octavius spoke as soon as they were in private.

"How do you find Naples?"

Agrippa pushed down the urge to shove him. "Wonderful."

Octavius raised a brow. "Really?"

They both knew Agrippa had always found Naples slightly distasteful, as it was the epicenter of the wealthiest Romans who liked to flock south in the summer for their leisure, wasting away on wine and women.

"Balbus has been very welcoming," Agrippa said at last. He did not wish to explain himself to Octavius. Besides, it was true, and Agrippa had no complaints about Balbus' hospitality. Attica, too, enjoyed the old man's company, and as a close friend to Cicero, they spoke often of the orator's legacy.

"I see." Octavius fiddled with the belt of his *gladius*. "And Attica?"

Agrippa was momentarily too surprised to answer. "She is well. The seaside agrees with her. But her father is in Rome, and she ultimately wishes to return to be near him."

Octavius nodded as if the question had simply been protocol. At one time, Agrippa would not have blinked an eye, considering it merely friendly. But they had long ceased being *friends*.

"Have you encountered any difficulties with the project?"

"None that we have not already resolved," Agrippa responded easily, as though he had rehearsed his answers. He supposed the hours he had wasted reliving their past conversations had come to good use after all.

"Good," Octavius said curtly, his tone sharpening as they turned to business. The commander was back. "Maecenas has confirmed that Antonius shall return to Rome, and he will bring three hundred ships to aid in the war against Sextus. Then we will draft our terms and renew our alliance. Only once the fleet is finished shall we launch an attack on Sextus."

"I am glad you have finally seen reason," Agrippa said dryly, recalling the many arguments they had when Agrippa tried to persuade him against fighting a hopeless war.

"Oh, there is much you don't know," Octavius said with a taunting smile. "I see beyond the horizon, not merely the limit of sea and sky."

Agrippa felt that familiar flame kindle within him, and he could not decide whether he wished to wrestle Octavius to the ground or kiss him. He settled on whichever would wipe that smile off his face. "That is because you sent me into exile. I no longer keep your closest counsel."

"An exile you wanted," Octavius shot back. "Or did you forget?"

"I thought we agreed that things had changed," Agrippa said in a low voice. "Or did you forget?"

They stood across from each other, silent, as if an ocean stood between them, and yet Agrippa only needed to take a few steps to touch him. How had they lost the very thing Agrippa had held close amidst all their enemies and friends, whether in life or in death?

I will always find you.

How had the world kept turning when Agrippa felt as though his own had stopped?

Octavius took a step forward, then paused. "Livia is pregnant."

Agrippa's heart dropped. Was this why he had come all this way? To bear him news of his wife? He forced the words past his throat. "The gods have blessed you."

"They have." Octavius' eyes looked far away, before settling on Agrippa again, who had the sudden feeling that there was another side of Octavius he had never seen before, and never would, and the thought was like death itself, terrible and cold.

"Do you love her?" He could not help himself, but he regretted asking the question once he had.

Octavius looked at him in mild surprise. "Yes."

"Then I suppose you have the life you always wanted," Agrippa said coldly, wishing that he had never crossed the sea from Apollonia all those years ago, wishing that he had died in his first battle, before he knew what love was, and before he knew what it meant to lose it.

"Agrippa," Octavius said quietly, and something in his voice made Agrippa stand still, his heart beating rapidly.

"Yes?"

"Livia...it is different." Pain flitted across his face, as if the words were impossible to say, though Agrippa had never seen Octavius run out of words before. "It is different...with you."

"Is it?"

"Yes, it is," Octavius whispered urgently, crossing the distance between them until he was close enough to kiss, eyes dark and dangerous. Agrippa felt the world slipping away from his grasp, and his head grew light. *Nothing has changed. I have always wanted you.* "It is not love with you. It is not even desire. It is something else. Something more. I cannot explain it."

Agrippa did not speak, looking at Octavius standing before him, his eyes searching Agrippa's face desperately. Octavius brought a hesitant hand up to touch him, and without thinking, Agrippa snatched his wrist in a tight grasp, a breath away from him.

"Why should I believe you?" Agrippa asked.

Octavius' brown eyes flickered with doubt. "It is the truth."

"Prove it."

Octavius moved forward and their lips brushed. The touch was so shocking after months of nothing that Agrippa nearly stepped back, if only to catch his breath.

But Octavius did not let him, taking a step forward to kiss him again, and Agrippa had to grasp Octavius' other wrist just to remain standing. Agrippa's pulse pounded in his ears, in his chest, a twin flame to the heartbeat in Octavius' wrists.

As they kissed they staggered back against the desk, Octavius' legs hitting the edge. Agrippa could not wait any longer, the year of nothing fading to oblivion, and he released Octavius' wrists and fumbled with the hem of his clothes, at the same time as Octavius struggled with trembling hands to unhook Agrippa's belt. Their breaths were heavy in the quiet as they cast their clothes aside and returned wordlessly to each other.

Octavius was pure heat against him, his muscles tensing in his embrace, lean and strong. Wherever skin kissed skin Agrippa felt those sparks of an undying flame, his breath gone as if he were drowning. Octavius placed his palms on Agrippa's abdomen, and he shuddered, circling those wrists again, keeping them in place. But the hands inched down, down, down—

Agrippa stumbled away. He stared wildly at Octavius leaning against the desk, his chest rising and falling rapidly. "Not here."

Octavius' brow hitched as if to ask, *Then where?*

"This was a mistake," Agrippa said, his voice rough. He walked to where his clothes had been strewn so carelessly on the ground, shrugging them on. "You must go."

"Now?" Octavius asked idly, glancing down at himself.

"After you dress," Agrippa said tersely, strapping his belt on and giving Octavius a hard look. "It is too dangerous. Anyone might have walked in."

Octavius' smile was nothing but sly. "I thought that was how you liked it."

Agrippa said nothing, merely watching as Octavius strode over to his pile of clothes and calmly pulled them over his head, taking his time adjusting the sleeves and buckling the belt. He wrapped a hand around the hilt of his *gladius*, his fingers flexing, and for a moment he looked like he was going to say something.

But he just shook his head and settled on, "Until next time, Agrippa."

"Goodbye, Caesar."

The corner of Octavius' smile twitched, and then he left.

꙳≫꙳ ꙳≪꙳

JULY 37 BC

"If you were not my brother," Octavia said angrily, "I would strangle you at this very moment."

Agrippa watched as Octavius raised a brow and smiled at his furious sister, who looked like a vengeful goddess descending to earth in fiery wrath.

They were in the triclinium of Octavius' Palatine house, discussing Antonius' arrival over dinner. Antonius had sent Maecenas and Octavia back to Rome to convince Octavius to meet in a conference, who thus far had continually delayed their meeting. Attica, who reclined beside Agrippa, looked between brother and sister in vague alarm.

"Has love addled your mind, sister?" Octavius asked curiously. "Or is it because you are pregnant?"

Octavia scowled. "Perhaps I *shall* strangle you."

She moved to stand and Maecenas just managed to catch her by the arm and stay her before she decided to actually murder her brother, her hands ready to pounce. Octavius sat amused and continued eating as if he had not just been in mortal danger.

"Fighting shall not solve anything," Maecenas drawled, then added hastily at a glare from Octavia, "but might I suggest a moderated debate?"

"I appreciate your efforts at peace, Maecenas," Octavius said with an exaggerated sigh, "but they are futile. Octavia cannot be reasoned with."

"And you can?" Octavia shot back, earning a stifled laugh from Livia, who had not deigned to interrupt this familial argument.

Livia was now very pregnant and would probably give birth in less than two months. Agrippa noticed that she had been less preoccupied with politics in conversation as of late, perhaps content for now to lie back and be doted upon.

Octavia, on the other hand, had become more prideful in her pregnancy, and quicker to anger, though that may as well be from her proximity to her brother.

"Antonius will not suffer too much if he must wait another month," Octavius said. "After all, he was content to delay much longer than that when it was *I* who called for *him*. It is important now that he remembers who has the upper hand here."

"If I remember correctly," Octavia replied slowly, "Sextus has the upper hand until Antonius arrives with his ships. Are you so sure Sextus shall not starve us all to death before then?"

Octavius' smile was undeniably smug. "Do not worry, sister. We will not starve. But I must wait until the last possible moment before I meet with Antonius. It is only fair that he receives a taste of his own medicine for once."

"It is difficult to marshal such a number of ships," Agrippa added, though he almost regretted speaking when Octavia turned her fierce gaze upon him. "Antonius knows Octavius has men he can spare for his Parthian campaign, so now he will be forced to wait, and more willing to do what we ask. It is merely politics."

"Merely politics?" Octavia asked angrily. "Tell that to the thousands of Romans half-starved to death!"

"It is either that," Octavius said sharply, "or the death of our family and friends. Do not forget, dear sister, how quick Antonius would be to abandon our alliance and join with Sextus. We must dangle a bone before the dog or else he will walk away."

But Octavia was stubborn, and she knew her brother and her husband better than they thought. "And you would not abandon Antonius likewise? Let us not play pretend, brother. We are too old for that now."

"That is precisely why I must delay," Octavius said impatiently. "If I wish to have an equal footing in our alliance, he must remember what it would cost to lose my aid, as I his. We must be at each other's mercy."

"You are my brother," Octavia said in a low voice, "so I yield to your counsel. But Antonius is the father of my children, and I am bound by my vows to aid him where I can."

Octavius frowned. "That is honorable of you, but we both know he would not do the same for you."

Octavia lifted her chin proudly. "Unlike you, my honor does not depend on his."

"Very well," Octavius muttered with a sigh. "We shall continue as planned. Antonius will remain at the ready until I say otherwise. You may tell him I am not available for the rest of the month, as the riots in the city do not allow me to depart any sooner."

The meeting concluded soon after, Livia wishing to sleep, Octavia to rest, and Octavius wishing to discuss something with Maecenas in private. While Agrippa could not prevent the small flare of jealousy, it quickly faded at the memory of Octavius' visit to Naples. *Until next time.*

After they said their goodbyes and walked into the atrium, Attica took his arm in hers. "I have been thinking."

"Yes?"

She stopped and turned towards him, her gray eyes kindled with hope. "I would like to have a baby."

Agrippa stared at her. Since the night of their marriage, Attica had been very clear that she would prevent a child in any way possible, both on her part and his. He had accepted it, even preferred it, but now everything could change in less than a year.

He could be a father.

"Attica—"

"I know what you are going to say about the risks of the upcoming war," Attica interrupted. "But I am sure. I realized today that there is no one I would rather have as the father of my children, and there is no one I would rather share my life with, however long it may be."

"All I was going to say," Agrippa whispered, taking her face gently in his hands, "is that I love you."

Then Attica beamed, and he kissed her.

When they returned home, Agrippa led them to bed. He brought her close as he always did. Later in the night, Agrippa kissed her cheek, and his fingertips grazed her bare stomach until they both fell asleep.

41

SEXTUS POMPEIUS MAGNUS PIUS

JULY 37 BC

E VER SINCE HE WAS a boy, Sextus had been on the run.

It was what he did best, just like his mother, Mucia Tertia. His father and older brother were the ones who stood and fought until their deaths. But he was his mother's youngest child by Pompeius, and she had taught him how to escape.

"Our scouts report that Antonius has set sail with no less than three hundred ships. If he comes to an agreement with Caesar, I am afraid our chances of defeating them will be slim," said his stepbrother, Scaurus.

Scaurus was the son of Mucia by her second marriage to Marcus Aemilius Scaurus, and he bore his name. Though he was still young, he had become useful in the wars against Caesar, having a keen mind for politics, like his father had been. But Sextus also sensed that Scaurus secretly resented him as the son of the man who had exiled his father ten years ago, tarnishing his legacy.

Sextus sighed at the bad news, ignoring the pang of his hurt pride. He had trusted Antonius despite his better sense, and the man had betrayed him without a second thought.

It was not as if Sextus had not known Antonius' shifty nature, but he had thought as the son of Pompeius the Great, he would have respected his name as he did that of Caesar. Alas, despite fame and fortune, the bold strokes of war, the vast territories conquered, his father was yet again defeated and diminished by a lesser man, and Sextus would forever live in the shadow cast by his father.

But if he was not as great as his father, Sextus was certainly the better sailor, and he would at least make Caesar suffer on the sea if he could not defeat him.

"We shall see about our chances when we have them on the water," Sextus said, dismissing Scaurus. There was still time before Caesar would launch his attack, and when the time came, Sextus would be ready.

He left the naval base, his bodyguard escorting him along the harbor of Messana, which yearned for the mainland of Italy across the strait as if it recalled a time when both lands were once joined. The waves were blue-green and calm, inviting him to explore the pathways to horizons yet unseen.

Sextus had always loved the sea, because the sea had always loved him, guiding him from danger to safer shores, and there was no sweeter, more beautiful sea than the bays and beaches of Sicily. He felt at home here, among a people who played much but fought more, and he respected their pride and honor of their island set apart from the rest of the world.

His carriage climbed up into the hills and eventually reached his villa overlooking the strait that connected the Tyrrhenian and Ionian seas, a hazy sliver of Italic land visible in the distance. The smoky peak of Etna was perched in the south, eternally watching over the land with her fiery red eye.

His mother, wife, and daughter, as well as his sister and her children, were all staying in his villa, since Rome had become far too hostile for his family. Sextus entered the house and found the three older women lounging in the courtyard, the children running about excitedly, with no care for the dangers ahead.

Sextus' mother looked at him anxiously as he walked in. "Have you any news?"

"Nothing good," he said quietly. Then he picked up his daughter, Pompeia, who was nearly six years old, kissing her bronze cheek and feeling his chest tighten. He wished to be a good father to her, but sometimes the tide pulled the ship in another direction no matter how hard one rowed. "But the future is not yet written."

His mother sighed. "It is not too late to sue for pardon, *mi fili*. Your father may have taught you that honor only lies in deeds of valor, but suicide is nothing more than cowardice. There is honor in living too, for your family, and for your wife and daughter." *And mother,* were the unspoken words.

Sextus glanced at his wife, Scribonia, daughter of Scribonius Libo, whose sister had once been married to Caesar before he cruelly divorced her on the very same day she had given birth.

Once that family tie had crumbled, Libo rescinded his support for Sextus in favor of Caesar, a decision Sextus' wife resented on the parts of both her husband and father. For according to their latest terms of peace, their daughter was to be married to Caesar's nephew, Marcellus, when they were of age. But that future had ended along with their alliance. Now they raised a child without knowing whether Sextus would be alive by the end of the year.

"My father and brother died in battle for our family," Sextus said finally. "I would be honored to do the same."

"Your father did not die for *this* family," his mother retorted, shaking her head. "I can assure you that."

"And you did not *live* for this family," Sextus said coldly. "You lived for another."

Many years ago his father had divorced his mother on his way back from the East after fighting King Mithridates VI of Pontus, when he was told that she was having an affair with Julius Caesar. Although his father had refused to acknowledge the rumors publicly, in private he had called Caesar by the name Aegisthus, the queen-seducer, and filed for divorce without speaking to Mucia ever again.

Sextus knew it was beneath him to bring up those rumors now, especially in front of his wife and sister, but he could not help it. At his words, Mucia stood up, looking at her son with a fury in her blue eyes, bright against her dark skin. "You know *nothing* of my life."

Then she left the room in anger and disappeared down the hall. Sextus sighed, running a hand over his face. His sister, Pompeia Magna, stood up and followed their mother.

Sextus ran after her. "Wait, sister."

He managed to stop her in the inner courtyard. Her son had waddled after them and clung to his mother's leg, pulling at her dress until she took his small hands in a stern grip.

Pompeia glanced at Sextus, and her eyes—a deeper blue than her mother, so different from Sextus' warm brown—were sad. They had been like this since her last husband, Cinna, had died, leaving her and their two children behind. But this time that sadness was directed at him.

"You ought not speak with Mother so. She is only trying to help," Pompeia said softly. She lifted up her son into her arms as they began strolling around the shaded colonnade, the sunlight dancing along the tiled floor.

"I know," Sextus said, his voice betraying his frustration. "But she would rather I surrender than fight. And I would rather die than surrender."

"But your wife—"

"—may marry again." He thought of Scribonia, his lovely Scribonia, holding their daughter in her arms for the first time. He had felt a bliss that day he had not thought possible, swiftly followed by the most terrible fear, knowing he was entirely responsible for their safety. "She shall be better off anyway. As would my daughter."

"It is as if you wish to punish us," Pompeia said in disbelief, almost angrily, though she still spoke calmly. "You wish to punish Mother for never telling you things, when she told me everything. I know you have always been envious of that. But she also told me things of our father that would make you ashamed, and for that I envy you. Be careful on whom you lay blame, brother. You might find yourself all alone."

Then she left him, walking in the same direction as their mother. Sextus went back to Scribonia, who raised her brows and looked at him silently, those eyes ever accusing as they watched him sit down opposite her.

"I suppose you have something to say as well?" Sextus asked warily.

Scribonia shook her head. "I have nothing to say."

"I know that is not true," Sextus said quietly. "You have not slept with me in months. If you wish to leave me, you know I would not stop you."

"Sextus," she said, pain in her voice, her eyes glimmering with tears. She was even more beautiful when she cried, her brown eyes soft, her face flushed, framed by those thick brown curls, so that Sextus had never been able to stay mad at her for long. "You shall never be your father. Why do you insist on trying?"

"Because otherwise, who am I?" he asked angrily. "Nothing. I am nothing."

Scribonia smiled, but it was sad and resigned. "My husband, Sextus. You are my husband, and I would not wish for any other. But you had best start acting like it."

Sextus felt the words as a sword in his side, and he knelt before her and kissed the tears as they fell down her face, though she sat very still and did not warm to him as she once did. He embraced her and young Pompeia in his arms nonetheless, shutting his eyes tightly, and wished that his choices were easier.

But even if his father was not the best of men, was he not a great man after all, and was that not what men were made for? To fight and die for their families, to defend their honor and gain glory for their name?

At last, his wife stirred in his arms and kissed him. She murmured his name against his lips. "Do you not love me? Is that not enough for you?"

If men were made for fighting, then women were made for loving, but Sextus longed for a world where men were made for loving too, and thought it would be a better world to live in.

"*Te amo, mea vita, ad finem maris.*"

I love you, my life, to the end of the sea.

But in the end, Sextus knew it would not be enough.

⟫⟫ ⟪⟪

Sextus woke up in a cold sweat, and threw the covers off his body, staring at the ceiling. He glanced at his side, where his wife slept, her brow furrowed as though in pain.

It was the first night in a long time that they had slept together. She made a small noise and he lightly kissed her hair before leaving the room. He walked out on the terrace that overlooked the sea, her rough, moonlit waves crashing up against the sheer cliffs.

He had been dreaming a terrible dream before he had forced himself awake. The ocean beneath his ship had borne him up and down, a black storm thundering across the skies as if the gods themselves were angry. The waves were rolling higher than he had ever seen, high enough to glimpse creatures of the deep in the water, arcing over his ship and plunging him into the salty depths below, when he had gasped and opened his eyes.

It was a bad omen, but Sextus still hoped his fleet would have a chance against the inexperienced soldiers of Caesar once they braved the open sea.

He looked further down the coast where the harbor of Messana lay calm and unbothered by the surging oceans about her. A lighthouse stood gleaming at her lip, visible even this far away. Sextus thought he spotted his own flagship amidst the rest of his fleet.

He recalled the meeting he had with Caesar and Antonius on that very ship, after their conference in Misenum, when he had entertained the two *Tresviri* on board. Sextus had his crew set up a banquet of sorts on deck, and they had reclined and drunk wine and eaten fresh seafood. The cables had kept the ship safely anchored to the harbor. Was it ironic or tragic that the very admiral who jokingly suggested to sail away with the two men as prisoners was the very admiral who later sold himself to Caesar?

Antonius had gotten drunk very quickly, his face flushed and grinning, enjoying the delicacies without a care, as if the tense debates they had only a day earlier were forgotten. Caesar, on the other hand, had barely eaten, watching Sextus carefully, too knowing for his age.

"You should pay me a visit in Athens," Antonius had boasted. "My cooks there make the best octopus you have ever eaten."

"I shall be sure to stop by," Sextus had said politely, much to the apparent amusement of Antonius, who had roared in laughter, though at his words or some private joke, Sextus did not know.

Caesar had glanced at Antonius, then, and Sextus had caught the slight distaste at the edges of his frown.

Antonius, also catching the look on Caesar's face, had smiled mockingly. "Why do you not enjoy yourself, Caesar? You eat like a bird. Nay, like a woman, which is worse!"

And he had roared again. Sextus had watched the interaction with interest, and Caesar had glanced at him sharply, as though he disliked Sextus noticing the strained relationship they clearly had. But it had not mattered, in the end. Antonius chose Caesar over Sextus, and they all knew this momentary peace would not last forever.

"If you must vomit after all that wine," Caesar had said idly, "please do so overboard."

Antonius' smile had curled in disgust. "It is not a crime to indulge in drink. But it certainly is a crime to deny the gifts of a host!"

Caesar had turned to Sextus. "Εἷσεν δ' εἰσαγαγοῦσα κατὰ κλισμούς τε θρόνους τε, ἐν δέ σφιν τυρόν τε καὶ ἄλφιτα καὶ μέλι χλωρὸν οἴνῳ Πραμνείῳ ἐκύκα."

She led them in and sat them down on couches and chairs, and stirred before them cheese, barley, groats, and yellow honey in Pramnian wine...

It was a well-known quote to anyone who had studied Greek, for it was about Circe, the cunning goddess, who welcomed Odysseus' men to food and drink only to imprison their pig forms in her garden after they feasted.

Caesar and Sextus had stared at each other in silence, while Antonius had ignored them, either not having heard or not even bothering to listen to Caesar's quotation. He continued eating his octopus, already reaching for the dish of clams before he finished.

"Your Greek is excellent," Sextus had said finally, inclining his head. For it was true, and he could not help wondering if Caesar had somehow divined what his admiral had said earlier.

Caesar had inclined his head in return. "So is the wine."

That was the day Sextus had learned not to underestimate the boy who claimed to be a son of a god. While Antonius could be brutish and mean, he was a simple man, and his fascination with the Egyptian queen marked him with a doom, as dark clouds gathered on the horizon before a storm.

But Sextus looked at Caesar and saw the same tempered steel, the same careless cruelty, that he had always seen in his own father, Pompeius the Great.

Caesar, like Sextus' father, knew the cost of greatness and did not flinch from it. If Sextus wanted to defeat him, he would have to risk more than he had ever bargained before. But when the time came and his life hung in the balance, would he stand and fight?

Your father did not die for this family.

Then Sextus would die for them instead.

42

OCTAVIA MINOR

I T TOOK THEM THREE weeks to reach Tarentum by carriage at a slow enough pace to accommodate the two pregnant women—herself and Livia—and by the end of the first week, Octavia decided she preferred the nausea of a rocking ship to the endless, cramped days in a carriage.

Octavius looked as if he agreed, his face pale and flushed across from her, resolutely staring out the small window. She had thought it was to avoid looking at her, but she quickly realized it was to prevent himself from growing sick. Livia sat beside Octavia, her hands resting on her heavily pregnant belly, fast asleep.

"You ought to leave me to do the talking," Octavia whispered. "The gods know he cannot stand you."

Octavius glanced at her, raising a brow. "This is purely politics, sister. There is no need to bring your marriage into it."

"Ah, but you see, my marriage *is* politics, as is everything in this world, and if you were a woman you would know that."

"Your willingness to fight on my behalf is admirable, but unnecessary," Octavius said, looking back out the window, his mind already on other things.

But Octavia only smiled. "Who said I was fighting on *your* behalf?"

She ignored his disapproving glance at her as the carriage rolled to a stop. Their bodyguards escorted them to the military camp Antonius had set up near the harbor.

Tarentum lay on the west side of the peninsula along the Via Appia, which continued east from there to Brundisium on the shores of the Adriatic Sea. It was an old town with an ancient history, where Greek colonists had once been conquered by Roman generals. She knew Octavius considered it a fitting setting for the renewal of his alliance with a man of Eastern habits.

Octavia felt her heart beat faster as they approached, and she pressed her palms against her stomach to keep them from shaking. They were a large group, much larger than she thought necessary for this kind of meeting. Along with Octavius and Livia, there was also Agrippa and Attica, Balbus and Maecenas, the last who had brought with him—to the apparent confusion of all except Octavius—two well-known poets, Quintus Horatius Flaccus and Publius Vergilius Maro.

She ignored all of them and went directly to her husband, who came forth from the camp with his own retinue of cavalry and foot soldiers.

When Antonius saw her, he put up a hand, and they came to a unified halt. She did as well, and they stood in silence for a few moments. Antonius looked at her with a strange air of confusion and contempt, as though he had expected to face an army but instead faced only a woman.

He was still handsome to her, his dark curls having grown wild at sea. Octavia felt that familiar desire deep within her, and she could not prevent the blush from forming on her cheeks. As if Antonius read her mind, his eyes narrowed, and the hand at his side twitched imperceptibly.

She lowered her face. "My dear husband, it is wonderful to see you."

"And you, my dear," Antonius said, but it sounded false to her ears.

Their marriage was on the brink of crumbling, and if she did not give birth to a boy, he would surely abandon her, if he had not planned to already.

Octavius stepped forward and met Antonius halfway between their two parties. They kissed in greeting, but neither looked the other in the eyes. "Shall we begin?"

Antonius nodded, sweeping a glance over Octavius' followers. "We shall."

They moved their meeting to a secure location within Antonius' camp. There, Pollio, Ventidius, and Ahenobarbus were waiting for them. Antonius had his attendants provide couches for all, and they reclined as food and drink were brought out. After the usual pleasantries and the second course was served, Antonius at last addressed her brother.

"Your delay, Caesar, is quite incomprehensible," Antonius said, raising a brow. He nodded at Octavia. "If I had not sent my wife, I wonder if we would have met at all."

Her brother only smiled. "If we have come to list our grievances, then might I add your abandonment of Brundisium when I had called for aid against Sextus?"

"No, you may not." Antonius returned his smile. "I left because you were not there to welcome me. My first priority is the safety and security of my men. But when you sent Maecenas to persuade me to return, I was under the impression we would meet immediately."

"Let us not squabble over the past," Octavia interrupted, unable to stand their bickering. Both Antonius and her brother looked at her angrily. She looked sternly at each of them in turn. "There are more important matters to discuss, such as your Parthian campaign, husband."

Antonius nodded reluctantly. "My wife is right. I have come to discuss the trade concerning my ships."

"Very well."

Octavius glanced at Agrippa and Maecenas, who reclined beside him. Livia had felt unwell and had asked Attica to remain behind with her to fetch a doctor. The two poets reclined on their own couch, silently watching the argument unfold. Octavia was not sure Antonius even knew who they were. Agrippa nodded in assent to the unspoken decision.

Octavia thought she sensed something different between her brother and Agrippa, but especially in Agrippa, who no longer seemed the desperate, loyal friend of her brother. She supposed he looked like a man now, calm, almost resigned, as though he had settled in reality and no longer believed in his youthful dreams.

"I am willing to give you one hundred ships in exchange for thirty thousand soldiers," Antonius said.

Octavius paused, pretending to ponder. "No."

"No?" Antonius asked, raising a brow.

"One hundred and thirty ships with their crews at the very least," Octavius said. "And I shall give you twenty thousand soldiers in return."

"One hundred ships is more than you deserve," Antonius spat.

Her brother smirked, and Octavia thought she saw her husband grimace. "One hundred and twenty or you do not get my soldiers."

Antonius' jaw clenched. He needed those soldiers as much as Octavius needed those ships, yet somehow they all knew Antonius needed them a little more.

Finally, Antonius nodded. "Agreed."

The negotiations continued in like manner, both Antonius and Octavius presenting offers and arguing until they reached an agreement, the others interjecting to retain order or debate the offer.

They agreed to renew their alliance for another five years, though their powers would not yet be ratified by any law. To solidify their alliance, Antonius offered his eldest son, Marcus Antonius Antyllus, in marriage to Octavius' daughter, Julia Caesaris filia.

When the meeting concluded and dinner had long since finished, Octavia drew her husband aside. Octavius had wished to return to Rome promptly, as it was still such a turbulent time to leave the seat of power to another. But Octavia would not leave without this.

Antonius did not meet her eyes, instead glancing at her pregnant stomach with a frown. She wondered if he had visited his Egyptian mistress while he was away, though none of her brother's scouts had heard any such rumors.

A part of her still longed to lure him back to Italy, to keep him rooted to the soil from which he had sprung, and grant him the empire he had always wanted. The other part of her only wanted to walk away.

"May I ask a favor of you, as my husband?" Octavia asked. "And let it be the last."

Antonius' eyes softened despite his obvious reluctance. "Of course. Anything you wish."

"I would like to present a gift to my brother," she said. "As a personal thanks."

While the exchanging of gifts was merely a formality, this time it felt personal. Antonius hesitated, but she knew he would relent on behalf of her if not on behalf of Roman custom, no matter how humiliating he considered it. For she sensed his guilt towards her, and he would consider this a form of penance.

He nodded. "I suppose."

They found Octavius speaking with Maecenas, Horatius, and Vergilius in hushed tones, followed by murmuring laughter.

When Antonius and Octavia approached, the poets went still under her husband's large shadow. But Octavius smiled, and Octavia understood it was a smile of triumph, for the terms of their agreement had favored him over Antonius. Octavia felt her husband stiffen beside her.

"Caesar," Octavia said. "Before we depart for Rome, allow me to present a gift for you, as a thanks for lending your ear towards my counsel, despite my womanly tendencies. My husband shall give you ten *phaseli* with triple bank oars. Please accept our gift."

Octavius bowed his head. "I shall only accept your gift if you accept mine. I shall give to you a bodyguard of no less than one thousand troops, to be picked personally by your husband."

Before Octavia could respond with her thanks, her husband interrupted. "I must begin the preparations for departure. We have a long journey at sea ahead of us. I am sure all shall be taken care of from your end, Caesar?"

Her brother looked at Antonius with a very thoughtful air, and Octavia had the sudden feeling that Octavius was seeing the future in her husband's hard glance, the hostility in his voice, before he smiled, and nodded.

"Until we meet again, Marcus Antonius," Octavius said.

Antonius grinned, but his eyes flashed with anger. "Until we meet again, Caesar Octavianus."

When they said their final goodbyes, Antonius looked at her carefully, and in that moment Octavia knew she would never see her husband again, and that if her husband ever did return to her, it would be in battle, as the conqueror of her family.

Octavia felt that familiar want rise in her, the want of a woman looking at the strong stature of her husband, the father of her children. But then he turned around and followed his men back to the harbor, and that feeling faded like a sun setting red on the open sea, burning brightest before it disappeared. Octavia had done her duty to her family, and now it was time he did his.

She just didn't know which family it would be.

⟫⟫⟫ ⟪⟪⟪

SEPTEMBER 37 BC

"Come now, Marcellus," Octavia said, gently pulling her son away from her leg, where he clung to her dress with tight fists. "Go out to the garden and play."

She stroked his blonde curls which had dulled to a dark golden color as he grew older, hoping the affection would sway him.

Marcellus turned his distressed face up to Octavia. "No."

It was his favorite word nowadays. She kissed the top of his head, breathing in that familiar scent of flowery soap and olive oil. Octavia thought there was nothing lovelier in the entire world. "Yes. Go, *mi aselle.*"

Marcellus' face scrunched up at this term of endearment—*my little donkey*—which was a special favorite of her brother.

"Phoebe, dear," Livia called out from her chair.

Octavia was visiting her at their house on the Palatine, as she hated her own husband's empty estate. Attica was also sitting with them, since Agrippa had some business to attend to with Octavius. They were in his office now with several other men, reviewing their project in Naples and planning their future war against Sextus.

"Phoebe," Livia said once the handmaiden entered the room. "Take Marcellus and Julia with you for a walk in the garden."

Phoebe took Marcellus by the hand and he waddled after her, glancing back at Octavia with a pout. Livia laughed, and even serious Attica smiled. The three of them had become quite close since Attica's marriage to Agrippa, and they spent much time together.

"He certainly loves his mother," Livia murmured, looking after Marcellus as he strained against Phoebe's arm, casting desperate pleading eyes back to Octavia. She glanced at Octavia. "I forgot to ask. How did Marcellus like Antonius?"

"Not at all," Octavia said with a grin.

"Who does?" Attica said under her breath, then looked up at Octavia with wide eyes. "I apologize. He is an honorable man."

355

Octavia laughed, whether at Attica or her statement, she did not know. "Honorable he is not. But between us women, he had his moments."

Livia's brows raised. "Had?"

"It is different now," Octavia said, glancing away. "We have children."

"I see," Livia said, nodding slowly. "Do you think he will return to Cleopatra?"

"Livia," Attica whispered in shock.

"It is not like it is much of a secret," Octavia said with an amused smile. She admired Attica's persistent propriety as much as she enjoyed Livia's intimate directness. They were like sisters to her, and she did not know how she would have endured her marriage to Antonius without them. "Perhaps it is for the best."

Livia nodded, her eyes sad but understanding. Octavius, too, was not the most attentive husband, but he was here, while Antonius was already somewhere in the East. At the thought of her husband lying with that Egyptian queen, something in Octavia's chest twisted, though she knew it was only her pride.

"At least our dear Attica has Agrippa," Livia said, smiling tenderly at the girl, who blushed. "We know he is good to you, my dear. No need to blush like that."

"Ah, yes, Agrippa is sweet," Octavia said, though she could not hide the bitterness in her words, remembering what her brother had said when he had returned from Apollonia, the doom she had seen woven between the two of them. *It is nothing.* She wondered if her brother had even known it was a lie. "Soon we shall have a little one, no?"

Attica looked at Octavia in surprise, her hands fluttering subconsciously to her stomach. Octavia raised a brow, but before she could speak, Livia gasped. They both looked at her, and Octavia saw that the front of her dress was wet.

She stood up. "Livia—"

"Get Phoebe," Livia whispered, holding her stomach and wincing. Her face was flushed and damp. "Quick."

Words died in her throat, and Octavia turned to Attica, who had gone very pale as she watched Livia groan aloud. The sound snapped Octavia back to the moment, and she pointed at Attica.

"Get Agrippa," Octavia commanded. "And my brother."

"No!" Livia cried, gasping as if she were struggling to breathe. "Not my husband."

Attica looked between Livia and Octavia, frozen by shock, but then Livia let out a whimpering cry, and Attica sprang to her feet and started down the hall.

"Go!" Octavia cried as she rushed forward and knelt by Livia, rubbing her palm over her stomach.

Livia shook her head, looking at Octavius with pained eyes. "No, no, no."

Octavia fetched Phoebe from the gardens, hoisting Marcellus on one hip and taking

Julia in the other arm until she found servants to take them away. By the time she returned, Phoebe was already tending to Livia in her room, and Octavius and Agrippa were waiting anxiously outside.

"What happened?" Octavius snapped at her.

"She went into labor," she said quietly. "It is early. I cannot promise—" Then she stopped. The fury on his face faded to dumb shock, and he looked at Octavia as if she had told him the world was ending. "You'd better send a message to Alfidia."

Octavius nodded slowly.

She shared a worried glance with Agrippa, who had Attica clinging to his arm tightly, a dazed look on her face. It would be best if she did not witness this.

Without another word, Octavia went inside the room, closing the door behind her. She knelt beside Livia, who was half-unconscious, her hair plastered to her forehead. There had been no time to prepare a birthing chair, and Octavia doubted Livia would have the strength to hold herself up.

Octavia smoothed the loose strands of her hair and patted a cool cloth on her burning skin which Phoebe had wordlessly handed her.

"It will be alright," Octavia whispered. "It will be alright."

Livia shook her head, breathing heavily, then groaned again, her body shaking as Phoebe stood between her legs and waited as the baby was pushed into her hands, quiet and still in her grasp. Octavia took Livia's hand and held it tightly as Phoebe leaned down and blew air into the small mouth, pumping the chest with her hands. Then she stood up abruptly, turning to find a cloth and cleaning the baby before wrapping it and setting it out of view.

For a moment, all was horribly silent, and Livia stared up at the ceiling, unseeing. Then she turned to her handmaiden, but Phoebe only shook her head, not meeting Livia's eyes.

Octavia felt her heart pang painfully, for her brother and her sister-in-law, watching as Livia's face went blank, her mouth slightly parted. Then she began to sob, heaving, messy sobs, and she squeezed Octavia's hand until it hurt.

"It will be alright," Octavia said, feeling numb. She did not know what else to say. "It will be alright."

"My husband," Livia said through a hiccup. "Is he here?"

Octavia nodded. "Yes. Outside."

Livia's brown eyes steeled themselves. "Do not let him in."

"Livia—"

"Don't." She turned to Octavia sharply, her cheeks tear-stained. "You do not understand."

"There will be more," Octavia whispered urgently. "Do not cry. He will understand."

Phoebe shook her head. "No more, my lady. Too dangerous."

Livia spoke through her dry sobs. "There will be no more children. The gods have cursed me, Octavia. I know it. They have cursed me for taking my fate into my own hands when it was never mine to choose."

Octavia felt herself go pale. "Do not say that, Livia."

"It is true," Livia said weakly. "If I cannot conceive a son...your brother..."

"You already have two strong boys who will grow up to be great men," Octavia said as firmly as she could, though she did not believe the words as she spoke them. "He shall love them like his own."

Livia managed a smile. "We both know he will not."

"My brother loves you. He will not abandon you." Octavia kissed Livia's knuckles. "I know him."

Her eyes were sad. "I know him too."

Octavia felt her heart harden against her brother, and a tear escaped down her cheek as she remembered his shocked face, the future pain they would endure that she could only imagine. "I promise he will not, because I will not let him."

Livia sighed, and brought Octavia's hand over her heart, her eyes closing tightly as more tears fell down her cheeks. "Thank you."

They remained like that for a long time.

43

GAIUS OCTAVIUS

OCTOBER 37 BC

"**A**RE YOU LISTENING TO me, brother?"

Octavius looked up. He had been lost in thought, staring at the ground. They had been talking in his office downstairs about the troops Octavius had promised Antonius in Tarentum. Octavia had received a letter from Antonius urging Octavius to action. Of course, Octavius did not plan on sending those troops any time soon.

"Yes," Octavius lied.

"You are not listening," Octavia said, sighing. "I do not blame you for it."

"I do not need your pity," he snapped, though he was too exhausted to sound truly angry.

Ever since Livia had given birth to a stillborn, Octavia had looked at him with a womanly sadness in her eyes that Octavius hated. It reminded him of the look his mother had given him whenever he had left home, and he had never understood it.

"You should talk to her," Octavia said gently. "She needs you now more than ever."

Octavius frowned. "She does not need me."

It was true. Livia had held aloof from him since the stillbirth, any of their previous intimacy dead before he could even revive it, as if their love had been the life of this child and their fates were bound up with it, doomed to die. He still remembered Livia's face afterward.

She had refused to see him, retiring to bed early, but Octavius had insisted on speaking with her and commanded Phoebe to allow him inside. To his surprise, she had already rested, bathed, and changed her clothes, and her brown hair had been combed and hung loose about her shoulders. She had never seemed more beautiful.

Then Livia had looked at him, and the pain on her face was deeper than any hurt, any mortal wound. It was Death itself etched into her very brows, darkening her eyes, kissing her mouth like a poison that killed from the inside.

He had known, then, that she had gone to a place he could not follow. She would not speak with him, and Octavius had finally given up. When he had left the room, he had called for Phoebe. He had to know. She had looked at him hesitantly.

"Was it a boy?"

Phoebe had hesitated, as if she had not wished to betray her mistress.

"Answer me."

"Yes," she had whispered. "It was a boy."

Then he had gone up to his study and remained there a long time, drinking several glasses of wine, until night had come and he slept alone.

Octavia shook her head. "It is not about you."

"I do not understand," Octavius said. "She may have another child."

That pity returned to Octavia's eyes, but this time mingled with a hardness he had never seen before. "And if she cannot?"

He paused, his heart dropping to his stomach. "I need an heir."

"Octavius," she said in disbelief. "She is your wife."

"Yes," he said, "she is."

"For the love of Jove, speak with her." Octavia's eyes gleamed with tears, and Octavius knew what she was going to say before she did. "And if it means anything to you, I offer Marcellus as your own, for you are like a father to him, and I know you love him dearly."

Octavius went still. He thought of Marcellus, the feeling he had when he held him in his arms for the first time, the warmth and movement of life in his small limbs, the miracle of it all like stars in his eyes.

He had grown much since then, but Octavius still felt that spark of life in his heart when he saw the boy, like watching a flame grow into a blazing fire and never knowing why.

But he was not his son, no matter how much he might wish it.

"It is not up to me whether we speak," Octavius said finally, sounding bitter. For at the end of the day, Livia *was* his wife, and he had grown accustomed to her advice and sharp wit. Octavius could no longer imagine his life without her.

Octavia smiled sadly. "Then you know much less than you think."

Once Octavia returned to Antonius' estate to see to her children's dinner, Octavius mustered up the courage to speak with Livia. He found her in the gardens despite the chilly weather, standing before the small laurel tree and staring at it silently.

She did not turn when he approached, but her shoulders stiffened.

Octavius stood beside her, as they had all those months ago when she had told him she was with child. It felt like an eternity had passed since then.

He sighed. "You must speak with me one of these days."

Livia remained still and silent.

Octavius turned towards her and grabbed her hand. He saw her jaw tighten. "You are my wife. I command you to speak with me."

Nothing. She continued to look at the tree, her hand unresponsive in his, as if he were not there at all. Octavius almost left, knowing in his heart that she would not speak with him, when his sister's words returned to him. *Then you know much less than you think.*

If she would not speak with him, then he would simply have to speak with her.

Octavius brought her hand up to his mouth and softly kissed the knuckles. "You know, I remember you at that dinner party, when I was still betrothed to Servilia."

Livia said nothing, but her hand twitched ever so slightly in his grasp.

He kissed the palm of her hand. "You were dressed in purple and gold, and I thought you looked like a goddess."

Still, she did not speak, but her mouth parted in surprise, and Octavius sensed her waiting, listening. Then he kissed the underside of her wrist, where the skin was softest, then higher, beneath the elbow, on her shoulder, and along the curve of her neck.

"Caesar," she whispered in warning. There were servants milling about the house, and surely one or two were patrolling the gardens, but Octavius found he did not care, not in the slightest.

Octavius kissed her neck again, then the tender skin below her jaw. "I was terrified of you. Your eyes saw right through me, even though it was only a glance." He lightly kissed her brows, and her eyelids as they closed.

Livia bit her lip, either to stop herself from speaking or from his touch, he did not know.

He brushed her cheek with his fingertips, and she looked at him, her brown eyes wavering with pain and love. "And when I heard footsteps by the office door, I saw a stola disappear around the corner. I cannot explain how, but I had the strangest feeling it was you."

Then he kissed her, and she stood frozen for a moment, before her arms curled around his neck and he wound his arms around her waist, pulling her in flush against him, their mouths seeking apologies and regrets that could not be said with words.

She surrendered against him, and he felt a fierce loyalty rise up in his chest, and he knew he would burn the entire world before he let anyone wrong her. Octavius lowered them to the ground until they were swallowed up by the tall rose bushes, the gray sky far above them.

He pulled up her dress between them, and she arched her neck, eyes closed tight. The earth anchored them to her bosom, Livia pinned beneath his embrace, and as she was a woman, her mouth a rose, her hair a lake, and her hips the gates to golden fields, she was also a goddess, an eternal flame, and Octavius knew he had found peace amidst the chaos.

When he rolled to her side, a tear slid down Livia's cheek. "I thought you would leave me," she whispered, her voice trembling.

"How could I?" Octavius asked softly, kissing the tear away. *"You are my destiny."*

Livia turned to him and smiled.

⤜⟫⟫ ⟪⟪⤛

NOVEMBER 37 BC

Octavius entered the house and was embraced by Balbus. He was visiting him in his villa at Baiae, where Balbus liked to enjoy the luxury of the seaside pleasure boats and vast hunting grounds.

Agrippa was also in Naples checking up on the progress of their fleet and agreed to join them for dinner. He was already in the atrium with Balbus when Octavius entered the house, his face tanned from working by the lake where the sun was harsher, and when he looked at Octavius his sea-green eyes seemed brighter.

"Thank you for visiting, son," Balbus said, slinging an arm around Octavius' shoulders affectionately. "And I send my love to your beautiful wife. It is a terrible thing to lose a child."

"Thank you, Balbus. I will."

Octavius thought he saw pain flash in Balbus' eyes before the old man smiled. He knew there was much about Balbus and his personal life that he did not know, but Octavius got the sense that Balbus preferred it that way. Octavius and Agrippa followed him to the triclinium, where dinner was already being laid out before the three plush couches.

"I requested that my cooks buy everything fresh from the docks," Balbus said with a grin. "Only the best for you, Caesar."

"You are too kind, Balbus."

They began speaking of the fleet and the difficulty of acquiring the necessary crews to man their ships. Dinner passed swiftly, the late hours of the night descending the house into shadows and halos of lamplight cast against the walls. As they ate dessert, Balbus turned to Octavius.

"I do have a question for you, Caesar, that I have been meaning to ask," Balbus said carefully. "As your financial advisor."

"Yes?"

362

Balbus cleared his throat. "Assuming you go to war with Sextus within this next year, it would be wise to have your affairs in order in the case of your death, Jove forbid it."

Agrippa looked startled, and Octavius was silent. He had thought about it, of course, as the inevitable wars ahead loomed ever closer. But to hear someone else voice those same realities aloud felt like discovering they had dreamed the same dream.

"But he has no sons," Agrippa said quietly.

Balbus glanced at him. "There are Livia's children. And his nephew. It would be dangerous to leave such a significant estate to chance. It would be best if you named an heir."

Octavius nodded, but his head felt light. He remembered what Octavia had said to him after his son had died. *I offer Marcellus as your own, for you are like a father to him.*

Yet to leave not only his estate but his legacy to a boy? To a child that was not even his son? There may come a day when Marcellus attained such heights, but until then, Octavius could only entrust his name and legacy to one person.

"Agrippa," Octavius whispered.

Agrippa looked at him. "Yes?"

"No." He turned to Balbus. "Agrippa will be named my heir."

Balbus raised a brow, and Agrippa stared at Octavius. While Balbus had certainly warmed up to Agrippa as Octavius' faithful friend if nothing else, Balbus still considered Agrippa an unusual choice in Octavius' closest circles. "And in the case that Agrippa fails to succeed?"

Octavius ignored Agrippa's heated gaze. "Then a third shall go to Livia, and the rest to the *potestas* of Marcellus."

"You will have to receive an exception for Livia," Balbus warned.

He nodded. "I shall take care of that."

Balbus sighed. "Very well."

When they retired to their rooms, Octavius stopped Agrippa in the hall. "Take a walk with me."

Agrippa met his eyes hesitantly, then nodded.

They walked along the shore, as they used to during their days at the Academy in Apollonia, after their long, grueling military training and even longer, tedious lessons with Athenodorus.

Balbus' estate was built on a cliff overlooking a natural harbor. The town itself was the most luxurious in all of Campania, with villas and parks housing the wealthiest of Romans who wished to escape the day-to-day business of the city and relax by the bay.

Octavius and Agrippa walked side by side until they reached a secluded stretch of the shore, the water calmly lapping the warm sand. They sat down and looked out at the ocean, its waves mild and peaceful, deceptively still, for when the moon was full the water had a mind of its own.

Agrippa glanced at him. "Why did you name me as your heir?"

"I trust you with my life," Octavius said softly.

Agrippa's eyes widened slightly, for it was what Octavius had told him when they had decided to return to Rome and claim his heirship, before they learned the true cost of those words.

"You remember."

Octavius nodded. "I remember a lot of things. I remember the first day I met you. I remember thinking that you were the smartest person I knew. I remember every illness, every night you stayed by my side. I even remember sailing to Apollonia, when I was still weak, and you had this worried look on your face, as if I were about to die."

Agrippa's mouth quirked into a smile. "I thought you would die before we reached the shore."

"Me too," Octavius admitted, and he could not help but laugh, remembering how his mother had bundled him up in thick layers of wool despite the heat.

"Really?" Agrippa asked. "You said you wouldn't."

Octavius smirked. "I lied."

Agrippa shook his head, but he was still smiling. "Of course you did."

"I remember loving how you looked at the ocean," Octavius said quietly, his heart pounding at the confession. "Because you seemed to forget the world around you, as if the waves spoke to you in a language I would never know."

"That's funny," Agrippa said, though his eyes were serious, "because I was only ever thinking about you."

"I think I knew," Octavius whispered. "That day. I knew."

"You knew what?" Agrippa asked suspiciously. "That you wanted me?"

"No." Octavius recalled that day, the ocean spraying salty water in his face, the fever he had already felt gripping his limbs, and those sea-green eyes, even brighter than the water surrounding them, and it was like he had seen the eyes of a god. "No. I never *wanted* you. I never had a choice."

Agrippa stared at him, incredulous. "You always have a choice."

"You are wrong," Octavius said, and his words fell with more confidence than he had ever felt because he knew the words were true. "I never had a choice with you."

"Octavius," he whispered.

"How could it be a choice, Agrippa?" Octavius took Agrippa's hand in his, lacing their fingers together. Agrippa glanced down at their joined hands as if it were the first time. "I cannot stay away from you, no matter how hard I try. And I do try. No, you were never a choice."

For had he not known then, that day on the ship? Had he not known the first time he had laid eyes on that quiet and strange boy from the countryside? Had Agrippa not looked at him and suddenly it was as if Octavius had found a gem at the bottom of the sea, and he was terrified of losing it?

And had every day since then not felt like swimming against the tide, only to find himself pulled back to shore, even closer in his arms than before?

Perhaps it was love, but the word always seemed to miss the mark, like being called by the wrong name. Octavius wished to reach into his chest and pull out his heart and read the words written there, to know what that whisper in his pulse spoke every time they kissed, like the ghost of Death after Life.

Look at me.

"I must tell you," Agrippa said hesitantly. "Before you find out elsewhere."

Octavius felt his heart skip a beat. "Yes?"

"Attica is pregnant."

"How long have you known?" Octavius asked, the words spoken from instinct, and he regretted how bitter they sounded.

"A little more than a month," Agrippa said. "I am sorry. I did not wish to tell you so soon after..."

"I know." Octavius laid back on the sand, staring up at the sky, the black now stained with blue and green as the sun began to rise. Agrippa followed suit, their hands still laced together between them. "Sometimes I dream we are still in Apollonia, and we are sleeping on the sand after swimming in the sea. But then I wake, and it is as if it were another life."

Agrippa sighed. "Everything seemed so simple back then."

"Because it was."

"I loved you. You knew, didn't you?"

"I did." It felt like the first truth he had ever told in his entire life.

Agrippa looked startled, then slightly embarrassed. He turned his head and looked at Octavius accusingly. "Why didn't you say anything?"

Octavius felt the words caught in his throat, and he tightened his hold on Agrippa's hand. "Because I was scared if I did, I would say I loved you too."

"Would that have been such a bad thing?" Agrippa asked. Octavius heard Livia's voice echo in his mind. *It is not so bad a thing to love someone, you know.*

"Yes."

"Why?"

Octavius closed his eyes. "Because if I loved you, I would be terrified to lose you."

The world was dark and silent, save for the cries of birds and the crash of the tide.

He wished that this moment would last for an eternity, Agrippa's hand in his, the cliffs sheltering them from the wars ahead, and his own heart, beating steady as if in time with the pulse of the earth below.

And for one single space between breaths, Octavius felt the civilizations of the world rise and fall about them like waves at sea, and the moon shone high for an endless night just before the dawn, and they passed into the stars like legends did, two lovers whose names were as old as time.

"If I were Patroclus, you would be Achilles."

Agrippa murmured the words, a long-forgotten memory on the wind, and Octavius turned to speak when he felt Agrippa's mouth on his, soft and gentle, and Octavius felt Agrippa's arms about his waist, bringing him closer, into the tender heat of his body. Yes, this was more than love. So much more than love.

For how could their love become less than memory when they were gone? How would history be told in years to come, when his body was no more and the sun shined on different greens of each new spring? What was life once their song stopped being sung?

If time simply forgot every kiss, every word, every love, why did Octavius find the answers to every question he had ever asked the gods in Agrippa's touch?

When the sun finally rose, and the faded blue sky above kindled with a faint rosy red, the stars disappearing in the light of a new day, they began the long walk back. The moon had since faded in the face of a chasing dawn, and the waves climbed up on the shore, searching steadily for an endless ocean.

Octavius ignored the pain in his heart, etched as if with a knife, spilling blood bitter-sweet, and listened to the voices whispering on the wind.

Look at me.

He knew then that he had seen eternity, and when he kissed Agrippa, he had known its name all along.

44

MARCUS ANTONIUS

DECEMBER 37 BC

ANTONIUS STOOD ON THE terrace of his sprawling villa, staring out at the city of Antioch on the far eastern edge of the Mediterranean Sea.

Its carefully gridded streets, hugged by the Orontes River—a deep blue framing the rich green parks and glades—reminded him of the city of Alexandria. He envisioned this city rising as the Eastern Rome, the center of trade and military power, when he would finally conquer the world with a queen by his side.

"Antonius, my love, there is a letter," came a voice from inside.

Antonius returned to his bedroom, where Cleopatra sat on his bed, Alexander Helios and Cleopatra Selene II crawling about her, shrieking as they fought with each other. Selene proved victorious when she pulled Alexander's hair and he began to cry.

Antonius scooped Alexander up and sat him down on his lap. "Now, Alexander, men do not cry."

"Only when they leave their lovers," Cleopatra said with a wry smile.

Antonius half-glared at her. "You are too funny, my love." Then he lowered Alexander to the ground, who climbed back onto the bed and into the arms of his mother. "Where is the letter?"

She motioned to a bound-up scroll left on a small table by the door. Antonius stood up and retrieved it, and read it silently to himself. The words were brief and to the point.

Cleopatra watched him carefully. "What does it say?"

"Let me finish," Antonius murmured. Then he took a deep breath. "It is from Octavia. She says Caesar is currently preoccupied with Sextus, but shall send the troops as soon as he can. Caesar is a liar. And so is she."

"Of course he is a liar," Cleopatra said lightly. "But you knew this."

"I thought perhaps Octavia would be enough to persuade him otherwise," Antonius muttered, shaking his head. "If there is someone he loves, it would be her."

Cleopatra laughed incredulously. "You do not seriously think your *wife* is fighting for you, do you? For I tell you, she is not."

"She loves me," Antonius countered, wondering why he felt so defensive.

"Women are not like men, my dear. Even when we are in love, we know when a battle is lost. She would first lose you before her brother. After all, you have not given her much hope to hold onto."

Antonius stared at her. "Do *you* know when a battle is lost?"

Cleopatra raised a brow, her eyes troubled. She remained quiet for a long time, as if she were put off that Antonius had asked her the question he had been so terrified to ask, the question that seemed to face them at all times.

"The battle is not yet lost," Cleopatra said slowly, "if that is what you are suggesting. We have amassed a larger army than has ever come before."

This, at least, was true. The combined Roman and Egyptian forces totaled over two hundred thousand men, not to mention forty thousand auxiliaries. They would invade Parthia and conquer their empire, leaving only Caesar or Sextus in Rome to oppose him. Then he and Cleopatra would rule, dividing the kingdom amongst their children, founding a unified empire of both East and West, and finally establishing peace throughout the world.

"I wish to marry you," Antonius said quietly, setting down the letter. Cleopatra looked at him in surprise, but she did not smile. "If I am to rule, I only want you by my side."

Her eyes lowered. "And your wife in Rome?"

"She is not my wife. I will divorce her." But his voice sounded desperate now.

"We both know you will not divorce her until there is no chance of returning," Cleopatra said, lifting her chin as if she dared him to defy her. Indeed, in the time that he had known her, she had never once been wrong. "There is no point pretending otherwise."

By the gods, she was right, and Antonius hated it. Even though she loved this Egyptian queen, her wine-dark eyes, her thick, black curls, those honeyed shoulders he loved to kiss in the dead of night, he was still a Roman, born and bred, and the thought of cutting off the last tie he had with his old life still felt too risky.

But the life he could have with Octavia would always mean surrendering to her brother, and after all, the marriage had been a pawn in the grand game they were playing. Yet he did not forget the hatred she stirred in him, the passion despite it, and the nights they spent awake and wrapped in each other's arms, whether warring or loving he did not know, her pale skin and fierce blue eyes merely the ghost of the first woman he had feared, and the first woman he had learned to respect.

Antonius wondered, of course, whether he would have changed his mind if Octavia had given birth to a boy instead of a girl, a Roman boy from an honorable Roman family.

But it was impossible to say, and Antonius knew that life did not live in the past.

Even with the possibility of a boy, Antonius had already begun to feel the distance between them, the passion reeling into dislike, even disgust, and they had not found that same intimacy again. Now Octavia has chosen her side, and Antonius his.

May I ask a favor of you, as my husband? And let it be the last.

They both knew the time had come to pick a side and now they found themselves, husband and wife, man and woman, on opposite sides of the same war. Antonius knew as well as she where his loyalties lay, so there was no need for him to preserve a vow that was already broken.

"I still wish to marry you," Antonius said finally. "I promised that if I returned alive, we would marry, and I intend to keep that promise."

"To my people, we are already married, for these are your children, and my home is your home," she said, gesturing to Alexander and Selene who were sprawled on her legs.

Antonius hesitated. "But not to my people."

Cleopatra looked at him for a long time, her lips pursed, and Antonius knew this promise had been as hard for her as it had been for him.

Then she nodded. "Very well. Let us marry."

⋙ ⋘

Antonius held Cleopatra in his arms, crossing the threshold of the estate. He had Asinius Pollio witness their marriage and provide the feast.

She held tightly to his neck as they entered. Antonius looked down at her face and smiled.

"Ubi tu Osiris, ibi ego Isis," she whispered.

Wherever you are, Osiris, I, Isis, am.

They were the Egyptian gods, the King and Queen of Egypt. It was a variation on the traditional vows, for Cleopatra had refused to call upon any Roman gods, even in the name of their love.

Antonius kissed her nonetheless, before he set her down gently. Then he took her hand and led her up the stairs to their bedroom. They had taken to sleeping in the same room, even though everything he had been taught would call it improper.

She was uncharacteristically quiet, and he ignored the warning in his heart that in vowing their love, he was sealing their fate as well.

Antonius removed his toga, which he had worn to remind his guests that he was still a Roman man and that this was his Roman wife. But Cleopatra had styled herself as she always did, in Egyptian gold and turquoise, her dress made of finely woven linen, and her

369

hair perfumed and oiled.

But she was beautiful, and when she looked at him Antonius thought she was from another time, when Egypt ruled the East, their tombs and temples piercing the sky ever higher, and their wealth of knowledge and magic as vast and glittering as the Nile.

Cleopatra stood before him, easily slipping out of her dress, the fabric clinging to each curve before it settled on the floor. Antonius lifted her up into his arms and their bodies melted in a familiar heat. They collapsed together on the bed, holding each other tightly, her thick hair falling over her bare shoulders.

He felt her nails skim his back, her mouth fitting against his. His fingertips dug into the soft skin of her waist, pulling her close until he called out her name.

All night they remained wrapped up in each other's arms, half-asleep, kissing slowly, their mouths going still against each other, only to move again in heated moments, when Antonius would bring her close against him, yearning for her, finding her wanting once more, and his smile would slip into a smirk.

It was near morning, after a brief rest, when Antonius finally spoke the words he had been meaning to tell her all this time.

"You shall be a queen of kings," he murmured.

Cleopatra ran a hand through his curls, still absorbed in his touch, not quite joined as one but not quite apart, not yet. "Oh?"

"Consider it my wedding gift to you," Antonius said. "Phoenicia, Coele-Syria, Nabatea, Ailana, and the lands circling Jericho, all shall be yours. You may do as you wish with them. You shall also rule Cyrene on the Libyan coast, and the cities Itanos and Olous. These are my gifts to you."

"And what gift shall *I* give to *you?*" Cleopatra asked archly, kissing his open mouth and twisting into his arms, which automatically found their way around her waist, sinking into her warm skin. She whispered into his ear. "I cannot hope to compete with yours."

He kissed her cheek. "You have already aided my war with the Parthians. If I wish for anything else, it is only you, here in my arms."

"Well that," Cleopatra said, moving her legs over his hips and forcing him flat against the bed until she sat above him, a smile hidden in the corner of her mouth, "I can do."

⟶⟫⟫ ⟪⟪⟵

JANUARY 36 BC

As winter waned with the passing of January, Antonius and his men began to finalize their plans of invasion.

They were holding a meeting with some of his army generals and advisors to discuss the next steps. He held a solid position for attack, with Roman client kingdoms of Anatolia, Syria, and Judea protecting his rear, while Cappadocia, Pontus, and Commagene would provide resources and supplies along their route.

His first attack was focused on the Kingdom of Armenia, ruled by King Artavasdes II. Antonius planned to send Publius Canidius Crassus to secure his surrender or defeat. Once they proved victorious, they would lead an invasion into Transcaucasus. Then Antonius would prepare his troops to invade the Parthian province of Media Atropatene.

"I would not trust King Artavasdes," Cleopatra said. "He is proud and calls himself king of kings. His father is a successor of Tigranes the Great, and on his mother's side, he is a descendant of Mithridates VI Eupator. He shall betray you if he can."

Cleopatra had insisted on attending all of his meetings, despite the obvious discomfort of Antonius' men. They would never dare criticize aloud, but it was clear they did not like the interference of the Egyptian Queen in what they considered purely Roman—and male—affairs. However, as Cleopatra was providing military aid and her invaluable knowledge of the ways of the East, Antonius did not ask her to leave.

"Let him try," Crassus sneered at her, and Antonius felt his face heat up, though Cleopatra bore his taunt stoically. "Our army shall crush him if he does."

"He will surrender," Antonius said dismissively.

"You think you know *the East,* as you Romans call it," Cleopatra said, smiling at Crassus, "simply because you come with horses and spears. But my people have ruled for three thousand years, and we have seen many kingdoms rise and fall in that time. Rome is but a child to our eyes. You ought to be careful, for when you are most powerful, you are also most vulnerable."

Crassus' nostrils flared, but he did not answer, perhaps out of respect for Antonius, and soon afterward the meeting concluded.

Antonius joined Cleopatra in their litter to retire for the rest of the day, but she refused to speak with him all the way to the house and once inside, she went upstairs furiously. He found her in their children's room, her eyes glistening with tears.

"Why must you rile him up?" Antonius asked. "You know he does not trust you."

"Do you think I care about him?" Cleopatra shook her head, a tear falling down her cheek. "I care for you. I need you alive. And if you invade Parthia listening to that fool you shall die."

"We have the larger army," Antonius said, but he still felt her words like a bad omen. "You said so yourself."

"Men do not understand," Cleopatra said bitterly as if she had not heard him. "They never do."

"Understand what?"

"I am pregnant!" Cleopatra cried out. "I have known for weeks now. And if you think I shall suffer you to die in Parthia because of another man's arrogance then you know even less than I think you do."

Antonius stared at her. He had never seen her so angry, so passionate, her face flushed and her hands trembling at her sides. It was terrible but beautiful, and he wished he could see the world through her eyes if only to understand why the sun and moon never failed in their course, and how life came to be like a flame sparked between them.

"I did not know," Antonius whispered. "I did not know."

Cleopatra cast her eyes to the ceiling, the tears spilling down her face. "If only I had never met you."

"Do not say that," he said, coming to her side and placing the palm of his hand on her belly. "You are a Queen of Kings now. We shall rule the world together."

She placed her hand over his and sighed shakily. "Then you must promise not to die without me, for a queen needs a king by her side in life and in death."

Antonius paused, his heart aflame at the foreign power of her words, like an ancient magic only known in myth. He lifted her hand and kissed the ring on her fourth finger. "I promise."

It was late in the night, Cleopatra fast asleep, when he heard the voice of one of his manservants outside the room. He went out in the hall, where a messenger had delivered a letter from Rome.

Octavia.

Antonius scanned the letter quickly. She had given birth to a girl, Antonia Minor. There was no news of the promised troops, and the message was brief, apparently written in her own hand, an elegant but firm script. Antonius returned to his room and burned the letter. When he slipped back into bed, he kissed Cleopatra's stomach, and she stirred, a hand resting on his arm.

But in the depths of his heart, he felt a small part of him die, as if the last shred of his Roman self was left behind in Octavia, and now that their daughter was born and he was to abandon her, he knew he would never be the same man again. He had staked his life on a foreign woman, a foreign queen, and it was too late to withdraw from the game.

Antonius has rolled the dice. Now he could only hope he had the numbers to win.

45

POMPONIA CAECILIA
ATTICA

FEBRUARY 36 BC

A TTICA HAD ALWAYS LOVED to read.

Her father had a private tutor, Epirota, teach her to read Homer in Greek from a very young age. She fell in love with Odysseus from the beginning, his wily ways, his clever deceit, and his delicate sensibilities. It seemed Homer had begun to describe a woman and had changed his mind and said he was a man. Attica thought he was better for it.

For Odysseus was a lover at heart, and even amidst the thrill of battle and the pleasure of beautiful goddesses, he always longed for his Penelope, far away across the dark and dangerous seas, sitting and weaving and waiting at home. She had her own battles to fight, of course, the greedy suitors and their uncontained lust, and in that way, they were alike. Man and woman, but warriors just the same.

Attica's favorite part would always be his return, when Penelope gave him one final test: to move their marriage bed which had been rooted to the ground. And when she read how Penelope and Odysseus embraced at last, the hurt and sorrow of the last decade fading in a single touch, she always cried.

She cried because of the years they lost, the love they shared despite it, and the certainty that she herself would never love like that.

For when she was fourteen, Attica had fallen in love with her tutor, or at least she thought she had. He was older and wiser, patient and kind, and Attica had no one else besides her father and Cicero, for her mother had died when she was twelve.

One day after their lessons, he had leaned over and kissed her. It was a frightening sensation, and she had run off and told her father, barely able to speak through the thick, shameful tears. For it had felt nothing like the kiss between Penelope and Odysseus, and all her dreams had been ruined.

Epirota had been dismissed that very day and she never saw him again. Attica forgot her dreams, read Plato and Aristotle instead, and her heart grew hard against the loveless world, as if the more she read and understood and saw, the more she wanted nothing to do with it, and now she dreamt of a long life alone caring for her father.

"You have your mother's melancholy," her father used to say when she would sit and read for hours, refusing to walk outside or in the gardens, wishing to disappear in the words, even if they held no feeling for her anymore.

He was right, though that had not always been the case. Her mother, Pilia, like Attica, had been eighteen when she had married her father, who had been thirty-five years older than her at the time. But to Attica's young eyes, they seemed to love each other, and her father had always given her mother gifts and she would smile and kiss his cheek tenderly.

While Attica looked like her mother—save for the eyes, which were gray like her father's—she always had her father's love of reading, and Cicero had been the one to give her the name *Attica,* after her father, and her favorite pet name *Atticula.*

Her mother, on the other hand, had a weariness, a seriousness to her smile which had always scared Attica away, and the reason why she had preferred her father's company, who liked to tease her.

Pilia was often cynical of the world and its petty politics and wars, and she often joked that she would never have married her father if he had been a politician. She fought Cicero at dinner over his meddling speeches in the Senate and disliked Attica's affection for the old man, perhaps worried that she could be used as leverage against him by his many enemies.

Since Attica had been young, her mother had also been plagued by bouts of fever, as if her hatred of the world had turned inwards, and many times Attica herself had succumbed to these illnesses as well.

When her mother had died, having taken ill swiftly and quietly in the night, Attica had felt a terrible sadness descend on her spirit, like the cloak of Death himself. She smiled less, read less, and found herself arguing with Cicero like her mother had, hating men like Julius Caesar who were merely tyrants wishing to be kings, hating the world that had stolen her mother, who only ever wanted to protect her.

Then she had married Agrippa, and her heart had warmed like ice as it thawed whenever he kissed her, and she felt the world open up to her as a flower in bloom, different than she had ever imagined. More intense, more painful, but it was hers.

She had found her Odysseus, despite the evil in this world, and she would hold onto it for as long as she lived, like Penelope had for twenty years.

"Reading the Odyssey again, *Atticula?*" Livia asked, smiling at her. Attica blushed as she set down the scroll, though not entirely because she was right.

Ever since Livia had lost her child, Attica had been heartbroken and terrified, but more than that, she felt ashamed, since she had just recently discovered her own pregnancy. But Livia had remained herself through it all, as if she had tucked away the sorrow Attica had heard through the door that day, never to be brought forth in the light of day.

"Now do not be shy, my dear," Octavia said, her eyes twinkling, though there was that ever-present unease in the steady blue, as if her mind was always elsewhere, on her husband far away in the East. She was holding their second daughter and her fifth child, Antonia Minor, in her arms, preparing to breastfeed her. "Who has not fancied Odysseus?"

"Oh, I always preferred Achilles," Livia said with a dismissive hand.

Octavia's eyes looked up briefly at the ceiling. "Of course you do."

Livia laughed. "He is the son of a goddess! And he defeated the Trojans."

"Odysseus defeated the Trojans!" Attica protested, then blushed again when Livia and Octavia both smirked at her. "Achilles only fights when Patroclus dies."

They all shared a brief, knowing look at that before Octavia cleared her throat. "I always preferred Hector myself. When I was a child, I would cry when he said goodbye to Andromache and their son."

"A true Roman, you are," Livia said, looking at Octavia fondly.

Suddenly Antonia Minor began to cry, and Octavia shook her head, exasperated. "Do not worry, child, you shall be fed." She sighed and stood up. "I will be back in a moment."

Then she left them, and Livia and Attica were alone for the first time since the death of Livia's child. Attica picked at a thread that had come loose from her stola, then put a hand swiftly to her belly when she felt a small kick, as had become habit, before feeling that familiar shame return when she saw that Livia had noticed.

Livia stood up and glanced at her stomach. "May I?"

Attica nodded silently, and Livia knelt beside her, placing a gentle palm on her belly, which was very large now. Her doctor had told her she would give birth in the next month, and she tried not to feel too terrified at the prospect. She remembered Livia's pale, flushed face when her water had broken, and Attica shivered.

"I am sorry," Attica said quietly.

Livia looked at her. "Why, my dear?"

When Attica did not answer, her throat tight, Livia sighed.

"My sorrow has nothing to do with your happiness," Livia whispered, though her eyes shone with tears. "Do not even think it for a moment."

"Are you not angry?" Attica asked, and she heard the fear in her voice.

"Not with you, *mea soror*." Livia smiled, and hearing the words Attica felt a deep gratitude she had never felt before. *My sister.* "I am angry with the gods."

It was so unexpected from someone whom Attica considered the most pious of women that her eyes widened and she lowered her voice, afraid someone might overhear them. "Do you not fear the gods?"

Livia shook her head firmly. "Nay, I do not. I love them, and that is why I am angered the more."

"I fear them," Attica whispered. "I fear I shall not survive."

Livia's eyes were sad. "Whether we love or fear them, the gods keep their own counsel, and so should we."

Attica glanced uneasily at her large belly, wondering how a living child could find its way out, doubting both the baby's and her own abilities. "Is it very painful?"

"Oh yes," Livia said, smiling. "But I shall be there, so you need not worry. I will make sure nothing happens to you."

Attica nodded, feeling her heart lighten ever more. "Thank you, Livia." She smiled. *"Mea soror."*

⟶⟫⟫ ⟪⟪⟵

MARCH 36 BC

The pain began in the morning while she was breaking her fast at her father's estate on the Quirinal Hill.

One moment she was smiling and talking with her father, the next her breath had been stolen from her and a wave of nauseating pain rolled through her body. The next thing she knew her water broke and the midwife was called.

She was set up downstairs in a spare bedroom, the midwife cooling her face with a damp cloth. A message had been sent to Agrippa, as well as Livia and Octavia, and within the hour they had abandoned whatever it was they had been doing and arrived at the house.

However, the baby did not come, and the midwife told them all to wait. The pain receded but would return in bursts at the base of her spine, then radiate as if her hips were about to crack open with the force of it.

When there were no signs of more intense labor, Livia and Octavia returned home and asked her to send a fast messenger when the pain worsened. One by one, the midwife, her handmaiden, some distant female relatives, and the few female slaves who lingered, having prepared the room for birth, all left.

But Agrippa remained, now allowed to be in the room to hold her hand and speak with her, ignoring messages from Caesar and other colleagues. Even her father had retired to his room and was reportedly asleep.

Agrippa stroked her forehead. There was a gentle worry in his eyes, but he was as calm as ever and spoke soothingly to her. "It is a long birth, that is all. My brother took almost an entire day to be born."

"What if the baby never comes?" Attica asked, her voice weak.

"The baby will come," Agrippa said firmly. "I promise." He paused. "What shall we name her?"

"Her?" Attica asked, smiling despite the pain pulsing in her hips.

"Or him, I suppose." Agrippa took one of her hands loosely in his. "Agrippina?"

"Vipsania Agrippina," Attica corrected, squeezing his hand. "You won't have our children forsake your father's name simply because you have."

It was a sensitive topic, as Agrippa loved his father dearly. But it also reminded him of his past, growing up on farms, far away from the upper classes of Rome. Attica loved Lucius Vipsanius, having brought Agrippa to her, and having given to her the beautiful gold wedding ring, two hands clasped, which now lay on the fourth finger of her left hand, the pathway to the heart.

"Vipsania Agrippina, then, in honor of my father," Agrippa said, "And Marcus Pomponius Agrippa if it is a boy, in honor of your father."

Attica nodded, and sighed, gritting her teeth together when she felt another cramp seize her belly. She tightened her hold on Agrippa's hand, who placed the other on her stomach and rubbed in soothing circles. He kissed her shoulder, then her neck, before kissing her mouth, and Attica relaxed into the familiar sensation, her eyes fluttering shut, sinking into the warmth of his touch as he placed both hands on her shoulders, and caressed down her arms.

Suddenly a piercing pain like a dagger shot up her spine, and she gasped, opening her eyes. Then another, less like a wave but a spasm, as if her very hips were being torn asunder and the muscles in her lower back clenched into the most violent pain.

Agrippa's eyes widened and he left the room wordlessly. A moment later the midwife appeared. She transferred her to the birthing chair, and Attica gripped the arms tightly, the wooden back digging into her spine, her legs shaking with the effort.

Attica groaned as she swore it was the end, her life at the brink of exploding into nothing, the world dark as if in a tunnel. Her skin stretched, her very bones snapped within, until she thought she might pass out or vomit.

It must have been hours, for Livia returned with several of her female relatives and knelt beside her, cooling her forehead with a wet cloth. Octavia arrived a few minutes later to murmur encouraging words, Attica's handmaiden fanning her neck from behind.

Then she felt her insides twist as if she were about to relieve herself right there in front of everyone, and she was not sure she hadn't. But the midwife kneeling before her only smiled, just as the baby's cries filled the room.

"It is over," Livia said, smiling and kissing Attica's cheek. "You gave birth to a little girl."

"Well done, Attica," Octavia breathed, wiping her own damp forehead.

Attica couldn't help but laugh, her body numb but somehow elated. She asked for Agrippa to be let inside once she was helped to the bed and cleaned up, and he entered immediately.

When he saw the baby, he stared at the small child with a quiet look of wonder.

"Well?" she asked. "Shall you accept our Vipsania Agrippina?"

The midwife placed the baby on the floor, the umbilical cord already cut and the baby wrapped carefully in soft linen bandages. They all looked at Agrippa.

He walked over to the baby slowly, who was now making small noises of protest, and in one smooth movement, he crouched to the ground and picked up the baby, raising her above his head.

And for a moment, he was not Agrippa, but Odysseus, the man Attica had long loved silently, quietly, behind stories and sorrow and pain, and she was Penelope, finally seeing her husband stand before her after so many long years of waiting.

"I claim you as my own, Vipsania Agrippina," he said softly, before kissing her cheek and cradling her in his strong arms. Then he brought the baby over to Attica, who held her as if it were the most natural thing in the world, a small hand clinging instantly to her finger.

"She is beautiful," Livia whispered, a single tear falling down her cheek, but she was smiling, proud and loving. She kissed Attica on the forehead and left with the rest of the women, including Octavia, who promised to check on her soon. Attica was alone with Agrippa once more.

Attica stared at the child, her child, and then at Agrippa, wondering how they could have made this small thing, this moving, living, breathing thing, that looked up with wide eyes at the two of them, mouth bubbling and cheeks red. Where one moment it was only the two of them, suddenly there was a third, but she felt as if they had finally become one. For if there was something that Caesar's love for her husband would never give, it was this.

"Promise me you will never leave me," Attica said, kissing his hand that rested on her shoulder, before looking at him seriously. "Promise me we will be a family, and you shall not go to war."

Agrippa's eyes turned sad, but he kissed their daughter's head, then Attica's. "You are my family. Always."

She did not say more, but she turned and kissed him, and when the midwife returned to put the baby in her crib, Attica fell into a deep sleep.

⋙ ⋘

JULY 36 BC

She held Vipsania Agrippina in her arms, now over four months old, having grown big and wild, always yearning to move about and tear at someone's hair, her eyes a bright sea-green in her pale, rosy face. Attica knew she would grow up to be beautiful, and very loved, but the thought terrified her.

"Do you want to hold her, Tiberius?" Livia asked, laughing. "Oh, I think he is in love!"

Since she had given birth, Attica had taken to visiting more often, if only so that her daughter could interact with Livia and Octavia's children.

Attica glanced over to where Tiberius sat beside his mother, quiet and serious as always, looking at little Agrippina with wide, entranced eyes. She laughed too, and went over to them, holding Agrippina in her arms.

Livia had an arm around Tiberius as Attica lowered Agrippina into his arms. He held her carefully, one small arm tucked behind her head, supported by Livia's hand. He looked at Attica with a pleased smile.

"She is so small," he muttered.

"Yes, so you must be careful," Livia said gently. She was always more gentle to her children than to others, and to Tiberius the most, who hardly left her mother's side, and disliked his stepfather, Caesar. "She will need you to protect her, as she grows older. Remember that, Tiberius."

Tiberius nodded gravely, then lowered his head and planted a soft kiss on her forehead. Agrippina shrieked happily and reached out, clinging to his shoulder, startling Tiberius, who gave a small gasp and sat up straight. But when he realized she was not crying, he relaxed and smiled again.

Just then the porter stepped into the inner courtyard where they had been lounging, bearing a message. Livia and Attica both looked at him worriedly.

At the beginning of July, Caesar and Agrippa had launched their attack against Sicily. This message could bring good news, but also bad, and Attica held her breath.

Livia was handed the scroll, and she hastily read through it, bringing a hand up to her mouth halfway.

"What is it?" Attica asked anxiously. "Is it bad? You must tell me, Livia."

"A storm broke out a few days ago, and Statilius Taurus was forced back to Tarentum. Caesar's ships were destroyed and it will take at least a month to repair them." Livia looked up, sighing in relief. "But Agrippa is safe, as is Caesar. They are alive. It was merely a misfortune of war."

Attica felt something within loosen, and she sat beside Tiberius, placing a hand over her chest as if she could keep her heart from beating wildly. She was trembling, and her eyes welled with tears. For she had been sure Agrippa was dead, and now that she knew he was not, she could not return to her previous state of calm.

"Agrippa shall return," Livia said, squeezing Attica's hand. "He is strong and capable."

Attica nodded quickly, her voice nearly failing her. "Yes, he is."

"They will return," Livia repeated firmly, but this time Attica did not know who she was trying to convince. "They will return."

Tiberius had not seemed to notice the interruption, however, looking with a happy intensity on Agrippina, only reverting to his usual quiet frown when Attica took Agrippina away.

It was time she returned home to rest, weave, and wait.

46

GAIUS OCTAVIUS

AUGUST 36 BC

*I*T WAS A TRAP.

The ship groaned beneath him, the shouts of men and the choppy sea loud as the battle grew like a storm around them, and they were in its very eye, spears flying, ships aflame, hulls crashing, soldiers heaved overboard.

Octavius clung to his post at the stern, salt water stinging his eyes as he watched the enemy—who had surprised them in the strait of Messana—sinking or capturing most of his ships.

He tried to pinpoint when things had gone so wrong.

Octavius had last seen Agrippa upon the isle of Strongyle, which they had seized as a stronghold off the northeast coast of Sicily, when their odds had looked better despite their earlier losses.

For only a month before they had suffered much damage by a violent southern storm which crushed six of his warships and even more of his Liburnian galleys. It took the rest of July to repair and rebuild his fleet, but Octavius was determined to win this war at all costs, and had sent Maecenas back to Rome in order to dispel any fear of invasion.

Octavius had then joined the legions of Valerius Messalla Corvinus stationed at Vibo on the western coast of Italy. They had planned for Agrippa to engage Sextus at sea and seize the city of Tyndaris in the north while Octavius and Corvinus would join the troops of Statilius Taurus across the strait near Rhegium before launching their coup on the southeastern side of Sicily.

Meanwhile, on the other side of the island, Lepidus would fight through Plennius and his legions on land and join them as soon as he could, penning Sextus on the island between their forces.

But Sextus had deceived them.

Though Agrippa had believed that Sextus' main fleet was at Mylae in the north, in truth, Sextus had left few ships at Mylae, or anywhere on the northern shore, and had slipped back to Messana as only a pirate knew how to do.

Hearing of Agrippa's easy victory at Tyndaris, Octavius had sailed to Sicily from the mainland to meet him. Yet no sooner had they landed when the fleet of Sextus—hiding in the strait along with his cavalry and infantry—had approached, trapping them both on land and at sea.

In the face of Sextus' formidable fleet, Octavius had hurriedly placed Lucius Cornificius in charge of infantry and went aboard his ship to face Sextus at sea, not knowing if Agrippa was safe, nor if he would live to see him again.

The thought was enough to weaken his knees as the waves playfully tossed his ship about the water. Was this to be his end, cut down by a nameless pirate? A rebel without a cause?

Look at me.

"Admiral Caesar!" shouted one of his generals, barely heard above the whistling wind and crashes of another ship captured, men's cries lost to the vast skies as enemy troops boarded and slew them as they stood. "We must retreat!"

Octavius turned reluctantly. "No!"

He would not surrender to a pirate, not when they were so close to defeating him, not when they had already lost so much. Octavius would rather be killed in battle than retreat and die in exile, the death of a coward.

Only men who cannot find honor in life wish to find honor in their death.

"Caesar! We shall die!"

Octavius stumbled, thinking he was nearly fainting, until he realized an enemy ship had sailed and crashed headlong into the side of their hull. His ship groaned loudly in protest, a large fissure running down the middle of the deck.

A man grunted across the way. Octavius looked and saw a *gladius* spear through one of his men, who then fell to his knees, revealing an enemy soldier behind him, blood and water swirling on the deck at their feet. More of Sextus' men jumped aboard, even as the deck tilted and began to fill up with water.

One enemy soldier began running towards Octavius, who was shoved away and dragged into an escape vessel before he realized what was happening. He could not speak, his breath snatched from him as they narrowly broke off from the ship's cables, enemy soldiers already crawling over the quickly sinking ship, their spears flying towards their boat, tearing up the wood and sinking into the waves around them.

Seawater spilled into their boat, which swayed perilously as they rowed furiously to shore, the burning of his arms all Octavius felt, the blood staining his captured ship all he could see, when suddenly the tide swallowed them in a wave, upturning the small boat, and Octavius was drowning, sucking in saltwater as he tumbled around and around, choking as he was spat ashore, coughing up water and vomit on the sand. His limbs trembled and his head pounded, blood splattering the sand, and he knew it was the end.

He was going to die.

The sky above spun in dizzying circles, and he gripped the wet sand, his fingers sinking into the muddy shore as a wave crashed over his head, dragging him back into the sea as if his body weighed nothing, his vision tunneling to black.

He wondered distantly if Agrippa had been trapped too, and whether he would see him in golden fields, or if his soul would forever wander the halls of Death, sad and alone for an eternity.

Octavius felt a hand grab his collar before all went dark.

⤞⤝

Voices, a weak sliver of light.

He struggled to breathe, gasping, choking, until he felt a strong hand slam his back and he felt acid dribble from his mouth, wincing at the sharpness in his throat.

There was more light as Octavius pried apart his eyelids, which were shut tight, encrusted with grime. He saw a familiar face swimming before him, forehead creased, with bright green eyes, though the features were hazy.

Octavius blinked slowly against the fog, his mouth moving as if stuffed with wool.

"Agrippa?" he asked brokenly, and the pounding in his head returned.

"No." The voice was deep and firm. There was something scalding against his eyes, and he groaned. Then it was gone and his vision cleared. A young man in military gear stood before him, eyeing Octavius warily. "Do you recognize me?"

He did. It was Lieutenant Corvinus, whom he and Cornificius had left behind at Vibo only a few days before they had sailed across the strait, though it felt like years since then. Corvinus had also been one of the many he had proscribed all those years ago, condemned to flee as an exile from his own home. He was surprised Corvinus had allowed him to live, knowing well what he would have done in his place.

"Yes. Lieutenant Corvinus." Octavius swallowed the bile he felt rise in his throat. "I thought I died."

"We did too," Corvinus said, his green eyes worried. "You took quite a hit to the head when your boat crashed. Luckily my men found you and brought you here. You were unconscious for an hour. The doctor recommends that you be watched."

"I must send a message to Agrippa," Octavius said, ignoring him. "He must aid

Cornificius."

He tried to get off the bed he was lying on when Corvinus laid a hand on his shoulder and pushed him back down with surprising strength. For a moment, Octavius wondered if Corvinus had rescued him only to kill him once he was awake.

"We have already sent a message to Agrippa and Cornificius," Corvinus said. "You must rest and restore your strength. War is not over yet, and I will not let you die on my watch."

"But Sextus," Octavius said haltingly. "We were deceived. All is lost."

"I do not believe that, Caesar. My scouts report that Sextus has concentrated all his forces at Pelorus and Messana. It is very likely Agrippa has not been defeated, and holds Tyndaris still, forcing Sextus to prepare for another attack."

"Then we must meet him." Octavius felt his heart beat faster, and a small flame of hope was kindled in his breast. But it was dangerous, and he forced himself to extinguish it. "They will need more men."

Corvinus hesitated. "I will transport you to the port of Tyndaris, but only if Agrippa has indeed captured it. We ought not to risk more men in a fight we cannot win."

Octavius wished to protest, but he held his tongue and nodded. He knew the lieutenant gave sane counsel, and he would be a fool to ignore it simply because of his personal feelings. Octavius ignored the soft, murmuring voice of Agrippa in the back of his mind. *Love makes all of us fools.*

It took another day and a half to receive any messages, and by then Octavius was much more rested, the throbbing in his head having lessened to a dull ache. He knew the toll on his body would be great, but it was a problem he could deal with if they survived. *When* they survived, Octavius corrected.

He met Corvinus in his tent, where the messages had been delivered. Corvinus rifled through several scrolls at his desk, while Octavius tried to hide his fear and waited impatiently for Corvinus to speak, unable to sit down until he knew the truth.

Finally, Corvinus looked at him steadily. "They are alive."

Octavius sank down in his seat and closed his eyes. Agrippa was alive. He had not known how much he had feared him dead until it was proven otherwise.

"Agrippa captured Tyndaris," Corvinus continued. "Cornificius and his men attempted to march across the mountains, and would have been utterly destroyed if the three legions Agrippa had sent with Laronius had not found them."

"Then we must sail to them," Octavius said, affecting a firmer voice of command. "Immediately."

Corvinus nodded, standing at attention. "Yes, Caesar."

Octavius stood up, his legs still shaky, but he forced himself to walk towards the exit.

He paused before he left the tent, glancing at the young man across from him, to whom Octavius had a hand in appointing death, and saw the loyalty and respect in his green eyes despite it.

"Your kindness shall not go unnoticed, Corvinus. Until we meet again."

Then he left and prepared for departure. They sailed from Vibo early the following morning and landed in the harbor of Tyndaris soon after.

Octavius walked across the docks swiftly, greeting his men with sparse words until he could politely pass on, walking until he saw the familiar tall figure ahead, standing with Cornificius in deep discussion, pausing and turning as if he sensed Octavius' approach.

They stared at each other.

Agrippa looked the same as he had left him, save a small red scratch across his cheek. Otherwise, he had bathed and rested, and had even shaved.

Octavius surely looked the worst, having sustained injuries to his head, his face peppered with light bruises, and scratched badly from forehead to chin on the left side. He wordlessly embraced Agrippa, then Cornificius.

"We were so glad to hear of your survival," Cornificius said, patting Octavius' shoulder, who winced, having nearly dislocated the joint in his crash to shore.

"As I of you," Octavius said quietly, but he could not help a glance at Agrippa, who only looked at him, his eyes dark and unreadable. "I and only a few others managed to escape and find safety ashore, as I am sure you heard."

I almost died, were the unsaid words, but Agrippa's eyes widened all the same.

"Let us meet inside and dine," Cornificius said, glancing around the docks with the suspicion of a well-trained general. "There is much we need to discuss."

In Cornificius' tent they ate hastily. Agrippa seemed to recover from his initial shocked silence and revealed his map of Sicily. He spread it across the desk, positioning small figurines on the locations of their legions in Tyndaris.

"Lepidus has crossed the island from Lilybaeum and plans to attack Messana," Agrippa said, positioning a figurine near the port city, next to Sextus' legions there. "Taurus has reached Sicilian shores and will raid the towns which Sextus relies upon for supplies." Another figurine was placed on the southeastern shores of Sicily near Messana. "We have twenty thousand legionaries and five thousand troops. We still have three hundred armed ships, which Sextus matches in number, but not in equipment." Agrippa paused, scanning the map with his expert glance. He moved the figurines of Sextus' fleet to the open ocean. "Sextus cannot afford to defeat us on land. He shall risk everything at sea, or surrender."

"He will not surrender," Octavius murmured, eyeing the map.

Sextus may be no better than a pirate and a traitor, but he was also the son of Pompeius, a great man who had always shadowed the lesser victories of his son. Octavius knew Sextus would rather die than surrender to a Caesar.

"Then we shall fight," Agrippa said gravely.

Octavius smirked. "Until he flees."

⤜⤛ ⤜⤛

SEPTEMBER 36 BC

The final battle was fought in the bay of Naulochus, and it was thoroughly underwhelming. Though it was long and grueling in the late summer heat of September, their fleet, under Agrippa's command and armed with his invention of the *harpax*, ultimately sank twenty-eight of Sextus' ships.

Though Octavius lost three ships in the battle, it was a decisive victory nonetheless, and it was not long before Sextus fled with seventeen ships and left the rest to be captured and burned.

Agrippa and Lepidus swiftly took hold of Sextus' former naval base in Messana, while Octavius remained in their camp at Naulochus in the north.

He had been reviewing the damages to his fleet when Cornificius entered his tent, looking worried. Octavius stood up, thinking wildly that Sextus had them deceived again, and Agrippa was now dead for good.

"You must sail to Messana," Cornificius said without delay. "A lieutenant of Sextus—Plennius—entered the city with eight legions. They have joined Lepidus' standard. We have been betrayed."

Octavius paused, his heart slowing at the words. He nearly smiled. "Lepidus, you say?"

Cornificius nodded hurriedly. "He is crazed and claims Sicily as his own, a spoil for his efforts in the war. Agrippa has urged you to come as quickly as possible."

It did not take long to sail to Messana, which lay very close to Naulochus. They entered the camp of Agrippa and found him in a hot debate with one of Lepidus' ambassadors.

When he saw Octavius, his face melted into relief, but he did not smile and ordered the ambassador to leave, who was escorted out by Cornificius. Agrippa approached Octavius and kissed him briefly in greeting, and the touch was alien, as if Octavius had truly died and come back to life, having forgotten what it felt like to kiss.

"The bastard wishes to fight," Agrippa said angrily. "But our men do not wish to, and neither do his. They will desert him if he does not cooperate."

"Let them," Octavius said dismissively. "I have no more need of him."

386

"He is one of the *Tresviri*," Agrippa countered, though his voice betrayed his doubt. "Antonius will see his dismissal as a threat."

"Then he should heed the warning," Octavius said coldly. "For he shall be next."

Agrippa went quiet, casting him a long glance. Octavius realized they were entirely alone at the moment, and he suddenly no longer cared for the war outside.

He looked at Agrippa steadily, the familiar dark curls and sea-green eyes, and he knew everything had changed between them that night before a rising dawn, the waves kissing the shore at their feet.

"I thought I was going to die," Octavius said quietly. "When I crashed on the shore."

"I thought you did," Agrippa whispered, his eyes strangely wide and fearful. "I thought I lost you forever."

"I was so afraid." Octavius swallowed, his head light. "I was so afraid I would not find you. That my soul would linger in dark places, alone forever."

Agrippa shook his head, his hands in fists at his side. "Never. *I will always find you.*"

Octavius nearly moved towards him when Cornificius entered the tent with one of Lepidus' soldiers, and they stood apart. Agrippa looked bewildered at the intrusion, and Octavius forced himself to focus on his lieutenant.

"Caesar, sir," Cornificius said. "This is one of Lepidus' men. He has deserted, and claims others will too."

The soldier nodded quickly, his eyes flicking nervously between Octavius and Agrippa. He was not young, his face creased with age, and his eyes shone with fear. Clearly he valued his life, Octavius thought, and would only risk it to come here if he felt certain.

"If you wait, sir, they will desert him," the soldier said quickly. "His men will not fight. They think he has gone mad. I was sent to warn you."

Octavius nodded, and he knew what he had to do. "Lead me to him."

Agrippa took a step forward. "Caesar—"

He cut Agrippa a sharp glance, and he fell silent. Even Cornificius looked at Octavius in disbelief, as if he too had gone mad. Octavius turned to the soldier, who stared at him anxiously. "Lead me to him. Alone. I shall not ask again."

The soldier nodded without another word, and quickly led him into Lepidus' camp, where his soldiers stood about, eyeing Octavius warily as he approached. Once they reached the middle of the camp, they waited.

A few moments later, Lepidus stormed out of a nearby tent, and looked at his men angrily, the lieutenant Plennius taking a hesitant place at his side.

"Well, somebody stop him!" Lepidus shouted, his eyes wild and defiant.

But his soldiers hesitated, looking at each other. Octavius walked towards him, and one soldier near Lepidus hoisted his spear, looking at Lepidus for instructions.

"What are you waiting for? Strike!" Lepidus commanded, a vein bulging in his forehead.

The spear flew, but it was a half-hearted throw and fell several yards away from Octavius. A belated grunt came from the same soldier, and he fell to his knees, his mouth open and a dagger stuck in his side.

Plennius stood beside him, saluting Octavius. He glanced at Lepidus in distaste. At this, Lepidus' eyes grew wide and terrified, and he immediately threw himself to the ground.

Octavius stopped before him and looked down at the man who had once served Julius Caesar, a traitor to Brutus and Cicero, a traitor to Octavius and Antonius, and now reduced to old age and pride, his very life at the mercy of a man he had always dismissed.

Lepidus supplicated him, grabbing his knees with trembling hands. "Please, Caesar, forgive me. Spare the life of an old man, who has always been a friend to your divine father."

"You are a coward," Octavius said in a low voice. "And a traitor. Many men have died for much less at your command. But I shall spare your life, so you may live the rest of it in shame."

"Thank you, Caesar, thank you," Lepidus said feverishly, his head bowed.

"Do not thank me," Octavius said, raising his voice, looking around at the soldiers who watched with grimaces at the lowly state of their general. "Thank *Divus Iulius* and his divine mercy. For otherwise, I would have killed you, and any who supported your betrayal."

Then he turned and left the old man prostrate on the ground, his soldiers already packing up the camp, prepared to join Octavius' standard. The battle was won, but it did not feel like victory. Instead, it felt like war had just begun.

When he returned to camp, Agrippa met him, searching his face for an answer.

Octavius smiled grimly. "We have work to do."

47

MARCUS VIPSANIUS AGRIPPA

DECEMBER 36 BC

T HERE WAS SOMETHING ABOUT a woman that always surprised Agrippa when he saw her up close.

He watched as Attica held Vipsania Agrippina on her lap, nearly eight months old now, full of energy as she flung her arms about wildly, her mother barely taking any notice as she continued to read at the same time as she spoke with Agrippa. If there was an earthquake, would she even flinch?

"You know, I do not want Agrippina to marry Tiberius before she is sixteen," Attica said, her eyes glancing up at Agrippa pointedly before returning to her reading. "Even sixteen is much too soon."

"Tiberius will be young as well," Agrippa said. "He shall take good care of her."

Tiberius already had a special affection for Agrippina after all, and it was amusing to watch them together. For he was very timid and serious, while she was a happy child and liked to yank at anything she managed to grasp, always followed by a laugh that sounded more like a mischievous cackle.

She seemed nothing like Attica and himself, who were calm in temper save on rare occasions. But then Agrippa remembered playing in the fields of his father's farm, chasing after birds and deer as soon as he could walk. He was the adventurer of the family, wanting to explore the mountains and valleys of the world, its many rivers and oceans. His father had sent him to Rome with the hopes that his dreams could come true.

But Agrippina was a girl, and she would be confined to the house for the rest of her life. Agrippa found himself wishing otherwise. Attica, however, was an anxious mother and disliked Agrippina's vigorous energy, fearful that she might harm herself in her more passionate moments.

"Caesar is a bad influence on the boy," Attica said. "Tiberius ought to be sent away."

"His livelihood shall depend on Caesar when his father dies," Agrippa replied, amused. "Tiberius ought to show some respect towards his stepfather."

"Respect?" Attica scoffed. "He is a child! And Caesar is too hard on him. You cannot expect the boy to know rhetoric at six years of age as if he were Plato!"

"Caesar only wants what is best for him," Agrippa said, but he knew Attica was right. While Tiberius was Livia's son, he was not Octavius', so that they resented each other, wishing the other was not in their life so that Livia might give him her full attention.

"Caesar only wants what is best for *himself*," Attica corrected, eyeing Agrippa meaningfully. "You ought to remember that."

"Trust me," Agrippa said coldly. "I never forget."

Attica sighed, setting her reading aside and looking at Agrippa sadly. She was never more beautiful than when she looked at him like this, but it was a terrible beauty, for in that look he knew that she was a woman and he was a man, and there were things within each other that they would never fully understand, that their love would never reach, like a tide that pulled back just before it reached the end of the beach. In that look, she revealed the secret truth that a woman's peculiar strength came from none other than a man's most intimate weakness.

"I must tell you something," Agrippa said reluctantly.

Attica looked at him sharply, sensing bad news. "What?"

"Caesar has declared war against the rebellious tribes in Illyricum." Agrippa paused, bracing himself for her reaction. "I am to go with him."

She stared at him. "But you have a family."

"So does he."

Attica glared. "It is different and you know it. He does not understand. I *need* you."

He tried to ignore the memory of a very different voice telling him the same thing, brown eyes dark and lowered, and it took all of him not to flush. *I need you here.*

"I cannot refuse," Agrippa whispered, a sharp pain in his heart as if it had broken, for he knew Attica would not understand. She could never understand. "I shall return as soon as possible."

Her eyes welled with tears. "I thought the wars had ended."

"Do wars ever truly end?" Agrippa asked, echoing what she had asked him five years ago before they were married, before they had a child, and before the world had begun doing everything it could to keep them apart.

"What if you...?" Attica shook her head and bit her lip.

Tears ran down her face, and Agrippa was frozen to the spot, ashamed of himself, so that he did not have the courage to move. But then Agrippina began to cry too. It was a rare occurrence, as Agrippina hardly ever cried, so that Attica was startled from her tears.

She kissed the baby's cheek nervously, her voice tremulous. "Are you alright, my love?"

Agrippina only wailed louder at the sound of her mother's weak voice, and Attica looked at Agrippa in panic, helpless, needing him, and he rose and sat beside her without thinking, taking Agrippina into his arms and rocking her gently against his chest.

"She does not like to see her mother cry," Agrippa said softly, kissing Attica's cheek, salty from her tears. Agrippina had already quieted down in his arms. "She needs you."

"She needs her father," Attica said shakily, her gray eyes shining blue. "I will not marry again." She reached out and grabbed his arm, holding it tightly. "Promise me, Agrippa. Swear to me. Swear to me, on our daughter's life, that you will come home to me. *Swear it.*"

Swear it.

I swear by Jupiter—

No. On me.

Agrippa had sworn that oath so long ago it might as well have been another lifetime, but the words always remained, as though they were seared on his heart. Perhaps they were.

All my life.

"I swear on our daughter's life," Agrippa said, "that I will come home to you."

"Alive," Attica whispered, her eyes wide and full of endless, endless pain. He had known the price of war, but it was always different to see it so clear and brutal in the eyes of the woman he loved.

"Alive," Agrippa repeated.

She rested her head wearily against his shoulder, breathing in deeply. Agrippa counted his heartbeats, closing his eyes and feeling the weight of her head on his arm, the strength within him as vital and eternal as Atlas holding up the sky. They remained like that until Agrippina fell fast asleep.

⟫⟫⟩ ⟨⟨⟨⟨

JANUARY 35 BC

The carriage rattled on the stone streets descending from the hills of Rome and across the vast, olive-green countryside towards the Adriatic coast. Agrippa looked at Octavius, who sat across from him, looking out the window.

Memories overlapped with memories, the many times they had traveled in this car-

391

riage, the silences and stolen glances, the touches and the insults, and all the spoken and unspoken confessions. It was like looking into a mirror, only to see his own face reflected into eternity, finding himself in the same places, wondering if he was still the same man as before.

Octavius looked at him keenly. "How was Attica?"

Agrippa did not understand why Octavius ever asked about her. They did not particularly get along. Attica certainly still blamed Octavius for the death of her father's dear friend Cicero, while Octavius secretly resented that he was not Agrippa's only concern. Agrippa loved them both, but if he had learned anything, it was that love was not always enough.

"She took it well, I suppose," he said.

"Then she did not want you to go."

I need you.

"No," Agrippa said reluctantly. "She did not."

"Did you?"

"What?"

Octavius' eyes were dark and challenging, just as they were before he rolled in a game of dice he knew he would win. Agrippa realized belatedly that he was testing him. "Did you wish to go?"

Agrippa stared at him. Finally, he said, "Well, there is the baby."

"Agrippina." Octavius raised a brow. "She is in good hands, surely."

"She is," Agrippa said. "But there is nothing like a father. You should know this better than anyone."

Octavius flushed. It was the wrong thing to say, and perhaps a low blow. Octavius had never really known his father, while Agrippa had only ever known his. But it was still true.

"Must I remind you why we are going?" Octavius asked tersely.

They had actually long planned to quell the rebellious tribes in Illyicum, so the summons had not exactly come as a surprise. The plan had been contingent on defeating Sextus, which would then leave tens of thousands of soldiers without occupation or housing.

Octavius had decided to bribe the soldiers with rich rewards if they chose to continue fighting alongside him in Illyricum, while the rest would be paid right then as promised. It had, of course, worked perfectly.

"It is as you said," Agrippa replied wearily. "The only thing worse than men at war are men at home, for they bring war with them."

"Precisely," Octavius said, his eyes hardened like metal. "If I allowed my men to remain idle in Rome, eating Roman food, living on Roman land, bearing weapons and complaining, it would not be long before riots broke out, if not an outright war." He sighed. "And we cannot afford to have another civil war."

"Not even with Antonius?" Agrippa asked with a smirk.

Octavius glared at him. "Antonius is no longer Roman, and the people know that. He is merely the puppet of an Egyptian queen."

"You had best hope the people remember it."

"*You* had best remember it," Octavius shot back. "I cannot have my best general abandon my cause for a child." *Or a woman,* Agrippa heard unsaid, and he knew Octavius thought it the worse of the two.

"Is that all you think of me?" Agrippa asked, only partly joking. "As your best general?"

It was his turn to test Octavius, who looked away, suddenly very quiet, watching the hilly countryside rise and fall outside the window. Agrippa wondered what he was thinking, whether he was remembering that night on the beach, the silence, the simple kiss.

If I loved you, I would be terrified to lose you.

"I am only joking," Agrippa said softly when Octavius did not speak.

Octavius looked at him sharply. "Are you?"

Agrippa smiled wryly, but inside he grew sad and lonely. If he was partly joking, it was only because it was partly true. "You didn't answer my question."

"If you were only my best general," Octavius said angrily, "would I have you in this carriage?"

Agrippa was silent.

Octavius raised a brow and took Agrippa's hand roughly in his, but the touch was cold and distant, as if he were merely proving a point. "Would I touch you? Would I kiss you?"

"You don't have to," Agrippa said, his voice chilly despite the sudden racing of his pulse, as it always did when Octavius touched him. "It is not an obligation."

Octavius huffed a laugh but his eyes flashed angrily, and he dropped Agrippa's hand. "Do not speak to me of *obligation.*"

Agrippa wondered if Octavius was still speaking about him, or someone else, someone from a past he would rather forget. *He always favored me.*

In Octavius' dark eyes, Agrippa saw a charming smile, a smooth voice, and clever eyes. Hirtius had been so worldly, so sophisticated, so unlike Agrippa. But Octavius had been young and impressionable, and despite his best efforts, the past did not always remain there.

While Agrippa felt a slight pity for a seventeen-year-old boy who did not know better, he also felt frustrated, and embarrassed, for he knew—of course he knew—that Octavius preferred to receive than give. Agrippa had known this from the very beginning and had not once demanded anything different until the day Octavius had sent him away to Gaul. He wanted Octavius to want him, but he felt ashamed to even have to ask. Did Octavius truly love him, or only the power he had over him?

"Octavius," Agrippa murmured. "Look at me."

Octavius' eyes fixed on him in surprise, like a deer caught in the woods, noticing too late the bow taught in the hunter's hand.

Agrippa wanted to reach out to him, but another part of him now shied away from this side of Octavius, the side that saw love as a weakness, as a submission, as if he would be less of a man beneath Agrippa, as if Agrippa were less of a man because he loved him.

"I will never beg for your love," Agrippa said, finally, softly. "You do not owe me anything."

Instead of fighting him, as Agrippa half-expected, Octavius was silent, crossing his arms and looking back out the window. They did not speak until the next rest stop, and when they did, Octavius pretended nothing had happened.

And since Agrippa loved him, he let him.

⤜⤛ ⤜⤛

APRIL 35 BC

A fog cloaked the rocky terrain about them as their army marched through the narrow valley towards Metulum, the capital of the territory home to the Iapodes, one of the most dangerous tribes in Illyricum.

During the dead of night, they had seized Terponus, a town south along the Colapis River which descended from the mountains in meandering, clear streams.

The men moved in silence. It was only just past first light, but the sun had not yet risen, and the valleys and ridges were quiet save for small birds waking up and calling to one another.

A thick, dark cloud of smoke curled into the sky far away, drifting over the wind in their direction. Agrippa spurred his horse on, moving forward and sidling up beside Octavius, who trotted on horseback ahead of him.

"We ought to split up and approach from both flanks," Agrippa said. "Our scouts report that the wall is heavily armed on all sides."

Octavius nodded and whistled to his generals.

There was no need for stealth any longer. If the city had not already received wind of their destruction on the outskirts of their territory, then they could certainly see the damage now.

Octavius pointed right, then left. *"Ad dextram! Ad sinistram!"*

Agrippa and Octavius led the remaining legions straight towards the city walls while the others broke off on either side.

The walls of the city were high and armed with men, some holding taut flaming arrows and spears, ready to fire once their men got within range. Circling the outer wall was a deep ditch. But that had been expected and would be no obstacle in a siege.

Their soldiers immediately began setting up camp, while others brought out the towers plated in metal and heavily armed with bolt-throwing *ballistae* and battering rams.

Agrippa always marveled at his men working in seamless order, silent except for the barked order and a whistle of a spear or stone from the walls as it fell short of their camp. Already weaponry was being loaded and carted up towards the wall, and men protected by *testudines*—vehicles shielded like a tortoise's shell—worked on piling mud, wood, and stone to build a ramp.

He called over one of his lieutenants. "We need more men working on the ramp. Our towers will not get close enough to the walls otherwise."

The lieutenant nodded and immediately relayed the orders to his subordinates, and soon more soldiers were dispatched to aid in the building of the ramp.

Octavius' horse stomped its foot impatiently as if it wished for battle. The ramp was quickly piling across the ditch, a siege tower rolling towards it, aloof to the arrows and spears raining down upon it. But the soldiers seemed to hesitate, moving slowly and dispirited, as if they were still unsure about the siege and had no desire to capture another city after so many years at war.

Indeed, news of Sextus Pompeius' capture and execution in Asia—having been betrayed by his stepbrother Scaurus—had spread like wildfire among the troops, and many perhaps longed for peace now that the true enemy was dead.

As if he had noticed the same thing, Octavius spurred his horse and galloped off towards one of the siege towers.

Agrippa stared in surprise for a moment before he rode after him. He dismounted his horse and followed Octavius up the ladders of the tower, his heart beating wildly, wondering what in Jove's name had gotten into his head this time.

At last, he reached the top of the tower. Octavius stood facing his men.

They looked at Octavius in surprise, but continued preparing their weapons, though many seemed weary, moving twice as slow as Agrippa knew they could in an emergency. While bribing the soldiers had worked to appease most of them, they had become no better than mercenaries—worse, for they once had a cause, and now appeared to have lost it.

"Ambula!" Octavius shouted angrily to the slaves on the ground.

The tower creaked, then began to wheel forward as hundreds of men pushed it below. They had to have been at least five stories above the ground, with men packed in each level and armed to the teeth. Yet they hardly seemed ready to fire on the enemy over the wall, let alone rush over the drawbridges once they reached the rampart, shifting uneasily on their feet.

Soon the tower was wheeled before the wall, across the hastily built earthen ramp that inclined so as to give them the best vantage point to shower the enemy with arrows from above.

Agrippa stood close to Octavius, who hardly glanced at him and continued to shout orders and spur his men forward. The ramparts were crowded with enemy soldiers who catapulted stones and flaming debris onto the tower. Its metal shielding withstood the onslaught, though the smoke and gas from the collision of firepower still stung Agrippa's eyes.

Finally, the level below them let down their drawbridge, banging harshly on the ramparts below, and a flood of their soldiers spilled onto the bridge and began marching into the city, killing anyone who stood in their way.

"Percute!" Octavius ordered, pointing his sword towards the city, and the soldiers listened and charged ahead with speed, encouraged by their commander so close to the battlefront.

But then a huge *snap* resounded, and the tower shook as the drawbridge groaned with the weight of the soldiers crossing. Many rushed back onto the tower, and other soldiers hesitated.

Octavius looked at Agrippa, his eyes glinting like metal. "Do not follow me."

Before Agrippa could protest, Octavius descended the ladder to the level below, and Agrippa followed, his body moving of its own accord. Octavius was already pushing his way through the soldiers.

"Ordinem servate!" Octavius called out, but the soldiers still hung back, flinching when another flying stone made the tower tremble, or a flash of fire caught a soldier from a level below and took him down in flames. "Are you afraid of the barbarians or the bridge? *Sequi me!*"

At the last order, Octavius ran across the drawbridge, and his men followed instinctively, running with a cry as they lifted their shields and swords alongside their commander.

Agrippa shoved his way onto the bridge, unthinking, his chest tight. The wood strained beneath them, already cleaving in the center, and Agrippa knew as if in a dream what would happen next.

Soldiers retreated, stumbling over each other, flinging themselves over the rampart or back onto the tower. Agrippa hardly made it back to the tower platform when the bridge caved in, slowly at first, before splitting clean in half. Octavius was swallowed up in the mass of falling soldiers as the bridge collapsed at last, sending the soldiers down the side of the tower in heaps and screams as many were impaled or pierced by broken shards of wood.

The world went completely silent. Then Agrippa turned, his head spinning, the chaos of the battle returning as more catapults and spears were thrown at the tower from the ramparts, the enemy encouraged at the collapse of the drawbridge.

Agrippa descended the tower with shaky hands, the metal and wood shuddering from the enemy's attacks. He ran over to the pile of collapsed planks and soldiers, shielded by his men who helped him reach the dirt ramp to extract their commander.

He found Octavius lying crookedly among the other soldiers, some of whom were dead, while others were bloodied and in pain, but alive. Agrippa shook Octavius' shoulders, and his eyes flew open.

"Agrippa," Octavius said hoarsely, and he smiled, before glancing down. "My leg."

With the help of a few soldiers, Agrippa heaved Octavius upright. His right leg was running with blood from where a broken piece of wood had left a deep cut. Both of his arms were scratched and bruised as well. He limped forward, and Agrippa slung one of his arms over his shoulders.

"I'm alright," Octavius said, wincing as they walked away from the tower, quickly sheltered by a *testudo* as they were led back to camp. "I was lucky."

Agrippa pushed down a wave of anger and did not respond. He *had* been lucky. The fall was high enough that if he had landed the wrong way he could have died, but as it was, Octavius had landed on a cushion of other soldiers, and at an angle where he rolled to a safe stop and avoided the ditch.

The siege tower had to be rolled away to be repaired, and many had died from the fall. But it had worked. Octavius' courage had revived the energy of the camp, and several more siege towers had already lined up against the wall, storming the city with terrifying speed and efficiency.

Once they were back inside his tent, Agrippa helped the doctors set him on a bed, where he was promptly cleaned and bandaged. The wounds had looked worse than they actually were, but Agrippa could still not stop his hands from trembling.

Octavius looked at him, his eyes dilated and glassy from the medicine the doctor had given him to ease the pain.

"Look at me," Octavius whispered once they were alone and in a deathly silence. Then Octavius half-smiled to himself, almost delirious.

But Agrippa was too angry to find it funny. "You could have died, Octavius."

"But I did not."

"That was unnecessary," Agrippa said harshly.

Octavius' face grew dark and serious. "On the contrary, that was *very* necessary."

"You cannot risk your life when so many depend on you. Your men need a champion, not a martyr." Agrippa took a deep breath, trying to calm himself. He still felt shaken, and not only because Octavius' life had been a narrow breath from death. *Swear to me, on our daughter's life, that you will come home to me. Swear it.* "You have nothing to prove, Octavius."

"I have everything to prove," Octavius said, closing his eyes. He sighed, then grimaced as he adjusted his bandaged leg. "Perhaps one day things will be different."

Agrippa wished Octavius was wrong, that the world demanded nothing from him, that the two of them could simply run away and forget the battles and wars that loomed on the horizon.

But they were no longer two boys in school, no longer racing the streets of Apollonia, drinking wine under a starlit sky, nameless in a wide, unknown world. Fate had cast her eyes upon them and had not looked away.

Then together we will conquer the world.

"One day," Agrippa echoed, but he did not know if he believed it anymore.

48

OCTAVIA MINOR

JULY 35 BC

HER HUSBAND—FOR MARCUS ANTONIUS was still her husband, despite their failed marriage—owned a large house on the Palatine Hill, overlooking the Velabrum, its marshy, green valley tucked between the Forum Boarium and the Capitoline Hill.

The house itself was grand and stately enough, but Octavia found it empty of a soul, the remnants of a great Roman man having abandoned his native country for a foreign woman and foreign wealth.

But it was the perfect house to entertain guests in, especially children, and between her, Livia, and Attica, there were a lot of them. For the house was much larger than either Octavius or Agrippa's estates, which were surprisingly modest, so that Octavia enjoyed inviting the two women and their children for a fun summer's day out in the gardens.

Attica had already arrived, very pregnant with her second child. Vipsania Agrippina was asleep in the arms of her handmaiden, already a year old. Soon after Livia arrived, Tiberius and Drusus burst out into the garden, finding Iullus—Antonius' second son by Fulvia—and Marcellus, who dragged his stepbrother and two cousins into a game of playing pretend, which usually involved much battle and multiple deaths and revivals.

Julia, now four years old, was holding Livia's hand, and she tried to run after the boys. Although Livia protested, Attica and Octavia convinced her that there really was no harm, and with a happy cry Julia joined the boys in their adventures.

Octavia asked her own daughters if they wished to join as well, but only Claudia Marcella Major, who was already in her eighth year, shyly walked over to Iullus and Drusus, who were looking under a bush, probably searching for strange bugs.

Her other daughters, Claudia Marcella Minor and Antonia Major, were content to play near their mother, braiding each other's hair and playing hand games. Octavia's youngest daughter, Antonia Minor, was hardly a year old, and remained on her mother's lap, more interested in undoing her mother's intricate braids than anything else.

"Very soon, my dear," Attica said to Agrippina, who was wide awake at the sounds of children playing and wished to join them, yearning towards Tiberius and Marcellus. They were pretending to be generals at war, while Iullus and Drusus were now examining a small caterpillar they had found crawling on a leaf. "But you are too young."

Agrippina, who seemed to understand, screamed angrily and caught the attention of Tiberius, who looked up at the noise worriedly. Tiberius said something quietly to Marcellus before he marched over to Agrippina.

"We were in the middle of our game!" Marcellus protested, but Tiberius did not seem to hear him, speaking with Attica and holding Agrippina's hand tenderly.

They would not know they were to be betrothed for many years, but it was already a good match. Livia, however, looked at them with a slight frown. While Agrippina might be a good match for her son, it was still an insult. For Julia was the more illustrious choice as Octavius' daughter, and she had been promised to Antyllus, Antonius' eldest son, instead of Tiberius.

"I can take his spot," Julia said, standing in front of Marcellus.

"But you're a girl!" Marcellus protested, a bit of wonder in his voice, perhaps surprised Julia had even thought to suggest it.

"Then I may play your wife," Julia suggested shyly. "And you have to save me from pirates."

Marcellus looked frightened at the thought and turned to Octavia in alarm. She could not help but laugh, and Julia's lip quivered as if she were about to cry or shout angrily.

"Come here, darling," Livia called to Julia, who was now quite embarrassed and willing to run back to her stepmother. "No need to bother the boys."

Tiberius then returned to Marcellus, and they pretended to be pirates and sailed across wild seas filled with monsters and sirens and explored strange isles of witches and one-eyed giants. Julia watched sullenly from beside Livia, but eventually she was put in charge of playing with Agrippina and Antonia Minor, who were so in awe of the older girl that all jealousy of the boys was forgotten.

"It is a lovely day, is it not?" Attica said suddenly, sighing. She bit her lip and then there were tears welling up in her gray eyes, though she wiped them away furiously.

"Oh, my love, what's wrong?" Livia asked, looking at Attica sadly, for they all knew what ailed her. Agrippa had been gone for nearly six months now fighting in Illyricum, and she was about to have another baby.

"Do not cry, my dear Attica," Octavia said. "They will return."

"I cannot," she said quietly. "I cannot have this child without him."

Livia shared an uneasy glance with Octavia. She knew as well as Octavia that Agrippa was loyal to Octavius first and foremost. "You have us. We shall take care of you."

This seemed to calm Attica for the most part, and they returned to amusing the children and watching as the boys played. Eventually, Marcellus felt pity for Julia and asked her to play in their games again, and she eagerly joined in the battles and sea voyages around the gardens.

A few hours later her porter appeared, bearing a message from her brother. She saw Attica and Livia turn to her anxiously. Octavia nodded at the porter, and he began to read the letter aloud.

"Gaius Julius Caesar sends his greetings to Octavia Minor. The war goes well. We laid siege to Metulum and were successful. I sustained injuries to my right leg and arm after we rushed over a drawbridge and it collapsed, but the doctor is confident in a full recovery. Many have died, many more are injured, but our supplies are well protected. We shall march to Segesta in the following weeks. Send my love to Marcellus, I do miss that little donkey. I shall see him again by the end of the year if he should ask. Vale."

Octavia sighed in relief. "They are alive."

"But Agrippa?" Attica asked worriedly. "He said nothing of Agrippa."

"Then nothing happened," Octavia said with a confidence she did not feel. "My brother would have mentioned it otherwise."

Livia was quiet, staring at the ground lost in thought. She was evidently not worried about her husband's injuries. Octavia knew she was thinking of his affection towards her son, Marcellus, which he had never once shown to Tiberius. It was an unspoken tension between them, for it was not in doubt *whom* Octavius favored—Marcellus or Tiberius—but *why*, for neither boy was his true son. However, it seemed her brother harbored a special love for Marcellus and a special hatred for Tiberius. While the former could be explained by Marcellus' relation by blood, the latter was a mystery.

After all, Octavia and Livia had both been given the same special honors this year. They were both granted *sacrosanctitas,* an honor previously reserved only for tribunes, which made it illegal to insult them. They were both excused from *tutela,* the customary male guardianship required for all women besides the Vestal Virgins, which also allowed them to manage their own finances. And they both had countless statues of themselves erected in public squares and buildings across Rome.

Octavia wished things were different, but she could not pretend she was not grateful that Marcellus was favored. For the alternative was dangerous, and she did not know what lengths she would go to protect her son, even against her own brother.

"The war is temporary," Octavia said finally, forcing a smile, glad the news was good at least. "It is only a precautionary measure. My brother would not risk his life for so little."

But Attica did not smile, and there was a darkness in her eyes that startled Octavia.

"No, not *his* life."

Octavia had no answer to that.

⇝⇝ ⇜⇜

NOVEMBER 35 BC

Octavia never thought she would return here.

As she wandered the empty, dark halls of her husband's villa in Athens, now coated in dust from disuse, Octavia could not help but reflect on how much her life had changed in only a few years.

She had been sent as an envoy to her husband by her brother, who had returned alone from Illyricum to attend to some affairs in Rome, leaving Agrippa in command of his legions while he was away. Her brother had decided to send only two thousand soldiers to Antonius, despite the fact that he had promised twenty thousand.

Antonius, meanwhile, currently resided in Alexandria, or at least he claimed to be using the Egyptian city as his base of operations while he campaigned in Armenia. That was the last Octavia had heard of him.

She knew she had become a pawn in the political game between her husband and her brother. The two thousand soldiers were nothing more than an insult, a test of Antonius' faith to the Roman people more so than to his wife.

Octavia had left her children in Rome, in case she never returned. Who knew what would become of her in Egypt? Octavius had assured her that he would allow no harm to befall her, but his reassurances fell flat as she looked at the dimly lit halls where she had spent most of her marriage with Antonius.

There had been a time of bliss, or at least, of willful ignorance. She had never been in love with Antonius, but the hatred that they seemed to mutually share, the kind of hatred that arose from an innate understanding, almost a similarity, between them, from the moment she had seen him at her mother's funeral, rapidly heated into a passion she had never felt before.

Antonius was, after all, only a man, solid and demanding, but surprisingly gentle and loving in a way only men could be.

She remembered one of the few real conversations they had together, before she knew she was pregnant with their first child. They had gone to sleep in the same bed, and Octavia had been warm at heart, for here she was, finally, a woman, and if she closed her eyes, here was her man, and that was all there was to the world.

402

But then she had opened them, and Antonius had looked at her silently, troubled.

"What?" she had asked.

He had shaken his head. "Nothing."

"No, tell me."

"It is nothing, really." Antonius had paused, leaning back. "You women always terrify me."

"Oh really?" Octavia had laughed. He could be amusing when he tried.

"I thought your mother could read every thought I had," he had murmured. "Your brother has those same eyes. And so do you."

"You truly knew my mother?"

"Well, yes," Antonius had answered uneasily. He had rarely liked to speak of their families. Though distant the connection, a connection there still was, and he seemed to despise it. "I remember the first time I met you."

"As do I," Octavia had said honestly.

And she had, though the memory had faded. It had been at her father's funeral. Antonius had been young, and ever so handsome. She had blushed at his voice alone. But she had been nothing more than a child, and soon she would come to hate him, if only because she had blushed all those years ago.

Antonius had looked at her in surprise, then frowned. "I was a scoundrel back then. Atia knew it. They all did."

"And now you are not?" Octavia had asked, raising a brow.

Instead of becoming angry, as she had expected, Antonius had grinned wickedly and rolled on top of her. "Why don't you tell me?"

Octavia sat down on what was once their bed, pushing the memory away. She secretly dreaded seeing him again, knowing he had returned to the Egyptian queen and made love to her. Though she knew it was not her fault, the small child in her wondered if somehow it had been. But that was a false logic, for Antonius would have had to abandon her regardless. Her brother would have made sure of it.

By the gods, to be a woman!

What a blessing, what a curse it was! Octavia knew she was a better person than Antonius, even a better man. As a woman, she longed for him, for his touch, but at the same time, she recoiled from it, from the touch of any man. Since the day she had lost the love of her life, her dear Marcellus, all men were cut off from her, their plights were false to her, their love and hate a mere shadow to the grief that had moved like mountains in her heart.

How she missed his smile, and those soft blue eyes! How she wished to return to that night when they first made love, those days of bliss and beginnings, of life and laughter!

Octavia knew her life was a mere footnote in the grand scheme of history. Men worshiped history and feared that it would forget them. But women knew there was no one to remember them, not even their children, who realized only too late to whom they owed their lives. History was a man's word, reserved for great deeds, conquests and triumphs, not marriage and children.

But what of it? She never cared for history. Let men believe their lives were worth something more than death. Octavia knew only herself, her love, and the children whom she bore, even if they did not bear her name. And she would never stop loving, for that was how life was made, and how life went on, whether men called it history or not.

"My lady."

Octavia whirled around, her heart beating frantically at the voice, wondering fearfully if her husband had come to meet her there. But it was only one of her servants. She had thought no one would interrupt her, so it had to be bad news.

"What is it?"

"A letter arrived." A pause. "From *Tresvir* Antonius."

Octavius' breath caught. "What does it say?"

"Only that he has accepted the two thousand soldiers, but demands that you do not go farther than Athens, and return home. He shall not welcome you in Egypt."

For a moment, all stood still, and the world was wide and filled with evil, and she was alone. Then the moment passed, and from one breath to the next Octavia felt relief flood through her body, and her head was lighter upon her shoulders, as if each step closer to her husband had been a weight upon her, dragging her down to earth when she had always been free to fly.

"Then I will return to Rome," Octavia said firmly, standing up. "Pack my things. I do not intend to stay the night."

She left their bedroom, the past settling in her soul like the dust in the house, and when her ship sailed away from the rocky Greek coastline, Octavia did not look back.

49

GAIUS OCTAVIUS

JANUARY 34 BC

"**P**LEASE, COME AGAIN SOON!" Livia called out the door as their decorated guests waved and descended the walkway to their carriages, their faces flushed from the wine, all careless smiles and easy laughter.

It was Livia's birthday, and as Octavius was luckily still in town, he had thrown a party for her. Most of the guests were senators, others wealthy private citizens, Balbus and Oppius among them. There were artists and poets, like Vergilius and Rufus, as well as sons of illustrious fathers, and daughters of the most well-respected matrons. Octavia and Attica had been present earlier, but both of them retired after dinner to care for the younger children, who were fussy by the late evening.

Octavius stood beside Livia as she closed the door and sighed, her smile falling into a slight frown.

"Finally," she said. "I was beginning to have trouble keeping my eyes open." It was nearing the early hours of the morning after all.

"Did you enjoy your birthday?" Octavius asked, taking her hand and reeling her into his arms.

She was now in her twenty-sixth year, while he was soon to be approaching his thirtieth. It seemed only yesterday they had met, when he was only nineteen, and the entire world felt like one war away.

Now they understood that the world was far larger and far more hostile than they had thought, and that accomplishing their dreams would take a lifetime, if not more.

"Yes, it was lovely," Livia said, kissing him briefly.

While time and distance certainly cooled whatever passion they had found in the early years after their hasty marriage, the love they felt for each other, sprung from a deep loyalty and understanding that Octavius had not expected to find, never wavered, and indeed, grew stronger with each passing year, as did the laurel tree in their garden, a symbol of the past as much as the future.

Octavius kissed her forehead. "I shall return to Illyricum in a few weeks."

"Very well," she said, though her brown eyes, usually so warm and kind, were troubled and did not meet his gaze.

"What is on your mind?" Octavius asked, touching her chin. "Tell me."

"Oh, it is nothing." She paused, eyeing him carefully. For a moment, Octavius did not know if she would tell him, but then she said, "I have only been thinking, ought not Julia be wed to Tiberius?"

The question was not exactly a surprise, but he went very still, for he had not thought she would ever ask it. "Julia is promised to Antyllus. And I have already arranged Tiberius' marriage to Agrippina. I thought you approved."

"Oh yes," Livia said carelessly, though her smile was tense. "When you needed to save your alliance with Antonius, I approved. But now we both know your alliance with Antonius will not last. Besides, Antyllus is living with him in Alexandria. He would be a bad influence on Julia."

"It is not worthwhile thinking of these things," Octavius said, turning away from her. "I cannot afford to break off my alliance with Antonius at such a delicate time. The public must be sure of peace."

"But when the time comes?" Livia challenged, and he knew she would not let him off so easily. "Shall you promise Julia to Tiberius?"

"They are too young to decide," Octavius said reluctantly. "They might die any day."

"Then you have chosen Marcellus," Livia said, raising her chin defiantly. "You wish Julia would wed him, and not Tiberius." When Octavius did not respond, she shook her head in disbelief. "Are not Tiberius and Drusus like your sons? Am I not their mother as I am your wife?"

"If they were my sons, they would bear my name."

Livia's eyes flashed angrily. "Then change their name. When their father dies, they will answer to you alone. What more could you ask of a son?"

Octavius stared at her, and when he realized she would not relent, he forced the words out. "Marcellus shares my blood. He is the only one who may inherit what I have built."

"So then you are a king now?" Livia asked, arching a brow. "Do you think the Senate shall ever approve it? Do you think the people will stand for it?"

Octavius bared a smile. "Those are two very different questions." He paused. "But I am no king. And you are no queen. We are Romans, and that is all."

"We both know that is not true," Livia murmured. "Not anymore. We may never be crowned, but when the wars are over, the people will look to us as the mother and father of all Romans and beyond."

"A father whose son is not even his?" Octavius asked, his voice rising. "I would be ridiculed! I would be humiliated. No, it cannot be."

"You are a liar," Livia said softly, but not with any spite, only pity, and somehow that was worse. "It is not because of blood that you favor Marcellus. It is because you hate Tiberius. You hate my son. I have known it since the day you met him. Perhaps you will not admit it. But it is the truth, whether you believe it or not."

"You are a better liar than me, Livia," Octavius said darkly. "I will not have my name insulted by the very woman who coerced me into this marriage!"

"Coerced?" Livia cried, and it was as if the word alone sparked a passion within her like a flaming sword, like Demeter in pursuit of her daughter Persephone. Octavius' eyes widened in surprise—and fear. "You and I both know very well you could have had me executed silently, without a whisper of falsehood said against your name. But you did not. Why?" Her eyes seemed to glow fiercely as if the sun shone through them. "Because you knew I was the answer. You knew I alone could give you what you wanted. My son is kind and loyal and intelligent. He will grow up and honor you properly, for he is not arrogant or ambitious. But you look at him and hate him, because you see in him a boy like yourself when you were too young to defend yourself, sensitive and quiet, and you think him *weak*."

Octavius was rooted to the spot, her persuasive voice like a spell, firm and compelling at the same time. He wanted to resist, to walk away and deny her, but at the same time a sudden fear gripped him, and he saw the shadow of Death looming at every corner, his breath rattling in his chest, a smooth voice, a clever smile, and he could not cry for help. He was utterly, utterly alone.

"Tiberius is nothing like me. He *is* weak. He is sheltered. When I was his age, you have no idea what I put up with, what I had to—"

He broke off. Livia watched him, and her eyes were kindled with triumph. "You look at Tiberius and you see yourself. That is why you hate him, and why you fear him. He could become what you have become, but only if you give him the chance." She walked over to him and took his hand gently, and it was as if she became mortal once more, looking up at him, the shadow of her lashes curved over her cheeks. "Please give my son a chance."

Octavius closed his eyes tightly, his will and his love wrestling within him. He sighed. "I will give Tiberius the same chances of success that I give Marcellus. If I deem him more deserving when the time comes, I shall wed him to Julia."

Livia kissed Octavius' cheek. "Thank you." She stepped back, then began to walk away. "And remember, I am always on your side. On *our* side. Goodnight, my love."

He said nothing as her stola swished and disappeared around the corner, an echo of that day so many years ago.

You are my destiny.
But Octavius thought that destiny was beginning to sound more like a curse.

⤐ ⥆

APRIL 34 BC

It was a cold day for late April, and Octavius wrapped his cloak tighter around his shoulders, holding back a shiver. His fighting at Metulum and Segesta had impressed the soldiers after his less-than-stellar showing at the battle of Philippi, and he could not afford to look ill during another war.

Agrippa glanced at him from across the tent. He said nothing, but he did not have to. They both knew how dangerous an illness would be. Octavius' generals did not seem to notice the perilous state of their commander, continuing to discuss strategy.

They planned to attack Promona, the stronghold of the Dalmatae, a tribe who had previously defeated General Gabinius in one of Rome's more embarrassing losses when their enemy had captured some standards. Therefore this was a matter of revenge as much as convenient military training for their troops.

"If we continue along the coast, the river shall provide us some cover from an easy ambush," said Publius, one of his generals, pointing to Agrippa's map which was spread on the desk.

"But fording the river may slow us down," said Varius, another general. "Any delay will surely give the Dalmatae the upper hand."

Agrippa stepped closer to the map, then circled the place where the ocean and river met. "It is no secret that we are here. Scouting has already reported an increased watch on their borders. Our supply ships may dock at this harbor. It is a worthwhile delay."

"Besides," Octavius added, "the only other option would be to go around the river, which would leave us vulnerable along the mountain passes."

While they discussed various strategies, a messenger arrived with news from Egypt. His scouts had gotten wind that Antonius wished to divide up the East for his children.

Octavius merely brushed it aside, but his generals were angry.

"You ought to challenge him, sir," said Publius—the older of the two—who had much more of that old Republican pride. "Handing off our land to some foreign bitch's litter? It is an outrage. It is a disgrace. And they even say he had a Roman triumph in the streets of Alexandria, dressed as Bacchus."

"It is only a rumor," Octavius said calmly. "We have no proof."

"You know it is true," the younger one, Varius, said, his eyes gleaming. "Challenge him to a fight and he will prove his traitorous ways."

"I will not be the first to draw blood," Octavius answered decidedly. "He will betray his people with no help from me. It is in his nature."

That was the end of the discussion, but he could sense their disapproval. They were not used to Antonius' open insults, whereas Octavius knew them all too well.

His generals retired for a meal and some much-needed rest before their long march south at daybreak. Agrippa remained, scrolling up his map and studiously avoiding Octavius' gaze. They had not spoken properly since Octavius had left Agrippa in command of his legions last autumn. The words Agrippa had told him in the carriage more than a year ago still rang in his ears. *I will never beg for your love.*

But they would have to speak of it eventually.

"Livia is upset with me," Octavius said quietly.

Agrippa looked at him in surprise. They rarely confided in each other about their wives. "Oh?"

"She wishes for me to wed Julia with Tiberius once I break my alliance with Antonius."

"I thought you planned to wed her to Marcellus," Agrippa said carefully.

"Yes. He shares my blood."

"I see." Agrippa eyed him warily. "But Livia does not agree."

"No, she does not." Octavius sighed. "She claims that I hate Tiberius because I think he is weak."

"Do you?"

"I do think he is weak," Octavius answered slowly. "But I do not hate him."

Agrippa hesitated. It was clear he had his own thoughts on the subject, but was debating whether it was wise to voice them. Finally, he said, "Livia is his mother. It is no surprise she advocates for him."

"I suppose," Octavius said, sounding sullen. He looked at Agrippa, who was watching him cautiously. A wave of defiance clenched Octavius' heart, and he spoke without thinking. "She said I see myself in him. That I think him weak because I think myself weak. But it is not true, you know. I am strong. Stronger than most people know. There were times—"

He broke off, the words halting in his throat. Agrippa kept very still, waiting, listening, until Octavius took in a deep breath, and calmed his racing heart. He did not know why he was saying anything at all, except that he had to speak now or keep the words until his death, and Agrippa was the only one who could hear them and bear witness to the past he had worked so hard to bury.

"There were times," Octavius said, his voice low and trembling, "when Hirtius would joke. With the other soldiers in Hispania. About me. He once said he would pay three hundred thousand *sesterces* to take me. I was young, and I bore it, and really no one thought anything of it. They knew Hirtius, they loved him, and I was protected by Caesar."

When he stopped, Agrippa was still standing, unmoving, his eyes like the Tiber on a moonless evening, calm and waveless as a lake. Octavius heard the words after they fell from his mouth, far away, as far away as the past.

"But when we were alone, he was different. Persistent. He wanted more. He offered me money. More than he ever joked about. I almost said yes just for him to stop. Then he kissed me. It was a test. To see if I would fight him." Octavius closed his eyes, having the strange urge to laugh, and it was like he was seventeen once more, wishing to prove himself, to be a man, but finding that he was only a boy after all. "It happened so quickly that sometimes I wonder if I had imagined it all. He led me to his private quarters. I was too drunk to notice. He pushed me over the desk, and—" He opened his eyes, clearing his throat. "It was a long time ago. But I never forgot that feeling, that I was helpless, powerless, and alone. I vowed never to allow myself to be so powerless again."

"Octavius," Agrippa whispered. "Why did you not tell me?"

"I could not bear to think that you saw me any differently," Octavius said stiffly. "That you thought me any less of a man."

"Any less of a man?" Agrippa repeated incredulously. He walked towards him slowly. Octavius tensed as Agrippa stood before him. He reached out and took Octavius' hand in his, loosely lacing their fingers together. "Am *I* less of a man? If you took me right now, would you think I am—what? A woman?"

Octavius nearly shivered, but said nothing. Agrippa shook his head, frowning.

"My wife is stronger than any man," Agrippa said quietly. "And I have fought in many battles. She has given everything for me, and risks her life to bear me children, knowing that even so, I will come back to *you* every time. Do you think that weak?"

His words stirred his heart, but Octavius could not simply forget the past. He imagined trying to touch Agrippa, to give something of himself, but he could not, he would not. For that night with Hirtius had been the last time he had given himself up, and ever since then, he had vowed never to give himself up like that again. He had vowed never to be weak with another man.

He pulled his hand from Agrippa's, and he stepped away, his heartbeat slow and distant, his skin prickling, his face hot as if with fever. The air in the tent was suffocating, closing in on his throat. "The rest of the world would think I am weak," he said. "Even if you do not."

"Oh, you and the rest of the world, Octavius," Agrippa said, sounding tired. "You could hardly touch me if we were the last two people on earth."

"You ask more of me than I am willing to give," Octavius said, his voice dropping to a whisper, a ghostly echo on the wind, an echo of himself ten years past, young and afraid and so utterly alone.

Agrippa's eyes flashed with pain. "Why must you always fight?"

He could not stop the harsh words from leaving his mouth. "I know *you* would not understand. You have nothing to lose. You never did."

A look of disbelief passed across his face, before Agrippa continued packing up his maps in silence. There was nothing more to say.

Octavius turned his back on him, unwilling to look him in the eyes and see the pity lingering there.

It was not long before Agrippa sighed and left the tent.

⋙ ⋘

SEPTEMBER 34 BC

The end of spring brought hot summer days and successful battles against the Dalmatae. Their legions captured Promona and Synodium, retrieving the stolen standards, and they continued to push deeper into enemy territory.

Octavius set down his tablet and stylus he had been using to calculate supply costs when Agrippa walked inside the tent. He ignored the pang of his heart at the sight.

"You called for me, Caesar?"

Octavius nearly winced at the name. It had been months of tiptoeing around each other, Octavius unwilling to surrender, Agrippa reluctant to ask any more of him. But Octavius thought that they were too old to play games any longer.

"You know it is only us here," he said quietly.

Agrippa's eyes shadowed. "You called for me?"

Octavius sighed. "Yes. You are going home."

"What?" It seemed despite the distance that had grown between them, Agrippa had not expected an outright dismissal.

"I am sending you home," Octavius repeated firmly. "Statilius Taurus has recently celebrated a triumph for his success in Africa. He shall be taking your position."

Agrippa stared at him. "I do not understand."

"It is an order, *general,*" Octavius said, wishing for him to feel the same hurt that he did. "There is nothing to understand, only follow."

"You are punishing me," Agrippa said, a tremor in his voice. "You are sending me away to punish me. But I have done nothing wrong. I have only ever loved you."

At the words, Octavius could not help but flinch, and he clenched his fists tightly. "Think of it as a reward, then. Livia has told me that Attica recently gave birth. To a girl."

Agrippa's eyes widened, and he said nothing. His anger quickly gave way to worry and excitement for his child, and he looked at Octavius without truly seeing him.

"I have already arranged your transportation," Octavius said. It was not jealousy, but longing, that settled on his heart, like sheets of packed snow ready to wait out a long winter. He was surprised to feel it, and could hardly focus on anything except Agrippa's eyes as they met his gaze once more. "You will leave at dawn."

Agrippa moved as if to come towards him. "Octavius—"

"Go home, Agrippa." Octavius tried to smile and failed. "Your family needs you."

50

Marcus Vipsanius Agrippa

NOVEMBER 34 BC

Browning trees shaded the entrance of his house, a chilly breeze rustling the leaves. The impluvium glittered under the waning afternoon sun as Agrippa walked into the house and passed the atrium to the inner courtyard.

He could just see Attica curled up on a seat in the last rays of sunlight, reading a scroll from his library, which was mostly borrowed from Atticus and his vast stores, as well as many of the late orator Cicero.

Agrippa paused before he walked into view. Her brown hair was swept into a bun, the top of her head almost golden in the sun, and her mouth was slightly parted, as if at any moment she might speak the words on the page and be swept into an enchanting world of monsters and magic.

She was beautiful, timeless, as a sunset never fails to illuminate the heart with its fading golden light. At that moment Agrippa knew she was the best woman on earth.

Then a loud shriek rang through the house, and little Agrippina burst into the courtyard, one of their servants trailing after her helplessly, a small baby already in her arms. Agrippina waddled excitedly over to Attica, who smiled at her daughter, though her eyes reluctantly looked away from her reading.

"Mama! Mama..." Agrippina threw herself onto her mother's legs, and Attica laughed and scooped up the little girl onto her lap.

"What is it, darling?" Attica asked, kissing her cheek.

"Mama, I want sweets," Agrippina mumbled against her chest.

"You want sweets?" Attica laughed.

"Yes." Agrippina pouted at her mother's amusement. "Sweets. Now."

Agrippa walked into the courtyard, and Attica looked up, startled, and then gasped

413

when she saw him. "Agrippa? But what are you doing here?"

"I wanted to surprise you," Agrippa said. Attica put Agrippina on the floor, who clung to her mother's dress. Agrippa walked over and embraced his wife. "I was sent home," he murmured into her hair, which smelled like roses and lemons, but mostly, like home.

Attica pulled away, her gray eyes worried. "Sent home?"

Agrippa nodded, then looked down at his daughter, who glanced up at him shyly, her eyelashes lowered. He crouched down and opened his arms. "Will you not give your father a kiss?"

Without a word, Agrippina barreled into his arms and kissed his cheek.

When Agrippa stood up, he looked at their servant, who was still cradling their younger daughter. "I have not yet met this little one, have I?"

He took the baby from the woman's arms, unable to hold back a smile at the small, yawning face, and gray-brown eyes that blinked up at him, curious and calm.

Attica walked over to him and kissed the baby's forehead. "Vipsania Agrippina Minor," she said proudly. "She is very healthy and quiet, thankfully. So different from this crazy girl."

She lifted Agrippina into her arms, who squealed delightfully and hugged her mother.

Agrippa sighed, feeling the weight of his world settle back on his shoulders. "I am so glad to be home."

"I am so glad you are back," Attica whispered, her eyes welling up with tears.

She shook her head, and the tears fell haphazardly down her cheek, and she tried to smile. Agrippina began to cry, as she always did when her mother cried, and Agrippa took their daughter in his arms.

"Everything is alright now, darling," he said, glancing at Attica with a teasing smile. "She still does not like to see her mother cry."

"But I do not understand," Attica said, drying her tears hastily. "How come he sent you home?"

For it was not a question whose orders he had followed. Agrippa tried not to frown. "Livia had sent him news of the birth. He had me replaced for the next year."

"Do you think he was punishing you?" Attica asked carefully. "I know—I know how he feels about you. About us."

Agrippa shook his head, recalling that meeting, and how Octavius had looked when he said it. *Go home, Agrippa.*

No, it had not been a punishment. Not for him at least.

"If anything, it was a reward," Agrippa said finally. "He told me that my family needed me."

"Oh, *mi vir.*" Attica reached for him and Agrippa was there, kissing her. It would never be the flame of passion he felt with Octavius, but it was also never the terrible, burning pain that came with it. Attica was the remedy to his broken heart, for she only needed him to be one thing, and that was himself. *"My husband."*

"I am home, my love," Agrippa said softly. "I am home."

⤜⤜ ⤛⤛

JANUARY 33 BC

Agrippa studied the map before him, the familiar seven hills rising like cresting waves, the city of Rome precisely drawn, its crooked alleys and hillside roads, its grand forums and parks, basilicas and stadiums.

He pointed to the Aqua Marcia snaking from the Anio valley along the Via Tiburtina into Rome. It was an old aqueduct, constructed over a hundred years ago by an ancestor of Julius Caesar from the spoils of the destroyed cities of Corinth and Carthage.

"We start with the Aqua Marcia," Agrippa said. "It definitely needs to be repaired. I have also sketched some plans for extending its pipes further across the city."

At the beginning of the year, Agrippa had been elected as one of the *aediles*, responsible for the upkeep of Rome—infrastructure, sewage, aqueducts, and street cleaning, as well as the oversight of the games and provisions such as grain.

It was not glorious work, not in comparison to his former consulship, but Agrippa found he rather looked forward to the rebuilding of Rome, the intimate understanding of the city which it required, and his own ideas and inventions he wished to put to the test.

Agrippa had invited the other *aediles* to his home office to discuss preliminary plans and sketch a program for the first six months of their term.

"An excellent idea, *magister*," said Aurelius, one of the *aediles plebis*.

The *aediles plebis* were quick to please him as the closest confidant to Caesar. Their careers relied on their connections after all, since they were not one of the *aediles curules*, which had only been open to the patrician class this year.

"Agreed," said Gracchus, the other *aedile plebis*. He spoke very little and was clearly nervous.

Agrippa's fellow *aedile curules*, Cethegus, nodded his head. He was over twice Agrippa's age, as the minimum age for this position was thirty-seven. Agrippa, of course, had been given an exception, due to his efforts in the recent wars and Octavius' influence in the Senate.

415

"Then if we are all in agreement," Agrippa continued, "let us consider the Cloaca Maxima."

"It must be cleansed," Cethegus said immediately. "Although that will take a lot of men."

"Cleansed and enlarged." Agrippa frowned. "And I would mention that the sewers must be cleaned out as well, otherwise it will all be for naught."

"Then the streets ought to be cleaned as well," suggested Aurelius. "Otherwise we will end up with the same problem as before."

"If there is something one learns when in charge of Rome," Agrippa said wryly, "it is that everything in this city is connected."

The meeting lasted all day until late afternoon, when the work day finished and most of them returned home or went to the baths. Agrippa himself considered spending a few hours in the baths, but he found himself too strung up to possibly relax.

He knew Octavius was due to arrive in Rome any day now, as he had assumed the consulship with a certain Lucius Volcatius Tullus. Agrippa could not decide if he dreaded his arrival or looked forward to it.

The feeling reminded him of those school breaks in Rome, when Octavius would go off with the rest of the rich boys and their families to their villas on the coast, summering in much cooler, more pleasant places than the stifling humidity of the city. Agrippa would long for Octavius to return, but at the same time, he would dread it, knowing deep down that he was destined to love and never be loved in return.

As dusk fell, Agrippa dined alone. Attica was staying with her father on the Esquiline Hill, as he had fallen ill, and the children were already asleep. With nothing more to do, and no one more to visit, Agrippa decided to retire to bed early.

He had finished washing up when his manservant entered his room.

"Pardon me, sir, I would not bother you with any more guests, only that it is the *Imperator* Caesar who bade me tell you that he awaits your presence in the atrium."

Agrippa paused, glancing at his reflection in the small mirror on his desk. He had decided to wait a day to shave his stubble and now regretted it. It was too late, as Octavius was already in the house. At the thought, his pulse raced and fell like a wave cresting at the thought.

His manservant waited for his reply, but he dismissed him, unsure of what to do. Of course, he must go and meet him. But what on earth was he doing at his house so late in the night? Had he just arrived today? Agrippa thought he must have since there had been no messages or news of his arrival otherwise.

After a long minute of debating, Agrippa knew there was no avoiding it. Octavius was, after all, his superior, and he always would be. He dressed in a simple tunic and made his way to the atrium.

Octavius stood near the pool, staring into its clear depths with an air of serene thoughtfulness that stopped Agrippa in his tracks.

As if sensing his eyes, Octavius looked up. "Agrippa."

"Octavius."

"Where is Attica?" Octavius asked, glancing around.

"Visiting her father," Agrippa said. "He is ill."

Octavius frowned. "I am very sorry to hear that. I hope he recovers soon."

Agrippa was silent. He did not know what to say or how to act around Octavius when he was like this, as if all the bad blood and tossed insults between them had fallen away like rain, as if the last ten years of wanting and loving and hating each other could all be brushed aside with an easy smile and a cold laugh.

If I were Achilles, you would be Patroclus.

But that had been a child's dream, for in real life, there were no heroes, and love was tragic only because it ended.

"May we speak in your office?" Octavius asked idly, but his brown eyes glanced quickly at Agrippa.

Agrippa's heart pounded once, like a premonition, and he struggled to swallow. He had not thought Octavius would come to see him at all when he returned, much less invite himself into his office, alone.

"Yes."

They walked to his office without speaking. It had been months since the last time they were alone together, and somehow those months felt too short and too long at the same time.

"What news?" Agrippa asked, more out of a need to speak than genuine curiosity.

Octavius raised a brow. "Nothing you did not already know, I am sure. The war goes well in Illyricum. But I must return soon to see to it that the Dalmatae surrender."

"You are a busy man," Agrippa said, only a touch mocking.

"So are you," Octavius countered, almost smirking. "Or you will be. The responsibilities of an *aedile* are much greater than perhaps they ought to be."

"I am to care for the city I love. What more could I ask for?"

Octavius' eyes lowered. "You could ask for a fair bit more, I suppose."

"Octavius," Agrippa said quietly.

"Yes?"

"Why did you come here?"

Octavius stared at him for a moment before speaking. "I came to apologize."

It was Agrippa's turn to stare at Octavius, his clear gaze, dark eyes, and firm jaw, ever so lightly shaded as if he too had not yet shaved. "Why?"

"Because I was wrong," Octavius said, taking a step closer. Agrippa could not help but tense. "You would never be less of a man to me. Ever."

Despite the sincerity of his words, the burning intensity of his eyes, Agrippa could not prevent the doubt from creeping into his heart. The cold laughter that had always followed in his dreams, the hand that dropped his the moment he got too close, the walls that had always encircled Octavius' heart, all of it warned him to turn around and leave.

Instead, he asked, "What has changed?"

"Nothing," Octavius said immediately, then flushed, and glanced away. "You. Leaving. I knew..."

"You knew what?"

Octavius looked him in the eyes, and his brown eyes caged a flame, small but bright, and Agrippa's breath caught. "I knew that I did not want to die not loving you."

His voice trembled, and Agrippa wished to touch him, to kiss him, but he held back, remembering his promise never to beg for love, never to break the walls Octavius had built so carefully to keep him out.

"Octavius, I—"

But he forgot what he was going to say because Octavius had moved forward and kissed him. "Don't." Octavius's hands trembled against his face, and he kissed him gently, almost haltingly, as if he were holding himself back somehow. His cheeks were flushed when he pulled away and murmured, "Don't speak."

Then he dropped to his knees, and Agrippa held his breath until he could not hold it anymore, and the only word he spoke in the quiet was Octavius' name.

⤜⤜⤜ ⤚⤚⤚

MAY 33 BC

"Here is to the *Imperator* Caesar *divi filius!*"

Maecenas lifted his glass high, and all of the guests raised theirs in unison. He had invited a large party to his home in Rome to celebrate the end of the wars in Illyricum.

By the end of spring, the Dalmatae had surrendered at last, followed by countless other tribes, and Octavius returned to Italy victorious. Today he had read out the impressive list of his achievements from the last year in a Senate speech, where he declared that the recovered standards which Gabinius had lost would be placed in the newly built Porticus Octavia.

"Say, Caesar, when shall you have your much-deserved triumph?" Balbus asked after they all drank.

Octavius smiled graciously. "You know very well it must be delayed. There is much work to be done before we celebrate victories."

The house was filled to the brim with the most notable names of Rome, so that Agrippa wondered how Maecenas had bribed all of them to come. Of course, no one would refuse an invitation from Caesar, but there were still those who might have supported Antonius—if he were here, at least. As it was, the rumors of Antonius wiling away his time in Egyptian debauchery increased each day, so that Octavius and his recent victories only raised him up more in the eyes of the Roman people.

If Agrippa closed his eyes, listening to the tinkle of laughter and clinking glasses around him, the murmured conversation and happy cries, all would seem perfect, as if the time that had passed since their brief, blissful days in Apollonia were always like this, carefree and happy.

But then he opened them and noticed the missing faces, as well as the new ones, and he was reminded of the truth. Rufus, who had been executed as a traitor. Livia, who sat beside Octavius with a smile, though there was a new sorrow in her eyes. Cicero, whose head and hands Antonius had cut off and nailed to the *rostra* in the forum. And Attica, reclining beside Agrippa and chatting with Octavia, whose husband's absence might have been the most noticeable of them all.

Agrippa caught Octavius' eyes from across the room, dark and unreadable. He thought that this time there was a shadow of a smirk on his mouth. Agrippa stood up, excusing himself for fresh air, and walked to the expansive gardens in the back of the house.

The fog of the night had already descended on the hills, and a misty rain fell as Agrippa strolled through the bushes, whose roses were speckled with water droplets.

A branch snapped behind him, but this time Agrippa did not turn around, not as the familiar figure stood beside him. Agrippa hid a smile, knowing this was dangerous, like standing on the edge of a cliff, and there was no turning back now if he jumped off.

"Agrippa, Agrippa, Agrippa," Octavius murmured, soft as the wind. "What am I going to do with you?"

His heart jumped to his throat. It took everything in him to remain still, staring out into the fog cloaking the endless gardens, clinging to the valley below, Rome nestled beneath like a baby in her cradle.

"I could not even look at you," Agrippa said, his voice no more than a breath. "By Jove, I wish I could kiss you."

Out of the corner of his eyes, he saw Octavius' hands tighten into fists, then loosen, and Agrippa felt something brush against the back of his hand. "If we were alone…"

There were footsteps, voices in the air, laughter. Agrippa turned, taking a step away, ignoring the heat blooming on his face.

Octavia walked beside Attica, arm in arm. When Octavia saw the two of them, her smile faltered, but she did not stop walking. Attica's face brightened when she saw Agrippa, and paid no mind to Octavius, though he did not miss the tense set of her shoulders as she joined them. Livia and Maecenas walked behind them, debating something enthusiastically, Livia laughing so much she had to wipe tears from her eyes.

"Hello brother," Octavia said coolly.

Beside him, Octavius stiffened ever so slightly, but he smiled. "My lovely sister."

"Now what were you two thinking?" Maecenas asked once he joined them. "Shall we tour the gardens at a time like this? We can hardly see through the fog!"

"Maecenas is right," Livia said, rubbing her hands down her arms, which were covered in a thin *palla*. "It is quite chilly too."

Maecenas clapped his hands together. "How about a game of dice!"

"Are you so sure you want to lose *more* money?" Octavius asked tauntingly. "Last time we played, you bet five hundred *aurei* and lost."

"Maecenas!" Livia gasped. "You did not."

Maecenas turned a little red. "You seem to be forgetting that Caesar matched the bet."

They all laughed, for it surprised no one, and Octavius grinned. He agreed to play one game of dice, and they all returned inside the house, finding that a table had already been set up and the guests were anxious for the game to begin.

Octavius had become somewhat notorious for his dice games and the outrageous bets he placed, though he was so willing to give money away that no one considered him a true gambler.

Agrippa took his place beside Octavius and across from Maecenas. Balbus took the usual place of Rufus, though no one acted as if they remembered him. As the guest of honor, Octavius was chosen to go first. He took the dice into his hands, closed his eyes, and shook them. The entire room held their breaths.

Octavius opened his eyes, his glance finding Agrippa's briefly, before he rolled. And for a moment, Agrippa had never felt happier.

Then call it fate.

51

LIVIA DRUSILLA

JULY 33 BC

LIVIA ENTERED THE HOUSE slowly, for her head was cloaked and she could hardly see in the darkness of the entryway.

Julia ran ahead of her, laughing happily as she was scooped up into the arms of her mother, Scribonia, who stood in the atrium with a smile, kissing her daughter's face over and over.

"Oh, my sweet, sweet girl," Scribonia cooed. *"Mea filia dulcissima."*

"Mama, stop it!"

Julia playfully craned her neck away as Scribonia hugged her close, burying her face against Julia's hair, as if to breathe her in entirely, and at last Julia gave up the struggle and allowed her mother to hold her close. It was one of the weeks during the month when Livia sent Julia to spend time with her mother.

After a few moments of tender silence, Livia stepped forward from her hiding spot among the servants and lifted her cloak.

Scribonia looked up and froze, hugging Julia tighter, before she realized who it was and set Julia on the ground, though very reluctantly. Then she stood up straight, shoulders back, her lips pressed tightly together, which Livia knew held back words she wished to say to her former husband's new wife.

"Livia Drusilla," Scribonia said at last when Livia did not speak, inclining her head, ever so proper, ever so cold and formal. "I had not expected the pleasure of your company."

Scribonia had always been more proud than Livia, though Livia had been raised in a more affluent household. While Livia's father had been born into a patrician family, Scribonia was of plebian birth. But Livia had only ever known the warmth of her father and the docile nature of her mother, whereas Scribonia had learned the harsh realities of a lesser family forced to marry their daughters to wealthy men.

"I apologize for the intrusion," Livia said. "But I had to speak with you." She glanced

421

at Julia meaningfully. "In private. I could see no other way."

Scribonia studied her carefully for another beat before she nodded. "Very well."

She left Julia with her handmaidens, leading Livia into the triclinium, where there were already platters of food set out, very simple dishes of soup and bread, only enough to feed one adult and a child.

"I was planning to dine with Julia when she arrived," Scribonia said, eyeing the plates with a strange look, disdain and sorrow mingled into a frown.

"Please, leave everything as is," Livia said hurriedly. "I already ate, and this will only take a moment."

"Nonsense." Scribonia called over one of her slaves to bring more food from the kitchen. The slave returned with platters of fruit and small cakes. "Now, what did you wish to speak with me about?"

"I actually wished to speak with you about Julia."

"Oh?" Scribonia raised a brow, but her blue eyes flickered with worry.

"I fear for her," Livia said quietly, as if Julia could hear from somewhere in the house. "She is not safe with Caesar. He will use her to his own ends, even if it makes her unhappy."

But Scribonia only laughed. "Is that not what happens to all little girls? Why should mine be any different?"

Livia felt a sudden anger, a defiance that came from somewhere deep within, an older part of her which only meant it was the younger part of her, the child in her, who had hated the thought of marriage and her future lack of freedom.

"She is the daughter of Caesar," Livia said. "Do you not see what she could become?"

"Oh, darling, I know," Scribonia said, and her smile was sharp and mocking. Livia suddenly understood why her husband had hated her, but she herself only felt a vague pity. "We women never learn, do we?"

"Learn what?" Livia asked warily.

"Men are only in power because they fear what we could become," Scribonia answered with a smooth, low persuasiveness that had Livia leaning forward to catch every word. "They use their strength because they know we would outsmart them. We are kept at home and forced to have children because if we refused they would be no more. It is a man's world, Livia, but women have it in the palm of their hands and always fail to see it."

"You speak in riddles," Livia said coolly. "I only seek your daughter's best interest."

"Now that is a lie," Scribonia said with a smile. "You seek your own best interest, and that of your son. Do you think I did not know you wished Julia for your own Tiberius? But I do not blame you. Oh no, quite the contrary. If I was still in your place, I would fight to the death for my children."

"What are you saying?"

Scribonia's blue eyes glittered as though holding some knowledge yet unknown. "You are young, but you will see as you grow older that you have much more influence than you think behind closed doors. Be his wife, be the mother of his children, be the *mater* of Rome. Let Caesar be Caesar, and let men fight and make laws. It is easier to get what you want when no one is looking."

"You think I will scheme behind my husband's back?" Livia asked angrily, though she was only angry because she had already thought the same thing. "Then you do not know much at all, and we are more different than I had thought."

"Do not come to my house and demand my sympathy," Scribonia said, her smile turning cold. "I know why you wished to speak with me, and it was not about my daughter. It was never about *her*. You came to me because I alone know what life you have chosen to live. I alone know whose home you share, and the burdens that come with the rewards of a man who will stop at nothing to get what he desires. You came to me because you wanted my advice as much as my approval. You came to me because I failed in what you wish to achieve." Scribonia paused. "Tell me I am wrong."

Livia could hardly speak, her throat closing up, and she stared at the woman Caesar had cast out so carelessly for herself, a woman who knew when to fight and when to retreat, how to demand as much as acquiesce.

She was powerful but powerless, and Livia saw her own doomed fate reflected in every crease on Scribonia's face, every gray streak in her hair, every mocking smile, as if it were herself ten years in the future, alone save her children, nothing ahead except Death itself, looking at her and saying, *Oh, darling, but what did you expect?*

"Thank you for the meal," Livia said quietly. "I must be getting home soon."

Scribonia sighed. "You are intelligent, Livia, and strong. I see much of myself in you. But never forget that you are alone, and that if you do not fight for yourself and your children, no one else will."

Livia looked at her one last time before she left. She no longer pitied Scribonia, and though she did not hate her and never had, Livia found herself slightly envious, for Scribonia had lost Caesar, but she had also escaped, and Livia did know which life she herself would rather live.

"Goodbye, Scribonia."

It was time she chose.

⟶≫⟩ ⟨≪⟵

SEPTEMBER 33 BC

Livia walked along the colonnades of her father's house, the house she had grown up in, the house she had loved, and the house she had lost when she had been married off to Tiberius all those years ago.

The house would have been sold and her mother abandoned had Caesar not bought the house and supported Alfidia as she lived the rest of her days in quiet comfort.

She remembered running along these very columns, lounging in the courtyard with her parents' guests. Her memories were all tinted by the hot summers, so that she forgot the rougher winters, the endless civil wars, the fights between her mother and father over politics at dinner. It was as if a fog had rolled in her mind, so that when she turned back to look at the past, most was lost before she even thought to remember.

But the long, nearly endless summers, the happy chatter, the walks in the forum, the festivals in the sun, and her father, chasing her across the house until she could not run any longer, remained untouched in her memory, cutting through the fog as clear as day.

"You know, your father would have been proud."

Her mother appeared from the hall that went to the kitchens, where she was overseeing the large dinner they were to host for some of their oldest acquaintances. Livia was visiting to help oversee the party and to keep her mother company, who was so often alone.

"I wonder what he would think of me now," Livia said uneasily. For her father had died at Philippi, having committed suicide as Brutus had, at the hands of her husband and Marcus Antonius. "Do you ever miss him?"

"Every day," Alfidia said, then smiled gently. "But he is still with me. Here." She placed an aged hand over her heart. "He would have thought you more beautiful than ever."

"Oh Mother, why was I born a girl?" Livia asked, and she had to close her eyes before the tears came. She refused to cry. "I could have been great. I could have done so much more with my life."

"You are a mother," Alfidia said, a hint of reproach in her voice. "Is that not something great?"

Livia's cheeks burned, and she felt ashamed. She was speaking with her own mother after all. "Of course it is."

Alfidia walked over to her and took Livia's hand, kissing her knuckles. "You know, your father never wanted a son."

"No?"

"No," her mother said, squeezing her hand. "He always thought boys were too rash, too careless. They went to war, they killed, they hated. No, your father wanted a girl, because he knew any daughter of ours would be worth more than any boy. He knew you would be great because you are Livia Drusilla, and no one else."

"What if I do it all wrong?" Livia asked, barely more than a whisper. "What if I die and all this will have been for nothing?"

"Then you will die proudly," her mother said sternly, the most confident Livia had ever heard her speak, and for the first time, Livia saw the strength in Alfidia, which was not as a mother, or a wife, but as a woman, who had the power to give life as Mother Earth herself. "Because life is not about what you have done, but who you have become."

⤜⤜⤜ ⤛⤛⤛

"War is coming," Caesar murmured, glancing at Livia as she wove by the water garden, his couch set up near her loom, the morning sun casting their inner courtyard in a hazy glow.

Livia liked when Caesar watched her weave, for she enjoyed his eyes watching her hands move steadily at the loom, hypnotized by her womanly deftness and precision. Julia was still with Scribonia, so they had all the house to themselves, a soft breeze floating through the house, a slight chill in the air that heralded a cold winter.

"Antonius is still living with the Egyptian queen?" Livia asked without breaking her movements.

"In Alexandria, yes." Her husband paused. "He has not moved any of his army. I suspect they will sail to Athens when the time comes."

"They will get support from the Greeks, then?"

"That is certainly his plan," Caesar said. He yawned, as if the slow morning routine were lulling him to sleep. "It does not matter. We are smarter than those Greeks. My only worry is that before war may begin, we will need a reason."

Livia arched her brow. Caesar had not voiced this worry until now. "Has not Antonius already bequeathed Roman lands to their children? Has he not already claimed Caesarion as the heir of *Divus Iulius?* What more reason could you need?"

"Those might be reasons enough for *me* to go to war," her husband replied wryly, "but not so for the Roman people. I would need some sort of proof of his treason. A document. Even a letter. Something that would truly scandalize every man who calls himself Roman."

Livia paused, thinking. "And what about a will?"

"A will?"

"It is better than a letter, for whatever is written there will be law. Nothing would terrify the Roman people into action more than if their master sold them into the slavery of Egyptian princelings."

425

Caesar's brow furrowed. "His will would be held secure in Egypt, or else stored with the Vestal Virgins. It is a crime to open such a sealed document."

Livia smirked. "Not if the contents hold a worse crime."

"But how can we be sure he has indeed written so damning a will?" Caesar asked pensively.

"We would need someone close to him to confirm our suspicions." She paused. "Or even fabricate them. Perhaps a witness, or someone who heard from one, so that our accusations are all the more credible."

"I think I know just the man," Caesar said with a sly smile. "I shall write to Plancus. If anyone could discover the contents of Antonius' will, it would be him."

"Are you so sure he would reveal them to you?" Livia asked cautiously.

Plancus had been the one to betray the Senate as Antonius grew in power, and she did not trust him. But sometimes the most untrustworthy people were more trustworthy by the very fact that one may be sure they were never loyal.

Caesar smirked. "At the right price." He pondered the plan silently, so that the only sound in the courtyard were the soft creaks of the loom and the distant trickle of water. "If I reveal his will, that might be enough to convince the Roman people of war. But it must not be war with Antonius, at least only as a supporter of Cleopatra. She is the true enemy. That is what Antonius has always mistaken. He may try his best to conquer the East, but there can only be one ruler of those people, and it is a queen."

Men are only in power because they fear what we could become.

"If Caesarion has been named his heir," Livia said quietly, "you ought to name yours."

Caesar glanced at her, and they both knew what she was thinking. But before he could answer, the porter appeared with an urgent message. It was addressed to Caesar, from the household of Tiberius, Livia's former husband.

He read the note carefully, without speaking, and stared at it for a long time. Then he looked up, his face calm, and he watched her carefully as he spoke. "Tiberius Claudius Nero...is dead."

Livia stopped weaving. Her heart beat steadily within her chest. The world seemed to be opened for her once more, and the weakness she had always felt since she was a little girl became her greatest strength, the same subtle strength she had seen in Alfidia.

She was no longer a wife or a mother, but the very vessel of the gods above, the author of her own fate, the woman she was always meant to become.

For she was Livia Drusilla, and that was enough.

"Send a message to my sons," Livia said, rising to her feet. Caesar looked at her warily but did not protest. "Tell them their mother welcomes them to their new home."

Her fate had just begun.

52

GAIUS OCTAVIUS

NOVEMBER 33 BC

O CTAVIUS LOVED ROME IN autumn. It was when the city eased her choking humidity at last, and rain fell, cooling the evenings. His health suffered in the summer heat and in too much cold, but as the leaves reddened and browned, the stone streets gleaming with a fresh shower, he felt he could endure the city a little longer.

But this year Rome had changed. Long gone were the famines, the poor spilling out into the streets, mobs protesting in the forum, the city slowing to a halt amidst civil war. His recent conquests in Sicily and Illyricum had brought back many spoils, and Agrippa's work as an *aedile curules* had breathed life back into Rome.

Grain once more flowed through the ports, and construction of new public baths and basilicas and forums could be heard from everywhere, metal breaking stone, the shouts of workers, the creaking of wooden pulleys. Restorations of the sewers and aqueducts had brought fresh water to every corner of the city as well as clean pipes and streets.

And this was only the beginning. Octavius knew there was much more work to be done if he planned to keep these improvements from crumbling into neglect and ruin as they had done for centuries. There needed new offices to be made, more specialization of tasks, and increased administration of the city's oversight.

His guidance would be needed, of course, for these new changes to be implemented in an organized manner. Through the Senate, Octavius planned to lead forth the city like a blind man by the arm, until he might hand off his creation to someone he trusted to continue the work he had begun.

He stepped out of the *curia*, his back aching from the many long hours sitting. Senate meetings tended to drag on more than was necessary, but Octavius understood the importance of appearing as if the old ways had not changed.

Indeed, today they voted to revive countless ancient festivals and rites that have died out or been forgotten in the past generations of civil war. He knew, of course, that many senators secretly considered it useless, and viewed these changes as resuscitating an archaic past that no longer existed. But Octavius merely considered it a reminder of Rome's divine origins and their right to rule.

His personal armed guard followed him wherever he went. Although some criticized it as a show of military strength, Octavius would not risk his vulnerable position of power to another assassination attempt.

The forum was busy today, with markets and stalls filled with bustling crowds, and senators pouring out of the *curia,* looking forward to relaxing in the baths.

Octavius himself was transported home, where he had installed his own modest, private baths. He spent much time here, especially since Tiberius and Drusus had moved in after their father passed away. Octavius tried to avoid encountering them, though he still held up his end of the deal, and both boys had been enrolled in the same education as Marcellus.

Once he became adjusted to the heat of the warm bath, Octavius moved from the *tepidarium* to the *caldarium.* He stepped into the scalding water of the hot bath and slipped under until the water level was below his chin.

Agrippa and Maecenas had always told him he spent too much time in the baths, but they did not understand the peace it brought him, the shelter from the outside world, where illness and war faded to witty lines of poetry and epic tragedies only found in stories.

His life made sense in the baths, when he closed his eyes, and the heat curled around him like a blanket, like a fog, so that his existence was as weightless as floating in water.

Footsteps at the door roused him.

He wondered who it was, for he had strict rules not to be bothered unless it was an emergency, or if he called for the *strigilis.* It could not be Livia, for she hated bathing, and never came near them. Besides, she would be occupied with the children or some other task of the house.

A shadowed, quiet figure filled the doorway.

"Hello," said the voice.

Agrippa.

Octavius felt his heart quicken its pulse immediately, but he forced himself to remain calm. He raised a brow at Agrippa, who watched him from the entryway, leaning against the frame of the door.

"How did you get in?" Octavius asked at last.

Agrippa's eyes traveled down his face, to the narrow strip of his chest above water, before reluctantly returning to his face. "Livia let me in."

They both stared at each other until Agrippa blushed. It was no secret why he was here.

Something had shifted between them since his return from Illyricum in January, when he had laid aside his pride and gave himself, bit by bit, to Agrippa. Not entirely, but it was enough for them to blush when they caught each other's eyes, even in a room full of people, and remember the stolen nights and hidden encounters over the past year.

"Do you want to join?" Octavius asked.

Agrippa hesitated, then walked inside, switching his sandals for the wooden ones so that he would not burn his feet. He came to the edge of the bath and stopped, still fully clothed.

Octavius held his breath as he waited, before Agrippa pulled his tunic over his head in a single motion, and his naked body seemed to quiver under Octavius' gaze, the broad shoulders and the indents of his hips more soft and inviting than ever before.

This was the first time they had ever been in the baths together since long before their first kiss. Octavius remembered bathing in Puteoli, near his stepfather's villa, when the wars ahead were as distant as stars on the horizon.

Nothing had seemed real then except Agrippa's hands on his skin, smoothing oil in painful, dizzying sweeps. Somehow, he had convinced himself it all had meant nothing. *Nothing, nothing, nothing.*

Agrippa climbed into the bath and sat down opposite him. His eyes did not quite reach Octavius', as if between them there were still oceans, as if he did not simply have to touch him and he would unravel beneath him. The thought sent his pulse lifting like the wings of a bird taking flight.

"I wish there was more time," Octavius murmured as Agrippa settled in the water.

"More time?"

But he seemed to understand what he meant, closing his eyes and leaning back until the water rose up his neck. Agrippa always wanted to hear him say it.

"For us," Octavius added reluctantly. "Before war with Antonius."

At the end of the year, the alliance of the *Tresviri* would legally expire, and there was no doubt that neither of them wished to renew any more dead promises. The time for false friendships had long passed, and now one of them must step up and become master of Rome.

For now, however, an uneasy peace held a spell over them, and Octavius would not dare declare war until he was certain the people would follow him into battle. Antonius, meanwhile, had not stirred his forces in the East, and whether this was on account of his ignorance of Octavius' growing support in Rome or simple indifference, it mattered not. Octavius would be ready when the time came, and Antonius would have to fight him to the death or surrender.

"You do not think we shall survive," Agrippa said with a hint of surprise.

Octavius hesitated. "Not exactly. There is always risk in war."

"Then what is different now?"

He looked away from Agrippa's keen glance. He saw too much in him, and it was too late to close himself up again. "Everything," Octavius said.

"Everything?"

"If I defeat Antonius," he replied, looking at him, "I shall be the savior of the Republic."

Agrippa shook his head, a sad smile on his face. "You will always be Octavius to me."

The words stung more than he had expected, and Octavius suddenly wished to cry, but he would not shed tears for a life he had so willingly left behind. "Not to the rest of the world."

"Since when does the rest of the world matter more than me?" Agrippa asked jokingly, but Octavius sensed that he was not joking, not in the slightest.

"Why must it be one or the other?" Octavius smirked, playing it off as he had always done. "Right now I have you, tomorrow I may have the world."

But the joke fell flat, and Octavius nearly winced at Agrippa's pained glance. How many times had he teased Agrippa since they were young, wanting to see his reaction if he pushed it too far? How many times had he wondered what would happen if he took Agrippa's face in his hands and kissed him, showing him that every lie he told had merely disguised the truth?

"Tomorrow we may die," Agrippa countered after a pause, and his sea-green eyes were dark, as dark as the depths of the sea. "The world would not so much as blink an eye."

"Perhaps," Octavius said, struggling to keep his voice level. "But if we live, the world will have no choice but to look at us. We will have no choice but to rule her."

"There is always a choice," Agrippa said with a wry smile. "You could leave it all behind. You could lay down your powers and appoint someone new. We could forget about politics and war and death and live our own lives, far away from the rest of the world, happy until the end of our days."

Octavius stared at him, his heart beating wildly in his chest. Agrippa was only joking, he knew, but at the same time, everything had come down to this. He felt deep in his bones that the life Agrippa described was nothing more than a dream, that could only happen in another life, or else in a story filled with other impossible things, like sirens and giants and heroes.

In this life, Octavius had only ever known one story, one ending, and it was more than a glorious death, more than endless conquering. *That is how you know, my child, whether you are destined for greatness.*

"You know it has never been a choice," Octavius said, his voice low. "You were never a choice, but neither was my fate. I cannot simply walk away from it." *Not like you,* were the unspoken words he did not say.

But Agrippa heard them anyway. He always did. "I know," he said softly.

"Do you?"

Agrippa nodded but did not speak.

Octavius stood up carefully and picked up the flask of oil left by the side of the bath. He flashed a half-hearted smile. "Would you?"

With a half-smile of his own, Agrippa stood up and came before him, taking the flask and pouring some oil on his hand. Octavius turned around so that Agrippa would not see how much he needed his touch, how much he desired it.

Hands gently touched his shoulders, moving down his arms, rubbing the oil down to the wrists. Octavius shut his eyes as Agrippa's hands returned between his shoulder blades, down the ridges of his spine, his knuckles brushing the small of his back.

Octavius turned around, facing him. He touched a hesitant hand on Agrippa's chest, the curling hair damp from the bath. Agrippa looked at him, startled, as if he had forgotten that Octavius could touch him, that they were both only a breath apart.

They seemed to start forward at the same time, Agrippa sliding his arms around Octavius' waist urgently, Octavius kissing the soft skin of his neck, the stubble on his jaw, his cheek. He rested his forehead against Agrippa's, their mouths pausing before they kissed, lips hardly touching. His heart was like a wild animal, trapped in his chest, and he felt his pulse everywhere at once, as hot and flaming as the furnaces working below the baths.

"Do you remember that night in the carriage?" Octavius asked in a whisper. "The oath you swore to me?"

"Yes." Agrippa tightened his hold on Octavius. *"All my life."*

"The rest of the world shall swear that oath to me," Octavius said, almost feverishly, and he felt that tug in his heart, the Weaver pulling taut at his thread. *Look at me.* "The world shall be loyal to us forever. We shall rule the people together."

He wanted to press his mouth to Agrippa's but he held himself back, their hands sliding across each other's skin slowly, still wet from the water mingled with oil. A calloused palm passed over his abdomen, settling into the indent of his hip. Octavius shut his eyes against the familiar rippling wave of want.

Agrippa was silent for a long moment, his fingertips grazing Octavius' shoulder, his eyes half-closed. "I will always love you, Octavius, beyond death. No oath can speak what is already written on my heart."

Octavius felt the impossibility of their love cloak him like Death, hiding a small, flickering flame between them. He shivered, pulling Agrippa close and kissing him, as if only then he could speak all the words he wished to say, unwilling to let go of this moment when it felt like it could be the last.

Look at me.

Octavius squeezed his eyes shut, ignoring the voice that was only the past, knowing that if he looked, if he opened the door, he would find all the memories he wished to forget, the hand on his chin, his back pressed down against his will, the helplessness he once felt and then never lost, like an iron chain around his neck.

Look at me.

Their kisses grew deeper and wild, Octavius threading one hand in Agrippa's thick curls as they sank down into the bath, tangled in each other's arms, one leg slipping between his like the day they had wrestled, which had always meant so much more than a fight.

And as the pleasure rose hot in his veins, and his legs shook, and they hardly kissed, the world turned white behind his eyelids, as white as the hottest flame, as blinding as staring straight into the sun, and he heard the voice as clear and bright as a song.

I am your destiny.

Octavius looked.

⠶⠶⠶⠶⠶ ⠶⠶⠶⠶⠶

JANUARY 32 BC

"This is dangerous," Agrippa said, eyeing Octavius warily from across the carriage. "They might have you killed."

The wheels rattled loudly across the stone street as they entered the outskirts of Rome on the Via Appia. Octavius wondered if they would survive the poorly maintained road, let alone the days ahead.

"If they have not killed me by now," Octavius said wryly, "they will not kill me today."

Agrippa shook his head, almost smiling before he frowned. "Then you have more faith in the Senate than me."

Octavius raised a brow. "It is not faith."

"Then what is it?"

"Call it friendship," Octavius said mockingly.

Agrippa's eyes briefly looked up at the ceiling, then settled on Octavius once more. There was a grudging fondness in those Tiber green eyes that were at once familiar and strange, the same eyes of the boy who had followed him from Apollonia, and the new ones of the man he loved, a life he had never dreamed could be true until now.

"The speech of Sosius has stirred Antonius' supporters in Rome," Agrippa said. "You are walking into the lion's den."

"But the lion is not there. And I am one of the *Tresviri*."

"Not anymore."

"Sosius has denounced me in front of the Senate," Octavius said, a touch angrily. "If I do not denounce Antonius, I might as well lay down my powers now."

Agrippa shook his head with a sigh. "You are inviting war."

Octavius smirked. "I am not inviting war. I am demanding it."

Agrippa sat back, looking out the window. They were passing into the center of the city, the temple of Jupiter rising on the top of the hill as they approached the forum.

"The people will not want to go to war against one of their own over nothing," Agrippa said. "Or worse than nothing—over power. For power benefits very few."

A fist clenched his heart. Octavius wished he could make Agrippa see what he saw, to draw back the veil on his eyes and reveal the destiny he saw for himself. But he knew Agrippa wanted little to do with destiny, and he would not understand why Octavius wished for more than the stars when they could already see them so well from Earth. Agrippa loved him, however, so he would never desert him, and for now that was all that mattered.

"This is not just about power," Octavius said firmly. "This is about Roman tradition, Roman values, *Roman* power. Antonius would hand it all over to an Egyptian queen simply because she fucks him."

Inexplicably, Agrippa flinched. "I suppose it all comes down to sex, then."

"Oh, *mi Agrippa,*" Octavius murmured. "Did you not know?"

The carriage slowed to a stop. Octavius and Agrippa remained in their seats as his armed bodyguard secured a route to the *curia*. They looked at each other in silence, as if it could be the last time.

"For the Republic," Agrippa said, hardly a whisper, his eyes almost mocking, almost sincere.

Octavius almost smiled. "For us."

He did not wait for Agrippa to answer, opening the carriage door and stepping out on the road. His guards surrounded him, each strapped with a sharp *gladius* and sword, their armor glittering under the early morning sun.

The Senate was meeting right now, and Octavius planned to attend. His guard led him down the Via Sacra, past the towering Basilica Aemilia and the gleaming temple of Vesta with her holy fire, through the parting crowds of people gathering in the forum, waiting for the end of the hearing. At the other end of the forum stood the *curia,* small and modest under the Temple of Jupiter's long shadow.

The tall wooden doors creaked as they opened, revealing the rows of white-robed senators seated around the shining marble floor in its rich greens and reds, the room quiet save for murmuring echoes as all eyes turned towards him. The current consuls, Gaius Sosius and Domitius Ahenobarbus, both loyal to Antonius, stood up in silent protest at the intrusion, their faces turning livid when they saw it was him.

Octavius walked across the floor, each step loud and measured, his entire body humming with anticipation but his mind calm and quiet, counting the steps it took to the seat placed between the two consuls. He looked around at the senators' faces as they waited impatiently for him to speak.

"Conscript Fathers," Octavius said, his voice ringing out clear and steady. He smiled, but it was not kind, and there was a shiver in the hall like wind rustling leaves. "Let us begin."

⟫⟫ ⟪⟪

FEBRUARY 32 BC

The torchlights of the courtyard flickered, casting dark shadows across Livia's face. She was more beautiful in the day when the light caught her dark eyes and lit them from the inside like gold right before it melted.

At night the darkness sharpened her features, so that the cut of her mouth, so soft in the sun, was harsh and cold, too cold to kiss, as though she no longer belonged to the world of the living. Her beauty at night was to be feared, and Octavius had to look away.

"There is not much time now that I have denounced Antonius publicly," he said quietly. "War must be declared."

"We have already decided to wait. It is pointless to discuss alternatives now," Livia answered calmly.

She was more distant lately, not bitter but not sweet either, as if some part of her had hardened away from him. Still, he could reach her if he tried, and they still found love in the long months between wars. But there was also an untouchable side to her now, in her womanhood, that he simply could not understand.

"I know," Octavius said sullenly. He had hoped Livia would hear his worries and indulge in a debate instead of returning his own cold logic, but it seemed her mind was elsewhere. "Antonius has assembled his troops in Ephesus. They say he has eight hundred ships."

"Does he have the men to man those ships?" Livia asked dubiously. It was the question everyone was discussing as the inevitable war loomed ever closer.

"Let us hope he does not." Octavius grinned with a humor he did not feel. "Maybe he will if everyone in the Senate defects to him."

Livia almost smiled. "You did say anyone may flee to Antonius if they wished."

Before Octavius could respond, there was an unusual commotion in the atrium, voices raised and feet hurrying on the floor. Livia raised a worried brow, as neither of them had expected more company.

But a few moments later Agrippa ran into the courtyard, escorted by his porter, who had express instructions to only welcome certain persons without permission, and even then quickly and quietly, lest the entire neighborhood be aware of who visited at such late hours.

Octavius was on his feet the instant Agrippa entered the room, his heart pounding. Bad news always took flight where one was not looking. "What is it?"

Agrippa glanced wildly at both of them. "It is Octavia. Antonius has divorced her. He sent men to evict her from his house. She is with Attica now. I believe she was too ashamed to come here."

At first, all was quiet. Octavius imagined his sister and all her children abandoned, dishonored, and Marcellus as well, the only hope for an heir of his blood, insulted by a man who would choose a false goddess over his own wife, his own family. He felt his chest heat up with a rage so hot and consuming it was completely calm, the still quiet before the most terrible storm.

Then he spoke, and the words fell ominously in the silence. "Antonius has declared war."

53

Marcus Vipsanius Agrippa

FEBRUARY 32 BC

Agrippa had never seen Octavius this angry in his life.

"He shall pay for his crimes," Octavius said in so low and measured a voice that even Livia glanced up at him in surprise. "I promise you that."

Octavius seemed to hardly notice anything, not the children milling about the atrium with all of their belongings, a few of them crying, nor Octavia who stood across from him, nor Agrippa and Livia at their sides, nor his entire household waiting for his instruction as the head of their family.

Octavia merely looked at him, her eyes dry and wintry cold. "I am done with promises."

"You are his wife," Octavius said, slowly, as if he were explaining something very important to a child. "And he has insulted you, and in so doing he has insulted me and the Roman people. It is not a promise but an oath, and it is an oath of vengeance."

"Do not blame me for your wars, brother," Octavia said, her voice chilly. "I am only a woman after all."

"Wars have been waged for much less," Agrippa murmured, earning him a sharp glare from both Octavia and her brother. He had the urge to laugh, but he knew he would earn more than a glare for that.

Livia barely hid a smile, then frowned, schooling her features. "Your brother is right. Come live with us, Octavia."

"No." Octavia stood tall, her skin glowing in the faint moonlight from above. "I shall not burden you with my lot."

"Nonsense!" Livia exclaimed, resting a tight hand on Octavia's arm. "You are my sister. Stay, for Jove's sake."

"Where shall you go otherwise?" Octavius asked quietly. "You will stay here. And that is not a request."

Octavia looked at her brother with such righteous defiance that Agrippa was surprised when Octavius did not burst into flames then and there. Finally, she nodded, and kissed her brother's cheek, then Livia's, though she was cool and distant as the stars.

"I shall forever be in your debt."

It sounded more resigned than grateful. She returned to her children and aided the servants in herding them to their new bedrooms.

Octavius sighed once she was gone.

Livia looked at Agrippa with a light smile. "And where is my sweet Attica?" she asked, clearly attempting to change the subject.

"She went to check on her father," Agrippa said quietly.

Livia eyed him worriedly. "How is he?"

Agrippa only shook his head. Atticus had not been doing well for many weeks now.

"Ah," Livia said, her voice sorrowful as a bird in the night. "If it is not war, it is age!"

"It is life," Octavius interrupted, not in the mood to philosophize. In fact, he seemed angrier than ever. "We ought to declare war tomorrow. Antonius is a traitor and a coward. The people shall be outraged at his treatment of my sister. Our troops are ready. They will follow us with or without the Senate's approval."

Agrippa placed a hand on his arm without thinking. "Octavius."

Livia glanced at the touch between them and raised a brow, but Octavius merely turned to Agrippa. "Yes?"

He quickly dropped his hand to his side, ignoring the way his cheeks burned at his momentary forgetfulness. "It would be rash to declare war now. The Senate needs only one reason to side with Antonius if you do not play your cards right."

"What other choice do I have?" Octavius asked, almost regretfully. "If I allow him to disrespect my sister, to mock our most ancient traditions in foreign streets, to claim the illegitimate child of Julius Caesar and an Egyptian queen as his heir, I am only proving to the world that I am as weak and cowardly as he says."

"It is not a crime to divorce your wife," Agrippa replied grimly. "He must commit a crime worthy of war, not merely disapproval, to move the Senate to action. You said it yourself that he has to be the one to draw first blood. Then you must wait for him to do so."

Octavius shared a knowing glance with Livia that Agrippa did not understand, though he was certain they were scheming something dangerous. "And when he does?"

Agrippa felt uneasy, but the answer was obvious, and despite wishing otherwise, there was no avoiding battle when there was hate between men. His eyes flickered to Livia, whose unforgiving presence as a woman in conversations of war had always surprised him. But she was smirking, her eyes glinting like newly sharpened steel, and when Agrippa did not speak, she spoke the words for him.

"We go to war."

⤜⟫⟫ ⟪⟪⤛

APRIL 32 BC

Quintus Caecilius Pomponianus Atticus died on the last day of March after three months of seriously failing health. Agrippa and Attica had attended the funeral and aided in the burial at the family tomb along the Via Appia.

At first, Attica had been inconsolable, refusing to speak, refusing to eat, and she did not interact with anyone except her children. But after a week, Attica began to look at Agrippa again, to truly see him instead of simply bearing him, and she would speak more often and eat a little.

"Do you wish to retire for a few weeks in Baiae?" Agrippa asked when he came home after the day's affairs. Attica was resting on a couch, her handmaiden pressing a cool cloth on her forehead, a slave fanning her body. The heat of the approaching summer was quickly growing each day. "It shall be cooler on the coast, and the sea breeze would do you good."

Attica sighed, and he saw an unwilling tear slide down the side of her face. It did not take much for her to cry these days. Her voice was thick and halting. "No, I do not. I wish to remain here, on this couch, and never leave."

Agrippa crouched beside her, taking one of her limp hands in his. Her skin was burning hot to the touch. He looked at her handmaiden worriedly, who refused to meet his eyes. "I know you are grieving—"

"No," Attica interrupted, pulling her hand away. "You do not know."

He sighed. It seemed the more he tried to reach her, the more she pushed her away, as if in tending for her father she had also helped him across the river Acheron in the Underworld, and while her body had returned among the living, her soul had remained below.

"I love you, Attica," Agrippa murmured, kissing her cheek, though she turned her head away resentfully. "Do not go where I cannot follow."

Just then the porter approached and announced the presence of the *Imperator* Caesar. Agrippa stood up, his heart suddenly pounding in his chest at the unexpected visit. A few

438

moments later Octavius strode into the house, in his hands a small wooden box.

"What are you doing here?" Agrippa asked, unable to help himself, his eyes glancing involuntarily to Attica.

Octavius raised a brow. "I came to pay my respects."

At this, Attica half-lifted her head, eyeing Octavius warily. She turned to Agrippa, then to Octavius, and nodded. Her handmaiden helped her sit up as Octavius approached her couch.

"May we speak alone?" Octavius asked her, without looking at Agrippa.

Agrippa almost started, for it was not usually allowed for women to be alone with men other than their husband. But Caesar, of course, was an exception, and he dared not refuse and anger both his wife and Octavius.

Attica stared at Octavius for a long time, so long that Agrippa thought she would never answer, until she finally spoke, her voice weak but sure. "Yes."

Agrippa looked between Attica and Octavius, sick at heart, but he would not disobey both their wishes at the same time. He left for his office and remained there, answering a few letters to keep himself occupied, but his mind kept wandering. He swore he heard faint voices from somewhere in the house, though he could not tell if they were in anger or not.

At last, there was a knock at the door.

Octavius entered. He looked solemn, but he glanced at Agrippa intently, walking over to where he sat at his desk. "Are you quite busy?"

Agrippa paused, setting down his stylus, his heart renewing its quick beat. "I thought you came to see Attica."

Octavius's expression was unreadable, staring at him. "I did."

"Then what news?" Agrippa knew Octavius did not come here simply to pay his respects.

He frowned, glancing away. "I am sure you heard of the slander Antonius' men have recently spread about me. He sent me a letter with the same accusations."

Agrippa almost winced. It was not uncommon for political rivals to demean their opponent by revealing their private affairs, but this felt more dangerous, as Octavius was already so vulnerable to such attacks.

"He claimed you have had multiple affairs," Agrippa said, remaining as calm and measured as he could. "That is not anything to fear." He paused, remembering the slander in previous years concerning Octavius' relations with Caesar and Hirtius. "It may even aid your cause."

"I do not fear what he said," Octavius said impatiently, guessing at Agrippa's thoughts. "I fear what he did *not* say. I fear he knows more than he says. I fear the woman."

"Cleopatra?" Agrippa asked in mild surprise.

"Yes. She is queen for a reason. Antonius may be blind in his love, but I assure you she is not."

"Well *I* assure you that if he knew about anything else, he would have already said it," Agrippa answered, trying to sound confident, though his heart held a sliver of doubt. "There is not much more time to sway the people to his side. They both know that."

"I suppose you are right, but I still worry," Octavius said pensively, a rare glimmer of insecurity in his eyes as he glanced at Agrippa, almost longingly, almost painfully. "That is all."

"I know." Agrippa wished to be close to him, to touch him, but he resisted. Attica was somewhere in the house, tearful and feverish, and he did not have the heart to betray her in grief.

Octavius seemed to sense this, and looked away, sighing. "There is something else."

Agrippa's heart dropped. There was always something else with Octavius. "What is it?"

"I have been in communication with Plancus and his nephew Titius," Octavius said. "They do not believe Antonius shall win. Plancus claims many will abandon him before the time comes. Death often makes honest men out of liars, after all."

"And you trust Plancus?"

"No," he said curtly. "But he has something that I want. He claims to have proof."

Agrippa almost did not want to ask. "Proof of what?"

A sly smile curved across Octavius' face. "That Antonius has drawn first blood."

He did not elaborate, promising more information in due time. Octavius left soon after with little other news to report besides the names of those who had fled to Antonius.

Agrippa gratefully rejoined Attica, who was no longer lying down but seated upright, the small wooden box Octavius had brought opened on her lap. Inside were small scrolls of parchment, the seals broken, piled in the box haphazardly. Attica turned to Agrippa as he approached, her face still flushed and pale but her eyes bright, nearly glowing.

"He gave me letters," Attica said breathlessly, her hands tightening possessively around the box. "Letters my father wrote to him."

"He did?" Agrippa could not contain his surprise. "What did he say to you?"

Attica glanced at him hesitantly, as if she were choosing her words carefully. "He said my father was a great man. And that he thought I might wish to read through his letters, as he wrote to Caesar about much of his thoughts and philosophies." Her fingertips brushed one of the scrolls. "Caesar was interested in his extensive knowledge of family histories, and they kept a close correspondence while my father was alive."

"I see." Agrippa watched as Attica closed the wooden box in slow, deliberate movements, and stroked the carvings on the lid reverently. "Was that all?"

Attica did not look at him, tracing the carved flowers and vines, the swords and shields, and the small figure of Athena at the center, the origin of her family name. He sensed that she was deciding whether to tell him or not.

Finally, she turned towards him, a calm fierceness in her eyes that Agrippa had not seen so clearly since their wedding day, as when the sun shone out of gray skies, and for a moment, he forgot to breathe.

"I think I understand now," she said, seeing him as one did a ghost, or as the dead saw the living, far, far away. "I think I see why you love him."

Agrippa was silent, his face hot. He did not know what to say, and for the first time in his life, he wished he had remained at home with his father all those years ago, exploring the vast rambling countryside—a simple life among simple people—so that he would never have known so much pain.

"Husband," Attica said tenderly. "Let us go to Baiae."

⟫⟫ ⟪⟪

JULY 32 BC

Octavius sat at his desk, hands crossed in front of him. Livia stood at his side, the hand she placed on his shoulder graced with a gold ring, inset with a large emerald stone.

A lamp in the corner burned, but the office remained dark, and Agrippa could hardly make out Octavius' expression as Lucius Munatius Plancus and his nephew, Marcus Titius, entered the office. Agrippa had been briefed before the meeting, but he was still skeptical of the plan.

Plancus bowed his head. *"Ave, Imperator Caesar divi fili, morituri te salutant."*

"There is no need for such formality, Plancus," Caesar said mildly. "Please, sit. We have much to discuss."

"Thank you, Caesar," Plancus said, clearing his throat nervously.

He sat down in the chair near Agrippa, who was reminded suddenly that Plancus and his nephew were quite at the mercy of Octavius. While Plancus was opportunistic at best and cowardly at worst, he was ultimately a military man and understood the risks of defecting to Octavius at so precarious a time.

"Well?" Octavius asked, raising a brow. "Have you secured the document?"

Plancus hesitated. He scratched at his chin, then glanced at his nephew, who was silent and watchful, waiting submissively for his uncle to speak. "Well, no."

"No?" Octavius repeated icily, and Plancus visibly winced.

"You see, Caesar, Antonius has entrusted the will with the Vestal Virgins," Plancus explained cautiously, not wishing to offend his new benefactor. "They shall not take orders from *me.*"

The implication was clear, and Octavius frowned.

"But the will is indeed with the Vestal Virgins?" Livia asked.

Plancus glanced at her in surprise, and his tone was nothing short of patronizing. "Naturally."

"He could have kept it stored in Egypt," Agrippa clarified quietly.

"Ah, yes," Plancus said, nodding at Agrippa, then frowned, as if the thought disturbed him. He had been, of course, one of Antonius' men long before he deserted him. "But no. He did not. His means may be Eastern but he has his eyes set on the West."

"And you have seen the contents of the will?" Octavius asked, leaning forward intently.

Plancus nodded hurriedly. "Of course. I witnessed it."

"When you last wrote to me," Octavius said slowly, "you claimed the will was criminal enough to turn the head of Jove himself." He paused, raising a brow, and Plancus had the grace to blush. "Is that still true?"

"I would not be here if it were not," Plancus replied, an ounce of pride returning to his voice. "I would not risk the wrath of the Roman people for nothing."

Titius shifted in his seat impatiently. "Tell him, uncle."

"Patience, Titius." For Plancus knew, as any good politician and gambler knew, when to hide his cards or reveal them, and the last will and testament of Marcus Antonius could be the best bargaining chip of all. "The will contained many of the usual technicalities of a man in love and at the brink of war, but there were three particular claims with which any sensible Roman would take issue. That was when I realized he was no longer the same man I knew and loved."

"Naturally," Octavius said with an edge of mockery.

Plancus ignored his tone and maintained an air of the gravest importance. "The first, as I am sure you heard, was the legitimacy of Caesarion, the illegitimate child of Queen Cleopatra and Julius Caesar. The second was the naming of his children by Cleopatra as his heirs. But in the end, it was the third clause that truly shocked me, for it goes against every shred of dignity and piety that a Roman citizen ought to hold dear, and shall convince the Roman people that Antonius is no longer a Roman man, but under the spell of a foreign witch."

Octavius nearly smiled at the theatrics. Plancus knew he only had one chance to sell his story, and it had yet to deliver its final act. "And what was that?"

Plancus looked Octavius dead in the eyes, and Agrippa knew then that everything was about to change. "He wished that his body be buried in the city of Alexandria, beside the

Egyptian queen Cleopatra."

54

CLEOPATRA VII
PHILOPATOR

NOVEMBER 32 BC

C LEOPATRA HAD ALWAYS LOVED libraries.

She would spend hours in the Mouseion of Alexandria when she was younger, the colonnades sparkling with marble, scrolls of papyrus piled up to the high ceilings, another world within a world.

Her tutor, Philostratos, had taught her oration and philosophy before she was ten years old, and she once could recite all twenty-four books of the Iliad without missing a single line. Dusty scrolls on arithmetic, astronomy, and alchemy had taught her everything from the precise measurements of the heavens and their movements to the fatal difference between medicine and poison.

Later she would teach herself Latin, Egyptian, Aramaic, as well as Syriac, Arabic, Median, Parthian, and even some Ethiopian. Not one person entered her court with whom she could not speak.

But it mattered not. Still, men did not respect her. At least, not as a woman.

As a queen, they respected her very much. Enough to wish to kill her, to send armies to her borders and threaten her power. But as a woman? No, they did not respect her, no matter how many languages she spoke, nor how many men she killed.

Cleopatra remembered returning home from the library one day, when her older sisters Berenice IV and Cleopatra VI were still alive. She had just memorized the lines of the Iliad where Menelaus and the other Greek war chiefs promised to avenge the abduction of Helen of Troy. Cleopatra did not understand, she told her sister Berenice. Why did Helen not simply escape?

Her sister had looked at her sadly, eyes old and wary beyond her years, and lay a soft hand against her cheek. She had been like a mother to her ever since theirs had died soon after Cleopatra was born. "Maybe she did not want to."

Cleopatra would only realize later how young her sister had been, and by then it was too late. Once she had left with her father into exile, Cleopatra would never see Berenice again.

Like her sister, Helen of Troy had been a woman surrounded by powerful men and trying to survive.

For that is what no one understood. Helen was a survivor. Menelaus married her after pillaging her town, and then Paris besieged her husband's city until she ran away with him. Was it love? Was it politics? Those were the questions of men; women asked very different ones.

Cleopatra had learned to survive ever since her father had been exiled from Egypt and dragged her along with him. They had spent the next year on the move, first in Rhodes, then in Athens, and finally in Italy. Pompeius the Great hosted them in his magnificent villa, tucked away in the ancient Alban hills near Praeneste, a lofty town overlooking breathtaking valleys of green.

She had been accustomed to the high-storied, bustling streets of Alexandria, where gods walked among mortals and knowledge was as old as the waters of the Nile. This rambling Italia was the wide wilderness, lurking with very different gods, and they had terrified her.

But it was the first time she had encountered the Romans, a people who loved war more than anything except for, perhaps, their sprawling villas in the countryside, whose splendor and solitude were prized above all else.

Cleopatra had thought them a rather tiresome lot, so concerned with morality that they could not even enjoy the pleasures of earth before they died. There was a rule for everything, for everyone, men, women, slaves—even the cattle and crops could not graze or grow for too long. They secretly detested her family's Greek heritage and their customs, though they were schooled in Greek philosophy and poetry. They begrudged her people's love of revelry, though they drank their wine.

Oh, those poor Romans! They believed themselves knowledgeable, but power was not knowledge in the end. And men! They knew so little. Cleopatra pitied them.

Worse were Roman men. They prided themselves on their manliness, their *virtus*, so different from the Greeks and their lovers, from Plato and his beloved symposium. Nay, the Romans were real men. They took women in marriage and in bed. Curious—for how little, how little they knew about women!

After all, what was Apollo to her Dionysus? A boy to a man!

Yet the Romans were powerful. She had known that from the moment she met

Pompeius the Great and her father had humbled himself before him. Her father was not a man to be humbled. He was hot-tempered, proud, a king of kings. And he had been worse since her sister Berenice had turned their people against him.

One night her father had taken her aside. They had not been there for three weeks. He was anxious but determined, and merciless. Her older sister Berenice IV had assumed the throne in Egypt and had sent an embassy to Rome opposing their father's rule. Cleopatra would learn later that her father had been the one to arrange the embassy leaders' assassinations.

She had had no choice in the matter—it was in her name, *Philopator*, to love her father—and so she had followed him. For Cleopatra had known the fight between her father and sister meant her own life or death. That was simply the cost of divinity, of power.

Everyone wanted it.

"Cleopatra, my daughter," he had said, glancing around as if someone might be eavesdropping. "Listen to me."

There had not been a soul awake this late, besides perhaps those pesky Roman household gods, the *Lares*. It was after dark and Pompeius had visited Rome on business, so the rest of the household had gone to sleep.

Maybe her father had been truly desperate, worried that his life would end soon, which could account for his following words to her that she would never forget. It was certainly a possibility. Her father, as she would find out as queen, owed the Romans over seventeen million *drachmae*. The Romans had continually refused her father an armed guard to invade Egypt and restore him to the throne. If the Romans had ever decided to support Berenice instead of her father, their lives would have been in great peril. No land was safe from those tireless Latins.

"Yes, father?"

"Pompeius the Great favors you," her father had said, almost accusing.

"The Roman king, father?" she had asked, startled, both at the statement and her father's tone.

"He is not a king," he had snapped. "But yes. He is quite enamored with you."

Cleopatra had not exactly understood, but she knew enough about men to know what this could mean, even at her tender age. "Am I to marry him, father?"

He eyed her with a strange, curious look. Her father was not a curious man, and she had the sudden urge to cry, as if she had said something terribly wrong. "No. You will not *marry* him."

Cleopatra had not known what to say, and apparently neither had her father, or he simply thought he had said enough on that subject for now. He had hastily sent her to the room where her younger sister and two brothers were already asleep. He would not, however, bring up the topic again, and they would leave Italy later that year to Ephesus with no help from the Romans.

Now she understood all too well what her father had been implying. For he had always intended her to marry her brother, Ptolemy XIII, as was custom, but that did not restrict her from the favor of a Roman general, king or not.

It would be another three years later when Cleopatra would meet another Roman general, Aulus Gabinius, whom her father had bribed to invade Egypt and restore him to power. But it was not he who would favor Cleopatra this time.

No, it was a young cavalry officer, tall and strong, sitting astride his horse with ease, all dark, curling hair, tanned skin, and a strong brow. He had introduced himself with a smile that had the edge of a self-satisfied smirk, and his men had shifted on their feet, forbidden laughter rustling among them.

He had taken her hand and kissed it. "Marcus Antonius greets you, Princess Cleopatra."

"A pleasure to meet you," she had said, in perfect Latin if only to annoy him, and she had seen a flicker of surprise in his eyes, for he had spoken in Greek.

His smile had faded, and he knelt before her. "My sword is yours to command, my lady. Please, accept my humble offer to a woman befit to be queen."

She had not known what to say, and looked to her father, who had stared at the young man in contempt. The soldiers had watched with scarcely concealed amusement.

"Another, Antonius?" one had shouted from the crowds, and laughter had erupted before it was forcibly calmed.

But Marcus had seemed unfazed, glancing at her with such singular intensity, as if she were seated naked before him, and she had to fight the urge to look down with a blush or burst out laughing too.

"By Jove, you are Isis herself—"

"Enough," her father had interrupted.

She had breathed a sigh of relief as the handsome man was escorted away amidst his men's tempered jostling and laughter, and she had retired to her rooms to rest. They would soon sail to Judea, where Hyrcanus II would hopefully acquire supplies for them.

Marcus would prove himself useful, however, even rescuing the fallen body of Berenice's husband in battle to bury him properly. She knew he had only done so for her, as a kind of courting gift. But her father would not have entertained her marriage to a Roman general, much less a mere cavalry officer.

And regardless, when her father had died and Cleopatra and her brother had assumed the throne together, she would find herself courting a very different Roman general.

Ten years after she had first followed her father in exile, she now faced her brother's greedy tutors and their allied military commander, Theodotus of Chios, who wished to eject her from the throne and gain power through her impressionable brother.

During the civil strife, Cleopatra had to flee to Thebes and then Syria with her sister Arsinoe. At the same time, Pompeius the Great—caught in his own civil strife—had sought refuge in Egypt and had been assassinated at the command of her brother's advisors, hoping to gain favor with his rival, the more powerful Roman general.

And sure enough, Julius Caesar arrived at the royal palace in Alexandria that October. Cleopatra had known, just as her father had, that her time was running out. Here she was, fighting not only for Egypt but her very life, and the only possible savior was a man—worse, a Roman man! And how could she escape it?

Then she remembered her sister's words all those years ago. *Maybe she did not want to.*

But it was her father's words at Pompeius' villa that echoed ominously in her mind, his accusation, his caution, as he stared at her not as a father to a daughter, but as a man when he realized his daughter was now a woman. *He is quite enamored with you.*

After Julius Caesar had failed to reply to her emissaries, she had been determined to speak with him herself. She had herself escorted by an armed guard to Alexandria from her army's camp near Pelousion, a city on the far eastern edges of the Nile Delta, and at last was given an audience.

He had been nothing like any Roman man she had ever met.

"So you are the famous Cleopatra Philopator," Caesar had said with a small, charming smile when she had been introduced to him.

He had been thin but wiry and muscled, already graying at his receding temples, and he moved with a subtle, languid affect that had struck her as quite feminine. He had not looked at her like Marcus Antonius had, all heated and bare. Instead, Caesar had watched her carefully, measuredly, more like a lion in wait than one ready to pounce.

"And you are the famous Julius Caesar," Cleopatra had answered, her Latin precise but fluid. Caesar had not been surprised. Apparently her love of languages had become known beyond the borders of Egypt. "Welcome to the city of Alexandria. I assure you, Caesar, there is no place in the world as beautiful."

"Tell me, Queen Cleopatra," Caesar had said with his curious, small smile, his eyes dark and amused. "Have you ever been to Rome?"

From that day many things happened very quickly.

When her brother had heard of her visit to Caesar and suspected that he would favor her, Ptolemy stirred the city into riots, and Julius Caesar had him arrested.

But a faction of the army had also supported her brother. Though Caesar did his best to restore peace between her and Ptolemy by placing Arsinoe IV and their youngest brother as rulers of Cyprus—a contested territory previously in Roman control—Ptolemy had quickly turned on them anyway. He then joined with Arsinoe's rebelling forces, so that in the end the palace was besieged, trapping her alone with Caesar.

Despite their change in fortune, Caesar had remained his same well-mannered, charming self. In fact, he had even seemed pleased, taking the time to dine with her and converse, not as a man with a woman, but as one scholar to another, discussing philosophy and rhetoric with her as if he had wished to know what she thought.

So it had come as a surprise when one evening after dinner he had leaned over and kissed her.

She had sat back, staring at him. It had not occurred to her that one could simply kiss someone, though she had known Romans kissed each other in greeting. But Cleopatra had never kissed anyone on the mouth before.

"Was it that bad?" Caesar had asked with mild amusement at her stunned silence.

He was never one to be embarrassed, and indeed, his ability to self-deprecate was his best quality. Cleopatra had not known what to say, so she had shaken her head. It had not been bad. But had she wanted it? Did it matter if she had or not? He was not handsome exactly, but there was a calm confidence, a self-assuredness to him, that had compelled Cleopatra to take him seriously as she had not any man before.

She had thought of her own sister and brother at the walls of the palace, waiting to murder her in cold blood. She had thought of Helen, swept away with Paris, ending one war by starting another.

Cleopatra had begun to see a plan forming in her mind, not love and not politics but something else, something more instinctual, something, she had thought ironically, more like marriage.

Am I to marry him, father?

"No," Cleopatra had answered, almost smiling to herself. "Not bad at all."

⤙⤙⤙ ⤚⤚⤚

Cleopatra watched her husband stand by the window and look out at the gulf extending west of Patrai, a city on the westernmost coast of Greece.

Marcus took an unconscious sip of his wine, his eyes focused far away. Ever since he had divorced his other wife, Octavia, he had taken to drinking more often. Cleopatra wondered why men always mourned for the very things they had a hand in killing. She felt her annoyance stir in her breast.

"There is talk of a letter you wrote to Caesar," Cleopatra said, stretching out on their bed, her voice teasing, though she felt a vague anger at his stiff figure standing so far away from her.

Marcus glanced at her, then back out the window. "I write many letters to Caesar."

"Did you really think I would not find out?" She spoke in her cold, sharp Latin, when she usually spoke to him in Greek. "Really, Marcus, it is all your men speak about these days."

"What of it?" Marcus asked, an edge to his voice, but it was telling that he did not deny it. "I wrote only the truth."

Cleopatra had not read the letter herself, but from the rumors floating about the camp, she had gathered that Marcus had accused Caesar of various affairs in order to justify having sex with other women outside of his own marriage. In other words, having sex with *her*.

She arched her brow. "Then I suppose it does not matter whether it is I in your bed or any other woman."

Marcus turned towards her, his eyes slightly narrowed. "Sex is only sex."

"Of course it is," Cleopatra said mockingly. "Then I suppose I may have sex with anyone I like as well."

His eyes glanced away. "That is different."

"Why?" she demanded. "Because I am a woman?"

"Because sex is different for women," Marcus said with a haughty but sincere calm, which only inflamed her anger against him more. "To a man, sex is only sex. To a woman, sex is more."

"Is that so," Cleopatra said, barely smirking.

"It is," Marcus insisted. "To a woman, sex is love."

"Do you even know what love is, Marcus?"

He stared at her, like she was suddenly a stranger, or perhaps someone he used to know. "Love is sacrifice."

Suddenly her anger died out. "And do you love me?"

Marcus spoke softly. "Yes."

"And do you still love me when you lie with me?" Cleopatra asked, her voice low, and now Marcus looked at her with the same burning eyes he had the first time they met all those years ago. It was easy to reach for that familiar desire in her, for it was safer than her love for him.

"Yes."

"Ah, but those are only words, my love," she said with a red-lipped smile.

She had returned to her familiar lilting Greek and Marcus relaxed in visible relief, joining her on the bed and taking her hand in his gently. With the other, he brushed aside her hair which hung loosely about her shoulders in dark, messy curls. Then he kissed her.

His mouth tasted of his bitter wine, and her body melted into the familiarity of his touch, the warmth of his skin, the pull deep within her towards his strong, steady arms. He was still ever so handsome, broad-chested, with thick brows and a sharp jaw. He was the man she loved, and that would never change.

Later in the night, Marcus turned to her. "Do you remember the first time we met?"

His eyes were cast down, almost embarrassed to be asking but desperately wanting to anyway. She was his world, Cleopatra knew, and his troubles lay with the fact that her world was much bigger than him.

"I loved you then," he said. "I know it."

"You did not even know me," Cleopatra teased, pushing him away softly, half-annoyed. While he liked to bring it up, she did not always wish to remember the time before she was queen, the days when her sisters were taken from her. "I was too young. It was improper."

"I was young too," Marcus countered. "But I knew I loved you. You spoke to me and I thought I had heard the voice of a goddess."

"You think all women are goddesses," she said with a laugh. "It is your nature."

"No," he said, shaking his head. "No. You alone I have loved."

She smiled and kissed his cheek. "I do not believe it."

"I love you," Marcus whispered against her skin. "I would die for you."

Her heart dropped at the thought. She knew he could only say this now that he had nothing left to lose except her. But still, her heart beat faster at the thought. "Do not speak of Death, Marcus."

His eyes were fierce and dark. "I would. I would die for you. You are everything to me. I do not care for Caesar or his wars or Rome or her people. I only care for you, my love. Until death. Even beyond death."

Cleopatra felt every word as a drop of poison in her blood. A part of her, the human part of her, yearned for him as her man, her lover, and the home they had found amidst all the chaos and bloodshed. But the other part of her, the divine blood that ran in her veins, feared that fierce look in his eyes, and knew it as a weakness. She herself would never betray her empire to a man, even if he was the man she loved.

For Marcus had been wrong about women. Sex was not about love at all. Sex was about power, and it was the moment when men were at their weakest.

"Do not speak so," Cleopatra said uneasily. "Let us defeat Caesar and we may live the rest of our days in peace."

"I would die for you," Marcus murmured as if he had not heard her, as if the words were an oath, kissing her neck, then her chest, his hands already slipping her dress off her shoulders. "I would die for you, *Cleopatra Philopator*."

"Kiss me, Marcus," she whispered, her hands trembling as she brought them to his chest. "Do not speak."

He did not speak for the rest of the night.

⟫⟫⟫ ⟪⟪⟪

DECEMBER 32 BC

"The boy asks for a conference?" Marcus asked angrily. "A conference! With his fleet at my very doorstep and he asks for a conference!"

Cleopatra sat silently in the corner of her tent as her husband shouted at his advisors, who had recently received news of Caesar's request for a conference. It was nothing more than an insult, for Caesar surely had to know Marcus would never accept. But Cleopatra considered it a mere nuisance and was surprised to find the men all worked up about it.

"The boy has gotten out of hand, sir," Ahenobarbus declared, knowing they were words Marcus wanted to hear. "He considers himself as powerful as a god."

"Oh does he now?" Marcus sneered. "He is as arrogant as his divine father."

Cleopatra raised a brow but did not interject. She knew her husband had always been jealous of Julius Caesar's natural charm and intellect, especially given that Caesar had not been as capable a soldier or military commander as Marcus.

But that is what Marcus had never understood. For Julius Caesar may not have been as manly, but he knew men better than they knew themselves, and therefore how to rule them.

"He will meet the same end," Quintus Dellius said grimly.

"Julius Caesar was betrayed by lesser men," Cleopatra said, her voice cold, and Dellius turned a sharp glare on her. Of all Marcus' friends, Dellius she hated most. He was an opportunist, a deserter, and Cleopatra did not trust him. But he was a good general, and Marcus could not now afford to make enemies out of friends. "Do you think this Caesar will make the same mistake? He may only be a boy, but he is dangerous, perhaps more than Julius Caesar had been. Do not underestimate him."

Dellius' lip curled. He hated her as much as she hated him, mostly because until her Dellius had been the closest advisor and friend of Marcus, and the two of them had encouraged all forms of debauchery in the other.

"We have twenty thousand more foot soldiers than Caesar and at least double the ships. He does not stand a chance," Dellius countered.

"And yet his fleet blocks us from sailing farther than Corcyra. He has us penned up like sheep waiting for slaughter."

Cleopatra turned to Marcus, wishing she could meet his eyes and persuade him with her look alone, but Marcus' mouth was firm and tense, and his eyes stubbornly eyed the map before him, unable to face her honestly when his men were near.

"Please, Marcus, let us return to Alexandria while there is still time."

Marcus glanced at her doubtfully.

Dellius nearly scoffed. "Sir, you cannot possibly—"

"Silence," Marcus interrupted.

Dellius and Ahenobarbus shared a glance that only Cleopatra noticed, and her stomach turned uneasily. These men did not respect her, and therefore they did not respect her husband when he listened to her. But she was a queen, a goddess, and would not be cowed by mere mortal men who knew less than her.

"There is too much coastline to defend in Greece. If we retreat we may buy ourselves time to attack," Cleopatra urged, but it was the wrong thing to say to a man who was quickly realizing that his plan of offense was looking more like defense with every passing day.

Marcus turned away from her, bristling, and Cleopatra felt her heart sink in her chest. "Retreat? We will not retreat. Our fleet is at the ready, and we hold the straight near Actium. His navy is outnumbered two to one. Let him come. We will be ready."

Satisfied with the answer, Dellius and Ahenobarbus left the tent.

Marcus sighed when they were gone, rubbing at his forehead. "You should leave these meetings to me. My men already wish me to send you back to Alexandria."

"Oh do they?" Cleopatra asked carelessly, though her heart beat angrily at how little, how very little men knew. "They also wish me dead. Shall you threaten to kill me as well?"

"I am not threatening you," Marcus said wearily. He walked over to her and took her hand in his, but she did not yield, and stood aloof from him, her pride hurt more than her heart. "Come, my love, you know I only care about you. But I must appease my men, lest they desert me."

"You appease men who would desert you *because* of me," Cleopatra whispered, her voice choking as her throat closed with unwilling tears. "Do you not see? It is not only my life at risk. They see you as they see me. But worse, for I was never a Roman, and have never pretended to be."

Marcus kissed her knuckles and pulled her close. She could not resist his strong arms wrapping around her, safe and familiar. But another part of her, the part she tucked away but never forgot, knew that their days were numbered. Caesar would not sit idle while Marcus whiled the winter away in Greece.

And for a moment, only a moment, she was Helen of Troy, besieged alongside her headstrong husband, and she could not stop the thought from flitting across her mind that there stood on the other side of the war a man of power, a man befit to be king, a man who may spare her life at the right price.

Am I to marry him, father?

No, Caesar would not marry her. He desired her empire, not her body. But was she willing to sacrifice the man she loved for the survival of her kingdom, her queenship? Was she, like Helen of Troy, willing to surrender everything to stay alive?

For the first time in her life, Cleopatra did not know.

55

GAIUS OCTAVIUS

MARCH 31 BC

T HE MAN ACROSS FROM him in the ship's cabin had the same dark curls and frown Octavius had once mistaken for Agrippa. But Valerius Messalla Corvinus was slightly younger, his face still soft and round as if he had not quite left his boyhood behind. His skin was paler too, a milky white, pronouncing a permanent red flush on his cheeks.

Octavius had appointed him to be his consular colleague for the new year, and Antonius and his supporters had not been in Rome to stop it.

In between them a map of Greece was spread on the table, carved wooden markers indicating where Octavius' fleet opposed Antonius' on the Ionian Sea. Octavius struggled to focus as his stomach churned with seasickness, bile rising up his throat, and he swallowed hard.

Agrippa stood beside Octavius, seemingly at ease despite the slow rocking of the ship on the water, threatening to toss the wooden markers off the table.

Also crammed in the cabin were Lucius Arruntius and Marcus Lurius, the commanders of the center and right wings of his fleet respectively, as well as Titus Statilius Taurus, the commander of Octavius' armies.

Before winter, they had sailed swiftly from Brundisium and had taken the island of Corcyra almost entirely unopposed. He had proposed a conference, knowing Antonius would refuse and hoping his rage and pride would do most of the work for him. Now their plan of attack had to be perfect, and with as little risk as possible, in order to win this war.

"Antonius has much of his fleet docked in the Ambracian Gulf, with only one entrance and exit," Agrippa said. He pointed to the small crooked opening of land linking the sea with the gulf. "The strait."

Octavius nearly flinched at the words, remembering another war fought on another precarious strait, and he swore he could still taste the saltwater and blood in his mouth as he tumbled to shore, knocked unconscious and left for dead if Corvinus had not saved him.

Arruntius frowned at the map, as if he too were recalling the Sicilian waters and their dangerous tides. He had sided with Sextus initially, but had joined Octavius after the Pact of Misenum nearly eight years ago. Arruntius knew the risks of war as well as anyone.

"If we allow them to escape, we lose our advantage," Arruntius said thoughtfully.

"Precisely," Agrippa said. "Which is why we must act, and we must do so quickly."

"But Antonius holds the strait," Taurus said suddenly, walking around the table with large strides. He was a sturdy man, a natural fighter, though his strengths lay on land and on horseback rather than at sea. "He mans a camp on the south side of the straight and a guarded tower in the north. It would be foolish to attempt an attack."

"The longer we wait, the more time we allow for his allies to send ships and supplies," Lurius said darkly. He had also seen much fighting against Sextus and Antonius. "It is dangerous not to act when Antonius has a much more reliable supply route than we do."

Unfortunately, it was true. Antonius pulled his supplies from nearby Egypt and Asia, whereas Octavius had to ship supplies across the sea from Italy. Neither of them, however, could survive the impoverished mainland of Greece without supplies, and Octavius did not intend to be starved to death.

"Then what should we do?" Octavius asked warily.

Corvinus peered over the map and pointed to a coastal city on the western shores of the Peloponnese. "If we take Methoni, we would be able to better intercept his supply ships."

Agrippa nodded. "It is the only way to make Antonius desperate."

Taurus swept a hand over the markers of Antonius' fleet scattered along the coast and in the gulf. "That is all well and good, but it does not change the fact that Antonius' forces are more than double our own. We shall need to impose ourselves on land as well if we wish to defeat him."

"Yes," Octavius murmured. "We must take the strait."

"You will not easily find a landing with Antonius watching it so closely," Arruntius warned.

Agrippa smirked. "You would need a distraction. I can handle that."

"And then..." Corvinus began, already smiling.

Taurus clapped his hands together, his grin feral. "We pounce."

The meeting concluded a few hours later once the details of their plan were decided and sketched down to the day and hour. Agrippa was to distract Antonius by raiding towns and diverting his attention until Octavius could find a pocket of coastline to land on and begin the fight for the strait. He trusted Taurus to defeat Antonius on dry land, or at the very least wear him down before their fleets met in battle.

Agrippa remained in their cabin as the rest of them filed out to prepare for the long days ahead.

Octavius studied Agrippa as he played with one of the wooden carvings, flipping it around with his fingers. They did not speak for a long time, the upcoming battle hanging over them like a thick fog.

Agrippa glanced at him, noticing his staring. "What?"

"Nothing."

He frowned. "You look troubled. Do you doubt the plan?"

Octavius hesitated, his gaze fixed on the deliberate movement of Agrippa's fingers as they flipped the wooden marker over and over. He tore his gaze away to find Agrippa smirking, and that look alone nearly made Octavius forget the war entirely.

"Antonius' fleet outnumbers us two to one," Octavius said finally. "I only worry it will not be enough."

"We can defeat him."

"How are you so sure?"

He had wanted to protest when Agrippa had offered himself up as a distraction, but he quickly checked himself. This was war, and all of their lives were at risk now. Agrippa was a general, but he was also a soldier, and his duty to Octavius and to the Republic was not to remain safely behind while others died in his stead.

"Just trust me. Besides, you were never the better strategist," Agrippa said with a crooked smile. "Athenodorus always said so."

Octavius shook his head, a strangled laugh escaping his mouth. "This is not the time for jokes."

"Come now," Agrippa said gently. "Have I ever failed you?"

He paused, pretending to think it over. "No, I suppose not."

"See?"

Octavius glanced at him, the dark brow, the broad shoulders, and wondered if this would be the last time he would look upon those Tiber green eyes. There were footsteps outside the cabin, his men moving to their posts, and Octavius was reminded of the world beyond them.

He stood up, taking a deep breath. "Do not fail me."

As he walked away Agrippa caught his hand.

Octavius went still, looking at their joined hands, the warmth of his touch as familiar and natural as sunlight. Agrippa leaned down and kissed his signet ring, as he had done all those years ago, his lips brushing against his knuckles.

"Never."

~»»»7 {{{«~

AUGUST 31 BC

The sea rocked violently beneath the ship, waves slapping the hull as if they wished to swallow them under that endless blue.

A strip of the coast along Epirus swayed on the horizon ahead of them. Agrippa was somewhere south of here, having successfully diverted Antonius' attention with small skirmishes and coastal raids. It seemed every other day they heard of another brilliant raid, another attack, so that Octavius wondered if Agrippa was proving to him just how better a strategist he was.

"*Praetor* Caesar!" called out one of his generals from across the deck. "We are close enough to land!"

Octavius nodded. "Start the rowers!"

This was not the first time they had tried to make a landing. For the past several months they had tried and failed to sneak past the heavily guarded coastline. The long summer days were almost unbearable at sea, but he had to trust that Agrippa would find a way to reel in Antonius' troops long enough to find a small opening, and now they were finally reaping the rewards.

"*Praetor* Caesar! We are approaching the seabed!"

"Cast anchor!"

Octavius had long ceased calling himself one of the *Tresviri*. He knew Antonius still refused to give up his powers despite having been divested of them by Senatorial decree. Now Octavius was merely a consul, alongside Corvinus, who had fought well against Sextus and would now fight alongside Taurus to secure a very different strait.

This was not unlike that day, however, surrounded by water, hostility on every shore. He remembered thinking he was going to die before the sea sank him beneath her strong tide and spat him back out on land, half alive.

Would this war end as the other had, victorious and final? Or would this be the war where they finally fell in defeat, and knew the name of Death as their own?

The ships anchored close to the shallows, and Octavius and his men quickly rowed to shore. Antonius would soon hear of Octavius' encampment so near to his own if he had not already been notified, and then time alone could tell how soon his forces would attack in retaliation.

"Send a messenger to Agrippa," Octavius said to one of his lieutenants. "Tell him we have landed. There is much work to do."

Now that Antonius' attention would return to Octavius, war was now days away instead of months. For despite Antonius' delayed defense, he still manned a tower with troops on this side of the strait. Octavius would not be able to rest until their forces met once and for all.

When your men see the forces they must fight against, they will flee.

Antonius had said it many years ago when neither of them knew the long road ahead. But Octavius had been young then, and he was no longer the boy aflame with vengeance, eager for triumph and a glorious death. He was a man now, and this war was not about his father. It was about the world as they knew it, and who would be its master.

"*Praetor* Caesar, sir! Our scouts have reported a cavalry unit approaching from the north!"

Octavius could not help but smile.

56

MARCUS VIPSANIUS AGRIPPA

AUGUST 31 BC

*H*EAT FLARED ACROSS AGRIPPA's *face, and for a moment, it was as if his face were on fire.*

Sweat beaded his brow, sliding down the sides of his temples. His forehead spasmed in pain, and then there was Attica, just as she had been all those months ago before he left for war, feverish and despondent from an illness, lying in bed and refusing to move.

"You cannot leave," Attica whispered, just as she had then, nearly choking on her tears. Always, always in tears.

Agrippa did not know what to say. He had to leave. That was the way of things with war. Attica knew this. But it did not lessen the guilt he felt when he saw the betrayal flash in her gray eyes.

"You know I must," Agrippa replied reluctantly.

Attica clutched at his hand, looking at him with wide, unseeing eyes. "Promise me."

Agrippa's heart twinged uneasily. It was not the first time she had asked this of him. "My love, please."

"Promise that you will not forget me," Attica whispered fervently. "Promise me that you will not get yourself killed for that man."

Octavius.

In her fever, Attica had hated him. Sometimes Agrippa had hated him a little too. For months he had sat beside her bed, Attica gripping his hand so tight his skin turned white, listening to all her delusional mutterings about Octavius and her father and the war.

"He only loves the power he has over you," Attica had hissed once when Agrippa had tried to leave her.

Octavius had summoned him to a meeting that day, and he had made the mistake of

460

mentioning it to her. Her words were nonsense, perhaps, but they still stung him as if she had meant them. Or as if they were true.

Usually, Attica nodded off to sleep as soon as she grew her most irate, but this time she did not. In his dreams, Attica never slept. Agrippa's heart clenched in fear as he saw Attica's gray eyes turn towards him, as clear and dry as if she had suddenly ceased crying.

"You promised me," she said calmly. Too calmly. Agrippa was rooted in place. He could not escape.

Then her face twisted into pure, blinding wrath and she sprung towards him, a dagger in her hand, aimed at his heart.

"You promised me!"

Agrippa gasped, opening his eyes. He winced as he blinked into bright sunlight.

His second-in-command was crouched beside him, roughly shaking his shoulder. Agrippa realized he had fallen asleep on deck. He passed a hand over his damp forehead as though he could wipe away the crazed look on Attica's face which he only saw in his dreams. He tried not to think it a bad omen.

"*Praetor* Caesar has called for you, sir." A pause. "It is time."

Agrippa's heart leaped, and he staggered to his feet. He was dizzy, almost nauseous. They had been waiting at sea for days since they captured the northern strait, defeating Antonius in cavalry skirmishes and forcing him to retreat to the southern side.

The sky was bright blue, the waves calm, a deceiving setting for the scenes about to unfold. But then a wind came gusting from the east and he felt the chill beneath his clothes, signaling more than a battle.

Agrippa took a deep breath as he entered the cabin.

Octavius stood by the desk, his arms crossed and a satisfied smile on his face. The map on the desk in the middle of the cabin held the markers of their fleet and that of Antonius' positioned for battle outside the Ambracian Gulf. He did not even look at Agrippa when he entered the cramped room.

Beside him stood Arruntius and Lurius, and next to them stood none other than Quintus Dellius, a personal friend and ally of Antonius, notorious for encouraging the worst kind of vices in his friends.

"Arruntius. Lurius," Agrippa said, nodding towards them. He paused. Octavius' eyes flickered over to him, ever so slightly. "Caesar. You say it is time?"

Octavius nodded, then jerked his chin towards Dellius. "Here is Quintus Dellius. Up until very recently, he was an ally of our enemies."

"And that has changed?" Agrippa asked with only a hint of sarcasm.

Dellius was also notorious for his knack of knowing when the tides of fortune were changing.

"Yes," Octavius said, and his smile was sly when he glanced at Dellius, who remained quiet and wary. "He has revealed to us Antonius' secret plan to return his main fleet to Alexandria. He has also positioned more garrisons along the coast. Antonius is retreating."

"Then we ought to attack," Agrippa said. Surprise flickered in Dellius' eyes. "There is no use waiting about while Antonius slinks off to Egypt."

"It would be a risk to attack." Octavius eyed the map, tapping the table unconsciously. "Even in retreat, Antonius is still dangerous. He has nearly twice as many ships."

Dellius stepped forward, clearing his throat. "Caesar, if I may. Antonius possesses more ships, it is true, but he does not have nearly enough men to row them. He hardly has enough to man a fifth of them. Besides, his ships are *quinqueremes,* and a few *quadriremes.* They are slow and hard to maneuver compared to your Liburnian galleys."

Octavius gave Dellius a sharp look. "What are you suggesting, Dellius?"

"You know what he is suggesting," Agrippa said gravely, coming towards the desk and rearranging the markers. He placed their fleet, left, right, and center, facing the mouth of the strait. Opposite them, he placed the three wings of Antonius' fleet, with Cleopatra's smaller squadron behind them. "He is saying that we can defeat him."

"It will not be easy to defeat Antonius," Arruntius said, stepping forward to take a closer look at the map. "He is still a Roman general. One of the best there ever was. We cannot underestimate him."

"He is not Roman anymore," Octavius said coldly. "Let Antonius retreat. I propose we attack from the rear when they believe they have escaped danger. He will not predict a delayed attack."

Agrippa recalled the wind he had felt on deck. "No."

Lurius raised a brow, looking between Octavius' surprised face and Agrippa. "No? I believe Caesar has spoken well. Antonius will see that he has escaped and believe that he successfully deceived us. There can be no better surprise attack."

"If he indeed intends to escape," Agrippa said, cutting a glance at Dellius, "then Antonius will use sails. I fear we shall be too slow in pursuit." He looked at Octavius, who stared back fiercely, though Agrippa knew him well enough to recognize it as fear. "There is a northwesterly wind. If we allow him to use it, his entire fleet may slip out of our hands for good. And from Egypt, he will have more time, more allies, and more resources. We could not besiege him then, nor attack him safely."

Octavius looked at him silently. The wind whistled against the small windows of the cabin like a whispered sign from the gods themselves. He sighed. "Then you think we can defeat Antonius in battle?"

Agrippa smiled. "I know it."

>>>> <<<<

SEPTEMBER 31 BC

The ship pitched side to side, waves cresting over the deck, tossing up stinging salt water. Dark clouds gathered to the east, hanging low in the sky.

Soldiers ran across the deck here and there in bright, glinting armor, hurrying to their posts as battle descended. To the west the sun still shone, gleaming through broken clouds, while Antonius' large warships dotted the eastern horizon, approaching along with the storm.

The large, armored ships of Antonius sailed swiftly with the wind at their backs, and Agrippa could sense the fear stifling their own men, eyes wide and frantically glancing around, the rowers hesitant, waiting for the impending chaos to break out.

For now, they were well out of range, but that would only last for so long. A loud clap of far-off thunder seemed to shake the very depths of the ocean itself.

"My brothers!"

Agrippa turned.

Octavius stood at the west end of the ship, elevated in the last rays of sunlight from above. His hair was lit as if with a golden crown, and his eyes were storming as the wine-dark sea around them.

Agrippa's breath caught. For this was no ordinary mortal standing before them.

This was the son of a god.

"My brothers in arms!" Octavius cried out, his voice ringing out clear above the rumbling of the storm. The crew turned, startled, staring at their commander half in fear, half in awe. "A foreign woman has threatened the peace of the Roman nation, the power of the Roman people. Shall we sit back and do nothing? Shall we surrender our customs, our women, our *livelihoods,* to a foreign queen and her lover, a traitor of his own people, Marcus Antonius?"

There was a resounding clamor of swords beating on shields and shouts of slander against Antonius and his supporters. Agrippa felt a shiver and realized distantly that a light shower had begun falling from the sky.

Octavius raised his sword up, the last light of the sun shining on the glittering waves on their side of the sea. "Then let us fight! Let us fight for Rome! *Ordinem servate!*"

And as they cried out and took their places, thunder clapped and lightning flashed across the sky. Rain poured upon them in heavy sheets, the dark clouds rolling in and blotting the last blue skies, the deck and the oars so slick that they nearly became one with the waves.

Agrippa met Octavius as he approached the stern. They stopped short, staring at each other, a strange look in Octavius' dark eyes. Agrippa did not know what to say. His heart beat painfully, out of fear or love he could not tell, and wondered if there was even a difference anymore.

"Do not die," Octavius warned. "Promise me, Agrippa, you will not do something stupid like that."

Promise me that you will not get yourself killed for that man.

Agrippa nodded, though his body was numb, as it always felt before battle, when instinct took over and all that mattered was the present moment, life or death only a breath away. Attica's gray eyes flashed through his mind like a warning, her face spasming in pain, the wrath of the gods in her twisting mouth as the dagger descended—

"Caesar!"

They both turned. A messenger hurriedly approached.

"What news?" Octavius asked darkly.

"We have news from General Lurius, sir," the messenger said, his chest heaving with deep breaths from rowing across the water. "General Sosius has attacked."

General Sosius commanded Antonius' left wing. They had successfully drawn them out into battle, but now they had to win. Octavius looked at Agrippa, and without a second thought, Agrippa stepped towards the messenger.

"Tell Lurius to stick to the plan," Agrippa said firmly. "Attack swiftly, target the men above deck and then retreat. Above all, be quick, and be nimble."

The messenger nodded frantically and hurried back to a small boat waiting at the side of their ship filled with rowers, which they used to send messages back and forth between commanders. He watched the small boat row speedily across the choppy waters, disappearing from view as the waves grew in size, rising over the sides of their ship and rushing across the deck.

Agrippa came close to Octavius. He placed a hand on his arm and tried to smile. "I will always find you."

Octavius nodded, silent as death. Then he stepped away and left Agrippa alone at the stern, looking out at Antonius' towering warships as the battle raged on.

The storm lasted all afternoon along with the battle, and when the sun dipped below the horizon, a lighter wind picked up from the shore, pressing the clouds onward, and as Agrippa listened he thought he heard a familiar sigh, a soft, gentle whisper, calling his name.

Agrippa.

He looked up, his heart clenched as if in sudden pain. There was a commotion behind him. Out of the corner of his eyes, he saw sails in the distance, specks of white on the frothing sea.

Promise me.

"He is fleeing! He is fleeing!"

The men were in disbelief, momentarily caught off guard at the news of Antonius' retreat. As they all stood and watched, a second pair of sails quickly followed the first. After a moment, there was cheering, and the news spread quick as wildfire across the water.

"He is fleeing with the queen! Antonius has surrendered!"

And just like that, the battle was won. Antonius' fleet would not fight for much longer without their commander. In the end, his queen had cast him under her spell, and bewitched by a woman, Antonius had, of course, retreated.

Or at least, that was what the men were saying. Agrippa could only recall Attica's panic when he had left for the war. It was as if the end of the war would be the end of their life together.

Agrippa had just not known how true that would be.

Oh, mi vir. My husband.

⤙⤙⤙ ⤚⤚⤚

Two weeks had passed since they had defeated Antonius at last. But suddenly, that did not matter anymore.

The tent nearly swayed before Agrippa's eyes. Octavius stood before him, his eyes lowered, the scroll of parchment held loosely in his hands. Agrippa wondered if he would ever not feel this pain, this deadly darkness within his very soul.

"I am sorry," Octavius said quietly. "She loved you very much."

Octavius held out the letter and Agrippa took it. It was from Livia, addressed to Octavius with an included note for Agrippa about Attica's death. She had died from her illness nearly two months ago.

The message had taken long to reach them, Octavius had said. But Agrippa knew Livia had probably withheld the information until after she had received news of the victory. He did not have the heart to be angry at her.

"You did not know her," Agrippa said, surprised at the coldness in his voice.

Octavius could not hide the flash of hurt on his face. "No, I did not."

Agrippa turned and left the tent. The night was cool but still, with no wind and no clouds in sight, the stars bright and colorful in the sky. He clutched the letter tightly in his hands until it crumpled as he made his way down the cliffside and to the narrow shore.

The water kissed the edge of the sand calmly, and Agrippa could not help but drop to his knees where the waves gently sunk into the earth.

He held up the letter in the white moonlight, hardly able to read the words but not needing to, having them already seared in his mind.

My dear, dear Agrippa,

There are no words for the pain I feel in writing this...

Livia would be taking care of the children until Agrippa returned home. He recalled Attica holding Agrippina when she was not even a year old, and he remembered the surprise, the utter awe he had felt watching her hold their child, a book in her other hand, talking distractedly with him, a woman like no other.

Poor Agrippina! Poor Vipsania! They would never know their mother. Their wonderful, clever, kind mother. They would never know her gray eyes, the intensity like a coming storm, the quick wit, the solemn, tender knowledge of a woman in a world of men.

Who shall kindle the memory of her? Who shall keep it burning? As the wars came and went, as the sun rose and set alongside the moon, as time kept its cruel count and history left even the best of humankind forgotten, who shall bear her torch and salvage her legacy from a nameless fate?

Pomponia Caecilia Attica, his wife, the mother of his children. But also, a woman, a woman of passion, ideas, and incredible strength. He thought of his own mother, already a shadow of a memory in his mind, a name gifted to sons and daughters and lost to death.

He felt the tides of time sinking in the past, and he could not help the tears that fell from his cheeks and into the water swirling about his knees, a drop in an endless ocean.

There were distant shouts carried across the waves. He looked up.

Small boats worked to sift through the burned ruins of their enemy, the wreckage of war. Various ships were still half-destroyed, smoldering on the sea, their crews either rescued or dead.

Antonius' entire fleet and army had surrendered after their commander had fled with his Egyptian queen. Rumor had already made her rounds, but it did not matter. Octavius had won the war, and without their fleet, it was only a matter of time before Antonius and Cleopatra were found and killed.

Everything was about to change. No. Everything had *already* changed. He felt familiar icy fear clutch his heart, and he held the letter close to his chest, shutting his eyes tightly.

"Ave atque vale, mea Attica," Agrippa whispered.

His hands released the letter, which fluttered in the air before settling on the water. The piece of parchment floated with the tide until it was swallowed in the waves, disappearing in the sea along with a part of his heart, forever.

Hail and farewell, my Attica.

57

MARCUS ANTONIUS

SEPTEMBER 31 BC

ANTONIUS HAD NEVER HEARD the streets of Alexandria so quiet.

The impending war had settled an eerie silence on the city like a blanket of snow in winter. Fear was palpable in the air as night descended, as if they might see the torches of battle glimmering on the horizon at any moment like ferrymen of the Underworld.

He wondered if the city would be ablaze by dawn, the treasures and knowledge of Alexandria devoured in the flames of war, the hot sun blotted by black smoke.

The last time the city was held under siege, Julius Caesar had occupied the palace. Antonius glanced at Cleopatra, lying in bed, her face untroubled in sleep. No matter how much Antonius wished to best his old general's legacy, it seemed he found himself unable to escape Caesar's shadow. Now here he was, in the same palace, under siege with the same woman, except Antonius was alive and Julius Caesar was dead. He did not know which fate was worse.

A part of him was surprised he did not feel ashamed. He knew well that in the eyes of the young Caesar, in the eyes of any Roman, his retreat was a coward's flight. And Antonius also knew well that the boy would return to Italy bearing the message of his defeat.

But there was no shame. No anger. No regret. How could he regret saving the life of the woman he loved?

Perhaps the battle could have been won, but there were too many risks. The desertions had not boded well, and one of them must have betrayed him. Greece was dangerous, poorly resourced, and Caesar had already managed to seize the northern side of the strait, leaving their army vulnerable.

Egypt, on the other hand, could supply and feed them, house them, but above all, protect them. The land and its people had survived many wars, many battles. And it was home.

For the gods knew his home was not Rome. After all, what had Rome ever done for him? What had the Roman people ever given him?

Antonius had always been alone, left to fend for himself, when his father had abandoned their family for a life of piracy and pleasure, when Rome had abandoned him gambling on the streets, chewing up every cent he had and spitting him back out to rot in Greece.

Even when Antonius had promised wealth, when he had promised fame and glory, Rome had not yielded, had not even offered up a thanks. Instead, she had chosen a boy whose only claim was a name and the arrogance to use it.

Now Cleopatra was his home, and he would protect her with his life.

He still remembered the first time he had seen her, a young princess, daughter to a king of kings. Her sharp nose, her dark curling hair, the too-perfect Latin spoken with the faintest air of an accent that she would rather die than admit she had. She had been young, too young for him, really, but he had been young too. Nineteen, a boy eager for war, eager to prove himself a man.

Egypt had been his first triumph, his first glimpse of glory, and it had felt like the entire world had opened up at his feet, all glimmering and gold.

He would never forget what Philippus had told him all those years ago, when Atia Balba had still been alive and terrifying, when his whole life had been gambling and girls, each drop of liquor, each drunken kiss, bringing him one step closer to outrunning his father's legacy.

Someone nobody remembers.

Antonius shivered and shut the window tightly. He used to fear death. He used to wake up in the middle of the night, still drunk from his escapades, quaking in fear, wondering if the black night would simply swallow him up into oblivion. But now that death was staring him in the face, Antonius did not fear it at all.

For he had love, and there was no one, not even Death himself, who could take that away from him.

"Marcus, my love."

He turned. Cleopatra stirred in their bed, her dark eyes heavy, watching him.

"Yes?"

"Come back to bed," she said gently. "Stop worrying."

"I am not worrying. I am thinking."

She sighed, her eyes sad. "Thinking is worse. It will not help us now."

"I do not understand you," Antonius said, raising a brow. "Have you surrendered already?"

Her eyes flashed like lightning in the night sky. "I never have and never will surrender to a man, much less a *Roman* man. I shall die before that day comes."

The words struck him like a blade to the heart, and he felt sick. He pushed the words out, but they rang false. "Then we must prepare for war."

Cleopatra glanced at him, hidden thoughts in her face. "Then we must prepare to lose. Caesar's forces are too strong. We cannot hope to defeat them in battle."

"Then what do you suggest?" Antonius asked angrily. "Flee? To where? All of Greece has surrendered to him. Judea as well. There is no distant shore that will be far enough to escape him."

She nearly spoke, then held back the words, looking away. A thought formed in his mind, more nauseating than defeat.

"Unless you think to negotiate." When she said nothing, he continued. "Ah, there is the woman in you. That is it, isn't it? You think he will spare your life if you fucked him?"

Cleopatra nearly flinched, and her voice turned cold. "No. I do not think he will spare my life." She paused. "Besides, it would not be for me. It would be for my children."

"Our children," Antonius corrected. "Or have you already forgotten?"

She sat up, looking very much awake, her narrowed eyes accusing. "You may negotiate too, you know. You are still a Roman, and he may feel merciful. It is not because I am a woman that I think to negotiate, but because I am a *queen.* Or have you already forgotten?"

Her taunts stung him more than he would like to admit. For he understood her position better than she knew, as any good gambler did. Here was the woman who had entertained Julius Caesar, who had captivated Antonius himself since the moment he had met her. Who was to say she would not do the same with the boy? Who was he to stop her?

After all, she was right. While Cleopatra had a kingdom to bargain, for the first time in his life, Antonius had nothing.

"Perhaps if we had not fled Actium we would have defeated him at sea," Antonius said, more resentful than regretful.

Cleopatra raised a brow. "Already Ahenobarbus and Dellius had defected to the boy, not to mention your Thracian kings and our Eastern allies. You know as well as I that if we had stayed, we would have died that day."

"Better to die in battle than in retreat," Antonius countered, though he only half meant it.

"Ah, there is the man in you," Cleopatra answered mockingly, getting up from the bed in her anger and standing across the room from him. Despite her tousled hair and night dress, she had never looked more like a queen to him. "I forget you Romans and your

senseless honor. Well, I have a people to protect, and I cannot do that from the grave. That, at least, is something the young Caesar understands. But tell me, Marcus, what has your precious honor ever gotten you?"

"Certainly more than you have gotten me!" The words came before he could stop them, but he did not regret saying them.

"Oh really?" Cleopatra stood tall, her eyes glowing fiercely at his raised voice. "Did you think if you fucked me I would hand you my kingdom? Did you think because I was a woman I would betray my people? Then I am sorry to disappoint you!"

"I wanted glory! I wanted fame! I wanted to make something of myself!" Antonius shouted, breathing heavily. "And I wanted you. I have wanted you since the moment I met you. And I will never stop wanting you, even if it makes me less of a general, less of a man, less of a Roman. That is what you do not understand. I would throw it all away for you! I have already thrown it all away. For you! And you have hardly done the same for me."

Cleopatra crossed the room, her face dark and livid. "Have I not? Tell me, have I not given you everything? Look!" She flung her arm wildly towards the window. "Look at my city! On the brink of war! On the brink of destruction!" She shoved him away, and Antonius stumbled back, staring dumbly at the tears in her eyes. "I have given up everything! My scepter, my children, my life! For what, Marcus? I already had glory! I already had fame! I already had everything! Everything! Do you not see? I knew all along, Marcus! One cannot be in love and hope to rule the world." She shook her head, her eyes glancing up at the ceiling, her voice trembling. "But I loved you anyway. And I knew my love for you would be my death. That, Marcus, is the difference between you and I. That is what *you* never understood."

Antonius could not look away from her tear-streaked face, her lashes dark around her shining eyes, and the love that set his heart aflame like a torch in the night. "Then what do you suggest we do?"

"Oh, we shall fight," Cleopatra said, lifting her chin haughtily, tears still clinging to her jaw, a picture of her righteous rule, the rule of a divine woman. "It is the only thing left to do."

"We hardly have the men for it," Antonius muttered.

"But we have you," she said softly, smirking faintly. "The best general west of the Nile."

Antonius reached out and loosely took one of her hands in his, pulling her into his arms and kissing her damp cheek. "The best general in the world."

"The best general I could ever ask for," Cleopatra whispered, looking up at him with sad, loving eyes. "I hope, on the last day of all days, that is enough. I hope I am enough."

"On the last day of all days, you are more than enough," Antonius said, lifting a curling strand of hair behind her ear. "You are everything to me."

Tears welled once more in her dark eyes. He felt his own eyes sting, and her fingertips brushed his cheek. "Marcus?"

"My love?"

"If all else fails, will you join me?" Her eyes held the world's constellations, they held eternity in a gaze, they held all the glory and fame he could ever ask for. "Will you join me in Death?"

"Whatever you ask of me, my love," Antonius whispered against her mouth. "And more."

Then he kissed her, his arms wrapping around her waist until their bodies were one, until he could not bring her any closer. She cried as she kissed him, her arms clinging to his neck. In a swift motion, he hoisted her up into his arms, and she kissed him harder, more desperately, as if this were the last time. Maybe it was.

He walked them to the bed and laid her down gently, reverently, wanting to remember all of her, the shape of her waist against his lips, the curve of her neck under his touch, and her eyes, dark and knowing like some goddess on earth.

Finally, he knew he had found the woman he had searched for all this time. A terrifying, beautiful, and proud woman whom he would die for on the last day of all days. If he had once wanted glory, fame, to make something of himself, then now all he wanted was this woman here, his woman, in his arms, forever.

Antonius wondered, distantly, what would be said of him, when his bones had long turned to dust, and a new sun shone on an earth he no longer knew. Would history remember him? Would they remember his name? His triumphs? His failures?

Or would they only remember a man who had given up everything for a woman? A Roman general who had surrendered to a foreign queen?

Cleopatra held his jaw in her hands, and kissed him slowly, tenderly, as if her lips spelled his name in a language that only they knew.

And Antonius realized then that he did not care. He did not care for his fame or his name or his honor. He did not know why he ever had. History, after all, was written by the victors, and the gods alone knew he had already won.

So little, so little.

At last, Antonius understood, at last he understood that it had all been a losing game, and only now that he ceased to play could he write his own rules.

Only now did he know anything at all.

58

GAIUS OCTAVIUS

SEPTEMBER 31 BC

"WE MAY AS WELL have defeated Scylla herself and the men would still demand their payment!" Statilius Taurus grumbled. "It is a pity the camps of Antonius were so depleted, or we might have won spoils enough to appease them. But I suppose this is what we call victory!"

Octavius could not help but smile at his army commander. They were still at their camp on the northern shore of the strait and would need to leave before winter made things difficult at sea, forcing his generals to plan rather than celebrate.

"Aye, Taurus, this is victory indeed. We shall find her sweeter when we are back in our homes, in the arms of our wives and children."

Lurius smirked, elbowing Taurus. "The arms of a wife are but another war, Caesar. Victory will be sweeter when I find myself in the arms of a—"

"Enough," Arruntius interrupted, though he could not suppress a smile. He was the eldest in the room and knew that while victory was had, the real work had just begun. "We are here on business, not pleasure."

"Thank you, Arruntius," Octavius said with a smile of his own. "We must begin discussing our plan of attack. While the battle has been won, the war will not be over until I drag that Egyptian queen through the streets of Rome."

"And Antonius?" Taurus asked warily. He had been a partisan of Antonius for many years before he chose Octavius' side when war broke out between them. But there was no room for mercy with that man.

"Dead," Octavius said. Antonius had dug his grave, and now he would have to lie in it.

"We have reports that he has secured Alexandria," Corvinus said cautiously. "No doubt he will put up a fight."

"He does not have the men," Octavius dismissed. "His best generals have already joined my cause. King Herod sent his emissaries to me before the blood of his allies had dried.

473

Even the Thracian kings have all but sworn their loyalty. He relies on his mistress' army, when Egypt already knows they do not stand a chance. Do you think they will throw away their lives for a deserted Roman?"

Corvinus frowned. "I suppose not."

"Unless their queen is prepared to throw away *her* life," Lurius countered.

"Then you do not know women very well, my friend," Octavius said with a smirk. "Women would throw away their honor before their lives. But Antonius will fight. He may be a traitor, but he was a Roman before that, and he would rather fight for his life than beg for it."

"Then what are we waiting for?" Taurus asked, thumping a fist on his thigh. "Let us sail to Egypt now and be done with it."

"No," Octavius said. "There is no rush. No one would be so foolish as to ally with a dead man. Besides, I have already sent a small contingent to keep an eye on him. Egypt may be dealt with in time. First, we must secure our own allies, and subdue the rest. I shall send Agrippa and Maecenas to Rome to oversee my affairs and prepare Brundisium for my arrival."

"Where *is* our dear Agrippa?" Lurius asked, glancing around. "He is not one to skirt his duties."

"No indeed." Octavius hesitated, remembering Agrippa's harsh words in the tent before he stormed out. "After the battle was ended he received news of his wife's death. He has been attending to his own affairs."

It was partly true. While Agrippa had met with someone sent from Rome to prepare for funeral arrangements, this meeting had happened three days ago, and Octavius had not seen Agrippa since.

"Ah, poor man," Taurus muttered. "So they shall be sent ahead to Rome? And where shall you go, Caesar?"

"First I will see to the laying of the foundation of my city, Nicopolis, on the spot where we first pitched camp along the strait. Then I shall make my rounds in Greece, and travel to Asia Minor. Not all battles need to end in death. I shall winter on Samos before I take Egypt."

"And once you have Egypt?" Arruntius asked, eyeing Octavius carefully.

Arruntius would not be the first to watch him closely with the ending of the war. Octavius knew many would be waiting to see how he returned, and what he would do next. He felt his heartbeat, the thread of his fate, pulled taut, as he drew ever closer to his destiny.

He smiled. "We close the doors of Janus. And then, peace."

Octavius picked a path carefully down the cliffside, the rocky coast of Epirus overlooking the Ionian Sea. The sun was setting over the horizon, casting the blue waves in a deep, bruising red.

Already a chill settled over the land as winter crept closer to the edges of Greece. Octavius could just make out a hunched figure where the tide broke on the shore, hands grabbing fistfuls of sand on either side of him, his broad back tense.

Even now Octavius' heart clenched and beat painfully. Would he ever cease feeling this way? Would they always be drawn to each other, like two stars in the night sky?

He came to a stop behind Agrippa, who had not yet noticed him. "If I were an enemy," Octavius said, and Agrippa spun around wildly, a hand on the hilt of his *gladius,* before he realized and relaxed, "you would already be dead."

"How did you find me?" Agrippa asked, glancing at him hesitantly as Octavius sat on the sand beside him. He knew he had done wrong to avoid Octavius and all his responsibilities, so now he wanted to know whether Octavius was angry or not.

"We have guards patrolling this entire coastline," Octavius said wryly. "You would not have been able to escape even if you wanted to."

Agrippa frowned. "I did not wish to escape."

Octavius raised a brow. "I have not seen you for three days."

"I know."

"You are grieving," Octavius said quietly, remembering the lost look in Agrippa's eyes when he had taken Livia's letter. "I understand."

"I was grieving many things." Agrippa avoided his gaze and looked out on the sea which was rapidly turning wine-dark and sparkling under the white moonlight.

"Like what?"

"Like us," Agrippa said, so softly Octavius wondered if he misheard. "My wife was not the only death of this war."

"What?"

"Come now, Octavius," he said, and his voice sounded tired. "Do you not think we are a little too old to play games?"

"This is no game, Agrippa," Octavius said steadily. "But if it were, it would be a very unfair game indeed."

"That is the way with most games." Agrippa gripped a handful of sand and watched with a bitter frown as it slipped through his fingers. "They favor those who cheat."

"What does that mean?"

He remembered that day in Apollonia when he had convinced Rufus to cheat on his behalf. Agrippa had looked so disappointed in him afterward that he could not bear it, and had laughed it off if only to make himself feel better.

"What I mean," Agrippa said, his eyes trained on the rolling tide, "is that I cannot pretend to be satisfied with half your love. I cannot pretend to be satisfied with our stolen nights and long, lonely days." He paused, his eyes half-closed. "I cannot pretend to be satisfied with a man who loves his own power more than me."

Octavius was silent and stared at the ocean. If he did not look at Agrippa, if he did not speak, it was almost as if they were back on the shores of Apollonia, when they were hardly nineteen years old, the future as far away and unknowable as the most distant horizon. Would he have done it all over again, if he knew how it would end?

"When did you decide this?" Octavius asked, for it was the only thing he could think to say.

Agrippa did not answer at first, then, "I think I knew for a long time, but I could not face it. Not until now."

Octavius took a deep breath past the tightness in his chest. "It was never a choice. You know that right? It was never a choice."

Agrippa gave him a sidelong glance. "It was never a choice for me either."

"In another life, perhaps it could have been different." His voice was bitter, almost mocking.

"There is no other life, Octavius," Agrippa said sadly. "Only this one."

Octavius swallowed, and a wind across the water made him shiver. "I do not believe that."

"You were always meant for greatness," Agrippa continued as if he had not heard him. "I knew from the day I met you that you were someone I could follow, someone I could look up to. I also knew I would love you, until the end of my days. But it had never occurred to me then that you would love me too. And yet, here we are now, and I am as close to having you as I was then."

Inexplicably, Octavius felt an anger that he had never felt before, an anger not only at himself, or Agrippa, but at the world. "You knew my fate from the beginning."

Agrippa smiled, but it was filled with irony and regret. "I suppose it was my fate to love you anyway."

"You may still love me," Octavius said without thinking, his voice low, his heart beating faster, more desperate. "You may still have me."

"Only what is left of you," Agrippa countered.

Octavius turned towards him and took his hand forcibly. Agrippa did not protest but he did not meet Octavius' eyes. "There is a way for me to love you still. Come to Samos for the winter. Be with me."

"And who shall you send ahead to Rome in my stead?"

"Anyone," Octavius said quickly, feeling that time was running out. "We have won the war. It is over. You know if you loved me, you would stay."

Agrippa looked at him. He touched Octavius' cheek with his fingertips, light as a feather, before his hand dropped. "I leave *because* I love you."

He stood up and began to walk away, his hand slipping from Octavius'. Without thinking, Octavius reached out and grabbed his wrist, holding it in a tight grip. Agrippa glanced down at his hand cautiously, then at Octavius.

"I will give you everything," Octavius whispered. "If that is what this is about, I will give you all of me."

Agrippa stared at him, his eyes wide, almost fearful. He said nothing and a panic seized Octavius, so that he felt he could not breathe, so that he thought he might die right then.

"You have waited for me to be ready, and here I am," Octavius said, his chest rising and falling rapidly. He was almost dizzy with fear. "I am ready. Is that not what you wanted?"

"No." Agrippa tugged his wrist away. "Not like this."

Octavius' arms were limp at his sides. It was as if all the desperation and panic had been spent in one fell swoop, and now he only felt empty.

Agrippa glanced at him uneasily, one last time, before he walked away. Octavius watched as he climbed up the rocky cliffside to the bluffs above until the small silhouette of his figure disappeared in the night.

He remained sitting on the sand until the wind dried the tears from his eyes.

⤞⤝

Octavius awoke deep in the night.

He had been sleeping fitfully once he had returned to his tent from the beach before some deep exhaustion had taken hold and pulled him into a death-like slumber, and only the sound of footsteps and someone's breath had startled him awake.

He reached for his dagger in the blind darkness and opened his mouth to shout when a finger pressed against his lips.

"Shh." The weight left his lips. "It is I."

Octavius sat up, bewildered, but a strong hand was placed on his chest and pressed him to the ground. "Agrippa?"

"Please, my love," he whispered. "Forgive me."

He nodded, unable to speak, and he felt Agrippa's mouth on his, slow and familiar, tasting of liquor and something almost like regret. Perhaps if he had been more awake, he would have protested more or asked him why, but Octavius found that Agrippa's warmth was like a new dawn and his touch a pleasant dream come to life.

Octavius closed his eyes. He felt Agrippa's mouth on his neck, his jaw, and his name was whispered like a prayer against his skin, like a promise—no, like an oath.

Their clothes fell away easily, and Agrippa's skin was burning against the cold air of the night. He placed a hand on Agrippa's arm, and he went still. Octavius only looked at him and nodded, but those sea-green eyes read the words he left unspoken.

He kissed him again, Agrippa's fingertips skating his inner thigh, and Octavius closed his eyes against the tender touch. A tremor as deep and dark as the moving earth seemed to flow from Agrippa's very pulse, so that they were not separate bodies but one, one heartbeat in the dead of night, beating together to the same fate, or as two fates when they crossed at one moment in time.

Octavius held onto Agrippa tightly as he surrendered, until his pleasure struck as blinding as lightning, and it was like touching the sun, it was like being a god, immortal for all days, this moment, this touch, and for the first time, Octavius knew the name of love and was not afraid.

59

Marcus Vipsanius Agrippa

OCTOBER 31 BC

THE OCEAN GLITTERED UNDER the sun like a sea of gems, as far as the eye could see. Agrippa remembered once wishing to become one with the waves and disappear into that unknown blue forever. Now that longing was replaced by a weariness that grew more familiar with each passing day.

Suddenly a cold wind off the ocean whipped across the deck, billowing the limp sails, and Agrippa's attention returned to the ship.

"Prepare to set sail!" Agrippa called out as he stalked across the deck. "Raise the anchor!"

"General Agrippa!"

He went still, then turned around. Octavius' strolling figure approached, surrounded by a small bodyguard. The crew stalled in their tasks as Octavius raised a hand to halt their preparations. His face was unconcerned, even smiling, but Agrippa knew him better.

Octavius was livid.

Once he was close enough, Octavius placed a firm hand on Agrippa's shoulder and guided him to the cabin on the pretense of privacy. His smile was tight, and his voice dropped to a hiss.

"What is the meaning of this?"

Agrippa returned the smile. "You know very well the meaning of this. For you were the one to order this ship to return to Italy, were you not?"

"Yes, but it was not meant for *you* to command. I had ordered Arruntius to go in your stead, or do you forget?"

The cabin door shut with a loud bang, and Agrippa stared at Octavius. Since that night, after their fight on the beach, they had not seriously spoken to each other. Octavius had been busy arranging his travel plans, and Agrippa had been busy executing them.

But they both knew that they were avoiding each other, delaying the inevitable. At least, what Agrippa knew to be inevitable. For he had intended that night to be the last, and it had taken every ounce of self-restraint he had to board this ship and not look back.

"Octavius," Agrippa said in a low, pained voice, glancing outside the cabin window at his men as they once more prepared to set sail. Their time had run out. "We both know I must go."

Octavius' gaze was hard but pleading. "Come with me to Samos for the winter. It is not too late. There we may be together. No one will disturb us. We shall live quietly for a time, at peace, before we must return to Italy. It is the only way, Agrippa, and you know it. I would rather have something than nothing."

"That is why it is impossible," Agrippa said, shaking his head. "You would rather have something than nothing, but I would rather have nothing than something."

"What do you want from me, Agrippa?" Octavius asked angrily.

"I want all of you," Agrippa said flatly, and Octavius flinched. "We can run away together, find an island or a city somewhere far away, pretend we are merchants, or exiles, or dead. It does not matter to me. Let us leave behind the world, Octavius. Rome, Egypt, everything. Let us give it all up for a life together. For *us*."

Octavius stared at him in deathly silence. Even though Agrippa knew what Octavius' answer would be, a small part of him had still hoped, the part of him that was still a ten-year-old boy, wanting to prove himself, wanting to be loved.

If I were Achilles, you would be Patroclus.

For his silence was answer enough.

"You see? That is the difference between you and me, Octavius. I would give up everything for you. And you would not."

"I gave you all of me that night," Octavius whispered, and angry tears welled in his eyes. Agrippa had never seen him so distraught, and he hoped no one entered the cabin. "Or did that mean nothing to you?"

"It meant everything," Agrippa said, his chest tightening. "But it only meant *something* to you."

"Then this is it?" Octavius asked, disbelieving. "You would give this up for nothing?"

Agrippa had to take a deep breath before he spoke, and it felt as though the very words held his own heart as he said them. "You must understand, Octavius. Every day in secret, every day I must pretend not to love you, every day apart, every day fighting for something, for something less than I feel for you, a part of me dies, until one day that something *would* become nothing. And I fear if that day ever came, our love would be the death of me."

Octavius stared at the ground, unmoving, his frown a bitter slash across his face. They stood in silence, save for the footsteps and shouts of his men and the clanking of iron as the sails fluttered in the wind.

Agrippa wished to reach out and touch him, to take him in his arms as he had that night, but a part of him now resisted, the part that knew it was over.

"It seems I shall not convince you," Octavius said at last. He flashed a twisted smile, and as he lifted his head high, the tears were almost dry. Octavius was proud and would not beg any longer. If there was something that had never changed since the first days Agrippa knew him, it was that. "Enjoy your voyage back to Rome."

He turned and walked towards the door.

"Octavius," Agrippa said before he left, though he immediately regretted it when Octavius paused, his shoulders tense. He did not turn around. He did not speak. "I will always love you. That will never change."

For a moment, so swift he thought he might have imagined it, Agrippa thought Octavius would turn around.

Then he opened the door and was gone.

⟶⟫⟫ ⟪⟪⟵

DECEMBER 31 BC

Agrippa stood in the courtyard of his house, the evening light weakly filtering through the red and white columns, shining on the waters of the impluvium.

The couch where Attica had spent so much time reading was empty and cold. There were other mourners gathered around, Livia, Octavia, and Attica's relatives. It was too cold outside to hold the ceremony in the gardens, though Attica would have preferred that.

He heard the indignant cries of Agrippina and Vipsania somewhere inside the house with their nurses. They did not really comprehend her death, though they knew now that their mother was gone.

"I do not understand, Livia," Agrippa said, his voice hardly more than a whisper. "How could she die? How could she leave me like this?"

Livia sighed beside him. Agrippa had never seen her so disheveled, her hair in loose strands and her face pallid. In many ways, she had lost a sister, as much as Agrippa had lost a wife. "She did not wish to."

Agrippa ran a hand down his face. "If only I had not gone to war. If only I had stayed."

"Do not blame yourself," Livia said gravely. "This was not your doing. Only the gods have the power to deal out death."

"I blame myself nonetheless," Agrippa replied, his throat tightening painfully. "She should have lived to see the end of all wars. She should have lived to see her husband return, to see her children grow old."

Livia turned towards him, her eyes sad. "Attica would not have wanted you to suffer on her behalf. She loved you in life, and she loves you in death. Her children must remember her as a strong and pious woman, and only you can give them those memories. You hide from them in grief, but that will only bring them more pain."

As if the words had heralded it, Vipsania suddenly waddled into the courtyard, crying, her distressed nurse following after her. Livia hurried towards the child and picked her up. She nodded towards Agrippa before going inside the house with the nurse and a few other women to calm the child. Vipsania was only four years old.

"You are not alone, you know."

Agrippa turned around.

Octavia stood tall and serene behind him, her hair loose in mourning, her eyes blue and distant. He saw that familiar pride, the same steel set to her jaw as her brother, but where Octavius was all dark, knowing glances and charming smiles, Octavia was colder in her politeness, having seen a different side of the world.

But Octavia had lost her husband, and she knew better his thoughts now.

"Yet I feel lonely all the same," Agrippa replied quietly.

"I know." Octavia smiled gently. "But you are loved by many. One day, this pain will be but a memory."

"What if I do not wish it to be a memory?"

Octavia studied his face closely. Too closely. It seemed every thought he ever had was now written there. He had the sudden feeling they were no longer speaking of Attica.

She sighed, shaking her head, as if she too had asked the same question and received the answer long ago. "It does not matter what you wish. Time takes no heed of us mortals. We shall all of us become memories."

Somehow her words were comforting. Agrippa smiled wryly. "Will you not marry again?"

Octavia gave a small smile. "No, I will not."

"Even if he asks it of you?"

"Even so." Octavia glanced around the room, her eyes perceptive and quick. "The war is over, Agrippa. I have done my duty. Any more life granted to me I shall devote to my children."

"That is a noble service," Agrippa said, inclining his head.

"Men take lives so that women may make them," Octavia said carelessly. "Who is to say what is noble?"

Agrippa raised a brow. "Regardless, I fear I shall still have to remarry."

"Yes, I suppose so," Octavia said, eyeing him carefully. "I hear Caesar sails for Brundisium. You and Maecenas called for him to come early."

It was true. While Octavius had been away, Agrippa and Maecenas had been in charge of his affairs in Rome. There had been a minor rebellion stirred up by the son of Lepidus, which they handled as discreetly as possible. But the more pressing issue was the soldiers, who demanded their pay and threatened mutiny. It was important for Octavius to show his face in Italy before his final conquest of Cleopatra, and remind the people of his loyalty to their cause.

"Yes," Agrippa said, though he would rather not talk about it. "Maecenas and I summoned him. There is some business which he must attend to in person."

Octavia nodded absently, still looking at him strangely. "You know, you shall never be the same."

"Pardon?" Agrippa asked, his heart beating fearfully. Octavia always seemed to speak words that held two meanings.

"When the other half of your soul is gone," Octavia said, her eyes distant, remembering something, or someone, long ago, "you shall never be the same. But why on earth would you want to be?"

⤞⤝

JANUARY 30 BC

The carriage rolled roughly down the stone road as they entered the town of Brundisium.

Agrippa caught the salty scent of the sea on the breeze. He closed his eyes, breathing deeply, but nothing he did could ease the tight knot forming in his stomach.

"You seem different, my friend."

Agrippa opened his eyes. Maecenas sat across from him, looking at him with his usual haughty gaze. A wave of hatred rose up in Agrippa and settled as swiftly as it came. While he would always find Maecenas ridiculous, his staunch loyalty to Octavius and his undeniable skill in collecting information had exonerated some of those qualities in Agrippa's eyes.

"How so?"

"More distant," Maecenas said, then smirked. "And you have a worse sense of humor."

"The last I might say of you," Agrippa said, glaring at him.

Maecenas laughed. "I suppose you are right. War changes us all for the worse."

"Some more than others, unfortunately."

"Are you speaking of me?" Maecenas asked mockingly. "Or someone else?"

Agrippa looked at him sharply. "What do you mean?"

Maecenas affected innocence. "Oh, nothing, really. I just get the sense that you and Caesar...are not on the best of terms at the moment."

"Why do you say so?" Agrippa asked, hating how his defensiveness betrayed him. He had never been as good with words as Octavius and Maecenas.

Maecenas' eyes glittered, for he knew he had struck a weak spot. "Should I not be the one asking questions?" Maecenas teased. "But I suppose if I must give an answer, it is written all over your face. You two were always so very close in school. If I am honest, I could always tell when you two were having some quarrel. The gods know you were much easier to read than he, but even then, he had his tell."

"And what was that?"

"He would go to the baths alone, and mope about until you found him and made amends," Maecenas said, half-smiling, though it faded quickly. He stared out the window and shook his head. "It was as clear as day, looking back now. But I suppose that is true with most things."

"We were children then," Agrippa said, surprised to find how bitter he sounded.

Maecenas raised a brow. "Ah, I see. This is more than a schoolboy squabble, is it?"

"Yes," Agrippa replied tersely, then sighed. "And no. I suppose not much has changed after all."

"Sometimes when everything changes," Maecenas said, "nothing really does. For it is only then that we truly see what stays the same."

"If I could do it all over again..." Agrippa ran a hand through his hair as he trailed off. He knew it was a useless thought now, but he said it anyway because it gave him more hope than looking toward the future.

"He loves you," Maecenas said suddenly, and Agrippa looked at him in surprise, for he thought he heard a tinge of jealousy. "He has always loved you. That has never changed."

Agrippa did not have time to reply, for just then the carriage jerked to a stop and they were escorted down the road by a retinue of guards. Already there were swarms of people awaiting Caesar's arrival, choking the streets so that their carriage could pass no more and they had to take the rest of the journey on foot.

There was an excitement stirring among the people, a strange anticipation, half-anxious, half-morbid, as if they expected the queen of Egypt herself to descend from the ship and walk all the way to Rome in chains.

Maecenas and Agrippa pushed their way to the docks, where most of the rioting soldiers were gathered to demand more money. Octavius' ship was already anchored, and a long line of guards marched down the quay.

They waited as Octavius himself disembarked the ship, surrounded by his heavily armed guard. He was fitted in shining armor, the cuirass on his breast engraved with gold, his face cleanly shaven. Octavius continued walking to a large platform built for his arrival, where thousands of people clamored for his attention.

Octavius swept his gaze over the crowds, his eyes dark and unreadable, but Agrippa knew, he knew that this was the moment he had been waiting for. He lifted his arms high as the crowd roared. Then the sunlight broke through the clouds, bathing the world in gold, and Octavius could not help but grin.

"My people!" he cried. "My people!"

Divi fili! Divi fili! Divi fili!

Maecenas laughed as the crowds riled themselves up to such a fervor, crying out to him in praise and prayer. He nudged Agrippa and shook his head.

"Now *there* is the son of a god."

60

CLEOPATRA VII PHILOPATOR

MARCH 30 BC

THE SIGNS OF DEATH were everywhere.

Winter had been much colder than usual but without storms. It had stopped raining for several weeks. The Nile was more dry than it ever had been for the past fifty years. Birds did not take to the skies, but huddled in trees and on the banks of the river. Animals were found dead in the countryside, picked apart by vultures. Her people knew war was coming and read many omens in the gloomy days that passed.

But Cleopatra did not need omens to tell her what she knew in her heart. Death drew near, and she would not outlive the year.

"Mother." Caesarion, her eldest, walked inside her room. "You called for me?"

At first, Cleopatra could only look at him. She has had these moments as of late while looking at her son, when her past memories rushed to the surface, and she was trapped in the palace with none other than Julius Caesar, and he smiled and asked her if she had ever been to Rome.

Though her son looked much like her and all the Ptolemys that came before, there was a sharpness to his eyes, a restlessness to him, that betrayed his Roman ancestry.

"Yes, my son," she said at last. "There is something we must speak about."

Caesarion looked worried as he sat beside his mother on the couch. "Is it about the war?"

"There will be no war," Cleopatra said sharply, and Caesarion's eyes widened. "The battle will be finished as soon as it begins, if it begins at all."

"But Antyllus told me—"

"You must forget Antyllus." She took up her son's hand when he was silent. "I am

486

sorry, my love, I know you two are like brothers, but I cannot promise you the fate of Antonius' son. I can only try to protect yours. You are the pharaoh of Egypt, and when I am gone, the people will look to you."

Tears shone in his eyes. "But mother—"

"No, listen to me, Caesarion." Cleopatra sighed, kissing his knuckles. "I have tried to negotiate with Caesar. I have sent him gold and treasure beyond count. He has not yet refused, but he is not like your father. His aim is Egypt, not just her queen. That is why you must flee. I have already arranged a ship at the port of Berenice on the Red Sea that will take you far away from here, as far as India if not farther. When it is safer, and you have gathered a strong enough force, then you may return, and reclaim the throne."

"I—I do not understand." Caesarion shook his head. "If I am to flee, you must flee with me! Why do you stay? Or do you stay because of *him?*"

Caesarion had never warmed up to Marcus, despite being Antyllus' close friend, and was often jealous that she had more children with him.

Cleopatra paused, and placed a hand against her son's cheek, stroking the soft skin as she used to do when he could not fall asleep as a little boy. "I stay because I am queen, and I have fled this country too many times. If it is my fate, I would rather die as her queen than be forced to flee as an exile of my own country."

Why did Helen not simply escape?

Maybe she did not want to.

"I want to stay," Caesarion said, angrily. "I want to fight! I am nearly in my seventeenth year. I am a man now."

"You are young," Cleopatra replied, keeping her voice calm. "And you are too important to throw your life away recklessly."

He turned away coldly and her hand dropped to her lap. "Antyllus wants to fight, and he is the same age as I."

"I do not command him, and he will not inherit a kingdom." She sighed. "These are things you would have learned in time. A leader must know when to sacrifice themselves and when to survive."

"And you are sacrificing yourself?" Caesarion asked in disbelief.

"Yes," Cleopatra said, smiling half-heartedly. "For you. For my people. It is my duty as a mother and a queen. One day I hope you will understand."

"I do not want to understand," he said bitterly, and he sounded much younger than he was, as if he were still a child and did not want anything besides his own mother. "I want to rule beside you, not alone. Nor all the way in India."

"Oh my love, I know. But that is not for us to decide. For now, you must focus on getting yourself to safety. That is your duty as king."

Caesarion hung his head, though Cleopatra saw his eyes narrow, thinking, searching secretly for a way out, just like his father. Just like his mother. "Then what will happen to Antyllus? Am I to leave him here to die?"

"I am afraid his fate is in the hands of Caesar, as is his father's. You cannot help them any more than I can." She thought of Marcus, her husband, preparing to fight a losing battle. Though she had no regrets about trying to bargain with Caesar, she pitied Marcus, who had only ever wanted to prove himself, to be someone worth remembering. "When the day comes for you to flee, you must be ready."

"Yes, mother."

"Good," she said, taking a deep breath and trying to smile. "Now you may leave."

Caesarion kissed her cheek and left.

Cleopatra did not fall asleep until very late in the night.

Rain fell for a week straight. It was springtime in Rome, and Cleopatra thought they would be drowned in this valley before the summer came.

She missed her desert heat, the winding Nile, the cool coast of Alexandria. Here she felt more mortal, closer to Death somehow, as if the divinity of her forefathers did not quite reach across the Mediterranean Sea.

"What do you think of so quietly, my lady?"

Cleopatra turned from the window overlooking the forum, startled.

Julius Caesar leaned against the door frame, watching her with his sharp brown eyes. She had not even heard him approach, and she wondered how long he had stood there, watching her.

"I am thinking of my country," she said, deciding not to lie. He had a knack for discovering the truth anyway.

"As a queen should," Caesar said, bowing his head. "Sometimes I wonder if Rome would not be better off with a queen as her leader, rather than a consul."

Cleopatra went still, unsure of his full meaning. "You forget yourself, Caesar. Rome had long ago ended her reign of royalty. If there would be any queen, it would be Roma herself."

Caesar had a faraway look which worried her. "Roma. She is as fickle as Fortuna. There is no man strong enough to rule her."

"Do you wish to?" Cleopatra asked, raising a brow.

Caesar's gaze fastened upon her. "What?"

"Do you wish to rule her?"

He stared at her, unseeing. At last, he looked away, troubled. He was a very troubled man,

THE SUN OF GOD

Cleopatra had learned, though to those he did not know well he hid it. Cleopatra wondered what he foresaw, what he knew, and if it would help or harm her in the end.

"Perhaps I do. There are those who would like to see me king."

"You mean Marcus Antonius," Cleopatra said, hiding her surprise. He had heard about the incident at the Lupercalia, when Marcus had tried to place a golden crown on Caesar's head, as it had become quite the scandal in Rome.

Caesar glanced at her quickly, frowning. "And others. But Rome has not had a king for many centuries. She will not suffer them now, I think."

"Perhaps not a king," she said, smiling. "Sometimes there is more power in a lesser title."

He raised a brow, a shadow of a smile flickering on his mouth. "You are too intelligent for your own good, my lady. And certainly too intelligent for him."

"Him?" Cleopatra feigned ignorance, but her pulse quickened.

"Oh, did you think I would not notice?" Caesar cocked his head to the side, like a sparrow, and Cleopatra nearly shivered. "Did you think I would not know if my closest friend was in love?"

"I do not know what you speak of," she said coldly.

A dislike lurked in Caesar's eyes, mingled with his amusement at her discomfort. She rather thought her time in Italy had come to an end.

"Do not worry, my dear," Caesar said, smiling, but it was harsh in his face. "I am not protective of my women, or my men. You may bring Antonius back to Egypt if you wish and he can play at being king. But just remember this." He looked her in the eyes and this time she did shiver. "He will never understand what it means to be king. You and I both know you are either born to rule, or you are not."

Before she could respond, Caesar grunted, and his eyes grew wide. He looked down at his chest, and she followed his gaze. Blood bloomed in dark red splotches, one above his heart, his stomach, all over his chest, as if a thousand daggers were thrusting into him.

He staggered back, then forward, until his knees buckled and he fell before her, gasping, blood dribbling over his white lips, and she opened her mouth to scream—

Cleopatra awoke, gasping. It was dark. She turned at a creaking noise beside her.

A figure approached from the door, shrouded in shadow. Her handmaiden. It was just a dream, no matter how mingled with memory. But her blood still ran cold when his dark eyes flashed in her mind.

"My lady."

"What is it?" she asked impatiently, still breathing hard. A bead of sweat rolled down her spine, and she shivered as a chilly draft from the windows cooled her hot skin.

"Marcus Antonius has called an emergency meeting. He has requested your presence."

He will never understand what it means to be king.

"Neither did you," Cleopatra muttered to herself. She took a deep breath. "Tell my husband I shall be there shortly."

The beginning of the end had come.

⊱⋙⋘⊰

AUGUST 30 BC

"Quick, my lady! While there is still time!"

Cleopatra stared out her balcony at the fires dotting the coast of her city. She thought she could see the roof of the Mouseion, the Library of Alexandria, the jewel of her childhood, alight in flames. Suddenly she was not seated on her couch, in her royal bedroom, but walking the dimly lit rooms of the library, the walls piled with scrolls towering as high as the sky itself.

"We must try to escape! My lady, please!"

"No." Cleopatra shook her head and felt distantly the tears which had not ceased flowing down her face cling to her jaw.

Will you join me in Death?

Whatever you ask of me, my love. And more.

"But my lady, your husband has already taken his own life," her handmaiden urged, and Cleopatra looked at her sharply so that she ceased her pleading.

"There is no escape for me," Cleopatra said steadily. "I shall always be hunted, even if I were to cross the unending ocean. My husband has chosen a noble end."

"Yes, my lady." But her handmaiden began to cry.

"Why do you cry? Do you fear the end is near?"

Her handmaid nodded silently, wiping at her tears with shaky hands.

"It is easy to fear death," Cleopatra said idly. "But just think what would become of you if Caesar were to take us alive."

A strangled sob came from across the room. "Let the gods forbid it, my lady!"

Suddenly there were shouts down the hall, and the sharp clang of swords, faintly heard but growing louder. The young Caesar had breached the palace sooner than she had expected.

She turned towards her handmaiden. "Quick! Bring me my wine."

"But—"

"Now!"

Her handmaiden hurried over to a large bronze chest tucked away in the corner of the room. She unlocked the latch with trembling fingers and pulled out a dusted pitcher of blood-red wine. She set it down hesitantly on the low table before Cleopatra, followed by a faïence-blue chalice, ornately engraved with the fanged serpent head of the Asp, whose poison already diluted the wine.

"Hide in the next room." Cleopatra listened for a moment as the guards in her corridor grunted and landed with a soft thud on the ground. "If he leaves me here to die, bury me with my husband. You must do that for me. It is the last earthly command of your queen."

Her handmaiden nodded frantically, and without another word scurried into the next room, locking the door behind her.

For a moment, everything was horribly silent.

Then the door to her room creaked open. Cleopatra held her breath, before a young man walked in, dressed in polished silver armor, a familiar, clean-shaven face beneath his helmet. His gait was uncanny in its similarity to his great-uncle, the lithe limbs, almost feminine, hiding a coiled strength.

His eyes found hers, and they held each other's stare in silence.

Then Cleopatra smiled, pouring herself a glass of wine. Caesar merely watched as she took the glass and raised it high. *"Ave, Caesar."*

He frowned. "Do you find this war amusing?"

"War? No." She took a small sip and relished in its bitterness. A single drop would be enough. "But you? Yes. Very amusing indeed."

Caesar raised a brow. "Then you may find it amusing to learn that your son, Caesarion, has been caught and killed."

Cleopatra went still, so still she thought the wine had already worked its magic. Distantly, she felt her heart skip a beat, and tears sprang unwillingly to her eyes as she thought of that face, still soft and round in its youth, the delicate brown curls falling over his forehead, killed by the man standing before her. Her hand clutched at the stem of her glass, and it seemed a long time until she could breathe again.

"Oh yes," Caesar said, a glint in his eyes. "You wanted him to escape. Pity, for he nearly did. But he had placed his trust in the wrong people. Just before Antyllus was killed, I asked if he knew where your son was, and though he did not wish to tell me, I can be very persuasive."

"You are cruel," Cleopatra said, hardly able to control the tremor in her voice.

"I only did what my divine father could not," Caesar replied coldly.

"And what is that?"

"What I must."

It was then that Cleopatra understood. While this man and her Caesar had much in common, in one thing they differed. Her Caesar had wanted to rule. This Caesar desired more, no matter the cost.

He shook his head ruefully. "Julius Caesar trusted too many, too much."

"He knew his own limits," Cleopatra countered. "You shall fly up, up, up, and like Icarus, you shall fly too close to the sun."

"Not if I *am* the sun," Caesar said with a smirk. "There are forces at work here that you do not understand. But soon you shall see. I am bringing you back to Rome. I shall show you what a true empire looks like. Alexandria shall seem a mere village beside it."

"Oh, men," Cleopatra said, and she took a long sip of her wine, wishing to bring it all to an end, though she already felt the poison stiffening her blood. "You know so much, and yet understand so little."

Caesar stared at her, his face unreadable, but she thought there was a flicker of doubt in his dark eyes. Where Julius Caesar had trusted in others, this Caesar trusted only in himself and his own knowledge, and it would cost him now. "I shall return soon. There is some business I must attend to. My guards will make sure you do not try to escape like your son."

"Do not worry, Caesar," she said, and the words already felt heavy in her mouth. "To me, my son has already escaped a worse fate."

Without another word, Caesar left the room.

A darkness descended on her vision, and she heard the cup clang on the floor as it slipped through her fingers. Minutes or hours passed, she could not tell, and then there were shouts, panic, hands on her face, her neck, but it was all shadow, a long-lost dream, slipping through the threads of time.

But she heard his voice, beckoning, beyond the veil, and she knew her ancestors would guide her in the everlasting night until she found him.

Until she was not a mother, not a queen, not even a woman, but someone more than that, someone more legendary, someone more eternal, someone, she thought ironically, more like Helen, who was really just a story.

Even beyond Death.

61

Gaius Octavius

AUGUST 30 BC

OCTAVIUS STARED AT THE bay hugging the city of Alexandria, the docks crawling with Roman soldiers, spilling out of large warships and heading into the streets in neat, organized squadrons.

The sky still held dark smoke from the fires which had burned in the city for days. On a small island off the coast towered a lighthouse, a bright flame visible at its top, which had remained untouched in the brief battle. As he gazed out on the harbor, the harsh summer sun suddenly glinted on the bright blue sea and nearly blinded him.

You shall fly up, up, up, and like Icarus, you shall fly too close to the sun.

Cleopatra had taken her own life shortly after he had left her. A part of Octavius thought he had known, somehow, and had let her die anyway. But why? Had he not wanted to bring her back to Rome, the emblem of his victory? Or had he wished to save her from that fate?

Or had he, perhaps, seen a part of himself in her, and hesitated?

Cleopatra had been the daughter of a god, after all, and she had always understood the world better than Antonius. Better than most men, even. They were alike in that way. But in one thing they were different, and always would be. Cleopatra had sacrificed everything for love, when Octavius never would.

Oh, men... You know so much and yet understand so little.

The words had made him pause. They had reminded him of his wife, in a place he had never expected to find her resemblance. Livia was a Roman woman, a pious and respectable matron. But here she was, her words echoed in the mouth of an Egyptian queen, casting a shadow on everything he thought he knew.

But they were only words, memories of words, and Octavius knew words meant little in the mouths of the dead. For Cleopatra and Antonius were both dead, while he and Livia were alive. That, in the end, would be the greatest difference of all.

"Caesar, sir."

It was Cornelius Gallus, commander of the legions which had marched into Egypt from the west, while Octavius and his legions had traveled through Syria all the way from Corinth and invaded from the east.

When Gallus was not soldiering, he was a poet, and in fact, he had been taught under the same tutelage as Vergilius and Varius Rufus, with whom Octavius was now very good friends. However, Gallus came from a much poorer family. At times, he rather reminded Octavius of Agrippa.

"What news, Gallus?"

"The palace has been emptied. No one remains, and most of the valuable items are already in the process of being transported to the ships," Gallus answered promptly. He was the same age as Octavius, but Gallus' intense admiration for him made him seem younger.

"Good." Octavius paused. "And the queen?"

"Buried alongside Marcus Antonius, as you requested," Gallus replied, though a hint of wariness found its way into the last few words.

While Octavius knew his men did not fully understand his decision, it was important that they respected it.

"At the end of the day, Marcus Antonius was a Roman," Octavius said sternly. "Our gods stand witness to his last will and testament."

"I meant no offense, sir."

"And I take none." Octavius turned to him and smiled, though Gallus eyed it uneasily, perhaps unsure of its sincerity. "But we should make sure the gods do not take any offense either."

"Of course, Caesar."

"Tell me, Gallus," Octavius said, glancing at him curiously. "You are a poet, are you not?"

"I try to be," Gallus said jokingly, then grew serious. "But yes, I suppose some call me that."

"What do you think I should do next?"

Gallus stared at him, and when Octavius did not elaborate, he laughed nervously. "I am not sure I understand your meaning, Caesar."

Octavius was beginning to be annoyed at his infuriating politeness. He was so accustomed to Agrippa's constant banter and critiques that to find only agreement was more off-putting than resistance.

"Come now," Octavius said. "You have surely studied Homer and his epics. You know how the Trojan War ends, the victories and deaths. They must have taught you something of value. Tell me what I should do next, as the victor of the Battle of Actium."

Gallus hesitated, then stared out at the sea, his eyes troubled. "I do not know for certain. But as the victor of war, you deserve a triumph."

"Is that so?" Octavius murmured, looking out at the soldiers loading the ships with gold and other treasures found deep within the palace.

He imagined wagons laden with those treasures, wheeling behind him as he rode in triumph through the streets of Rome. It was not the first time he had imagined what it would be like when at last he had the entire world at his feet. But something always held him back, something always cut his thoughts short.

"And after the triumph?" he asked.

"Well, I suppose there would be everlasting peace."

Octavius glanced at him. "Do you believe that?"

Gallus offered an ironic smile. "I would prefer to believe in peace than in war." He paused. "Do you believe it, sir?"

Octavius was silent. For the first time, he allowed his imagination to continue, to follow the carriage as he rode in triumph to the heart of his city, the eternal city, where war had ravaged and raged for centuries past, where he now had the power to raise it like a star among the heavens.

"When the doors of Janus close, I will know it," he said at last. "But only when I have restored Rome to her former glory shall I believe it."

⤜⤜⤜ ⟫⟫⟫

DECEMBER 30 BC

Winter on the island of Samos was mild, but Octavius still found his days too cold for his liking. Perhaps there was no place in the world that would ever rid himself of the ever-present chills that crept into his very bones.

Already he felt hints of a fever weighing down his head, small shivers running through his body, which no amount of Muscat wine could quell. When the fever grew worse, Octavius nearly panicked and was preparing a letter to call for Agrippa when he stopped himself. He remembered Agrippa's words the last time they spoke truly with one another.

And I fear that if that day ever came, our love would be the death of me.

Instead, Octavius took to exercising, then bathing. He would work up a sweat, plunge into the cold bath, then immediately soak in the *caldarium* for hours. No one was permitted to enter the baths when he was there unless he called for a slave to scrape his skin. Then the metal strigil, firm but skillful, would follow the curves of his muscles, the hot oil thick and smooth like honey as it scraped the dirt and grime from his skin.

Today the steam coming off the water fogged the room until Octavius could hardly see. He allowed himself to relax, close his eyes, and sink into the water until his chin touched the surface. When his skin began to prune, he left the baths and retired to his villa, where he went to bed and tried to sleep.

At some point in the night, he felt a cool cloth on his forehead and murmuring words. Octavius understood belatedly that he had succumbed to his illness. He opened his eyes, but he found that a film covered his eyes, and he saw nothing but shadows moving around his bed.

"Agrippa?"

But even to his own ears, his voice sounded weak. The shadows left and he was alone once more.

Memories rose like dreams in his sleep. The Adriatic Sea, glittering before him, a bird flying up, up, up, until it was swallowed by the sun. Agrippa, always, always Agrippa, bloodied but alive. Apollo and his eternal glance, carved in stone, and Livia's knowing eyes.

A field of flowers unfolded before him. There was laughter in the wind, and voices in song, like a chorus of maidens. A scream suddenly tore apart the air and Octavius stumbled as the earth gaped before him, her dark, hideous depths yawning beneath him.

Look at me.

Octavius' eyes flew open. Sweat beaded his brow and stung his eyes. There was a cool cloth patting his forehead, but when he turned the face was unfamiliar, wrinkled and bearded, and he realized they had called a local doctor.

"Do not touch me," Octavius said quietly, and the doctor's arm froze, then silently withdrew. "I am fine."

The doctor glanced at him hesitantly. He was Greek, but he seemed to understand him. "Unconscious," he muttered in Latin. "Three days, three nights." His accent reminded him of his old tutor, and it made him slightly petulant.

"And I shall make it seven days and seven nights if I please," Octavius retorted, then sighed at the alarm on the doctor's face. "I have had these illnesses before. No mention of this shall leave the shores of this island, let alone this room. You will be adequately compensated for it, and well punished otherwise."

The doctor nodded hurriedly. "Yes, Καῖσαρ."

"That will be all," Octavius said when the doctor still did not leave.

The doctor hesitated, then held out a scroll of parchment. "Letter. For you."

Octavius sat up, snatching it quickly. "From whom?"

The doctor shook his head as if he did not understand the question. Octavius looked at the top of the page. *Livia Drusilla.* His wife.

"I see." Octavius hated the sinking feeling which he knew to be disappointment. "I will read it myself. You are dismissed."

The doctor nodded silently and left the room. Octavius let the scroll drop unopened onto his lap. Though he felt better than before, his mind was still foggy, and he had no desire to read his wife's letter. But then the thought occurred to him that she would have seen and spoken to Agrippa, and his fingers quickly unrolled the scroll.

It was brief, much briefer than he had expected for the distance it had traveled, though Livia had always written to the point.

My dearest Octavianus,

Your wife misses you very much. I hope Samos is good for your health, which is of the utmost importance, not only to me but to Rome herself. Rumor has it you will be voted consul again in January, and that the doors of Janus will close at long last. The people miss you, and await your triumphant return.

It feels as though everything has changed, though I still do my weaving, visit friends as usual, and take care of the children, so that it seems nothing has changed at the same time. Only Agrippa seems truly changed, though I suppose that is natural when one loses their spouse, especially one as lovely as poor Attica. Perhaps there is something more, but I dare not press him. That was always your task, after all. Until you return, Tiberius and Drusus send their love and eagerly await their father. Vale.

Octavius nearly smiled but frowned instead. Livia was all too perceptive of Agrippa, and perhaps of Octavius himself. She had seen them that night, many years ago, and like a single stone dropped in the ocean it had shaped the course of his fate.

It did not escape Octavius' notice, however, that while she wove and visited friends and took care of the children, in the back of her mind she thought over her future plans carefully, and envisioned her own son as his successor.

But that was a problem for the future. For now, there were much more pressing issues, and the most important ones lay firmly in the East.

Egypt had quickly been dealt with. Octavius had appointed Gallus as governor of the newly formed province, despite his low equestrian rank. Octavius valued loyalty and honor above mere titles, which were qualities even age could not teach. It was important, also, that Egypt remained far away from the prying hands of greedy senators.

Now there remained the rest of the East which would require much more thought and tact. Parthia had been in turmoil ever since war had broken out between himself and Antonius, who up until very recently had been meddling with their politics. It would take time for the disputes to settle. Kings were proud, after all, and disliked compromise.

There were other provinces scattered beyond the borders of Italy, whose governments were disorganized and disunified. Constant rebellions in the north required more men and more money to keep at a distance. If Octavius had inherited an empire, it was a fragmented one on the brink of chaos, and it was now up to him to restore it to something worth remembrance.

For who would now step forward to purify the city of its long, generational wars? Who would settle the veterans and pay them their dues? Who would repair the countryside, the poor farmers? Who would bring clean water to the city, and establish a dependable food supply? Or a central administration for the city and its amenities, which easily succumbed to crimes and fires? Who would remind the Roman people of their ancient traditions, their sacred customs, forgotten in the many years of warfare?

It would not be the Senate, long ago divided by squabbling noble families and upstart *novi homines*. The gods knew Octavius would need to exercise much patience to bring any sense of order and stability to *that* corrupted institution. They could not be entirely done away with, however, given their ancient history, their wealth and pride, but nor could they yet be entrusted with as much power as they had before. It was time for change, but it must happen slowly, so slowly that most would go unnoticed.

His title was yet another thing to take into account. Since he had relinquished the powers of the *Tresviri*, he only named himself consul, and called himself so when dealing with the embassies of Eastern cities as they scrambled to do him honor.

While Egypt and other Eastern provinces were more willing to declare him their leader, he would not be called a king, and certainly not a dictator. He would not take any title indefinitely, lest he make the same mistake as his divine father. If Rome must change, then he would simply have to change with her, and take on the role that was most needed.

And if Octavius were to be able to take on these roles, he would need to stay alive, and stay healthy, and he would need an heir.

All these thoughts, in the end, were mere shadows of the future. He could not be sure, no matter how hard he tried, that all of his plans would go according to his wishes. There were so many uncertainties, so many variables. If he did not perish from one of his illnesses, or was not killed by one of his many enemies, then he could find resistance in the Senate, or else his men or the people could revolt. Even earthquakes and fires posed a threat.

The only thing he could control was himself.

He remembered his tutor's advice back in Rome, when it seemed that Antonius would attack the city at any moment and Octavius needed to choose whether to back the Senate or retreat.

σπεῦδε βραδέως

Make haste slowly.

Octavius would not return to Rome for many months. Let the doors of Janus close. Let the people remember what peace was supposed to feel like, and forget the horrors of war. He would return when the East was settled, and the West was ready to welcome him home. He would return like the dawn of a new age, after centuries of darkness.

Not if I am the sun.

He would return like the son of a god.

62

MARCUS VIPSANIUS
AGRIPPA

MARCH 29 BC

O CTAVIUS HAD BEEN GONE for over a year now since his last brief visit to Brundisium.

Rome was still excited about the end of the war and the closing of the doors of Janus,
signifying that peace had come at last. Now that the original uproar had settled for the
most part, daily life in the city—to Agrippa's complete surprise— returned to normal.

Agrippa sighed deeply as he approached the large doors of Octavius' house on the
Palatine Hill. The doors opened wide, and this time Livia stood on the other side, a smile
on her face.

She looked much more lively than she had for many months, her hair styled back in a
modest bun, her dress adorned very simply with dark red and purple borders. Her only
jewelry was the emerald ring she wore on her left hand, as well as a matching necklace and
gold earrings.

"Agrippa," she said, beckoning him inside. "The others have just arrived."

It was a small, intimate celebration for the victory at Actium and the peace that was to
come, though Octavius was still far away.

Agrippa followed Livia into the house where he already heard the familiar voice of
Octavia calling out to the younger children. For indeed, the house would be full of
children this evening.

After Cleopatra and Antonius were defeated, and Antyllus and Caesarion executed
as potential rivals, the rest of Cleopatra and Antonius' children were sent to live with
Octavia, who had agreed—as much as she could agree to her brother's commands—to
take care of them.

Iullus, Antyllus' younger brother, had already been living with Octavia during the war, while twins Alexander Helios and Cleopatra Selene, along with their younger brother Ptolemy Philadelphus, were sent to Rome from Alexandria at the end of last October. Once Octavius returned for his triumphs, they would be paraded in the streets as a symbol of his victory.

"It has been a little chaotic with everyone in the house," Livia said apologetically.

And just as she finished speaking a young girl ran out from the back of the house, shrieking in delight. She came to a sudden stop when she saw Livia and Agrippa ahead of her, her grin dropping immediately.

"Julia!" Livia exclaimed. "What is all this running about?"

Julia stood tall, and though she could not have been older than ten years of age, she took on a ladylike aspect. She glanced at Agrippa, her eyes narrowed, before she turned to her stepmother.

"It is Tiberius! He is chasing me."

A boy burst forth into the room and grabbed Julia's shoulders from behind, who cried out in fright and tripped forward. She would have fallen flat on her face if Agrippa had not rushed to catch her.

"Are you alright?" Agrippa asked, lifting her up from the ground.

Julia nodded silently, her cheeks red. She glanced at Tiberius, who had hastily stepped away from her when he saw his mother's disapproving gaze.

"You mustn't let the boys chase you around," Agrippa said. "You may tell them to stop, you know."

But Julia only smiled, looking at Tiberius. It was clear she rather enjoyed being chased by the boys. "Oh, he didn't mean any harm. It was just a bit of fun. Right, Tiberius?"

Tiberius nodded but avoided the eyes of both his mother and Agrippa. His happy smile while chasing Julia had vanished the instant he had seen the two of them, and his countenance had turned sullen. Even though his father had died when he was young, he had a strenuous relationship with Octavius as his stepfather, and therefore with anyone who supported him. He was nearly in his thirteenth year and had begun to understand the world better, and the responsibilities which he would soon be obligated to fulfill.

"You ought to behave, Tiberius," Livia said, though her admonishing tone was mild. "Your stepfather will not allow you to behave like a child at twelve years of age."

"But Caesar is not here, Mother," Tiberius said very quietly.

"Tiberius," Livia warned.

Before he could reply, another boy ran towards them and threw an arm around Tiberius. It was Marcellus, the eldest son of Octavia, his curling blonde hair nearly falling into his eyes. He had a good-natured smile like his father, as well as his soft blue eyes, which held none of the cold distance of his mother.

"Here you are," Marcellus said. "We were looking everywhere for you two." Then he noticed Agrippa and his eyes lit up. "General Agrippa! It is nice to see you, sir."

"And you as well, Marcellus," Agrippa said. "You have grown since last I saw you."

Marcellus grinned. "See? Tiberius thinks I have not grown at all. He is taller than me, though *I* am older, which I would argue matters more."

Tiberius did not answer, and looked slightly miserable, though he glanced at Marcellus in reluctant fondness. It was hard to dislike a boy who loved others so openly and easily, even if Tiberius could not help his jealousy at the other boy's natural charm and good looks.

"Where are the others, my dear?" Livia asked.

"This way," Marcellus said, and he led them to the gardens in the back of the house, where the children had gathered despite the coolness of the evening. The spring rain had left the ground muddy, but now small buds of flowers dotted the bushes and trees.

Octavia approached with Claudia Marcella Major, her eldest daughter, now in her twelfth year, and Iullus, who trailed after them solemnly. Apparently he had taken the news of his father and brother's deaths better than expected, but it clearly weighed on his mind. He was now fourteen years of age, making him the oldest of all the children there.

"Agrippa, it is nice to see you again," Octavia said, inclining her head.

"And you as well, Octavia."

She rested a hand on Marcella's arm. "I would like you to say hello to my eldest daughter, Marcella."

Marcella looked at him carefully. She had soft blonde hair like her brother, twisted into braids and lifted high on her head. But where Marcellus was more like their father, Marcella had taken most after her mother, with those wintry blue eyes. She did, however, smile at Agrippa.

"Hello Marcella," Agrippa said, surprised to see her blush when he said her name. "You have become quite the young lady."

"Thank you, sir." Her voice was quiet but steady, and she glanced at her mother nervously.

Agrippa looked at Octavia, whose lips were pressed together tightly. *Any more life granted to me I shall devote to my children.*

Suddenly he understood the meaning of this interaction, and a shot of anger ran through him. Had Octavius planned this all along? Why did he tell Octavia before himself? Was Agrippa ever going to have a say in who he married?

But then Marcella's eyes grew worried, and Agrippa took pity on the poor girl despite himself.

"Please, you may call me Agrippa. I am too young for such an address." Though just then he felt very old indeed.

"Papa!"

"Papa! Papa!"

He turned, just in time to catch his two daughters hurtling into his arms. They had been sent ahead to the house while Agrippa finished some business with Maecenas.

"I hope you two have not caused any trouble," Agrippa warned, though his tone was playful.

"Oh nonsense, they have been wonderful," Livia said, smiling at them. She then glanced at Julia, who had begun chasing Tiberius, while Drusus watched and threw small rocks and fallen nuts at them. "I cannot say the same for mine."

"They are still children," Agrippa reminded her gently.

Livia looked at him worriedly. "Not for long."

"Marcella! Come quick!" Julia called from across the garden. She was running from both Tiberius and Marcellus now, who had vicious grins on their faces, though Julia looked as happy as could be with the boys hot on her tail. "Iullus, do help!"

Marcella looked at her mother, who watched as Julia dodged the quick hands of the boys, and at last, Octavia sighed. "Go on. You too, Iullus. Keep an eye on them for me."

Then Marcella and Iullus ran off, and Octavia stood beside Agrippa as they watched the children run about, playing with each other. Livia quietly excused herself and returned inside the house to check up on the dinner.

Eventually Agrippa's daughters ran off, chasing Drusus, for whom they had a special affection. Even the children of Antonius and Cleopatra, who were standing by shyly, were induced to join the chase.

"He did not tell me," Agrippa said, now that he and Octavia were alone. "I did not know he had arranged our marriage."

"He would not have told *me* if he could get away with it," Octavia replied wryly. "But I cannot refuse his wishes. Not in this, at least."

Agrippa shook his head, looking at Marcella as she laughed at something the other children did. "She is young. Too young to be married."

Octavia half-smiled. "I was the same age when I married Marcellus."

"It does not make it right."

She looked at him curiously, her eyes kind. "You are a good man, Agrippa. And you will be a good husband for my daughter. That is all a mother can hope for."

They were both silent for a long time. At last, Agrippa said softly, "Your brother loves you. Even if it does not always seem like it."

Octavius smiled, though her eyes were sad. "I know." She paused. "I am glad he has you. I am glad he found you."

Agrippa stared out at the garden, his heart heavy. "Me too, Octavia. Me too."

⤜⤛⤛

AUGUST 29 BC

A roar of laughter rose in the room.

Maecenas was at the front of the triclinium, pretending to trudge through a marsh. "And we march through the mud in complete darkness. And who do we find hiding in the reeds? None other than Caesar himself!"

Everyone laughed again, looking around in happy surprise. Vergilius, who lay near Maecenas, could barely contain his laughter. Even Livia smiled. Agrippa was the only one who had trouble joining in the banter. *I will always find you.*

Maecenas briefly made eye contact with him and frowned as if he read Agrippa's thoughts. "Of course, he was much younger then," Maecenas continued carelessly, reclining on the couch once more. "We all were."

"And the victim of this jest is not even here to defend himself," Agrippa pointed out, ignoring Maecenas' narrowing eyes.

"Actually," said a voice from the doorway, "he is."

They all turned and began talking at once when they saw Octavius enter the room. He had invited everyone to stay at Livia's villa outside of Rome to wait for his return, but his journey from Brundisium had been delayed—whether from illness or something else Agrippa did not know—and they had not known when to expect him.

For soon he would be celebrating not one but *three* triumphs in Rome. Until then he would not be allowed into the city by law, so he wished to meet with everyone beforehand.

Octavius looked at Maecenas. For a moment, everyone hesitated, wondering if he would be angry, before Octavius smiled. "That was not one of my finest moments, I admit. But beware, my friend, for I have many a story to tell about *you*."

Maecenas looked fearful but relieved to find Octavius unbothered by his joke. "Naturally, Caesar, I only make fun of others because I myself am the more worthy of embarrassment."

"Oh, I do not doubt it," Octavius said mockingly. "Come now, do not cease the festivities on account of me. Bring more wine! More food!"

He then took his place beside Livia, who smiled at him. Agrippa realized too late that he was trying to catch his eye as he was always accustomed to. He forced himself to look at the small fountain in the center of the couches instead.

"Vergilius," Octavius said later on in the night after most of the wine had been passed around. "I hear your latest work is nothing short of a masterpiece."

Vergilius had the grace to blush, glancing at Maecenas, who appeared equally innocent and delightfully guilty. "I dare say that is a high compliment, Caesar. But truthfully, it is nothing more than the fancies of a country boy."

"Well go on, then," Octavius said, raising his glass. "Let us hear some of it now."

After the cheers and encouragement of the guests Vergilius at last agreed to sing the first book.

He then stood up in front of the room and his eyes grew determined. "Alright then, you asked for it. I call this piece *Georgica...*

"Quid faciat laetas segetes, quo sidere terram
vertere, Maecenas—"

What makes the cornfield smile, by what star
it is proper to plow the earth, Maecenas—

At his name Maecenas cheered, raising his glass and taking a sip, and everyone laughed.

"—ulmisque adiungere vitis
conveniat, quae cura boum, qui cultus habendo
sit pecori, apibus quanta experientia parcis,
hinc canere incipiam..."

—and bind vines to elms,
what care oxen need, what tending cattle
require, how much skill for thrifty bees,
from here I will begin to sing...

He sang well into the night, as more food and wine were brought out to the guests, who grew tired as the night wore on. But Octavius listened attentively to the soft chanting voice of Vergilius, as he prayed to the gods and to Octavius himself, and described everything from the various agricultural techniques, to the different ages of man, to the storms which destroy the crops of mankind. He finally ended the first book of his poem with a prayer to Octavius as the savior amidst much war, earning him a great round of applause.

Once many of the guests retired to bed, Agrippa said goodnight as well, but walked outside to the grounds stretching around the villa. The modest house was situated atop a sloping hill and overlooked a wide and green valley. It was nearly dawn, the sky deep hues of purple and blue, and Agrippa wondered if he would forever feel this alone.

Leaves crunched behind him. Even without looking, Agrippa already knew who it was.

"I thought I might find you here," Octavius said quietly, standing beside him and looking out at the creeping light beyond the far-off hills.

Agrippa glanced at him. "I did not think you would speak with me."

"Why wouldn't I?"

He did not answer. For a time, they were silent. Sometimes silence spoke more than words. Octavius remained at his side, unspeaking, waiting. When the chill of the night crept under his clothes, at last Agrippa spoke.

"You did not tell me." Octavius raised a questioning brow. "You did not tell me I was to marry Marcella."

"Ah, she told you then."

"I would have found out eventually, Octavius. You still should have told me. I know it is too much to expect you to *ask* me."

Octavius frowned. "I was not sure you would agree so soon after Attica's death. But it has already been over a year, Agrippa. The time has come for you to think of the future, and the future of the Roman people." He gave Agrippa a sidelong glance. "But I did not come here to argue."

"Then why did you come?"

Octavius sighed. "I wanted to make sure that your oath to me still stood." He paused. "After everything."

The force of the memory was nearly enough for Agrippa to feel faint. It was as if fifteen years had come and gone in a single breath, in a blink of an eye, and here they were, no longer hunted by enemies on all sides, no longer on the brink of death, no longer two boys hoping to rule the world, but victors of an empire in the making.

Agrippa turned to him, and Octavius mirrored him, his dark eyes wary.

"I swear by you, Gaius Julius Caesar Octavianus, that I will be loyal to you and only you. Regarding your friends as my friends, and your enemies as my enemies. And who you regard as enemies I will by land and sea, with weapons and sword, pursue and punish."

As if in a dream, Agrippa reached out and took Octavius' hand in his, who went very still but did not stop him. He lifted his hand and kissed the signet ring, as he had done all those years ago, though now it meant more than they could ever have imagined then.

"All my life."

Then Agrippa pulled him close and kissed him.

It was nothing more than a brush of their lips before Agrippa stepped away, so swiftly that anyone who saw might have thought they had imagined it.

Octavius did not move, as still as a marble statue, but before Agrippa walked away he thought he saw a glimmer of tears in his eyes. For they both knew the kiss would be their last.

"Goodnight, Octavius."

Agrippa went back inside.

⠶⠶⠶ ⠶⠶⠶

There was no feeling like seeing Rome again, her noble temples rising above the rolling hills like a ship at sea.

Octavius led the army ahead, mounted on horseback instead of riding in the usual triumphal chariot, and dressed in gleaming, colorful armor. He had been fighting a mild illness ever since returning to Italy, but Livia had been there to care for him, and he had even requested that Vergilius sing the rest of his *Georgica* to him while he rested in bed. Now he looked as strong and impenetrable as ever.

His nephew, Marcellus, rode on his right with a proud grin, while his stepson, Tiberius, rode on his left, serious and frowning.

The magistrates followed behind them instead of at their traditional place in front of the procession, along with the captives from Egypt, Selene and Alexander at the head, bound in chains. At the rear was Octavius' army, with whom Agrippa and Maecenas walked, cheering and singing their bawdy songs as they marched into the city.

Agrippa took a deep breath as they began their descent.

They started in the Campus Martius, a marshy green field just outside of the city, before entering through the triumphal gate and passing the forum until they approached the towering temple of Jupiter Optimus Maximus, as tall and proud as the god himself.

All around them the people of the city flocked, staring at Octavius, crying out to him as their hero, their victor, the son of a god, as young and strong as Apollo. The summer sun shone brightly upon him as he rode to the base of the steps, looking out at the crowds of people who chanted his name in the streets, over and over again.

Divi fili! Divi fili! Divi fili!

Agrippa could not help it. He smiled.

Just then Octavius found Agrippa in the crowd, his eyes still half-lidded and smirking as the day he had met him. Agrippa felt the circles of time envelope them in a story that ended where it began.

If I were Achilles, you would be Patroclus.

For Agrippa would never forget the boy he had loved, before he was the man he had

507

followed, and the love he had lost. In some ways, nothing had changed. Octavius had been right, after all.

Together they had conquered the world.

63

OCTAVIA MINOR

JUNE 28 BC

"LET THE FEAST BEGIN!" Octavius called out, raising his glass of grape juice. "Bring out the *mustaceum!*"

It was late in the night, and the guests were just as excited as ever. Even her brother, who had been very busy lately with his work as consul alongside Agrippa, smiled and drank until his cheeks were flushed and he leaned a little too close to Livia.

Octavius hushed the room, raising his glass again, but this time he looked very serious. "Let us make a toast."

"Oh no," Octavia muttered, earning a glare from her brother and a stifled laugh from Livia.

"We are gathered here today to celebrate the union of two people who are very close to my heart," Octavius began, and the room grew quiet as his voice turned softer. "Here is to my good friend, Marcus Agrippa, without whom I would hardly be alive and here today." Agrippa raised his own glass, his eyes grudgingly fond, a love bellied by a deeper sorrow. Octavia understood. It was not an easy thing to love her brother. "And to my beautiful niece, Claudia Marcella. May your life be as sweet as your smile. You could not have a better husband, nor shall there be a better wife. I wish your marriage all the blessings in the world."

Marcella glanced at Agrippa with a blush, and Agrippa smiled back.

"To Agrippa and Marcella!" Octavius exclaimed.

"To marriage!" someone added.

"To love!" another cried.

And they all drank, laughing happily, the men wearing their best *togae viriles* and the women in their *tunicae rectae,* their hair done up and veiled in yellow just as the bride herself.

Octavia tried to eat a slice of cake but found herself without an appetite. She sat beside

Octavius and Livia but she might as well have been in a room alone.

She felt a nudge against her arm.

"Sister, why do you look so sad?" Octavius asked with a grin. "It is your daughter's wedding, after all, and her husband is not unfit for her, I think."

"It is not that," Octavia said, not wishing to speak about it. "It is nothing."

"Ah, ah, ah." Octavius poked her arm as he used to when they were younger and he wished to annoy her. "Now you must tell me." Then he leaned in closer, lowering his voice. "You know you are not the only one to find this night bittersweet."

Octavia stared in surprise at her brother. Then she sighed, knowing she would have to tell him eventually. "It is only that Marcellus is not here to see our daughter marry. And now all I can think about is the night that I married him, how happy we were, and how young I was. It makes me sad."

"I see," Octavius said, nodding slowly. "I remember that night. You were very beautiful."

"If I could live it all over again with him," Octavia whispered, her throat closing with tears, "I would."

A strange look passed over Octavius' face, and Octavia realized it was pain. "I understand."

Pity stirred in her breast for her brother, and she rested a hand on his. "I know."

It was several hours later when Dawn began to lift her rosy fingers above the horizon, and the party settled into low conversation. At some point in the night, Octavius had moved across the room to speak with Maecenas and Agrippa, while Livia reclined closer to Octavia. They both tried not to think of Attica, who would have loved the wedding, having always considered herself an aunt to Marcella.

"Do you remember your first wedding night?" Octavia asked.

"Oh yes," Livia said, smiling. "I was already sixteen years of age, but Tiberius was nearly forty. It was a strange time, too, full of rumor and doubt. But I knew I had to marry if I wished to survive the wars ahead."

"Marriage is strange, is it not?" Octavia shook her head wryly. "You bind yourself to another person for life. You bear them children and name them after him. And then they die! Just like that, it is all over, except *we* still have to care for the children."

Livia laughed. "Well, when you put it like that!"

Octavia leaned in conspiratorially, realizing distantly that she must be quite drunk, and muttered, "But I daresay I would not want to be a man."

"No," Livia agreed. "But sometimes I think I'd rather make a better man than most if I were."

"Oh my dear Livia," Octavia said with a hardly stifled laugh, "you already *are* a better man. If it were not for you, I doubt my brother would have gotten very far at all."

"Do not tell *him* that," Livia murmured, but she smiled, the kind of smile that was at once innocent and knowing, looking at her husband.

Octavius caught her gaze across the room and raised a brow, sensing mischief. This only sent Octavia and Livia into another bout of laughter.

"But Livia," Octavia said between laughs, "he already knows."

Just then Agrippa stepped forward, and the room quieted, waiting. The time had come. Marcella lay very still, watching Agrippa carefully, her eyes following him beneath her yellow veil as he made his way across the room to her.

Marcella glanced at her mother, half-excitement, half-fear in her eyes, and then Agrippa lifted her up in his arms and Marcella shrieked, smiling, holding out her arms to her mother as Agrippa carried her out of the room.

The guests cheered as they scrambled to follow, forming the trailing procession behind the bride and groom. They walked down the meandering road from Octavius and Livia's house on the Palatine, down and down through the forum and around until they reached the modest house of Agrippa.

The bride and groom paused on the threshold, glancing back at the crowd which had formed behind them.

Octavius stood beside Octavia, and it seemed at that moment Marcella and Agrippa found them in the crowd, holding their gaze. She felt Octavius stiffen beside her, and she slipped her arm through his as Agrippa stepped over the threshold and the door closed behind them.

"I was wrong, you know, that day," Octavia said quietly. "Love is worth all the sacrifice in the world."

"What?" Octavius looked at her slowly, as if he were being pulled from a dream.

Octavia recalled that day long ago, when Octavius had returned from the wars against Decimus and marched on Rome, demanding the consulship. From a single glance, Octavia had known. She had seen the love between them and had warned her brother against it. She often wondered if it had been her fault, if she could have protected him from the pain of love, but she knew now that there were powers in this world that were even greater than love, which only the gods could wield.

"I was wrong to tell you who to love," she said, squeezing his arm. "It is too seldom found to be thrown away."

"But that is the thing about love, my sister," Octavius said, looking at the house once more. "Love never truly leaves us."

Octavia stared at him, and for the first time, she saw the man her little brother had become. He was nothing like that boy returning from Apollonia, rough-shaven and reckless, his eyes gleaming with revenge.

Here was a man fit to be the leader of their people, a man who knew what it meant to risk everything he loved for what he believed in.

"Mother would have been proud of you, brother."

"And you as well," Octavius said, turning to her with a fond smile. "She lives on in you, *mater omnium matrum.*"

Mother of all mothers.

Octavia smiled despite her tears, and they turned and walked back home under the shining sun of a new day.

⟫⟫ ⟪⟪

AUGUST 28 BC

It had been three years since the Battle of Actium, and two years since Marcus Antonius had fallen, deciding the fate of the world and proving her brother victorious. A year ago Octavius had ridden through the streets of Rome in triumph, her son, Marcellus, riding on his right-hand side like the image of Hope itself.

Much had changed, though it was not always apparent. The doors of Janus were closed, and war had begun to seem more like a dream than real memory. Octavius and Agrippa had taken to reforming and rebuilding the city, though Octavia hardly concerned herself with politics these days, and she heard most of the latest news from Livia.

Shortly after her daughter's wedding, Octavius bought Octavia a new home to raise her children, and though she had no man to call her own, Octavia found herself quite busy.

Iullus, Marcellus, Alexander Helios, and Ptolemy Philadelphus were educated together by Athenodorus, who used to teach her brother and his friends back in Apollonia. He was growing very old now, but his mind was still sharp, and under his tutelage, the boys were learning rhetoric and philosophy in both Latin and Greek.

Cleopatra Selene spent time with her three remaining daughters, Claudia Marcella Minor, Antonia Major, and Antonia Minor, though she suspected that Octavius would want to marry off the daughter of Cleopatra as soon as he could.

They all frequently visited Agrippa and Marcella as well as Livia and her brother, and their children played with each other while the adults dined.

It seemed, at last, that peace had come to Rome.

She sat and wove by the window, warmed by a patch of sunlight. Then she heard her name from across the room, and for a moment, she was back in the house she shared with

512

Marcellus, and she would turn and find him staring at her, his blue eyes soft and loving.

Octavia turned.

It was Iullus, standing awkwardly across the room.

"Should you not be studying with your brothers?" Octavia asked, raising a brow.

Iullus looked down at his feet, frowning. He looked much like his father, but at the same time, there was a sensitivity to him that Octavia had never seen either in Antonius or Fulvia. She wondered where it had come from, and if it had ever been in his father when he was a young boy.

"I do not like to study," he said quietly. "I would rather write."

"Write?"

"Yes," Iullus said, blushing. "Poetry."

"I see," Octavia said slowly. "And do you think your education will not help you write poetry? You know even the greatest poets went to school."

His mouth twisted into a bitter frown. "I know. But I don't want to. I don't want to learn Greek. I don't want to be like my father."

Octavia stared at the boy and felt her heart swell with pity, even love, though he was not her child by blood. "Come here, Iullus."

Iullus walked over to her loom hesitantly. Though she had been like a mother to the boy since Fulvia died, he did not come to her as Marcellus did. Perhaps now that he no longer had his father, he could only come to her.

"Look out at the city," Octavia said, sweeping her gaze over the narrow, winding streets that crisscrossed Rome, the crowds pushing through as they went about their day. "Your father grew up on those streets. He was a Roman man, just like you shall be soon when you don your *toga virilis*."

"He was a traitor," Iullus said angrily, his eyes welling with tears. "And my brother is dead because of him. I *hate* him."

"Do not judge your father so harshly," Octavia said, taking his hands in hers. "He was a good man, and your brother died fighting for him. Do you know, when my mother died, he attended the funeral? For all his faults, he had always respected my mother, and me. He was quick to love and very brave. If you grow to be a man like him, it would not be anything shameful."

Iullus frowned, but he looked more at peace. "I still hate school."

Octavia laughed. "It will be over before you know it, and then you can write poetry all day long. Now go back to your studies!"

"Thank you," Iullus said quietly, before he flashed a grateful smile and ran off.

With a sigh, Octavia sat back down at her loom and began to weave once more. She looked out at the vast city of Rome, her brightly colored temples rising high in the sky, the forums and shops, the circuses and stadiums, all moving, all alive, weaving all their lives together in one large tapestry as if Roma were, indeed, a woman.

Octavia had lived and loved in this city, the city of her mother, and her mother before her—strong, beautiful, and pious Roman women—and that would never change. Even when she was no longer on this earth, even when the city crumbled into dust, even when no one remembered her name and the life she led and the love she gave, even when the gods brought an end to all the world.

Even then, Octavia would forever be her mother's daughter, the wife of the man she loved, and the mother of her children, and that was all that mattered.

64

GAIUS OCTAVIUS

JANUARY 27 BC

"I BET TWENTY *AUREI* I roll a Canis," Maecenas said, dropping the coins noisily on the table and raising a brow.

Agrippa sighed and placed his coins alongside his. After a moment's consideration, Balbus did the same, and Octavius followed.

Maecenas shook his hands, then threw the dice across the table, watching eagerly as they bounced and rolled to a stop, reading them quickly. "One, one, three, four—damn you!"

He handed the dice over to Agrippa with a huff, who scooped them up gingerly. "I raise the bet to fifty *aurei* that I roll a Canis."

He threw the coins in, and the rest of them did the same. Then Agrippa gave the dice a practiced shake and let them fly on the table.

"Not even close," Maecenas said, eyeing the dice which did not have a single one amongst them. Agrippa rolled his eyes as he pushed the dice toward Balbus. "I nearly had all four ones at least three times now! It is very unfair."

"Quiet, Maecenas," Balbus said gruffly, grabbing the dice while he took a sip of his wine. The many years that Octavius had known Balbus had aged him too, and his black curls were now streaked with gray. "It is my turn. I bet three hundred *aurei* that I roll a Senio."

"Three *hundred!*" Maecenas exclaimed. "By Jove, Balbus, do you have that on you?"

"It is New Year's Day," Balbus replied curtly. "And you do not know your Caesar very well if you expected the stakes to be a mere twenty *aurei*."

Balbus called his attendant over, who presented a small iron safe and opened it to reveal a silk pillow piled carefully with gold bars. He took one out and placed it at the center of the table, glancing questioningly at the rest of them.

Maecenas slipped off a large gold ring inset with an even larger ruby, placing it beside

515

the coins. "It is worth at least four hundred *aurei,* but let it stand for now."

Agrippa raised a brow. "I must yield. You know I do not have an ounce of luck when it comes to dice."

They all looked at Octavius. In answer, he picked up a similar box near his feet and opened it away from their view, though they all knew what lay inside. A gold bar of the same weight was placed beside the others.

"Go on, Balbus."

Balbus rolled the dice and peered over the table. "Three, four, six—and six! I have won! I have won!"

Maecenas swore under his breath.

"Not so fast," Octavius said, smirking. "It is my turn."

He carefully counted out three gold bars, setting them on the table. "I raise the bet to a thousand *aurei* that I roll a Venus."

All of them stared at him. Even Balbus raised a brow. It was the highest sequence that could be rolled because it was the hardest to roll, though he had beaten more impossible odds before. Agrippa looked relieved to have backed out when he did.

Maecenas shook his head as if he too recalled the last time he had bet against him and a Venus roll. "I am out, my friends. Good luck, Balbus."

"And what should happen if you lose?" Balbus asked curiously.

"If I lose," Octavius said, "I yield the pot to you, Balbus. But if I win, it's all mine."

Balbus hesitated.

"Come now, Balbus," Agrippa said, taunting. "I thought you knew Caesar's love of gambling."

At this, Balbus narrowed his eyes. "So be it!"

"Very well," Octavius said.

He waited for Balbus to count his gold bars and place them onto the already-growing pile before them. Then Octavius picked up the dice and rubbed them between his hands, sending a quick prayer to Venus, whom his family had always considered their ancestor. Then he rolled.

Six, four, three...four.

"Aha!" Balbus cried, standing up in his excitement. "I cannot believe it! I have beaten Caesar! I have won! I have won!"

"Won what?"

They all turned.

Livia was standing behind Octavius, raising a sharp brow. Balbus laughed nervously and looked at Octavius, who merely gestured to the pile of gold as if it explained everything.

"Gambling all our money away, my love?" Livia asked.

Octavia approached, arm in arm with her daughter, Marcella, and stood beside Livia, looking down at their gambling table in distaste. The three of them were as beautiful and terrifying as goddesses, as if they were Hera, Venus, and Artemis themselves, though this time they were not awaiting judgment, but dealing it.

"Nonsense," Octavius said, smiling easily. "I am merely giving it away. Think of it as a New Year's gift to our dear friend Balbus."

"Ah yes," Octavia said, her eyes flashing with amusement. "My brother is always so generous."

"It is just a game, sister," Octavius said. "I do not mind losing because I love all of my friends, and I love to see them win as much as myself."

"Now that the game has ended," Livia interrupted, "perhaps you all may join us for food and drink. We have hired a very famous—and dare I say, *expensive*—mime, who has come all the way from Hispania!"

The four of them followed the three women into the gardens, covered with a tarp to shield them from the rain, where most of the guests had already been herded in to watch the performance. Drinks were passed around, as well as various traditional dishes and delicate sweets. All of the children were running about, laughing and stealing as many sweets as possible, bargaining them away to the younger ones for toys and favors.

Agrippa took a seat beside Marcella, and they spoke to each other in hushed voices, smiling and laughing. Octavia was charged with keeping the children in order, and could be heard berating the boys as they tried to wrestle each other about the house. Guests of all kinds were gathered here today, both family and friends, who had supported Octavius throughout his campaigning years.

At last, the mime began his performance, changing his face from comically sad to absurdly happy, then angry, then in love, and as he morphed from one face to the next, even dragging them out into clever sketches, the audience laughed and applauded, throwing coins and food at the stage.

Livia sat beside Octavius, as beautiful and charming as the day they married, thirteen years ago now. By the end of January, Livia would be thirty-two years of age, while Octavius would be nearly thirty-six.

While so much time had passed, looking into her knowing eyes Octavius felt that it was only yesterday she had spoken to him at Tiberius' house, sealing their fate forever as husband and wife, as a father and mother, not merely for Romans, but for the world.

"Can you believe how far we have come, my love?" Livia asked, eyeing Octavius with a smile, as pure as sunlight, as secretive as Venus. "I daresay you nearly laughed in my face when I told you all those years ago."

"The gods were watching us," Octavius said softly. "It was our fate to find each other."

"The gods watch us still," Livia countered, her smile turning sly. "Our fate has just begun."

Perhaps it was the new year, or the drink, or the years spent away from her touch, which rekindled some of the fire of that love and made him dip his head and kiss her right then amid all their guests.

But Livia smiled as he kissed her, and she said his name softly, like a prayer—no, like a promise.

I am your destiny.

⤞⤜ ⤛⤝

Octavius sat beside Agrippa in their consular chairs, the *curia* falling silent as the last senator who spoke took his seat.

It was a long meeting, the worst kind of meeting, really, when the senators had the chance to bring forth motions for the Senate to vote on. He had thus far been accorded all kinds of honors and distinctions, and now the meeting was, thankfully, coming to an end.

The weak light of the morning filtered through the high windows above, gleaming across the polished marble floor. A chair scraped in the silence, and footsteps filled the room as Lucius Munatius Plancus took center stage.

There was a rustling amongst the rows of senators, who were all too familiar with the shifty, scheming Plancus. Even if they supported him now, they disliked him anyway.

"Conscript Fathers," Plancus said, in his rather theatrical but soft-spoken voice. "Since I am the last man to speak today, I will state my thoughts very clearly. We are gathered here today on account of one man, and one man only. When the Republic fell at the hands of those whom *Divus Iulius* considered friends, when this very Senate was stormed and besieged by mobs, when Marcus Antonius seized power in hopes of handing it over to an Egyptian queen, only one man stepped forth with the courage necessary to guide this nation, a light in the dark. Only one man had the wits and wisdom to fight for what was right and just, and he was then only nineteen years old."

There was a murmuring throughout the crowd. Not everyone gathered had fully supported Octavius and his cause at the time, though none openly rebelled against him anymore. But there were others who nodded, their eyes hardened after years of war, after watching the Senate's prestige crumble to the whims of wealthy families and their rivals.

"This man alone knew our true enemy, Queen Cleopatra Philopator, and did everything in his power to conquer her. This man alone pursued the fleeing enemy into Egypt

518

and returned victorious. But that is not all this man has done, not only concerned with ending war but establishing peace and prosperity for the ages to come. Already roads are being repaved and temples rebuilt. Already peace has flourished in Rome. It was not long ago when this would have seemed impossible. We owe our very lives to this man."

Plancus extended his hand toward Octavius, and everyone's eyes settled upon him, some in respect, some warily. Octavius welcomed them all with a smile.

"Conscript Fathers, I am not here to wax on the praises of a man more than deserving of them. Rather, I am here to propose an honor be bestowed upon a man who merits our greatest thanks, an honor which shall forever be a reminder that this man saved the people of Rome, that he restored the Republic."

Octavius glanced at Agrippa. He saw those sea green eyes—just like the Tiber on a summer's day he remembered thinking once. The world was theirs at last, no longer just a dream, no longer just an oath, and it had only come at the greatest cost of all.

"I propose that henceforth, Gaius Julius Caesar shall be named..."

Agrippa's eyes were steady and sure, like his own heartbeat, his own fate marching to the same rhythm for eternity.

"*Augustus.*"

EPILOGUE
LIVIA DRUSILLA

JULY AD 14

T HE LARGE LAUREL TREE with its twisting branches and bright green leaves stood regal as ever in the middle of the garden. It had been a hot summer, and already the flowers and foliage were wilting in the heat, ready to turn brown with the changing seasons.

Livia had long tended to their gardens atop the Palatine Hill, overlooking the bustling and crowded forum. She was too old now to do more than trim dead leaves, but she still liked to walk the rows of flower bushes, and roam the grounds of their estate, recalling fond memories, and darker ones.

Her children had long grown up and left her care, and their children as well. It had been many years since the days when children ran amongst the flowers and trees every day, playing with their cousins, not yet knowing the cruelties and tragedies of the world.

"Augusta."

Livia turned. Her handmaiden stood at the edge of the garden, and at once Livia felt her heart leap into her throat. "What is it?"

"Your husband asks for you."

She let out a breath and returned to the house silently.

Augustus was in his office, which to this day he lovingly called *Syracuse.* This past year, as his health gradually declined, he had taken to writing in his office all through the night. It seemed that was all he did these days, ceaselessly, desperately, as if his life depended upon it. Perhaps it did.

He sat at his desk. Her husband had grown very thin in his old age, his cheekbones harsh in his now pale face, making his eyes flash darkly under his gray brows. But beneath the wrinkled skin and silver-white hair was the same sharpness to his gaze, the same charming smile, that he always had in youth, and that restlessness that would never sleep until his death.

"Livia," he said gravely. "I must speak with you about something."

"Anything," she said quickly.

It was not as if they did not know he was dying. But time was a question, and they could only prepare for when. Augustus himself did not cease his work in Rome and abroad, and had even tried to travel with Tiberius to the Eastern provinces, but his health had failed him and he had reluctantly remained at home.

"I have amended my will," Augustus said, watching her carefully. "Tiberius shall be named my heir."

"He would not have it so," Livia said defensively, hearing the accusation in his words, though she was only airing an age-old argument.

Augustus raised a brow. "No. But *you* would."

"Well, *you* would not have chosen him, if you had any other choice," Livia replied, though she spoke without real resentment.

For Marcellus, his true favorite and the princeling of Rome, had died young and tragically. She could still hear Octavia's sobs as they clawed out of her throat, her body draped over her son's dead body. Only when her own son, Drusus, had died from a fatal accident many years ago did she truly understand her pain.

Then there were the sons of Agrippa, whom Augustus had hoped would continue his legacy, who had all died young, scattered across the empire. Tiberius alone had remained suitable for the job, and Augustus had only very reluctantly accepted him as his heir.

"It is not easy to rule an empire," he said coldly. "I only wish to preserve what I have worked so long and hard to build."

"If the Republic fails," Livia answered, matching his chilly tone, "it will not be on account of my son."

"It does not matter," Augustus said with a labored sigh. His old age had made him impatient, and cynical, and he no longer put up with their usual banter for long. "People are weak and corrupt. If it is not him, it shall be another who fails."

His eyes scanned the wax tablets upon which he had been writing, though he seemed unusually pensive today, almost distracted, as if his mind were being pulled to other things, other places.

"Do not doubt yourself now," Livia said more gently. She felt keenly that her husband thought less of the world and more of his death these days. "You have come all this way."

"It is not doubt," Augustus said, then hesitated, glancing at her. "It is fear."

"I see." Livia reached out and covered his hand in hers. He sighed at her touch, and his eyes closed in exhaustion. "But fear is a kind of doubt, is it not? Fear is not knowing."

"I fear that everything I thought I knew shall be false." Augustus paused, as though the words took much effort to speak. "I fear the loves I have lost will never be found again."

521

Livia sighed. So many had died over the years. Marcellus, Octavia, Drusus, Agrippa. Some had died young, the others old. Agrippa had died rather unexpectedly, when Julia—who had been forced to marry him after Marcellus passed away—was still pregnant with their fifth child.

Something had changed in Augustus that day. He turned colder, quieter, and more private. They never spoke of Agrippa again, but somehow their silence said more than words ever could.

"Have you learned nothing, *mi Octaviane?*" Livia asked, and at her old endearment, Augustus glanced at her with a fond smile. "Love can never be lost. It stays with us, even beyond death. Always."

⤜⟫⟫ ⟪⟪⤛

AUGUST AD 14

Over the next few weeks, Augustus grew seriously ill and had to remain in his bed. They moved him to their villa at Nola, near Naples, hoping that the milder climate by the sea would do him good, though she knew it would not.

She recalled with a sense of dread that Augustus' own father, his true father, Gaius Octavius, had also died at Nola on his return to Rome from wounds that had never healed, and she wondered if Augustus had planned this all along.

Time felt very short and sudden, and the horizon appeared dark, looming ever closer like an impending storm. Now was the test of all that they had built together. Now Augustus left behind the greatest legacy of all, and she was the one who must preserve it. An empire built by the hands of men, to be passed on by the hands of a woman.

For Rome was no longer a city on the brink of chaos, but a city made of marble, her temples rising higher and more noble than ever. Livia had seen the city grow from grimy streets and war-riddled families to the flourishing flower of the West. She had survived wars and famines, death and disease, and had lived to see the day when Rome was finally at peace. A hard-won peace, and no one knew that better than her.

Where Augustus' fate ended, Livia saw her life unfold in front and behind her like the ever-changing waters of the Tiber, the roots of the laurel tree above and below, planting the seeds of her life beyond birth and death, when her children's children would have children of their own, and their children would inherit a Rome she had only ever known in dreams.

When Livia had been but a child, her father had told her that she would accomplish great things one day. At last, she believed him. She thought of her mother, long since passed away, and the subtle strength she had found in all the things Livia used to think were weak.

Life is not about what you have done, but who you have become.

She was Livia Drusilla, and this was her fate.

Finis

Acknowledgements

First, I would like to thank my family, whose love and support keep me grounded even while I am far away. Thank you especially to my dad, who read the first draft of this novel in its entirety before a much-needed rewrite. His belief in this story and my writing career in general is unmatched, and I am eternally grateful.

A huge thank you to my close friend and fellow Classicist, Grace DeAngelis, who read each chapter as I wrote them, leaving edits, encouragement, and invaluable expertise in all things Classics. Not only would my Latin be worse without her help, but so would the story itself, which owes so much to our discussions of and journeys into the Classical world.

I would also like to thank the Centro class of Fall 2021 for all their enthusiasm while reading this story in between long, rigorous days of travel and classwork. Their devotion to the field of Classics inspired me from the start, and I can only hope that this story has reflected some of that passion which runs as deep as the oldest ruins.

On that note, thank you to my Centro professor of Ancient Greek, Matt Panciera, for introducing me to Augustus' riveting *Res Gestae* (the bilingual edition!) and for our many debates which sparked my curiosity about the enigmatic and ambitious nineteen-year-old, Gaius Octavius.

I must mention Pat Southern's *Augustus,* whose careful documentation of Augustus' younger, private self and his rise to power in impressive chronological detail were vital to the creation of this story.

A special thanks to my 12th-grade English literature teacher, Mr. Beckman, who told me that I was a writer before I knew it myself. That prophecy has haunted me all these years in the most beautiful way.

Thank you to my cousin, Alexis, who made my beautiful cover. And thank you to all of my friends who have shown their support for my writing career in any way they can, it means the world to me.

Lastly, I want to thank all the mothers, sisters, daughters, and wives of the great men in history. Nothing could be written without you.

HISTORICAL NOTES

The Sun of God is based on real historical events, places, and people. However, the forbidden romance between Gaius Octavius and Marcus Agrippa is not attested to in any historical source. My decision to weave this love affair among the historically proven events coincided with the inception of this story, so that their fictional romance and the story itself are inextricably bound.

When I first began reading Augustus' *Res Gestae* for my Ancient Greek class at the Intercollegiate Center for Classical Studies in Rome, I was immediately drawn to the enigmatic Augustus and his younger, private self, Gaius Octavius, whose character and thoughts are shrouded in lost history, propaganda, and rumor. At nineteen he raised an army and rose to absolute power in a little over a decade. And as I began researching more, I was only more impressed, and more confused, as to how this happened.

For when one studies the events after the fall of the Republic, it is clear that who would emerge victorious was less than certain. But Octavius was the one who survived, who proved victorious, and he accomplished this with surprising tact, ruthlessness, and foresight for both his age and experience. But what was he like as a person to have become the Emperor Augustus? Who did he love? Who loved him? Who were his closest friends, his most bitter enemies? What did he fear? What did he believe in? These questions followed me as I began researching primary sources, such as Appian, Suetonius, Cassius Dio, as well as well-researched biographies like Pat Southern's *Augustus* and various academic articles.

In my research, I then discovered some key facts that inspired the forbidden romance between Octavius and Agrippa. First of all, Marcus Agrippa is always mentioned as one of Octavius' childhood friends, as well as his best general and closest confidant. Despite this, and despite Agrippa's impressive feats as his second-in-command, he never attempts to gain more power than Octavius, and remains a devoted follower his entire life. Moreover, when Octavius falls seriously ill in 23 BC, he gives his signet ring to Agrippa as a sign that he would succeed him if he died. This was a scandal even in his day because everyone expected him to claim Marcellus, his sister's son and the princeling of Rome, as his heir.

Octavius also legally adopted Agrippa's children in the hopes that they would be his heirs after Marcellus died. And when Agrippa died at around fifty years old, Augustus put on a lavish funeral and was in mourning for over a month. He also deposited Agrippa's remains in his family mausoleum.

While all of these historical events do not prove a romance, they do testify to an intense love and friendship between Octavius and Agrippa that has, in many ways, withstood the tests of time. Octavius' mausoleum—where both of their remains were buried—still stands, and Agrippa's many public works under Augustus' command, like the Pantheon, are revered today. My hope in writing their love story was to bring them—and those around them—closer to us, as living, breathing people who loved, hated, feared, and dreamed as intensely as we do. I believe the love they share in my story helped me to do that.

In historical fact, Augustus' past will always be obscure, a list of achievements and dates with no clue as to the person behind the mask. Only fiction can bring the past to life, even if it cannot be considered fact. That, at least, the ancient historians knew well, and the Appians and Suetoniuses and Livys of those days had no qualms in telling history as, well, it always is—a story—fully equipped with invented speeches, murderous plots, and rumored love affairs.

In response to the anticipated critique of why I included a romance that has no historical backing, I would also like to point to the inclusion of the female narratives in the story, whose lives, marriages, and children are hardly mentioned in history, and if they are, as a mere footnote. But their lives were incredible and surprising too.

For example, Octavia Minor had five children. She married the infamous Marcus Antonius. She took care of Antonius' four other children. What a life she lived! Then there was Livia, who had a miscarriage. She was married to Augustus, the first Emperor of Rome, until his death. How can you not wonder at that? Then there was Attica, who married Agrippa. She disappears from historical records by the Battle of Actium. What was Attica like, the daughter of Atticus and a favorite of the famous Cicero? And how did she die? In learning about their scarcely recorded lives, I knew I had to write their stories, about their love and hate for their husbands, their hopes and aspirations, their children and friendships, even though I had no ancient source to prove that any of it existed.

In other words, I wanted to show that these women had full lives too. A marriage is not a small thing, even today, and neither is having children. Now imagine having Marcus Antonius' children! Nor are their friendships, their family relationships, or their daily lives worth less than that of the great men of history, like Cicero and Brutus, Antonius and Augustus, whose lives were, after all, mainly lived through their daily relationships too. Perhaps the point is not whether Attica loved Agrippa or not, or whether Livia really schemed for more power, or whether Octavia felt anything for Antonius in their politically-arranged marriage. The point is that it *might* be true, and that is the most important fact of all.

In the end, the bare facts of history only get one so far in understanding the past, the people who lived it, the decisions they made, and the relationships they formed day after day. In that sense, this novel is simply about living history, in the only way we can, and that is through story, and taking a moment to wonder what it would have been like to live and love in such a monumental time. They were only human like us, after all, and for that reason alone, I believe their stories are worth telling.

ABOUT THE AUTHOR

Zoë Tavares Bennett is a writer based in Los Angeles, California. She is also the author of the YA novel *My Sister's Best Friend*. She has a degree in Classics from Williams College, specializing in Ancient Greek and Latin.

To learn more about the author or subscribe to her newsletter, visit her website: https://www.zoetavaresbennett.com/

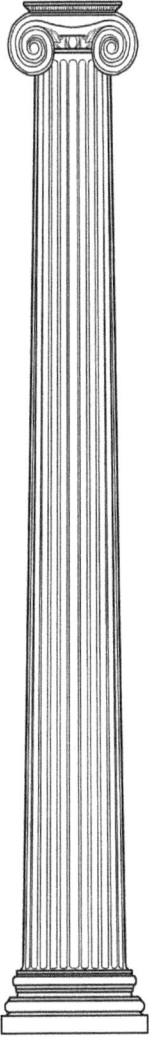

APPENDICES

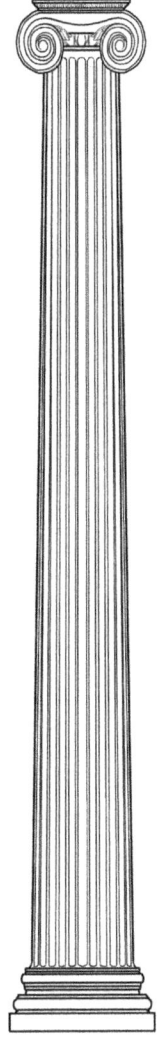

Julio-Claudian Family Tree

son/daughter   Emp. = emperor
1,2... = number of
affair   marriages
marriage

Calpurnia
Pompeia Sulla
Cornelia Cinna
Gaius Julius Caesar
Mucia Tertia
Sextus Pompeius
Gnaeus Pompeius (Pompeius the Great)
Julia Caesaris
Tiberius Claudius Nero
Livia Drusilla Augusta
Tiberius Claudius Nero (Emp. 14-37 AD)
Nero Claudius Drusus
Vipsania Agrippina Major
Attica
Marcus Vipsanius Agrippa
Vipsania Agrippina Minor
Julia Caesaris
Clodia
Fulvia
Scribonia
Gaius Julius Caesar
Octavianus Augustus (Gaius Octavius Thurinus) Emp. 27BC-14AD
Julia Minor
Marcus Atius Balbus
Atia Balba
Gaius Octavius
Cleopatra
Caesaris
Octavia Minor
Claudius Marcellus
Claudius Marcellus
Claudia Marcella Major
Marcella Minor
Marcus Antonius Antyllus
Iullus Antonius
Marcus Antonius
Antonia Major
Antonia Minor
Cleopatra
Nero Claudius Drusus

Timeline of Historical Events

63 B. C.	September 23	BIRTH OF AUGUSTUS, at Rome
59		Gaius Octavius, wife of Atia and father of Octavius, dies from battle wounds at Nola.
ca. 50		Funeral Oration for his grandmother Julia
48	October 18	Toga virilis (ceremony: became a man in law)
45	October	In Spain with Julius Caesar: Battle of Munda At Apollonia in Macedonia, with troops assembling for Caesar's eastern expedition.
44	March 15	Assassination of Julius Caesar, young Octavius' grandmother's brother.
	April 18	Back in Italy, at Naples.
	April 19	Meeting with Cicero and Balbus. Puteoli, at Philippus' villa. Cumae, at Cicero's Villa.
	early May	In Rome: Meeting with Antonius.
44-43?		Atia Balba, mother of Octavius, dies.
43	April 14	Battle at Forum Gallorum. Antonius defeated.

	April 14-27	Battle at Mutina (April 21): Antonius defeated.
	May 24	Antonius and Lepidus join forces.
	August 19	First Consulate of Caesar, with his cousin Pedius.
	October	Meeting with Antonius and Lepidus at the Island of Reni (near Bononia).
	November 27	Second Triumvirate legislated into existence for 5 years at Rome: Lex Titia. Proscriptions: 130+ senators (Livy) or 200 senators and 2000+ Equites (Appian) –Only one ex-consul known (Cicero).
42		The Campaign against the "Liberators" (Brutus and Cassius).
	October 23	Battle of Philippi. Young Caesar was ill.
41		Perusine War.
40	by July 5	Capture of Perusia; Caesar returns to Rome. Antonius marries Caesar's full-sister Octavia.
39		Caesar marries Scribonia (child: Julia).
38	January 17	Caesar marries Livia, the pregnant wife of Tiberius Claudius Nero (children: Tiberius and Drusus). Livia finally died in A. D. 29 at the age of 86.
36	September 3	Battle of Naulochus (off the coast of Sicily). The end of Lepidus' importance.
32-29?		Attica, wife of Agrippa, dies of unknown causes.

31	September 2	Battle of Actium: Defeat of Antonius and Cleopatra.
30	August	Alexandria: Suicide of Antonius and Cleopatra.
29	August 13-15	Triple triumph of Caesar on his return to Rome.
27	January 13 & 16	Restoration of the Republic. Constitutional Settlement; name of Augustus awarded by Senate.
26		Augustus leads the Spanish campaign.
23	June	Augustus ill. Gave signet ring to Agrippa as a sign that he would succeed him if he died. Assassination attempt (led by Maecenas' brother-in-law). Augustus gave up the consulship, and was given Tribunician Power. Marcellus, Octavia's son, dies at 19 years old.
22		Augustus tours the East.
18		Lectio Senatus (revision of membership of the Senate).
17		Adoption of Gaius and Lucius Agrippa (sons of Marcus Agrippa and Julia Caesaris filia).
16–13		Tour of Gaul and Tour of Spain (Augustus accompanied by Livia, Tiberius and Terentia).
12	March 6	Augustus elected Pontifex Maximus, in succession to Lepidus.
	March 19-23	Augustus travels to Campania with Agrippa.

	April 3	Augustus wrote his Last Will and Testament and the Res Gestae Divi Augusti.
	July 24-25	Augustus and Tiberius leave Rome for the East.
	August 9	Departure of Tiberius for the Balkans.
	August 16	Return of Tiberius to Brundisium, summoned by Livia.
	August 19	Death of Imperator Caesar Augustus, at his villa at Nola, aged 76.
	September	Augustus deified by Senatorial Decree.

Real Names of History Mentioned

Alfidia
Alexander Helios
Antonia (first daughter of Antonius)
Antonia Major
Antonia Minor
Apollodorus
Arsinoe IV
Athenodorus
Atia Balba
Aulus Gabinius
Aulus Hirtius
Berenice IV
Caesarion
Cinna
Claudia Marcella Major
Claudia Marcella Minor
Cleopatra VI
Cleopatra VII Philopator
Cleopatra Selene II
Clodia
Cocceius Nerva
Cornelius Gallus
Decimus Brutus
Decimus Carfulenus
Epirota
Fulvia
Gaius Asinius Pollio

Gaius Cassius Longinus

Gaius Julius Caesar

Gaius Maecenas

Gaius Matius

Gaius Norbanus Flaccus

Gaius Octavius Thurinus/Gaius Julius Caesar Octavianus Augustus

Gaius Oppius

Gaius Sosius

Gaius Trebonius

Gaius Vibius Pansa Caetronianus

Glyco

Gnaeus Cornelius Lentulus Marcellinus

Gnaeus Domitius Ahenobarbus

Gnaeus Pompeius Magnus (son of Pompeius Magnus)

Hyrcanus II

Iullus Antonius

Julia Caeseris filia

Julia Minor

King Artavasdes II

King Mithridates VI of Pontus

Quintus Laronius

Livia Drusilla

Lucius Antonius

Lucius Arruntius

Lucius Cornelius Balbus

Lucius Cornificius

Lucius Decidius Saxa

Lucius Marcius Philippus

Lucius Varius Rufus

Lucius Vipsanius (Agrippa's father)

Lucius Volcatius Tullus

Lysippos

Marcus Aemilius Lepidus

Marcus Aemilius Lepidus Minor (son)

Marcus Aemilius Scaurus (father)

Marcus Aemilius Scaurus (Mucia's son)

Marcus Antonius

Marcus Antonius Antyllus

Marcus Calpurnius Bibulus

Marcus Favonius

Marcus Junius Brutus

Marcus Licinius Crassus

Marcus Livius Drusus Claudianus

Marcus Lurius

Marcus Titius (Plancus' nephew)

Marcus Tullius Cicero

Marcus Valerius Messalla Corvinus

Marcus Vipsanius Agrippa

Marius (pretender)

Marius (procurator to Marcus Antonius)

Menas, the freedman (also known as Menodorus)

Mithridates VI Eupator

Mucia Tertia

Murcus (admiral of fleet alongside Ahenobarbus)

Nero Claudius Drusus (son)

Octavia Minor

Philostratos (or Philostratus the Egyptian, Cleopatra's tutor)

Phoebe

Pilia (wife of Atticus)

Plennius

Pompeia (Sextus' daughter)

Pompeia Magna (Sextus' sister)

Pompeius Magnus

Pomponia Caecilia Attica

Porcia

Ptolemy XIV Philopator

Ptolemy XIII Theos Philopator

Publius Canidius Crassus

Publius Cornelius Dolabella

Publius Cornelius Scipio Africanus

Publius Decius

Publius Servilius Isauricus

Publius Silicius Corona

Publius Ventidius Bassus

Publius Vergilius Maro

Quintus Dellius

Quintus Horatius Flaccus

Quintus Laronius

Quintus Pedius

Quintus Salvius Salvidienus Rufus

Rhascupolis

Scribonia (Sextus' wife)

Scribonius Libo

Scribonius Curio

Servilia

Sentia

Sextus Pompeius Magnus Pius

Tertia (Tertulla)

Theodotus of Chios

Tiberius Claudius Nero

Tiberius Julius Caesar Augustus (son)

Tigranes the Great

Titus Pomponius Atticus/Quintus Caecilius Pomponianus Atticus

Titus Statilius Taurus

Vipsania Agrippina Major

Vipsania Agrippina Minor

Latin & Greek Words

Ad dextram! Ad sinistram! - To the right! To the left!

Ad latus stringe! - Close the ranks!

Ambula! - advance!

Ἀριστολοχία (Aristolochia)- a plant mostly known for its use in childbirth, can be healing or poisonous

Atrium - first room of the house after entering

Ave, Caesar - Hail, Caesar

Ave, Imperator Caesar divi fili, morituri te salutant. - Formal greeting of a master/commander/tyrant. "Hail Imperator Caesar son of god, we who are about to die salute you"

Avia/Auia - grandmother

Augustus - august, revered, holy

Aurei (sg. Aureus) - gold coin

Ballistae - a large crossbow used in ancient warfare for firing a spear

Caldarium - hot room/bath

Ciringite frontem! - Hold the front!

Conspiratores - the negative word for who plotted to murder Julius Caesar

Consul - the elected heads (two) of Rome and the Senate

Consul suffectus - the consul to replace the dead or removed consul previous

Contendite vestra sponte! - Go forth by your own will! (To attack each enemy as they came)

Cum ordine seque! - Follow in good order!

Cuneum formate! - Form a wedge!

Curia - the Senate courthouse

Cursu mina! - Gallop! Charge!

Curules - relating to or being a high-ranking person

Dirige frontem! - Adjust the front!

Divus Iulius - Divine Julius

543

Drachma/ae - a silver coin of ancient Greece.

Dulcissima - Sweetest

Equaliter ambula! Invenite Antonium! - Advance uniformly! Follow Antonius!

Equites - cavalry

Imperium - legal command of an army among other things

Fasces - a bundle of rods with a projecting axe blade, carried by a lictor in ancient Rome as a symbol of a magistrate's power

Filia - daughter

Fili canes - son of a bitch/dog

Filius Divi Iulii - son of Divine Julius

Forum - main square in the city for commerce and business and public speeches

Frigidarium - cold room/plunge pool

Gallia Transalpina - Latin for Transalpine Gaul

Garum - a delicacy in Ancient Rome that is essentially a fish paste

Gens - race, tribe, or clan

Gladius - a short sword

Gustatio - The first course of a dinner in Ancient Rome, intended to stimulate the appetite.

Harpax - a Roman catapult-shot grapnel that allowed an enemy vessel to be harpooned and then winched alongside for boarding.

Hostis - enemy of the state

Impluvium - small shallow fountain in the middle of an atrium

Καῖσαρ - Caesar (Greek)

Lares - Roman household gods

Laudatio - funeral song

Legio - the chief unit of the Roman army consisting of 3000 to 6000 foot soldiers with cavalry

Luperci - the male priests in charge of the Lupercalia festival

Magister - master, chief, boss, etc.

Mater - mother

Mater omnium matrum - Mother of all mothers

Mea filia dulcissima. - my sweetest daughter

Mea soror - my sister

Mea Tertulla - my Tertulla (nickname of Tertia)

Mi Agrippa - my Agrippa

Mi aselle - my little donkey

Mi fili - my son

Mi vir - my husband

Morere! Morere! Morere! - Die! Die! Die!

Mustaceus - the traditional Roman wedding cake

Novi homines - lit. "New men," the term in ancient Rome for a man who was the first in his family to serve in the Roman Senate or, more specifically, to be elected as consul.

Octavianus - lit. "formerly Octavius"

Optiones - An *optio* was stationed at the rear of the ranks to keep the troops in order

Ordinem servate! - Maintain the formation!

Palla - a loose outer garment formed by wrapping or draping a large square of cloth and worn by women

Pankration - an unarmed combat sport introduced into the Greek Olympic Games in 648 BC. The athletes used boxing and wrestling techniques but also others, such as kicking, holds, joint-locks, and chokes on the ground, making it similar to modern mixed martial arts.

Parati equites! - Get ready cavalry!

Pater - father

Patientia - patience

Percute! - Charge!

Phaseli - sailing passenger ferries first centuries BCE and CE

Philopator - father-lover

Plebis - of the plebs

Potestas - The male guardians of a child who had power over them

Praetor - title for consuls

Proconsul - a governor of a province

Propraetor - A magistrate of ancient Rome who governed a province after serving as a praetor in Rome.

Proscripti - those listed to be executed

Quadriremes - a galley with four banks of oars.

Quaestor - any of a number of officials who had charge of public revenue and expenditure

Quinqueremes - an ancient galley propelled by five banks of oars.

Rostra - part of the Forum in Rome, which was decorated with the beaks of captured galleys, and was used as a platform for public speakers

Sacrosanctitas - an honor reserved only for tribunes that makes it illegal to insult them

Salve - hello

Seclusus - secluded

Sequi me! - follow me!

σπεῦδε βραδέως (speude bradeus)- make haste slowly

Sponsus/sponsa - betrothed (m/f)

Strigilis - a tool for the cleansing of the body by scraping off dirt, perspiration, and oil that was applied before bathing in Ancient Greek and Roman cultures.

Te amo, mea vita, ad finem maris. - I love you, my life, to the end of the sea.

Tepidarium - warm room/pool

Testudines - a type of military shelter in the shape of a tortoise shell

Toga virilis - the toga assumed by a youth at the age of 14 as a symbol of manhood and citizenship

Triclinium - dining room

Tunicae rectae - typical Roman bride dress

Tutela - male guardianship required for all women

Vale - farewell

Via - road

Virtus - a specific concept in Ancient Rome. It carries connotations of valor, masculinity, excellence, courage, character, and worth, perceived as masculine strengths.

Χαῖρε, (Kaire)- hello

Milton Keynes UK
Ingram Content Group UK Ltd.
UKHW041208051024
449245UK00016B/116/J

9 798991 580229